Praise for The Tales of Alvin Maker

"The best fantasy s ... ekly

"Card brings to buil ... st of well-wrought characters, formidable scholarship in history, religion, and folklore. . . . We are talking about the most important work of American fantasy since Stephen Donaldson's original Thomas Covenant trilogy."

—*Chicago Sun-Times*

"With delicacy and insight, incorporating folktales and folk magic with mountain lore and other authentic details, Orson Scott Card has evoked a different vision of America as it might have been."

—*Tribune-Review* (Greensburg, PA)

"Card has created a uniquely American fantasy."

—*The Charlotte Observer*

Praise for Volume One: *Seventh Son*

"*Seventh Son* begins what may be a significant recasting in fantasy terms of the tall tale of America. . . . There is something dee ... ut an America come true, ever ... ntasy novel. . . . The first volume ... ker is sharp and clean and braci ...

—... *ost Book World*

"In *Se* ... bring-ing s ... bodes extra ... some-thing ...

—*Locus*

"The mixture of folk magic and the frontier setting is a comfortable one that allows Card to insert all manner of insights, ranging from philosophical parables to outdoor lore. The characters, even the bad guys, are irresistible and Card's polished storytelling keeps the plot thick, yet subtle, throughout." —*The Houston Post*

"Card's blend of folklore, historical research, and religion adds depth and power to a consistently exciting narrative." —*Detroit Free Press*

Praise for Volume Two: *Red Prophet*

"Harsher, bleaker, and more mystical than *Seventh Son*, *Red Prophet* superbly demonstrates Card's solid historical research and, most of all, his mastery of the art of storytelling." —*Booklist*

"*Red Prophet* is the logical and emotional continuation of *Seventh Son*, surpassing the earlier volume in power and compassion, in cruelty and love. At times the starkness and beauty are nearly unendurable; at times the evocation of human failures and cruelty are equally unendurable. But always *Red Prophet* moves us one step nearer to (and in fact provides the first fleeting glimpses of) the Crystal City—and somehow that instant of vision is enough to convince that, in spite of all, in spite of death and fear and horror, there is a purpose . . . and that purpose will be greater than anything Alvin Miller can yet imagine." —*West Coast Review of Books*

SEVENTH SON

• AND •

RED PROPHET

ORSON SCOTT CARD

A TOM DOHERTY ASSOCIATES BOOK | NEW YORK

This is a work of fiction. All of the characters, organizations, and events portrayed in these novels are either products of the author's imagination or are used fictitiously.

SEVENTH SON AND RED PROPHET

Seventh Son copyright © 1987 by Orson Scott Card

Red Prophet copyright © 1988 by Orson Scott Card

All rights reserved.

Maps by Alan McKnight

A Tor Book
Published by Tom Doherty Associates, LLC
175 Fifth Avenue
New York, NY 10010

www.tor-forge.com

Tor® is a registered trademark of Tom Doherty Associates, LLC.

ISBN 978-0-7653-8587-1

Our books may be purchased in bulk for promotional, educational, or business use. Please contact your local bookseller or the Macmillan Corporate and Premium Sales Department at 1-800-221-7945, extension 5442, or by e-mail at MacmillanSpecialMarkets@macmillan.com.

First Edition: February 2016

Printed in the United States of America

0 9 8 7 6 5 4 3 2

CONTENTS

NORTH AMERICA
POLITICAL FEATURES
National Boundaries
Duchy Boundaries
State/Colony/Territory
Scale of Miles
0 50 100 150 200 250 300

CANADA
(FRANCE)

ACADIA

QUEBEC

WEST
ANGLIA

HURON

Fort
Detroit

NEW HOLLAND

NEW HAMPSHIRE

NEW ENGLAND

EAST HAMPSHIRE

IRRAKWA

Boston

MASS
ACHUSETTS

PLYMOUTH

NETICUT

RHODE
ISLAND

Hatrack
River

HIO
TERR.

PENNSYLANIA

NEW ORANGE

Crystal
City

Vigor
Church

NOISY
RIVER
TERR.

WOBBISH
TERR.

Carthage
City

UNITED STATES

SUSKWA
HENNY

Dekane

NEW AMSTERDAM

New Amsterdam

Philadelphia

Luther

NEW SWEDEN

RAPPAHANNOCK

DUCHY OF
VIRGINIA

ROANOKE

APPALACHEE

Franklin

SPENSER

RALEIGH

NEW
DOVER

NEW
KENT

NEW
WALES

CROWN COLONIES

DUCHY
OF
CAROLINA

DRYDEN

Camelot

DUCHY OF
JACOBIA

NUEVA
BARCELONA
(SPAIN)

FLORIDA
(SPAIN)

NORTH AMERICA
PHYSICAL FEATURES

Alvin Miller's Road ....
(Wobbish Road)

Scale of Miles

0   50 100 150 200 250 300

HIGH WATER LAKE

LAKE MIZOGAN

HURON LAKE

Osh-Kontsy R.

Mizzipy R.

R. Seine

R. St. Denis

R. Rhine

Scoggin

Merrimuck

Notthaull River

LAKE CANADA

IRRAKWA

Mo-Hawk

Algony R.

River

River

Hudson River

Boston

Cape Faith

Fort Detroit

St. Joseph

Tippy-Canoe

Maw-Mee

Dekane

Hatrack

Eight-face Mound

Harrow

Kenky

Susquahenny

New Amsterdam

Philadelphia

Crystal City

Pan-Nee River

Nany River

Springfield

Woobbish River

Vigor Church

Carthage City

Picketwee

Mym-Mee

Virgin R.

Potomac

Shenandoah

Luther

R. Mizeray

Hio River

Kenituck River

Cree-ek

River

Smoky

River Hio

James River

Bay of St. Olaf

Hat R.

Ozark R.

Ar-Kansies R.

Tenny R.

R. Noche

R. Santa Maria

Cherriky

Franklin

Tenny R.

APPALACHEE MOUNTAINS

Roanoke River

Yadkin River

Ann River

River Mersey

Camelot

Mizzipy R.

Red River

Yazoo River

Pearl River

Bammy

River Tweed

Savannah River

Rio de Hispana

Barcy

Santa Isabela

SEVENTH SON

To Emily Jan,
who knows all the magic
that she'll ever need

Acknowledgments

I owe thanks to Carol Breakstone, for her help in researching folk magic of the American frontier. The material she found became a rich mine of story ideas and details of life in the frontier period of the Northwest Territories. I also made extensive use of information contained in Douglass L. Brownstone's *A Field Guide to America's History* (Facts on File, Inc.) and John Seymour's *The Forgotten Crafts* (Knopf).

Scott Russell Sanders contributed by putting in my hands a copy of his exquisite story cycle *Wilderness Plots: Tales About the Settlement of the American Land* (Quill). His work showed me what could be achieved through realistic handling of frontier life and helped keep me on the right track with my ongoing Alvin Maker project. And, though he is long dead, I owe a considerable debt to William Blake (1757–1827), for writing poems and proverbs that came so perfectly to Taleswapper's lips.

Above all, I am grateful to Kristine A. Card, for the incalculable value of her criticism, encouragement, editing, and proofreading, and for single-handedly turning our children into wise, kind, well-mannered human beings, who readily forgive their father when he is not a fit example of those virtues.

1

BLOODY MARY

Little Peggy was very careful with the eggs. She rooted her hand through the straw till her fingers bumped something hard and heavy. She gave no never mind to the chicken drips. After all, when folk with babies stayed at the roadhouse, Mama never even crinkled her face at their most spetackler diapers. Even when the chicken drips were wet and stringy and made her fingers stick together, little Peggy gave no never mind. She just pushed the straw apart, wrapped her hand around the egg, and lifted it out of the brood box. All this while standing tiptoe on a wobbly stool, reaching high above her head. Mama said she was too young for egging, but little Peggy showed her. Every day she felt in every brood box and brought in every egg, every single one, that's what she did.

Every one, she said in her mind, over and over. I got to reach into every one.

Then little Peggy looked back into the northeast corner, the darkest place in the whole coop, and there sat Bloody Mary in her brood box, looking like the devil's own bad dream, hatefulness shining out of her nasty eyes, saying Come here little girl and give me nips. I want nips of

finger and nips of thumb and if you come real close and
try to take my egg I'll get a nip of eye from you.

Most animals didn't have much heartfire, but Bloody
Mary's was strong and made a poison smoke. Nobody else
could see it, but little Peggy could. Bloody Mary dreamed
of death for all folks, but most specially for a certain little
girl five years old, and little Peggy had the marks on her
fingers to prove it. At least one mark, anyway, and even if
Papa said he couldn't see it, little Peggy remembered how
she got it and nobody could blame her none if she sometimes forgot to reach under Bloody Mary who sat there like
a bushwhacker waiting to kill the first folks that just *tried*
to come by. Nobody'd get mad if she just sometimes forgot to look there.

I forgot. I looked in every brood box, every one, and if
one got missed then I forgot forgot forgot.

Everybody knew Bloody Mary was a lowdown chicken
and too mean to give any eggs that wasn't rotten anyway.

I forgot.

She got the egg basket inside before Mama even had the
fire het, and Mama was so pleased she let little Peggy put
the eggs one by one into the cold water. Then Mama put
the pot on the hook and swung it right on over the fire.
Boiling eggs you didn't have to wait for the fire to slack,
you could do it smoke and all.

"Peg," said Papa.

That was Mama's name, but Papa didn't say it in his
Mama voice. He said it in his little-Peggy-you're-in-dutch
voice, and little Peggy knew she was completely found out,
and so she turned right around and yelled what she'd been
planning to say all along.

"I forgot, Papa!"

Mama turned and looked at little Peggy in surprise.
Papa wasn't surprised though. He just raised an eyebrow.
He was holding his hand behind his back. Little Peggy

knew there was an egg in that hand. Bloody Mary's nasty egg.

"What did you forget, little Peggy?" asked Papa, talking soft.

Right that minute little Peggy reckoned she was the stupidest girl ever born on the face of the earth. Here she was denying before anybody accused her of anything.

But she wasn't going to give up, not right off like that. She couldn't stand to have them mad at her and she just wanted them to let her go away and live in England. So she put on her innocent face and said, "I don't know, Papa."

She figgered England was the best place to go live, cause England had a Lord Protector. From the look in Papa's eye, a Lord Protector was pretty much what she needed just now.

"What did you forget?" Papa asked again.

"Just say it and be done, Horace," said Mama. "If she's done wrong then she's done wrong."

"I forgot one time, Papa," said little Peggy. "She's a mean old chicken and she hates me."

Papa answered soft and slow. "One time," he said.

Then he took his hand from behind him. Only it wasn't no single egg he held, it was a whole basket. And that basket was filled with a clot of straw—most likely all the straw from Bloody Mary's box—and that straw was mashed together and glued tight with dried-up raw egg and shell bits, mixed up with about three or four chewed-up baby chicken bodies.

"Did you have to bring that in the house before breakfast, Horace?" said Mama.

"I don't know what makes me madder," said Horace. "What she done wrong or her studying up to lie about it."

"I didn't study and I didn't lie!" shouted little Peggy. Or anyways she meant to shout. What came out sounded espiciously like crying even though little Peggy had decided only yesterday that she was done with crying for the rest of her life.

"See?" said Mama. "She already feels bad."

"She feels bad being caught," said Horace. "You're too slack on her, Peg. She's got a lying spirit. I don't want my daughter growing up wicked. I'd rather see her dead like her baby sisters before I see her grow up wicked."

Little Peggy saw Mama's heartfire flare up with memory, and in front of her eyes she could see a baby laid out pretty in a little box, and then another one only not so pretty cause it was the second baby Missy, the one what died of pox so nobody'd touch her but her own mama, who was still so feeble from the pox herself that she couldn't do much. Little Peggy saw that scene, and she knew Papa had made a mistake to say what he said cause Mama's face went cold even though her heartfire was hot.

"That's the wickedest thing anybody ever said in my presence," said Mama. Then she took up the basket of corruption from the table and carried it outside.

"Bloody Mary bites my hand," said little Peggy.

"We'll see what bites," said Papa. "For leaving the eggs I give you one whack, because I reckon that lunatic hen looks fearsome to a frog-size girl like you. But for telling lies I give you ten whacks."

Little Peggy cried in earnest at that news. Papa gave an honest count and full measure in everything, but most especially in whacks.

Papa took the hazel rod off the high shelf. He kept it up there ever since little Peggy put the old one in the fire and burnt it right up.

"I'd rather hear a thousand hard and bitter truths from you, Daughter, than one soft and easy lie," said he, and then he bent over and laid on with the rod across her thighs. Whick whick whick, she counted every one, they stung her to the heart, each one of them, they were so full of anger.

Worst of all she knew it was all unfair because his heart-fire raged for a different cause altogether, and it always did. Papa's hate for wickedness always came from his most secret memory. Little Peggy didn't understand it all, because it was twisted up and confused and Papa didn't remember it right well himself. All little Peggy ever saw plain was that it was a lady and it wasn't Mama. Papa thought of that lady whenever something went wrong. When baby Missy died of nothing at all, and then the next baby also named Missy died of pox, and then the barn burnt down once, and a cow died, everything that went wrong made him think of that lady and he began to talk about how much he hated wickedness and at those times the hazel rod flew hard and sharp.

I'd rather hear a thousand hard and bitter truths, that's what he said, but little Peggy knew that there was one truth he didn't ever want to hear, and so she kept it to herself. She'd never shout it at him, even if it made him break the hazel rod, cause whenever she thought of saying aught about that lady, she kept picturing her father dead, and that was a thing she never hoped to see for real. Besides, the lady that haunted his heartfire, she didn't have no clothes on, and little Peggy knew that she'd be whipped for sure if she talked about people being naked.

So she took the whacks and cried till she could taste that her nose was running. Papa left the room right away, and Mama came back to fix up breakfast for the blacksmith and the visitors and the hands, but neither one said boo to her, just as if they didn't even notice. She cried even harder and louder for a minute, but it didn't help. Finally she picked up her Bugy from the sewing basket and walked all stiff-legged out to Oldpappy's cabin and woke him right up.

He listened to her story like he always did.

"I know about Bloody Mary," he said, "and I told your

papa fifty times if I told him once, wring that chicken's neck and be done. She's a crazy bird. Every week or so she gets crazy and breaks all her own eggs, even the ones ready to hatch. Kills her own chicks. It's a lunatic what kills its own."

"Papa like to killed *me*," said little Peggy.

"I reckon if you can walk somewhat it ain't so bad altogether."

"I can't walk *much*."

"No, I can see you're nigh crippled forever," said Oldpappy. "But I tell you what, the way I see it your mama and your papa's mostly mad at each other. So why don't you just disappear for a couple of hours?"

"I wish I could turn into a bird and fly."

"Next best thing, though," said Pappy, "is to have a secret place where nobody knows to look for you. Do you have a place like that? No, don't tell me—it wrecks it if you tell even a single other person. You just go to that place for a while. As long as it's a safe place, not out in the woods where a Red might take your pretty hair, and not a high place where you might fall off, and not a tiny place where you might get stuck."

"It's big and it's low and it ain't in the woods," said little Peggy.

"Then you go there, Maggie."

Little Peggy made the face she always made when Oldpappy called her that. And she held up Bugy and in Bugy's squeaky high voice she said, "Her name is Peggy."

"You go there, *Piggy*, if you like that better—"

Little Peggy slapped Bugy right across Oldpappy's knee.

"Someday Bugy'll do that once too often and have a rupture and die," said Oldpappy.

But Bugy just danced right in his face and insisted, "Not piggy, *Peggy*!"

"That's right, Puggy, you go to that secret place and if

anybody says, We got to go find that girl, I'll say, I know where she is and she'll come back when she's good and ready."

Little Peggy ran for the cabin door and then stopped and turned. "Oldpappy, you're the nicest grown-up in the whole world."

"Your papa has a different view of me, but that's all tied up with another hazel rod that I laid hand on much too often. Now run along."

She stopped again right before she closed the door. "You're the *only* nice grown-up!" She shouted it real loud, halfway hoping that they could hear it clear inside the house. Then she was gone, right across the garden, out past the cow pasture, up the hill into the woods, and along the path to the spring house.

2

WAGON PEOPLE

They had one good wagon, these folks did, and two good horses pulling it. One might even suppose they was prosperous, considering they had six big boys, from mansize on down to twins that had wrestled each other into being a good deal stronger than their dozen years. Not to mention one big daughter and a whole passel of little girls. A big family. Right prosperous if you didn't know that not even a year ago they had owned a mill and lived in a big house on a streambank in west New Hampshire. Come down far in the world, they had, and this wagon was all they had left of everything. But they were hopeful, trekking west along the roads that crossed the Hio, heading for open land that was free for the taking. If you were a family with plenty of strong backs and clever hands, it'd be good land, too, as long as the weather was with them and the Reds didn't raid them and all the lawyers and bankers stayed in New England.

The father was a big man, a little run to fat, which was no surprise since millers mostly stood around all day. That softness in the belly wouldn't last a year on a deepwoods homestead. He didn't care much about that, anyway—he had no fear of hard work. What worried him today was his wife, Faith. It was her time for that baby, he knew it. Not that she'd ever talk about it direct. Women just don't speak about things like that with men. But he knew how big she was and how many months it had been. Besides, at the noon stop she murmured to him, "Alvin Miller, if there's a road house along this way, or even a little broken-down cabin, I reckon I could use a bit of rest." A man didn't have to be a philosopher to understand her. And after six sons and six daughters, he'd have to have the brains of a brick not to get the drift of how things stood with her.

So he sent off the oldest boy, Vigor, to run ahead on the road and see the lay of the land.

You could tell they were from New England, cause the boy didn't take no gun. If there'd been a bushwhacker the young man never would've made it back, and the fact he came back with all his hair was proof no Red had spotted him—the French up Detroit way were paying for English scalps with liquor and if a Red saw a White man alone in the woods with no musket he'd own that White man's scalp. So maybe a man could think that luck was with the family at last. But since these Yankees had no notion that the road wasn't safe, Alvin Miller didn't think for a minute of his good luck.

Vigor's word was of a road house three miles on. That was good news, except that between them and that road house was a river. Kind of a scrawny river, and the ford was shallow, but Alvin Miller had learned never to trust water. No matter how peaceful it looks, it'll reach and try to take you. He was halfway minded to tell Faith that they'd spend the night this side of the river, but she gave just the tiniest groan and at that moment he knew that there was no chance of that. Faith had borne him a dozen living children, but it was four years since the last one and a lot of women took it bad, having a baby so late. A lot of women died. A good road house meant women to help with the birthing, so they'd have to chance the river.

And Vigor did say the river wasn't much.

Whatever they didn't like most about theirself they tried to tuck away in some dark corner but they didn't know how all them dark places burned in little Peggy's eyes. Even when she was so little that she spit out her corn mash cause she was still hoping for a suck, she knew all the stories that the folks around her kept all hid. She saw the bits of their past that they most wished they could bury, and she saw the bits of their future that they most feared.

And that was why she took to coming up here to the spring house. Here she didn't have to see those things. Not even the lady in Papa's memory. There was nothing here but the heavy wet dark cool air to quench the fire and dim the light so she could be—just for a few minutes in the day—a little five-year-old girl with a straw poppet named Bugy and not even have to *think* about any of them grown-up secrets.

I'm not wicked, she told herself. Again and again, but it didn't work because she knew she was.

All right then, she said to herself, I *am* wicked. But I won't be wicked anymore. I'll tell the truth like Papa says, or I'll say nothing at all.

Even at five years old, little Peggy knew that if she kept *that* vow, she'd be better off saying nothing.

So she said nothing, not even to herself, just lay there on a mossy damp table with Bugy clenched tight enough to strangle in her fist.

Ching ching ching.

Little Peggy woke up and got mad for just a minute.

Ching ching ching.

Made her mad because nobody said to her, Little Peggy, you don't mind if we talk this young blacksmith feller into settling down here, do you?

Not at all, Papa, she would've said if they'd asked. She knew what it meant to have a smithy. It meant your village would thrive, and folks from other places would come,

3

SPRING HOUSE

The air in the spring house was cool and heavy, dark and wet. Sometimes when little Peggy caught a nap here, she woke up gasping like as if the whole place was under water. She had dreams of water even when she wasn't here—that was one of the things that made some folks say she was a seeper instead of a torch. But when she dreamed outside, she always knew she was dreaming. Here the water was real.

Real in the drips that formed like sweat on the milkjars setting in the stream. Real in the cold damp clay of the spring house floor. Real in the swallowing sound of the stream as it hurried through the middle of the house.

Keeping it cool all summer long, cold water spilling right out of the hill and into this place, shaded all the way by trees so old the moon made a point of passing through their branches just to hear some good old tales. That was what little Peggy always came here for, even when Papa didn't hate her. Not the wetness of the air, she could do just fine without that. It was the way the fire went right out of her and she didn't have to be a torch. Didn't have to see into all the dark places where folks hid theirselfs.

From her they hid theirselfs as if it would do some good.

dusk. The air was all a-prickle with lightning just waiting
to flash. She knew that feeling, knew that it meant the
lightning'd hit close.

She looked down to see if the blacksmith's stable was
still full of horses. It was. The shoeing wasn't done, the
road would turn to muck, and so the farmer with his two
sons from out West Fork way was stuck here. Not a chance
they'd head home in *this*, with lightning ready to put a fire
in the woods, or knock a tree down on them, or maybe just
smack them a good one and lay them all out dead in a circle like them five Quakers they still was talking about
and here it happened back in '90 when the first White folks
came to settle here. People talked still about the Circle of
Five and all that, some people wondering if God up and
smashed them flat so as to shut the Quakers up, seeing how
nothing else ever could, while other people was wondering if God took them up into heaven like the first Lord
Protector Oliver Cromwell who was smote by lightning at
the age of ninety-seven and just disappeared.

No, that farmer and his big old boys'd stay another night.
Little Peggy was an innkeeper's daughter, wasn't she?
Papooses learnt to hunt, pickaninnies learnt to tote, farmer
children learnt the weather, and an innkeeper's daughter
learnt which folks would stay the night, even before they
knew it right theirselfs.

Their horses were champing in the stable, snorting and
warning each other about the storm. In every group of
horses, little Peggy figgered, there must be one that's remarkable dumb, so all the others have to tell him what all's
going on. Bad storm, they were saying. We're going to get
a soaking, if the lightning don't smack us first. And the
dumb one kept nickering and saying, What's that noise,
what's that noise?

Then the sky just opened right up and dumped water on
the earth. Stripped leaves right off the trees, it came down

and when they came there'd be trade, and where there was
trade then her father's big house could be a forest inn, and
where there was a forest inn then all the roads would kind
of bend a little just to pass the place, if it wasn't too far
out of the way—little Peggy knew all that, as sure as the
children of farmers knew the rhythms of the farm. A road
house by a smithy was a road house that would prosper.
So she would've said, Sure enough, let him stay, deed him
land, brick his chimney, feed him free, let him have my
bed so I have to double up with Cousin Peter who keeps
trying to peek under my nightgown, I'll put up with all
that—just as long as you don't put him near the spring
house so that all the time, even when I want to be alone
with the water, there's that whack thump hiss roar, noise
all the time, and a fire burning up the sky to turn it black,
and the smell of charcoal burning. It was enough to make a
body wish to follow the stream right back into the mountain just to get some peace.

Of course the stream was the smart place to put the
blacksmith. Except for water, he could've put his smithy
anywheres at all. The iron came to him in the shipper's
wagon clear from New Netherland, and the charcoal—
well, there was plenty of farmers willing to trade charcoal
for a good shoe. But water, that's what the smith needed
that nobody'd bring him, so of course they put him right
down the hill from the spring house where his ching ching
ching could wake her up and put the fire back into her in
the one place where she had used to be able to let it burn
low and go almost to cold wet ash.

A roar of thunder.

She was at the door in a second. Had to see the lightning. Caught just the last shadow of the light but she knew
that there'd be more. It wasn't much after noon, surely, or
had she slept all day? What with all these blackbelly clouds
she couldn't tell—it might as well be the last minutes of

so hard. Came down so thick, too, that little Peggy couldn't even see the smithy for a minute and she thought maybe it got washed right away into the stream. Oldpappy told her how that stream led right down to the Hatrack River, and the Hatrack poured right into the Hio, and the Hio shoved itself on through the woods to the Mizzipy, which went on down into the sea, and Oldpappy said how the sea drank so much water that it got indigestion and gave off the biggest old belches you ever heard, and what came up was clouds. Belches from the sea, and now the smithy would float all that way, get swallered up and belched out, and someday she'd just be minding her own business and some cloud would break up and plop that smithy down as neat as you please, old Makepeace Smith still ching ching chinging away.

Then the rain slacked off a mite and she looked down to see the smithy still there. But that wasn't what she saw at all. No, what she saw was sparks of fire way off in the forest, downstream toward the Hatrack, down where the ford was, only there wasn't a chance of taking the ford today, with this rain. Sparks, lots of sparks, and she knew every one of them was folks. She didn't hardly think of doing it anymore, she only had to see their heartfires and she was looking close. Maybe future, maybe past, all the visions lived together in the heartfire.

What she saw right now was the same in all their hearts. A wagon in the middle of the Hatrack, with the water rising and everything they owned in all the world in that wagon.

Little Peggy didn't talk much, but everybody knew she was a torch, so they listened whenever she spoke up about trouble. Specially this kind of trouble. Sure the settlements in these parts were pretty old now, a fair bit older than little Peggy herself, but they hadn't forgotten yet that anybody's wagon caught in a flood is everybody's loss.

She fair to flew down that grassy hill, jumping gopher holes and sliding the steep places, so it wasn't twenty seconds from seeing those far-off heartfires till she was speaking right up in the smithy's shop. That farmer from West Fork at first wanted to make her wait till he was done with telling stories about worse storms he'd seen. But Makepeace knew all about little Peggy. He just listened right up and then told those boys to saddle them horses, shoes or no shoes, there was folks caught in the Hatrack ford and there was no time for foolishness. Little Peggy didn't even get a chance to see them go—Makepeace already sent her off to the big house to fetch her father and all the hands and visitors there. Wasn't a one of them who hadn't once put all they owned in the world into a wagon and dragged it west across the mountain roads and down into this forest. Wasn't a one of them who hadn't felt a river sucking at that wagon, wanting to steal it away. They all got right to it. That's the way it was then, you see. Folks noticed other people's trouble every bit as quick as if it was their own.

4

HATRACK RIVER

Vigor led the boys in trying to push the wagon, while Eleanor hawed the horses. Alvin Miller spent his time carrying the little girls one by one to safety on the far shore. The current was a devil clawing at him, whispering, I'll have your babies, I'll have them all, but Alvin said no, with every muscle in his body as he strained shoreward he said no to that whisper, till his girls stood all bedraggled on the bank with rain streaming down their faces like the tears from all the grief in the world.

He would have carried Faith, too, baby in her belly and all, but she wouldn't budge. Just sat inside that wagon, bracing herself against the trunks and furniture as the wagon tipped and rocked. Lightning crashed and branches broke; one of them tore the canvas and the water poured into the wagon but Faith held on with white knuckles and her eyes staring out. Alvin knew from her eyes there wasn't a thing he could say to make her let go. There was only one way to get Faith and her unborn baby out of that river, and that was to get the wagon out.

"Horses can't get no purchase, Papa," Vigor shouted. "They're just stumbling and bound to break a leg."

"Well we can't pull out without the horses!"

"The horses are *something*, Papa. We leave 'em in here and we'll lose wagon and horses too!"

"Your mama won't leave that wagon."

He saw understanding in Vigor's eyes. The *things* in the wagon weren't worth a risk of death to save them. But Mama was.

"Still," Vigor said. "On shore the team could pull strong. Here in the water they can't do a thing."

"Set the boys to unhitching them. But first tie a line to a tree to hold that wagon!"

It wasn't two minutes before the twins Wastenot and Wantnot were on the shore making the rope fast to a stout tree. David and Measure made another line fast to the rig that held the horses, while Calm cut the strands that held them to the wagon. Good boys, doing their work just right, Vigor shouting directions while Alvin could only watch, helpless at the back of the wagon, looking now at Faith who was trying not to have the baby, now at the Hatrack River that was trying to push them all down to hell.

Not much of a river, Vigor had said, but then the clouds came up and the rain came down and the Hatrack became something after all. Even so it looked passable when they got to it. The horses strode in strong, and Alvin was just saying to Calm, who had the reins, "Well, we made it not a minute to spare," when the river went insane. It doubled in speed and strength all in a moment, and the horses got panicky and lost direction and started pulling against each other. The boys all hopped into the river and tried to lead them to shore but by then the wagon's momentum had been lost and the wheels were mired up and stuck fast. Almost as if the river knew they were coming and saved up its worst fury till they were already in it and couldn't get away.

"Look out! Look out!" screamed Measure from the shore.

Alvin looked upstream to see what devilment the river had in mind, and there was a whole tree floating down the river, endwise like a battering ram, the root end pointed at the center of the wagon, straight at the place where Faith was sitting, her baby on the verge of birth. Alvin couldn't think of anything to do, couldn't think at all, just screamed his wife's name with all his strength. Maybe in his heart he thought that by holding her name on his lips he could keep her alive, but there was no hope of that, no hope at all.

Except that Vigor didn't know there was no hope. Vigor leapt out when the tree was no more than a rod away, his body falling against it just above the root. The momentum of his leap turned it a little, then rolled it over, rolled it and turned it away from the wagon. Of course Vigor rolled with it, pulled right under the water—but it worked, the root end of the tree missed the wagon entirely, and the shaft of the trunk struck it a sidewise blow.

The tree bounded across the stream and smashed up against a boulder on the bank. Alvin was five rods off, but in his memory from then on, he always saw it like as if he'd been right there. The tree crashing into the boulder, and Vigor between them. Just a split second that lasted a lifetime, Vigor's eyes wide with surprise, blood already leaping out of his mouth, spattering out onto the tree that killed him. Then the Hatrack River swept the tree out into the current. Vigor slipped under the water, all except his arm, all tangled in the roots, which stuck up into the air for all the world like a neighbor waving good-bye after a visit.

Alvin was so intent on watching his dying son that he didn't even notice what was happening to his own self. The blow from the tree was enough to dislodge the mired wheels, and the current picked up the wagon, carried it downstream, Alvin clinging to the tailgate, Faith weeping inside, Eleanor screaming her lungs out from the driver's seat, and the boys on the bank shouting something. Shouting, "Hold! Hold! Hold!"

The rope held, one end tied to a strong tree, the other end tied to the wagon, it held. The river couldn't tumble the wagon downstream; instead it swung the wagon in to shore the way a boy swings a rock on a string, and when it came to a shuddering stop it was right against the bank, the front end facing upstream.

"It held!" cried the boys.

"Thank God!" shouted Eleanor.

"The baby's coming," whispered Faith.

But Alvin, all he could hear was the single faint cry that had been the last sound from the throat of his firstborn son, all he could see was the way his boy clung to the tree as it rolled and rolled in the water, and all he could say was a single word, a single command. "Live," he murmured. Vigor had always obeyed him before. Hard worker, willing companion, more a friend or brother than a son. But this time he knew his son would disobey. Still he whispered it. "Live."

"Are we safe?" said Faith, her voice trembling.

Alvin turned to face her, tried to strike the grief from his face. No sense her knowing the price that Vigor paid to save her and the baby. Time enough to learn of that after the baby was born. "Can you climb out of the wagon?"

"What's wrong?" asked Faith, looking at his face.

"I took a fright. Tree could have killed us. Can you climb out, now that we're up against the bank?"

Eleanor leaned in from the front of the wagon. "David and Calm are on the bank, they can help you up. The rope's holding, Mama, but who can say how long?"

"Go on, Mother, just a step," said Alvin. "We'll do better with the wagon if we know you're safe on shore."

"The baby's coming," said Faith.

"Better on shore than here," said Alvin sharply. "Go *now*."

Faith stood up, clambered awkwardly to the front. Alvin climbed through the wagon behind her, to help her if she should stumble. Even he could see how her belly had dropped. The baby must be grabbing for air already.

On the bank it wasn't just David and Calm, now. There were strangers, big men, and several horses. Even one small wagon, and that was a welcome sight. Alvin had no notion who these men were, or how they knew to come and help, but there wasn't a moment to waste on introductions. "You men! Is there a midwife in the road house?"

"Goody Guester does with birthing," said a man. A big man, with arms like oxlegs. A blacksmith, surely.

"Can you take my wife in that wagon? There's not a moment to spare." Alvin knew it was a shameful thing, for men to speak so openly of birthing, right in front of the woman who was set to bear. But Faith was no fool—she knew what mattered most, and getting her to a bed and a competent midwife was more important than pussyfooting around about it.

David and Calm were careful as they helped their mother toward the waiting wagon. Faith was staggering with pain. Women in labor shouldn't have to step from a wagon seat up onto a riverbank, that was sure. Eleanor was right behind her, taking charge as if she wasn't younger than all the boys except the twins. "Measure! Get the girls together. They're riding in the wagon with us. You too, Wastenot and Wantnot! I know you can help the big boys but I need you to watch the girls while I'm with Mother." Eleanor was never one to be trifled with, and the gravity of the situation was such that they didn't even call her Eleanor of Aquitaine as they obeyed. Even the little girls mostly gave over their squabbling and got right on.

Eleanor paused a moment on the bank and looked back

to where her father stood on the wagon seat. She glanced downstream, then looked back at him. Alvin understood the question, and he shook his head no. Faith was not to know of Vigor's sacrifice. Tears came unwelcome to Alvin's eyes, but not to Eleanor's. Eleanor was only fourteen, but when she didn't want to cry, she didn't cry.

Wastenot hawed the horse and the little wagon lurched forward, Faith wincing as the girls patted her and the rain poured. Faith's gaze was somber as a cow's, and as mindless, looking back at her husband, back at the river. At times like birthing, Alvin thought, a woman becomes a beast, slack-minded as her body takes over and does its work. How else could she bear the pain? As if the soul of the earth possessed her the way it owns the souls of animals, making her part of the life of the whole world, unhitching her from family, from husband, from all the reins of the human race, leading her into the valley of ripeness and harvest and reaping and bloody death.

"She'll be safe now," the blacksmith said. "And we have horses here to pull your wagon out."

"It's slacking off," said Measure. "The rain is less, and the current's not so strong."

"As soon as your wife stepped ashore, it eased up," said the farmer-looking feller. "The rain's dying, that's sure."

"You took the worst of it in the water," said the blacksmith. "But you're all right now. Get hold of yourself, man, there's work to do."

Only then did Alvin come to himself enough to realize that he was crying. Work to do, that's right, get hold of yourself, Alvin Miller. You're no weakling, to bawl like a baby. Other men have lost a dozen children and still live their lives. You've had twelve, and Vigor lived to be a man, though he never did get to marry and have children of his own. Maybe Alvin had to weep because Vigor died so nobly; maybe he cried because it was so sudden.

David touched the blacksmith's arm. "Leave him be for a minute," he said softly. "Our oldest brother was carried off not ten minutes back. He got tangled in a tree floating down."

"It wasn't no *tangle*," Alvin said sharply. "He jumped that tree and saved our wagon, and your mother inside it! That river paid him back, that's what it did, it punished him."

Calm spoke quietly to the local men. "It run him up against that boulder there." They all looked. There wasn't even a smear of blood on the rock, it seemed so innocent.

"The Hatrack has a mean streak in it," said the blacksmith, "but I never seen this river so riled up before. I'm sorry about your boy. There's a slow, flat place downstream where he's bound to fetch up. Everything the river catches ends up there. When the storm lets up, we can go down and bring back the—bring him back."

Alvin wiped his eyes on his sleeve, but since his sleeve was soaking wet it didn't do much good. "Give me a minute more and I can pull my weight," said Alvin.

They hitched two more horses and the four beasts had no trouble pulling the wagon out against the much weakened current. By the time the wagon was set to rights again on the road, the sun was even breaking through.

"Wouldn't you know," said the blacksmith. "If you ever don't like the weather hereabouts, you just set a spell, cause it'll change."

"Not this one," said Alvin. "This storm was laid in wait for us."

The blacksmith put his arm across Alvin's shoulder and spoke real gentle. "No offense, mister, but that's crazy talk."

Alvin shrugged him off. "That storm and that river wanted us."

"Papa," said David, "you're tired and grieving. Best be still till we get to the road house and see how Mama is."

"My baby is a boy," said Papa. "You'll see. He would have been the seventh son of a seventh son."

That got their attention, right enough, that blacksmith and the other men as well. Everybody knew a seventh son had certain gifts, but the seventh son of a seventh son was about as powerful a birth as you could have.

"That makes a difference," said the blacksmith. "He'd have been a born dowser, sure, and water hates that." The others nodded sagely.

"The water had its way," said Alvin. "Had its way, and all done. It would've killed Faith and the baby, if it could. But since it couldn't, why, it killed my boy Vigor. And now when the baby comes, he'll be the sixth son, cause I'll only have five living."

"Some says it makes no difference if the first six be alive or not," said a farmer.

Alvin said nothing, but he knew it made all the difference. He had thought this baby would be a miracle child, but the river had taken care of that. If water don't stop you one way, it stops you another. He shouldn't have hoped for a miracle child. The cost was too high. All his eyes could see, all the way home, was Vigor dangling in the grasp of the roots, tumbling through the current like a leaf caught up in a dust devil, with the blood seeping from his mouth to slake the Hatrack's murderous thirst.

5

CAUL

Little Peggy stood in the window, looking out into the storm. She could see all those heartfires, especially one, one so bright it was like the sun when she looked at it. But there was a blackness all around them. No, not even black—a nothingness, like a part of the universe God hadn't finished making, and it swept around those lights as if to tear them from each other, sweep them away, swallow them up. Little Peggy knew what that nothingness was. Those times when her eyes saw the hot yellow heartfires, there were three other colors, too. The rich dark orange of the earth. The thin grey color of the air. And the deep black emptiness of water. It was the water that tore at them now. The river, only she had never seen it so black, so strong, so terrible. The heartfires were so tiny in the night.

"What do you see, child?" asked Oldpappy.

"The river's going to carry them away," said little Peggy.

"I hope not."

Little Peggy began to cry.

"There, child," said Oldpappy. "It ain't always such a grand thing to see afar off like that, is it."

She shook her head.

"But maybe it won't happen as bad as you think."

Just at that moment, she saw one of the heartfires break away and tumble off into the dark. "Oh!" she cried out, reaching as if her hand could snatch the light and put it back. But of course she couldn't. Her vision was long and clear, but her reach was short.

"Are they lost?" asked Oldpappy.

"One," whispered little Peggy.

"Haven't Makepeace and the others got there yet?"

"Just now," she said. "The rope held. They're safe now."

Oldpappy didn't ask her how she knew, or what she saw. Just patted her shoulder. "Because you told them. Remember that, Margaret. One was lost, but if you hadn't seen and sent help, they might all have died."

She shook her head. "I should've seen them sooner, Oldpappy, but I fell asleep."

"And you blame yourself?" asked Oldpappy.

"I should've let Bloody Mary nip me, and then Father wouldn't've been mad, and then I wouldn't've been in the spring house, and then I wouldn't've been asleep, and then I would've sent help in time—"

"We can all make daisy chains of blame like that, Maggie. It don't mean a thing."

But she knew it meant something. You don't blame blind people cause they don't warn you you're about to step on a snake—but you sure blame somebody with eyes who doesn't say a word about it. She knew her duty ever since she first realized that other folks couldn't see all that she could see. God gave her special eyes, so she'd better see and give warning, or the devil would take her soul. The devil or the deep black sea.

"Don't mean a thing," Oldpappy murmured. Then, like he just been poked in the behind with a ramrod, he went all straight and said, "Spring house! Spring house, of course." He pulled her close. "Listen to me, little Peggy.

It wasn't none of your fault, and that's the truth. The same water that runs in the Hatrack flows in the spring house brook, it's all the same water, all through the world. The same water that wanted them dead, it knew you could give warning and send help. So it sang to you and sent you off to sleep."

It made a kind of sense to her, it sure did. "How can that be, Oldpappy?"

"Oh, that's just in the nature of it. The whole universe is made of only four kinds of stuff, little Peggy, and each one wants to have its own way." Peggy thought of the four colors that she saw when the heartfires glowed, and she knew what all four were even as Oldpappy named them. "Fire makes things hot and bright and uses them up. Air makes things cool and sneaks in everywhere. Earth makes things solid and sturdy, so they'll last. But water, it tears things down, it falls from the sky and carries off everything it can, carries it off and down to the sea. If the water had its way, the whole world would be smooth, just a big ocean with nothing out of the water's reach. All dead and smooth. That's why you slept. The water wants to tear down these strangers, whoever they are, tear them down and kill them. It's a miracle you woke up at all."

"The blacksmith's hammer woke me," said little Peggy.

"That's it, then, you see? The blacksmith was working with iron, the hardest earth, and with a fierce blast of air from the bellows, and with a fire so hot it burns the grass outside the chimney. The water couldn't touch him to keep him still."

Little Peggy could hardly believe it, but it must be so. The blacksmith had drawn her from a watery sleep. The smith had *helped* her. Why, it was enough to make you laugh, to know the blacksmith was her friend this time.

There was shouting on the porch downstairs, and doors

opened and closed. "Some folks is here already," said Old-pappy.

Little Peggy saw the heartfires downstairs, and found the one with the strongest fear and pain. "It's their mama," said little Peggy. "She's got a baby coming."

"Well, if that ain't the luck of it. Lose one, and here already is a baby to replace death with life." Oldpappy shambled on out to go downstairs and help.

Little Peggy, though, she just stood there, looking at what she saw in the distance. That lost heartfire wasn't lost at all, and that was sure. She could see it burning away far off, despite how the darkness of the river tried to cover it. He wasn't dead, just carried off, and maybe somebody could help him. She ran out then, passed Oldpappy all in a rush, clattered down the stairs.

Mama caught her by the arm as she was running into the great room. "There's a birthing," Mama said, "and we need you."

"But Mama, the one that went downriver, he's still alive!"

"Peggy, we got no time for—"

Two boys with the same face pushed their way into the conversation. "The one downriver!" cried one.

"Still alive!" cried the other.

"How do you know!"

"He can't be!"

They spoke so all on top of each other that Mama had to hush them up just to hear them. "It was Vigor, our big brother, he got swept away—"

"Well he's alive," said little Peggy, "but the river's got him."

The twins looked to Mama for confirmation. "She know what she's talking about, Goody Guester?"

Mama nodded, and the boys raced for the door, shouting, "He's alive! He's still alive!"

"Are you sure?" asked Mama fiercely. "It's a cruel thing, to put hope in their hearts like that, if it ain't so."

Mama's flashing eyes made little Peggy afraid, and she couldn't think what to say.

By then, though, Oldpappy had come up from behind. "Now Peg," he said, "how would she know one was taken by the river, lessun she saw?"

"I know," said Mama. "But this woman's been holding off birth too long, and I got a care for the baby, so come on now, little Peggy, I need you to tell me what you see."

She led little Peggy into the bedroom off the kitchen, the place where Papa and Mama slept whenever there were visitors. The woman lay on the bed, holding tight to the hand of a tall girl with deep and solemn eyes. Little Peggy didn't know their faces, but she recognized their fires, especially the mother's pain and fear.

"Someone was shouting," whispered the mother.

"Hush now," said Mama.

"About him still alive."

The solemn girl raised her eyebrows, looked at Mama. "Is that so, Goody Guester?"

"My daughter is a torch. That's why I brung her here in this room. To see the baby."

"Did she see my boy? Is he alive?"

"I thought you didn't tell her, Eleanor," said Mama.

The solemn girl shook her head.

"Saw from the wagon. Is he alive?"

"Tell her, Margaret," said Mama.

Little Peggy turned and looked for his heartfire. There were no walls when it came to this kind of seeing. His flame was still there, though she knew it was afar off. This time, though, she drew near in the way she had, took a close look. "He's in the water. He's all tangled in the roots."

"Vigor!" cried the mother on the bed.

"The river wants him. The river says, Die, die."

Mama touched the woman's arm. "The twins have gone off to tell the others. There'll be a search party."

"In the dark!" whispered the woman scornfully.

Little Peggy spoke again. "He's saying a prayer, I think. He's saying—seventh son."

"Seventh son," whispered Eleanor.

"What does that mean?" asked Mama.

"If this baby's a boy," said Eleanor, "and he's born while Vigor's still alive, then he's the seventh son of a seventh son, and all of them alive."

Mama gasped. "No wonder the river—" she said. No need to finish the thought. Instead she took little Peggy's hands and led her to the woman on the bed. "Look at this baby, and see what you see."

Little Peggy had done this before, of course. It was the chief use they had for torches, to have them look at an unborn baby just at the birthing time. Partly to see how it lay in the womb, but also because sometimes a torch could see who the baby was, what it would be, could tell stories of times to come. Even before she touched the woman's belly, she could see the baby's heartfire. It was the one that she had seen before, that burned so hot and bright that it was like the sun and the moon, to compare it to the mother's fire. "It's a boy," she said.

"Then let me bear this baby," said the mother. "Let him breathe while Vigor still breathes!"

"How's the baby set?" asked Mama.

"Just right," said little Peggy.

"Head first? Face down?"

Little Peggy nodded.

"Then why won't it come?" demanded Mama.

"She's been telling him not to," said little Peggy, looking at the mother.

"In the wagon," the mother said. "He was coming, and I did a beseeching."

"Well you should have told me right off," said Mama sharply. "Speck me to help you and you don't even tell me he's got a beseeching on him. You, girl!"

Several young ones were standing near the wall, wide-eyed, and they didn't know which one she meant.

"Any of you, I need that iron key from the ring on the wall."

The biggest of them took it clumsily from the hook and brought it, ring and all.

Mama dangled the large ring and the key over the mother's belly, chanting softly:

"Here's the circle, open wide,
Here's the key to get outside,
Earth be iron, flame be fair,
Fall from water into air."

The mother cried out in sudden agony. Mama tossed away the key, cast back the sheet, lifted the woman's knees, and ordered little Peggy fiercely to *see*.

Little Peggy touched the woman's womb. The boy's mind was empty, except for a feeling of pressure and gathering cold as he emerged into the air. But the very emptiness of his mind let her see things that would never be plainly visible again. The billion billion paths of his life lay open before him, waiting for his first choices, for the first changes in the world around him to eliminate a million futures every second. The future was there in everyone, a flickering shadow that she could only sometimes see, and never clearly, looking through the thoughts of the present moment; but here, for a few precious moments, little Peggy could see them sharp.

And what she saw was death down every path. Drowning, drowning, every path of his future led this child to a watery death.

"Why do you hate him so!" cried little Peggy.

"What?" demanded Eleanor.

"Hush," said Mama. "Let her see what she sees."

Inside the unborn child, the dark blot of water that surrounded his heartfire seemed so terribly strong that little Peggy was afraid he would be swallowed up.

"Get him out to breathe!" shouted little Peggy.

Mama reached in, even though it tore the mother something dreadful, and hooked the baby by the neck with strong fingers, drawing him out.

In that moment, as the dark water retreated inside the child's mind, and just before the first breath came, little Peggy saw ten million deaths by water disappear. Now, for the first time, there were some paths open, some paths leading to a dazzling future. And all the paths that did not end in early death had one thing in common. On all those paths, little Peggy saw herself doing one simple thing.

So she did that thing. She took her hands from the slackening belly and ducked under her mother's arm. The baby's head had just emerged, and it was still covered with a bloody caul, a scrap of the sac of soft skin in which he had floated in his mother's womb. His mouth was open, sucking inward on the caul, but it didn't break, and he couldn't breathe.

Little Peggy did what she had seen herself do in the baby's future. She reached out, took the caul from under the baby's chin, and pulled it away from his face. It came whole, in one moist piece, and in the moment it came away, the baby's mouth cleared, he sucked in a great breath, and then gave that mewling cry that birthing mothers hear as the song of life.

Little Peggy folded the caul, her mind still full of the visions she had seen down the pathways of this baby's life. She did not know yet what the visions meant, but they made such clear pictures in her mind that she knew she would never forget them. They made her afraid, because so much would depend on her, and how she used the birth caul that was still warm in her hands.

"A boy," said Mama.

"Is he," whispered the mother. "Seventh son?"

Mama was tying the cord, so she couldn't spare a glance at little Peggy. "Look," she whispered.

Little Peggy looked for the single heartfire on the distant river. "Yes," she said, for the heartfire was still burning.

Even as she watched, it flickered, died.

"Now he's gone," said little Peggy.

The woman on the bed wept bitterly, her birthwracked body shuddering.

"Grieving at the baby's birth," said Mama. "It's a dreadful thing."

"Hush," whispered Eleanor to her mother. "Be joyous, or it'll darken the baby all his life!"

"Vigor," murmured the woman.

"Better nothing at all than tears," said Mama. She held out the crying baby, and Eleanor took it in competent arms—she had cradled many a babe before, it was plain. Mama went to the table in the corner and took the scarf that had been blacked in the wool, so it was night-colored clear through. She dragged it slowly across the weeping woman's face, saying, "Sleep, Mother, sleep."

When the cloth came away, the weeping was done, and the woman slept, her strength spent.

"Take the baby from the room," said Mama.

"Don't he need to start his sucking?" asked Eleanor.

"She'll never nurse this babe," said Mama. "Not unless you want him to suck hate."

"She can't hate him," said Eleanor. "It ain't his fault."

"I reckon her milk don't know that," said Mama. "That right, little Peggy? What teat does the baby suck?"

"His mama's," said little Peggy.

Mama looked sharp at her. "You sure of that?"

She nodded.

"Well, then, we'll bring the baby in when she wakes up. He doesn't need to eat anything for the first night, anyway." So Eleanor carried the baby out into the great room, where the fire burned to dry the men, who stopped trading stories about rains and floods worse than this one long enough to look at the baby and admire.

Inside the room, though, Mama took little Peggy by the chin and stared hard into her eyes. "You tell me the truth, Margaret. It's a serious thing, for a baby to suck on its mama and drink up hate."

"She won't hate him, Mama," said little Peggy.

"What did you see?"

Little Peggy would have answered, but she didn't know words to tell most of the things she saw. So she looked at the floor. She could tell from Mama's quick draw of breath that she was ripe for a tongue-lashing. But Mama waited, and then her hand came soft, stroking across little Peggy's cheek. "Ah, child, what a day you've had. The baby might have died, except you told me to pull it out. You even reached in and opened up its mouth—that's what you did, isn't it?"

Little Peggy nodded.

"Enough for a little girl, enough for one day." Mama turned to the other girls, the ones in wet dresses, leaning against the wall. "And you, too, you've had enough of a day. Come out of here, let your mama sleep, come out and get dry by the fire. I'll start a supper for you, I will."

But Oldpappy was already in the kitchen, fussing around, and refused to hear of Mama doing a thing. Soon enough she was out with the baby, shooing the men away so she could rock it to sleep, letting it suck her finger.

Little Peggy figured after a while that she wouldn't be

missed, so she snuck up the stairs to the attic ladder and up the ladder into the lightless, musty space. The spiders didn't bother her much, and the cats mostly kept the mice away, so she wasn't afraid. She crawled right to her secret hiding place and took out the carven box that Oldpappy gave her, the one he said his own papa brought from Ulster when he came to the colonies. It was full of the precious scraps of childhood—stones, strings, buttons—but now she knew that these were nothing compared to the work before her all the rest of her life. She dumped them right out, and blew into the box to clear away the dust. Then she laid the folded caul inside and closed the lid.

She knew that in the future she would open that box a dozen dozen times. That it would call to her, wake her from her sleep, tear her from her friends, and steal from her all her dreams. All because a baby boy downstairs had no future at all but death from the dark water, excepting if she used that caul to keep him safe, the way it once protected him in the womb.

For a moment she was angry, to have her own life so changed. Worse than the blacksmith coming, it was, worse than Papa and the hazel wand he whupped her with, worse than Mama when her eyes were angry. Everything would be different forever and it wasn't fair. Just for a baby she never invited, never asked to come here, what did she care about any old baby?

She reached out and opened the box, planning to take the caul and cast it into a dark corner of the attic. But even in the darkness, she could see a place where it was darker still: near her heartfire, where the emptiness of the deep black river was all set to make a murderer out of her.

Not me, she said to the water. You ain't part of me.

Yes I am, whispered the water. I'm all through you, and you'd dry up and die without me.

You ain't the boss of me, anyway, she retorted.

She closed the lid on the box and skidded her way down the ladder. Papa always said that she'd get splinters in her butt doing that. This time he was right. It stung something fierce, so she walked kind of sideways into the kitchen where Oldpappy was. Sure enough, he stopped his cooking long enough to pry the splinters out.

"My eyes ain't sharp enough for this, Maggie," he complained.

"You got the eyes of an eagle. Papa says so."

Oldpappy chuckled. "Does he now."

"What's for dinner?"

"Oh, you'll like this dinner, Maggie."

Little Peggy wrinkled up her nose. "Smells like chicken."

"That's right."

"I don't like chicken soup."

"Not just soup, Maggie. This one's a-roasting, except the neck and wings."

"I hate *roast* chicken, too."

"Does your Oldpappy ever lie to you?"

"Nope."

"Then you best believe me when I tell you this is one chicken dinner that'll make you *glad*. Can't you think of any way that a partickler chicken dinner could make you glad?"

Little Peggy thought and thought, and then she smiled. "Bloody Mary?"

Oldpappy winked. "I always said that was a hen born to make gravy."

Little Peggy hugged him so tight that he made choking sounds, and then they laughed and laughed.

Later that night, long after little Peggy was in bed, they brought Vigor's body home, and Papa and Makepeace set to making a box for him. Alvin Miller hardly looked alive, even when Eleanor showed him the baby. Until she said, "That torch girl. She says that this baby is the seventh son of a seventh son."

Alvin looked around for someone to tell him if it was true.

"Oh, you can trust her," said Mama.

Tears came fresh to Alvin's eyes. "That boy hung on," he said. "There in the water, he hung on long enough."

"He knowed what store you set by that," said Eleanor.

Then Alvin reached for the baby, held him tight, looked down into his eyes. "Nobody named him yet, did they?" he asked.

"Course not," said Eleanor. "Mama named all the other boys, but you always said the seventh son'd have—"

"My own name. Alvin. Seventh son of a seventh son, with the same name as his father. Alvin Junior." He looked around him, then turned to face toward the river, way off in the nighttime forest. "Hear that, you Hatrack River? His name is Alvin, and you didn't kill him after all."

Soon they brought in the box and laid out Vigor's body with candles, to stand for the fire of life that had left him. Alvin held up the baby, over the coffin. "Look on your brother," he whispered to the infant.

"That baby can't see nothing yet, Papa," said David.

"That ain't so, David," said Alvin. "He don't *know* what he's seeing, but his eyes can see. And when he gets old enough to hear the story of his birth, I'm going to tell him that his own eyes saw his brother Vigor, who gave his life for this baby's sake."

It was two weeks before Faith was well enough to travel. But Alvin saw to it that he and his boys worked hard for their keep. They cleared a good spot of land, chopped the winter's firewood, set some charcoal heaps for Makepeace Smith, and widened the road. They also felled four big trees and made a strong bridge across the Hatrack River, a covered bridge so that even in a rainstorm people could cross that river without a drop of water touching them.

Vigor's grave was the third one there, beside little Peggy's two dead sisters. The family paid respects and prayed there on the morning that they left. Then they got in their wagon and rode off westward. "But we leave a part of ourselves here always," said Faith, and Alvin nodded.

Little Peggy watched them go, then ran up into the attic, opened the box, and held little Alvin's caul in her hand. No danger—for now, at least. Safe for now. She put the caul away and closed the lid. You better be something, baby Alvin, she said, or else you caused a powerful lot of trouble for nothing.

6

RIDGEBEAM

Axes rang, strong men sang hymns at their labor, and Reverend Philadelphia Thrower's new church building rose tall over the meadow commons of Vigor Township. It was all happening so much faster than Reverend Thrower ever expected. The first wall of the meetinghouse had hardly been erected a day or so ago, when that drunken one-eyed Red wandered in and was baptized, as if the mere sight of the churchhouse had been the fulcrum on which he could be levered upward to civilization and Christianity. If a Red as benighted as Lolla-Wossiky could come unto Jesus, what other miracles of conversion might not be wrought in this wilderness when his meetinghouse was finished and his ministry firmly under way?

Reverend Thrower was not altogether happy, however, for there were enemies of civilization far stronger than the barbarity of the heathen Reds, and the signs were not all so hopeful as when Lolla-Wossiky donned White man's clothing for the first time. In particular what somewhat darkened this bright day was the fact that Alvin Miller was not among the workers. And his wife's excuses for him had run out. The trip to find a proper millstone quarry had

ended, he had rested for a day, and by rights he should
be here.

"What, is he ill?" asked Thrower.

Faith tightened her lips. "When I say he *won't* come,
Reverend Thrower, it's not to say he *can't* come."

It confirmed Thrower's gathering suspicions. "Have I
offended him somewise?"

Faith sighed and looked away from him, toward the
posts and beams of the meetinghouse. "Not you yourself,
sir, not the way a man treads on another, as they say."
Abruptly she became alert. "Now what is that?"

Right up against the building, most of the men were
tying ropes to the north half of the ridgebeam, so they
could lift it into place. It was a tricky job, and all the
harder because of the little boys wrestling each other in
the dust and getting underfoot. It was the wrestlers that
had caught her eye. "Al!" cried Faith. "Alvin Junior, you
let him up this minute!" She took two strides toward the
cloud of dust that marked the heroic struggles of the six-
year-olds.

Reverend Thrower was not inclined to let her end the
conversation so easily. "Mistress Faith," said Reverend
Thrower sharply. "Alvin Miller is the first settler in these
parts, and people hold him in high regard. If he's against
me for some reason, it will greatly harm my ministry. At
least you can tell me what I did to give offense."

Faith looked him in the eye, as if to calculate whether
he could stand to hear the truth. "It was your foolish
sermon, sir," she said.

"Foolish?"

"You couldn't know any better, being from England,
and—"

"From Scotland, Mistress Faith."

"And being how you're educated in schools where they
don't know much about—"

"The University of Edinburgh! Don't know much indeed, I—"

"About hexes and doodles and charms and beseechings and suchlike."

"I know that claiming to use such dark and invisible powers is a burning offense in the lands that obey the Lord Protector, Mistress Faith, though in his mercy he merely banishes those who—"

"Well looky there, that's my point," she said triumphantly. "They're not likely to teach you about that in university, now, are they? But it's the way we live here, and calling it a superstition—"

"I called it hysteria—"

"That don't change the fact that it works."

"I understand that you *believe* that it works," said Thrower patiently. "But everything in the world is either science or miracles. Miracles came from God in ancient times, but those times are over. Today if we wish to change the world, it is not magic but science that will give us our tools."

From the set of her face, Thrower could see that he wasn't making much impression on her.

"Science," she said. "Like feeling head bumps?"

He doubted she had tried very hard to hide her scorn. "Phrenology is an infant science," he said coldly, "and there are many flaws, but I am seeking to discover—"

She laughed—a girlish laugh, that made her seem much younger than a woman who had borne fourteen children. "Sorry, Reverend Thrower, but I just remembered how Measure called it 'dowsing for brains,' and he allowed as how you'd have slim luck in these parts."

True words, thought Reverend Thrower, but he was wise enough not to say so. "Mistress Faith, I spoke as I did to let people understand that there are superior ways of thought in the world today, and we need no longer be bound by the delusions of—"

It was no use. Her patience had quite run out. "My boy looks about to get himself smacked with a spare joist if he don't let up on them other boys, Reverend, so you'll just have to excuse me." And off she went, to fall on six-year-old Alvin and three-year-old Calvin like the vengeance of the Lord. She was a champion tongue-lasher. He could hear the scolding from where he stood, and that with the breeze blowing the other way, too.

Such ignorance, said Thrower to himself. I am needed here, not only as a man of God among near heathens, but also as a man of science among superstitious fools. Somebody whispers a curse and then, six months later, something bad happens to the person cursed—it always does, something bad happens to everybody at least twice a year—and it makes them quite certain that their curse had malefic effect. Post hoc ergo propter hoc.

In Britain, students learned to discard such elementary logic errors while yet studying the trivium. Here it was a way of life. The Lord Protector was quite right to punish practitioners of magic arts in Britain, though Thrower would prefer that he do it on grounds of stupidity rather than heresy. Treating it as heresy gave it too much dignity, as if it were something to be feared rather than despised.

Three years ago, right after he earned his Doctor of Divinity degree, it had dawned on Thrower what harm the Lord Protector was actually doing. He remembered it as the turning point of his life; wasn't it also the first time the Visitor had come to him? It was in his small room in the rectory of St. James Church in Belfast, where he was junior assistant pastor, his first assignment after ordination. He was looking at a map of the world when his eye strayed to America, to where Pennsylvania was clearly marked, stretching from the Dutch and Swedish colonies westward until the lines faded in the obscure country beyond the Mizzipy. It was as if the map then came alive, and he saw the flood of people arriving in the New World. Good Puritans, loyal churchmen, and sound businessmen all went to New England; Papists, Royalists, and scoundrels all went to the rebellious slave country of Virginia, Carolina, and Jacobia, the so-called Crown Colonies. The sort of people who, once they found their place, stayed in it forever.

But it was another kind of people went to Pennsylvania. Germans, Dutchmen, Swedes, and Huguenots fled their countries and turned Pennsylvania Colony into a slop pot, filled with the worst human rubbish of the continent. Worse yet, they would *not* stay put. These dimwitted country people would debark in Philadelphia, discover that the settled—Thrower did not call them "civilized"—portions of Pennsylvania were too crowded for them, and immediately head westward into the Red country to hew out a farm among the trees. Never mind that the Lord Protector specifically forbade them to settle there. What did such pagans care for law? Land was what they wanted, as if the mere ownership of dirt could turn a peasant into a squire.

Then Thrower's vision of America turned from bleak to black indeed. He saw that war was coming to America with the new century. In his vision, he foresaw that the King of France would send that obnoxious Corsican colonel, Bonaparte, to Canada, and his people would stir up the Reds from the French fortress town in Detroit. The Reds would fall upon the settlers and destroy them; scum they might be, but they were mostly English scum, and the vision of the Reds' savagery made Thrower's skin crawl.

Yet even if the English won, the overall result would be the same. America west of the Appalachees would never be a Christian land. Either the damned Papist French and Spanish would have it, or the equally damned heathen Reds would keep it, or else the most depraved sort of Englishmen would thrive and thumb their noses at Christ and the Lord Protector alike. Another whole continent would be lost to the knowledge of the Lord Jesus. It was such a fearsome vision that Thrower cried out, thinking none would hear him in the confines of his little room.

But someone did hear him. "There's a life's work for a man of God," said someone behind him. Thrower turned at once, startled; but the voice was gentle and warm, the face old and kindly, and Thrower was not afraid for more than a moment, despite the fact that the door and window were both locked tight, and no natural man could have come inside his little room.

Thinking that this man was surely a part of the manifestation he had just seen, Thrower addressed him reverently. "Sir, whoever you are, I have seen the future of North America, and it looks like the victory of the devil to me."

"The devil takes his victories," the man replied, "wherever men of God lose heart, and leave the field to him."

Then the man simply was not there.

Thrower had known in that moment what the work of his life would be. To come to the wilds of America, build a country church, and fight the devil in his own country. It had taken him three years to get the money and the permission of his superiors in the Scottish Church, but now he was here, the posts and beams of his church were rising, their white and naked wood a bright rebuke to the dark forest of barbarism from which they had been hewn.

Of course, with such a magnificent work under way, the devil was bound to take notice. And it was obvious that the devil's chief disciple in Vigor Township was Alvin Miller. Even though all his sons were here, helping to build the churchhouse, Thrower knew that this was Faith's doing. The woman had even allowed as how she was probably Church of Scotland in her heart, even though she was born in Massachusetts; her membership would mean that Thrower could look forward to having a congregation—

provided Alvin Miller could be kept from wrecking everything.

And wreck it he would. It was one thing if Alvin had been offended by something Thrower had inadvertently said and done. But to have the quarrel be about belief in sorcery, right from the start—well, there was no hiding from this conflict. The battle lines were laid. Thrower stood on the side of science and Christianity, and on the other side stood all the powers of darkness and superstition; the bestial, carnal nature of man was on the other side, with Alvin Miller as its champion. I am only at the beginning of my tournament for the Lord, thought Thrower. If I can't vanquish this first opponent, then no victory will ever be possible for me.

"Pastor Thrower!" shouted Alvin's oldest boy, David. "We're ready to raise the ridgebeam!"

Thrower started toward them at a trot, then remembered his dignity and walked the rest of the way. There was nothing in the gospels to imply that the Lord ever ran—only walked, as befitted his high station. Of course, Paul had his comments about running a good race, but that was allegory. A minister was supposed to be a shadow of Jesus Christ, walking in His way and representing Him to the people. It was the closest these people would ever come to beholding the majesty of God. It was Reverend Thrower's duty to deny the vitality of his youth and walk at the reverent pace of an old man, though he was only twenty-four.

"You mean to bless the ridgebeam, don't you?" asked one of the farmers. It was Ole, a Swedish fellow from the banks of the Delaware, and so a Lutheran at heart; but he was willing enough to help build a Presbyterian Church here in the Wobbish valley, seeing how the nearest church besides that was the Papist Cathedral in Detroit.

"I do indeed," said Thrower. He laid his hand on the heavy, axehewn beam.

"Reverend Thrower." It was a child's voice behind him, piercing and loud as only a child's voice can be. "Ain't it a kind of a charm, to give a blessing to a piece of wood?"

Thrower turned around to see Faith Miller already hushing the boy. Only six years old, but Alvin Junior was obviously going to grow up to be just as much trouble as his father. Maybe more—Alvin Senior had at least had the good grace to stay away from the church-raising.

"You go on," said Faith. "Never mind him. I haven't learned him yet when to speak and when to keep silence."

Even though his mother's hand was tight-clamped over his mouth, the boy's eyes were steady, looking right at him. And when Thrower turned back around, he found that all the grown men were looking at him expectantly. The child's question was a challenge that he had to answer, or he'd be branded a hypocrite or fool before the very men he had come to convert.

"I suppose that if you think my blessing actually does something to change the nature of the ridgebeam," he said, "that might be akin to ensorcelment. But the truth is that the ridgebeam itself is just the *occasion*. Whom I'm really blessing is the congregation of Christians who'll gather under this roof. And there's nothing magic about that. It's the power and love of God we're asking for, not a cure for warts or a charm against the evil eye."

"Too bad," murmured a man. "I could use a cure for warts."

They all laughed, but the danger was over. When the ridgebeam went up, it would be a Christian act to raise it, not a pagan one.

He blessed the ridgebeam, taking care to change the usual prayer to one that specifically did *not* confer any special properties upon the beam itself. Then the men tugged on the rope, and Thrower sang out "O Lord Who on the Mighty Sea" at the top of his magnificent baritone voice, to give them the rhythm and inspiration for their labors.

All the time, however, he was acutely aware of the boy Alvin Junior. It was not just because of the boy's embarrassing challenge a moment ago. The child was as simple-minded as most children—Thrower doubted he had any dire purpose in mind. What drew him to the child was something else entirely. Not any property in the boy himself, but rather something about the people near him. They always seemed to keep him in attention. Not that they always *looked* at him—that would be a full-time occupation, he ran about so much. It was as if they were always aware of him, the way the college cook had always been aware of the dog in the kitchen, never speaking to it, but stepping over and around it without so much as pausing in his work.

It wasn't just the boy's family, either, that was so careful of him. Everyone acted the same way—the Germans, the Scandinavians, the English, newcomers and old-timers alike. As if the raising of this boy were a community project, like the raising of a church or the bridging of a river.

"Easy, easy, easy!" shouted Wastenot, who was perched near the east ridgepole to guide the heavy beam into place. It had to be just so, for the rafters to lean evenly against it and make a sturdy roof.

"Too far your way!" shouted Measure. He was standing on scaffolding above the crossbeam on which rested the short pole that would support the two ridgebeams where they butted ends in the middle. This was the most crucial point of the whole roof, and the trickiest to get right; they had to lay the ends of two heavy beams onto a pole top that was barely two palms wide. That was why Measure stood there, for he had grown into his name, keen-eyed and careful.

"Right!" shouted Measure. "More!"

"My way again!" shouted Wastenot.

"Steady!" shouted Measure.

"Set!" shouted Wastenot.

Then "Set!" from Measure, too, and the men on the ground relaxed the tension on the ropes. As the lines went slack, they let out a cheer, for the ridgebeam now went half the length of the church. It was no cathedral, but it was still a mighty thing to achieve in this benighted place, the largest structure anyone had dared to think of for a hundred miles around. The mere fact of building it was a declaration that the settlers were here to stay, and not French, not Spanish, not Cavaliers, not Yankees, not even the savage Reds with their fire arrows, no man would get these folks to leave this place.

So of course Reverend Thrower went inside, and so did all the others, to see the sky blocked for the first time by a ridgebeam no less than forty feet in length—and that only half of what it would finally be. My church, thought Thrower, and already finer than most I saw in Philadelphia itself.

Up on the flimsy scaffolding, Measure was driving a wooden pin through the notch in the end of the ridge-beam and down into the hole in the top of the ridgepole. Wastenot was doing the same at his end, of course. The pins would hold the beam in place until the rafters could be laid. When that was done, the ridgebeam would be so strong that they could almost remove the crossbeam, if it weren't needed for the chandelier that would light the church at night. At night, so that the stained glass would shine out against the darkness. That's how grandiose a place Reverend Thrower had in mind. Let their simple minds stand in awe when they see this place, and so reflect upon the majesty of God.

Those were his thoughts when, suddenly, Measure let out a shout of fear, and all saw in horror that the center ridgepole had split and shivered at the blow of Measure's mallet against the wooden pin, bouncing the great heavy ridgebeam some six feet into the air. It pulled the beam out of Wastenot's hands at the other end, and broke the scaffolding like tinderwood. The ridgebeam seemed to hover in the air a moment, level as you please, then rushed downward as if the Lord's own foot were stomping it.

And Reverend Thrower knew without looking that there would be someone directly under that beam, right under the midpoint of it when it landed. He knew because he was *aware* of the boy, of how he was running just exactly the wrong direction, of how his own shout of "Alvin!" brought the boy to a stop in just exactly the wrong place.

And when he looked, it was exactly as he knew it would be—little Al standing there, looking up at the shaven tree that would grind him into the floor of the church. Nothing else would be damaged—because the beam was level, its impact would be spread across the whole floor. The boy was too small even to slow the ridgebeam's fall. He would be broken, crushed, his blood spattering the white wood of the church floor. I'll never get that stain out, thought Thrower—insanely, but one could not control one's own thoughts in the moment of death.

Thrower saw the impact as if it were a blinding flash of light. He heard the crash of wood on wood. He heard the screams. Then his eyes cleared and he saw the ridgebeam lying there, the one end exactly where it should be, the other too, but in the middle, the beam split in two parts, and between the two parts little Alvin standing, his face white with terror.

Untouched. The boy was untouched.

Thrower didn't understand German or Swedish, but he knew what the muttering near him meant, well enough. Let them blaspheme—I must understand what has happened here, thought Thrower. He strode to the boy, placed his hands on the child's head, searching for injury. Not a hair out of place, but the boy's head felt warm, very warm, as if he had been standing near a fire. Then Thrower knelt and looked at the wood of the ridgebeam. It was cut as smooth as if the wood had grown that way, just exactly wide enough to miss the boy entirely.

Al's mother was there only a moment later, scooping up her boy, sobbing and babbling with relief. Little Alvin also cried. But Thrower had other things on his mind. He *was* a man of science, after all, and what he had seen was not possible. He made the men step off the length of the ridgebeam, measuring it again. It lay exactly its original length along the floor—the east end just as far from the west end as it should be. The boy-sized chunk in the middle had simply disappeared. Vanished in a momentary flash of fire that left Alvin's head and the butt ends of the wood as hot as coals, yet not marked or seared in any way.

Then Measure began yelling from the crossbeam, where he dangled by his arms, having caught himself after the collapse of the scaffolding. Wantnot and Calm climbed up and got him down safely. Reverend Thrower had no thought for that. All he could think about was a six-year-old boy who could stand under a falling ridgebeam, and the beam would break and make room for him. Like the Red Sea parting for Moses, on the right hand and the left.

"Seventh son," murmured Wastenot. The boy sat astride the fallen ridgebeam, just west of the break.

"What?" asked Reverend Thrower.

"Nothing," said the young man.

"You said 'Seventh son,'" said Thrower. "But it's little Calvin who's the seventh."

Wastenot shook his head. "We had another brother. He died a couple minutes after Al was born." Wastenot shook his head again. "Seventh son of a seventh son."

"But that makes him devil's spawn," said Thrower, aghast.

Wastenot looked at him with contempt. "Maybe in England you think so, but around here we look on such to be a healer, maybe, or a doodlebug, and a right good one of whatever he is." Then Wastenot thought of something and grinned. "'Devil's spawn,'" he repeated, maliciously savoring the words. "Sounds like hysteria to me."

Furious, Thrower stalked out of the church.

He found Mistress Faith sitting on a stool, holding Alvin Junior on her lap and rocking him as he continued to whimper. She was scolding him gently. "Told you not to run without looking, always underfoot, can't never hold still, makes a body go plumb lunatic looking after you—" Then she saw Thrower standing before her, and fell silent.

"Don't worry," she said. "I'll not bring him back here."

"For his safety, I'm glad," said Thrower. "If I thought my churchhouse had to be built at the cost of a child's life, I'd sooner preach in the open air all the days of my life."

She looked close at him and knew that he meant it with his whole heart. "It's no fault of yourn," she said. "He's always been a clumsy boy. Seems to live through scrapes that'd kill an ordinary child."

"I'd like—I'd like to understand what happened in there."

"Ridgepole shivered, of course," she said. "It happens sometimes."

"I mean—how it happened to miss him. The beam split—before it touched his head. I want to feel his head, if I may—"

"Not a mark on him," she said.

"I know. I want to feel it to see if—"

She rolled her eyes upward and muttered, "Dowsing for brains," but she also moved her hands away so he could feel the child's head. Slowly now, and carefully, trying to understand the map of the boy's skull, to read the ridges and bumps, the troughs and depressions. He had no need to consult a book. The books were nonsense, anyway. He had found that out quite quickly—they all spouted idiotic generalities, such as, "The Red will always have a bump just over the ear, indicating savagery and cannibalism," when of course Reds had just as much variety in their heads as Whites. No, Thrower had no faith in those books—but he *had* learned a few things about people with particular skills, and head bumps they had in common. He had developed a knack of understanding, a map of the shapes of the human skull; he knew as his hands passed over Al's head what it was he found there.

Nothing remarkable, that's what he found. No one trait that stood out above all others. Average. As average as can be. So utterly average that it could be a virtual textbook example of normality, if only there were any textbook worth reading.

He lifted his fingers away, and the boy—who had stopped crying under his hands—twisted on his mother's lap to look at him. "Reverend Thrower," he said, "your hands are so cold I like to froze." Then he squirmed off his mother's lap and ran off, shouting for one of the German boys, the one he had been wrestling so savagely before.

Faith laughed ruefully. "You see how quickly they forget?"

"And you, too," he said.

She shook her head. "Not me," she said. "I don't forget a thing."

"You're already smiling."

"I *go on*, Reverend Thrower. I just go on. That's not the same as forgetting."

He nodded.

"So—tell me what you found," she said.

"Found?"

"Feeling his bumps. Brain-dowsing. Does he got any?"

"Normal. Absolutely normal. Not a single thing unusual about his head."

She grunted. "*Nothing* unusual?"

"That's right."

"Well, if you ask me, that's pretty unusual right there, if a body was smart enough to notice it." She picked up the stool and carried it off, calling to Al and Cally as she went.

After a moment, Reverend Thrower realized she was right. Nobody was so perfectly average. Everybody had *some* trait that was stronger than the others. It wasn't normal for Al to be so well balanced. To have every possible skill that could be marked by the skull, and to have it in exactly even proportions. Far from being average, the child was extraordinary, though Thrower had no notion what it would mean in the child's life. Jack of all trades and master of none? Or master of all?

Superstition or not, Thrower found himself wondering. A seventh son of a seventh son, a startling shape to the head, and the miracle—he could think of no other word—of the ridgebeam. An ordinary child would have died this day. Natural law demanded it. But someone or something was protecting this child, and natural law had been overruled.

Once the talk had subsided, the men resumed work on the roof. The original beam was useless, of course, and they carried the two sections of it outside. After what had happened, they had no intention of using the beams for anything at all. Instead they set to work and completed another beam by midafternoon, rebuilt the scaffolding, and by nightfall the whole roof ridge was set in place. No one spoke of the incident with the ridgebeam, at least not in Thrower's presence. And when he went to look for the shivered ridgepole, he couldn't find it anywhere.

7

ALTAR

Alvin Junior wasn't scared when he saw the beam falling, and he wasn't scared when it crashed to the floor on either side. But when all the grown-ups started carrying on like the Day of Rapture, a-hugging him and talking in whispers, *then* he got scared. Grown-ups had a way of doing things for no reason at all.

Like the way Papa was setting on the floor by the fire, just studying the split pieces of the shivered ridgepole, the piece of wood that sprung under the weight of the ridgebeam and sent it all crashing down. When Mama was being herself, not Papa or nobody could bring big old pieces of split and dirty wood into her house. But today Mama was as crazy as Papa, and when he showed up toting them big old splinters of wood, she just bent over, rolled up the rug, and got herself out of Papa's way.

Well, anybody who didn't know to get out of Papa's way when he had that look on his face was too dumb to live. David and Calm was lucky, they could go off to their own houses on their own cleared land, where their own wives had their own suppers cooking and they could decide whether to be crazy or not. The rest of them weren't so lucky. With Papa and Mama being crazy, the rest of them had to be crazy, too. Not one of the girls fought with any of the others, and they all helped fix supper and clean up after without a word of complaint. Wastenot and Wantnot went out and chopped wood and did the evening milking without so much as punching each other in the arm, let alone getting in a wrestling match, which was right disappointing to Alvin Junior, seeing as how he always got to wrestle the loser, which was the best wrestling he ever got to do, them being eighteen years old and a real challenge, not like the boys he usually hunkered down with. And Measure, he just sat there by the fire, whittling out a big old spoon for Mama's cooking pot, never so much as looking up—but he was waiting, just like the others, for Papa to come back to his right self and yell at somebody.

The only normal person in the house was Calvin, the three-year-old. The trouble was that normal for him meant tagging along after Alvin Junior like a kitten on a mouse's trail. He never came close enough to *play* with Alvin Junior, or to touch him or talk to him or anything useful. He was just there, always there at the edge of things, so Alvin would look up just as Calvin looked away, or catch a glimpse of his shirt as he ducked behind a door, or sometimes in the dark of night just hear a faint breathing that was closer than it ought to be, which told him Calvin wasn't lying on his cot, he was standing right there by Alvin's bed, *watching*. Nobody ever seemed to notice it. It had been more than a year since Alvin gave up trying to get him to stop. If Alvin Junior ever said, "Ma, Cally's pestering me," Mama would just say, "Al Junior, he didn't say a thing, he didn't touch you, and if you don't like him just standing quiet as a body could ask, well, that's just too bad for you, because it suits me fine. I wish certain other of my children could learn to be as still." Alvin figured that it wasn't that Calvin was *normal* today, it's that the rest of the family had just come up to his regular level of craziness.

Papa just stared and stared at the split wood. Now and then he'd fit it together the way it was. Once he spoke, real quiet. "Measure, you sure you got all them pieces?"

Measure said, "Ever single bit, Pa, I couldn't've got more with a broom. I couldn't've got more if I'd bent down and lapped it up like a dog."

Ma was listening, of course. Papa once said that when Ma was paying attention, she could hear a squirrel fart in the woods a half mile away in the middle of a storm with the girls rattling dishes and the boys all chopping wood. Alvin Junior wondered sometimes if that meant Ma knew more witchery than she let on, since one time he sat in the woods not three yards away from a squirrel for more than an hour, and he never heard it so much as belch.

Anyway, she was right there in the house tonight, so of course she heard what Papa asked, and she heard what Measure answered, and her being as crazy as Papa, she lashed out like as if Measure had just taken the name of the Lord. "You mind your tongue, young man, because the Lord said unto Moses on the mount, honor your father and mother that your days may be long on the land which the Lord your God has given you, and when you speak fresh to your father then you are taking days and weeks and even *years* off your own life, and your soul is not in such a condition that you should welcome an early visit to the judgment bar to meet your Savior and hear him say your eternal fate!"

Measure wasn't half so worried about his eternal fate as he was worried about Mama being riled at him. He didn't try to argue that he wasn't talking smart or being sassy—only a fool would do that when Mama was already hot. He just started in looking humble and begging her pardon, not to mention the forgiveness of Papa and the sweet mercy of the Lord. By the time she was done with ragging him, poor Measure had already apologized a half a dozen times, so that she finally just grumped and went back to her sewing.

Then Measure looked up at Alvin Junior and winked.

"I saw that," said Mama, "and if you don't go to hell, Measure, I'll get up a petition to Saint Peter to send you there."

"I'd sign that petition myself," said Measure, looking meek as a puppy dog that just piddled on a big man's boot.

"That's right you would," said Mama, "and you'd sign it in blood, too, because by the time I'm through with you there'll be enough open wounds to keep ten clerks in bright red ink for a year."

Alvin Junior couldn't help himself. Her dire threat just struck him funny. And even though he knew he was taking his life in his hands, he opened up his mouth to laugh. He knew that if he laughed he'd have Mama's thimble hard on his head, or maybe her hand clapped hard on his ear, or even her hard little foot smashed right down on his bare foot, which she did once to David the time he told her she should have learnt the word *no* sometime before she had thirteen mouths to cook for.

This was a matter of life and death. This was more frightening than the ridgebeam, which after all never hit him, which was more than he could say for Mama. So he caught that laugh before it got loose, and he turned it into the first thing he could think of to say.

"Mama," he said, "Measure can't sign no petition in blood, cause he'd already be dead, and dead people don't bleed."

Mama looked him in the eye and spoke slow and careful. "They do when I tell them to."

Well, that did it. Alvin Junior just laughed out loud. And that set half the girls to laughing. Which made Measure laugh. And finally Mama laughed, too. They all just laughed and laughed till they were mostly crying and Mama started sending people upstairs to bed, including Alvin Junior.

All the excitement had Alvin Junior feeling pretty spunky, and he hadn't figured out yet that sometimes he ought to keep all that jumpiness locked up tight. It happened that Matilda, who was sixteen and fancied herself a lady, was walking up the stairs right in front of him. Everybody hated walking anywhere behind Matilda, she took such delicate, ladylike steps. Measure always said he'd rather walk in line behind the moon, cause it moved faster. Now Matilda's backside was right in Al Junior's face, swaying back and forth, and he thought of what Measure said about the moon, and reckoned how Matilda's backside was just about as round as the moon, and then he got to wondering what it would be like to *touch* the moon, and whether it would be hard like a beetle's back or squishy as a slug. And when a boy six years old who's already feeling spunky gets a thought like that in his head, it's not even half a second till his finger is two inches deep in delicate flesh.

Matilda was a real good screamer.

Al might have got slapped right then, except Wastenot and Wantnot were right behind him, saw the whole thing, and laughed so hard at Matilda that she started crying and fled on up the stairs two steps at a time, not ladylike at all. Wastenot and Wantnot carried Alvin up the stairs between them, so high up he got a little dizzy, singing that old song about St. George killing the dragon, only they sang it about St. Alvin, and where the song usually said something about poking the old dragon a thousand times and his sword didn't melt in the fire, they changed *sword* to *finger* and made even Measure laugh.

"That's a filthy filthy song!" shouted ten-year-old Mary, who stood guard outside the big girls' door.

"Better stop singing that song," said Measure, "before Mama hears you."

Alvin Junior could never understand why Mama didn't like that song, but it was true that the boys never sang it where she could hear. The twins stopped singing and clambered up the ladder to the loft. At that moment the door to the big girls' room was flung open and Matilda, her eyes all red from crying, stuck her head out and shouted, "You'll be sorry!"

"Ooh, I'm sorry, I'm sorry," Wantnot said in a squeaky voice.

Only then did Alvin remember that when the girls set out to get even, he would be the main victim. Calvin was still considered the baby, so he was safe enough, and the twins were older and bigger and there was always two of them. So when the girls got riled, Alvin was first in line for their deadly wrath. Matilda was sixteen, Beatrice was fifteen, Elizabeth was fourteen, Anne was twelve, Mary was ten, and they all preferred picking on Alvin to practically any other recreation that the Bible would permit. One time when Alvin was tormented past endurance and only Measure's strong arms held him back from hot-blooded murder with a hayfork, Measure allowed as how the punishments of hell would most likely consist of living in the same house with five women who were all about twice a man's size. Ever since then, Alvin wondered what sin he committed before he was born to make him deserve to grow up half-damned to start with.

Alvin went into the little room he shared with Calvin and just set there, waiting for Matilda to come and kill him. But she didn't come and didn't come, and he realized that she was probably waiting till after the candles were all out, so that no one would know which of his sisters snuck in and snuffed him out. Heaven knew he'd given them all ample reason to want him dead in the last two months alone. He was trying to guess whether they'd stifle him with Matilda's goosedown pillow—which would be the first time he was ever allowed to touch it—or if he'd die with Beatrice's precious sewing scissors in his heart, when all of a sudden he realized that if he didn't get outside to the privy in about twenty-five seconds he'd embarrass himself right in his trousers.

Somebody was in the privy, of course, and Alvin stood outside jumping and yelling for three minutes and still they wouldn't come out. It occurred to him that it was probably one of the girls, in which case this was the most devilish plan they'd ever come up with, keeping him out of the privy when they knew he was scared to go into the woods after dark. It was a terrible vengeance. If he messed himself he'd be so ashamed he'd probably have to change his name and run away, and that was a whole lot worse than a poke in the behind. It made him mad as a constipated buffalo, it was so unfair.

Finally he was mad enough to make the ultimate threat. "If you don't come out I'll do it right in front of the door so you'll step in it when you come out!"

He waited, but whoever was in there *didn't* say, "If you do I'll make you lick it off my shoe," and since that was the customary response, Al realized for the first time that the person inside the privy might not be one of his sisters after all. It was certainly not one of the boys. Which left only two possibilities, each one worse than the other. Al was so mad at himself he smacked his own head with his fist, but it didn't make him feel no better. Papa would probably give him a lick, but even worse would be Mama. She might give him a tongue-lashing, which was bad enough, but if she was in a real vile temper, she'd get that cold look on her face and say real soft, "Alvin Junior, I used to hope that at least one of my boys would be a born gentleman, but now I see my life was wasted," which always made him feel about as low as he knew how to feel without dying.

So he was almost relieved when the door opened and

Papa stood there, still buttoning his trousers and looking none too happy. "Is it safe for me to step out this door?" he asked coldly.

"Yup," said Alvin Junior.

"What?"

"Yes sir."

"Are you sure? There's some wild animals around here that think it's smart to leave their do on the ground outside privy doors. I tell you that if there's any such animal I'll lay a trap and catch it by the back end one of these nights. And when I find it in the morning, I'll stitch up its bung hole and turn it loose to bloat up and die in the woods."

"Sorry, Papa."

Papa shook his head and started walking toward the house. "I don't know what's wrong with your bowel, boy. One minute you don't need to go and the next minute you're about to die."

"Well if you'd just build another outhouse I'd be fine," Al Junior muttered. Papa didn't hear him, though, because Alvin didn't actually say it till the privy door was closed and Papa'd gone back to the house, and even then he didn't say it very loud.

Alvin rinsed his hands at the pump a long time, because he feared what was waiting for him back in the house. But then, alone outside in the darkness, he began to be afraid for another reason. Everybody said that a White man never could hear when a Red man was walking through the woods, and his big brothers got some fun out of telling Alvin that whenever he was alone outside, especially at night, there was Reds in the forest, watching him, playing with their flint-bladed tommy-hawks and itching to have his scalp. In broad daylight, Al didn't believe them, but at night, his hands cold with the water, a chill ran through him, and he thought he even knew where the Red was standing. Just over his shoulder, back over near the pigsty, moving so quiet that the pigs didn't even grunt and the dogs didn't bark or nothing. And they'd find Al's body, all hairless and bloody, and *then* it'd be too late. Bad as his sisters were—and they were *bad*—Al figured they'd be better than dying from a Red man's flint in his head. He fair to flew from the pump to the house, and he *didn't* look back to see if the Red was really there.

As soon as the door was closed, he forgot his fears of silent invisible Reds. Things were right quiet in the house, which was pretty suspicious to start with. The girls were never quiet till Papa shouted at them at least three times each night. So Alvin walked up real careful, looking before every step, checking over his shoulder so often he started getting a crick in his neck. By the time he was inside his room with the door closed he was so jittery that he almost hoped they'd do whatever they were planning to do and get it over with.

But they didn't do it and they didn't do it. He looked around the room by candlelight, turned down his bed, looked into every corner, but there was nothing there. Calvin was asleep with his thumb in his mouth, which meant that if they *had* prowled around his room, it had been a while ago. He began to wonder if maybe, just this once, the girls had decided to leave him be or even do their dirty tricks to the twins. It would be a whole new life for him, if the girls started being nice. Like as if an angel came down and lifted him right out of hell.

He stripped off his clothes quick as he could, folded them, and put them on the stool by his bed so they wouldn't be full of roaches in the morning. He had kind of an agreement with the roaches. They could get into anything they wanted if it was on the floor, but they didn't climb into Calvin's bed or Alvin's neither, and they didn't climb onto his stool. In return, Alvin never stomped them. As a result Alvin's room was pretty much the roach sanctuary of the house, but since they kept the treaty, he and Calvin were the only ones who never woke up screaming about roaches in the bed.

He took his nightgown off its peg and pulled it on over his head.

Something bit him under the arm. He cried out from the sharp pain. Something else bit him on the shoulder. Whatever it was, it was all over inside his nightgown, and as he yanked it off, it kept right on nipping him everywhere. Finally it was off, and he stood there stark naked slapping and brushing with his hands to try to get the bugs or whatever they were off him.

Then he reached down and carefully picked up his nightgown. He couldn't see anything scurrying away from it, and even when he shook it and shook it, nary a bug fell off. Something else fell off. It glinted for a moment in the candlelight and made a tiny twinking sound when it hit the floor.

Only then did Alvin Junior notice the stifled giggling from the room next door. Oh, they got him, they got him sure. He sat on the edge of his bed, picking pins out of his nightgown and poking them into the bottom corner of his quilt. He never thought they'd be so mad they'd risk losing one of Mama's precious steel pins, just to get even with him. But he should have known. Girls never did have any bounds of fair play, the way boys did. When a boy knocked you down in a wrestling match, why, he'd either jump on you or wait for you to get back up, and either way you'd be even—both up or both down. But Al knew from painful experience that girls'd kick you when you were down and gang up on you whenever they had the chance. When they fought, they fought in order to end the fight as quick as they could. Took all the fun out of it.

Just like tonight. It wasn't a fair punishment, him poking

her with his finger, and them getting him all jabbed up with pins. A couple of those places were bleeding, they stabbed so deep. And Alvin didn't reckon Matilda had so much as a bruise, though he wished she did.

Alvin Junior wasn't mean, no sir. But sitting there on the edge of the bed, taking pins out of his nightgown, he couldn't help but notice the roaches going about their business in the cracks of the floor, and he couldn't help imagining what it would be like if all those roaches just happened to go a-calling in a certain room full of giggles.

So he knelt down on the floor and set the candle right there, and he began whispering to the roaches, just the way he did the day he made his peace treaty with them. He started telling them all about nice smooth sheets and soft squishy skin they could scamper on, and most of all about Matilda's satin pillowcase on her goosedown pillow. But they didn't seem to care about that. Hungry, that's all they are, thought Alvin. All they care about is food, food and fear. So he started telling them about food, the most perfectly delicious food they ever ate in their life. The roaches perked right up and came close to listen, though nary one of them climbed on him, which was right in keeping with the treaty. All the food you ever wanted, all over that soft pink skin. And it's safe, too, not a speck of danger, nothing to worry about, you just go on in there and find the food on that soft pink squishy smooth skin.

Sure enough, a few of the roaches started skittering under Alvin's door, and then more and more of them, and finally the whole troop went off in a single great cavalry charge under the door, through the wall, their bodies shiny and glowing in the candlelight, guided by their eternal insatiable hunger, fearless because Al had told them there wasn't nothing to fear.

It wasn't ten seconds before he heard the first whoop from the room next door. And within a minute the whole house was in such an uproar you'd've thought it was on fire. Girls screaming, boys shouting, and big old boots stomping as Papa rushed up the stairs and squashed roaches. Al was about as happy as a pig in mud.

Finally things started calming down in the next room. In a minute they'd come in to check on him and Calvin, so he blew out the candle, ducked under the covers, and whispered for the roaches to hide. Sure enough, here came Mama's footsteps in the hall outside. Just at the last moment, Alvin Junior remembered that he wasn't wearing his nightgown. He snaked out his hand, snatched the nightgown, and pulled it under the covers just as the door opened. Then he concentrated on breathing easy and regular.

Mama and Papa came in, holding up candles. He heard them pull down Calvin's covers to check for roaches, and he feared they might pull down his as well. That would be such a shameful thing, to sleep like an animal without a stitch on. But the girls, who knew he couldn't possibly be asleep so soon after getting stuck with so many pins, they were naturally afraid of what Alvin might tell Mama and Papa, so they made sure to hustle them out of the room before they could do more than shine a candle in Alvin's face to make sure he was asleep. Alvin held his face absolutely still, not even twitching his eyelids. The candle went away, the door softly closed.

Still he waited, and sure enough, the door opened again. He could hear the padding of bare feet across the floor. Then he felt Anne's breath against his face and heard her whisper in his ear. "We don't know how you did it, Alvin Junior, but we know you set those roaches onto us."

Alvin pretended not to hear anything. He even snored a little.

"You don't fool me, Alvin Junior. You better not go to sleep tonight, because if you do, you'll never wake up, you hear me?"

Outside the room, Papa was saying, "Where's Anne got to?"

She's in here, Papa, threatening to kill me, thought Alvin. But of course he didn't say it out loud. Anyway, she was just trying to scare him.

"We'll make it look like an accident," said Anne. "You always have accidents, nobody will think it's murder."

Alvin was beginning to believe her, more and more.

"We'll carry your body out and stuff it down the privy hole, and they'll all think you went to relieve yourself and fell in."

That would work, thought Alvin. Anne was just the one to think of something so devilish clever, since she was the very best at secretly pinching people and being a good ten feet away before they screamed. That was why she always kept her fingernails so long and sharp. Even now, Alvin could feel one of those sharp nails scraping along his cheek.

The door opened wider. "Anne," whispered Mama, "you come out of there this instant."

The fingernail quit scratching. "I was just making sure little Alvin was all right." Her bare feet padded back out of the room.

Soon all the doors were closed, and he heard Papa's and Mama's shoes clattering down the stairs.

He knew that by rights he should still be scared to death by Anne's threats, but it wasn't so. He had won the battle. He pictured the roaches crawling all over the girls, and he started to laugh. Well, that wouldn't do. He had to stifle that, breathe calm as could be. His whole body shook from trying to hold in the laughter.

There was somebody in the room.

He couldn't hear anything, and when he opened his eyes he couldn't see anybody. But he knew somebody was there. Hadn't come in the door, so they must've come in the open window. That's plain silly, Alvin told himself, there isn't a soul in here. But he lay still, all laughter gone out of him, because he could *feel* it, somebody standing there. No, it's a nightmare, that's all, I'm still spooked from thinking about Reds watching me outside, or maybe from Anne's threat, something like that, if I just lie here with my eyes closed it'll go away.

The blackness inside Al's eyelids turned pink. There was a light in his room. A light as bright as daylight. There wasn't no candle in the world, no, not even a lantern that could burn so bright as that. Al opened his eyes, and all his dread turned into terror, for now he saw that what he feared was real.

There was a man standing at the foot of his bed, a man shining as if he was made of sunlight. The light in the room was coming from his skin, from his chest where his shirt was tore open, from his face, and from his hands. And in one of those hands, a knife, a sharp steel knife. I am going to die, thought Al. Just like Anne promised me, only there wasn't no way his sisters could conjure up such an awful apparition as this one. This bright Shining Man had come on his own, that was sure, and planned to kill Alvin Junior for his own sins and not cause somebody else had set him on.

Then it was like as if the light from the man pushed right through Alvin's skin and came inside him, and the fear just went right out of him. The Shining Man might have him a knife, and he might've snuck on into the room without so much as opening a door, but he didn't mean no harm to Alvin. So Alvin relaxed a little and wriggled up in his bed till he was mostly sitting, leaning up against the wall, watching the Shining Man, waiting to see what all he'd do.

The Shining Man took his bright steel knife and brought the blade against his other palm—and cut. Alvin saw the

gleaming crimson blood flow from the wound in the Shining Man's hand, stream down his forearm, and drip from
his elbow onto the floor. He hadn't seen four drops, though,
before he came to see a vision in his mind. He could see
his sisters' room, he knew the place, but it was different.
The beds were up high, and his sisters were giants, so all
he could see clear was big old feet and legs. Then he realized he was seeing a little creature's view of the room. A
roach's view. In his vision he was scurrying, filled with
hunger, absolutely fearless, knowing that if he could get
up onto those feet, those legs, there'd be food, all the food
he'd ever want. So he rushed, he climbed, he scurried,
searching. But there wasn't no food, not a speck of it,
and now huge hands reached and swept him off, and then
a great huge shadow loomed over him, and he felt the hard
sharp crushing agony of death.

Not once, but many times, dozens of times, the hope
of food, the confidence that no harm would come; then
disappointment—nothing to eat, nothing at all—and after
disappointment, terror and injury and death. Each small
trusting life, betrayed, crushed, battered.

And then in his vision he was one who lived, one who
got away from the looming, stomping boots, under the
beds, into the cracks in the walls. He fled from the room
of death, but not into the old place, not into the safe room,
because now that was no longer safe. That was where the
lies came from. That was the place of the betrayer, the liar,
the killer who had sent them into this place to die. There
were no words in this vision, of course. There could be
no words, no clarity of thought in a roach's brain. But Al
had words and thoughts, and he knew more than any
roach what the roaches had learned. They had been promised something about the world, they had been made *sure*
of it, and then it was a lie. Death was a fearful thing, yes,
flee that room; but in the other room, there was worse

than death—there the world had gone crazy, it was a place where anything could happen, where nothing could be trusted, where nothing was certain. A terrible place. The worst place.

Then the vision ended. Alvin sat there, his hands pressed against his eyes, sobbing desperately. They suffered, he cried out silently, they suffered, and I did it to them, I betrayed them. That's what the Shining Man came to show me. I made the roaches trust me, but then I cheated them and sent them to die. I've done murder.

No, not murder! Who ever heard of roach-killing being murder? Nobody in the whole world would call it that.

But it didn't matter what other folks thought of it, Al knew that. The Shining Man had come to show him that murder was murder.

And now the Shining Man was gone. The light was gone from the room, and when Al opened his eyes, there was no one in the room but Cally, fast asleep. Too late even to beg forgiveness. In pure misery Al Junior closed his eyes and cried some more.

How long was it? A few seconds? Or did Alvin doze off and not notice the passage of a much longer time? Never mind how long—the light came back. Once again it came into him, not just through his eyes, but piercing clear to his heart, whispering to him, calming him. Again Alvin opened his eyes and looked at the face of the Shining Man, waiting for him to speak. When he said nothing, Alvin thought it was *his* turn, and so he stammered out the words, so weak compared to the feelings in his heart. "I'm sorry, I'll never do it again, I'll—"

He was babbling, he knew it, couldn't even hear himself speak he was so upset. But the light grew brighter for a moment, and he felt a question in his mind. Not a word was spoke, mind you, but he knew that the Shining Man wanted him to say what it was he was sorry *for*.

And when he thought about it, Alvin wasn't altogether sure what all was wrong. Sure it wasn't the killing itself— you could starve to death if you didn't slaughter a pig now and then, and it wasn't hardly murder when a weasel killed himself a mouse, was it?

Then the light pushed at him again, and he saw another vision. Not roaches this time. Now he saw the image of a Red man, kneeling before a deer, calling it to come and die; the deer came, all trembling and its eyes wide, the way they are when they're scared. It knew it was coming to die. The Red loosed him an arrow, and there it stood, quivering in the doe's flank. Her legs wobbled. She fell. And Alvin knew that in this vision there wasn't no sin at all, because dying and killing, they were both just a part of life. The Red was doing right, and so was the deer, both acting according to their natural law.

So if the evil he done wasn't the death of the roaches, what was it? The power he had? His knack for making things go just where he wanted, making them break just in the right place, understanding how things ought to be and helping them get that way? He'd found that right useful, as he made and fixed the things a boy makes and fixes in a rough country household. He could fit the two pieces of a broken hoe handle, fit them so tight that they joined forever without glue or tack. Or two pieces of torn leather, he didn't even have to stitch them; and when he tied a knot in string or rope, it stayed tied. It was the same knack he used with the roaches. Making them understand how things was supposed to be, and then they did what he wanted. Was that his sin, that knack of his?

The Shining Man heard his question before he even found words for it. Here came the push of light, and another vision. This time he saw himself pressing his hands against a stone, and the stone melted like butter under his hands, came out in just the shape he wanted, smooth and whole, fell from the side of the mountain and rolled away, a perfect ball, a perfect sphere, growing and growing until it was a whole world, shaped just the way his hands had made it, with trees and grass springing up on its face, and animals running and leaping and flying and swimming and crawling and burrowing on and above and within the ball of stone that he had made. No, it wasn't a terrible power, it was a glorious one, if he only knew how to use it.

Well if it ain't the dying and it ain't the knack, what did I do wrong?

This time the Shining Man didn't show him a thing. This time Alvin didn't see no burst of light, there wasn't a vision at all. Instead the answer just came, not from the Shining Man but from inside his own self. One second he felt too stupid ever to understand his own wickedness, and then the next second he saw it all as clear as could be.

It wasn't the roaches dying, and it wasn't the fact he made them do it. It was the fact that he made them do it just to suit his own pleasure. He told them it was for their own good, but it wasn't so, it was for Alvin's benefit alone. Harming his sisters, more than harming the roaches, and all so Alvin could lie in his bed shaking with laughter because he got *even*—

The Shining Man heard the thoughts of Alvin's heart, yes sir, and Al Junior saw a fire leap from his gleaming eye and strike him in the heart. He had guessed it. He was right.

So Alvin made the most solemn promise of his whole life, right then and there. He had a knack, and he'd use it, but there was rules in things like that, rules that he would follow even if it killed him. "I'll never use it for myself again," said Alvin Junior. And when he said the words he felt like his heart was on fire, it burned so hot inside.

The Shining Man disappeared again.

Alvin lay back, slid down under the blanket, exhausted

from weeping, weary with relief. He'd done a bad thing, that was so. But as long as he kept this oath he made, as long as he only used his knack to help other people and never ever used it to help himself, why then he would be a good boy and didn't need to be ashamed. He felt lightheaded the way you do coming out of a fever, and that was about right, he had been healed of the wickedness that grew inside him for a spell. He thought of himself laughing when he'd just caused death for his own pleasure, and he was ashamed, but that shame was tempered, it was softened, cause he knew that it would never happen again.

As he lay there, Alvin once again felt the light grow in the room. But this time it didn't come from a single source. Not from the Shining Man at all. This time when he opened his eyes he realized the light was coming from himself. His own hands were shining, his own face must be glowing the way the Shining Man had. He threw off his covers and saw that his whole body glowed with light so dazzling he couldn't hardly bear to look at himself, except that he also couldn't bear to look anywhere else. Is this me? he thought.

No, not me. I'm shining like this because I've also got to do something. Just like the Shining Man did something for me, I've got something to do, too. But who am I supposed to do it for?

There was the Shining Man, visible again at the foot of his bed, but not shining no more. Now Al Junior realized that he knew this man. It was Lolla-Wossiky, that one-eyed whisky-Red who got himself baptized a few days ago, still wearing the White man's clothes they gave him when he turned Christian. With the light inside him now, Alvin saw clearer than he ever did before. He saw that it wasn't likker that poisoned this poor Red man, and it wasn't losing one eye that crippled him. It was something much darker, something growing like a mold inside his head.

The Red man took three steps and knelt beside the bed, his face only a little way from Alvin's eyes. What do you want from me? What am I supposed to do?

For the first time, the man opened his eyes and spoke. "Make all things whole," he said. A second later, Al Junior realized that the man had said it in his Red language— Shaw-Nee, he remembered, from what the grown-ups said when he was baptized. But Al had understood it plain as if it was the Lord Protector's own English. Make all things whole.

Well, that was Al's knack, wasn't it? Fixing things, making things go the way they were supposed to. Trouble was, he didn't even half understand how he did it, and he surely had no idea how to fix something that was alive.

Maybe, though, he didn't have to understand. Maybe he just had to *act*. So he lifted his hand, reached out as careful as he could, and touched Lolla-Wossiky's cheek, under the broken eye. No, that wasn't right. He raised his finger until it touched the slack eyelid where the Red man's other eye was supposed to be. Yes, he thought. Be whole.

The air crackled. Light sparked. Al gasped and pulled his hand away.

All the light was gone from the room. Just the moonlight now coming in the window. Not even a glimmer of the brightness was left. Like as if he just woke up from a dream, the strongest dream he ever had in his life.

It took a minute for Alvin's eyes to change so he could see. It wasn't no dream, that was sure. Cause there was the Red man, who had once been the Shining Man. You ain't dreaming when you got a Red man kneeling by your bed, tears coming out of his one good eye, and the other eye, where you just touched him—

That eyelid was still loose, hanging over nothing. The eye wasn't healed. "It didn't work," whispered Alvin. "I'm sorry."

It was a shameful thing, that the Shining Man had saved him from awful wickedness, and he hadn't done a thing for him in return. But the Red man said nary a word of reproach. Instead he reached out and took Alvin's naked shoulders in both his large strong hands and pulled him close, kissed him on the forehead, hard and strong, like a father to a son, like brothers, like true friends the day before they die. That kiss and all it held—hope, forgiveness, love—let me never forget that, Alvin said silently.

Lolla-Wossiky sprang to his feet. Lithe as a boy he was, not staggering drunk at all. Changed, he *was* changed, and it occurred to Alvin that maybe he *had* healed something, set something right, something deeper than his eyes. Cured him of the whisky-lust, maybe.

But if that was so, Al knew it wasn't himself that done it, it was the light that was in him for a time. The fire that had warmed him without burning.

The Red man rushed to the window, swung over the sill, hung for a moment by his hands, then disappeared. Alvin didn't even hear his feet touch the ground outside, he was that quiet. Like the cats in the barn.

How long had it been? Hours and hours? Would it be daylight soon? Or had it taken only a few seconds since Anne had whispered in his ear and the family had quieted down?

Didn't matter much. Alvin couldn't sleep, not now, not with all that had just happened. Why had this Red man come to him? What did it all mean, the light that filled Lolla-Wossiky and then came to fill him? He couldn't just lie here in bed, all full of wonder. So he got up, slithered into his nightgown as fast as he could, and slipped out of his door.

Now that he was in the hall, he heard talking from downstairs. Mama and Papa were still up. At first he wanted to rush down and tell them what all happened to him. But then he heard the tone of their voices. Anger, fear, all upset. Not a good time to come to them with a tale of a dream. Even if Alvin knew it wasn't a dream at all, that it was real, *they'd* treat it like a dream. And now that he was thinking straight, he couldn't tell them at all. What, that he sent the roaches into his sisters' room? The pins, the pokes, the threats? All of that would come out too, even though it felt like months, *years* ago to Alvin. None of it mattered now, compared to the vow he had taken and the future he thought might be in store for him—but it would matter to Mama and Papa.

So he tiptoed down the hall and down the stairs, just close enough to hear, just far enough to be around the corner and out of sight.

After just a few minutes, he forgot about being out of sight, too. He crept farther down, until he could see into the big room. Papa sat on the floor, surrounded with wood. It surprised Al Junior that Papa was still doing that, even after coming upstairs to kill roaches, even after so much time had passed. He was bent over now, his face buried in his hands. Mama knelt in front of him, the biggest hunks of wood between them.

"He's alive, Alvin," said Mama. "All the rest ain't worth never mind."

Papa lifted his head and looked at her. "It was water that seeped into the tree and froze and thawed, long before we even cut it down. And we happened to cut it in just such a way that the flaw never showed on the surface. But it was split three ways inside, just waiting for the weight of the ridgebeam. It was water done it."

"Water," said Mama, and there was derision in her voice.

"This is fourteen times the water's tried to kill him."

"Children always get in scrapes."

"The time you slipped on a wet floor when you were holding him. The time David knocked down the boiling

cauldron. Three times when he was lost and we found him
on the bank of the river. Last winter when the ice broke on
the Tippy-Canoe River—"

"You think he's the first child to fall into the water?"

"The poison water that made him throw up blood. The
mud-covered buffalo that charged him in that meadow—"

"Mud-covered. Everybody knows that buffaloes wallow
like pigs. It had nothing to *do* with water."

Papa slapped his hand down hard on the floor. The
sound rang like a gunshot through the house. It startled
Mama, and of course she started to look toward the stairs
to where the children would be sleeping. Alvin Junior
scampered right back up the stairs and waited out of sight
for her to order him back to bed. But she must not have
seen him, cause she didn't shout anything and nobody
came up after him.

When he tiptoed back down, they were still going at it,
only a little quieter.

Papa whispered, but there was fire in his eyes. "If you
think this *doesn't* have to do with water, then *you're* the
one that's a lunatic."

Mama was icy now. Alvin Junior knew that look—it
was the maddest Mama knew how to get. No slaps then,
no tongue-lashings. Just coldness and silence, and any
child who got that treatment from her began to long for
death and the tortures of hell, because at least it would be
warmer.

With Papa she wasn't silent, but her voice was terrible
cold. "The Savior himself drank water from the Samari-
tan well."

"I don't recollect that Jesus fell down that well, neither,"
said Papa.

Alvin Junior thought of hanging onto the well bucket,
falling down into the darkness, until the rope bound up on
the windlass and the bucket stopped just above the water,

where he would have drowned for certain. They told him he wasn't yet two years old when that happened, but he still dreamed sometimes about the stones that lined the inside of the well, getting darker and darker as he went down. In his dreams the well was ten miles deep and he fell forever before waking up.

"Then think of this, Alvin Miller, since you think you know scripture."

Papa started to protest that he didn't think nothing of the kind—

"The devil hisself said to the Lord in the desert that the angels would bear Jesus up lest he dash his foot against a stone."

"I don't know what that has to do with water—"

"It's plain that if I married you for brains I was plumb cheated."

Papa's face turned red. "Don't you call me no simpleton, Faith. I know what I know and—"

"He has a guardian angel, Alvin Miller. He has someone watching out for him."

"You and your scriptures. You and your angels."

"You tell me why else he had those fourteen accidents and not one of them so much as gave him a scrape on his arm. How many other boys get to six years old without no injury?"

Papa's face looked strange then, twisted up a little, as if it was hard for him to speak at all. "I tell you that there's something wants him dead. I *know* it."

"You don't know any such thing."

Papa spoke even slower, biting out the words as if each one caused him pain. "I *know.*"

He had such a hard time talking that Mama just went on and talked right over him. "If there's some devil plot to kill him—which I ain't saying, Alvin—then there's an even stronger heavenly plan to preserve him."

Then, suddenly, Papa didn't have no trouble talking at all. Papa just gave up saying the hard thing, and Alvin Junior felt let down, like when somebody said uncle before they even got throwed. But he knew, the minute he thought about it, that his papa wouldn't give up like that lessen it was some terrible force stopping him from speaking up. Papa was a strong man, not a bit cowardly. And seeing Papa beat down like that, well, it made the boy afraid. Little Alvin knew that Mama and Papa were talking about him, and even though he didn't understand half what they said, he knew that Papa was saying somebody wanted Alvin Junior dead, and when Papa tried to tell his real proof, the thing that made him *know*, something stopped his mouth and kept him still.

Alvin Junior knew without a word being said that whatever it was stopped Papa's mouth, it was the plain opposite of the shining light that had filled Alvin and the Shining Man tonight. There was something that wanted Alvin to be strong and good. And there was something else that wanted Alvin dead. Whatever the good thing was, it could bring visions, it could show him his terrible sin and teach him how to be shut of it forever. But the bad thing, it had the power to shut Papa's mouth, to beat down the strongest, best man Al Junior ever knew or heard of. And that made Al afraid.

When Papa went on with his arguments, his seventh son knew that he wasn't using the proof that counted. "Not devils, not angels," said Papa, "it's the elements of the universe, don't you see that he's an offense against nature? There's power in him like you nor I can't even guess. So much power that one part of nature itself can't bear it— so much power that he protects hisself even when he don't know he's doing it."

"If there's so much power in being seventh son of a seventh son, then where's *your* power, Alvin Miller? You're a seventh son—that ain't nothing, supposedly, but I don't see you doodlebugging or—"

"You don't know what I do—"

"I know what you *don't* do. I know that you don't believe—"

"I believe in every true thing—"

"I know that every other man is down at the commons building that fine church, except for you—"

"That preacher is a fool—"

"Don't you ever think that maybe God is using your precious seventh son to try to wake you up and call you to repentance?"

"Oh, is that the kind of God you believe in? The kind what tries to kill little boys so their papas will go to meeting?"

"The Lord has *saved* your boy, as a sign to you of his loving and compassionate nature—"

"The love and compassion that let my Vigor die—"

"But someday his patience will run out—"

"And then he'll murder another of my sons."

She slapped his face. Alvin Junior saw it with his own eyes. And it wasn't the offhand kind of cuffing she gave her sons when they lipped or loafed around. It was a slap that like to took his face off, and he fell over to sprawl on the floor.

"I'll tell you this, Alvin Miller." Her voice was so cold it burned. "If that church is finished, and there's none of your handiwork in it, then you will cease to be my husband and I will cease to be your wife."

If there were more words, Alvin Junior didn't hear them. He was up in his bed a-trembling that such a terrible thought could be thought, not to mention being spoke out loud. He had been afraid so many times tonight, afraid of pain, afraid of dying when Anne whispered murder in his ear, and most of all afraid when the Shining Man came to him and named his sin. But this was something else. This was the end of the whole universe, the end of the one sure thing, to hear Mama talk about not being with Papa anymore. He lay there in his bed, all kinds of thoughts dancing in his head so fast he couldn't lay hold of any one of them, and finally in all that confusion there wasn't nothing for it but to sleep.

IN THE MORNING he thought maybe it was all a dream, it had to be a dream. But there were new stains on the floor at the foot of his bed, where the blood of the Shining Man had dripped, so that wasn't a dream. And his parents' quarrel, that wasn't no dream neither. Papa stopped him after breakfast and told him, "You stay up here with me today, Al."

The look on Mama's face told him plain as day that what was said last night was still meant today.

"I want to help on the church," Alvin Junior said. "I ain't afraid of no ridgebeams."

"You're going to stay here with me, today. You're going to help me build something." Papa swallowed, and stopped himself from looking at Mama. "That church is going to need an altar, and I figure we can build a right nice one that can go inside that church as soon as the roof is on and the walls are up." Papa looked at Mama and smiled a smile that sent a shiver up Alvin Junior's back. "You think that preacher'll like it?"

That took Mama back, it was plain. But she wasn't the kind to back off from a wrestling match just because the other guy got one throw, Alvin Junior knew that much. "What can the boy do?" she asked. "He ain't no carpenter."

"He's got a good eye," said Papa. "If he can patch and tool leather, he can put some crosses onto the altar. Make it look good."

"Measure's a better whittler," said Mama.

"Then I'll have the boy *burn* the crosses in." Papa put his hand on Alvin Junior's head. "Even if he sits here all day and reads in the Bible, this boy ain't going down to that church till the last pew is in."

Papa's voice sounded hard enough to carve his words in stone. Mama looked at Alvin Junior and then at Alvin Senior. Finally she turned her back and started filling the basket with dinner for them as was going to the church.

Alvin Junior went outside to where Measure was hitching the team and Wastenot and Wantnot were loading roof shakes onto the wagon for the church.

"You aim to stand inside the church again?" asked Wantnot.

"We can drop logs down on you, and you can split them into shakes with your head," said Wastenot.

"Ain't going," said Alvin Junior.

Wastenot and Wantnot exchanged identical knowing looks.

"Well, too bad," said Measure. "But when Mama and Papa get cold, the whole Wobbish Valley has a snowstorm." He winked at Alvin Junior, just the way he had last night, when it got him in so much trouble.

That wink made Alvin figure he could ask Measure a question that he wouldn't normally speak right out. He walked over closer, so his voice wouldn't carry to the others. Measure caught on to what Alvin wanted, and he squatted down right there by the wagon wheel, to hear what Alvin had to say.

"Measure, if Mama believes in God and Papa doesn't, how do I know which one is right?"

"I think Pa believes in God," said Measure.

"But if he don't. That's what I'm asking. How do I know about things like that, when Mama says one thing and Papa says another?"

Measure started to answer something easy, but he

stopped himself—Alvin could see in his face how he made up his mind to say something serious. Something true, instead of something easy. "Al, I got to tell you, I wisht I knew. Sometimes I figure ain't nobody knows nothing."

"Papa says you know what you see with your eyes. Mama says you know what you feel in your heart."

"What do *you* say?"

"How do *I* know, Measure? I'm only six."

"I'm twenty-two, Alvin, I'm a growed man, and I still don't know. I reckon Ma and Pa don't know, neither."

"Well, if they don't *know*, how come they get so mad about it?"

"Oh, that's what it means to be married. You fight all the time, but you never fight about what you think you're fighting about."

"What are they really fighting about?"

Alvin could see just the opposite thing this time. Measure thought of telling the truth, but he changed his mind. Stood up tall and tousled Alvin's hair. That was a sure sign to Alvin Junior that a grown-up was going to lie to him, the way they always lied to children, as if children weren't reliable enough to be trusted with the truth. "Oh, I reckon they just quarrel to hear theirselfs talk."

Most times Alvin just listened to grown-ups lie and didn't say nothing about it, but this time it was Measure, and he especially didn't like having Measure lie to him.

"How old will I have to be before you tell me straight?" asked Alvin.

Measure's eyes flashed with anger for just a second—nobody likes being called a liar—but then he grinned, and his eyes were sharp with understanding. "Old enough that you already guess the answer for yourself," he said, "but young enough that it'll still do you some good."

"When's that?" Alvin demanded. "I want you to tell me the truth now, all the time."

Measure squatted down again. "I can't always do that, Al, cause sometimes it'd just be too hard. Sometimes I'd have to explain things that I just don't know how to explain. Sometimes there's things that you have to figure out by living long enough."

Alvin was mad and he knew his face showed it.

"Don't you be so mad at me, little brother. I can't tell you some things because I just don't know myself, and that's not lying. But you can count on this. If I *can* tell you, I will, and if I can't, I'll just say so, and won't pretend."

That was the most fair thing a grown-up ever said, and it made Alvin's eyes fill up. "You keep that promise, Measure."

"I'll keep it or die, you can count on that."

"I won't forget, you know." Alvin remembered the vow he had made to the Shining Man last night. "I know how to keep a promise, too."

Measure laughed and pulled Alvin to him, hugged him right against his shoulder. "You're as bad as Mama," he said. "You just don't let up."

"I can't help it," said Alvin. "If I start believing you, then how'll I know when to stop?"

"Never stop," said Measure.

Calm rode up on his old mare about then, and Mama came out with the dinner basket, and everybody that was going, went. Papa took Alvin Junior out to the barn and in no time at all Alvin was helping notch the boards, and his pieces fit together just as good as Papa's. Truth to tell they fit even better, cause Al could use his knack for *this*, couldn't he? This altar was for everybody, so he could make the wood fit so snug that it wouldn't ever come apart, not at the joints or nowhere. Alvin even thought of making Papa's joints fit just as tight, but when he tried, he saw that Papa had something of a knack at this himself. The wood didn't join together to make one continuous piece, like Alvin's did—but it fit good enough, yes sir, so there wasn't no need to fiddle.

Papa didn't say much. Didn't have to. They both knew Alvin Junior had a knack for making things fit right, just like his Papa did. By nightfall the whole altar was put together and stained. They left it to dry, and as they walked into the house Papa's hand was firm on Alvin's shoulder. They walked together just as smooth and easy as if they were both parts of the same body, as if Papa's hand just growed there right out of Alvin's neck. Alvin could feel the pulse in Papa's fingers, and it was beating right in time with the blood pounding in his throat.

Mama was working by the fire when they came in. She turned and looked at them. "How is it?" she asked.

"It's the smoothest box I ever seen," said Alvin Junior.

"There wasn't a single accident at the church today," said Mama.

"Everything went real good here, too," said Papa.

For the life of him Alvin Junior couldn't figure out why Mama's words sounded like "I ain't going nowhere," and why Papa's words sounded like "Stay with me forever." But he knew he wasn't crazy to think so, cause right then Measure looked up from where he lay all sprawled out afore the fire and winked so only Alvin Junior could see.

8

VISITOR

Reverend Thrower allowed himself few vices, but one was to eat Friday supper with the Weavers. Friday *dinner* was more accurate, since the Weavers were shopkeepers and manufacturers, and didn't stop work for more than a snack at noon. It wasn't the quantity so much as the quality that brought Thrower back every Friday. It was said that Eleanor Weaver could take an old tree stump and make it taste like sweet rabbit stew. And it wasn't just the food, either, because Armor-of-God Weaver was a churchgoing man who knew his Bible, and conversation was on a higher plane. Not so elevated as conversation with highly educated churchmen, of course, but the best that could be had in this benighted wilderness.

They would eat in the room back of the Weavers' store, which was part kitchen, part workshop, and part library. Eleanor stirred the pot from time to time, and the smell of boiled venison and the day's bread baking mingled with the odors from the soapmaking shed out back and the tallow they used in candlemaking right here. "Oh, we're some of everything," said Armor, the first time Reverend Thrower visited. "We do things that every farmer hereabouts can do for himself—but we do it better, and when they buy it from us it saves them hours of work, which gives them time to clear and plow and plant more land."

The store itself, out front, was shelved to the ceiling, and the shelves were filled with dry goods brought in by wagon from points east. Cotton cloth from the spinning jennies and steam looms of Irrakwa, pewter dishes and iron pots and stoves from the foundries of Pennsylvania and Suskwahenny, fine pottery and small cabinets and boxes from the carpenters of New England, and even a few precious bags of spices shipped into New Amsterdam from the Orient. Armor Weaver had confessed once that it took all his life savings to buy his stock, and it was no sure bet that he'd prosper out here in this thinly settled land. But Reverend Thrower had noticed the steady stream of wagons coming up from the lower Wobbish and down the Tippy-Canoe, and even a few from out west in the Noisy River country.

Now, as they waited for Eleanor to announce that the venison stew was ready, Reverend Thrower asked him a question that had bothered him for some time.

"I've seen what they haul away," said Reverend Thrower, "and I can't begin to guess what they use to pay you. Nobody makes cash money around here, and not much they can trade that'll sell back east."

"They pay with lard and charcoal, ash and fine lumber, and of course food for Eleanor and me and—whoever else might come." Only a fool wouldn't notice that Eleanor was thickening enough to be about halfway to a baby. "But mostly," said Armor, "they pay with credit."

"Credit! To farmers whose scalps might well be traded for muskets or liquor in Fort Detroit next winter?"

"There's a lot more talk of scalping than there is scalping going on," said Armor. "The Reds around here aren't stupid. They know about the Irrakwa, and how they have seats in Congress in Philadelphia right along with White men, and how they have muskets, horses, farms, fields, and towns just like they do in Pennsylvania or Suskwahenny or New Orange. They know about the Cherriky people of Appalachee, and how they're farming and fighting right alongside Tom Jefferson's White rebels to keep their country independent from the King and the Cavaliers."

"They might also have noticed the steady stream of flatboats coming down the Hio and wagons coming west, and the trees falling down and the log houses going up."

"I reckon you're half right, Reverend," said Armor. "I reckon the Reds might go either way. Might try to kill us all, or might try to settle down and live among us. Living with us wouldn't be exactly easy for them—they aren't much used to town living, whereas it's the most natural way for White folks to live. But fighting us has got to be worse, cause if they do that they'll end up dead. They may think that killing White folks might scare the others into staying away. They don't know how it is in Europe, how the dream of owning land will bring people five thousand mile to work harder than they ever did in their lives and bury children who might have lived in the home country and risk having a tommyhock mashed into their brains cause it's better to be your own man than to serve any lord. Except the Lord God."

"And that's how it is with you, too?" asked Thrower. "Risk everything, for land?"

Armor looked at his wife Eleanor and smiled. She didn't smile back, Thrower noticed, but he also noticed that her eyes were beautiful and deep, as if she knew secrets that made her solemn even though she was joyful in her heart.

"Not land the way farmers own it, I'm no farmer, I'll tell you that," said Armor. "There's other ways to own land. You see, Reverend Thrower, I give them credit now because I believe in this country. When they come to trade with me, I make them tell me the names of all their neighbors, and make rough maps of the farms and streams where they live, and the roads and rivers along their way here. I make them carry letters that other folks writ, and I write their letters for them and ship them on back east to folks they left behind. I know where everything and everybody in the whole upper Wobbish and Noisy River country is and how to get there."

Reverend Thrower squinted and smiled. "In other words, Brother Armor, you're the government."

"Let's just say that if there comes a time when a government would come in handy, I'll be ready to serve," said Armor. "And in two years, three years, when more folks come through, and some more start making things, like bricks and pots and blackware, cabinets and kegs, beer and cheese and fodder, well, where do you think they'll come to sell it or to buy? To the store that gave them credit when their wives were longing for the cloth to make a bright-colored dress, or they needed an iron pot or a stove to keep out the winter cold."

Philadelphia Thrower chose not to mention that he had somewhat less confidence in the likelihood of grateful people staying loyal to Armor-of-God Weaver. Besides, thought Thrower, I might be wrong. Didn't the Savior say that we should cast our bread upon the waters? And even if Armor doesn't achieve all he dreams of, he will have done a good work, and helped to open this land to civilization.

The food was ready. Eleanor dished out the stew. When she set a fine white bowl in front of him, Reverend Thrower had to smile. "You must be right proud of your husband, and all that's he's doing."

Instead of smiling demurely, as Thrower expected that she would, Eleanor almost laughed aloud. Armor-of-God wasn't half so delicate. He just plain guffawed. "Reverend Thrower, you're a caution," said Armor. "When I'm up to my elbows in candle tallow, Eleanor's up to hers in soap. When I'm writing up folks' letters and having them delivered, Eleanor's drawing up maps and taking down names for our little census book. There ain't a thing I do that Eleanor isn't beside me, and not a thing she does that I'm not beside her. Except maybe her herb garden, which she cares for more than me. And Bible reading, which I care for more than her."

"Well, it's good she's a righteous helpmeet for her husband," said Reverend Thrower.

"We're helpmeets for each other," said Armor-of-God, "and don't you forget it."

He said it with a smile, and Thrower smiled back, but the minister was a little disappointed that Armor was so henpecked that he had to admit right out in the open that he wasn't in charge of his own business or his own home. But what could one expect, considering that Eleanor had grown up in that strange Miller family? The oldest daughter of Alvin and Faith Miller could hardly be expected to bend to her husband as the Lord intended.

The venison, however, was the best that Thrower had ever tasted. "Not gamy a bit," he said. "I didn't think wild deer could taste like this."

"She cuts off the fat," said Armor, "and throws in some chicken."

"Now you mention it," said Thrower, "I can taste it in the broth."

"And the deer fat goes into the soap," said Armor. "We never throw anything away, if we can think of any use for it."

"Just as the Lord intended," said Thrower. Then he fell to eating. He was well into his second bowl of stew and his third slice of bread when he made a comment that he thought was a jesting compliment. "Mrs. Weaver, your cooking is so good that it almost makes me believe in sorcery."

Thrower was expecting a chuckle, at the most. Instead, Eleanor looked down at the table just as ashamed as if he had accused her of adultery. And Armor-of-God sat up stiff and straight. "I'll thank you not to mention that subject in this house," he said.

Reverend Thrower tried to apologize. "I wasn't serious about it," he said. "Among rational Christians that sort of thing is a joke, isn't it? A lot of superstition, and I—"

Eleanor got up from the table and left the room.

"What did I say?" Thrower asked.

Armor sighed. "Oh, there's no way you could know," he said. "It's a quarrel that goes back to before we were married, when I first come out to this land. I met her when she came with her brothers to help build my first cabin—the soapmaking shed, now. She started to scatter spearmint on my floor and say some kind of rhyme, and I shouted for her to stop it and get out of my house. I quoted the Bible, where it says, You shall not suffer a witch to live. It made for a right testy half hour, you may be sure."

"You called her a witch, and she married you?"

"We had a few conversations in between."

"She doesn't believe in that sort of thing anymore, does she?"

Armor knitted his brows. "It ain't a matter of believing, it's a matter of doing, Reverend. She doesn't do it anymore. Not here, not anywhere. And when you sort of halfway accused her of it, well, it made her upset. Because it's a promise to me, you see."

"But when I apologized, why did she—"

"Well, there you are. You have your way of thinking, but you can't tell her that come-hithers and herbs and incantations got no power, because she's seen some things herself that you can't just explain away."

"Surely a man like you, well read in the scripture and

acquainted with the world, surely you can convince your wife to give up the superstitions of her childhood."

Armor gently laid his hand on Reverend Thrower's wrist. "Reverend, I got to tell you something that I didn't think I'd ever have to tell a grown man. A good Christian refuses to allow that stuff in his life because the only proper way to bring the hidden powers into your life is through prayer and the grace of the Lord Jesus. It ain't because it doesn't *work*."

"But it *doesn't*," said Thrower. "The powers of heaven are real, and the visions and visitations of angels, and all the miracles attested in the scripture. But the powers of heaven have nothing at all to do with young couples falling in love, or curing the croup, or getting chickens to lay, or all the other silly little things that the ignorant common people do with their so-called hidden wisdom. There's not a thing that's done by doodlebugging or hexing or whatever that can't be explained by simple scientific investigation."

Armor didn't answer for the longest while. The silence made Thrower quite uncomfortable, but he had no idea what more he could say. It hadn't occurred to him before that Armor could possibly *believe* in such things. It was a startling perspective. It was one thing to abstain from witchery because it was nonsense, and quite another to believe in it and abstain because it was unrighteous. It occurred to Thrower that this latter view was actually more ennobling: for Thrower to disdain witching was a matter of mere common sense, while for Armor and Eleanor it was quite a sacrifice.

Before he could find a way to express this thought, however, Armor leaned back on his chair and changed the subject entirely.

"Reckon your church is just about done."

With relief, Reverend Thrower followed Armor onto safer ground. "The roof was finished yesterday, and today they were able to clap all the boards on the walls. It'll be watertight tomorrow, with shutters on the windows, and when we get them glazed and the doors hung it'll be tight as a drum."

"I've got the glass coming by boat," said Armor. Then he winked. "I solved the problem of shipping on Lake Erie."

"How did you manage that? The French are sinking every third boat, even from Irrakwa."

"Simple. I ordered the glass from Montreal."

"French glass in the windows of a British church!"

"An American church," said Armor. "And Montreal's a city in America, too. Anyway, the French may be trying to get rid of us, but in the meantime we're a market for their manufactured goods, so the Governor, the Marquis de La Fayette, he doesn't mind letting his people turn a profit from our trade as long as we're here. They're going to ship it clear around and down into Lake Mizogan, and then barge it up the St. Joseph and down the Tippy-Canoe."

"Will they make it before the bad weather?"

"I reckon so," said Armor, "or they won't get paid."

"You're an amazing man," said Thrower. "But I wonder that you have so little loyalty to the British Protectorate."

"Well, you see, that's how it is," said Armor. "You grew up under the Protectorate, and so you still think like an Englishman."

"I'm a Scot, sir."

"A Brit, anyway. In your country, everybody who was even rumored to be practicing the hidden arts got exiled, right away, hardly even bothered with a trial, did they?"

"We try to be just—but the ecclesiastical courts are swift, and there is no appeal."

"Well, now, think about it. If everybody who had any gift for the hidden arts got shipped off to the American colonies, how would you ever see a lick of witchery while you were growing up?"

"I didn't see it because there's no such thing."

"There's no such thing *in Britain*. But it's the curse of good Christians in America, because we're up to our armpits in torches, doodlebugs, bog-stompers and hexifiers, and a child can't hardly grow to be four feet tall without bumping headlong into somebody's go-away or getting caught up in some prankster's speak-all spell, so he says everything that comes to mind and offends everybody for ten miles around."

"A speak-all spell! Now, Brother Armor, surely you can see that a touch of liquor does as much."

"Not to a twelve-year-old boy who never touched a drop of liquor in his life."

It was plain that Armor was talking from his own experience, but that didn't change the facts. "There is always another explanation."

"There's a powerful lot of explanations you can think up for anything that happens," said Armor. "But I tell you this. You can preach against conjuring, and you'll still have a congregation. But if you keep on saying that conjuring don't *work*, well, I reckon most folks'll wonder why they should come all the way to church to hear the preaching of a plumb fool."

"I have to tell the truth as I see it," said Thrower.

"You may see that a man cheats in his business, but you don't have to name his name from the pulpit, do you? No sir, you just keep giving sermons about honesty and hope it soaks in."

"You're saying that I should use an indirect approach."

"That's a right fine church building, Reverend Thrower, and it wouldn't be half so fine if it wasn't for your dream of how it ought to be. But the folks here figure it's *their* church. They cut the wood, they built it, it's on common land. And it'd be a crying shame if you were so stubborn that they up and gave your pulpit to another preacher."

Reverend Thrower looked at the remnants of dinner for a long time. He thought of the church, not unpainted raw lumber the way it was right now, but finished, pews in place, the pulpit standing high, and the room bright with sunlight through clean-glazed windows. It isn't just the place, he told himself, but what I can accomplish here. I'd be failing in my Christian duty if I let this place fall under the control of superstitious fools like Alvin Miller and, apparently, his whole family. If my mission is to destroy evil and superstition, then I must dwell among the ignorant and superstitious. Gradually I will bring them to knowledge of the truth. And if I can't convince the parents, then in time I can convert the children. It is the work of a lifetime, my ministry, so why should I throw it away for the sake of speaking the truth for a few moments only?

"You're a wise man, Brother Armor."

"So are you, Reverend Thrower. In the long run, even if we disagree here and there, I think we both want the same thing. We want this whole country to be civilized and Christian. And neither one of us would mind if Vigor Church became Vigor City, and Vigor City became the capital of the whole Wobbish territory. There's even talk back in Philadelphia about inviting Hio to become a state and join right in, and certainly they'll make such an offer to Appalachee. Why not Wobbish someday? Why not a country that stretches from sea to sea, White man and Red, every soul of us free to vote the government we want to make the laws we'll be glad to obey?"

It was a good dream. And Thrower could see himself within it. The man who had the pulpit of the greatest church in the greatest city of the territory would become the spiritual leader of a whole people. For a few minutes he believed so intensely in his dream that when he thanked Armor kindly for the meal and stepped outside, it made him gasp to see that right now Vigor Township consisted entirely of Armor's big store and its outbuildings, a fenced common with a dozen sheep grazing on it, and the raw wood shell of a big new church.

Still, the church was real enough. It was almost ready, the walls were *there*, the roof was on. He was a rational man. He had to see something solid before he could believe in a dream, but that church was solid enough now, and between him and Armor they could make the rest of the dream come true. Bring people to this place, make this the center of the territory. This church was big enough for town meetings, not just church meetings. And what about during the week? He'd be wasting his education if he didn't start a school for the children hereabouts. Teach them to read, to write, to cipher, and, above all, to *think*, to expunge all superstition from their minds, and leave behind nothing but pure knowledge and faith in the Savior.

He was so caught up in these thoughts that he didn't even realize he wasn't heading for Peter McCoy's farm downriver, where his bed would be waiting for him in the old log cabin. He was walking back up the slope to the meetinghouse. Not till he lit a couple of candles did he realize that he actually meant to spend the night here. It was his home, these bare wooden walls, as no other place in the world had ever been home to him. The sappish smell was like a madness in his nostrils, it made him want to sing hymns he'd never even heard before, and he sat there humming, thumbing through the pages of the Old Testament without so much as noticing that there were words on the paper.

He didn't hear them until they stepped onto the wooden floor. Then he looked up and saw, to his surprise, Mistress

Faith carrying a lantern, followed by the eighteen-year-old twins, Wastenot and Wantnot. They were carrying a large wooden box between them. It took a moment before he realized that the box was meant to be an altar. That in fact it was a rather fine altar, the wood was tightly fitted as any master cabinetmaker could manage, beautifully stained. And burnt into the boards surrounding the top of the altar were two rows of crosses.

"Where do you want it?" asked Wastenot.

"Father said we had to bring it down tonight, now that the roof and walls were done."

"Father?" asked Thrower.

"He made it for you special," said Wastenot. "And little Al burnt in the crosses hisself, seeing how he wasn't allowed down here no more."

By now Thrower was standing with them, and he could see that the altar had been lovingly built. It was the last thing he expected from Alvin Miller. And the perfectly even crosses hardly looked like the work of a six-year-old child.

"Here," he said, leading them to the place where he had imagined his altar would stand. It was the only thing in the meetinghouse besides the walls and the floor, and being stained, it was darker than the new-wood floor and walls. It was perfect, and tears came to Thrower's eyes. "Tell them that it's beautiful."

Faith and the boys smiled as broad as could be. "You see he ain't your enemy," said Faith, and Thrower could only agree.

"I'm not his enemy, either," he said. And he didn't say: I will win him over with love and patience, but I *will* win, and this altar is a sure sign that in his heart he secretly longs for me to set him free from the darkness of ignorance.

They didn't linger, but headed home briskly through the

night. Thrower set his candlestick on the floor near the altar—never *on* it, since that would smack of Papistry—and knelt in a prayer of thanksgiving. The church mostly built, and a beautiful altar already inside it, built by the man he had most feared, the crosses burnt into it by the strange child who most symbolized the compelling superstitions of these ignorant people.

"You're so full of pride," said a voice behind him.

He turned, already smiling, for he was always glad when the Visitor appeared.

But the Visitor was not smiling. "So full of pride."

"Forgive me," said Thrower. "I repent of it already. Still, can I help it if I rejoice in the great work that is begun here?"

The Visitor gently touched the altar, his fingers seeking out the crosses. "*He* made this, didn't he?"

"Alvin Miller."

"And the boy?"

"The crosses. I was so afraid they were servants of the devil—"

The Visitor looked at him sharply. "And because they built an altar, you think that proves they're not?"

A thrill of dread ran through him, and Thrower whispered, "I didn't think the devil could use the sign of the cross—"

"You're as superstitious as any of the others," said the Visitor coldly. "Papists cross themselves all the time. Do you think it's a hex against the devil?"

"How can I know anything, then?" asked Thrower. "If the devil can make an altar and draw a cross—"

"No, no. Thrower, my dear son, they aren't devils, either of them. You'll know the devil when you see him. Where other men have hair on their heads, the devil has the horns of a bull. Where other men have feet, the devil has the cloven hooves of a goat. Where other men have hands, the devil has the great paws of a bear. And be sure of this: he'll make no altars for you when he comes." Then the Visitor laid both his hands on the altar. "This is *my* altar now," he said. "No matter who made it, I can turn it to my purpose."

Thrower wept in relief. "Consecrated now, you've made it holy." And he reached out a hand to touch the altar.

"Stop!" whispered the Visitor. Even voiceless, though, his word had the power to set the walls a-trembling. "Hear me first," he said.

"I always listen to you," said Thrower. "Though I can't guess why you should have chosen such a lowly worm as me."

"Even a worm can be made great by a touch from the finger of God," said the Visitor. "No, don't misunderstand me—I am not the Lord of Hosts. Don't worship me."

But Thrower could not help himself, and he wept in devotion, kneeling before this wise and powerful angel. Yes, angel, Thrower had no doubt of it, though the Visitor had no wings and wore a suit of clothes one might expect to see in Parliament.

"The man who built this is confused, but there is murder in his soul, and if he is provoked enough, it will come forth. And the child who made the crosses—he is as remarkable as you suppose. But he is not yet ordained to a life of good or evil. Both paths are set before him, and he is open to influence. Do you understand me?"

"Is this my work?" asked Thrower. "Should I forget all else, and devote myself to turning the child to righteousness?"

"If you seem too devoted, his parents will reject you. Rather you should conduct your ministry as you have planned. But in your heart, you'll bend everything toward this remarkable child, to win him to my cause. Because if he does not serve me by the time he's fourteen years of age, then I'll destroy him."

The mere thought of Alvin Junior being hurt or killed was unbearable to Thrower. It filled him with such a sense of loss that he could not imagine a father or even a mother feeling more. "All that a weak man can do to save the child, I will do," he cried, his voice wrung almost to a scream by his anguish.

The Visitor nodded, smiled his beautiful and loving smile, and reached out his hand to Thrower. "I trust you," he said softly. His voice was like healing water on a burning wound. "I know you will do well. And as for the devil, you must feel no fear of *him*."

Thrower reached for the proffered hand, to cover it with kisses; but when he should have touched flesh, there was nothing there, and in that moment the Visitor was gone.

9

TALESWAPPER

There was once a time, Taleswapper well remembered, when he could climb a tree in these parts and look out over a hundred square miles of undisturbed forest. A time when oaks lived a century or more, with ever-thickening trunks making mountains out of wood. A time when leaves were so thick overhead that there were places where the forest ground was bare from lack of light.

That world of eternal dusk was slipping away now. There still were reaches of primeval wood, where Red men wandered more quietly than deer and Taleswapper felt himself to be in the cathedral of the most well-worshipped God. But such places were so rare that in this last year of wandering, Taleswapper had not journeyed a single day in which he could climb a tree and see no interruption in the forest roof. All the country between the Hio and the Wobbish was being settled, sparsely but evenly, and even now, from his perch atop a willow at the crest of a rise, Taleswapper could see three dozen cookfires sending pillars of smoke straight up into the cold autumn air. And in every direction, great swatches of forest had been cleared, the land plowed, crops planted, tended, harvested, so that where once great trees had shielded the earth from the sky's eye, now the stubbled soil was naked, waiting for winter to cover its shame.

Taleswapper remembered his vision of drunken Noah. He had engraved it for an edition of Genesis for Scottish Rite Sunday schools. Noah, nude, his mouth lolling open, a cup half-spilled still dangling from his curled fingers; Ham, not far off, laughing derisively; and Japheth and Shem, walking backward to draw a robe over their father, so they would not see what their father had exposed in his stupefaction. With an electric excitement, Taleswapper realized that this, now, is what that prophetic moment foreshadowed. That he, Taleswapper, perched atop a tree, was seeing the naked land in its stupor, awaiting the modest covering of winter. It was prophecy fulfilled, a thing which one hoped for but could not expect in one's own life.

Or, then again, the story of drunken Noah might not be a figure of this moment at all. Why not the other way around? Why not cleared land as a figure for drunken Noah?

Taleswapper was in a foul mood by the time he reached the ground. He thought and thought, trying to open his mind to see visions, to be a good prophet. Yet every time he thought he had got something firm and tight, it shifted, it changed. He thought one thought too many, and the whole fabric came undone, and he was left as uncertain as ever before.

At the base of the tree he opened his pack. From it he took the Book of Tales that he had first made for Old Ben back in '85. Carefully he unbuckled the sealed portion, then closed his eyes and riffled the pages. He opened his eyes and found his fingers resting among the Proverbs of Hell. Of course, at a time like this. His finger touched two proverbs, both written by his own hand. One meant nothing, but the other seemed appropriate. "A fool sees not the same tree that a wise man sees."

Yet the more he tried to study out the meaning of that proverb at this moment, the less connection he saw, except that it included mention of trees. So he tried the first proverb after all. "If the fool would persist in his folly he would become wise."

Ah. This was speaking to him, after all. This was the voice of prophecy, recorded when he lived in Philadelphia, before he ever began his journey, on a night when the Book of Proverbs came alive for him and he saw as if in letters of flame the words that should have been included. That night he had stayed up until dawn's light killed the fires of the page. When Old Ben came thumping down the stairs to grouch his way in for breakfast, he stopped and sniffed the air. "Smoke," he said. "You haven't been trying to burn down the house, have you, Bill?"

"No sir," answered Taleswapper. "But I saw a vision of what God meant the Book of Proverbs to say, and wrote them down."

"You are obsessed with visions," said Old Ben. "The only true vision comes not from God but from the inmost recesses of the human mind. Write that down as a proverb, if you want. It's far too agnostic for me to use it in Poor Richard's Almanac."

"Look," said Taleswapper.

Old Ben looked, and saw the last flames as they died. "Well, now, if that's not the most remarkable trick to do with letters. And you told me you weren't a wizard."

"I'm not. God gave this to me."

"God or the devil? When you're surrounded by light, Bill, how do you know whether it's the glory of God or the flames of hell?"

"I don't know," said Taleswapper, growing confused.

Being young then, not yet thirty, he was easily confused in the presence of the great man.

"Or perhaps you, wanting truth so badly, gave it to yourself." Old Ben tilted his head to examine the pages of Proverbs through the lower lenses of his bifocals. "The letters have been burned right in. Funny, isn't it, that I'm called a wizard, who am not, and you, who are, refuse to admit it."

"I'm a prophet. Or—want to be."

"If one of your prophecies comes true, Bill Blake, then I'll believe it, but not until."

In the years since then, Taleswapper had searched for the fulfilment of even one prophecy. Yet whenever he thought he had found such a fulfilment, he could hear Old Ben's voice in the back of his mind, providing an alternate explanation, scoffing at him for thinking that any connection between prophecy and reality could be true.

"Never *true*," Old Ben would say. "Useful—now, there's something. Your mind might make a connection that is useful. But *true* is another matter. True implies that you have found a connection that exists independent of your apprehension of it, that would exist whether you noticed it or not. And I must say that I have never seen such a connection in my life. There are times when I suspect that there are no such connections, that all links, bonds, ties, and similarities are creatures of thought and have no substance."

"Then why doesn't the ground dissolve beneath our feet?" asked Taleswapper.

"Because we have managed to persuade it not to let our bodies by. Perhaps it was Sir Isaac Newton. He was such a persuasive fellow. Even if human beings doubt him, the ground does not, and so it endures." Old Ben laughed. It was all a lark to him. He never could bring himself to believe even his own skepticism.

Now, sitting at the base of the tree, his eyes closed, Taleswapper connected again: The tale of Noah with Old Ben. Old Ben was Ham, who saw the naked truth, limp and shameful, and laughed at it, while all the loyal sons of church and university walked backward to cover it up again, so the silly truth would not be seen. Thus the world continued to think of the truth as firm and proud, never having seen it in a slack moment.

That is a true connection, thought Taleswapper. That is the meaning of the story. That is the fulfilment of the prophecy. The truth when we see it is ridiculous, and if we wish to worship it, we must never allow ourselves to see it.

In that moment of discovery, Taleswapper sprang to his feet. He must find someone at once, to tell of this great discovery white he still believed it. As his own proverb said, "The cistern contains: the fountain overflows." If he did not speak his tale, it grew dank and musty, it shrank inside him, while with the telling the tale stayed fresh and virtuous.

Which way? The forest road, not three rods off, led toward a large white church with an oak-high steeple—he had seen it, not a mile away, while up the tree. It was the largest building Taleswapper had seen since he last visited in Philadelphia. Such a large building for people to gather in implied that folks in this part of the land felt they had plenty of room for newcomers. A good sign for an itinerant teller of tales, since he lived by the trust of strangers, who might take him in and feed him when he brought nothing with him to pay with, except his book, his memory, two strong arms, and sturdy legs that had carried him ten thousand miles and were good for at least five thousand more.

The road was rutted with wagon tracks, which meant it was often used, and in the low places it was firmed up with rails, making a good strong corduroy so that wagons wouldn't mire in rain-soaked soil. So this was on its way to being a town, was it? The large church might not mean openness at all—it might speak more of ambition. That's the danger of judging anything, thought Taleswapper: There are a hundred possible causes for every effect, and a hundred possible effects from every cause. He thought of writing down that thought, but decided against it. It had no traces on it save the prints of his own soul—neither the marks of heaven nor of hell. By this he knew that it hadn't been given to him. He had forced the thought himself. So it couldn't be prophecy, and couldn't be true.

The road ended in a commons not far from a river. Taleswapper knew that from the smell of rushing water— he had a good nose. Around the commons were scattered several buildings, but the largest of all was a white-washed clapboard two-story building with a small sign that said "Weaver's."

Now when a house has a sign on it, Taleswapper knew, that generally means the owners want people to recognize the place though they've never been shown the way, which is the same as to say that the house is open to strangers. So Taleswapper went right up and knocked.

"Minute!" came a shout from inside. Taleswapper waited on the porch. Toward one end were several hanging baskets, with the long leaves of various herbs dangling. Taleswapper recognized many of them as being useful in various arts, such as healing, finding, sealing, and reminding. He also recognized that the baskets were arranged so that, seen from a spot near the base of the door, they would form a perfect hex. In fact, this was so pronounced an effect that Taleswapper squatted and finally lay prone on the porch to see it properly. The colors daubed on the baskets at exactly the correct points proved that it was no accident. It was an exquisite hex of protection, oriented toward the doorway.

Taleswapper tried to think of why someone would put up such a powerful hex, and yet seek to conceal it. Why, Taleswapper was probably the only person around likely to feel the whiff of power from something as passive as a hex, and so be drawn to notice it. He was still lying there on the floor, puzzling about it, when the door opened and a man said, "Are you so tired, then, stranger?"

Taleswapper leapt to his feet. "Admiring your arrangement of herbs. Quite an aerial garden, sir."

"My wife's," said the man. "She fusses over them all the time. Has to have them just so."

Was the man a liar? No, Taleswapper decided. He wasn't trying to hide the fact that the baskets made a hex and the trailing leaves intertwined to bind them together. He simply didn't know. Someone—his wife, probably, if it was her garden—had set up a protection on his house, and the husband didn't have a clue.

"They look just right to me," said Taleswapper.

"I wondered how someone could arrive here, and me not hear the wagon nor the horse. But from the looks of you, I'd guess you came afoot."

"That I did, sir," said Taleswapper.

"And your pack doesn't look full enough to hold many articles to trade."

"I don't trade in *things*, sir," said Taleswapper.

"What, then? What but things can be traded?"

"Work, for one thing," said Taleswapper. "I work for food and shelter."

"You're an old man, to be a vagrant."

"I was born in fifty-seven, so I still have a good seventeen years until I've used up my three-score and ten. Besides, I have a few knacks."

At once the man seemed to shrink away. It wasn't in his body. It was his eyes that got more distant, as he said, "My wife and I do our own work here, seeing how our sons are right small yet. We've no need of help."

There was a woman behind him now, a girl still young enough that her face hadn't grown hard and weathered, though she was solemn. She held a baby in her arms. She spoke to her husband. "We have enough to spare another place for dinner tonight, Armor—"

At that the husband's face went firm and set. "My wife is more generous than I am, stranger. I'll tell you straight out. You spoke of having a few knacks, and in my experience that means you make some claim to hidden powers. I'll have no such workings in a Christian house."

Taleswapper looked hard at him, and then looked a bit softer at the wife. So that was the way of it here: she working such hexes and spells as she could hide from her husband, and he flat rejecting any sign of it. If her husband ever realized the truth, Taleswapper wondered what would happen to the wife. The man—Armor?—seemed not to be the murderous kind, but then, there was no telling what violence would flow in a man's veins when the flood of rage came undammed.

"I understand your caution, sir," said Taleswapper.

"I know you have protections on you," said Armor. "A lone man, afoot in the wild for all this way? The fact that your hair is still on your head says that you must have warded off the Reds."

Taleswapper grinned and swept his cap off his head, letting his bald crown show. "Is it a true warding, to blind them with the reflected glory of the sun?" he asked. "They'd get no bounty for *my* scalp."

"Truth to tell," said Armor, "the Reds in these parts are more peaceable than most. The one-eyed Prophet has built him a city on the other side of the Wobbish, where he teaches Reds not to drink likker."

"That's good advice for any man," said Taleswapper. And he thought: A Red man who calls himself a prophet. "Before I leave this place I'll have to meet that man and have words with him."

"He won't talk to *you*," said Armor. "Not unless you can change the color of your skin. He hasn't spoke to a White man since he had his first vision a few years back."

"Will he kill me if I try?"

"Not likely. He teaches his people not to kill White men."

"That's also good advice," said Taleswapper.

"Good for White men, but it may not have the best result for Reds. There's folks like so-called Governor Harrison down in Carthage City who mean naught but harm for all Reds, peaceable or not." The truculence had not left Armor's face, but he was talking anyway, and from his heart, too. Taleswapper put a great deal of trust in the sort of man who spoke his mind to all men, even strangers, even enemies. "Anyway," Armor went on, "not all Reds are believers in the Prophet's peaceable words. Them as follow Ta-Kumsaw are stirring up trouble down by the Hio, and a lot of folks are moving north to the upper Wobbish country. So you won't lack for houses willing to take a beggar in—you can thank the Reds for that, too."

"I'm no beggar, sir," said Taleswapper. "As I told you, I'm willing to work."

"With knacks and hidden shiftiness, no doubt."

The man's hostility was the plain opposite of his wife's gentle welcoming air. "What *is* your knack, sir?" asked the wife. "From your speech you're an educated man. You'd not be a teacher, would you?"

"My knack is spoken with my name," he said. "Taleswapper. I have a knack for stories."

"For making them up? We call that lying, hereabouts."

The more the wife tried to befriend Taleswapper, the colder her husband became.

"I have a knack for remembering stories. But I tell only those that I believe are true, sir. And I'm a hard man to convince. If you tell me your stories, I'll tell you mine, and we'll both be richer for the trade, since neither one of us loses what we started with."

"I've got no stories," said Armor, even though he had already told a tale of the Prophet and another of Ta-Kumsaw.

"That's sad news, and if it's so, then I've come to the wrong house indeed." Taleswapper could see that this truly wasn't the house for him. Even if Armor relented and let him in, he would be surrounded by suspicion, and Taleswapper couldn't live where people looked sharp at him all the time. "Good day to you."

But Armor wasn't letting him go so easily. He took Taleswapper's words as a challenge. "Why should it be sad? I live a quiet, ordinary life."

"No man's life is ordinary to himself," said Taleswapper, "and if he says it is, then that's a story of the kind that I never tell."

"You calling me a liar?" demanded Armor.

"I'm asking if you know a place where my knack might be welcome."

Taleswapper saw, though Armor didn't, how the wife did a calming with the fingers of her right hand, and held her husband's wrist with her left. It was smoothly done, and the husband must have become quite attuned to it, because he visibly relaxed as she stepped a bit forward to reply. "Friend," she said, "if you take the track behind that hill yonder, and follow it to the end, over two brooks, both with bridges, you'll reach the house of Alvin Miller, and I know he'll take you in."

"Ha," said Armor.

"Thank you," said Taleswapper. "But how can you know such a thing?"

"They'll take you in for as long as you want to stay, and never turn you away, as long as you show willingness to help out."

"Willing I always am, milady," said Taleswapper.

"*Always* willing?" said Armor. "Nobody's *always* willing. I thought you always spoke true."

"I always tell what I believe. Whether it's true, I'm no more sure than any man."

"Then how do you call me 'sir,' when I'm no knight, and call her 'milady,' when she's as common as myself?"

"Why, I don't believe in the King's knightings, that's why. He calls a man a knight because he owes him a favor, whether he's a true knight or not. And all his mistresses are called 'ladies' for what they do between the royal sheets. That's how the words are used among the Cavaliers—lies half the time. But your wife, sir, acted like a true lady, gracious and hospitable. And you, sir, like a true knight, protecting your household against the dangers you most fear."

Armor laughed aloud. "You talk so sweet I bet you have to suck on salt for half an hour to get the taste of sugar out of your mouth."

"It's my knack," said Taleswapper. "But I have other ways to talk, and not sweetly, when the time is right. Good afternoon to you, and your wife, and your children, and your Christian house."

Taleswapper walked out onto the grass of the commons. The cows paid him no mind, because he *did* have a warding, though not of the sort that Armor would ever see. Taleswapper sat in the sunlight for a little while, to let his brain get warm and see if it could come up with a thought. But it didn't work. Almost never had a thought worth having, after noon. As the proverb said, "Think in the morning, Act in the noon, Eat in the evening, Sleep in the night." Too late for thinking now. Too early for eating.

He headed up the pathway to the church, which stood well back from the commons, atop a good-sized hill. If I were a true prophet, he thought, I'd know things now. I'd know whether I'd stay here for a day or a week or a month. I'd know whether Armor would be my friend, as I hope, or my enemy, as I fear. I'd know whether his wife would someday win herself free to use her powers in the open. I'd know whether I'd ever meet this Red Prophet face to face.

But that was nonsense, he knew. That was the sort of seeing that a torch would do—he'd seen them doing it before, more than a few of them, and it filled him with dread, because it wasn't good, he knew, for a man to know too much of the path of his own life ahead. No, for him the knack he wanted was prophecy, to see, not the small doings of men and women in their little corners of the world, but rather the great sweep of events as directed by God. Or by Satan—Taleswapper wasn't particular, since both of them had a good idea of what they planned to do in the world, and so either one was likely to know a few things about the future. Of course, it was likely to be more *pleasant* to hear from God. What traces of the devil he had touched so far in his life had all been painful, each in its own way.

The church door stood open, this being a warmish day for autumn, and Taleswapper buzzed right in along with the flies. It was as fine a church inside as out—obviously Scottish Rite, so it was plain—but all the more cheerful for that, a bright and airy place, with whited walls and glass-paned windows. Even the pews and pulpit were of light wood. The only thing dark in the whole place was the altar. So naturally his eye was drawn to it. And, because he had a knack for this sort of thing, he saw traces of a liquid touch upon the surface of it.

He walked slowly toward the altar. Toward it, because he had to know for sure; slowly, because this sort of thing ought not to be in a Christian church. Up close, though, there was no mistaking. It was the same trace he had seen on the face of the man in DeKane who tortured his own children to death and blamed it on the Reds. The same trace he had seen lingering on the sword that beheaded George Washington. It was like a thin film of filthy water, invisible unless you looked at a certain angle, in a certain light. But to Taleswapper it was always visible now—he had an eye for it.

He reached out his hand and set his forefinger carefully on the clearest trace. It took all his strength just to hold it there for a moment, it burned so, setting his whole arm to trembling and aching, right to the shoulder.

"You're welcome in God's house," said a voice.

Taleswapper, sucking on his burnt finger, turned to face the speaker. He was robed as a Scottish Rite preacher—Presbyterian, they called them here in America.

"You didn't get a splinter, did you?" asked the preacher.

It would have been easier just to say Yes, I got a splinter. But Taleswapper only told stories he believed. "Preacher," said Taleswapper, "the devil has set his hand upon this altar."

At once the preacher's lugubrious smile disappeared. "How do you know the devil's handprint?"

"It's a gift of God," said Taleswapper. "To see."

The preacher looked at him closely, unsure whether or not to believe. "Then can you also tell where angels have touched?"

"I could see traces, I think, if goodly spirits had intervened. I've seen such marks before."

The preacher paused, as if he wanted to ask a very important question but was afraid of the answer. Then he shuddered, the desire to learn plainly fled from him, and the preacher spoke now with contempt. "Nonsense. You can fool the common people, but I was educated in England, and I am not deluded by talk of hidden powers."

"Oh," said Taleswapper. "You're an educated man."

"And so are you, by your speech," said the preacher. "The south of England, I would say."

"The Lord Protector's Academy of Art," said Taleswapper. "I was trained as an engraver. Since you're Scottish Rite, I daresay you've seen my work in your Sunday school book."

"I never notice such things," said the preacher. "Engravings are a waste of paper that could be given over to words of truth. Unless they illustrate matters that the artist's eye has actually seen, like anatomies. But what the artist conceives in his imagination has no better claim on my eyes than what I imagine for myself."

Taleswapper followed that notion to its root. "What if the artist were also a prophet?"

The preacher half-closed his eyes. "The day of prophets is over. Like that apostate heathen one-eyed drunken Red man across the river, all who claim to be prophets now are charlatans. And I have no doubt that if God granted the gift of prophecy even to one artist, we would soon have a surplus of sketchers and daubers wishing to be taken for prophets, especially if it would bring them better pay."

Taleswapper answered mildly, but he did not let the preacher's implicit accusation stand. "A man who preaches the word of God for a salary ought not to criticize others who seek to earn a living by revealing the truth."

"I was ordained," said the preacher. "No one ordains artists. They ordain themselves."

Just as Taleswapper had expected. The preacher retreated to authority as soon as he feared his ideas could not stand on their own merit. Reasonable argument was impossible when authority became the arbiter; Taleswapper returned to the immediate matter. "The devil laid his fingers on this altar," said Taleswapper. "It burned my finger to touch the place."

"It never burned mine," said the preacher.

"I expect not," said Taleswapper. "*You* were ordained."

Taleswapper made no effort to hide the scorn in his voice, and it plainly irked the preacher, who lashed back. It did not bother Taleswapper when people got angry at him. It meant they were listening, and at least half believing him. "Tell me, then, if you have such keen eyes," said the preacher. "Tell me if a messenger from God has ever touched the altar."

Plainly the preacher regarded this question as a test. Taleswapper had no idea which answer the preacher thought was correct. It hardly mattered; Taleswapper would answer truthfully, no matter what. "No," he said.

It was the wrong answer. The preacher smirked. "Just like that? You can say that he has not?"

Taleswapper thought for a moment that the preacher might believe his own ordained hands had left the marks of God's will. He would lay that notion to rest at once. "Most preachers don't leave tracks of light on things they touch. Only a few are ever holy enough."

But it wasn't himself the preacher had in mind. "You've said enough now," said the preacher. "I know that you're a fraud. Get out of my church."

"I'm no fraud," said Taleswapper. "I may be mistaken, but I never lie."

"And I never believe a man who says he never lies."

"A man always assumes that others are as virtuous as himself," said Taleswapper.

The preacher's face flushed with anger. "Get out of here, or I'll throw you out."

"I'll go gladly," said Taleswapper. He walked briskly to

the door. "I never hope to return to a church whose preacher is not surprised to learn that Satan has touched his altar."

"I wasn't surprised because I don't believe you."

"You believed me," said Taleswapper. "You also believe an angel has touched it. That's the story you think is true. But I tell you that no angel could touch it without leaving a trace that I could see. And I see but one trace there."

"Liar! You yourself are sent by the devil, trying to do your necromancy here in the house of God! Begone! Out! I conjure you to leave!"

"I thought churchmen like you didn't practice conjurings."

"Out!" The preacher screamed the last word, the veins standing out in his neck. Taleswapper put his hat back on and strode away. He heard the door slam closed behind him. He walked across a hilly meadow of dried-out autumn grass until he struck the track that led up toward the house that the woman had spoken of. Where she was sure they'd take him in.

Taleswapper wasn't so sure. He never made more than three visits in a place—if he hadn't found a house to take him in by the third try, it was best to move on. This time, the first stop had been unusually bad, and the second had gone even worse.

Yet his uneasiness wasn't just that things were going badly. Even if at this last place they fell on their faces and kissed his feet, Taleswapper felt peculiar about staying around here. Here was a town so Christian that the leading citizen wouldn't allow hidden powers in his house—yet the altar in the church had the devil's mark on it. Even worse was the pattern of deception. The hidden powers were being used right under Armor's nose, and by the person he loved and trusted most; while in the church, the preacher was convinced that God, not the devil, had claimed his altar. What could Taleswapper expect, in this place up the hill, but more madness, more deception? Twisted people entwined each other, Taleswapper knew that much from the evidence of his own past.

The woman was right—the brooks were bridged. Even this, though, wasn't a good sign. To bridge a river was a necessity; to bridge a broad stream, a kindness to travelers. But why did they build such elaborate bridges over brooks so narrow that even a man as old as Taleswapper could leap them without wetting a foot? The bridges were sturdy, anchored into the earth far to either side of the stream, and both had roofs, well thatched. People pay money to stay in inns that aren't as tight and dry as these bridges, thought Taleswapper.

Surely this meant that the people at the end of the track were at least as strange as those he had met so far. Surely he ought to turn away. Prudence demanded that he leave.

But prudence was not strong in Taleswapper's character. It was as Old Ben told him, years before. "You'll go into the mouth of hell someday, Bill, just to find out why the devil has such bad teeth." There was a reason for the bridges, and Taleswapper sensed that it would mean a story worth remembering in his book.

It was only a mile, after all. Just when it seemed the track was about to wander into impenetrable wood, it took a sharp northward turn and opened into as pretty a holding as Taleswapper had seen, even in the placid settled lands of New Orange and Pennsylvania. The house was large and fine, with shaped logs, to show that they meant it to last, and there were barns and sheds and pens and coops that made it almost a village in itself. A wisp of smoke rising a half mile on up the track told him that his guess wasn't all wrong. There was another household nearby, sharing the road, which meant it was probably kin. Married children, no doubt, and all farming together, for the better prosperity of all. That was a good thing, Taleswapper knew, when brothers could grow up liking each other well enough to plow each other's fields.

Taleswapper always headed for the house—best to announce himself at once, rather than skulking about and being taken for a robber. Yet this time, when he meant to walk toward the house, he felt himself become stupid all at once, unable to remember what it was he was about to do. It was a warding so powerful that he did not realize he had been pushed away until he was halfway down the hill toward a stone building beside a brook. He stopped abruptly, frightened, for no one had power enough, he thought, to back him off without him realizing what was happening. This place was as strange as the other two, and he wanted no part of it.

Yet as he tried to turn back the way he had come, the same thing happened again. He found himself going down the hill toward the stone-walled building.

Again he stopped, and this time muttered, "Whoever you are, and whatever you want, I'll go of my own free will or I'll not go at all."

All at once it was like a breeze behind him, pushing him toward the building. But he knew he could go back if he wanted. Against the breeze, yes, but he could do it. That eased his mind considerably. Whatever constraints had been placed upon him, they were not meant to enslave him. And that, he knew, was one of the marks of a goodly spell—not the hidden chains of a tormentor.

The path rounded to the left a bit, along the brook, and now he could see that the building was a mill, for it had a millrace and the frame of a tall wheel standing where the water would flow. But no water flowed in the race today, and as he came close enough to see through the large barn-size door, he discovered why. It wasn't just closed up for the winter. It had never been used as a mill. The gears were in place, but the great round millstone wasn't there. Just a foundation of rammed cobbles, level and ready and waiting.

Waiting a long time. This construction was at least five years old, from the vines and the mosses on the building. It had been a lot of work to build this millhouse, and yet it was being used as a common haybarn.

Just inside the large door, a wagon was rocking back and forth as two boys grappled together atop a half-load of hay. It was a friendly bout; the boys were obviously brothers, the one about twelve years old, the other perhaps nine, and the only reason the young one wasn't thrown off the wagon and out the door was because the older boy couldn't keep himself from laughing. They didn't notice Taleswapper, of course.

They also didn't notice the man standing at the edge of the loft, pitchfork in hand, looking down at them. Taleswapper thought at first that the man was watching in pride, like a father. Then he came close enough to see how he held the fork. Like a javelin, ready to cast. For a single moment, Taleswapper saw in his mind's eye just what would happen—the fork thrown, burying itself in the flesh of one of the boys, surely killing him, if not immediately, then soon enough, with gangrene or belly bleeding. It was murder that Taleswapper saw.

"No!" he shouted. He ran through the doorway, fetching up alongside the wagon, looking up at the man in the loft.

The man plunged the pitchfork into the hay beside him and heaved the hay over the edge onto the wagon, half-burying the two boys. "I brought you here to work, you two bearcubs, not to tie each other in knots." The man was smiling, teasing. He winked at Taleswapper. Just as if there hadn't been death in his eyes a moment before.

"Howdy, young feller," said the man.

"Not so young," said Taleswapper. He doffed his hat, letting his bare pate give away his age.

The boys dug themselves out of the hay. "What were you shouting at, Mister?" asked the younger one.

"I was afraid someone might come to harm," said Taleswapper.

"Oh, we wrassle like that all the time," said the older boy. "Put her there, friend. My name's Alvin, same as my pa." The boy's grin was contagious. Scared as he'd been, with so much dark dealing going on today, Taleswapper had no choice but to smile back and take the proffered hand. Alvin Junior had a handshake like a grown man, he was that strong. Taleswapper commented on it.

"Oh, he gave you his fish hand. When he gets to wringing and wrenching on you, he like to pops your palm like a razzleberry." The younger boy shook hands, too. "I'm seven years old, and Al Junior, he's ten." Younger than they looked. They both had that nasty bitter body stench that young boys get when they've been playing hard. But Taleswapper never minded that. It was the father who puzzled him. Was it just a fancy in his own mind, that Taleswapper thought he meant to kill the boys? What man could take a murderous hand to boys as sweet and fine as these?

The man had left the pitchfork in the loft, clambered down the ladder, and now strode toward Taleswapper with his arms out as if to hug him. "Welcome here, stranger," said the man. "I'm Alvin Miller, and these are my two youngest sons, Alvin Junior and Calvin."

"Cally," corrected the younger boy.

"He doesn't like the way our names rhyme," said Alvin Junior. "Alvin and Calvin. See, they named him like me hoping he'd grow up to be as fine a specimen of manhood as I am. Too bad it ain't working."

Calvin gave him a shove of mock anger. "Near as I can

tell, he was the first try, and when I came along they finally got it right!"

"Mostly we call them Al and Cally," said the father.

"Mostly you call us 'shutup' and 'get over here,'" said Cally.

Al Junior gave him a whack on the shoulder and sent him sprawling in the dirt. Whereupon his father placed a boot on his backside and sent him head over heels out the door. All in fun. Nobody was hurt. How could I have thought there was murder going on here?

"You come with a message? A letter?" asked Alvin Miller. Now that the boys were outside, yelling at each other across the meadow, the grown men could get a word in.

"Sorry," said Taleswapper. "Just a traveler. A young lady in town said I might find a place to sleep up here. In exchange for whatever good hard work you might have for my arms."

Alvin Miller grinned. "Let me see how much work those arms can do." He thrust out an arm, but it wasn't to shake hands. He gripped Taleswapper by the forearm and braced his right foot against Taleswapper's right foot. "Think you can throw me?" asked Alvin Miller.

"Just tell me before we start," said Taleswapper, "whether I'll get a better supper if I throw you, or if I don't throw you."

Alvin Miller leaned back his head and whooped like a Red. "What's your name, stranger?"

"Taleswapper."

"Well, Mr. Taleswapper, I hope you like the taste of dirt, cause that's what you'll eat before you eat anything else here!"

Taleswapper felt the grip on his forearm tighten. His own arms were strong, but not like this man's grip. Still, a game of throws wasn't all strength. It was also wit, and

Taleswapper had a bit of that. He let himself slowly flinch under Alvin Miller's pressure, long before he had forced the man to use his full strength. Then, suddenly, he pulled with all his might in the direction Miller was pushing. Usually that was enough to topple the bigger man, using his own weight against him—but Alvin Miller was ready, pulled the other way, and flung Taleswapper so far that he landed right among the stones that formed the foundation for the missing millstone.

There had been no malice in it, though, just the love of the contest. No sooner was Taleswapper down than Miller was helping him up, asking him if anything was broken.

"I'm just glad your millstone wasn't in place yet," said Taleswapper, "or you'd be stuffing brains back into my head."

"What? You're in Wobbish country, man! There ain't no need for brains out *here*."

"Well, you threw me," said Taleswapper. "Does that mean you won't let me earn a bed and a meal?"

"Earn it? No sir. I won't allow such a thing." But the grin on his face denied the harshness of his words. "No, no, you can work if you like, because a man likes to feel that he pays his way in the world. But truth is I'd let you stay even if you had two legs broke and couldn't help a lick. We've got a bed all ready for you, just off the kitchen, and I'll bet a hog against a huckleberry that them boys already told Faith to set another bowl for supper."

"That's kind of you, sir."

"Not at all," said Alvin Miller. "You sure nothing got broke? You hit them stones awful hard."

"Then I imagine you ought to check to make sure none of those stones got split, sir."

Alvin laughed again, slapped him on the back, and led him up to the house.

Such a house it was. There couldn't be more screeching

and shouting in hell. Miller tried to sort out all the children for him. The four older girls were his daughters, busy as could be at half a dozen jobs, each one carrying on separate arguments with each of her sisters, at the top of her voice, passing from quarrel to quarrel as her work took her from room to room. The screaming baby was a grandchild, as were the five toddlers playing Roundheads and Cavaliers on and under the dining table. The mother, Faith, seemed oblivious to it all as she labored in the kitchen. Occasionally she'd reach out to cuff a nearby child, but otherwise she didn't let them interrupt her work—or her steady stream of orders, rebukes, threats, and complaints. "How do you keep your wits together, in all this?" Taleswapper asked her.

"Wits?" she asked him sharply. "Do you think anyone with wits would put up with this?"

Miller showed him to his room. That's what he called it, "your room, as long as you care to stay." It had a large bed and a feather pillow, and blankets, too, and half of one wall was the back of the chimney, so it was warm. Taleswapper hadn't been offered a bed like this in all his wandering. "Promise me that your name isn't really Procrustes," he said.

Miller didn't understand the allusion, but it didn't matter, he knew the look on Taleswapper's face. No doubt he'd seen it before. "We don't put our guests in the worst room, Taleswapper, we put them in the best. And no more talk about *that*."

"You have to let me work for you tomorrow, then."

"Oh, there's jobs to do, if you're good with your hands. And if you ain't ashamed of women's work, my wife could use a help or two. We'll see what happens." At that, Miller left the room and closed the door behind him.

The noise of the house was only partly dampened by the closed door, but it was a music that Taleswapper didn't mind hearing. It was only afternoon, but he couldn't help himself. He swung off his pack and pried off his boots and eased himself down on the mattress. It rustled like a straw tick, but there was a feather mattress on top of that, so it was deep and soft. And the straw was fresh, and dried herbs hung by the hearthstones to give it the smell of thyme and rosemary. Did I ever lie upon so soft a bed in Philadelphia? Or before that, in England? Not since I left my mother's womb, he thought.

There was nothing shy about the use of powers in this house; the hex was right in the open, painted above the door. But he recognized the pattern. It wasn't a peacemaker, designed to quell any violence in the soul that slept here. It wasn't a warning, and it wasn't a fending. Not a bit of it was designed to protect the house from the guest, or the guest from the house. It was for comfort, pure and simple. And it was perfectly, exquisitely drawn, exactly the right proportions. An exact hex wasn't easy to draw, being made of threes. Taleswapper couldn't remember seeing a more perfect one.

So it didn't surprise him, as he lay on the bed, to feel the muscles of his body unknotting, as if this bed and this room were undoing the weariness of twenty-five years of wandering. It occurred to him that when he died, he hoped the grave was as comfortable as this bed.

When Alvin Junior rocked him awake, the whole house smelled of sage and pepper and simmered beef. "You've just got time to use the privy, wash up, and come eat," said the boy.

"I must have fallen asleep," said Taleswapper.

"That's what I made that hex to do," said the boy. "Works good, don't it?" Then he charged out of the room.

Almost immediately Taleswapper heard one of the girls yelling the most alarming series of threats at the boy. The quarrel continued at top volume as Taleswapper went out to the privy, and when he came back inside, the yelling was still going on—though Taleswapper thought perhaps now it was a different sister yelling.

"I swear tonight in your sleep Al Junior I'll sew a skunk to the soles of your feet!" Al's answer was muffled by distance, but it caused another bout of screaming. Taleswapper had heard yelling before. Sometimes it was love and sometimes it was hate. When it was hate, he got out as quickly as he could. In this house, he could stay.

Hands and face washed, he was clean enough that Goody Faith allowed him to carry the loaves of bread to the table—"as long as you don't let the bread touch that gamy shirt of yours." Then Taleswapper took his place in line, bowl in hand, as the whole family trooped into the kitchen and emerged with the majority of a hog parceled out among them.

It was Faith, not Miller himself, who called on one of the girls to pray, and Taleswapper took note that Miller didn't so much as close his eyes, though all the children had bowed heads and clasped hands. It was as if prayer was a thing he tolerated, but didn't encourage. Without having to ask, Taleswapper knew that Alvin Miller and the preacher down in that fine white church did not get along at all. Taleswapper decided Miller might even appreciate a proverb from his book: "As the caterpillar chooses the fairest leaves to lay her eggs on, so the priest lays his curse on the fairest joys."

The meal was not a time of chaos, to Taleswapper's surprise. Each child in turn reported what he did that day, and all listened, sometimes giving advice or praise. Finally, when the stew was gone and Taleswapper was dabbing at the last traces in his bowl with a sop of bread, Miller turned to him, just like he had to everyone else in the family.

"And your day, Taleswapper. Was it well spent?"

"I walked some miles before noon, and climbed a tree," said Taleswapper. "There I saw a steeple, which led me to a town. There a Christian man feared my hidden powers, though he saw none of them, and so did a preacher, though he said he didn't believe I had any. Still, I was looking for a meal and a bed, and a chance to work to earn them, and a woman said that the folks at the end of a particular wagon track would take me in."

"That would be our daughter Eleanor," said Faith.

"Yes," said Taleswapper. "I see now that she has her mother's eyes, which are always calm no matter what is happening."

"No, friend," said Faith. "It's just that these eyes have seen such times that since then it hasn't been easy to alarm me."

"I hope before I leave to hear the story of such times," Taleswapper said.

Faith looked away as she put another slab of cheese on a grandchild's bread.

Taleswapper went right on with his account of the day, however, not wishing to show that she might have embarrassed him by not answering. "That wagon track was most peculiar," he said. "There were covered bridges over brooks that a child could wade in, and a man could step over. I hope to hear the story of those bridges before I go."

Again, no one would meet his gaze.

"And when I came out of the woods, I found a mill with no millstone, and two boys wrestling on a wagon, and a miller who gave me the worst throw of my life, and a family that took me in and gave me the best room in the house even though I was a stranger, and they didn't know me to be good or evil."

"Of course you're good," said Al Junior.

"Do you mind my asking? I've met many hospitable people in my time, and stayed in many a happy home, but not one happier than this, and no one quite so glad to see me."

All were still around the table. Finally, Faith raised her head and smiled at him. "I'm glad you found us to be happy," she said. "But we all remember other times as well, and perhaps our present happiness is sweeter, from the memory of grief."

"But why do you take in a man like me?"

Miller himself answered. "Because once we were strangers, and good folk took us in."

"I lived in Philadelphia for a time, and it strikes me to ask you, are you of the Society of Friends?"

Faith shook her head. "I'm Presbyterian. So are many of the children."

Taleswapper looked at Miller.

"I'm nothing," he said.

"A Christian isn't nothing," said Taleswapper.

"I'm no Christian, either."

"Ah," said Taleswapper. "A Deist, then, like Tom Jefferson." The children murmured at his mention of the great man's name.

"Taleswapper, I'm a father who loves his children, a husband who loves his wife, a farmer who pays his debts, and a miller without a millstone." Then the man stood up from the table and walked away. They heard a door close. He was gone away outside.

Taleswapper turned to Faith. "Oh, milady, I'm afraid you must regret my coming to your house."

"You ask a powerful lot of questions," she said.

"I told you my name, and my name is what I do. Whenever I sense that there's a story, one that matters, one that's true, I hunger for it. And if I hear it, and believe it, then I remember it forever, and tell it again wherever I go."

"That's how you earn your way?" asked one of the girls.

"I earn my way by helping mend wagons and dig ditches and spin thread and anything else that needs doing. But my life work is tales, and I swap them one for one. You may think right now that you don't want to tell me any of your stories, and that's fine with me, because I never took a story that wasn't willingly told. I'm no thief. But you see, I've already got a story—the things that happened to me today. The kindest people and the softest bed between the Mizzipy and the Alph."

"Where's the Alph? Is that a river?" asked Cally.

"What, you want a story?" asked Taleswapper.

Yes, clamored the children.

"But not about the river Alph," said Al Junior. "That's not a real place."

Taleswapper looked at him in genuine surprise. "How did you know? Have you read Lord Byron's collection of Coleridge's poetry?"

Al Junior looked around in bafflement.

"We don't get much bookstuff here," said Faith. "The preacher gives them Bible lessons, so they can learn to read."

"Then how did you know the river Alph isn't real?"

Al Junior scrunched his face, as if to say, Don't ask me questions when I don't even know the answer myself. "The story I want is about Jefferson. You said his name like you met him."

"Oh, I did. And Tom Paine, and Patrick Henry before they hanged him, and I saw the sword that cut off George Washington's head. I even saw King Robert the Second, before the French sank his ship back in naught one and took him to the bottom of the sea."

"Where he belonged," murmured Faith.

"If not deeper," said one of the older girls.

"I'll say amen to that. They say in Appalachee that he had so much blood on his hands that even his bones are stained brown with it, and even the most indiscriminate fish won't gnaw at them."

The children laughed.

"Even more than Tom Jefferson," said Al Junior, "I want a tale of the greatest American wizard. I bet you knew Ben Franklin."

Again, the child had startled him. How did he guess that of all tales, those about Ben Franklin were the ones he best loved to tell? "Know him? Oh, a little," said Taleswapper, knowing that the way he said it promised them all the stories they could hope for. "I lived with him only half a dozen years, and there were eight hours every night that I wasn't with him—so I can't say I know *much*."

Al Junior leaned over the table, his eyes bright and unblinking. "Was he truly a maker?"

"All those stories, each in its own time," said Taleswapper. "As long as your father and mother are willing to have me around, and as long as I believe I'm being useful, I'll stay and tell stories night and day."

"Starting with Ben Franklin," insisted Alvin Junior. "Did he really pull lightning out of the sky?"

10

VISIONS

Alvin Junior woke up sweating from the night-mare. It was so real, and he was panting just as if he had been trying to run away. But there was no running away, he knew that. He lay there with his eyes closed, afraid to open them for a while, knowing that when he did, it would still be there. A long time ago, when he was still little, he used to cry out when this nightmare came. But when he tried to explain it to Pa and Mama, they always said the same thing. "Why, that's just *nothing*, son. You're telling me you're so a-scared of *nothing*?" So he learned himself to stifle and never cry when the dream came.

He opened his eyes, and it fled away to the corners of the room, where he didn't have to look right at it. That was good enough. Stay there and let me be, he said silently.

Then he realized that it was full daylight, and Mama had laid out his black broadcloth pants and jacket and a clean shirt. His Sunday go-to-meeting clothes. He'd almost rather go back to the nightmare than wake up to this.

Alvin Junior hated Sunday mornings. He hated getting all dressed up, so he couldn't set on the ground or kneel in the grass or even bend over without something getting messed up and Mama telling him to have some respect for the Lord's day. He hated having to tiptoe around the house all morning because it was the Sabbath and there wasn't to be no playing or making noise on the Sabbath. Worst of all he hated the thought of sitting on a hard bench down front, with Reverend Thrower looking him in the eye while he preached about the fires of hell that were waiting for the ungodly who despised the true religion and put their faith in the feeble understanding of man. Every Sunday, it seemed like.

And it wasn't that Alvin really despised religion. He just despised Reverend Thrower. It was all those hours in school, now that harvest was over. Alvin Junior was a good reader, and he got right answers most of the time in his ciphering. But that wasn't enough for old Thrower. He also had to teach religion right along with it. The other children—the Swedes and Knickerbockers from upriver, the Scotch and English from down—only got a licking when they sassed or got three wrong answers in a row. But Thrower took his cane to Alvin Junior every chance he got, it seemed like, and it wasn't over book-learning, it was always about religion.

Of course it didn't help much that the Bible kept striking Alvin funny at all the wrong times. That's what Measure said, the time that Alvin ran away from school and hid in David's house till Measure found him nigh onto suppertime. "If you just didn't laugh when he reads from the Bible, you wouldn't get whupped so much."

But it was *funny*. When Jonathan shot all those arrows in the sky and they missed. When Jeroboam didn't shoot enough arrows out his window. When Pharaoh kept finding tricky ways to keep the Israelites from leaving. When Samson was so dumb he told his secret to Delilah after she already betrayed him twice. "How can I keep from laughing?"

"Just think about getting blisters on your butt," said Measure. "That ought to take the smile off your face."

"But I never remember till after I already laughed."

"Then you'll probably never need a chair till you're fifteen years old," said Measure. "Cause Mama won't ever let you out of that school, and Thrower won't ever let up on you, and you can't hide in David's house forever."

"Why not?"

"Because hiding from your enemy is the same as letting him win."

So Measure wouldn't keep him safe, and he had to go back—and take a licking from Pa, too, for scaring everybody by running away and hiding so long. Still, Measure *had* helped him. It was a comfort to know that somebody else was willing to say that Thrower was his enemy. All the others were so full of how wonderful and godly and educated Thrower was, and how *kind* he was to teach the children from his fount of wisdom, that it like to made Alvin puke.

Even though Alvin mostly kept his face under control during school, and so got less lickings, Sunday was the most terrible struggle of all, because he sat there on that hard bench listening to Thrower, half the time wanting to bust out laughing till he fell on the floor, and half the time wanting to stand up and shout, "That's just about the stupidest thing I ever heard a growed man say!" He even had a feeling Pa wouldn't lick him very hard for saying that to Thrower, since Pa never had much of an opinion of the man. But Mama—she'd never forgive him for doing blasphemy in the house of the Lord.

Sunday morning, he decided, is designed to let sinners have a sample of the first day of eternity in hell.

Probably Mama wouldn't even let Taleswapper tell so much as the tiniest story today, lessen it came from the Bible. And since Taleswapper never seemed to tell stories from the Bible, Alvin Junior guessed that nothing good would come today.

Mama's voice blasted up the stairs. "Alvin Junior, I'm so sick and tired of you taking three hours to get dressed on Sunday morning that I'm about to take you to church naked!"

"I ain't naked!" Alvin shouted down. But since what he was wearing was his nightgown, it was probably *worse* than being naked. He shucked off the flannel nightgown, hung it on a peg, and started dressing as fast as he could.

It was funny. On any other day, he only had to reach out for his clothes without even thinking, and they'd be there, just the piece he wanted. Shirt, trousers, stockings, shoes. Always there in his hand when he reached. But on Sunday morning, it was like the clothes ran away from his hand. He'd go for his shirt and come back with his pants. He'd reach for a sock and come up with a shoe, time after time. It was like as if the clothes didn't want to get put on his body any more than he wanted them there.

So when Mama banged open the door, it wasn't altogether Alvin's fault that he didn't even have his pants on yet.

"You've missed breakfast! You're still half-naked! If you think I'm going to make the whole family parade into church late on account of you, you've got—"

"Another think coming," said Alvin.

It wasn't *his* fault that she always said the same thing. But she got mad at him as if he should have pretended to be *surprised* to hear her say it for the ninetieth time since summer. Oh, she was all set to give him a licking, all right, or call for Pa to do it even worse, when there was Taleswapper, come to save him.

"Goody Faith," said Taleswapper, "I'd be glad to see to it he comes to church, if you want to go on ahead with the others."

The minute Taleswapper spoke, Mama whirled around and tried to hide how mad she'd been. Alvin right away started doing a calming on her—with his right hand, where she couldn't see it, since if she saw him doing a spell on her, she'd break his arm, and that was one threat Alvin Junior truly believed. A calming didn't work so well without touching, but since she was trying so hard to *look* calm in front of Taleswapper, it worked all right.

"I hate to put you to any trouble," said Mama.

"No trouble, Goody Faith," said Taleswapper. "I do little enough to repay your kindness to me."

"Little enough!" The fretfulness was almost gone from Mama's voice now. "Why, my husband says you do the work of two grown men. And when you tell stories to the little ones I get more peace and quiet in this house than I've had since—since *ever*." She turned back to Alvin, but now her anger was more an act than real. "Will you do what Taleswapper tells you, and come to church right quick?"

"Yes, Mama," said Alvin Junior. "Quick as I can."

"All right then. Thank you kindly, Taleswapper. If you can get that boy to obey, that's more than anybody else has managed since he learned to talk."

"He's a real brat," said Mary, from the hallway outside.

"Shut your mouth, Mary," Mama said, "or I'll stuff your lower lip up your nose and tack it there to *keep* it shut."

Alvin sighed in relief. When Mama made impossible threats it meant she wasn't all that angry anymore. Mary put her nose in the air and flounced down the hall, but Alvin didn't even bother with it. He just grinned at Taleswapper, and Taleswapper grinned at him.

"Having trouble getting dressed for church, lad?" asked Taleswapper.

"I'd rather dress myself in lard and walk through a herd of hungry bears," said Alvin Junior.

"More people live through church than survive encounters with bears."

"Not by much, though."

Soon enough he got dressed. But he was able to talk Taleswapper into taking the shortcut, which meant walking through the woods up over the hill behind the house, instead of going around by way of the road. Since it was right cold outside, and hadn't rained in a while, and wasn't about to snow yet, there'd be no mud and Mama'd probably not even guess. And what Mama didn't know wouldn't hurt him.

"I noticed," said Taleswapper as they climbed up the leaf-covered slope, "that your father didn't go with your mother and Cally and the girls."

"He doesn't go to that church," said Alvin. "He says Reverend Thrower is a jackass. Course, he don't say that where Mama can hear."

"I suppose not," said Taleswapper.

They stood at the top of the hill, looking down across open meadowland toward the church. The church's own hill hid the town of Vigor Church from view. The frost was just beginning to melt off the brown autumn grass, so that the church looked to be the whitest thing in a world of whiteness, and the sun flashed on it like it was another sun. Alvin could see wagons still pulling into place, and horses being tied to the posts on the meadow. If they hurried right now, they'd probably be in their places before Reverend Thrower started up the hymn.

But Taleswapper didn't start down the hill. He just set himself on a stump and started to recite a poem. Alvin listened tight, because Taleswapper's poems often had a real bite to them.

> *"I went to the Garden of Love,*
> *And saw what I never had seen:*

A chapel was built in the midst,
Where I used to play on the green.

And the gates of this chapel were shut,
And 'Thou shalt not' writ over the door,
So I turned to the Garden of Love,
That so many sweet flowers bore,

And I saw it was filled with graves,
And tomb-stones where flowers should be:
And priests in black gowns were walking their rounds,
And binding with briars my joys and desires."

Oh, Taleswapper had a knack, he did, for as he recited, the very world changed before Alvin's eyes. The meadows and trees looked like the loudest shout of spring, vivid yellow-green with ten thousand blossoms, and the white of the chapel in the midst of it was no longer gleaming, but instead the dusty, chalky white of old bones. "Binding with briars my joys and desires," Alvin repeated. "You ain't got much use for religion."

"I breathe religion with my every breath," said the Taleswapper. "I long for visions, I search for the traces of God's hand. But in this world I see more traces of the other. A trail of glistening slime that burns me when I touch it. God is a bit standoffish these days, Al Junior, but Satan has no fear of getting down in the muck with mankind."

"Thrower says his church is the house of God."

Taleswapper, he just sat there and said nothing for the longest time.

Finally Alvin asked him right out: "Have you seen devil traces in that church?"

In the days that Taleswapper had been with them, Alvin had come to know that Taleswapper never exactly lied.

But when he didn't want to get pinned down with the true answer, he'd say a poem. He said one now.

> *"O Rose, thou art sick.*
> *The invisible worm*
> *That flies in the night*
> *In the howling storm*
>
> *Has found out thy bed*
> *Of crimson joy,*
> *And his dark secret love*
> *Does thy life destroy."*

Alvin was impatient with such twisting answers. "If I want to hear something I don't understand, I can read Isaiah."

"Music to my ears, my lad, to compare me to the greatest of prophets."

"He ain't much of a prophet if nobody can understand a thing he wrote."

"Or perhaps he meant us all to become prophets."

"I don't hold with prophets," said Alvin. "Near as I can tell, they end up just as dead as the next man." It was something he had heard his father say.

"Everybody ends up dead," said Taleswapper. "But some who are dead live on in their words."

"Words never stay straight," said Alvin. "Now, when I *make* a thing, then it's the thing I made. Like when I make a basket. It's a basket. When it gets tore, then it's a tored-up basket. But when I say words, they can get all twisted up. Thrower can take those same very words I said and bend them back and make them mean just contrary to what I said."

"Think of it another way, Alvin. When you make one basket, it can never be more than one basket. But when you say words, they can be repeated over and over, and fill men's hearts a thousand miles from where you first spoke them. Words can magnify, but things are never more than what they are."

Alvin tried to picture that, and with Taleswapper saying it, the picture came easy to his mind. Words as invisible as air, coming out of Taleswapper's mouth and spreading from person to person. Growing larger all the time, but still invisible.

Then, suddenly, the vision changed. He saw the words coming from the preacher's mouth, like a trembling in the air, spreading out, seeping into everything—and suddenly it became his nightmare, the terrible dream that came on him, waking or sleeping, and spiked his heart to his spine till he like to died. The world filling up with an invisible trembling *nothing* that seeped into everything and shook it apart. Alvin could see it, rolling toward him like a huge ball, growing all the time. He knew from all the nightmares before that even if he clenched his fists it would thin itself out and seep between his fingers, and even when he closed his mouth and his eyes it would press on his face and ooze into his nose and ears and—

Taleswapper shook him. Shook him hard. Alvin opened his eyes. The trembling air retreated back to the edges of his sight. That's where Alvin saw it most of the time, waiting just barely out of sight, wary as a weasel, ready to flit away if he turned his head.

"What's wrong with you, lad?" asked Taleswapper. His face looked afraid.

"Nothing," said Alvin.

"Don't tell me nothing," said Taleswapper. "All of a sudden I saw a fear come over you, as if you were seeing a terrible vision."

"It wasn't a vision," said Alvin. "I had a vision once, and I know."

"Oh?" said Taleswapper. "What vision was that?"

"A Shining Man," said Alvin. "I never told nobody about it, and I don't reckon to start now."

Taleswapper didn't press him. "What you saw now, if it wasn't a vision—well, what was it?"

"It was nothing." It was a true answer, but he also knew it was no answer at all. But he didn't *want* to answer. Whenever he told people, they just scoffed at him for being such a baby about nothing.

But Taleswapper wouldn't let him slough off his question. "I've been longing for a true vision all my life, Al Junior, and you saw one, here in broad daylight, with your eyes wide open, you saw something so terrible it made you stop breathing, now tell me what it was."

"I told you! It was nothing!" Then, quieter: "It's *nothing*, but I can see it. Like the air gets wobbly wherever it goes."

"It's nothing, but not invisible?"

"It gets into everything. It gets into all the smallest cracks and shakes everything apart. Just shivers and shivers until there's nothing left but dust, and then it shivers the dust, and I try to keep it out, but it gets bigger and bigger, it rolls over everything, till it like to fills the whole sky and the whole earth." Alvin couldn't help himself. He was shaking with cold, even though he was bundled up thick as a bear.

"How many times have you seen this before?"

"Ever since I can remember. Just now and then it'll come on me. Most times I just think about other things and it stays back."

"Where?"

"Back. Out of sight." Alvin knelt down and then sat down, exhausted. Sat right in the damp grass with his Sunday pants, but he didn't hardly notice. "When you talked about words spreading and spreading, it made me see it again."

"A dream that comes again and again is trying to tell you the truth," said Taleswapper.

The old man was so plainly eager about the whole thing that Alvin wondered if he really understood how frightening it was. "This ain't one of your stories, Taleswapper."

"It will be," said Taleswapper, "as soon as I understand it."

Taleswapper sat beside him and thought in silence for the longest time. Alvin just sat there, twisting grass in his fingers. After a while he got impatient. "Maybe you can't understand everything," he said. "Maybe it's just a craziness in me. Maybe I get lunatic spells."

"Here," said Taleswapper, taking no notice that Alvin had even spoke. "I've thought of a meaning. Let me say it, and see if we believe it."

Alvin didn't like being ignored. "Or maybe *you* get lunatic spells, you ever think of that, Taleswapper?"

Taleswapper brushed aside Alvin's doubt. "All the universe is just a dream in God's mind, and as long as he's asleep, he believes in it, and things stay real. What you see is God waking up, gradually waking up, and his wakefulness sweeps through the dream, undoes the universe, until finally he sits up, rubs his eyes, and says, 'My, what a dream, I wish I could remember what it was,' and in that moment we'll all be gone." He looked eagerly at Alvin. "How was that?"

"If you believe that, Taleswapper, then you're a blamed fool, just like Armor-of-God says."

"Oh, he says that, does he?" Taleswapper suddenly snaked out his hand and took Alvin by the wrist. Alvin was so surprised he dropped what he was holding. "No! Pick it up! Look what you were doing!"

"I was just fiddling, for pete's sake."

Taleswapper reached down and picked up what Alvin had dropped. It was a tiny basket, not an inch across, made from autumn grasses. "You made this, just now."

"I reckon so," said Alvin.

"Why did you make it?"

"Just made it."

"You weren't even thinking about it?"

"It ain't much of a basket, you know. I used to make them for Cally. He called them bug baskets when he was little. They just fall apart pretty soon."

"You saw a vision of *nothing*, and then you had to make *something*."

Alvin looked at the basket. "Reckon so."

"Do you always do that?"

Alvin thought back to other times he'd seen the shivering air. "I'm always making things," he said. "Don't mean much."

"But you don't feel right again until you've made something. After you see the vision of nothing, you aren't at peace until you put something together."

"Maybe I've just got to work it off."

"Not just *work*, though, is it, lad? Chopping wood doesn't do the job for you. Gathering eggs, toting water, cutting hay, that doesn't ease you."

Now Alvin began to see the pattern Taleswapper had found. It was true, near as he could remember. He'd wake up after such a dream at night, and couldn't stop fidgeting until he'd done some weaving or built a haystack or done up a doll out of corn shucks for one of the nieces. Same thing when the vision came on him in the day—he wasn't no good at whatever chore he was doing, until he built something that hadn't been there before, even if it was nothing more than a pile of rocks or part of a stone wall.

"It's true, isn't it? You do that every time, don't you?"

"Mostly."

"Then let me tell you the name of the nothing. It's the Unmaker."

"Never heard of it," said Alvin.

"Neither did I, till now. That's because it likes to keep itself secret. It's the enemy of everything that exists. All it wants is to break everything into pieces, and break those pieces into pieces, until there's nothing left at all."

"If you break something into pieces, and break the pieces into pieces, you don't get *nothing*," said Alvin. "You just get lots of little pieces."

"Shut up and listen to the story," said Taleswapper.

Alvin was used to him saying that. Taleswapper said it to Alvin Junior more often than to anybody else, even the nephews.

"I'm not talking about good and evil," said Taleswapper. "Even the devil himself can't afford to break everything down, can he, or he'd cease to be, just like everything else. The most evil creatures don't desire the destruction of everything—they only desire to exploit it for themselves."

Alvin had never heard the word *exploit* before, but it sounded nasty.

"So in the great war between the Unmaker and everything else, God and the devil should be on the same side. But the devil, he doesn't know it, and so he serves the Unmaker as often as not."

"You mean the devil's out to beat himself?"

"My story isn't about the devil," said Taleswapper. He was steady as rain when a story was coming out of him. "In the great war against the Unmaker of your vision, all the men and women of the world should be allies. But the great enemy remains invisible, so that no one guesses that they unwittingly serve him. They don't realize that war is the Unmaker's ally, because it tears down everything it touches. They don't understand that fire, murder, crime, cupidity, and concupiscence break apart the fragile bonds that make human beings into nations, cities, families, friends, and souls."

"You must be a prophet right enough," said Alvin Junior, "cause I can't understand a thing you said."

"A prophet," murmured Taleswapper, "but it was your eyes that saw. Now I know the agony of Aaron: to speak the words of truth, yet never have the vision for himself."

"You're making a big lot out of my nightmares."

Taleswapper was silent, sitting on the ground, his elbows on his knees, his chin propped all dismal on his palms. Alvin tried to figure out what the man was talking about. It was a sure thing that what he saw in his bad dreams wasn't a thing of any kind, so it must be poetical to talk about the Unmaker like a person. Maybe it was true, though, maybe the Unmaker wasn't just something he imagined up in his brain, maybe it was real, and Al Junior was the only person who could see it. Maybe the whole world was in terrible danger, and it was Alvin's job to fight it off, to beat it back, to keep the thing at bay. It was sure enough that when the dream was on him, Alvin couldn't bear it, wanted to drive it away. But he never could figure out how.

"Sposing I believe you," said Alvin. "Sposing there's such a thing as the Unmaker. There ain't a blame thing I can do."

A slow smile crept over Taleswapper's face. He tipped himself to one side, to free up his hand, which slowly reached down to the ground and picked up the little bug basket where it lay in the grass. "Does that look like a blamed thing?"

"That's just a bunch of grass."

"It *was* a bunch of grass," said Taleswapper. "And if you tore it up it'd be a bunch of grass again. But now, right now, it's something more than that."

"A little bug basket is all."

"Something that you made."

"Well, it's a sure thing grass don't grow that way."

"And when you made it, you beat back the Unmaker."

"Not by much," said Alvin.

"No," said Taleswapper. "But by the making of one bug basket. By that much, you beat him back."

It came together in Alvin's mind. The whole story that the Taleswapper was trying to tell. Alvin knew all kinds of opposites in the world: good and evil, light and dark, free and slave, love and hate. But deeper than all those opposites was making and unmaking. So deep that hardly anybody noticed that it was the most important opposite of all. But *he* noticed, and so that made the Unmaker his enemy. That's why the Unmaker came after him in his sleep. After all, Alvin had his knack. His knack for setting things in order, putting things in the shape they ought to be in.

"I think my *real* vision was about the same thing," said Alvin.

"You don't have to tell me about the Shining Man," said Taleswapper. "I never mean to pry."

"You mean you just pry by accident?" said Alvin.

That was the kind of remark that got him a slap across the face at home, but Taleswapper only laughed.

"I did something evil and I didn't even know it," said Alvin. "The Shining Man came and stood by the foot of my bed, and first he showed me a vision of what I done, so I knowed it was bad. I tell you I cried, to know I was so wicked. But then he showed me what my knack was for, and now I see it's the same thing you're talking about. I saw a stone that I pulled out of a mountain, and it was round as a ball, and when I looked close I saw it was the whole world, with forests and animals and oceans and fish and all on it. That's what my knack is for, to try to put things in order."

Taleswapper's eyes were gleaming. "The Shining Man showed you such a vision," he said. "Such a vision as I'd give my life to see."

"Only cause I'd used my knack to cause harm to others, just for my own pleasure," said Alvin. "I made a promise then, my most solemn vow, that I'd never use my knack for my own good. Only for others."

"A good promise," said Taleswapper. "I wish all men and women in the world would take such an oath and keep it."

"Anyway, that's how I know that the—the Unmaker, it isn't a vision. The Shining Man wasn't even a vision. What he *showed* me, *that* was a vision, but him standing there, he was *real*."

"And the Unmaker?"

"Real, too. I don't just see it in my head, it's *there*."

Taleswapper nodded, his eyes never leaving Alvin's face.

"I've got to make things," said Alvin. "Faster than he can tear them down."

"Nobody can make things fast enough for that," said Taleswapper. "If all the men in all the world made all the earth into a million million million million bricks, and built a wall all the days of their lives, the wall would crumble faster than they could build it. Sections of the wall would fall apart even before they built them."

"Now that's silly," said Alvin. "A wall can't fall down before you build it up."

"If they keep at it long enough, the bricks will crumble into dust when they pick them up, their own hands will rot and slough like slime from their bones, until brick and flesh and bone alike all break down into the same indistinguishable dust. Then the Unmaker will sneeze, and the dust will be infinitely dispersed so that it can never come together again. The universe will be cold, still, silent, dark, and at last the Unmaker will be at rest."

Alvin tried to make sense out of what Taleswapper was saying. It was the same thing he did whenever Thrower talked about religion in school, so Alvin thought of it as kind of a dangerous thing to do. But he couldn't stop himself from doing it, and from asking his questions, even if they made people mad. "If things are breaking down faster than they're getting made, then how come anything's still around? Why hasn't the Unmaker already won? What are we doing here?"

Taleswapper wasn't Reverend Thrower. Alvin's question didn't make him angry. He just knit his brow and shook his head. "I don't know. You're right. We *can't* be here. Our existence is impossible."

"Well we *are* here, in case you didn't notice," said Alvin. "What kind of stupid tale is that, when we just have to look at each other to know it isn't true?"

"It has problems, I admit."

"I thought you only told stories you believe."

"I believed it while I was telling it."

Taleswapper looked so mournful that Alvin reached out and laid his hand on the man's shoulder, though his coat was so thick and Alvin's hand so small that he wasn't altogether sure Taleswapper felt his touch. "I believed it, too. Parts of it. For a while."

"Then there *is* truth in it. Maybe not much, but some." Taleswapper looked relieved.

But Alvin couldn't leave well enough alone. "Just because you believe it doesn't make it so."

Taleswapper's eyes went wide. Now I've done it, thought Alvin. Now I've made him mad, just like I make Thrower mad. I do it to everbody. So he wasn't surprised when Taleswapper reached out both arms toward him, took

Alvin's face between his hands, and spoke with such force as to drive the words deep into Alvin's forehead. "Everything possible to be believed is an image of truth."

And the words *did* pierce him, and he understood them, though he could not have put in words what it was he understood. Everything possible to be believed is an image of truth. If it feels true to me, then there is something true in it, even if it isn't all true. And if I study it out in my mind, then maybe I can find what parts of it are true, and what parts are false, and—

And Alvin realized something else. That all his arguments with Thrower came down to this: that if something just plain didn't make sense to Alvin, he didn't believe it, and no amount of quoting from the Bible would convince him. Now Taleswapper was telling him that he was *right* to refuse to believe things that made no sense. "Taleswapper, does that mean that what I *don't* believe *can't* be true?"

Taleswapper raised his eyebrows and came back with another proverb. "Truth can never be told so as to be understood, and not be believed."

Alvin was fed up with proverbs. "For once would you tell me straight!"

"The proverb *is* the straight truth, lad. I refuse to twist it up to fit a confused mind."

"Well, if my mind's confused, it's all your fault. All your talk about bricks crumbling before the wall is built—"

"Didn't you believe that?"

"Maybe I did. I reckon if I set out to weave all the grass of this meadow into bug baskets, before I got to the far end of the meadow the grass would all have died and rotted to nothing. I reckon if I set out to turn all the trees from here to Noisy River into barns, the trees'd all be dead and fell before I ever got to the last of them. Can't build a house out of rotted logs."

"I was going to say, 'Men cannot build permanent things

out of impermanent pieces.' That is the law. But the way you said it was the proverb of the law: 'You can't build a house out of rotted logs.' "

"I said a proverb?"

"And when we get back to the house, I'll write it in my book."

"In the sealed part?" asked Alvin. Then he remembered that he had only seen that book by peeking through a crack in his floor late at night when Taleswapper was writing by candlelight in the room below him.

Taleswapper looked at him sharp. "I hope you never tried to conjure open that seal."

Alvin was offended. He might peek through a crack, but he'd never *sneak*. "Just knowing you don't want me to read that part is better than any old seal, and if you don't know that, you ain't my friend. I don't pry into your secrets."

"My secrets?" Taleswapper laughed. "I seal that back part because that's where my own writings go, and I simply don't want anyone else writing in that part of the book."

"Do other people write in the front part?"

"They do."

"Well, what do they write? Can I write there?"

"They write one sentence about the most important thing they ever did or ever saw with their own eyes. That one sentence is all I need from then on to remind me of their story. So when I visit in another city, in another house, I can open the book, read the sentence, and tell the story."

Alvin thought of a remarkable possibility. Taleswapper had lived with Ben Franklin, hadn't he? "Did Ben Franklin write in your book?"

"He wrote the very first sentence."

"He wrote down the most important thing he ever did?"

"That he did."

"Well, what *was* it?"

Taleswapper stood up. "Come back to the house with me, lad, and I'll show you. And on the way I'll tell you the story to explain what he wrote."

Alvin sprang up spry, and took the old man by his heavy sleeve, and fairly dragged him toward the path back down to the house. "Come on, then!" Alvin didn't know if Taleswapper had decided not to go on to church, or if he plumb forgot that's where they were supposed to go— whatever the reason, Alvin was happy enough with the result. A Sunday with no church at all was a Sunday worth being alive. Add to that Taleswapper's stories and Maker Ben's own writing in a book, and it was well nigh to being a perfect day.

"There's no hurry, lad. I won't die before noon, nor will you, and stories take some time to tell."

"Was it something he made?" asked Alvin. "The most important thing?"

"As a matter of fact, it was."

"I knew it! The two-glass spectacles? The stove?"

"People used to say to him all the time, Ben, you're a true Maker. But he always denied it. Just like he denied he was a wizard. I've got no knack for hidden powers, he said. I just take pieces of things and put them together in a better way. There were stoves before I made my stove. There were spectacles before I made my spectacles. I never really *made* anything in my life, in the way a true Maker would do it. I give you two-glass spectacles, but a *Maker* would give you new eyes."

"He figured he never made *anything*?"

"I asked him that one day. The very day that I was starting out with my book. I said to him, Ben, what's the most important thing you ever made? And he started in on what I just told you, about how he never really made anything, and I said to him, Ben, you don't believe that, and I don't believe that. And he said, Bill, you found me out.

There's one thing I made, and it's the most important thing I ever did, and it's the most important thing I ever saw."

Taleswapper fell silent, just shambling down the slope through leaves that whispered loud underfoot.

"Well, what was it?"

"Don't you want to wait till you get home and read it for yourself?"

Alvin got real mad then, madder than he meant to. "I hate it when people know something and they won't say!"

"No need to get your dander up, lad. I'll tell you. What he wrote was this: The only thing I ever truly made was Americans."

"That don't make sense. Americans are *born*."

"Well, now, that's not so, Alvin. *Babies* are born. In England the same as in America. So it isn't being born that makes them American."

Alvin thought about that for a second. "It's being born *in* America."

"Well, that's true enough. But along about fifty years ago, a baby born in Philadelphia was never called an American baby. It was a Pennsylvanian baby. And babies born in New Amsterdam were Knickerbockers, and babies born in Boston were Yankees, and babies born in Charleston were Jacobians or Cavaliers or some such name."

"They still are," Alvin pointed out.

"They are indeed, lad, but they're something else besides. All those names, Old Ben figured, those names divided us up into Virginians and Orangemen and Rhode Islanders, into Whites and Reds and Blacks, into Quakers and Papists and Puritans and Presbyterians, into Dutch, Swedish, French, and English. Old Ben saw how a Virginian could never quite trust a man from Netticut, and how a White man could never quite trust a Red, because they were *different*. And he said to himself, If we've got all these names to hold us apart, why not a name to bind us together? He toyed with a lot of names that already were used. Colonials, for instance. But he didn't like calling us all Colonials because that made us always turn our eyes back to Europe, and besides, the Reds aren't Colonials, are they! Nor are the Blacks, since they came as slaves. Do you see the problem?"

"He wanted a name we could all share the same," said Alvin.

"Just right. There was one thing we all had in common. We all lived on the same continent. North America. So he thought of calling us North Americans. But that was too long. So—"

"Americans."

"That's a name that belongs to a fisherman living on the rugged coast of West Anglia as much as to a baron ruling his slavehold in the southwest part of Dryden. It belongs as much to the Mohawk chief in Irrakwa as to the Knicker-bocker shopkeeper in New Amsterdam. Old Ben knew that if people could once start thinking of themselves as Americans, we'd become a nation. Not just a piece of some tired old European country, but a single new nation here in a new land. So he started using that word in everything he wrote. Poor Richard's Almanac was full of talk about Americans this and Americans that. And Old Ben wrote letters to everybody, saying things like, Conflict over land claims is a problem for Americans to solve together. Europeans can't possibly understand what Americans need to survive. Why should Americans die for European wars? Why should Americans be bound by European precedents in our courts of law? Inside of five years, there was hardly a person from New England to Jacobia who didn't think of himself as being, at least partly, an American."

"It was just a name."

"But it is the name by which we call ourselves. And it includes everyone else on this continent who's willing to accept the name. Old Ben worked hard to make sure that name included as many people as possible. Without ever holding any public office except postmaster, he single-handedly turned a name into a nation. With the King ruling over the Cavaliers in the south, and the Lord Protector's men ruling over New England in the north, he saw nothing but chaos and war ahead, with Pennsylvania smack in the middle. He wanted to forestall that war, and he used the name 'American' to fend it off. He made the New Englanders fear to offend Pennsylvania, and made the Cavaliers bend over backward trying to woo Pennsylvanian support. He was the one who agitated for an American Congress to establish trade policies and uniform land law.

"And finally," Taleswapper continued, "just before he invited me over from England, he wrote the American Compact and got the seven original colonies to sign it. It wasn't easy, you know—even the number of states was the result of a great deal of struggle. The Dutch could see that most of the immigrants to America were English and Irish and Scotch, and they didn't want to be swallowed up—so Old Ben allowed them to divide New Netherland into three colonies so they'd have more votes in the Congress. With Suskwahenny split off from the land claimed by New Sweden and Pennsylvania, another squabble was put to rest."

"That's only six states," said Alvin.

"Old Ben refused to allow anyone to sign the Compact unless the Irrakwa were included as the seventh state, with firm borders, with Reds governing themselves. There were plenty of people who wanted a White man's nation, but Old Ben wouldn't hear of it. The only way to have peace, he said, was for all Americans to join together as equals. That's why his Compact doesn't allow slavery or even bonding. That's why his Compact doesn't allow any religion to have authority over any other. That's why his

Compact doesn't let the government close down a press or silence a speech. White, Black, and Red; Papist, Puritan, and Presbyterian; rich man, poor man, beggarman, thief— we all live under the same laws. One nation, created out of a single word."

"American."

"Now do you see why he calls it his greatest deed?"

"How come the Compact itself ain't more important?"

"The Compact was just the words. The name 'American' was the idea that made the words."

"It still doesn't include the Yankees and the Cavaliers, and it didn't stop war, neither, cause the Appalachee folk are still fighting against the King."

"But it *does* include all those people, Alvin. Remember the story of George Washington in Shenandoah? He was Lord Potomac in those days, leading King Robert's largest army against that poor ragtag band that was all Ben Arnold had left. It was plain to see that in the morning, Lord Potomac's Cavaliers would overrun that little fort and seal the doom of Tom Jefferson's free-mountain rebellion. But Lord Potomac had fought beside those mountain men in the wars against the French. And Tom Jefferson had been his friend in days gone by. In his heart he could not bear to think of the morrow's battle. Who was King Robert, that so much blood should be shed for him? All these rebels wanted was to own their land, and not have the King set barons over them, to tax them dry and turn them into slaves as surely as any Black in the Crown Colonies. He didn't sleep at all that night."

"He was praying," said Alvin.

"That's the way Thrower tells it," Taleswapper said sharply. "But no one knows. And when he spoke to the troops the next morning, he didn't say a word about *prayer*. But he did speak about the word Ben Franklin made. He wrote a letter to the King, resigning from his command

and rejecting his lands and titles. He didn't sign it 'Lord Potomac,' he signed it 'George Washington.' Then he rose up in the morning and stood before the blue-coat soldiers of the King and told them what he had done, and told them that they were free to choose, all of them, whether to obey their officers and go into battle, or march instead in defense of Tom Jefferson's great Declaration of Freedom. He said, 'The choice is yours, but as for me—' "

Alvin knew the words, as did every man, woman, and child on the continent. Now the words meant all the more to him, and he shouted them out: " 'My American sword will never shed a drop of American blood!' "

"And then, when most of his army had gone and joined the Appalachee rebels, with their guns and their powder, their wagons and their supplies, he ordered the senior officer of the men loyal to the King to arrest him. 'I broke my oath to the King,' he said. 'It was for the sake of a higher good, but still I broke my oath, and I will pay the price for my treason.' He paid, yes sir, paid with a blade through his neck. But how many people outside the court of the King think it was really treason?"

"Not a one," said Alvin.

"And has the King been able to fight a single battle against the Appalachees since that day?"

"Not a one."

"Not a man on that battlefield in Shenandoah was a citizen of the United States. Not a man of them lived under the American Compact. And yet when George Washington spoke of American swords and American blood, they understood the name to mean themselves. Now tell me, Alvin Junior, was old Ben wrong to say that the greatest thing he ever made was a single word?"

Alvin would have answered, but right then they stepped up onto the porch of the house, and before they could get to the door, it swung open, and Ma stood there looking down at him. From the look on her face, Alvin knew that he was in trouble this time, and he knew why.

"I meant to go to church, Ma!"

"Lots of dead people meant to go to heaven," she answered, "and they didn't get there, neither."

"It was my fault, Goody Faith," said Taleswapper.

"It surely was not, Taleswapper," she said.

"We got to talking, Goody Faith, and I'm afraid I distracted the boy."

"The boy was born distracted," said Ma, never taking her eyes from Alvin's face. "He takes after his father. If you don't bridle and saddle him and ride him to church, he never gets there, and if you don't nail his feet to the floor of the church he's out that door in a minute. A ten-year-old boy who hates the Lord is enough to make his mother wish he'd never been born."

The words struck Alvin Junior to the heart.

"That's a terrible thing to wish," said Taleswapper. His voice was real quiet, and Ma finally lifted her gaze to the old man's face.

"I *don't* wish it," she finally said.

"I'm sorry, Mama," said Alvin Junior.

"Come inside," she said. "I left church to come and find you, and now there's not time to get back before the sermon ends."

"We talked about a lot of things, Mama," Alvin said. "About my dreams, and about Ben Franklin, and—"

"The only story I want to hear from you," said Ma, "is the sound of hymn singing. If you won't go to the church, then you'll sit in the kitchen with me and sing me hymns while I fix the dinner."

So Alvin didn't get to see Old Ben's sentence in Taleswapper's book, not for hours. Ma kept him singing and working till dinnertime, and after dinner Pa and the big boys and Taleswapper sat around planning tomorrow's expedition to bring a millstone down from the granite mountain.

"I'm doing it for you," Pa said to Taleswapper, "so you better come along."

"I never asked you to bring a millstone."

"Not a day since you've been here that you haven't said something about what a shame it is that such a fine mill gets used as nothing but a haybarn, when people hereabouts need good flour."

"I only said it the once, that I remember."

"Well, maybe so," said Pa, "but every time I see you, I think about that millstone."

"That's because you keep wishing the millstone had been there when you threw me."

"He don't wish that!" shouted Cally. "Cause then you'd be dead!"

Taleswapper just grinned, and Papa grinned back. And they went on talking about this and that. Then the wives brought the nephews and nieces over for Sunday supper, and they made Taleswapper sing them the laughing song so many times that Alvin thought he'd scream if he heard another chorus of "Ha, Ha, Hee."

It wasn't till after supper, after the nephews and nieces were all gone, that Taleswapper brought out his book.

"I wondered if you'd ever open that book," Pa said.

"Just waiting for the right time." Then Taleswapper explained about how people wrote down their most important deed.

"I hope you don't expect *me* to write in there," Pa said.

"Oh, I wouldn't let you write in it, not yet. You haven't even told me the story of your most important deed." Taleswapper's voice got even softer. "Maybe you didn't actually *do* your most important deed."

Pa looked just a little angry then, or maybe a little afraid.

Whichever it was, he got up and came over. "Show me what's in that book, that other people thought was so all-fired important."

"Oh," said Taleswapper. "Can you read?"

"I'll have you know I got a Yankee education in Massachusetts before I ever got married and set up as a miller in West Hampshire, and *long* before I ever came out here. It may not amount to much compared to a *London* education like you got, Taleswapper, but you don't know how to write a word I can't read, lessen it's Latin."

Taleswapper didn't answer. He just opened the book. Pa read the first sentence. "The only thing I ever truly made was Americans." Pa looked up at Taleswapper. "Who wrote *that*?"

"Old Ben Franklin."

"The way I heard it the only American he ever made was illegitimate."

"Maybe Al Junior will explain it to you later," said Taleswapper.

While they said this, Alvin wormed his way in front of them, to stare at Old Ben's handwriting. It looked no different from other men's writing. Alvin felt a little disappointed, though he couldn't have said what he expected. Should the letters be made of gold? Of course not. There was no reason why a great man's words should look any different on a page than the words of a fool.

Still, he couldn't rid himself of frustration that the words were so plain. He reached out and turned the page, turned many pages, riffling them with his fingers. The words were all the same. Grey ink on yellowing paper.

A flash of light came from the book, blinding him for a moment.

"Don't play with the pages like that," said Papa. "You'll tear one."

Alvin turned around to look at Taleswapper. "What's

the page with light on it?" he asked. "What does it say *there*?"

"Light?" asked Taleswapper.

Then Alvin knew that he alone had seen it.

"Find the page yourself," said Taleswapper.

"He'll just tear it," said Papa.

"He'll be careful," said Taleswapper.

But Papa sounded angry. "I said stand away from that book, Alvin Junior."

Alvin started to obey, but felt Taleswapper's hand on his shoulder. Taleswapper's voice was quiet, and Alvin felt the old man's fingers moving in a sign of warding. "The boy saw something in the book," said Taleswapper, "and I want him to find it again for me."

And, to Alvin's surprise, Papa backed down. "If you don't mind getting your book ripped up by that careless lazy boy," he murmured, then fell silent.

Alvin turned to the book and carefully thumbed the pages, one at a time. Finally one fell into place, and from it came a light, which at first dazzled him, but gradually subsided until it came only from a single sentence, whose letters were on fire.

"Do you see them burning?" asked Alvin.

"No," said Taleswapper. "But I smell the smoke of it. Touch the words that burn for you."

Alvin reached out and gingerly touched the beginning of the sentence. The flame, to his surprise, was not hot, though it did warm him. It warmed him through to the bone. He shuddered as the last cold of autumn fled from his body. He smiled, he was so bright inside. But almost as soon as he touched it, the flame collapsed, cooled, was gone.

"What does it say?" asked Mama. She was standing now, across the table from them. She wasn't such a good reader, and the words were upside down to her.

Taleswapper read. "A Maker is born."

"There hasn't been a Maker," said Mama, "since the one who changed the water into wine."

"Maybe not, but that's what she wrote," said Taleswapper.

"Who wrote?" demanded Mama.

"A slip of a girl. About five years ago."

"What was the story that went with her sentence?" asked Alvin Junior.

Taleswapper shook his head.

"You said you never let people write unless you knew their story."

"She wrote it when I wasn't looking," said Taleswapper. "I didn't see it till the next place I stopped."

"Then how did you know it was her?" asked Alvin.

"It was her," he answered. "She was the only one there who could have opened the hex I kept on the book in those days."

"So you don't know what it means? You can't even tell me why I saw those letters burning?"

Taleswapper shook his head. "She was an innkeeper's daughter, if I remember rightly. She spoke very little, and when she did, what she said was always strictly truthful. Never a lie, even to be kind. She was considered to be something of a shrew. But as the proverb says, If you always speak your mind, the evil man will avoid you. Or something like that."

"Her name?" asked Mama. Alvin looked up in surprise. Mama hadn't seen the glowing letters, so why did she look so powerful eager to know about who wrote them?

"Sorry," said Taleswapper. "I don't remember her name right now. And if I remembered her name, I wouldn't tell it, nor will I tell whether I know the place where she lived. I don't want people seeking her out, troubling her for answers that she may not want to give. But I will say this.

She was a torch, and saw with true eyes. So if she wrote that a Maker was born, I believe it, and that's why I let her words stay in the book."

"I want to know her story someday," said Alvin. "I want to know why the letters were so bright."

He looked up and saw Mama and Taleswapper looking steadily into each other's eyes.

And then, around the fringes of his own vision, where he could almost but not quite see it, he sensed the Unmaker, trembling, invisible, waiting to shiver the world apart. Without even thinking about it, Alvin pulled the front of his shirt out of his pants and knotted the corners together. The Unmaker wavered, then retreated out of sight.

11

MILLSTONE

Taleswapper woke up to somebody shaking him. Still full dark outside, but it was time to be moving. He sat, flexed himself a little, and took some pleasure in how few knots and pains he had these days, sleeping on a soft bed. I could get used to this, he thought. I could enjoy living here.

The bacon was so fat he could hear it sizzling clear from the kitchen. He was just about to pull his boots on when Mary knocked at the door. "I'm presentable, more or less," he said.

She came in, holding out two pair of long thick stockings. "I knotted them myself," she said.

"I couldn't buy socks this thick in Philadelphia."

"Winter gets right cold here in the Wobbish country, and—" She didn't finish. Got too shy, ducked her head, and scampered out of the room.

Taleswapper pulled on the stockings, and his boots over them, and grinned. He didn't feel bad about accepting a few things like this. He worked as hard as anybody, and he'd done a lot to help ready this farm for winter. He was a good roof man—he liked climbing and didn't get dizzy.

So his own hands had made sure the house and barns and coops and sheds all were tight and dry.

And, without anybody ever deciding to do it, he had prepared the millhouse to receive a millstone. He had personally loaded all the hay from the mill floor, five wagons full. The twins, who really hadn't got their two farms going yet, since they married only that summer, did the unloading up in the big barn. It was all done without Miller himself ever touching a pitchfork. Taleswapper saw to that, without making a fuss over it, and Miller never insisted.

Other things, though, weren't going so well. Ta-Kumsaw and his Shaw-Nee Reds were driving off so many folks from down Carthage way that everybody had the jitters. It was fine for the Prophet to have his big town of thousands of Reds across the river, all talking about how they'd never again raise their hands in war for any reason. But there were a lot of Reds who felt the way Ta-Kumsaw did, that the White man ought to be forced to the shores of the Atlantic and floated back to Europe, with or without boats. There was war talk, and word was that Bill Harrison down in Carthage was only too happy to fan that particular flame, not to mention the French in Detroit, always urging the Reds to attack the American settlers in land the French claimed was part of Canada.

Folks in the town of Vigor Church talked about this all the time, but Taleswapper knew that Miller didn't take it all that seriously. He thought of Reds as country clowns that wanted nothing more than to guzzle such whisky as they could find. Taleswapper had seen that attitude before, but only in New England. Yankees never seemed to realize that New England Reds with any gumption had long since moved to the state of Irrakwa. It would surely open Yankee eyes to see that the Irrakwa were working heavily with steam engines brought straight from England, and up in the Finger Lakes country a White named Eli Whitney was helping them make a factory that could turn out guns about twenty times faster than it had ever been done before. Someday those Yankees were going to wake up and find out that the Reds weren't all likker-mad, and some White folks were going to have to scramble fast to catch up.

In the meantime, though, Miller didn't take the war talk very seriously. "Everybody knows there's Reds in the woods. Can't stop them from skulking around, but I haven't missed any chickens so it's no problem yet."

"More bacon?" asked Miller. He shoved the bacon board across the table toward Taleswapper.

"I'm not used to eating so much in the morning," said Taleswapper. "Since I've been here I've had more food at every meal than I used to eat in a whole day."

"Put some meat on your bones," said Faith. She slapped down a couple of hot scones with honey smeared on them.

"I can't eat another bite," protested Taleswapper.

The scones slid right off Taleswapper's plate. "Got em," said Al Junior.

"Don't reach across the table like that," said Miller. "And you can't eat both those scones."

Al Junior proved his father wrong in an alarmingly short time. Then they washed the honey off their hands, put on their gloves, and went out to the wagon. The first light was just showing in the east as David and Calm, who lived townward from the farm, rode up. Al Junior climbed in the back of the wagon, along with all the tools and ropes and tents and supplies—it would be a few days before they came back.

"So—do we wait for the twins and Measure?" asked Taleswapper.

Miller swung up onto the wagon seat. "Measure's on ahead, felling trees for the sledge. And Wastenot and

Wantnot are staying back here, riding circuit from house to house." He grinned. "Can't leave the womenfolk unprotected, with all the talk of wild Reds prowling around, can we?"

Taleswapper grinned back. Good to know that Miller wasn't as complacent as he seemed.

It was a good long way up to the quarry. On the road they passed the ruins of a wagon with a split millstone right in the middle of it. "That was our first try," said Miller. "But an axle dried out and jammed up coming down this steep hill, and the whole wagon fell in under the weight of the stone."

They came near a good-sized stream, and Miller told about how they had tried to float two millstones down on a raft, but both times the raft just up and sank. "We've had bad luck," said Miller, but from the set of his face he seemed to take it personally, as if someone had set out to make things fail.

"That's why we're using a sledge and rollers this time," said Al Junior, leaning over the back of the seat. "Nothing can fall off, nothing can break, and even if it does, it's all just logs, and we got no shortage of replacements."

"As long as it don't rain," said Miller. "Nor snow."

"Sky looks clear enough," said Taleswapper.

"Sky's a liar," said Miller. "When it comes to anything I want to do, water always gets in my way."

They got to the quarry when the sun was full up, but still far from noon. Of course, the trip back would be much longer. Measure had already felled six stout young trees and about twenty small ones. David and Calm set right to work, stripping off branches and rounding them smooth as possible. To Taleswapper's surprise, it was Al Junior who picked up the sack of stonecutting tools and headed up into the rocks.

"Where are you going?" asked Taleswapper.

"Oh, I've got to find a good place for cutting," said Al Junior.

"He's got an eye for stone," said Miller. But he wasn't saying all he knew.

"And when you find the stone, what'll you do then?" asked Taleswapper.

"Why, I'll cut it." Alvin sauntered on up the path with all the arrogance of a boy who knows he's about to do a man's job.

"Got a good hand for stone, too," said Miller.

"He's only ten years old," said Taleswapper.

"He cut the first stone when he was six," said Miller.

"Are you saying it's a knack?"

"I ain't saying nothing."

"Will you say this, Al Miller? Tell me if by chance you are a seventh son."

"Why do you ask?"

"It's said, by those who know such things, that a seventh son of a seventh son is born with the knowledge of how things look under the surface. That's why they make such good dowsers."

"Is that what they say?"

Measure walked up, faced his father, put his hands on his hips, and looked plain exasperated. "Pa, what harm is there in telling him? Everybody in the whole country roundabout here knows it."

"Maybe I think Taleswapper here knows more than I want him to know already."

"That's a right ungracious thing to say, Pa, to a man who's proved himself a friend twice over."

"He doesn't have to tell me anything he doesn't want me to know," said Taleswapper.

"Then *I'll* tell you," said Measure. "Pa is a seventh son, all right."

"And so is Al Junior," said Taleswapper. "Am I right?

You've never mentioned it, but I'd guess that when a man gives his own name to a son other than his firstborn, it's bound to be his seventh born."

"Our oldest brother Vigor died in the Hatrack River only a few minutes after Al Junior was born," said Measure.

"Hatrack," said Taleswapper.

"Do you know the place?" asked Measure.

"I know *every* place. But for some reason that name makes me think I should have remembered it before now, and I can't think why. Seventh son of a seventh son. Does he conjure the millstone out of the rock?"

"We don't talk about it like that," said Measure.

"He cuts," said Miller. "Just like any stonecutter."

"He's a *big* boy, but he's still just a boy," said Taleswapper.

"Let's just say," said Measure, "that when *he* cuts the stone it's a mite softer than when *I* cut it."

"I'd appreciate it," said Miller, "if you'd stay down here and help with the rounding and notching. We need a nice tight sledge and some smooth true rollers." What he didn't say, but Taleswapper heard just as plain as day, was, Stay down here and don't ask too many questions about Al Junior.

So Taleswapper worked with David and Measure and Calm all morning and well into the afternoon, all the time hearing a steady chinking sound of iron on stone. Alvin Junior's stonecutting set the rhythm for all their work, though no one commented on it.

Taleswapper wasn't the sort of man who could work in silence, though. Since the others weren't too conversational at first, he told stories the whole time. And since they were grown men instead of children, he told stories that weren't all adventure and heroics and tragic death.

Most of the afternoon, in fact, he devoted to the saga of John Adams: How his house was burnt down by a Boston mob after he won the acquittal of ten women accused of witchcraft. How Alex Hamilton invited him to Manhattan Island, where the two of them set up a law practice together. How in ten years they managed to maneuver the Dutch government to allow unlimited immigration of non-Dutch-speaking people, until English, Scotch, Welsh, and Irish were a majority in New Amsterdam and New Orange, and a large minority in New Holland. How they got English declared a second official language in 1780, just in time for the Dutch colonies to become three of the seven original states under the American Compact.

"I'll bet the Dutchmen hated those boys, by the time they were through," said David.

"They were better politicians than *that*," said Taleswapper. "Why, both of them learned to speak Dutch better than most Dutchmen, and had their children grow up speaking Dutch in Dutch schools. They were so dad-gum Dutch, boys, that when Alex Hamilton ran for governor of New Amsterdam and John Adams ran for president of the United States, they both did better in the Dutch parts of New Netherland than they did among the Scotch and Irish."

"Reckon if I run for mayor, I could get those Swedes and Dutchmen downriver to vote for me?" said David.

"*I* wouldn't even vote for you," said Calm.

"*I* would," said Measure. "And I hope someday you *do* run for mayor."

"He can't run for mayor," said Calm. "This ain't even a proper town."

"It will be," said Taleswapper. "I've seen it before. Once you get this mill working, it won't be long before three hundred people dwell between your mill and Vigor Church."

"You think so?"

"Right now people come in to Armor's store maybe three or four times a year," said Taleswapper. "But when they can get flour, they'll come in much more often. They'll prefer your mill to any other around here for some time, too, since you've got a smooth road and good bridges."

"If the mill makes money," Measure said, "Pa's sure to send for a Buhr Stone from France. We had one back in West Hampshire, before the flood broke up the mill. And a Buhr Stone means fine white flour."

"And white flour means good business," said David. "We older ones, we remember." He smiled wistfully. "We were almost rich there, once."

"So," said Taleswapper. "With all that traffic here, it won't be just a store and a church and a mill. There's good white clay down on the Wobbish. Some potter's bound to go into business, making redware and stoneware for the whole territory."

"Sure wish they'd hurry with *that*," said Calm. "My wife is sick unto death, she says, of having to serve food on tin plates."

"That's how towns grow," said Taleswapper. "A good store, a church, then a mill, then a pottery. Bricks, too, for that matter. And when there's a town—"

"David can be mayor," said Measure.

"Not me," said David. "All that politics business is too much. It's Armor wants that, not me."

"Armor wants to be king," said Calm.

"That's not kind," said David.

"But it's true," said Calm. "He'd try to be God, if he thought the job was open."

Measure explained to Taleswapper. "Calm and Armor don't get along."

"It ain't much of a husband that calls his wife a witch," said Calm bitterly.

"Why would he call her that?" asked Taleswapper.

"It's sure he doesn't call her that *now*," said Measure. "She promised him to give them up. All her knacks in the kitchen. It's a shame to make a woman run a household with just her own two hands."

"That's enough," David said. Taleswapper caught just a corner of his warning look.

Obviously they didn't trust Taleswapper enough to let him in on the truth. So Taleswapper let them know that the secret was already in his possession. "It seems to me that she uses more than Armor guesses," said Taleswapper. "There's a clever hex out of baskets on the front porch. And she used a calming on him before my eyes, the day I arrived in town."

Work stopped then, for just a moment. Nobody looked at him, but for a second they did nothing. Just took in the fact that Taleswapper knew Eleanor's secret and hadn't told about it to outsiders. Or to Armor-of-God Weaver. Still, it was one thing for him to know, and something else for them to confirm it. So they said nothing, just resumed notching and binding the sledge.

Taleswapper broke the silence by returning to the main topic. "It's just a matter of time before these western lands have enough people in them to call themselves states, and petition to join the American Compact. When that happens, there'll be need for honest men to hold office."

"You won't find no Hamilton or Adams or Jefferson out here in the wild country," said David.

"Maybe not," said Taleswapper. "But if you local boys don't set up your own government, you can bet there'll be plenty of city men willing to do it for you. That's how Aaron Burr got to be governor of Suskwahenny, before Daniel Boone shot him dead in ninety-nine."

"You make it sound like murder," said Measure. "It was a fair duel."

"To my way of thinking," said Taleswapper, "a duel is just two murderers who agree to take turns trying to kill each other."

"Not when one of them is an old country boy in buckskin and the other is a lying cheating city man," said Measure.

"I don't want no Aaron Burr trying to be governor over the Wobbish country," said David. "And that's what kind of man Bill Harrison is, down there in Carthage City. I'd vote for Armor before I'd vote for him."

"And I'd vote for you before I'd vote for Armor," said Taleswapper.

David grunted. He continued weaving rope around the notches of the sledge logs, binding them together. Taleswapper was doing the same thing on the other side. When he got to the knotting place, Taleswapper started to tie the two ends of the rope together.

"Wait on that," said Measure. "I'll go fetch Al Junior." Measure took off at a jog up the slope to the quarry.

Taleswapper dropped the ends of the rope. "Alvin Junior ties the knots? I would have thought grown men like you could tie them tighter."

David grinned. "He's got a knack."

"Don't any of you have knacks?" asked Taleswapper.

"A few."

"David's got a knack with the ladies," said Calm.

"Calm's got dancing feet at a hoedown. Ain't nobody fiddles like him, neither," said David. "It ain't on tune all the time, but he keeps that bow busy."

"Measure's a true shot," said Calm. "He's got an eye for things too far off for most folks to see."

"We got our knacks," said David. "The twins have a way of knowing when trouble's brewing, and getting there just about in time."

"And Pa, he fits things together. We have him do all the wood joints when we're building furniture."

"The womenfolk got women's knacks."

"But," said Calm, "there ain't nobody like Al Junior."

David nodded gravely. "Thing is, Taleswapper, he don't seem to know about it. I mean, he's always kind of surprised when things turn out good. He's right proud when we give him a job to do. I never seen him lord it over nobody because he's got more of a knack than they do."

"He's a good boy," said Calm.

"Kind of clumsy," said David.

"Not *clumsy*," said Calm. "Most times it isn't his *fault*."

"Let's just say that accidents happen more common around him."

"I wouldn't say jinx or nothing," said Calm.

"No, I wouldn't say jinx."

Taleswapper noted that in fact they both had said it. But he didn't comment on their indiscretion. After all, it was the third voice that made bad luck true. His silence was the best cure for their carelessness. And the other two caught on quickly enough. They, too, held their silence.

After a while, Measure came down the hill with Alvin Junior. Taleswapper dared not be the third voice, since he had taken part in the conversation before. And it would be even worse if Alvin himself spoke next, since he was the one who had been linked with a jinx. So Taleswapper kept his eye on Measure, and raised his eyebrows, to show Measure that he was expected to speak.

Measure answered the question that he thought Taleswapper was asking. "Oh, Pa's staying up by the rock. To watch."

Taleswapper could hear David and Calm breathe a sigh of relief. The third voice didn't have jinx in his mind, so Alvin Junior was safe.

Now Taleswapper was free to wonder *why* Miller felt he had to keep watch at the quarry. "What could happen to a rock? I've never heard of Reds stealing rocks."

Measure winked. "Powerful strange things happen sometimes, specially with millstones."

Alvin was joking with David and Calm now, as he tied the knots. He worked hard to get them as tight as he could, but Taleswapper saw that it wasn't in the knot itself that his knack was revealed. As Al Junior pulled the ropes tight, they seemed to twist and bite into the wood in all the notches, drawing the whole sledge tighter together. It was subtle, and if Taleswapper hadn't been watching for it, he wouldn't have seen. But it was real. What Al Junior bound was bound tight.

"That's tight enough to be a raft," said Al Junior, standing back to admire.

"Well, it's floating on solid earth this time," said Measure. "Pa says he won't even piss into water no more."

Since the sun was low in the west, they set to laying the fire. Work had kept them warm today, but tonight they'd need the fire to back off the animals and keep the autumn cold at bay.

Miller didn't come down, even at supper, and when Calm got up to carry food up the hill to his father, Taleswapper offered to come along.

"I don't know," said Calm. "You don't need to."

"I want to."

"Pa—he don't like lots of people gathered at the rock face, time like this." Calm looked a little sheepish. "He's a miller, and it's his stone getting cut there."

"I'm not a lot of people," said Taleswapper. Calm didn't say anything more. Taleswapper followed him up among the rocks.

On the way, they passed the sites of two early stonecuttings. The scraps of cut stone had been used to make a smooth ramp from the cliff face to ground level. The cuts were almost perfectly round. Taleswapper had seen plenty of stone cut before, and he'd never seen one cut this way—perfectly round, right in the cliff. Most times it was a whole slab they cut, then rounded it on the ground. There were several good reasons for doing it that way, but the best of all was that there was no way to cut the back of the stone unless you took a whole slab. Calm didn't slow down for him, so Taleswapper didn't have a chance to look closely, but as near as he could tell there was no possible way that the stonecutter in *this* quarry could have cut the back of the stone.

It looked just the same at the new site, too. Miller was raking chipped rock into a level ramp in front of the mill-stone. Taleswapper stood back and, in the last specks of daylight, studied the cliff. In a single day, working alone, Al Junior had smoothed the front of the millstone and chipped away the whole circumference. The stone was practically polished, still attached to the cliff face. Not only that, but the center hole had been cut to take the main shaft of the mill machinery. It was fully cut. And there was no way in the world that anybody could get a chisel in position to cut away the back.

"That's some knack the boy has," said Taleswapper.

Miller grunted assent.

"Hear you plan to spend the night up here," said Taleswapper.

"Heard right."

"Mind company?" asked Taleswapper.

Calm rolled his eyes.

But after a little bit, Miller shrugged. "Suit yourself."

Calm looked at Taleswapper with wide eyes and raised eyebrows, as if to say, Miracles never cease.

When Calm had set down Miller's supper, he left. Miller set aside the rake. "You et yet?"

"I'll gather wood for tonight's fire," said Taleswapper. "While there's still light. You eat."

"Watch out for snakes," said Miller. "They're mostly shut in for the winter now, but you never know."

Taleswapper watched out for snakes, but he never saw

any. And soon they had a good fire, laid with a heavy log that would burn all night.

They lay there in the firelight, wrapped in their blankets. It occurred to Taleswapper that Miller might have found softer ground a few yards away from the quarry. But apparently it was more important to keep the millstone in plain sight.

Taleswapper began talking. Quietly, but steadily, he talked about how hard it must be for fathers, to watch their sons grow, so full of hope for the boys, but never knowing when death would come and take the child away. It was the right thing to talk about, because soon it was Alvin Miller doing the talking. He told the story of how his oldest boy Vigor died in the Hatrack River, only a few minutes after Alvin Junior was born. And from there, he turned to the dozens of ways that Al Junior had almost died. "Always water," Miller said at the end. "Nobody believes me, but it's so. Always water."

"The question is," said Taleswapper, "is the water evil, trying to destroy a good boy? Or is it good, trying to destroy an evil power?"

It was a question that might have made some men angry, but Taleswapper had given up trying to guess when Miller's temper would flare. This time it didn't. "I've wondered that myself," said Miller. "I've watched him close, Taleswapper. Of course, he has a knack for making people love him. Even his sisters. He's tormented them unmerciful since he was old enough to spit in their food. Yet there's not a one of them who doesn't find a way to make him something special, and not just at Christmas. They'll sew his socks shut or smear soot on the privy bench or needle up his nightshirt, but they'd also die for him."

"I've found," said Taleswapper, "that some people have a knack for winning love without ever earning it."

"I feared that, too," said Miller. "But the boy doesn't

know he has that knack. He doesn't trick people into doing what he wants. He lets me punish him when he does wrong. And he could stop me, if he wanted."

"How?"

"Because he knows that sometimes when I see him, I see my boy Vigor, my firstborn, and then I can't do him any harm, even harm that's for his own good."

Maybe that reason was partly true, Taleswapper thought. But it certainly wasn't the whole truth.

A bit later, after Taleswapper stirred the fire to make sure the log caught well, Miller told the story that Taleswapper had come for.

"I've got a story," he said, "that might belong in your book."

"Give it a try," said Taleswapper.

"Didn't happen to me, though."

"Has to be something you saw yourself," said Taleswapper. "I hear the craziest stories that somebody heard happened to a friend of a friend."

"Oh, I saw this happen. It's been going on for years now, and I've had some discussions with the fellow. It's one of the Swedes downriver, speaks English good as I do. We helped him put up his cabin and his barn when he first come here, the year after us. And I watched him a little bit even then. See, he has a boy, a blond Swede boy, you know how they get."

"Hair almost white?"

"Like frost in the first morning sun, white like that, and shiny. A beautiful boy."

"I can see him in my mind," said Taleswapper.

"And that boy, his papa loved him. Better than his life. You know that Bible story, about that papa who gave his boy a coat of many colors?"

"I've heard tell of it."

"He loved his boy like that. But I saw them two walking alongside the river, and the father all of a sudden lurched kind of, just bumped his boy, and sent the lad tumbling down into the Wobbish. Now, it happened that the boy caught onto a log and his father and I helped pull him in, but it was a scary thing to see that the father might have killed his own best-loved child. It wouldn't've been a-purpose, mind you, but that wouldn't make the boy any less dead, or the father any less blameful."

"I can see the father might never get over such a thing."

"Well, of course *not*. Yet not long after that, I seen him a few more times. Chopping wood, and he swung that axe wild, and if the boy hadn't slipped and fell right at that very second, that axe would've bit into the boy's head, and I never seen nobody live after something like that."

"Nor I."

"And I tried to imagine what must be happening. What that father must be thinking. So I went to him one day, and I said, 'Nels, you ought to be more careful round that boy. You're likely to take that boy's head off someday, if you keep swinging that axe so free.'

"And Nels, he says to me, 'Mr. Miller, that wasn't no accident.' Well, you could've blowed me down with a baby's burp. What does he mean, no accident? And he says to me, 'You don't know how bad it is. I think maybe a witch cursed me, or the devil takes me, but I'm just working there, thinking how much I love the boy, and suddenly I have this wish to kill him. It came on me first when he was just a baby, and I stood at the top of the stairs, holding him, and it was like a voice inside my head, it said, "Throw him down," and I wanted to do it, even though I also knew it would be the most terrible thing in the world. I was hungry to throw him off, like a boy gets when he wants to smash a bug with a stone. I *wanted* to see his head break open on the floor.

"'Well, I just fought off that feeling, just swallowed it

back and held that boy so tight I like to smothered him. Finally when I got him back into his cradle, I knew that from then on I wasn't going to carry him up those stairs no more.

" 'But I couldn't just leave him alone, could I? He was my boy, and he grew up so bright and good and beautiful that I had to love him. If I stayed away, he cried cause his papa didn't play with him. But if I stayed with him, then those feelings came back, again and again. Not every day, but many a day, sometimes so fast that I did it afore I even knew what I was doing. Like the day I bumped him into the river, I just took a wrong step and tripped, but I knew even as I took that step that it was a wrong step, and that I'd trip, and that I'd bump him, I *knew* it, but I didn't have time to stop myself. And someday I know that I won't be able to stop myself, I won't mean to do it, but someday when that boy is under my hand, I'll kill him.' "

Taleswapper could see Miller's arm move, as if to wipe tears away from his cheek.

"Ain't that the strangest thing?" Miller asked. "A man having that kind of feeling for his own son."

"Does that fellow have any other sons?"

"A few. Why?"

"I just wondered if he ever felt a desire to kill them."

"Never, not a speck. I asked him that, matter of fact. I asked him, and he said not a speck."

"Well, Mr. Miller, what did you tell him?"

Miller breathed in and out a few times. "I didn't know what to tell him. Some things are just too big for a man like me to understand. I mean, the way that water is out to kill my boy Alvin. And then this Swede fellow with his son. Maybe there's some children that wasn't meant to grow up. Do you think so, Taleswapper?"

"I think there are some children that are so important, that someone—some force in the world—may want them dead. But there are always other forces, maybe stronger forces, that want them alive."

"Then why don't those forces show theirselves, Taleswapper? Why don't some power from heaven come and say— come to that poor Swedish man and say, 'Don't you fear no more, your boy is safe, even from you!' "

"Maybe those forces don't speak out loud in words. Maybe those forces just show you what they're doing."

"The only force that shows itself in this world is the one that kills."

"I don't know about that Swedish boy," said Taleswapper, "but I'd guess that there's a powerful protection on *your* son. From what you said, it's a miracle he isn't dead ten times over."

"That's the truth."

"I think he's being watched over."

"Not well enough."

"The water never got him, did it?"

"It came so close, Taleswapper."

"And as for that Swedish boy, I *know* he's got somebody watching over him."

"Who?" asked Miller.

"Why, his own father."

"His father is the enemy," said Miller.

"I don't think so," said Taleswapper. "Do you know how many fathers kill their sons by accident? They're out hunting, and a shot goes wrong. Or a wagon crushes the boy, or he takes a fall. Happens all the time. Maybe those fathers just didn't *see* what was happening. But this Swedish man is sharp, he sees what's happening, and he watches himself, catches himself in time."

Miller sounded a little more hopeful. "You make it sound like maybe the father ain't all bad."

"If he were all bad, Mr. Miller, that boy would be dead and buried long ago."

"Maybe. Maybe."

Miller thought for a while more. So long, in fact, that Taleswapper dozed a little. He snapped awake with Miller already talking.

"—and it's just getting worse, not better. Harder to fight off those feelings. Not all that long ago, he was standing up in a loft in the—in his barn—and he was pitching down hay. And there below him was his boy, and all it would take is to let fly with the pitchfork, easiest thing in the world, he could say the pitchfork slipped and no one would ever know. Just let it fly, and stick that boy right through. And he was going to do it. Do you understand me? It was so hard to fight off those feelings, harder than ever before, and he just *gave up*. Just decided to have it done with, to give in. And in that very moment, why, a stranger appeared in the doorway, and shouted, 'No,' and I set down the pitchfork—that's what he said, 'I set down the pitchfork, but I was shaking so bad I could hardly walk, knowing that the stranger saw me with murder in my heart, he must think I'm the most terrible man in the world to think of killing my own boy, he can't even guess how hard I've struggled all those years before—'"

"Maybe that stranger knew something about the powers that can work inside a man's heart," said Taleswapper.

"Do you think so?"

"Oh, I can't be sure, but maybe that stranger also saw how much that father loved the boy. Maybe the stranger was confused for a long time, but finally began to realize that the child was extraordinary, with powerful enemies. And then maybe he came to understand that no matter how many enemies the boy had, his father wasn't one of them. Wasn't an enemy. And he wanted to say something to that father."

"What did he want to say?" Miller brushed his eyes with

his sleeve again. "What do you think that stranger might want to say?"

"Maybe he wanted to say, 'You've done all you can do, and now it's too strong for you. Now you ought to send that boy away. To relatives back east, maybe, or as a prentice in some town.' That might be a hard thing for the father to do, since he loves the boy so much, but he'll do it because he knows that real love is to take the boy out of danger."

"Yes," said Miller.

"For that matter," said Taleswapper, "maybe you ought to do something like that with your own boy, Alvin."

"Maybe," said Miller.

"He's in some danger from the water around here, wouldn't you say? Somebody's protecting him, or some-*thing*. But maybe if Alvin weren't living here—"

"Then some of the dangers would go away," said Miller.

"Think about it," said Taleswapper.

"It's a terrible thing," said Miller, "to send your boy away to live with strangers."

"It's a worse thing, though, to put him in the ground."

"Yes," said Miller. "That's the worst thing in the world. To put your child in the ground."

They didn't talk any more, and after a while they both slept.

The morning was cold, with a heavy frost, but Miller wouldn't even let Al Junior come up to the rock until the sun burned it away. Instead they all spent the morning preparing the ground from the cliff face to the sledge, so they could roll the stone down the mountain.

By now, Taleswapper was sure that Al Junior used a hidden power to get the millstone away from the cliff face, even if he didn't realize it himself. Taleswapper was curious. He wanted to see just how powerful this power was, so he could understand more about its nature. And since Al Junior didn't realize what he was doing, Taleswapper's experiment had to be subtle, too. "How do you dress your stone?" asked Taleswapper.

Miller shrugged. "Buhr Stone is what I used before. They all come with sickle dress."

"Can you show me?" asked Taleswapper.

Using a corner of the rake, Miller drew a circle in the frost. Then he drew a series of arcs, radiating from the center of the circle out to the edges. Between each pair of arcs he drew a shorter arc, which began at the edge but never came closer than two-thirds of the way toward the center. "Like that," said Miller.

"Most millstones in Pennsylvania and Suskwahenny are quarter dress," said Taleswapper. "You know that cut?"

"Show me."

So Taleswapper drew another circle. It didn't show up as well, since the frost was burning off now, but it was good enough. He drew straight lines instead of curved ones from the center to the edge, and the shorter lines branched directly from the long ones and ran straight to the edge. "Some millers like this better, because you can keep it sharp longer. Since all the lines are straight, you get a nice even draw when you're tooling the stone."

"I can see that," said Miller. "I don't know, though. I'm used to those curvy lines."

"Well, suit yourself," said Taleswapper. "I've never been a miller, so I don't know. I just tell stories about what I've seen."

"Oh, I don't mind you showing me," said Miller. "Don't mind a bit."

Al Junior stood there, studying both circles.

"I think if we once get this stone home," said Miller, "I'll try that quarter dress on it. Looks to me like it might be easier to keep up a clean grind."

Finally the ground was dry, and Al Junior walked to the

cliff face. The other boys were all down below, breaking camp or bringing the horses up to the quarry. Only Miller and Taleswapper watched as Al Junior finally carried his hammer to the cliff face. He had a little more cutting to do, to get the circle to its full depth all around.

To Taleswapper's surprise, when Al Junior set the chisel in place and gave a whang with the hammer, a whole section of stone, some six inches long, split away from the cliff face and crumbled to the ground.

"Why, that stone's as soft as coal," said Taleswapper. "What kind of millstone can it make, if it's as weak as that?"

Miller grinned and shook his head.

Al Junior stepped away from the stone. "Oh, Taleswapper, it's *hard* stone, unless you know just the right place to crack it. Give it a try, you'll see."

He held out the chisel and hammer. Taleswapper took them and approached the rock. Carefully he laid the chisel onto the stone, a slight angle away from perpendicular. Then, after a few trial taps, he laid on a blow with the hammer.

The chisel practically jumped out of his left hand, and the shock of impact was so great that he dropped the hammer. "Sorry," he said, "I've done this before, but I must have lost the skill—"

"Oh, it's just the stone," said Al Junior. "It's kind of temperamental. It only likes to give in certain directions."

Taleswapper inspected the place where he had tried to cut. He couldn't find the spot. His mighty blow had left no mark at all.

Al Junior picked up the tools and laid the chisel against the stone. It looked to Taleswapper as though he put it in exactly the same place. But Al acted as though he had placed it quite differently. "See, it's getting just the angle on it. Like this."

He whanged with the hammer, the iron rang out, there was a cracking of stone, and once again crumbled stone pattered on the ground.

"I can see why you have him do all the cutting," Taleswapper said.

"Seems like the best way," said Miller.

In only a few minutes, the stone was fully rounded. Taleswapper said nothing, just watched to see what Al would do.

He set down his tools, walked to the millstone, and embraced it. His right hand curled around the lip of it. His left hand probed back into the cut on the other side. Alvin's cheek pressed against the stone. His eyes were closed. It looked for all the world as though he were listening to the rock.

He began to hum softly. A mindless little tune. He moved his hands. Shifted his position. Listened with the other ear.

"Well," Alvin said, "I can't hardly believe it."

"Believe what?" asked his father.

"Those last few cuts must have set up a real shiver in the rock. The back is already split right off."

"You mean that millstone is standing free?" asked Taleswapper.

"I think we can rock it forward now," said Alvin. "It takes a little rope work, but we'll get it out of there without too much trouble."

The brothers arrived with the ropes and horses. Alvin passed a rope back behind the stone. Even though not a single cut had been made against the back, the rope dropped easily into place. Then another rope, and another, and soon they were all tugging, first left, then right, as they slowly walked the heavy stone out of its bed in the cliff face.

"If I hadn't seen it," murmured Taleswapper.

"But you did," said Miller.

It was only a few inches clear when they changed the ropes, passing four lines through the center hole and hitching them to a team of horses uphill of the stone. "It'll roll on downhill just fine," Miller explained to Taleswapper. "The horses are there as a drag, pulling against it."

"It looks heavy."

"Just don't lie down in front of it," said Miller.

They started it rolling, very gently. Miller took hold of Alvin's shoulder and kept the boy well back from the stone—and uphill of it, too. Taleswapper helped with the horses, so he didn't get a good look at the back surface of the stone until it was down on level ground by the sledge.

It was smooth as a baby's backside. Flat as ice in a basin. Except that it was scored in a quarter dress pattern, straight lines radiating from the lip of the center hole to the edge of the stone.

Alvin came up to stand beside him. "Did I do it right?" he asked.

"Yes," said Taleswapper.

"It was the luckiest thing," said the boy. "I could just feel that stone ready to split right along those lines. It just wanted to split, easy as you please."

Taleswapper reached out and drew his finger gently along the edge of a dress cut. It stung. He brought his finger to his mouth, sucked, and tasted blood.

"Stone holds a nice sharp edge, don't it?" said Measure. He sounded as if this sort of thing happened every day. But Taleswapper could see the awe in his eyes.

"Good cut," said Calm.

"Best one yet," said David.

Then, with horses bracing against a rapid fall, they gently tipped it to lie on the sledge, dress side up.

"Will you do me a favor, Taleswapper?" asked Miller.

"If I can."

"Take Alvin back home with you now. His work's done."

"No, Papa!" Alvin shouted. He ran over to his father. "You can't make me go home *now*."

"Don't need no ten-year-old boys underfoot while we're manhandling a stone that size," said his father.

"But I've got to watch the stone, to make sure it don't split or chip, Pa!"

The older sons looked at their father, waiting. Taleswapper wondered what they hoped for. They were too old now, surely, to resent their father's particular love for his seventh son. They also must hope to keep the boy safe from harm. Yet it meant much to all of them that the stone arrive safely, unbroken, to begin its service in the mill. There could be no doubt that young Alvin had the power to keep it whole.

"You can ride with us till sundown," Miller finally said. "By then we'll be close enough to home that you and Taleswapper can head back and spend the night in beds."

"Fine with me," said Taleswapper.

Alvin Junior plainly wasn't satisfied, but he didn't answer back.

They got the sledge under way before noon. Two horses in front and two behind, for stopping, were hitched to the stone itself. The stone rested on the wooden raft of the sledge, and the sledge rode atop seven or eight of the small rollers at a time. The sledge moved forward, passing over new rollers waiting in front. As the rollers emerged from the back, one of the boys immediately yanked the roller out from under the ropes hitched to the trailing team, raced to the front, and laid it in place directly behind the lead team. It meant that each man ran about five miles for every mile the stone traveled.

Taleswapper tried to take his turn, but David, Calm, and Measure wouldn't hear of it. He ended up tending the trailing team, with Alvin perched atop one of the horses.

Miller drove the leading team, walking backward half the time to make sure he wasn't going too fast for the boys to keep up.

Hour after hour they went on. Miller offered to let them stop and rest, but they seemed not to tire, and Taleswapper was amazed to see how the rollers held up. Not a one split on a rock or from the sheer weight of the stone. They got scuffed and dented, but that was about all.

And as the sun sank to about two fingers above the horizon, awash in the ruddy clouds of the western sky, Taleswapper recognized the meadow opening up before them. They had made the whole journey in a single afternoon.

"I think I got the strongest brothers in the whole world," Alvin murmured.

I have no doubt of it, Taleswapper said silently. You who can cut a stone from the mountain without hands, because you "find" the right fractures in the rock, it's no surprise that your brothers find in themselves exactly as much strength as you believe they have. Taleswapper tried again, as he had tried so many times before, to puzzle out the nature of the hidden powers. Surely there was some natural law that governed their use—Old Ben had always said so. And yet here was this boy who, by mere belief and desire, could cut stone like butter and give strength to his brothers. There was a theory that the hidden power came from friendship with a particular element, but which was it that could do all that Alvin did? Earth? Air? Fire? Certainly not water, for Taleswapper knew that Miller's stories were all true. Why was it that Alvin Junior could wish for something, and the earth itself would bend to his will, while others could long for things and never cause so much as a breeze to blow?

They needed lanterns inside the millhouse by the time they rolled the stone through the doors. "Might as well lay it in place tonight," said Miller. Taleswapper imagined the fears that ran through Miller's mind. If he left the stone upright, it would surely roll in the morning and crush a particular child as he innocently carried water up to the house. Since the stone had miraculously come down from the mountain in a single day, it would be foolish to leave it anywhere but in its proper place, on the foundation of rammed earth and stone in the millhouse.

They brought a team inside and hitched it to the stone, as they had when they lowered it on the sledge back by the quarry. The team would pull against the weight of the stone as they levered it downward onto the foundation.

At the moment, though, the stone was resting on built-up earth just outside the circle of foundation stones. Measure and Calm were working their lever poles under the outside edge of the stone, ready to pry it up and make it fall into place. The stone rocked a little as they worked. David was holding the horses, since it would be a disaster if they pulled too soon and rocked the stone over the wrong way, to lie on its dress face in the plain dirt.

Taleswapper stood aside, watching as Miller directed his sons with useless calls of "Careful there" and "Steady now." Alvin had been beside him ever since they brought the millstone inside. One of the horses got jumpy. Miller reacted at once. "Calm, go help your brother with the horses!" Miller also took a step that way.

At that moment, Taleswapper realized that Alvin was *not* beside him, after all. He was carrying a broom, walking briskly toward the millstone. Perhaps he had seen some loose stones lying on the foundation; he had to sweep them away, didn't he? The horses backed up; the lines went slack. Taleswapper realized, just as Alvin got behind the stone, that with ropes so slack there'd be nothing to keep the stone from falling all the way over, if it should fall at just this moment.

Surely it would not fall, in a reasonable world. But Taleswapper knew by now that it was *not* a reasonable world at all. Alvin Junior had a powerful, invisible enemy, and it would not miss such a chance as this.

Taleswapper bounded forward. Just as he came level with the stone, he felt a lurching in the earth under his feet, a collapse of the firm dirt. Not much, just a few inches, but it was enough to let the inside lip of the millstone fall that much, which rocked the top of the great wheel more than two feet, and so quickly that the momentum could not be stopped. The millstone would fall all the way down, right into its proper place on the foundation, with Alvin Junior underneath, ground like grain under the stone.

With a shout, Taleswapper caught hold of Alvin's arm and yanked him back, away from the stone. Only then did Alvin see the great stone falling upon him. Taleswapper had enough force in his movement to carry the boy several feet back, but it was not quite enough. The boy's legs still lay in the stone's shadow. It was falling fast now, too fast for Taleswapper to respond, to do anything but watch it crush Alvin's legs. He knew that such an injury was the same as death, except that it would take longer. He had failed.

In that moment, though, as he watched the stone in its murderous fall, he saw a crack appear in the stone and, in less than an instant, it became a clean split right through the stone. The two halves leapt apart from each other, each with such a movement that it would fall beside Alvin's leg, not touching him.

No sooner had Taleswapper seen lantern light through the middle of the stone than Alvin himself cried, "No!"

To anyone else, it would seem the boy was shouting at the fall of the stone, at his impending death. But to Taleswapper, lying on the ground beside the boy, with the light of the lantern dazzling through the split in the millstone, the cry meant something else altogether. Heedless of his own danger, as children usually are, Alvin was crying out against the breaking of the millstone. After all his work, and the labors in bringing the stone home, he could not bear to see it breaking.

And because he could not bear it, it did not happen. The halves of the stone jumped back together like a needle jumping at a magnet, and the stone fell in one piece.

The shadow of the stone had exaggerated its footprint on the ground. It did not crush both Alvin's legs. His left leg, in fact, was completely clear of the stone, tucked up under him as it was. The right leg, however, lay so that the rim of the stone overlapped his shin by two inches at the widest point. Since Alvin was still pulling his legs away, the blow from the stone pushed it further in the direction it was already going. It peeled off all the skin and muscle, right down to the bone, but it did not catch the leg directly when it came to rest. The leg might not even have broken, had the broom not been lying crosswise under it. The stone drove Alvin's leg downward against the broom handle, just hard enough to snap both bones of the lower leg clean in half. The sharp edges of the bone broke the skin and came to rest like two sides of a vise, gripping the broom handle. But the leg was not under the millstone, and the bones were broken cleanly, not ground to dust under the rock.

The air was filled with the crash of stone on stone, the great-throated shouts of men surprised by grief, and above all the piercing cry of agony from one boy who was never so young and frail as now.

By the time anyone else could get there, Taleswapper had seen that both Alvin's legs were free of the stone. Alvin tried to sit up and look at his injury. Either the sight or the pain of it was too much for him, and he fainted. Alvin's father reached him then; he had not been nearest, but he had moved faster than Alvin's brothers. Taleswapper tried to reassure him, for with the bones gripping the broom handle, the leg did not look broken. Miller lifted his son, but the leg would not come, and even unconscious the pain wrung a cruel moan from the boy. It was Measure who steeled himself to pull on the leg and free it from the broom handle.

David already held a lantern, and as Miller carried the boy, David ran alongside, lighting the way. Measure and Calm would have followed, but Taleswapper called to them. "The womenfolk are there, and David, and your father," he said. "Someone needs to see to all this."

"You're right," said Calm. "Father won't be eager to come down here soon."

The young men used levers to raise the stone enough that Taleswapper could pull out the broom handle and the ropes that were still tied to the horses. The three of them cleared all the equipment out of the millhouse, then stabled the horses and put away the tools and supplies. Only then did Taleswapper return to the house to find that Alvin Junior was sleeping in Taleswapper's bed.

"I hope you don't mind," said Anne anxiously.

"Of course not," said Taleswapper.

The other girls and Cally were clearing away the supper dishes. In the room that had been Taleswapper's, Faith and Miller, both ashen and tight-lipped, sat beside the bed, where Alvin lay with his leg splinted and bandaged.

David stood near the door. "It was a clean break," he whispered to Taleswapper. "But the cuts in the skin—we fear infection. He lost all the skin off the front of his shin. I don't know if bare bone like that can ever heal."

"Did you put the skin back?" asked Taleswapper.

"Such as was left, we pressed into place, and Mother sewed it there."

"That was well done," said Taleswapper.

Faith lifted her head. "Do you know aught of physicking, then, Taleswapper?"

"Such as a man learns after years trying to do what he can among those who know as little as he."

"How could this happen?" Miller said. "Why now, after so many other times that did him no injury?" He looked up at Taleswapper. "I had come to think the boy had a protector."

"He has."

"Then the protector failed him."

"It did not fail," said Taleswapper. "For a moment, as the stone fell, I saw it split, wide enough that it wouldn't have touched him."

"Like the ridgebeam," whispered Faith.

"I thought I saw it too, Father," said David. "But when it came down whole, I decided I must have seen what I wished for, and not what was."

"There's no split in it now," said Miller.

"No," said Taleswapper. "Because Alvin Junior refused to let it split."

"Are you saying he knit it back together? So it would strike him and wreck his leg?"

"I'm saying he had no thought of his leg," said Taleswapper. "Only of the stone."

"Oh, my boy, my good boy," murmured his mother, gently caressing the arm that extended thoughtlessly toward her. As she moved his fingers, they limply bent as she pushed them, then sprang back.

"Is it possible?" asked David. "That the stone split and was made whole again, as quickly as that?"

"It must be," said Taleswapper, "because it happened."

Faith moved her son's fingers again, but this time they did not spring back. They extended even further, then flexed into a fist, then extended flat again.

"He's awake," said his father.

"I'll fetch some rum for the boy," said David. "To slack the pain. Armor'll have some in his store."

"No," murmured Alvin.

"The boy says no," said Taleswapper.

"What does he know, in pain as he is?"

"He has to keep his wits about him, if he can," said Taleswapper. He knelt by the bed, just to the right of Faith, so he was even nearer to the boy's face. "Alvin, do you hear me?"

Alvin groaned. It must have meant yes.

"Then listen to me. Your leg is very badly hurt. The bones are broken, but they've been set in place—they'll heal well enough. But the skin was torn away, and even though your mother has sewn it back in place, there's a good chance the skin will die and take gangrene, and kill you. Most surgeons would cut off your leg to save your life."

Alvin tossed his head back and forth, trying to shout. It came out as a moan: "No, no, no."

"You're making things worse!" Faith said angrily.

Taleswapper looked at the father for permission to go on.

"Don't torment the boy," said Miller.

"There's a proverb," said Taleswapper. "The apple tree never asks the beech how he shall grow, nor the lion the horse, how he shall take his prey."

"What does that mean?" asked Faith.

"It means that I have no business trying to teach *him* how to use powers that I can't begin to understand. But since he doesn't know how to do it himself, I'll have to try, won't I?"

Miller pondered a moment. "Go ahead, Taleswapper. Better for him to know how bad it is, whether he can heal himself or not."

Taleswapper held the boy's hand gently between his own. "Alvin, you want to keep your leg, don't you? Then you have to think of it the way you thought of the stone.

You have to think of the skin of your leg, growing back, attaching to the bone as it should. You have to study it out. You'll have plenty of time for it, lying here. Don't think about the pain, think about the leg as it should be, whole and strong again."

Alvin lay there, squinting his eyes closed against the pain.

"Are you doing that, Alvin? Can you try?"

"No," said Alvin.

"You have to fight against the pain, so you can use your own knack to make things right."

"I never will," said Alvin.

"Why not!" cried Faith.

"The Shining Man," said Alvin. "I promised him."

Taleswapper remembered Alvin's oath to the Shining Man, and his heart sank.

"What's the Shining Man?" asked Miller.

"A—visitation he had, when he was little," said Taleswapper.

"How come we never heard of this afore now?" Miller asked.

"It was the night the ridgebeam split," said Taleswapper. "Alvin promised the Shining Man that he'd never use his power for his own benefit."

"But Alvin," said Faith. "This isn't to make you rich or nothing, this is to save your *life*."

The boy only winced against the pain and shook his head.

"Will you leave me with him?" said Taleswapper. "Just for a few minutes, so I can talk to him?"

Miller was rushing Faith out the door of the room before Taleswapper even finished his sentence.

"Alvin," said Taleswapper. "You must listen to me, listen carefully. You know I won't lie to you. An oath is a terrible thing, and I'd never counsel a man to break his word, even to save his own life. So I won't tell you to use your power for your own good. Do you hear me?"

Alvin nodded.

"Just think, though. Think of the Unmaker going through the world. Nobody sees him as he does his work, as he tears down and destroys things. Nobody but one solitary boy. Who is that boy, Alvin?"

Alvin's lips formed the word, though no sound came out. Me.

"And that boy has been given a power that he can't even begin to understand. The power to build against the enemy's unbuilding. And more than that, Alvin, the *desire* to build as well. A boy who answers every glimpse of the Unmaker with a bit of making. Now, tell me, Alvin, those who help the Unmaker, are they the friend or the enemy of mankind?"

Enemy, said Alvin's lips.

"So if you help the Unmaker destroy his most dangerous foe, you're an enemy of mankind, aren't you?"

Anguish wrung sound from the boy. "You're twisting it," he said.

"I'm straightening it," said Taleswapper. "Your oath was never to use your power for your own benefit. But if you die, only the Unmaker benefits, and if you live, if that leg is healed, then that's for the good of all mankind. No, Alvin, it's for the good of the world and all that's in it."

Alvin whimpered, more against the pain in his mind than the pain in his body.

"But your oath was clear, wasn't it? Never to your own benefit. So why not satisfy one oath with another, Alvin? Take an oath now, that you will devote your whole *life* to building up against the Unmaker. If you keep *that* oath— and you will, Alvin, you're a boy who keeps his word—if you keep that oath, then saving your own life is truly for the benefit of others, and not for your private good at all."

Taleswapper waited, waited, until at last Alvin nodded slightly.

"Do you take an oath, Alvin Junior, that you will live your life to defeat the Unmaker, to make things whole and good and right?"

"Yes," whispered the boy.

"Then I tell you, by the terms of your own promise, you must heal yourself."

Alvin gripped Taleswapper's arm. "How," he whispered.

"That I don't know, boy," said Taleswapper. "How to use your power, you have to find that out inside yourself. I can only tell you that you must try, or the enemy has his victory, and I'll have to end your tale with your body being lowered into a grave."

To Taleswapper's surprise, Alvin smiled. Then Taleswapper understood the joke. His tale would end with the grave no matter what he did today. "Right enough, boy," said Taleswapper. "But I'd rather have a few more pages about you before I put finis to the Book of Alvin."

"I'll try," whispered Alvin.

If he tried, then surely he would succeed. Alvin's protector had not brought him this far only to let him die. Taleswapper had no doubt that Alvin had the power to heal himself, if he could only figure out the way. His own body was far more complicated than the stone. But if he was to live, he had to learn the pathways of his own flesh, bind the fissures in the bones.

They made a bed for Taleswapper out in the great room. He offered to sleep on the floor beside Alvin's bed, but Miller shook his head and answered, "That's my place."

Taleswapper found it hard to sleep, though. It was the middle of the night when he finally gave up, lit a lantern with a match from the fire, bundled on his coat, and went outside.

The wind was brisk. There was a storm coming, and

from the smell in the air, it would be snow. The animals were restless in the big barn. It occurred to Taleswapper that he might not be alone outside tonight. There might be Reds in the shadows, or even wandering among the buildings of the farm, watching him. He shuddered once, then shrugged off the fear. It was too cold a night. Even the most bloodthirsty, White-hating Choc-Taws or Cree-Eks spying from the south were too smart to be outside with such a storm coming.

Soon the snow would fall, the first of the season, but it would be no slight trace. It would snow all day tomorrow, Taleswapper could feel it, for the air behind the storm would be even colder than this, cold enough for the snow to be fluffy and dry, the kind of snow that piled deeper and deeper, hour after hour. If Alvin had not hurried them home with the millstone in a single day, they would have been trying to sledge the stone home in the midst of the snowfall. It would have become slippery. Something even worse might have happened.

Taleswapper found himself in the millhouse, looking at the stone. It was so solid-looking, it was hard to imagine anyone ever moving it. He touched the face of it again, being careful not to cut himself. His fingers brushed over the shallow dress cuts, where flour would collect when the great water wheel turned the shaft and made the grindstone roll around and around atop the millstone, as steadily as the Earth rolled around and around the sun, year after year, turning time into dust as surely as the mill turned grain into flour.

He glanced down, to the place where the earth had given way slightly under the millstone, tipping it and nearly killing the boy. The bottom of the depression glistened in the lantern light. Taleswapper knelt and dipped his finger into a half-inch of water. It must have collected there, weakening the ground, carrying away the soil. Not so that it would ever be visibly moist. Just enough that when great weight was placed on it, it would give way.

Ah, Unmaker, thought Taleswapper, show yourself to me, and I'll build such a building that you'll be trussed up and held captive forever. But try as he might, he could not make his eyes see the trembling air that had shown itself to Alvin Miller's seventh son. Finally Taleswapper took up the lantern and left the millhouse. The first flakes were falling. The wind had almost died. The snow came faster and faster, dancing in the light of his lantern. By the time he reached the house, the ground was grey with snow, the forest invisible in the distance. He went inside the house, lay down on the floor without removing even his boots, and fell asleep.

12

BOOK

They kept a three-log fire, night and day, so the
stones of the wall seemed to glow with heat, and
the air in his room was dry. Alvin lay unmoving
on his bed, his right leg heavy with splints and bandages,
pressing into the bed like an anchor, the rest of his body
afloat, adrift, pitching and rolling and yawing. He was
dizzy, and a little sick.

But he hardly noticed the weight of his leg, or the dizziness. The pain was his enemy, throbs and stabs of it taking his mind away from the task that Taleswapper had set
him: to heal himself.

Yet the pain was his friend, too. It built a wall around
him so he scarce knew he was in a house, in a room, on a
bed. The outside world could burn up and turn to ash and
he'd never notice it. It was the world inside that he was exploring now.

Taleswapper didn't know half what he was talking
about. It wasn't a matter of making pictures in his mind.
His leg wouldn't get better from just pretending it was
all healed up. But Taleswapper still had the right idea. If
Alvin could feel his way through the rock, could find the
weak and strong places and teach them where to break and

where to hold firm, why couldn't he do it with skin and bone?

Trouble was, skin and bone was all mixed up. The rock was pretty much the same thing through and through, but the skin changed with every layer, and it wasn't no easy trick figuring where everything went. He lay there with his eyes closed, looking into his own flesh for the first time. At first he tried following the pain, but that didn't get nowhere, just led him to where everything was mashed and cut and messed up so he couldn't tell up from down. After a long while he tried a different tack. He listened to his heart beating. At first the pain kept tearing him away, but after a while he closed in on that sound. If there was noise in the world outside he didn't know about it, because the pain shut all that out. And the rhythm of the heartbeat, that shut out the pain, or mostly, anyway.

He followed the tracks of his blood, the big strong stream, the little streams. Sometimes he got lost. Sometimes a stab from his leg just broke in and demanded to be heard. But by and by he found his way to healthy skin and bone in the other leg. The blood wasn't half so strong there, but it led him where he wanted to go. He found all the layers, like the skin of an onion. He learned their order, saw how the muscle was tied together, how the tiny veins linked up, how the skin stretched taut and bonded tight.

Only then did he find his way to the bad leg. The patch of skin Mama sewed on was pretty much dead, just turning to rot. Alvin Junior knew what it needed, though, if any part of it was to live. He found the mashed-off ends of the arteries around the wound, and began to urge them to grow, just the way he made cracks travel through stone. The stone was easy, compared to this—to make a crack, it just had to let go, that's all. The living flesh was slower to do what he wanted, and pretty soon he gave up on all but the strongest artery.

He began to see how it was using bits and pieces of this and that to build with. A lot was happening that was far too small and fast and complicated for Alvin to get hold of with his mind. But he could get his body to free up what the artery needed in order to grow. He could send it where it was needed, and after a while the artery linked up with the rotted tissue. It took some doing, but he finally found the end of a shriveled artery and linked them up, and sent the blood flowing into the sewn-on patch.

Too soon, too fast. He felt the heat on his leg from blood pouring out of the dead flesh at a dozen points; it couldn't hold in all the blood he sent. Slow, slow, slow. He followed the blood, now seeping instead of pumping, and again linked up blood vessels, arteries to veins, trying to match it, as best he could, to the other leg.

Finally it was done, or well enough. The normal flow of blood could be contained. Many parts of the patch of skin came back to life as the blood returned. Other parts stayed dead. Alvin kept going around and around with the blood, stripping away the dead parts, breaking them up into bits and pieces too small for him to recognize. But the living parts recognized them well enough, took them up, put them to work. Wherever Alvin explored, he made the flesh grow.

Until he was so weary in his mind from thinking so small and working so hard that he fell asleep in spite of himself.

"I don't want to wake him."

"No way to change the bandage without touching it, Faith."

"All right, then—oh, be careful, Alvin! No, let me!"

"I've done this before—"

"On cows, Alvin, not on little boys!"

Alvin Junior felt pressure on his leg. Something pulling at the skin there. The pain wasn't as bad as yesterday. But he was still too tired even to open his eyes. Even to make a sound to let them know he was awake, he could hear them.

"Good laws, Faith, he must have bled something awful in the night."

"Mama, Mary says I have to—"

"Hush up and get on out of here, Cally! Can't you see your ma's worried about—"

"No need to yell at the boy, Alvin. He's only seven."

"Seven's old enough to keep his mouth shut and leave grown-ups alone when we've got things to—look at that."

"I can hardly believe it."

"I thought to see pus coming out like cream from a cow's tit."

"Clean as can be."

"And skin growing back, will you look at that? Your sewing must've took."

"I hardly dared to hope that skin would live."

"Can't even see no bone under there."

"The Lord is blessing us. I prayed all night, Alvin, and look what God has done."

"Well, you should've prayed harder, then, and got it healed up tight. I need this boy for chores."

"Don't you get blasfemious with me, Alvin Miller."

"It just gripes me hollow, the way God always sneaks in to take the credit. Maybe Alvin's just a good healer, you ever think of that?"

"Look, your nastiness is waking the boy."

"See if he wants a drink of water."

"He's getting one whether he wants it or not."

Alvin wanted it badly. His body was dry, not just his mouth; it needed to make back what it lost in blood. So he swallowed as much as he could, from a tin cup held to his mouth. A lot of it spilled around his face and neck but he didn't hardly notice that. It was the water that trickled into his belly that mattered. He lay back and tried to find out from the inside how his wound was doing. But it was too hard to get back there, too hard to concentrate. He dropped off before he was halfway there.

He woke again, and thought it must be night again, or maybe the curtains were drawn. He couldn't find out cause it was too hard to open his eyes, and the pain was back, fierce again, and something maybe even worse: the wound was a-tickling till he could hardly keep himself from reaching down to scratch. After a while, though, he was able to find the wound and once again help the layers to grow. By the time he slept, there was a thin, complete layer of skin over the whole wound. Underneath, the body was still working to renew the ravaged muscles and knit the broken bones. But there'd be no more loss of blood, no more open wound to get infected.

"Look at this, Taleswapper. You ever seen the like of this?"

"Skin like a newborn baby."

"Maybe I'm crazy, but except for the splint I can't see no reason to leave this leg bound up no more."

"Not a sign of a wound. No, you're right, there's no need for a bandage now."

"Maybe my wife is right, Taleswapper. Maybe God just rared back and passed a miracle on my boy."

"Can't prove anything. When the boy wakes up, maybe he'll know something about it."

"Not a chance of that. He hasn't even opened his eyes this whole time."

"One thing's certain, Mr. Miller. The boy isn't about to die. That's more than I could have guessed yesterday."

"I was set to build him a box to hold him underground,

that I was. I didn't see no chance him living. Will you look at how healthy he is? I want to know what's protecting him, or who."

"Whatever is protecting him, Mr. Miller, the boy is stronger. That's something to think about. His protector split that stone, but Al Junior put it back together and not a thing his protector could do about it."

"Reckon he even knew what he was doing?"

"He must have some notion of his powers. He knew what he could do with the stone."

"I never heard of a knack like this, to tell you straight. I told Faith what he did with that stone, dressing it on the backside without ever laying on a tool, and she starts reading from the Book of Daniel and crying about fulfilment of the prophecy. Wanted to rush in here and warn the boy about clay feet. Don't that beat all? Religion makes them crazy. Not a woman I ever met wasn't crazy with religion."

The door opened.

"Get out of here! Are you so dumb I have to tell you twenty times, Cally? Where's his mother, can't she keep one seven-year-old boy away from—"

"Be easy on the lad, Miller. He's gone now, anyway."

"I don't know what's wrong with him. As soon as Al Junior is down, I see Cally's face wherever I look. Like an undertaker hoping for a fee."

"Maybe it's strange to him. To have Alvin hurt."

"As many times as Alvin's been an inch from death—"

"But never injured."

A long silence.

"Taleswapper."

"Yes, Mr. Miller?"

"You've been a good friend to us here, sometimes in spite of ourselfs. But I reckon you're still a walking man."

"That I am, Mr. Miller."

"What I'm saying is, not to rush you off, but if you go

anytime soon, and you happen to be heading generally eastward, do you think you could carry a letter for me?"

"I'd be glad to. And no fee, to sender or receiver."

"That's right kind of you. I been thinking on what you said. About a boy needing to be sent far off from certain dangers. And I thought, in all the world where's there some folks I can trust to look after the boy? We got no kin worth speaking of back in New England—I don't want the boy raised Puritan on the brink of hell anyway."

"I'm relieved to hear that, Mr. Miller, because I have no great longing to see New England again myself."

"If you just follow back on the road we made coming west, sooner or later you come along to a place on the Hatrack River, some thirty miles north of the Hio, not all that far downriver from Fort Dekane. There's a road house there, or leastwise there was, with a graveyard out back where a stone says 'Vigor he died to save his kin.'"

"You want me to take the boy?"

"No, no, I'll not send him now that the snow's come. Water—"

"I understand."

"There's a blacksmith there, and I thought he might want a prentice. Alvin's young, but he's big for his age, and I reckon he'll be a bargain for the smith."

"Prentice?"

"Well, I sure won't make him a bond slave, now, will I? And I got no money to send him off to school."

"I'll take the letter. But I hope I can stay till the boy is awake, so I can say good-bye."

"I wasn't going to send you out tonight, was I? Nor tomorrow, with new snow deep enough to smother bunnies."

"I didn't know if you had noticed the weather."

"I always notice when there's water underfoot." He laughed wryly, and they left the room.

Alvin Junior lay there, trying to figure why Pa wanted

to send him away. Hadn't he done right all his life, as best he could? Hadn't he tried to help all he knew how? Didn't he go to Reverend Thrower's school, even though the preacher was out to make him mad or stupid? Most of all, didn't he finally get a perfect stone down from the mountain, holding it together all the time, teaching it the way to go, and at the very end risking his leg just so the stone wouldn't split? And now they were going to send him away.

Prentice! To a blacksmith! In his whole life he never even saw a blacksmith up to now. They had to ride three days to the nearest smithy, and Pa never let him go along. In his whole life he never even been ten mile from home one way or any other.

In fact, the more he thought about it the madder he got. Hadn't he been begging Mama and Papa just to let him go out walking in the woods alone, and they wouldn't let him. Had to have somebody with him all the time, like he was a captive or a slave about to run off. If he was five minutes late getting somewhere, they came to look for him. He never got to go on long trips—the longest one ever was to the quarry a few times. And now, after they kept him penned up like a Christmas goose all his life, they were set to send him off to the end of the whole earth.

It was so blame unfair that tears come to his eyes and squeezed out and tickled down his cheeks right into his ears, which felt so silly it made him laugh.

"What you laughing at?" asked Cally.

Alvin hadn't heard him come in.

"Are you all better now? It ain't bleeding nowhere, Al." Cally touched his cheek.

"You crying cause it hurts so bad?"

Alvin probably could have spoke to him, but it seemed like too much work to open up his mouth and push words out, so he kind of shook his head, slow and gentle.

"You going to die, Alvin?" asked Cally.

He shook his head again.

"Oh," said Cally.

He sounded so disappointed that it made Alvin a little mad. Mad enough to get his mouth working after all. "Sorry," he croaked.

"Well it ain't fair, anyhow," said Cally. "I didn't want you dead, but they all said you was going to die. And I got to thinking what it'd be like if *I* was the one they all took care of. All the time, everybody watching out for you, and when I say one little thing they just say, Get out of here, Cally, Just shut up, Cally. Nobody asked you, Cally, Ain't you spose to be in bed, Cally? They don't care what I do. Except when I start hitting *you*, then they all say, Don't get in fights, Cally."

"You wrestle real good for a field mouse." At least that was what Alvin meant to say, but he didn't know for sure if his lips even moved.

"You know what I did one time when I was six? I went out and got myself lost in the woods. I just walked and walked. Sometimes I closed my eyes and spun around a few times so I'd sure not know where I was. I must have been lost half the day. Did one soul come looking for me? I finally had to turn around and find my own way home. Nobody said, Where you been all day, Cally? Mama just said, Your hands are dirty as the back end of a sick horse, go wash yourself."

Alvin laughed again, near silently, his chest heaving.

"It's funny for *you*. Everybody looks after *you*."

Alvin worked hard to make a sound this time. "You want me gone?"

Cally waited a long time to answer. "No. Who'd play with me then? Just the dumb old cousins. There ain't a good wrassler in the bunch of them."

"I'm going," whispered Alvin.

"No you ain't. You're the seventh son and they'll never let you go."

"Going."

"Course the way I count up it's *me* that's number seven. David, Calm, Measure, Wastenot, Wantnot, Alvin Junior that's you, and then me, that's seven."

"Vigor."

"He's dead. He's been dead a long time. Somebody ought to tell that to Ma and Pa."

Alvin lay there, near wore out from the few things he said. Cally didn't say anything much after that. Just sat there, still as could be. Holding Alvin's hand real tight. Pretty soon Alvin started drifting, so he wasn't sure altogether whether Cally really spoke or it was in a dream. But he heard Cally say, "I don't never wish you dead, Alvin." And then he might have said, "I wish I was you." But anyway Alvin drifted off to sleep, and when he woke up again there was nobody with him and the house was still except for nightsounds, the wind rattling the shutters, the timbers popping as they shrunk from the cold, the log snapping in the hearth.

One more time Alvin went inside himself and worked his way down to the wound. Only this time he didn't have much to do with the skin and muscle. It was the bones he worked on now. It surprised him how lacy it was, pocked with little hollows all over, not solid straight through like the millstone was. But he learned the way of it soon enough, and it was easy after a while to knit the bones up tight.

Still, there was something wrong with that bone. Something in his bad leg just wouldn't get exactly like the good leg. But it was so small he couldn't see it clear. Just knew that whatever it was, it made the bone sick inside, just a little patch of sickness, but he couldn't figure how to make it better. Like trying to pick up snowflakes off the ground, whenever he thought he had ahold of something, it turned out to be nothing, or maybe just too small to see.

Maybe, though, it would just go away. Maybe if everything else got better, that sick place on his bone would get better by itself.

ELEANOR WAS LATE getting back from her mother's house. Armor believed that a wife should have strong ties with her family, but coming home at dusk was too dangerous.

"There's talk of wild Reds up from the south," said Armor-of-God. "And you traipsing about after dark."

"I hurried home," she said. "I know the way in the dark."

"It's not a question of knowing the way," he said sternly. "The French are giving guns as bounty on White scalps now. It won't tempt the Prophet's people, but there's many a Choc-Taw who'd be glad to come up to Fort Detroit, gathering scalps along the way."

"Alvin isn't going to die," said Eleanor.

Armor hated it when she turned the subject like that. But it was such news that he couldn't very well not ask after it. "They decide to take off the leg, then?"

"I saw the leg. It's getting better. And Alvin Junior was awake late this afternoon. I talked to him awhile."

"I'm glad he was awake, Elly, I truly am, but I hope you don't expect the leg to get better. A big wound like that may look to be healing for a while, but the rot'll set in pretty soon."

"I don't think so this time," she said. "You want supper?"

"I must have gnawed down two loaves just pacing back and forth wondering whether you were even coming home."

"It isn't good for a man to get a belly."

"Well, I got one, and it calls out for food just like any other man's."

"Mama gave me a cheese to bring home." She set it out on the table.

Armor had his doubts. He figured half the reason Faith Miller's cheeses turned out so good was because she *did* things to the milk. At the same time, there wasn't no better cheese on the banks of the Wobbish, nor up Tippy-Canoe Creek neither.

It put him out of sorts when he caught himself compromising with witchery. And being out of sorts, he wasn't about to let anything lie, even though he knew Elly plain didn't want to talk about it. "Why don't you think the leg will rot?"

"It's just getting better so fast," she said.

"How much better?"

"Oh, pert near fixed."

"How near?"

She turned around, rolled her eyes, and turned back away from him. She started cutting up an apple to eat with the cheese.

"I said *how* near, Elly? How near fixed?"

"Fixed."

"Two days after a millstone rips off the front half of his leg, and it's fixed?"

"Only two days?" she said. "Seems like a week to me."

"Calendar says it's two days," said Armor. "Which means there's been witchery up there."

"As I read the gospels, the one that healed people wasn't no witch."

"Who did it? Don't tell me your pa or ma suddenly figured out something as strong as that. Did they conjure up a devil?"

She turned around, the knife in her hands still poised for

cutting. There was a flash in her eyes. "Pa may be no kind of church man, but the devil never set foot in our house."

That wasn't what Reverend Thrower said, but Armor knew better than to bring *him* into the conversation. "It's that beggar, then."

"He works for his room and board. Hard as anyone."

"They say he knew that old wizard Ben Franklin. And that atheist from Appalachee, Tom Jefferson."

"He tells good stories. And he didn't heal the boy neither."

"Well, *somebody* did."

"Maybe he just healed up himself. Anyway, the leg's still *broke*. So it ain't a miracle or nothing. He's just a fast healer."

"Well maybe he's a fast healer cause the devil takes care of his own."

From the look in her eye when she turned around, Armor kind of wished he hadn't said it. But dad-gum it, Reverend Thrower as much as said the boy was as bad as the Beast of the Apocalypse.

But beast or boy, he was Elly's brother, and whereas she might be as quiet as you please most of the time, when she got her dander up she could be a terror.

"Take that back," she said.

"Now, that's about as silly a thing as I ever heard. How can I take back what I said?"

"By saying you know it ain't so."

"I don't know it is and I don't know it ain't. I said maybe, and if a man can't say his maybes to his wife then he might as well be dead."

"I reckon that's about true," she said. "And if you don't take that back you'll wish you was dead!" And she started coming after him with two chunks of apple, one in each hand.

Now, most times she came for him like that, even if

she was really mad, if he let her chase him around the house awhile she usually ended up laughing. But not this time. She mushed one apple in his hair and threw the other one at him, and then just sat down in the upstairs bedroom, crying her eyes out.

She wasn't one to cry, so Armor figured this had got right out of hand.

"I take it back, Elly," he said. "He's a good boy, I know that."

"Oh, I don't care what you think," she said. "You don't know a thing about it anyway."

There weren't many husbands who'd let their wife say such a thing without slapping her upside the head. Armor wished sometimes that Elly'd appreciate how him being a Christian worked to her advantage.

"I know a thing or two," he said.

"They're going to send him off," she said. "Once spring comes, they're going to prentice him out. He's none too happy about it, I can tell, but he don't argue none, he just lies there in his bed, talking real quiet, but looking at me and everybody else like he was saying good-bye all the time."

"What are they wanting to send him off for?"

"I told you, to prentice him."

"The way they baby that boy, I can't hardly believe they'd let him out of their sight."

"They ain't talking about nothing close by, neither. Clear back at the east end of Hio Territory, near Fort Dekane. Why, that's halfway to the ocean."

"You know, it just makes sense, when you think about it."

"It does?"

"With Red trouble starting up, they want him plumb gone. The others can all stick around to get an arrow in their face, but not Alvin Junior."

She looked at him with withering contempt. "Sometimes you're so suspicious you make me want to puke, Armor-of-God."

"It ain't suspicion to say what's really happening."

"You can't tell real from a rutabaga."

"You going to wash this apple out of my hair, or do I have to make you lick it out?"

"I expect I'll have to do something, or you'll rub it all over the bed linen."

TALESWAPPER FELT ALMOST like a thief, to take so much with him as he left. Two pair of thick stockings. A new blanket. An elkhide cloak. Jerky and cheese. A good whetstone.

And things they couldn't even know they gave him. A rested body, free of aches and bruises. A jaunty step. Kind faces fresh in his mind. And stories. Stories jotted in the sealed-up part of the book, the ones he wrote down himself. And true stories painfully inscribed by their own hands.

Still, he gave them fair return, or tried to. Roofs patched for winter, other jobs here and there. More important, they'd seen a book with Ben Franklin's own handwriting in it, with sentences from Tom Jefferson, Ben Arnold, Pat Henry, John Adams, Alex Hamilton—even Aaron Burr, from before the duel, and Daniel Boone, from after. Before Taleswapper came they were part of their family, and part of the Wobbish country, and that's all. Now they belonged to much larger stories. The War of Appalachee Independence. The American Compact. They saw their own trek through the wilderness as one thread among many, and felt the strength of the whole tapestry woven from those threads. Not a tapestry, really. A rug. A good, thick, solid rug that generations of Americans after them could tread on. There was a poem in that; he'd work that into a poem sometime.

He left them a few other things, too. A beloved son he pulled from under a falling millstone. A father who now had the strength to send away his son before he killed him. A name for a young man's nightmare, so he could understand that his enemy was real. A whispered encouragement for a broken child to heal himself.

And a single drawing, burnt into a fine slab of oakwood with the tip of a hot knife. He'd rather have worked with wax and acid on metal, but there was neither to be had in this place. So he burnt lines into the wood, making of it what he could. A picture of a young man caught in a strong river, bound up in the roots of a floating tree, gasping for breath, his eyes facing death fearlessly. It would have earned nothing but scorn at the Lord Protector's Academy of Art, being so plain. But Goody Faith cried out when she saw it, and hugged it to her, dropping her tears over it like the last drips from the eaves after a rainstorm. And Father Alvin, when he saw it, nodded and said, "That's your vision, Taleswapper. You got his face perfect, and you never even saw him. That's Vigor. That's my boy." Then he cried, too.

They set it right up on the mantel. It might not be great art, thought Taleswapper, but it was true, and it meant more to these folks than any portrait could mean to some fat old lord or parliamentarian in London or Camelot or Paris or Vienna.

"It's fair morning now," said Goody Faith. "You've got long to go before dark."

"You can't blame me for being reluctant to leave. Though I'm glad you trusted me with this errand, and I won't fail you." He patted his pocket, wherein lay the letter to the blacksmith of Hatrack River.

"You can't go without you say good-bye to the boy," said Miller.

He'd put it off as long as it could be delayed. He nodded once, then eased himself from the comfortable chair by the fire and went on into the room where he'd slept the best nights of his life. It was good to see Alvin Junior's eyes wide open, his face lively, no longer slack the way it was for a while, or winced up with pain. But the pain was still there, Taleswapper knew.

"You going?" asked the boy.

"I'm gone, except for saying good-bye to you."

Alvin looked a little angry. "So you ain't even going to let me write in your book?"

"Not everybody does, you know."

"Pa did. And Mama."

"And Cally, too."

"I bet that looks good," said Alvin. "He writes like a, like a—"

"Like a seven-year-old." It was a rebuke, but Alvin had no intention of squirming.

"Why not me, then? Why Cally and not me?"

"Because I only let people write the most important thing they ever did or ever saw with their own eyes. What would *you* write?"

"I don't know. Maybe about the millstone."

Taleswapper made a face.

"Then maybe my vision. That's important, you said so yourself."

"And that got written up somewhere else, Alvin."

"I want to write in the book," he said. "I want my sentence in there along with Maker Ben's."

"Not yet," said Taleswapper.

"When!"

"When you've whipped that old Unmaker, lad. That's when I'll let you write in this book."

"What if I don't ever whip him?"

"Then this book won't amount to much, anyway."

Tears sprang to Alvin's eyes. "What if I die?"

Taleswapper felt a thrill of fear. "How's the leg?"

The boy shrugged. He blinked back the tears. They were gone.

"That's no answer, lad."

"It won't stop hurting."

"It'll be that way till the bone knits."

Alvin Junior smiled wanly. "Bone's all knit."

"Then why don't you walk?"

"It pains me, Taleswapper. It never goes away. It's got a bad place on the bone, and I ain't figured out yet how to make it right."

"You'll find a way."

"I ain't found it yet."

"An old trapper once said to me, 'It don't matter if you start at the bung or the breastbone, any old way you get the skin off a panther is a good way.'"

"Is that a proverb?"

"It's close. You'll find a way, even if it isn't what you expect."

"Nothing's what I expect," said Alvin. "Nothing turns out like anything I figured."

"You're ten years old, lad. Weary of the world already?"

Alvin kept rubbing folds of the blanket between his thumb and fingers. "Taleswapper, I'm dying."

Taleswapper studied his face, trying to see death there. It wasn't. "I don't think so."

"The bad place on my leg. It's growing. Slow, maybe, but it's growing. It's invisible, and it's eating away at the hard places of the bone, and after a while it'll go faster and faster and—"

"And Unmake you."

Alvin started to cry for real this time, and his hands were shaking. "I'm scared to die, Taleswapper, but it got inside me and I can't get it out."

Taleswapper laid a hand on his, to still the trembling. "You'll find a way. You've got too much work to do in this world, to die now."

Alvin rolled his eyes. "That's about as dumb a thing as I've heard this year. Just because somebody's got things to do don't mean he won't die."

"But it does mean he won't die *willingly*."

"I ain't willing."

"That's why you'll find a way to live."

Alvin was silent for a few seconds. "I've been thinking. About if I do live, what I'll do. Like what I done to make my leg get mostly better. I can do that for other folks, I bet. I can lay hands on them and feel the way it is inside, and fix it up. Wouldn't that be good?"

"They'd love you for it, all the folks you healed."

"I reckon the first time was the hardest, and I wasn't partickler strong when I done it. I bet I can do it faster on other people."

"Maybe so. But even if you heal a hundred sick people every day, and move on to the next place and heal a hundred more, there'll be ten thousand people die behind you, and ten thousand more ahead of you, and by the time you die, even the ones you healed will almost all be dead."

Alvin turned his face away. "If I know how to fix them, then I got to fix them, Taleswapper."

"Those you can, you must," said Taleswapper. "But not as your life's work. Bricks in the wall, Alvin, that's all they'll ever be. You can never catch up by repairing the crumbling bricks. Heal those who chance to fall under your hand, but your life's work is deeper than that."

"I know how to heal people. But I don't know how to beat down the Un—the Unmaker. I don't even know what it is."

"As long as you're the only one that can see him, though, you're also the only one who has a hope of beating him."

"Maybe."

Another long silence. Taleswapper knew it was time to go.

"Wait."

"I've got to leave now."

Alvin caught at his sleeve. "Not yet."

"Pretty soon."

"At least—at least let me read what the others wrote."

Taleswapper reached into his bag and pulled out the book pouch. "I can't promise I'll explain what they mean," he said, sliding the book out of its waterproof cover.

Alvin quickly found the last, newest writings.

In his mother's hand: "Vigor he push a log and he don die til the boy is bornd."

In David's hand: "A mil ston splits in two then it suks bak not a crak."

In Cally's hand: "A sevent sunn."

Alvin looked up. "He ain't talking about me, you know."

"I know," said Taleswapper.

Alvin looked back at the book. In his father's hand: "He dont kil a boy cus a stranjer com in time."

"What's Pa talking about?" asked Alvin.

Taleswapper took the book from his hands and closed it. "Find a way to heal your leg," he said. "There's a lot more souls than you who need it to be strong. It's not for yourself, remember?"

He bent over and kissed the boy on the forehead. Alvin reached up and held him with both arms, hanging on him so that he couldn't stand up without lifting the boy clear out of bed. After a while, Taleswapper had to reach up and pull the boy's arms away. His cheek was wet with Alvin's tears. He didn't wipe them away. He let the breeze dry them as he trudged along the cold dry path, with fields of half-melted snow stretching left and right.

He paused a moment on the second covered bridge. Just

long enough to wonder if he'd ever come back here, or see them again. Or get Alvin Junior's sentence for his book. If he were a prophet, he'd know. But he hadn't the faintest idea.

He walked on, setting his feet toward morning.

13

❧

SURGERY

The Visitor sat comfortably upon the altar, leaning casually on his left arm, so that his body had a jaunty tilt. Reverend Thrower had seen just such an informal pose taken by a dandy from Camelot, a rake-hell who clearly despised everything that the Puritan churches of England and Scotland stood for. It made Thrower more than a little uncomfortable to see the Visitor in such an irreverent pose.

"Why?" asked the Visitor. "Just because the only way you can maintain control over your bodily passions is to sit straight in your chair, knees together, hands delicately arranged in your lap, fingers tightly intertwined, does not mean that I am required to do the same."

Thrower was embarrassed. "It isn't fair to chastise me for my thoughts."

"It is, when your thoughts chastise me for my actions. Beware of hubris, my friend. Do not fancy yourself so righteous that *you* can judge the acts of angels."

It was the first time the Visitor had ever called himself an angel.

"I did not call myself *anything*," said the Visitor. "You

must learn to control your thoughts, Thrower. You leap to conclusions far too easily."

"Why have you come to me?"

"It's a matter of the maker of this altar," said the Visitor. He patted one of the crosses Alvin Junior had burnt into the wood.

"I've done my best, but the boy is unteachable. He doubts everything, and contests each point of theology as if it were required to meet the same tests of logic and consistency that prevail in the world of science."

"In other words, he expects your doctrines to make sense."

"He is unwilling to accept the idea that some things remain mysteries, comprehensible only to the mind of God. Ambiguity makes him saucy, and paradox causes open rebellion."

"An obnoxious child."

"The worst I have ever seen," said Thrower.

The Visitor's eyes flashed. Thrower felt a stab in his heart.

"I've tried," said Thrower. "I've tried to turn him to serve the Lord. But the influence of his father—"

"It is a weak man who blames his failures on the strength of others," said the Visitor.

"I haven't failed yet!" said Thrower. "You told me I had until the boy was fourteen—"

"No. I told you *I* had until the boy was fourteen. *You* only have him as long as he lives here."

"I've heard nothing about the Millers moving. They just got their millstone in place, they're going to start grinding in the spring, they wouldn't leave without—"

The Visitor stood up from the altar. "Let me put a case to you, Reverend Thrower. Purely hypothetical. Let us suppose you were in the same room with the worst enemy of all that I stand for. Let us suppose that he were ill, and lay helpless in his bed. If he recovered, he would be removed from your reach, and would thus go on to destroy all that you and I love in this world. But if he died, our great cause would be safe. Now suppose that someone put a knife into your hand, and begged you to perform a delicate surgery upon the boy. And suppose that if you were to slip, just the tiniest bit, your knife could cut a great artery. And suppose that if you simply delayed, his lifeblood would flow out so quickly that in moments he would die. In that case, Reverend Thrower, what would be your duty?"

Thrower was aghast. All his life he had prepared to teach, persuade, exhort, expound. Never to perform a bloody-handed act like the one the Visitor suggested. "I'm not suited for such things," he said.

"Are you suited for the kingdom of God?" asked the Visitor.

"But the Lord said Thou shalt not kill."

"Oh? Is that what he said to Joshua, when he sent him into the promised land? Is that what he said to Saul, when he sent him against the Amalekites?"

Thrower thought of those dark passages in the Old Testament, and trembled with fear at the thought of taking part in such things himself.

But the Visitor did not relent. "The high priest Samuel commanded King Saul to kill all the Amalekites, every man and woman, every *child*. But Saul hadn't the stomach for it. He saved the king of the Amalekites and brought him back alive. For that crime of disobedience, what did the Lord do?"

"Chose David to be king in his place," murmured Thrower.

The Visitor stood close to Thrower, his eyes wounding him with their fire. "And then Samuel, the high priest, the *gentle* servant of God, what did he do?"

"He called for Agag the king of the Amalekites to be brought before him."

The Visitor would not relent. "And what did Samuel *do*?"

"Killed him," whispered Thrower.

"*What does the scripture say that he did!*" roared the Visitor. The walls of the meetinghouse shook, the glass of the windows rattled.

Thrower wept in fear, but he spoke the words that the Visitor demanded: "Samuel hacked Agag in pieces—in the presence of the Lord."

Now the only sound in the church was Thrower's own ragged breath as he tried to control his hysterical weeping. The Visitor smiled at him, his eyes filled with love and forgiveness. Then he was gone.

Thrower sank to his knees before the altar and prayed. O Father, I would die for Thee, but do not ask me to kill. Take away this cup from my lips, I am too weak, I am unworthy, do not lay this burden upon my shoulders.

His tears fell on the altar. He heard a sizzling sound and jumped back from the altar, startled. His tears skittered along the surface of the altar like water on a hot skillet, until finally they were consumed.

The Lord has rejected me, he thought. I pledged to serve Him however He required, and now, when He asks something difficult, when He commands me to be as strong as the great prophets of old, I discover myself to be a broken vessel in the hands of the Lord. I cannot contain the destiny He wanted to pour into me.

The door of the church opened, letting in a wave of freezing air that rushed along the floor and sent a chill through the minister's flesh. He looked up, fearing that it was an angel sent to punish him.

It was no angel, though. Merely Armor-of-God Weaver.

"I didn't mean to interrupt you in prayer," said Armor.

"Come in," said Thrower. "Close the door. What can I do for you?"

"Not for me," said Armor.

"Come here. Sit down. Tell me."

Thrower hoped that perhaps it was a sign from God that Armor had come just now. A member of the congregation, coming to him for help, right after he prayed—surely the Lord was letting him know that he was accepted after all.

"It's my wife's brother," said Armor. "The boy, Alvin Junior."

Thrower felt a thrill of dread run through him, freezing him to the bone. "I know him. What about him?"

"You know he got his leg mashed."

"I heard of it."

"You didn't happen to go visit and see him afore it healed up?"

"I've been given to believe that I'm not welcome in that house."

"Well, let me tell you, it was bad. A whole patch of skin tore off. Bones broke. But two days later, it was healed right up. Couldn't even see no scar. Three days later he was *walking.*"

"It must not have been as bad as you thought."

"I'm telling you, that leg was *broke* and the wound was *bad*. The whole family figured the boy was bound to die. They asked me about buying nails for a coffin. And they looked so bad from grieving that I wasn't sure but what we'd bury the boy's ma and pa, too."

"Then it can't be as fully healed as you say."

"Well, it ain't *fully* healed, and that's why I come to you. I know you don't believe in such things, but I tell you they witched the boy's leg to heal somehow. Elly says the boy did the witching himself. He was even walking on the leg for a few days, no splint even. But the pain never let up, and now he says there's a sick place on his bone. He's got a fever, too."

"There's a perfectly natural explanation for everything," said Thrower.

"Well, be that as you like, the way I see it the boy invited the devil with his witchery, and now the devil's eating him alive inside. And seeing how you're an ordained minister of God, I thought maybe you could cast out that devil in the name of the Lord Jesus."

Superstitions and sorceries were nonsense, of course, but when Armor brought up the possibility of a devil being in the boy, it made sense, it fit with what he knew from the Visitor. Maybe the Lord wanted him to exorcise the child, to purge the evil from him, not to kill the boy at all. It was a chance for him to redeem himself from his failure of will a few minutes before.

"I'll go," he said. He reached for his heavy cloak and whipped it around his shoulders.

"I better warn you, nobody up at their house asked me to bring you."

"I'm prepared to deal with the anger of the unfaithful," said Thrower. "It's the victim of deviltry that concerns me, not his foolish and superstitious family."

ALVIN LAY ON his bed, burning with the heat of his fever. Now, in the daylight, they kept his shutters closed, so the light wouldn't hurt his eyes. At night, though, he made them open things up, let some of the cold air in. He would breathe it in relief. During the few days when he could walk, he had seen the snow covering the meadow. Now he tried to imagine himself lying under that blanket of snow. Relief from the fire burning through his body.

He just couldn't see small enough inside himself. What he did with the bone, with the strands of muscle and layers of skin, it was harder than ever it was to find the cracks in the quarry stone. But he could feel his way through the labyrinth of his body, find the large wounds, help them to close. Most of what went on, though, was too small and fast for him to comprehend. He could see the result, but he couldn't see the pieces, couldn't make out how it happened.

That's how it was with the bad place in his bone. Just a patch of it that was weakening, rotting away. He could feel the difference between the bad place and the good healthy bone, he could find the borders of the sickness. But he couldn't actually see what was happening. He couldn't undo it. He was going to die.

He wasn't alone in the room, he knew. Someone always sat at his bedside. He would open his eyes and see Mama, or Papa, or one of the girls. Sometimes even one of the brothers, even though it meant he had left his wife and his chores. It was a comfort to Alvin, but it was also a burden. He kept thinking he ought to hurry up and die so they could all get back to their regular lives.

This afternoon it was Measure sitting there. Alvin said howdy to him when he first came, but there wasn't much to talk about. Howdy do? I'm dying, thanks, and you? Kind of hard to keep chatting. Measure talked about how he and the twins had tried to cut a grindstone. They chose a softer stone than what Alvin worked with, and still they had a devil of a time cutting. "We finally gave right up," said Measure. "It's just going to have to wait till you can go up the mountain and get us a stone yourself."

Alvin didn't answer that, and they neither one said a word since then. Alvin just lay there, sweating, feeling the rot in his bone as it slowly, steadily grew. Measure sat there, lightly holding his hand.

Measure started to whistle.

The sound of it startled Alvin. He'd been so caught up inside himself that the music seemed to come from a great distance, and he had to travel some distance to discover where it was coming from.

"Measure," he cried; but the sound of his voice was a whisper.

The whistling stopped. "Sorry," said Measure. "Does it bother you?"

"No," said Alvin.

Measure started in whistling again. It was a strange tune, one that Alvin didn't recollect he ever heard before. In fact it didn't sound like any kind of tune at all. It never did repeat itself, just went on with new patterns all the time, like as if Measure was making it up on the way. As Alvin lay there and listened, the melody seemed like it was a map, winding through a wilderness, and he started to follow it. Not that he *saw* anything, the way he would following a real map. It just seemed always to show him the center of things, as if he was standing in that place. Almost like he could see all the thinking he had done before, trying to figure out a way to fix the bad place on his bone, only now he was looking from a ways off, maybe higher up a mountain or in a clearing, somewhere that he could see *more*.

Now he thought of something he never thought of before. When his leg was first broke, with the skin all tore up, everybody could see how bad off he was, but nobody could help him, only himself. He had to fix it all from inside. Now, though, nobody else could see the wound that was killing him. And even though *he* could see it, he couldn't do a blame thing to make it better.

So maybe this time, somebody else could fix him up. Not using any kind of hidden power at all. Just plain old bloody-handed surgery.

"Measure," he whispered.

"I'm here," said Measure.

"I know a way to fix my leg," he said.

Measure leaned in close. Alvin didn't open his eyes, but he could feel his brother's breath on his cheek.

"The bad place on my bone, it's growing, but it ain't spread all over yet," Alvin said. "I can't make it better, but I reckon if somebody cut off that part of my bone and took it right out of my leg, I could heal it up the rest of the way."

"Cut it out?"

"Pa's bone saw that he uses when he's cutting up meat, that'd do the trick I think."

"But there ain't a surgeon in three hundred mile."

"Then I reckon somebody better learn how real quick, or I'm dead."

Measure was breathing quicker now. "You think cutting your bone would save your life?"

"It's the best I can think of."

"It might mess up your leg real bad," said Measure.

"If I'm dead, I won't care. And if I live, it'll be worth a messed-up leg."

"I'm going to fetch Pa." Measure scuffed back his chair and thumped out of the room.

THROWER LET ARMOR lead the way onto the Millers' porch. They couldn't very well turn away their daughter's husband. His concern was unfounded, however. It was Goody Faith who opened the door, not her pagan husband.

"Why, Reverend Thrower, if you ain't being too kind to us, stopping up here," she said. The cheerfulness of her voice was a lie, though, if her haggard face was telling the truth. There hadn't been much good sleep in this house lately.

"I brought him along, Mother Faith," said Armor. "He come only cause I asked him."

"The pastor of our church is welcome in my home whenever it pleases him to come by," said Faith.

She ushered them into the great room. A group of girls making quilt squares looked up at him from their chairs near the hearth. The little boy, Cally, was doing his letters on a board, writing with charcoal from the fire.

"I'm glad to see you doing your letters," said Thrower.

Cally just looked at him. There was a hint of hostility in his eyes. Apparently the boy resented having his teacher look at his work here at home, which he had supposed was a sanctuary.

"You're doing them well," said Thrower, trying to put the boy at ease. Cally said nothing, just looked down again at his makeshift slate and kept on scrawling out words.

Armor brought up their business right away. "Mother Faith, we come cause of Alvin. You know how I feel about witchery, but I never before said a word against what you folks do in your house. I always reckoned that was your business and none of mine. But that boy is paying the price for the evil ways that you've let go on here. He witched his leg, and now there's a devil in him, killing him off, and I brought Reverend Thrower here to wring that devil on out of him."

Goody Faith looked puzzled. "There ain't no devil in this house."

Ah, poor woman, said Thrower silently. If you only knew how long a devil has dwelt here. "It is possible to become so accustomed to the presence of a devil as not to recognize that it is present."

A door by the stairs opened up, and Mr. Miller stepped backward through the doorway. "Not me," he said, talking to whoever was in that room. "I'll not lay a knife to the boy."

Cally jumped up at the sound of his father's voice and ran to him. "Armor brung old Thrower here, Papa, to kill the devil."

Mr. Miller turned around, his face twisted with unidentified emotion, and looked at the visitors as if he hardly recognized them.

"I've got good strong hexes on this house," said Goody Faith.

"Those hexes are a summons for the devil," said Armor. "You think they protect your house, but they drive away the Lord."

"No devil ever came in here," she insisted.

"Not by itself," said Armor. "You called it in with all your conjuring. You forced the Holy Spirit to leave your house by your witchery and idolatry, and having swept goodness from your home, the devils naturally come right in. They always come in, where they see a fair chance to do mischief."

Thrower became a little concerned that Armor was saying too much about things he didn't really understand. It would have been better had he simply asked if Thrower could pray for the boy at Alvin's bedside. Now Armor was drawing battle lines that should never have been drawn.

And whatever was going on in Mr. Miller's head right now, it was plain to see that this wasn't the best of times to provoke the man. He slowly walked toward Armor. "You telling me that what comes into a man's house to do mischief is the devil?"

"I bear you my witness as one who loves the Lord Jesus," Armor began, but before he could get any further into his testimony, Miller had him by the shoulder of his coat and the waist of his pants, and he turned him right toward the door.

"Somebody better open this door!" roared Miller. "Or there's going to be a powerful big hole right in the middle of it!"

"What do you think you're doing, Alvin Miller!" shouted his wife.

"Casting out devils!" cried Miller. Cally had swung the door open by then, and Miller walked his son-in-law to the edge of the porch and sent him flying. Armor's cry of outrage ended up muffled by the snow on the ground, and there wasn't much chance to hear his yelling after that because Miller closed and barred the door.

"Ain't you a big man," said Goody Faith, "throwing out your own daughter's husband."

"I didn't do but what he said the Lord wanted done," said Miller. Then he turned his gaze upon the pastor.

"Armor didn't speak for me," said Thrower mildly.

"If you lay a hand on a man of the cloth," said Goody Faith, "you'll sleep in a cold bed for the rest of your life."

"Wouldn't think of touching the man," said Miller. "But the way I figure it, I stay out of his place, and he ought to stay out of mine."

"You may not believe in the power of prayer," said Thrower.

"I reckon it depends on who's doing the praying, and who's doing the listening," said Miller.

"Even so," said Thrower, "your wife believes in the religion of Jesus Christ, in the which I have been called and ordained a minister. It is her belief, and my belief, that for me to pray at the boy's bedside might be efficacious in his cure."

"If you use words like that in your praying," said Miller, "it's a wonder the Lord even knows what you're talking about."

"Though you don't believe such prayer will help," Thrower went on, "it certainly can't hurt, can it?"

Miller looked from Thrower to his wife and back again. Thrower had no doubt that if Faith had not been there, he would have been eating snow alongside Armor-of-God. But Faith *was* there and had already uttered the threat of Lysistrata. A man does not have fourteen children if his wife's bed holds no attraction to him. Miller gave in. "Go on in," he said. "But don't pester the boy too long."

Thrower nodded graciously. "No more than a few hours," he said.

"Minutes!" Miller insisted. But Thrower was already headed for the door by the stairs, and Miller made no move to stop him. He could have hours with the boy, if he wanted to. He closed the door behind him. No sense in letting any of the pagans interfere with this.

"Alvin," he said.

The boy was stretched out under a blanket, his forehead beaded with sweat. His eyes were closed. After a while, though, he opened his mouth a little. "Reverend Thrower," he whispered.

"The very same," said Thrower. "Alvin, I've come to pray for you, so the Lord will free your body of the devil that is making you sick."

Again a pause, as if it took a while for Thrower's words to reach Alvin and just as long again for his answer to return. "Ain't no devil," he said.

"One can hardly expect a child to be well-versed in matters of religion," said Thrower. "But I must tell you that healing comes only to those who have the faith to be healed." He then devoted several minutes to recounting the story of the centurion's daughter and the tale of the woman who had an issue of blood and merely touched the Savior's robe. "You recall what he said to her. Thy faith hath made thee whole, he said. So it is, Alvin Miller, that your faith must be strong before the Lord can make you whole."

The boy didn't answer. Since Thrower had used his considerable eloquence in the telling of both stories, it offended him a bit that the boy might have fallen asleep. He reached out a long finger and poked Alvin's shoulder.

Alvin flinched away. "I heard you," he muttered.

It wasn't good that the boy could still be sullen, after

hearing the light-giving word of the Lord. "Well?" asked Thrower. "Do you believe?"

"In what," murmured the boy.

"In the gospel! In the God who would heal you, if you only soften your heart!"

"Believe," he whispered. "In God."

That should have been enough. But Thrower knew too much of the history of religion not to press for more detail. It was not enough to confess faith in a deity. There were so many deities, and all but one were false. "*Which* God do you believe in, Al Junior?"

"God," said the boy.

"Even the heathen Moor prays toward the black stone of Mecca and calls it God! Do you believe in the true God, and do you believe in Him correctly? No, I understand, you're too weak and fevered to explain your faith. I will help you, young Alvin. I'll ask you questions, and you tell me, yes or no, whether you believe."

Alvin lay still, waiting.

"Alvin Miller, do you believe in a God without body, parts, or passions? The great Uncreated Creator, Whose center is everywhere, yet Whose circumference can never be found?"

The boy seemed to ponder this for a while before he spoke. "That don't make a bit of sense to me," he said.

"He isn't supposed to make sense to the carnal mind," Thrower said. "I merely ask if you *believe* in the One who sits atop the Topless Throne; the self-existing Being who is so large He fills the universe, yet so penetrating that He lives in your heart."

"How can he sit on the top of something that ain't got no top?" the boy asked. "How can something that big fit inside my heart?"

The boy was obviously too uneducated and simple-minded to grasp sophisticated theological paradox. Still, it was more than a life or even a soul at stake here—it was all the souls that the Visitor had said this boy would ruin if he could not be converted to the true faith. "That's the beauty of it," said Thrower, letting emotion fill his voice. "God is beyond our comprehension; yet in His infinite love He condescends to save us, despite our ignorance and foolishness."

"Ain't love a passion?" asked the boy.

"If you have trouble with the idea of God," said Thrower, "then let me pose another question, which may be more to the point. Do you believe in the bottomless pit of hell, where the wicked writhe in flames, yet are never burned up? Do you believe in Satan, the enemy of God, who wishes to steal your soul and take you captive into his kingdom, to torment you through all eternity?"

The boy seemed to perk up a little, turning his head toward Thrower, though he still didn't open his eyes. "I might believe in something like that," he said.

Ah, yes, thought Thrower. The boy *has* had some experience with the devil. "Have you seen him, child?"

"What's *your* devil look like?" whispered the boy.

"He is not *my* devil," said Thrower. "And if you had listened in services, you would have known, for I have described him many times. Where a man has hair on his head, the devil has the horns of a bull. Where a man has hands, the devil has the claws of a bear. He has the hooves of a goat, and his voice is the roar of a ravening lion."

To Thrower's amazement, the boy smiled, and his chest bounced silently with laughter. "And you call *us* superstitious," he said.

Thrower would never have believed how firm a grip the devil could have on a child's soul, had he not seen the boy laugh with pleasure at the description of the monster Lucifer. That laughter must be stopped! It was an offense against God!

Thrower slapped his Bible down on the boy's chest, causing Alvin to wheeze out his breath. Then, with his hand pressing on the book, Thrower felt himself fill up with inspired words, and he cried out with more passion than he had ever felt before in his life: "Satan, in the name of the Lord I rebuke you! I command you to depart from this boy, from this room, from this house forever! Never again seek to possess a soul in this place, or the power of God will wreak destruction unto the uttermost bounds of hell!"

Then silence. Except for the boy's breathing, which seemed labored. There was such peace in the room, such exhausted righteousness in Thrower's own heart, that he felt convinced the devil had heeded his peroration and retreated forthwith.

"Reverend Thrower," said the boy.

"Yes, my son?"

"Can you take that Bible off my chest now? I reckon if there was any devils here, they're all gone now."

Then the boy began to laugh again, causing the Bible to jump up and down under Thrower's hand.

In that moment Thrower's exultation turned to bitter disappointment. Indeed, the fact that the boy could laugh so devilishly with the Bible itself resting on his body was proof that no power could purge him of evil. The Visitor had been right. Thrower should never have refused the mighty work that the Visitor had called him to do. It had been in his power to be the slayer of the Beast of the Apocalypse, and he had been too weak, too sentimental to accept the divine calling. I could have been a Samuel, hewing to death the enemy of God. Instead I am a Saul, a weakling, who cannot kill what the Lord commands must die. Now I will see this boy rise up with the power of Satan in him, and I will know that he thrives only because I was weak.

Now the room was stifling hot, choking him. He had not realized until now how his clothing sogged with sweat. It was hard to breathe. But what should he expect? The hot breath of hell was in this room. Gasping, he took the Bible, held it out between him and the satanic child who lay giggling feverishly under the blanket, and fled.

In the great room he stopped, breathing heavily. He had interrupted a conversation, but he scarcely took notice of it. What did the conversations of these benighted people amount to, compared to what he had just experienced? I have stood in the presence of Satan's minion, masquing it as a young boy; but his mockery revealed him to me. I should have known what the boy was years ago, when I felt his head and found it to be so perfectly balanced. Only a counterfeit would be so perfect. The child was never *real*. Ah, that I had the strength of the great prophets of old, so I could confound the enemy and bear the trophy back to my Lord!

Someone was tugging at his sleeve. "Are you well, Reverend?" It was Goody Faith, but Reverend Thrower did not think to answer her. Her tugging pulled him around, though, so he faced the fireplace. There on the mantel he saw a carven image, and in his distracted state he could not at once determine what it was. It seemed to be the face of a soul in torment, surrounded by writhing tendrils. Flames, that's what they are, he thought, and that is a soul drowning in brimstone, burning in hellfire. The image was a torment to him, and yet it was also satisfying, for its presence in this house signified how closely bound this family was to hell. He stood in the midst of his enemies. A phrase from the Psalmist came to his mind: Bulls of Bashan stare upon me, and I can tell all my bones. My God, my God, why hast Thou forsaken me?

"Here," said Goody Faith. "Sit down."

"Is the boy all right?" demanded Miller.

"The boy?" asked Thrower. Words could hardly come to his mouth. The boy is a fiend from Sheol, and you ask how he is? "As well as can be expected," said Thrower.

They turned away from him then, back to their conversation. Gradually he came to understand what they were discussing. It seemed that Alvin wanted someone to cut away the diseased portion of his bone. Measure had even brought a fine-toothed bone saw from the butchery shed. The argument was between Faith and Measure, because Faith didn't want anyone cutting her son, and between Miller and the other two, because Miller refused to do it, and Faith would only consent if Alvin's father did the cutting.

"If you think it ought to be done," said Faith, "then I don't see how you'd be willing to have anyone but yourself cut into him."

"Not me," said Miller.

It struck Thrower that the man was afraid. Afraid to lay the knife against his own son's flesh.

"He asked for you, Pa. He said he'd draw the marks for cutting right on his own leg. You just cut a flap of skin and peel it back, and right under it there's the bone, and you just cut a wedge in the bone that takes out the whole bad place."

"I'm not the fainting kind," said Faith, "but my head is getting light."

"If Al Junior says it's got to be done, then do it!" said Miller. "But not me!"

Then, like a rush of light into a dark room, Reverend Thrower saw his redemption. The Lord was clearly offering him exactly the opportunity that the Visitor had prophesied. A chance to hold a knife in his hand, to cut into the boy's leg, and *accidently* sever the artery and spill the blood until the life was gone. What he had shrunk to do in the church, thinking of Alvin as a mere boy, he would do gladly, now that he had seen the evil that disguised itself in child-shape.

"I'm here," he said.

They looked at him.

"I'm no surgeon," he said, "but I have some knowledge of anatomy. I *am* a scientist."

"Head bumps," said Miller.

"You ever butchered cattle or pigs?" asked Measure.

"Measure!" said his mother, horrified. "Your brother is not a beast."

"I just wanted to know if he was going to throw up when he saw blood."

"I've seen blood," said Thrower. "And I have no fear, when the cutting is for salvation."

"Oh, Reverend Thrower, it's too much to ask of you," said Goody Faith.

"Now I see that perhaps it *was* inspiration that brought me up here today, after so long being away from this house."

"It was my pebble-headed son-in-law brought you here," said Miller.

"Well," said Thrower, "it was just a thought. I can see that you don't want me to do it, and I can't say that I blame you. Even if it means saving your son's life, it's still a dangerous thing to let a stranger cut into your own child's body."

"You're no stranger," insisted Faith.

"What if something went wrong? I might slip. His previous injury might have changed the path of certain blood vessels. I might cut an artery, and he could bleed to death in moments. Then I'd have the blood of your child on my hands."

"Reverend Thrower," said Faith, "we can't blame you for chance. All we can do is try."

"It's sure that if we don't do something he'll die," said

Measure. "He says we got to cut right away, before the bad place spreads too far."

"Perhaps one of your older sons," said Thrower.

"We got no time to fetch them!" cried Faith. "Oh, Alvin, he's the boy you chose to have your name. Are you set to let him die, just cause you can't abide the preacher here?"

Miller shook his head miserably. "Do it, then."

"He'd rather *you* did, Pa," said Measure.

"No!" said Miller vehemently. "Better anyone than me. Better even him than me."

Thrower saw disappointment, even contempt, on Measure's face. He stood and walked to where Measure sat, holding a knife and the bone saw in his hands. "Young man," he said, "do not ajudge any man to be a coward. You cannot guess what reasons he hides in his heart."

Thrower turned to Miller and saw a look of surprise and gratitude on the man's face. "Give him them cutting tools," Miller said.

Measure held out the knife and the bone saw. Thrower pulled out a handkerchief, and had Measure lay the implements carefully within it.

It had been so easy to do. In just a few moments he had them all asking him to take the knife, absolving him in advance of any accident that might happen. He had even won the first scrap of friendship from Alvin Miller. Ah, I have deceived you all, he thought triumphantly. I am a match for your master the devil. I have deceived the great deceiver, and will send his corrupt progeny back to hell within the hour.

"Who will hold the boy?" asked Thrower. "Even with wine in him, the pain will make him jump if he isn't held down."

"I'll hold him," said Measure.

"He won't take no wine," said Faith. "He says he has to have his head clear."

"He's a ten-year-old boy," said Thrower. "If you insist that he drink it, he's bound to obey you."

Faith shook her head. "He knows what's best. He bears up right smart under pain. You never seen the like."

I imagine not, said Thrower silently. The devil within the boy no doubt revels in the pain, and doesn't want the wine to dim the ecstasy. "Very well, then," he said. "There's no reason to delay further." He led the way into the bedroom and boldly pulled the blanket off Alvin's body. The boy immediately began trembling in the sudden cold, though he continued sweating from the fever. "You say that he has marked the place to cut?"

"Al," said Measure. "Reverend Thrower here is going to do the cutting."

"Papa," said Alvin.

"It's no use asking him," said Measure. "He just plain won't."

"Are you sure you won't have some wine?" asked Faith.

Alvin started to cry. "No," he said. "I'll be all right if Pa holds me."

"That does it," said Faith. "He may not do the cutting, but he'll be here with the boy or he'll be stuffed up the chimney, one or the other." She stormed out of the room.

"You said the boy would mark the place," Thrower said.

"Here, Al, let me set you up here. I got some charcoal, and you mark right on your leg here just exactly where you want that flap of skin took up."

Alvin moaned as Measure lifted him to a sitting position, but his hand was steady as he marked a large rectangle on his shin. "Cut it from the bottom, and leave the top attached," he said. His voice was thick and slow, each word an effort. "Measure, you hold that flap back out of the way while he cuts."

"Ma'll have to do that," said Measure. "I got to hold you down so you don't jump."

"I won't jump," said Alvin. "If Pa's holding me."

Miller came slowly into the room, his wife right behind. "I'll be holding you," he said. He took Measure's place, sitting behind the boy with his arms wrapped clear around him. "I'm holding you," he said again.

"Very well, then," said Thrower. He stood there, waiting for the next step.

He waited for a good little while.

"Ain't you forgetting something, Reverend?" asked Measure.

"What?" asked Thrower.

"The knife and the saw," he said.

Thrower looked at his handkerchief, wadded in his left hand. Empty. "Why, they were right here."

"You set them down on the table on the way in," said Measure.

"I'll fetch them," said Goody Faith. She hurried out of the room.

They waited and waited and waited. Finally Measure got up. "I can't guess what's keeping her."

Thrower followed him out of the room. They found Goody Faith in the great room, piecing together quilt squares with the girls.

"Ma," said Measure. "What about the saw and the knife?"

"Good laws," said Faith, "I can't imagine what's got into me. I clean forgot why I come out here." She picked up the knife and saw and marched back to the room. Measure shrugged at Thrower and followed her. Now, thought Thrower. Now I'll do all that the Lord ever expected of me. The Visitor will see that I am a true friend to my Savior, and my place in heaven will be assured. Not like this poor, miserable sinner caught up in the flames of hell.

"Reverend," said Measure. "What are you doing?"

"This drawing," said Thrower.

"What about it?"

Thrower looked closely at the drawing over the hearth. It wasn't a soul in hell at all. It was a depiction of the family's oldest boy, Vigor, drowning. He had heard the story at least a dozen times. But why was he standing here looking at it, when he had a great and terrible mission to perform in the other room?

"Are you all right?"

"Perfectly all right," said Thrower. "I just needed a moment of silent prayer and meditation before I undertook this task."

He strode boldly into the room and sat down on the chair beside the bed where Satan's child lay trembling, waiting for the knife. Thrower looked around for his tools of holy murder. They were nowhere in sight. "Where is the knife?" he asked.

Faith looked at Measure. "Didn't you bring them back in with you?" she asked.

"You're the one brought them in here," said Measure.

"But when you went back out to get the preacher, you took them," she said.

"Did I?" Measure looked confused. "I must have set them down out there." He got up and left the room.

Thrower began to realize that something strange was going on here, though he couldn't quite put his finger on it. He walked to the door and waited for Measure to return.

Cally was standing there, holding his slate, looking up at the minister. "You going to kill my brother?" he asked.

"Don't even think of such a thing," Thrower answered.

Measure looked sheepish as he handed the implements to Thrower. "I can't believe I just set them on the mantel like that." Then the young man pushed past Thrower into the room.

A moment later, Thrower followed him into Alvin's

room and took his place beside the exposed leg, with the box drawn in black.

"Well where'd you put them?" asked Faith.

Thrower realized that he didn't have the knife or the saw. He was completely confused. Measure handed them to him just outside the door. How could he have lost them?

Cally stood in the doorway. "Why'd you give me these?" he asked. He was, in fact, holding both blades.

"That's a good question," said Measure, eyeing the pastor with a frown. "Why'd you give them to Cally?"

"I didn't," said Thrower. "*You* must have given them to him."

"I put them right in your hands," said Measure.

"The preacher give them to me," said Cally.

"Well, bring them here," said his mother.

Cally obediently started into the room, brandishing the blades like trophies of war. Like the attack of a great army. Ah, yes, a great army, like the army of the Israelites that Joshua led into the promised land. This is how they held their weapons, high above their heads, as they marched around and around the city of Jericho. Marched and marched. Marched and marched. And on the seventh day they stopped and blew their trumpets and gave a great shout, and *down* came the walls, and they held their swords and knives high over their heads and charged into the city, hacking men, women, and children, all the enemies of God, so the promised land would be purged of their filthiness and be ready to receive the people of the Lord. They were spattered in blood by the end of the day, and Joshua stood in their midst, the great prophet of God, holding a bloody sword above his head, and he shouted. What did he shout?

I can't remember what he shouted. If I could only remember what he shouted, I'd understand why I'm standing here on the road, surrounded by snow-covered trees.

Reverend Thrower looked at his hands, and looked at the trees. He had somehow walked half a mile away from the Millers' house. He wasn't even wearing his heavy cloak.

Then the truth came clear. He hadn't fooled the devil at all. Satan had transported him here, in the twinkling of an eye, rather than let him kill the Beast. Thrower had failed in his one opportunity for greatness. He leaned against a cold black trunk and cried bitterly.

CALLY WALKED INTO the room, holding the blades above his head. Measure was all set to get a grip on the leg, when all of a sudden old Thrower stood right up and walked out of the room just as quick as if he was trotting to the privy.

"Reverend Thrower," cried Ma. "Where are you going?"

But Measure understood now. "Let him go, Ma," he said.

They heard the front door of the house open, and the minister's heavy steps on the porch.

"Go shut the front door, Cally," said Measure.

For once Cally obeyed without a speck of backsass. Ma looked at Measure, then at Pa, then at Measure again. "I don't understand why he left like that," she said.

Measure gave her a little half-smile and looked at Pa. "*You* know, don't you, Pa?"

"Maybe," he said.

Measure explained to his mother. "Them knives and that preacher, they can't be in this room with Al Junior at the same time."

"But why not!" she said. "He was going to do the surgery!"

"Well, he sure ain't going to do it now," said Measure.

The knife and the bone saw lay on the blanket.

"Pa," said Measure.

"Not me," said Pa.

"Ma," said Measure.

"I can't," Faith said.

"Well then," said Measure, "I reckon I just turned surgeon." He looked at Alvin.

The boy's face had a deathly pallor to it that was even worse than the ruddiness of the fever. But he managed a sort of smile, and whispered, "Reckon so."

"Ma, you're going to have to hold back that flap of skin."

She nodded.

Measure picked up the knife and brought the blade to rest against the bottom line.

"Measure," Al Junior whispered.

"Yes, Alvin?" Measure asked.

"I can stand the pain and hold right still, iffen you whistle."

"I can't keep no tune, if I'm trying to cut straight at the same time," said Measure.

"Don't want no tune," said Alvin.

Measure looked into the boy's eyes and had no choice but to do as he asked. It was Al's leg, after all, and if he wanted a whistling surgeon, he'd get one. Measure took a deep breath and started in whistling, no kind of tune at all, just notes. He put the knife on the black line again and began to cut. Shallow at first, cause he heard Al take a gasp of air.

"Keep whistling," Alvin whispered. "Right to the bone."

Measure whistled again, and this time he cut fast and deep. Right to the bone in the middle of the line. A deep slit up both sides. Then he worked the knife under the two corners and peeled the skin and muscle right back. At first it bled more than a little bit, but almost right away the bleeding stopped. Measure figured it must be something Alvin did inside himself, to stop the bleeding like that.

"Faith," said Pa.

Ma reached over and laid her hand on the bloody flap

of skin. Al reached out a trembling hand and traced a wedge on the red-streaked bone of his own leg. Measure laid down the knife and picked up the saw. It made an awful, squeaky sound as he cut. But Measure just whistled and sawed, sawed and whistled. And pretty soon he had a wedge of bone in his hand. It didn't took no different from the rest of the bone.

"You sure that was the right place?" he asked.

Al nodded slowly.

"Did I get it all?" Measure asked.

Al sat for a few moments, then nodded again.

"You want Ma to sew this back up?" Measure asked.

Al didn't say a thing.

"He fainted," said Pa.

The blood started to flow again, just a little, seeping into the wound. Ma had a needle and thread on the pincushion she wore around her neck. In no time she had that flap of skin right back down, and she was stitching away at it, making a fine tight seam.

"You just keep on whistling, Measure," she said.

So he kept right on whistling and she kept right on sewing, till they had the wound all bandaged up and Alvin was laying back sleeping like a baby. They all three stood up to go. Pa laid a hand on the boy's forehead, as gentle as you please.

"I think his fever's gone," he said.

Measure's tune got downright jaunty as they slipped on out the door.

14

CHASTISEMENT

As soon as Elly saw him, she was sweet as could be, brushing snow off him, helping with his cloak, and never so much as whispering a question of how it happened.

Didn't make no difference how kindly she might be. He was shamed afore his own wife, cause sooner or later she'd hear the tale from one of those children. Soon enough the tale would be all up and down the Wobbish. How Armor-of-God Weaver, storekeeper for the western country, future governor, got throwed right off a porch into the snow by his old father-in-law. They'd be laughing behind their hands, all right. They'd laugh him up and down. Never to his face, of course, cause there was hardly a soul between Lake Canada and the Noisy River who didn't owe him money or need his maps to prove their claims. Come the time when the Wobbish country was made a state, they'd tell that story at every polling place. They might like a man they laughed at, but they wouldn't respect him, and they wouldn't vote for him.

It was the death of his plans he was facing, and his wife just had too much of that Miller family look about her. She was pretty enough, for a frontier woman, but he didn't care about pretty right now. He didn't care about sweet nights and gentle mornings. He didn't care about her working alongside him in the store. All he cared about was shame and rage.

"Don't do that."

"You got to get that wet shirt off. How'd you get snow clear down your shirt?"

"I said get your hands off me!"

She stepped back, surprised. "I was just—"

"I know what you 'was just.' Poor little Armor, you just pat him like a little boy and he'll feel better."

"You could catch your death—"

"Tell that to your pa! If I cough my guts out, you tell him what it means to throw a man in the snow!"

"Oh no!" she cried. "I can't believe Papa would—"

"See? You don't even believe your own husband."

"I *do* believe you, it just ain't like Pa—"

"No ma'am, it's like the devil himself, that's what it's like! That's what fills that house of yours up there! The spirit of evil! And when a body tries to speak the words of God in that house, they throw him right out in the snow!"

"What were you doing up at the house?"

"Trying to save your brother's life. He's no doubt dead by now."

"How could *you* save him?"

Maybe she didn't mean to sound so contemptuous. It didn't matter. He knew what she meant. That him having no hidden power, there wasn't a thing he could do to help anybody. After years of being married, she still put her faith in witchery, just like her kin. He hadn't changed her a bit. "You're just the same," he said. "Evil's in you so deep that I can't *pray* it out of you, and I can't *preach* it out of you, and I can't *love* it out of you, and I can't *yell* it out of you!" When he said "pray," he shoved her a little, just to make his point. When he said "preach," he shoved her harder, and she stumbled back. When he said "love," he took her by the shoulders and gave her such a shake her hair broke right out of the bun she'd made of it, and fluttered around her head. When he said "yell," he knocked her back so far she stumbled down on the floor.

Seeing her falling, even before she hit the floor, he felt such a shame go through him, even worse than when her father threw him in the snow. A strong man makes me feel weak, so I go home and shove around my wife, what a big man that makes me. Here I been a Christian who never hit or hurt a man or woman, and I knock my own wife, flesh of my flesh, right down on the floor.

That was his thinking, and he was about to throw himself on his knees and bawl like a baby and beg forgiveness. He would've done it, too, except that when she saw the look on his face, all twisted up with shame and rage, she didn't know that he was angry at himself, she just knew that he was hurting her, and so she did what come natural to a woman who grew up like she did. She moved her fingers to make a fending, and whispered a word to hold him back.

He couldn't fall on his knees before her. He couldn't take one step toward her. He couldn't even *think* of taking a step toward her. Her fending was so strong he staggered back, he headed for the door, he opened it and ran outside in just his shirt. Everything he'd been afraid of came true today. He probably lost his future in politics, but that was nothing compared to this: his own wife did witchery in his own home, and she did it against *him*, and he had no defense against it. She was a witch. She was a witch. And his house was unclean.

It was cold. He had no coat, not even his waistcoat. His shirt was already wet, and now it clung to him and froze him to the bone. He had to get indoors, but he couldn't bear to knock on anybody's door. There was only one place he could go. Up the hill to the church. Thrower had firewood there, so he'd be warm. And in the church he could pray and try to understand why the Lord didn't help him. Haven't I served you, Lord?

REVEREND THROWER OPENED the door of the church and walked slowly, fearfully inside. He could not bear to face the Visitor, knowing how he had failed. For it had been his own failure, he knew that now. Satan should have had no power over him, to drive him from the house that way. An ordained minister, acting as the emissary of the Lord, following instructions given to him by an angel— Satan should not have been able to thrust him out of the house like that, before he even knew what was happening.

He stripped off his cloak, and his topcoat as well. The church was hot. The fire in the stove must have burned longer than he expected. Or maybe he felt the heat of shame.

It could not be that Satan was stronger than the Lord. The only possible explanation was that Thrower himself was too weak. It was his own faith that faltered.

Thrower knelt at the altar and cried out the name of the Lord. "Forgive thou my unbelief!" he cried. "I held the knife, but Satan stood against me, and I had no strength!" He recited a litany of self-excoriation, he rehearsed all his failures of the day, until at last he was exhausted.

Only then, with his eyes sore from crying, his voice feeble and hoarse, did he realize the moment when his faith was undermined. It was when he stood in Alvin's room, asking the boy to confess his faith, and the boy scoffed at the mysteries of God. "How can he be on top of something that ain't got no top?" Even though Thrower had rejected the question as the result of ignorance and evil, the question had nevertheless pierced his heart and penetrated to the core of his belief. Certainties that had sustained him most of his life were suddenly split through by the questions of an ignorant boy. "He stole my faith," said Thrower. "I went into his room a man of God, and came out as a doubter."

"Indeed," said a voice behind him. A voice he knew.

A voice that now, in his moment of failure, he both feared and longed for. Oh, forgive me, comfort me, my Visitor, my friend! Yet do not fail also to chastise me with the terrible wrath of a jealous God.

"Chastise you?" asked the Visitor. "How could I chastise you, such a glorious specimen of humanity?"

"I am not glorious," said Thrower miserably.

"You're barely human, for that matter," said the Visitor. "In whose image were you made? I sent you to bring my word into that house, and instead they have nearly converted you. What do I call you now? A heretic? Or merely a skeptic?"

"A Christian!" cried Thrower. "Forgive me and call me once again a Christian."

"You had the knife in your hand, but you set it down."

"I didn't mean to!"

"Weak, weak, weak, weak, weak . . ." Each time the Visitor repeated the word, he stretched it longer and longer, until each repetition became a song in itself. As he sang, he began to walk around the church. He did not run, but he walked quickly, far faster than any man could walk. "Weak, weak . . ." He was moving so fast that Thrower had to turn constantly just to keep him in sight. The Visitor was no longer walking on the floor. He was skittering along the walls, as smooth and fast in his motion as a cockroach, then even faster, until he became a blur, and Thrower could not keep up with him by turning. Thrower leaned on the altar, facing the empty pews, watching the Visitor race by again and again and again.

Gradually Thrower realized that the Visitor had changed shape, that he had stretched himself, like a long slender beast, a lizard, an alligator, bright-scaled and shining, longer and longer, until finally the Visitor's body was so long that it circled the room, a vast worm that gripped its own tail between its teeth.

And in his mind Thrower realized how very small and worthless he was, compared to this glorious being that sparkled with a thousand different colors, that glowed with inner fire, that breathed in darkness and exhaled light. I worship thee! he shouted inside himself. Thou art all that I desire! Kiss me with your love, so I may taste your glory!

Suddenly the Visitor stopped, and the great jaws came toward him. Not to devour, for Thrower knew he was unworthy even to be consumed. He saw now the terrible predicament of man: he saw that he dangled over the pit of hell like a spider on a slender thread, and the only reason God did not let him fall was because he was not even worthy of destruction. God did not hate him. He was so vile that God disdained him.

Thrower looked into the Visitor's eyes and despaired. For there was neither love, nor forgiveness, nor anger, nor contempt. The eyes were utterly empty. The scales dazzled, scattering the light of an inner fire. But that fire did not shine through the eyes. They were not even black. They simply were not there at all, a terrible emptiness that trembled, that would not hold still, and Thrower knew that this was his own reflection, that he was nothing, that for him to continue to exist was a cruel waste of precious space, that the only choice left to him was to be annihilated, uncreated, to restore the world to the greater glory it would have had if Philadelphia Thrower had never been born.

IT WAS THROWER'S praying that woke Armor up. He was curled up by the Franklin stove. Maybe he stoked that stove a mite too hot, but that's what it took to beat back the cold. Why, by the time he got to the church his shirt was solid ice. He'd get more charcoal to pay back the parson.

Armor meant to speak right up and let Thrower know he was there, but when he heard the words that Thrower was praying, he couldn't find no words to say. Thrower was talking about knives and arteries, and how he should've cut up the enemies of God. After a minute it came clear: Thrower hadn't gone up there to save that boy, he'd gone up to kill him! What's wrong around here, thought Armor, when a Christian man beats his wife, and a Christian wife witches her husband, and a Christian minister plots murder and prays for forgiveness cause he failed to commit the crime!

All of a sudden, though, Thrower stopped praying. He was so hoarse and his face so red that Armor thought he might have had the apoplexy. But no. Thrower lifted his head like he was listening to somebody. Armor listened, too, and he could hear something, like people talking in a windstorm, so you couldn't never hear what they were saying.

I know what this is, thought Armor. Reverend Thrower's having himself a vision.

Sure enough, Thrower talked, and the faint voice answered, and pretty soon Thrower started turning around and around, faster and faster, like he was watching something on the walls. Armor tried to see what it was he was watching, but he couldn't never make it out. It was like a shadow passing across the sun—you couldn't see it coming and you couldn't see it go, but for a second it was darker and colder. That's what Armor saw.

Then it stopped. Armor saw a shimmering in the air, a dazzle here and there like when a pane of glass catches the sunlight. Was Thrower seeing the glory of God, like Moses saw? Not likely, looking at the parson's face. Armor never did see such a face as that before. Like a man's face might look if he had to watch his own baby being killed.

The shimmering and dazzle went away. The church was quiet. Armor wanted to run to Thrower and ask him, What did you see! What was your vision! Was it a prophecy?

But Thrower didn't look much like he wanted to answer questions. That look of wishing to die was still on his face. The preacher walked real slow away from the altar. He wandered around among the pews, bumping into them sometimes, not watching or caring where his body went. Finally he ended up by the window, facing the glass, but Armor knew he didn't see nothing, he was just standing there, his eyes wide open, looking like death.

Reverend Thrower lifted up his right hand, the fingers spread, and he laid his palm on a pane of glass. He pressed. He pressed and pushed so hard that Armor could see the glass bowing outward. "Stop it!" shouted Armor. "You'll cut yourself!"

Thrower didn't even make a sign that he heard. Just kept pressing. Armor started walking toward him. Got to make that man stop before he breaks the glass and cuts up his arm.

With a crash the glass shattered. Thrower's arm went right through, up to the shoulder. The preacher smiled. He pulled his arm partway back into the church. Then he began to slide his arm around the frame, jamming it right into the shards of glass that hung there in the putty.

Armor tried to pull Thrower away from the window, but the man had a strength on him like Armor never seen before. Finally Armor had to take a run at him and knock him right down to the floor. Blood was spattered everywhere. Armor grabbed at Thrower's arm, which was dripping all over with blood. Thrower tried to roll away from him. Armor didn't have no choice. For the first time since he became a Christian man he made his hand into a fist and popped Thrower right on the chin. It slammed the preacher's head back into the floor and knocked him silly.

Got to stop the bleeding, Armor thought. But first he had to get the glass out. Some of the big pieces were only stuck in a little way, and he could brush them right off. But other pieces, some of the little pieces, were in deep, only a bit of their top showing, and that was slimy with blood so he couldn't get much of a grip on it. Finally, though, he got all the glass he could find. Lucky enough there wasn't a single cut a-pumping blood, which told Armor that the big veins hadn't been cut. He stripped off his shirt, which left him naked to the waist with that cold draft coming in from the broken window, but he didn't hardly notice. He just ripped up the shirt and made bandages. He bound up the wounds and stopped the bleeding. Then he sat there and waited for Thrower to wake up.

THROWER WAS SURPRISED to find he wasn't dead. He was lying on his back on a hard floor, covered up with heavy cloth. His head hurt. His arm hurt worse. He remembered trying to cut up that arm, and he knew he ought to try again, but he just couldn't work up the same wish for death that he had felt before. Even remembering the Visitor in the form of a great lizard, even remembering those empty eyes, Thrower just couldn't remember how it felt. He only knew that it was the worst feeling in the world.

His arm was bandaged tight. Who had bandaged him?

He heard the sloshing of water. Then the flopping sound of wet rags slapping against wood. In the winter twilight coming through the window, he could make out somebody washing the wall. One of the window panes was covered over with a piece of wood.

"Who is it?" asked Thrower. "Who are you?"

"Just me."

"Armor-of-God."

"Washing down the walls. This is a church, not a butcher shed."

Of course there'd be blood all over. "Sorry," said Thrower.

"I don't mind cleaning up," said Armor. "I think I got all the glass out of your arm."

"You're naked," said Thrower.

"Your arm is wearing my shirt."

"You must be cold."

"Maybe I was, but I got the window covered and the stove het up. You're the one with a face so white you look like you been dead a week."

Thrower tried to sit up, but he couldn't. He was too weak; his arm hurt too bad.

Armor pushed him back down. "Now, you just lay back, Reverend Thrower. You just lay back. You been through a lot."

"Yes."

"I hope you don't mind, but I was here in the church when you come in. I was asleep by the stove—my wife threw me out of the house. I been thrown out twice today." He laughed, but there was no mirth in it. "So I saw you."

"Saw?"

"You were having a vision, weren't you?"

"Did you see him?"

"I didn't see much. I mostly saw *you*, but there was a few glimpses, if you know what I mean. Running around the walls."

"You saw," said Thrower. "Oh, Armor, it was terrible, it was beautiful."

"Did you see God?"

"See *God*? God has no body to be seen, Armor. No, I saw an angel, an angel of chastisement. Surely this was what Pharaoh saw, the angel of death that came through the cities of Egypt and took the firstborn."

"Oh," said Armor, sounding puzzled. "Was I spose to let you die, then?"

"If I were supposed to die, you could not have saved me," said Thrower. "Because you saved me, because you were here at the moment of my despair, it is a sure sign that I am meant to live. I was chastised, but not destroyed. Armor-of-God, I have another chance."

Armor nodded, but Thrower could see that he was worried about something. "What is it?" Thrower asked. "What is it that you want to ask me?"

Armor's eyes widened. "Can you hear what I'm thinking?"

"If I could, I wouldn't have to ask you."

Armor smiled. "Reckon not."

"I'll tell you what you want to know, if I can."

"I heard you praying," said Armor. He waited, as if that were the question.

Since Thrower didn't know what the question was, he wasn't sure what to answer. "I was in despair, because I failed the Lord. I was given a mission to perform, but at the crucial moment my heart was filled with doubt." With his good hand he reached out and clutched at Armor. All he could touch was the cloth of Armor's trousers, where he knelt beside him. "Armor-of-God," he said, "never let doubt enter your heart. Never question what you know is true. It's the doorway to let Satan have power over you."

But that wasn't the answer to Armor's question.

"Ask me what you want to ask me," said Thrower. "I'll tell you the truth, if I can."

"You prayed about killing," said Armor.

Thrower had not thought to tell anyone about the burden the Lord had placed upon him. Yet if the Lord had wanted the secret kept from Armor, He would not have allowed the man to be there in the church to overhear. "I believe," said Thrower, "that it was the Lord God that brought you to me. I am weak, Armor, and I failed at what the Lord required. But now I see that you, a man of faith, have been given to me as a friend and helper."

"What did the Lord require?" asked Armor.

"Not murder, my brother. The Lord never asked me to kill a man. It was a devil I was sent to kill. A devil in man-shape. Living in that house."

Armor pursed his lips, deep in thought. "The boy ain't just possessed, is that what you're saying? It ain't something you can cast right out?"

"I tried, but he laughed at the Holy Book and mocked my words of exorcism. He is not possessed, Armor-of-God. He is the devil's own kin."

Armor shook his head. "My wife ain't a devil, and she's his own sister."

"She has given up witchcraft, and so she has been made pure," said Thrower.

Armor gave one bitter laugh. "I thought so."

Thrower understood, now, why Armor had taken refuge in the church, in the house of God: His own house had been polluted.

"Armor-of-God, will you help me purge this country, this town, that house, that *family*, of the evil influence that has corrupted them?"

"Will it save my wife?" asked Armor. "Will it end her love of witchery?"

"It may," said Thrower. "Perhaps the Lord has brought us together so we can purify both our houses."

"Whatever it takes," said Armor. "I'm with you against the devil."

15

PROMISES

The blacksmith listened as Taleswapper read the letter from beginning to end.

"Do you remember the family?" asked Taleswapper.

"I do," said Makepeace Smith. "The graveyard almost began with their oldest boy. I pulled his body from the river with my own hands."

"Well then, will you take him as your prentice?"

A youth, perhaps sixteen years old, walked into the forge carrying a bucket of snow. He glanced at the visitor, ducked his head, and walked to the cooling barrel that stood near the hearth.

"You see I have a prentice," said the smith.

"He looks like a big one," said Taleswapper.

"Getting on," the smith agreed. "Ain't that right, Bosey? You ready to go on your own?"

Bosey smiled a bit, stifled it, nodded. "Yes, sir," he said.

"I'm not an easy master," said the smith.

"Alvin's a good-hearted boy. He'll work hard for you."

"But will he obey me? I like to be obeyed."

Taleswapper looked again at Bosey. He was busy scooping snow into the barrel.

"I said he's a good-hearted boy," said Taleswapper. "He'll obey you if you're fair with him."

The smith met his gaze. "I give honest measure. I don't beat the boys I take on. Have I ever laid hand on you, Bosey?"

"Never, sir."

"You see, Taleswapper, a prentice can obey out of fear, and he can obey out of greed. But if I'm a good master, he'll obey me cause he knows that's how he'll learn."

Taleswapper grinned at the smith. "There's no fee," said Taleswapper. "The boy will earn it out. And he gets his schooling."

"No need for a smith to have letters, as I should know."

"Won't be long before Hio's part of the United States," said Taleswapper. "The boy's got to vote, I think, and read the newspapers. A man who can't read only knows what other folks tell him."

Makepeace Smith looked at Taleswapper with a grin half-hid on his face. "That so? And ain't it you telling me? So don't I only know this cause other folks, namely you, is telling me so?"

Taleswapper laughed and nodded. The smith had shot the head clean off the turkey with that one. "I make my way in the world telling tales," said Taleswapper, "so I know you can get much with just the sound of a man's voice. He already reads above his years, so it won't do him harm to miss a bit of school. But his ma is set on him having letters and ciphering like a scholar. So just promise me you won't stand between him and schooling, if he wants it, and we'll leave it at that."

"Got my word on that," said Makepeace Smith. "And you don't have to write it down. A man who keeps his word doesn't have to read and write. But a man who has to write down his promises, you got to watch him all morning. I know that for a fact. We got lawyers in Hatrack these days."

"The curse of civilized man," said Taleswapper. "When a man can't get folks to believe his lies anymore, then he hires him a professional to lie in his place."

They laughed together over that one, setting there on two stout stumps just inside the door of the forge, the fire smoldering in its brick chimney place behind them, the sun shining on half-melted snow outside. A redbird flew across the grassy, trampled, dunged-up ground in front of the forge. It dazzled Taleswapper's eyes for a moment, it was such a startlement against the whites and greys and browns of late winter.

In that moment of amazement at the redbird's flight, Taleswapper knew for certain, though he couldn't say why, that it would be a while yet before the Unmaker let young Alvin come to this place. And when he came he'd be like a redbird out of season, to dazzle folks all hereabouts, them thinking he was just as natural as a bird flying, not knowing what a miracle it was every minute that the bird stayed in the air.

Taleswapper shook himself, and the moment's clear vision passed. "Then it's done, and I'll write to them to send the boy."

"I'll look for him the first of April. No later!"

"Unless you expect the boy to control the weather, you'd best be flexible about the date."

The smith grumbled and waved him away. All in all, a successful meeting. Taleswapper left feeling good—he had discharged his duty. It'd be easy to send a letter with a westbound wagon—several groups passed through the town of Hatrack every week.

Though it had been a long time since he passed through this place, he still knew the way from the forge to the inn. It was a well-traveled road, and not a long one. The inn was much larger now than it had been, and there were several shops a bit farther up the road. An outfitter, a saddler, a cobbler. The kind of service traveling folk could use.

He hardly set foot on the porch when the door opened and Old Peg Guester came out, her arms spread wide to embrace him. "Ah, Taleswapper, you've been away too long, come in, come in!"

"It's good to see you again, Peg," he said.

Horace Guester growled at him from behind the bar in the common room, where he was serving several thirsty visitors. "What I don't need here is another teetotaling man!"

"Good news, then, Horace," Taleswapper answered cheerfully. "I gave up tea as well."

"What do you drink, *water*?"

"Water and the blood of greasy old men," said Taleswapper.

Horace gestured to his wife. "You keep that man away from me, Old Peg, you hear?"

Old Peg helped him strip off a few layers of clothing. "Look at you," said Old Peg, sizing him up. "There ain't enough meat on you to make a stew."

"The bears and panthers pass me by in the night, looking for richer fare," said Taleswapper.

"Come in and tell me stories while I fix up a mess of supper for the company."

There was talk and chatter, especially once Oldpappy came in to help. He was getting feeble now, but he still had a hand in the kitchen, which was all to the benefit of those who ate here; Old Peg meant well and worked hard, but some folks had the knack and some folks didn't. But it wasn't food that Taleswapper came for, nor conversation either, and after a while he realized he'd have to bring it up himself. "Where's your daughter?"

To his surprise, Old Peg stiffened, and her voice went cold and hard. "She ain't so little no more. She's got a mind of her own, she's the first to tell you."

And you don't much like it, thought Taleswapper. But his business with the daughter was more important than any family squabbles. "Is she still a—"

"A torch? Oh, yes, she does her duty, but it's no pleasure for folks to come for her. Snippy and cold, that's what she is. It's got her a name for being sharp-tongued." For a moment Old Peg's face softened. "She used to be such a soft-hearted child."

"I've never seen a soft heart turn hard," said Taleswapper. "At least not without good reason."

"Well, whatever her reason, she's one whose heart has crusted up like a waterbucket on a winter's night."

Taleswapper held his tongue and didn't sermonize, didn't talk about how if you chip the ice it'll freeze up again right away, but if you take it inside, it'll warm up fresh as you please. No use stepping in the middle of a family squabble. Taleswapper knew enough of the way people lived that he took this particular quarrel as a natural event, like cold winds and short days in autumn, like thunder after lightning. Most parents didn't have much use for a half-grown child.

"I have a matter to discuss with her," said Taleswapper. "I'll take the risk of having my head bitten off."

HE FOUND HER in Dr. Whitley Physicker's office, working on his accounts. "I didn't know you were a bookkeeper," he said.

"I didn't know you held much with physicking," she answered. "Or did you just come to see the miracle of a girl who does sums and ciphers?"

Oh, yes, she was as sharp as could be. Taleswapper could see how a wit like that might discommode a few folks who expected a young woman to cast down her eyes and speak softly, glancing upward only now and then under heavy-lidded eyes. There was none of that young ladyness about Peggy. She looked Taleswapper in the face, plain as could be.

"I didn't come to be healed," said Taleswapper. "Or to have my future told. Or even to have my accounts added up."

And there it was. The moment a man answered her right back instead of getting his dander up, why, she flashed a smile fit to charm the warts off a toad. "I don't recollect you having much to add or subtract anyhow," she said. "Naught plus naught is naught, I think."

"You've got it wrong, Peggy," said Taleswapper. "I own this whole world, and folks haven't been keeping up too well on the payments."

She smiled again, and set aside the doctor's account book. "I keep his records for him, once a month, and he brings me things to read from Dekane." She talked about the things she read, and Taleswapper began to see that her heart yearned for places far beyond Hatrack River. He also saw other things—that she, being a torch, knew the folks around here too well, and thought that in faraway places she'd find people with jewel-like souls that would never disappoint a girl who could see clean into their heart.

She's young, that's all. Give her time, and she'll learn to love such goodness as she finds, and forgive the rest.

After a while the doctor came in, and they chatted a bit, and it was well into the afternoon by the time Taleswapper was alone with Peggy again and could ask her what he came to ask.

"How far off can you see, Peggy?"

He could almost see wariness fall across her face like a thick velvet curtain. "I don't reckon you're asking me whether I need spectacles," she said.

"I just wonder about a girl who once wrote in my book, A Maker is born. I wonder if she still keeps an eye on that Maker, now and then, so she can see how he fares."

She looked away from him, gazing at the high window above where the curtain gave privacy. The sun was low and the sky outside was grey, but her face was full of light, Taleswapper saw that right enough. Sometimes you didn't have to be a torch to know full well what was in a person's heart.

"I wonder if that torch saw a ridgebeam falling on him one time," said Taleswapper.

"I wonder," she said.

"Or a millstone."

"Could be."

"And I wonder if somehow she didn't have some way to split that ridgebeam clean in twain, and crack that millstone so a certain old taleswapper could see lantern light right through the middle of that stone."

Tears glistened in her eyes, not like she was about to cry, but like she was looking into the sun straight on, and it made her water up. "A scrap of his birth caul, rubbed into dust, and a body can use the boy's own power to work a few clumsy makings," she said softly.

"But now he knows something of his own knack, and he undid what you did for him."

She nodded.

"Must be lonely, watching out for him from so far away," said Taleswapper.

She shook her head. "Not to me. I got folks all around me, all the time." She looked at Taleswapper and smiled wanly. "It's almost a relief to spend time with that one boy who doesn't want a thing from me, because he doesn't even know that I exist."

"I know, though," said Taleswapper. "And I don't want a thing from you, either."

She smiled. "You old fraud," she said.

"All right, I *do* want something from you, but not something for myself. I've met that boy, and even if I can't see into his heart the way you can, I think I know him. I think I know what he might be, what he might do, and I want you to know that if you ever need my help for anything, just send me word, just tell me what to do, and if it's in my power I'll do it."

She didn't answer, nor did she look at him.

"So far you didn't need help," said Taleswapper, "but now he has a mind of his own, and you can't always do for him the things he'll need. The dangers won't come just from things that fall on him or hurt him in the flesh. He's in as much danger from what he decides to do himself. I'm just telling you that if you see such danger and you need me to help, I'll come no matter what."

"That's a comfort," she said. That was honest enough, Taleswapper knew; but she was feeling more than she said, he knew that too.

"And I wanted to tell you he was coming here, first of April, to prentice with the smith."

"I know he's coming," she said, "but it won't be the first of April."

"Oh?"

"Or even this year at all."

Fear for the boy stabbed at Taleswapper's heart. "I guess I did come to hear the future after all. What's in store for him? What's to come?"

"All kinds of things might happen," she said, "and I'd be a fool to guess which one. I see it open like a thousand roads before him, all the time. But there's precious few of those roads that bring him here by April, and a whole lot more that leave him dead with a Red man's hatchet in his head."

Taleswapper leaned across the doctor's writing table and rested his hand on hers. "Will he live?"

"As long as I have breath in my body," she said.

"Or I in mine," he answered.

They sat in silence for a moment, hand on hand, eye to eye, until she burst into laughter and looked away.

"Usually when folks laugh I get the joke," said Taleswapper.

"I was just thinking we're a poor excuse for a conspiracy, the two of us, against the enemies that boy will face."

"True," said Taleswapper, "but then, our cause is good, and so all nature will conspire with us, don't you think?"

"And God, too," she added firmly.

"I can't say about that," said Taleswapper. "The preachers and priests seem to have him so fenced up with doctrine that the poor old Father hardly has room to act anymore. Now that they've got the Bible safely interpreted, the last thing they ever want is for him to speak another word, or show his hand of power in this world."

"I saw his hand of power in the birth of a seventh son of a seventh son, some years back," she said. "Call it nature if you want to, since you've got all kinds of learning from philosophers and wizards. I just know that he's tied as tight to my life as if we was born from the same womb."

Taleswapper didn't plan his next question, it just came unthought-of from his lips. "Are you glad of it?"

She looked at him with terrible sadness in her eyes. "Not often," she said. She looked so weary then that Taleswapper couldn't help himself, he walked around the table and stood beside her chair and held her tight like a father holds his daughter, held her for a good long while. If she was crying or just holding on, he couldn't say. They spoke not a word. Finally she let go of him and turned back to the account book. He left without breaking the silence.

Taleswapper wandered on over to the inn to take his supper. There were tales to tell and chores to do in order to earn his keep. Yet all the stories seemed to pale beside the one story that he could *not* tell, the one story whose end he didn't know.

ON THE MEADOW around the millhouse were a half dozen farm wagons, watched over by farmers who had come a good long way to get high-quality flour. No more would their wives sweat over a mortar and pestle to make coarse meal for hard and lumpy bread. The mill was in business, and everyone for miles around would bring their grain to the town of Vigor Church.

The water poured through the millrace, and the great wheel turned. Inside the millhouse, the force of the wheel was carried by interlocking gears, to make the grindstone roll around and around, riding on the face of a quarter dress millstone.

The miller poured out the wheat upon the stone. The grindstone passed over it, crushing it to flour. The miller swept it smooth for a second pass, then brushed it off into a basket held by his son, a ten-year-old boy. His son poured the flour into a sieve, and shook the good flour into a cloth sack. He emptied what stayed in the sieve into a silage barrel. Then he returned to his father's side for the next basket of wheat.

Their thoughts were remarkably alike, as they worked silently together. This is what I want to do forever, each one thought. Rise in the morning, come to the mill, and work all day with him beside me. Never mind that the wish was impossible. Never mind that they might never see each other again, once the boy left for his apprenticeship back in the place of his birth. That only added to the sweetness of the moment, which would soon become a memory, would soon become a dream.

RED
PROPHET

In memory of my grandfather,
Orson Rega Card (1891–1984),
whose life was saved by Indians of the Blood tribe
when he was a child on the Canadian frontier.

AUTHOR'S NOTE

This story takes place in an America whose history is often similar to, but often quite different from our own. You should not assume that the portrayal in this book of a person who shares a name with a figure from American history is an accurate portrayal of that historical figure. In particular, you should be aware that William Henry Harrison, famed in our own history for having the briefest presidency and for his unforgettable election slogan "Tippecanoe and Tyler too," was a somewhat nicer person than his counterpart in this book.

My thanks to Carol Breakstone for American Indian lore; to Beth Meacham for Octagon Mound and Flint Ridge; to Wayne Williams for heroic patience; and to my great-great-grandfather Joseph for the stories behind the story in this book.

As always with my work, Kristine A. Card has influenced and improved every page in this book.

1

HOOCH

Not many flatboats were getting down the Hio these days, not with pioneers aboard, anyway, not with families and tools and furniture and seed and a few shoats to start a pig herd. It took only a couple of fire arrows and pretty soon some tribe of Reds would have themselves a string of half-charred scalps to sell to the French in Detroit.

But Hooch Palmer had no such trouble. The Reds all knew the look of *his* flatboat, stacked high with kegs. Most of those kegs sloshed with whisky, which was about the only musical sound them Reds understood. But in the middle of the vast heap of cooperage there was one keg that didn't slosh. It was filled with gunpowder, and it had a fuse attached.

How did he use that gunpowder? They'd be floating along with the current, poling on round a bend, and all of a sudden there'd be a half-dozen canoes filled with painted-up Reds of the Kicky-Poo persuasion. Or they'd see a fire burning near shore, and some Shaw-Nee devils dancing around with arrows ready to set alight.

For most folks that meant it was time to pray, fight, and die. Not Hooch, though. He'd stand right up in the middle of that flatboat, a torch in one hand and the fuse in the other, and shout, "Blow up whisky! Blow up whisky!"

Well, most Reds didn't talk much English, but they sure knew what "blow up" and "whisky" meant. And instead of arrows flying or canoes overtaking them, pretty soon them canoes passed by him on the far side of the river. Some Red yelled, "Carthage City!" and Hooch hollered back, "That's right!" and the canoes just zipped on down the Hio, heading for where that likker would soon be sold.

The poleboys, of course, it was their first trip downriver, and they didn't know all that Hooch Palmer knew, so they about filled their trousers first time they saw them Reds with fire arrows. And when they saw Hooch holding his torch by that fuse, they like to jumped right in the river. Hooch just laughed and laughed. "You boys don't know about Reds and likker," he said. "They won't do nothing that might cause a single drop from these kegs to spill into the Hio. They'd kill their own mother and not think twice, if she stood between them and a keg, but they won't touch *us* as long as I got the gunpowder ready to blow if they lay one hand on me."

Privately the poleboys might wonder if Hooch really would blow the whole raft, crew and all, but the fact is Hooch *would*. He wasn't much of a thinker, nor did he spend much time brooding about death and the hereafter or such philosophical questions, but this much he had decided: when he died, he supposed he wouldn't die alone. He also supposed that if somebody killed him, they'd get no profit from the deed, none at all. Specially not some half-drunk weak-sister cowardly Red with a scalping knife.

The best secret of all was, Hooch wouldn't need no torch and he wouldn't need no fuse, neither. Why, that fuse didn't even go right into the gunpowder keg, if the truth be known—Hooch didn't want a chance of that powder going off by accident. No, if Hooch ever needed to blow up his flatboat, he could just set down and think about it for a while. And pretty soon that powder would start to hotten up right smart, and maybe a little smoke would come off it, and then pow! it goes off.

That's right. Old Hooch was a spark. Oh, there's some folks says there's no such thing as a spark, and for proof they say, "Have you ever *met* a spark, or knowed anybody who did?" but that's no proof at all. Cause if you happen to be a spark, you don't go around telling everybody, do you? It's not as if anybody's hoping to hire your services— it's too easy to use flint and steel, or even them alchemical matches. No, the only value there is to being a spark is if you want to start a fire from a distance, and the only time you want to do that is if it's a *bad* fire, meant to hurt somebody, burn down a building, blow something up. And if you hire out *that* kind of service, you don't exactly put up a sign that says Spark For Hire.

Worst of it is that if word once gets around that you're a spark, every little fire gets blamed on you. Somebody's boy lights up a pipe out in the barn, and the barn burns down—does that boy ever say, "Yep, Pa, it was me all right." No sir, that boy says, "Must've been some spark set that fire, Pa!" and then they go looking for *you,* the neighborhood scapegoat. No, Hooch was no fool. He didn't ever tell nobody about how he could get things het up and flaming.

There was another reason Hooch didn't use his sparking ability too much. It was a reason so secret that Hooch didn't rightly know it himself. Thing was, fire scared him. Scared him deep. The way some folks is scared of water, and so they go to sea; and some folks is scared of death, and so they take up gravedigging; and some folks is scared of God, and so they set to preaching. Well Hooch feared the fire like he feared no other thing, and so he was always drawn to it, with that sick feeling in his stomach;

but when it was time for him to lay a fire himself, why, he'd back off, he'd delay, he'd think of reasons why he shouldn't do it at all. Hooch had a knack, but he was powerful reluctant to make much use of it.

But he would have done it. He would have blown up that powder and himself and his poleboys and all his likker, before he'd let a Red take it by murder. Hooch might have his bad fear of fire, but he'd overcome it right quick if he got mad enough.

Good thing, then, that the Reds loved likker so much they didn't want to risk spilling a drop. No canoe came too close, no arrow whizzed in to thud and twang against a keg, and Hooch and his kegs and casks and firkins and barrels all slipped along the top of the water peaceful as you please, clear to Carthage City, which was Governor Harrison's high-falutin name for a stockade with a hundred soldiers right smack where the Little My-Ammy River met the Hio. But Bill Harrison was the kind of man who gave the name first, then worked hard to make the place live up to the name. And sure enough, there was about fifty chimney fires outside the stockade this time, which meant Carthage City was almost up to being a village.

He could hear them yelling before he hove into view of the wharf—there must be Reds who spent half their life just setting on the riverbank waiting for the likker boat to come in. And Hooch knew they were specially eager this time, seeing as how some money changed hands back in Fort Dekane, so the other likker dealers got held up this way and that until old Carthage City must be dry as the inside of a bull's tit. Now here comes Hooch with his flatboat loaded up heavier than they ever saw, and he'd get a price this time, that's for sure.

Bill Harrison might be vain as a partridge, taking on airs and calling himself governor when nobody elected him and nobody appointed him but his own self, but he knew his business. He had those boys of his in smart-looking uniforms, lined up at the wharf just as neat as you please, their muskets loaded and ready to shoot down the first Red who so much as took a step toward the shore. It was no formality, neither—them Reds looked mighty eager, Hooch could see. Not jumping up and down like children, of course, but just standing there, just standing and watching, right out in the open, not caring who saw them, half-naked the way they mostly were in summertime. Standing there all *humble,* all ready to bow and scrape, to beg and plead, to say, Please Mr. Hooch one keg for thirty deerskins, oh that would sound sweet, oh indeed it would; Please Mr. Hooch one tin cup of likker for these ten muskrat hides. "Whee-haw!" cried Hooch. The poleboys looked at him like he was crazy, cause they didn't know, they never saw how these Reds used to look, back before Governor Harrison set up shop here, the way they never deigned to look at a White man, the way you had to crawl into their wicky-ups and choke half to death on smoke and steam and sit there making signs and talking their jub-jub until you got permission to trade. Used to be the Reds would be standing there with bows and spears, and you'd be scared to death they'd decide your scalp was worth more than your trade goods.

Not anymore. Now they didn't have a single weapon among them. Now their tongues just hung out waiting for likker. And they'd drink and drink and drink and drink and drink and *whee-haw!* They'd drop down dead before they'd ever stop drinking, which was the best thing of all, best thing of all. Only good Red's a dead Red, Hooch always said, and the way he and Bill Harrison had things going now, they had them Reds dying of likker at a good clip, and paying for the privilege along the way.

So Hooch was about as happy a man as you ever saw when they tied up at the Carthage City Wharf. The sergeant even saluted him, if you could believe it! A far cry from the way the U.S. Marshals treated him back in Suskwahenny, acting like he was scum they just scraped off the privy seat. Out here in this new country, free-spirited men like Hooch were treated most like gentlemen, and that suited Hooch just fine. Let them pioneers with their tough ugly wives and wiry little brats go hack down trees and cut up the dirt and raise corn and hogs just to live. Not Hooch. He'd come in after, after the fields were all nice and neat looking and the houses were all in fine rows on squared-off streets, and then he'd take his money and buy him the biggest house in town, and the banker would step off the sidewalk into the mud to make way for him, and the mayor would call him sir—if he didn't decide to be mayor himself by then.

This was the message of the sergeant's salute, telling his future for him, when he stepped ashore.

"We'll unload here, Mr. Hooch," said the sergeant.

"I've got a bill of lading," said Hooch, "so let's have no privateering by your boys. Though I'd allow as how there's probably one keg of good rye whisky that somehow didn't exactly get counted on here. I'd bet that one keg wouldn't be missed."

"We'll be as careful as you please, sir," said the sergeant, but he had a grin so wide it showed his hind teeth, and Hooch knew he'd find a way to keep a good half of that extra keg for himself. If he was stupid, he'd sell his half-keg bit by bit to the Reds. You don't get rich off a half keg of whisky. No, if that sergeant was smart, he'd *share* that half keg, shot by shot, with the officers that seemed most likely to give him advancement, and if he kept that up, someday that sergeant wouldn't be out greeting flatboats, no sir, he'd be sitting in officers' quarters with a pretty wife in his bedroom and a good steel sword at his hip.

Not that Hooch would ever tell this to the sergeant. The

way Hooch figured, if a man had to be told, he didn't have brains enough to do the job anyway. And if he had the brains to bring it off, he didn't need no flatboat likker dealer telling him what to do.

"Governor Harrison wants to see you," said the sergeant.

"And I want to see *him*," said Hooch. "But I need a bath and a shave and clean clothes first."

"Governor says for you to stay in the old mansion."

"*Old* one?" said Hooch. Harrison had built the official mansion only four years before. Hooch could think of only one reason why Bill might have upped and built another so soon. "Well, now, has Governor Bill gone and got his-self a new wife?"

"He has," said the sergeant. "Pretty as you please, and only fifteen years old, if you like that! She's from Manhattan, though, so she don't talk much English or anyway it don't *sound* like English when she does."

That was all right with Hooch. He talked Dutch real good, almost as good as he talked English and a lot better than he talked Shaw-Nee. He'd make friends with Bill Harrison's wife in no time. He even toyed with the idea of—but no, no, it wasn't no good to mess with another man's woman. Hooch had the desire often enough, but he knew things got way too complicated once you set foot on that road. Besides, he didn't really need no White woman, not with all these thirsty squaws around.

Would Bill Harrison bring his children out here, now he had a second wife? Hooch wasn't too sure how old them boys would be now, but old enough they might relish the frontier life. Still, Hooch had a vague feeling that the boys'd be a lot better off staying in Philadelphia with their aunt. Not because they shouldn't be out in wild country, but because they shouldn't be near their father. Hooch liked Bill Harrison just fine, but he wouldn't pick him as the ideal guardian for children—even for Bill's own.

Hooch stopped at the gate of the stockade. Now, there was a nice touch. Right along with the standard hexes and tokens that were supposed to ward off enemies and fire and other such things, Governor Bill had put up a sign, the width of the gate. In big letters it said

CARTHAGE CITY

and in smaller letters it said

CAPITAL OF THE STATE OF WOBBISH

which was just the sort of thing old Bill would think of. In a way, he expected that sign was more powerful than any of the hexes. As a spark, for instance, Hooch knew that the hex against fire wouldn't stop him, it'd just make it *harder* to start a fire up right near the hex. If he got a good blaze going somewhere else, that hex would burn up just like anything else. But that sign, naming Wobbish a state and Carthage its capital, why, that might actually have some power in it, power over the way folks thought. If you say a thing often enough, people come to expect it to be true, and pretty soon it *becomes* true. Oh, not something like "The moon is going to stop in its tracks and go backward tonight," cause for that to work the moon'd have to hear your words. But if you say things like "That girl's easy" or "That man's a thief," it doesn't much matter whether the person you're talking about believes you or not—everybody *else* comes to believe it, and treats them like it was true. So Hooch figured that if Harrison got enough people to see a sign that named Carthage as the capital of the state of Wobbish, someday it'd plumb come to be.

Fact is, though, Hooch didn't much care whether it was Harrison who got to be governor and put his capital in

Carthage City, or whether it was that teetotaling self-righteous prig Armor-of-God Weaver up north, where Tippy-Canoe Creek flowed into the Wobbish River, who got to be governor and make Vigor Church the capital. Let those two fight it out; whoever won, Hooch intended to be a rich man and do as he liked. Either that or see the whole place go up in flames. If Hooch ever got completely beat down and broken, he'd make sure nobody else profited. When a spark had no hope left, he could still get even, which is about all the good Hooch figured he got out of being a spark.

Well, of course, as a spark he made sure his bathwater was always hot, so it wasn't a total loss. Sure was a nice change, getting off the river and back into civilized life. The clothes laid out for him were clean, and it felt good to get that prickly beard off his face. Not to mention the fact that the squaw who bathed him was real eager to get an extra dose of likker, and if Harrison hadn't sent a soldier knocking on his door telling him to hurry it up, Hooch might have collected the first installment of her trade goods. Instead, though, he dried and dressed.

She looked real concerned when he started for the door. "You be back?" she asked.

"Look here, of course I will," he said. "And I'll have a keg with me."

"Before dark though," she said.

"Well maybe yes and maybe no," he answered. "Who cares?"

"After dark, all Reds like me, outside fort."

"Is that so," murmured Hooch. "Well, I'll try to be back before dark. And if I don't, I'll remember you. May forget your face, but I won't forget your hands, hey? That was a real nice bath."

She smiled, but it was a grotesque imitation of a real smile. Hooch just couldn't figure out why the Reds didn't die out years ago, their women were so ugly. But if you kind of closed your eyes, a squaw would do well enough until you could get back to real women.

It wasn't just a new mansion Harrison had built—he had added a whole new section of stockade, so the fort was about twice the size it used to be. And a good solid parapet ran the whole length of the stockade. Harrison was ready for war. That made Hooch pretty uneasy. The likker trade didn't thrive too good in wartime. The kind of Reds who fought battles weren't the kind of Reds who drank likker. Hooch saw so much of the latter kind that he pretty much forgot the former kind existed. There was even a cannon. No, two cannons. This didn't look good at all.

Harrison's office wasn't in the mansion, though. It was in another building entirely, a new headquarters building, and Harrison's office was in the southwest corner, with lots of light. Hooch noticed that besides the normal complement of soldiers on guard and officers doing paperwork, there were several Reds sprawling or sitting in the headquarters building. Harrison's tame Reds, of course—he always kept a few around.

But there were more tame Reds than usual, and the only one Hooch recognized was Lolla-Wossiky, a one-eyed Shaw-Nee who was always about the drunkest Red who wasn't dead yet. Even the other Reds made fun of him, he was so bad, a real lickspittle.

What made it even funnier was the fact that Harrison himself was the man who shot Lolla-Wossiky's father, some fifteen years ago, when Lolla-Wossiky was just a little tyke, standing right there watching. Harrison even told the story sometimes right in front of Lolla-Wossiky, and the one-eyed drunk just nodded and laughed and grinned and acted like he had no brains at all, no human dignity, just about the lowest, crawliest Red that Hooch ever seen. He didn't even care about revenge for his dead papa, just so long as he got his likker. No, Hooch wasn't a bit sur-prised to see that Lolla-Wossiky was lying right on the floor outside Harrison's office, so every time the door opened, it bumped him right in the butt. Incredibly, even now, when there hadn't been new likker in Carthage City in four months, Lolla-Wossiky was pickled. He saw Hooch come in, sat up on one elbow, waved an arm in greeting, and then rocked back onto the floor without a sound. The handkerchief he kept tied over his missing eye was out of place, so the empty socket with the sucked-in eyelids was plainly visible. Hooch felt like that empty eye was look-ing at him. He didn't like that feeling. He didn't like Lolla-Wossiky. Harrison was the kind of man who liked having such squalid creatures around—made him feel real good about himself, by contrast, Hooch figured—but Hooch didn't like seeing such miserable specimens of humanity. Why hadn't Lolla-Wossiky died yet?

Just as he was about to open Harrison's door, Hooch looked up from the drunken one-eyed Red into the eyes of another man, and here's the funny thing: He thought for a second it was Lolla-Wossiky again, they looked so much alike. Only it was Lolla-Wossiky with both eyes, and not drunk at all, no sir. This Red must be six feet from sole to scalp, leaning against the wall, his head shaved except his scalplock, his clothing clean. He stood *straight*, like a sol-dier at attention, and he didn't so much as look at Hooch. His eyes stared straight into space. Yet Hooch knew that this boy saw *everything*, even though he focused on noth-ing. It had been a long time since Hooch saw a Red who looked like that, all cold and in control of things.

Dangerous, dangerous, is Harrison getting careless, to let a Red into his own headquarters with eyes like those? With a bearing like a king, and arms so strong he looks like he could pull a bow made from the trunk of a six-year-old oak? Lolla-Wossiky was so contemptible it made Hooch sick. But this Red who looked like Lolla-Wossiky, he was the opposite. And instead of making Hooch sick, he made Hooch mad, to be so proud and defiant as if he thought he was as good a man as any White. No, better. That's how he looked—like he thought he was *better*.

Then he realized he was just standing there, his hand on the latch pull, staring at the Red. Hadn't moved in how long? That was no good, to let folks see how this Red made him uncomfortable. He pulled the door open and stepped inside.

But he didn't talk about that Red, no sir, that wouldn't do at all. It wouldn't do to let Harrison know how much that one proud Shaw-Nee bothered him, made him angry. Because there sat Governor Bill behind a big old table, like God on his throne, and Hooch realized things had changed around here. It wasn't just the fort that had got bigger—so had Bill Harrison's vanity. And if Hooch was going to make the profit he expected to on this trip, he'd have to make sure Governor Bill came down a peg or two, so they could deal as equals instead of dealing as a tradesman and a governor.

"Noticed your cannon," said Hooch, not bothering even to say howdy. "What's the artillery *for,* French from Detroit, Spanish from Florida, or Reds?"

"No matter who's buying the scalps, it's always Reds, one way or another," said Harrison. "Now sit down, relax, Hooch. When my door is closed there's no ceremony between us." Oh, yes, Governor Bill liked to play his games, just like a politician. Make a man feel like you're doing him a favor just to let him sit in your presence, flatter him by making him feel like a real *chum* before you pick his pocket. Well, thought Hooch, I have some games of my own to play, and we'll see who comes out on top.

Hooch sat down and put his feet up on Governor Bill's desk. He took out a pinch of tobacco and tucked it into his cheek. He could see Bill flinch a little. It was a sure sign that his wife had broke him of some manly habits. "Care for a pinch?" asked Hooch.

It took a minute before Harrison allowed as how he wouldn't mind a bit of it. "I mostly swore off this stuff," he said ruefully.

So Harrison still missed his bachelor ways. Well, that was good news to Hooch. Gave him a handle to get the Gov off balance. "Hear you got yourself a White bed-warmer from Manhattan," said Hooch.

It worked: Harrison's face flushed. "I married a *lady* from New Amsterdam," he said. His voice was quiet and cold. Didn't bother Hooch a bit—that's just what he wanted.

"A *wife!*" said Hooch. "Well, I'll be! I beg your pardon, Governor, that wasn't what I heard, you'll have to forgive me, I was only going by what the—what the rumors said."

"Rumors?" asked Harrison

"Oh, no, you just never mind. You know how soldiers talk. I'm ashamed I listened to them in the first place. Why, you've kept the memory of your first wife sacred all these years, and if I was any kind of friend of yours, I would've known any woman you took into your house would be a lady, and a properly married wife."

"What I want to know," said Harrison, "is who told you she was anything *else*?"

"Now, Bill, it was just loose soldiers' talk; I don't want any man to get in trouble because he can't keep his tongue. A likker shipment just came in, for heaven's sake, Bill! You won't hold it against them, what they said with their minds on whisky. No, you just take a pinch of this tobacky and remember that your boys all like you fine."

Harrison took a good-sized chaw from the offered to-bacco pouch and tucked it into his cheek. "Oh, I know, Hooch, they don't bother me." But Hooch knew that it *did* bother him, that Harrison was so angry he couldn't spit straight, which he proved by missing the spittoon. A spittoon, Hooch noticed, which had been sparkling clean. Didn't *anybody* spit around here anymore, except Hooch?

"You're getting civilized," said Hooch. "Next thing you know you'll have lace curtains."

"Oh, I do," said Harrison. "In my house."

"And little china chamber pots?"

"Hooch, you got a mind like a snake and a mouth like a hog."

"That's why you love me, Bill—cause you got a mind like a hog and a mouth like a snake."

"Keep that in mind," said Harrison. "You just keep that in mind, how I might bite, and bite deep, and bite with poison in it. You keep that in mind before you try to play your diddly games with me."

"Diddly games!" cried Hooch. "What do you mean, Bill Harrison! What do you accuse me of!"

"I accuse you of arranging for us to have no likker at all for four long months of springtime, till I had to hang three Reds for breaking into military stores, and even my soldiers ran out!"

"Me! I brought this load here as fast as I could!"

Harrison just smiled.

Hooch kept his look of pained outrage—it was one of his best expressions, and besides it was even partly true. If even one of the other whisky traders had half a head on him, he'd have found a way downriver despite Hooch's efforts. It wasn't *Hooch's* fault if he just happened to be the sneakiest, most malicious, lowdown, competent skunk in a business that wasn't none too clean and none too bright to start with.

Hooch's look of injured innocence lasted longer than

Harrison's smile, which was about what Hooch figured would happen.

"Look here, Hooch," said Harrison.

"Maybe you better start calling me Mr. Ulysses Palmer," said Hooch. "Only my *friends* call me Hooch."

But Harrison did not take the bait. He did not start to make protests of his undying friendship. "Look here, *Mr. Palmer*," said Harrison, "you know and I know that this hasn't got a thing to do with friendship. You want to be rich, and I want to be governor of a real state. I need your likker to be governor, and you need my protection to be rich. But this time you pushed too far. You understand me? You can have a monopoly for all I care, but if I don't get a steady supply of whisky from you, I'll get it from someone else."

"Now Governor Harrison, I can understand you might've started fretting along in there sometime, and I can make it right with you. What if you had six kegs of the best whisky all on your own—"

But Harrison wasn't in the mood to be bribed, either. "What you forget, Mr. Palmer, is that I can have *all* this whisky, if I want it."

Well, if Harrison could be blunt, so could Hooch, though he made it a practice to say things like this with a smile. "Mr. Governor, you can take all my whisky *once*. But then what trader will want to deal with you?"

Harrison laughed and laughed. "Any trader at all, Hooch Palmer, and you know it!"

Hooch knew when he'd been beat. He joined right in with the laughing.

Somebody knocked on the door. "Come in," said Harrison. At the same time he waved Hooch to stay in his chair. A soldier stepped in, saluted, and said, "Mr. Andrew Jackson here to see you, sir. From the Tennizy country, he says."

"Days before I looked for him," said Harrison. "But I'm delighted, couldn't be more pleased, show him in, show him in."

Andrew Jackson. Had to be that lawyer fellow they called Mr. Hickory. Back in the days when Hooch was working the Tennizy country, Hickory Jackson was a real country boy—killed a man in a duel, put his fists into a few faces now and then, had a name for keeping his word, and the story was that he wasn't exactly completely married to his wife, who might well have another husband in her past who wasn't even dead. That was the difference between Hickory and Hooch—Hooch would've made sure the husband was dead and buried long since. So Hooch was a little surprised that this Jackson was big enough now to have business that would take him clear from Tennizy up to Carthage City.

But that was nothing to his surprise when Jackson stepped through the door, ramrod straight with eyes like fire. He strode across the room and offered his hand to Governor Harrison. Called him *Mr.* Harrison, though. Which meant he was either a fool, or he didn't figure he needed Harrison as much as Harrison needed *him.*

"You got too many Reds around here," said Jackson. "That one-eyed drunk by the door is enough to make a body puke."

"Well," said Harrison, "I think of him as kind of a pet. My own pet Red."

"Lolla-Wossiky," said Hooch helpfully. Well, not really helpfully. He just didn't like how Jackson hadn't noticed him, and Harrison hadn't bothered to introduce him.

Jackson turned to look at him. "What did you say?"

"Lolla-Wossiky," said Hooch.

"The one-eyed Red's name," said Harrison.

Jackson eyed Hooch coldly. "The only time I need to

know the name of a horse," he said, "is when I plan to ride it."

"My name's Hooch Palmer," said Hooch. He offered his hand.

Jackson didn't take it. "Your name is Ulysses Brock," said Jackson, "and you owe more than ten pounds in unpaid debts back in Nashville. Now that Appalachee has adopted U.S. currency, that means you owe two hundred and twenty dollars in gold. I bought those debts and it happens that I have the papers with me, since I heard you were trading whisky up in these parts, and so I think I'll place you under arrest."

It never occurred to Hooch that Jackson would have that kind of memory, or be such a skunk as to buy a man's paper, especially seven-year-old paper, which by now should be pretty much forgot. But sure enough, Jackson took a warrant out of his coat pocket and laid it on Governor Harrison's desk.

"Since I appreciate your already having this man in custody when I arrived," said Jackson, "I am glad to tell you that under Appalachee law the apprehending officer is entitled to ten percent of the funds collected."

Harrison leaned back in his chair and grinned at Hooch. "Well, Hooch, maybe you better set down and let's all get better acquainted. Or I guess maybe we don't have to, since Mr. Jackson here seems to know you better than I did."

"Oh, I know Ulysses Brock all right," said Jackson. "He's just the sort of skunk we had to get rid of in Tennizy before we could lay claim to being civilized. And I expect you'll be rid of his sort soon enough here, too, as you get the Wobbish country ready to apply for admission to the United States."

"You take a lot for granted," said Harrison. "We might try to go it alone out here, you know."

"If Appalachee couldn't make a go of it alone, with Tom Jefferson as President, you won't do any better here, I reckon."

"Well maybe," said Harrison, "just maybe we've got to do something that Tom Jefferson didn't have the guts to do. And maybe we've got a need for men like Hooch here."

"What you have need for is soldiers," said Jackson. "Not rummers."

Harrison shook his head. "You're a man who forces me to come to the point, Mr. Jackson, and I can calculate right enough why the folks in Tennizy sent you on up here to meet with me. So I'll come to the point. We've got the same trouble up here that you've got down there, and that trouble can be summed up in one word: Reds."

"Which is why I'm perplexed that you let drunken Reds sit around here in your own headquarters. They all belong west of the Mizzipy, and that's as plain as day. We won't have peace and we won't have civilization until that's done. And since Appalachee and the U.S. alike are convinced that Reds can be treated like human beings, we've got to solve our Red problem *before* we join the Union. It's as simple as that."

"Well, you see?" said Harrison. "We already agree completely."

"Then why is it that you keep your headquarters as full of Reds as Independence Street in Washington City? They have Cherriky men acting as clerks and even holding government offices in Appalachee, right in the capital, jobs that White men ought to have, and then I come here and find you keep Reds around you, too."

"Cool down, Mr. Jackson, cool right down. Don't the King keep his Blacks there in his palace in Virginia?"

"His Blacks are slaves. Everybody knows you can't make slaves out of Reds. They aren't intelligent enough to be properly trained."

"Well, you just set yourself there in that chair, Mr. Jackson, and I'll make my point the best way I know how, by showing you two prime Shaw-Nee specimens. Just set down."

Jackson picked up the chair and moved it to the opposite side of the room from Hooch. It made something gnaw in Hooch's gut, the way Jackson acted. Men like Jackson were so upright and honest-seeming, but Hooch knew that there wasn't no such thing as a good man, just a man who wasn't bought yet, or wasn't in deep enough trouble, or didn't have the guts to reach out and take what he wanted. That's all that virtue ever boiled down to, so far as Hooch ever saw in his life. But here was Jackson, putting on airs and calling for Bill Harrison to arrest him! Think of that, a stranger from Tennizy country coming up here and waving around a warrant from an Appalachee judge, of all things, which didn't have no more force in Wobbish country than if it was written by the King of Ethiopia. Well, Mr. Jackson, it's a long way home from here, and we'll just see if you don't have some kind of accident along the way.

No, no, no, Hooch told himself silently. Getting even don't amount to nothing in this world. Getting even only gets you behind. The best revenge is to get rich enough to make them all call you sir, that's how you get even with these boys. No bushwhacking. If you ever get a name for bushwhacking, that's the end of you, Hooch Palmer.

So Hooch sat there and smiled, as Harrison called for his aide. "Why don't you invite Lolla-Wossiky in here? And while you're at it, tell his brother he can come in, too."

Lolla-Wossiky's brother—had to be the defiant Red who was standing up against the wall. Funny, how two peas from the same pod could grow up so different.

Lolla-Wossiky came in fawning, smiling, looking quickly from one White face to the next, wondering what they wanted, how he could make them happy enough to reward him with whisky. It was written all over him, how thirsty he was, even though he was already so drunk he didn't walk straight. Or had he already drunk so much likker that he couldn't walk straight even when he was sober? Hooch wondered—but soon enough he knew the answer. Harrison reached into the bureau behind him and took out a jug and a cup. Lolla-Wossiky watched the brown liquid splash into the cup, his one eye so intense it was like he could taste the likker by vision alone. But he didn't take even a single step toward the cup. Harrison reached out and set the cup on the table near the Red, but still the man stood there, smiling, looking now at the cup, now at Harrison, waiting, waiting.

Harrison turned to Jackson and smiled. "Lolla-Wossiky is just about the most civilized Red in the whole Wobbish country, Mr. Jackson. He never takes things that don't belong to him. He never speaks except when spoken to. He obeys and does whatever I tell him. And all he ever asks in return is just a cup of liquid. Doesn't even have to be good likker. Corn whisky or bad Spanish rum are just fine with him, isn't that right, Lolla-Wossiky?"

"Very so right, Mr. Excellency," said Lolla-Wossiky. His speech was surprisingly clear, for a Red. Especially a drunken Red.

Hooch saw Jackson study the one-eyed Red with disgust. Then the Tennizy lawyer's gaze shifted to the door, where the tall, strong, defiant Red was standing. Hooch enjoyed watching Jackson's face. From disgust, his expression plainly changed to anger. Anger and, yes, fear. Oh, yes, you aren't fearless, Mr. Jackson. You know what Lolla-Wossiky's brother is. He's your enemy, and my enemy, the enemy of every White man who ever wants to have this land, because sometime this uppity Red is going to put his tommy-hawk in your head and peel off your scalp real slow, and he won't sell it to no Frenchman, neither, Mr. Jackson, he'll keep it and give it to his children, and say to them, "This is the only good White man. This is the only White man who doesn't break his word. This is what you do to White men." Hooch knew it, Harrison knew it, and Jackson knew it. That young buck by the door was death. That young buck was White men forced to live east of the mountains, all crammed into the old towns with all their lawyers and professors and high-toned people who never gave you room to breathe. People like Jackson himself, in fact. Hooch gave one snort of laughter at that idea. Jackson was exactly the sort of man that folks moved west to get away from. How far west will I have to go before the lawyers lose the trail and get left behind?

"I see you've noticed Ta-Kumsaw. Lolla-Wossiky's older brother, and my very, very dear friend. Why, I've known that lad since before his father died. Look what a strong buck he's grown into!"

If Ta-Kumsaw noticed how he was being ridiculed, he showed no sign of it. He looked at no person in the room. Instead he looked out the window on the wall behind the governor. Didn't fool Hooch, though. Hooch knew what he was watching, and had a pretty good idea what Ta-Kumsaw was feeling, too. These Reds, they took family real serious. Ta-Kumsaw was secretly watching his brother, and if Lolla-Wossiky was too likkered up to feel any shame, that just meant Ta-Kumsaw would feel it all the more.

"Ta-Kumsaw," said Harrison. "You see I've poured a drink for you. Come, sit down and drink, and we can talk."

At Harrison's words, Lolla-Wossiky went rigid. Was it possible that the drink wasn't for him, after all? But Ta-Kumsaw did not twitch, did not show any sign that he heard.

"You see?" said Harrison to Jackson. "Ta-Kumsaw isn't

even civilized enough to sit down and have a convivial drink with friends. But his younger brother is civilized, isn't he? Aren't you, Lolly? I'm sorry I don't have a chair for you, my friend, but you can sit on the floor under my table here, sit right at my feet, and drink this rum."

"You are remarkable kind," said Lolla-Wossiky in that clear, precise speech of his. To Hooch's surprise, the one-eyed Red did not scramble for the cup. Instead he walked carefully, each step a labor of precision, and took the cup between only slightly trembling hands. Then he knelt down before Harrison's table and, still balancing the cup, sank into a seated position, his legs crossed.

But he was still out in front of the table, not under it, and Harrison pointed this out to him. "I'd like you to sit under my table," said the governor. "I'd regard it as a great courtesy to me if you would."

So Lolla-Wossiky bent his head almost down into his lap and waddled on his buttocks until he was under the table. It was very hard for him to drink in that position, since he couldn't lift his head straight up, let alone tip it back to drain the cup. But he managed anyway, drinking carefully, rocking from one side to the other.

All this time, Ta-Kumsaw said nary a word. Didn't even show that he saw how his brother was being humiliated. Oh, thought Hooch, oh, the fire that burns in that boy's heart. Harrison's taking a real risk here. Besides, if he's Lolla-Wossiky's brother, he must know Harrison shot his daddy during the Red uprisings back in the nineties sometime, when General Wayne was fighting the French. A man doesn't forget that kind of thing, especially a Red man, and here Harrison was testing him, testing him right to the limit.

"Now that everybody's comfortable," said Harrison, "why don't you set down and tell us what you came for, Ta-Kumsaw."

Ta-Kumsaw didn't sit. Didn't close the door, didn't take a step farther into the room. "I speaking for Shaw-Nee, Caska-Skeeaw, Pee-Orawa, Winny-Baygo."

"Now, Ta-Kumsaw, you know that you don't even speak for all the Shaw-Nee, and you sure don't speak for the others."

"All tribes who sign General Wayne's treaty." Ta-Kumsaw went on as if Harrison hadn't said a thing. "Treaty says Whites don't sell whisky to Reds."

"That's right," said Harrison. "And we're keeping that treaty."

Ta-Kumsaw didn't look at Hooch, but he lifted his hand and pointed at him. Hooch felt the gesture as if Ta-Kumsaw had actually touched him with that finger. It didn't make him mad this time, it plain scared him. He heard that some Reds had a come-hither so strong that didn't no hex protect you, so they could lure you off into the woods alone and slice you to bits with their knives, just to hear you scream. That's what Hooch thought of, when he felt Ta-Kumsaw point to him with hatred.

"Why are you pointing at my old friend Hooch Palmer?" asked Harrison.

"Oh, I reckon nobody likes me today," Hooch said. He laughed, but it didn't dispel his fear after all.

"He bring his flatboat of whisky," said Ta-Kumsaw.

"Well, he brought a lot of things," said Harrison. "But if he brought whisky, it'll be delivered to the sutler here in the fort and not a drop of it will be sold to the Reds, you can be sure. We uphold that treaty, Ta-Kumsaw, even though you Reds aren't keeping it too good lately. It's got so flatboats can't travel alone down the Hio no more, my friend, and if things don't let up, I reckon the army's going to have to take some action."

"Burn a village?" asked Ta-Kumsaw. "Shoot down our babies? Our old people? Our women?"

"Where do you get these ideas?" said Harrison. He sounded downright offended, even though Hooch knew right well that Ta-Kumsaw was describing the typical army operation.

Hooch spoke right up, in fact. "You Reds burn out helpless farmers in their cabins and pioneers on their flatboats, don't you? So why do you figure your villages should be any safer, you tell me that!"

Ta-Kumsaw still didn't look at him. "English law says, Kill the man who steals your land, you are not bad. Kill a man to steal his land, and you are very bad. When we kill White farmers, we are not bad. When you kill Red people who live here a thousand years, you are very bad. Treaty says, stay all east of My-Ammy River, but they don't stay, and you help them."

"Mr. Palmer here spoke out of turn," said Harrison. "No matter what you savages do to our people—torturing the men, raping the women, carrying off the children to be slaves—we don't make war on the helpless. We are civilized, and so we behave in a civilized manner."

"This man will sell his whisky to Red men. Make them lie in dirt like worms. He will give his whisky to Red women. Make them weak like bleeding deer, do all things he says."

"If he does, we will arrest him," said Harrison. "We will try him and punish him for breaking the law."

"If he does, you *not* will arrest him," said Ta-Kumsaw. "You will share pelts with him. You will keep him safe."

"Don't call me a liar," said Harrison.

"Don't lie," said Ta-Kumsaw.

"If you go around talking to White men like this, Ta-Kumsaw, old boy, one of them's going to get real mad at you and blast your head off."

"Then I know you will arrest him. I know you will try him and punish him for breaking the law." Ta-Kumsaw said it without cracking a smile, but Hooch had traded with the Reds enough to know their kind of joke.

Harrison nodded gravely. It occurred to Hooch that Harrison might not realize it was a joke. He might think Ta-Kumsaw actually believed it. But no, Harrison knew he and Ta-Kumsaw was lying to each other; and it came into Hooch's mind that when both parties are lying and they both know the other party's lying, it comes powerful close to being the same as telling the truth.

What was really hilarious was that Jackson actually *did* believe all this stuff. "That's right," said the Tennizy lawyer. "Rule of law is what separates civilized men from savages. Red men just aren't advanced enough yet, and if you aren't willing to be subject to White man's law, you'll just have to make way."

For the first time, Ta-Kumsaw looked one of them in the eye. He stared coldly at Jackson and said, "These men are liars. They know what is true, but they say it is not true. You are not a liar. You believe what you say."

Jackson nodded gravely. He looked so vain and upright and godly that Hooch couldn't resist it, he hottened up the chair under Jackson just a little, just enough that Jackson had to wiggle his butt. That took off a few layers of dignity. But Jackson still kept his airs. "I believe what I say because I tell the truth."

"You say what you believe. But still it is not true. What is your name?"

"Andrew Jackson."

Ta-Kumsaw nodded. "Hickory."

Jackson looked downright surprised and pleased that Ta-Kumsaw had heard of him. "Some folks call me that." Hooch hottened up his chair a little more.

"Blue Jacket says, Hickory is a good man."

Jackson still had no idea why his chair was so uncomfortable, but it was too much for him. He popped right up, stepped away from the chair, kind of shaking his legs with each step to cool himself off. But still he kept talking with all the dignity in the world. "I'm glad Blue Jacket feels that way. He's chief of the Shaw-Nee down in Tennizy country, isn't he?"

"Sometimes," said Ta-Kumsaw.

"What do you mean sometimes?" said Harrison. "Either he's a chief or he isn't."

"When he talks straight, he is chief," said Ta-Kumsaw.

"Well, I'm glad to know he trusts me," said Jackson. But his smile was a little wan, because Hooch was busy hotting up the floor under his feet, and unless old Hickory could fly, he wasn't going to be able to get away from *that*. Hooch didn't plan to torment him long. Just until he saw Jackson take a couple of little hops, and then try to explain why he was dancing right there in front of a young Shaw-Nee warrior and Governor William Henry Harrison.

Hooch's little game got spoiled, though, cause at that very moment, Lolla-Wossiky toppled forward and rolled out from under the table. He had an idiotic grin on his face, and his eyes were closed. "Blue Jacket!" he cried. Hooch took note that drink had finally slurred his speech. "Hickory!" shouted the one-eyed Red.

"You are my enemy," said Ta-Kumsaw, ignoring his brother.

"You're wrong," said Harrison. "I'm your friend. Your enemy is up north of here, in the town of Vigor Church. Your enemy is that renegade Armor-of-God Weaver."

"Armor-of-God Weaver sells no whisky to Reds."

"Neither do I," said Harrison. "But he's the one making maps of all the country west of the Wobbish. So he can parcel it up and sell it after he's killed all the Reds."

Ta-Kumsaw paid no attention to Harrison's attempt to turn him against his rival to the north. "I come to warn you," said Ta-Kumsaw.

"Warn me?" said Harrison. "You, a Shaw-Nee who doesn't speak for anybody, you *warn* me, right here in my stockade, with a hundred soldiers ready to shoot you down if I say the word?"

"Keep the treaty," said Ta-Kumsaw.

"We *do* keep the treaty! It's you who always break the treaties!"

"Keep the treaty," said Ta-Kumsaw.

"Or what?" asked Jackson.

"Or every Red west of the mountains will come together and cut you to pieces."

Harrison leaned back his head and laughed and laughed. Ta-Kumsaw showed no expression.

"*Every* Red, Ta-Kumsaw?" asked Harrison. "You mean, even Lolly here? Even my pet Shaw-Nee, my tame Red, even *him?*"

For the first time Ta-Kumsaw looked at his brother, who lay snoring on the floor. "The sun comes up every day, White man. But is it tame? Rain falls down every time. But is it tame?"

"Excuse me, Ta-Kumsaw, but this one-eyed drunk here is as tame as my horse."

"Oh yes," said Ta-Kumsaw. "Put on the saddle. Put on the bridle. Get on and ride. See where this tame Red goes. Not where you want."

"Exactly where I want," said Harrison. "Keep that in mind. Your brother is always within my reach. And if you ever get out of line, boy, I'll arrest him as your conspirator and hang him high."

Ta-Kumsaw smiled thinly. "You think so. Lolla-Wossiky thinks so. But he will learn to see with his other eye before you ever lay a hand on him."

Then Ta-Kumsaw turned around and left the room. Quietly, smoothly, not stalking, not angry, not even closing the door behind him. He moved with grace, like an animal, like a very dangerous animal. Hooch saw a cougar once, years ago, when he was alone in the mountains. That's what Ta-Kumsaw was. A killer cat.

Harrison's aide closed the door.

Harrison turned to Jackson and smiled. "You see?" he said.

"What am I supposed to see, Mr. Harrison?"

"Do I have to spell it out for you, Mr. Jackson?"

"I'm a lawyer. I like things spelled out. If you can spell."

"I can't even *read*," said Hooch cheerfully.

"You also can't keep your mouth shut," said Harrison. "I'll spell it out for you, Jackson. You and your Tennizy boys, you talk about moving the Reds west of the Mizzipy. Now let's say we do that. What are you going to do, keep soldiers all the way up and down the river, watching all day and all night? They'll be back across this river whenever they want, raiding, robbing, torturing, killing."

"I'm not a fool," said Jackson. "It will take a great bloody war, but when we get them across the river, they'll be broken. And men like that Ta-Kumsaw—they'll be dead or discredited."

"You think so? Well, during that great bloody war you talk about, a lot of White boys will die, and White women and children, too. But I have a better idea. These Reds suck down likker like a calf sucks down milk from his mama's tit. Two years ago there was a thousand Pee-Ankashaw living east of the My-Ammy River. Then they started getting likkered up. They stopped working, they stopped eating, they got so weak that the first little sickness came through here, it wiped them out. Just wiped them out. If there's a Pee-Ankashaw left alive here, I don't know about it. Same thing happened up north, to the Chippy-Wa, only it was French traders done it to them. And the best thing about likker is, it kills off the Reds and not a White man dies."

Jackson rose slowly to his feet. "I reckon I'll have to take three baths when I get home," he said, "and even then I still won't feel clean."

Hooch was delighted to see that Harrison was really mad. He rose to his feet and shouted at Jackson so loud that Hooch could feel his chair shake. "Don't get high and mighty with me, you hypocrite! You want them all dead, just like I do! There's no difference between us."

Jackson stopped at the door and eyed the governor with disgust. "The assassin, Mr. Harrison, the *poisoner*, he can't see the difference between himself and a soldier. But the soldier can."

Unlike Ta-Kumsaw, Jackson was not above slamming the door.

Harrison sank back down onto his chair. "Hooch, I've got to say, I don't much like that fellow."

"Never mind," said Hooch. "He's with you."

Harrison smiled slowly. "I know. When it comes to war, we'll all be together. Except for maybe that Red-kisser up in Vigor Church."

"Even him," said Hooch. "Once a war starts, the Reds won't be able to tell one White man from another. Then his people will start dying just like ours. Then Armor-of-God Weaver will fight."

"Yeah, well, if Jackson and Weaver would likker up their Reds the way we're doing ours, there wouldn't have to *be* a war."

Hooch aimed a mouthful at the spittoon and didn't miss by much. "That Red, that Ta-Kumsaw."

"What about him?" asked Harrison.

"He worries me."

"Not me," said Harrison. "I've got his brother here passed out on my floor. Ta-Kumsaw won't do nothing."

"When he pointed at me, I felt his finger touch me from across the room. I think he's maybe got a come-hither. Or a far-touch. I think he's dangerous."

"You don't believe in all that hexery, do you, Hooch? You're such an educated man, I thought you were above that kind of superstition."

"I'm not and neither are you, Bill Harrison. You had a doodlebug tell you where firm ground was so you could build this stockade, and when your first wife had her babies, you had a torch in to see how the baby was laying in the womb."

"I warn you," said Harrison, "to make no more comment about my wife."

"Which one, now, Bill? The hot or the cold?"

Harrison swore a good long string of oaths at that. Oh, Hooch was delighted, Hooch was pleased. He had such knack for hotting things up, yes sir, and it was more fun hotting up a man's temper, because there wasn't no *flame* then, just a lot of steam, a lot of hot air.

Well, Hooch let old Bill Harrison jaw on for a while. Then he smiled and raised his hands like he was surrendering. "Now, you know I didn't mean no harm, Bill. I just didn't know as how you got so prissy these days. I figured we both know where babies grow, how they got in there, and how they come out, and your women don't do it any different than mine. And when she's lying there screaming, you know you've got a midwife there who knows how to cast a sleep on her, or do a pain-away, and when the baby's slow to come you've got a torch telling where it lays. And so you listen to me, Bill Harrison. That Ta-Kumsaw, he's got some kind of knack in him, some kind of power. He's more than he seems."

"Is he now, Hooch? Well maybe he is and maybe he ain't. But he said Lolla-Wossiky would see with his other eye before I laid a hand on him, and it won't be long before I prove that he's no prophet."

"Speaking of old one-eye, here, he's starting to fart something dreadful."

Harrison called for his aide. "Send in Corporal Withers and four soldiers, at once."

Hooch admired the way Harrison kept military discipline. It wasn't thirty seconds before the soldiers were there, Corporal Withers saluting and saying, "Yes, sir, General Harrison."

"Have three of your men carry this animal out to the stable for me."

Corporal Withers obeyed instantly, pausing only to say, "Yes sir, General Harrison."

General Harrison. Hooch smiled. He knew that Harrison's only commission was as a colonel under General Wayne during the last French war, and he didn't amount to much even then. General. Governor. What a pompous—

But Harrison was talking to Withers again, and looking at Hooch as he did so. "And now you and Private Dickey will kindly arrest Mr. Palmer here and lock him up."

"Arrest me!" shouted Hooch. "What are you talking about!"

"He carries several weapons, so you'll have to search him thoroughly," said Harrison. "I suggest stripping him here before you take him to the lock-up, and leave him stripped. Don't want this slippery old boy to get away."

"What are you arresting me for!"

"Why, we have a warrant for your arrest for unpaid debts," said Harrison. "And you've also been accused of selling whisky to Reds. We'll naturally have to seize all your assets—those suspicious-looking kegs my boys've been hauling into the stockade all day—and sell them to make good the debt. If we can sell them for enough, and we can clear you of those ugly charges of likkering up the Reds, why, we'll let you go."

Then Harrison walked on out of his office. Hooch cussed and spit and made remarks about Harrison's wife and mother, but Private Dickey was holding real tight to a musket, and that musket had a bayonet attached to the business end; so Hooch submitted to the stripping and the search. It got worse, though, and he cussed again when Withers marched him right across the stockade, stark naked, and didn't give him so much as a blanket when he locked him into a storage room. A storage room filled with empty kegs from the *last* shipment of likker.

He sat in that lock-up room for two days before his trial, and for the first while there was murder in his heart. He had a lot of ideas for revenge, you can bet. He thought of setting fire to the lace curtains in Harrison's house, or burning the shed where the whisky was kept, starting all kinds of fire. Cause what good is it to be a spark if you can't use it to get even with folks who pretend to be your friends and then lock you into jail?

But he didn't start no fires, because Hooch was no fool. Partly, he knew that if a fire once got started anywhere in the stockade, there was a good chance it'd spread from one end to the other inside half an hour. And there was a good chance that while everybody's rushing around to save their wives and children and gunpowder and likker, they might not remember about one whisky trader locked up in a storage room. Hooch didn't hanker to die in a fire of his own setting—that wasn't no kind of vengeance. Time enough to start fires when he had a noose around his neck someday, but he wasn't going to risk burning to death just to get even over something like this.

But the main reason he didn't start a fire wasn't fear, it was plain business sense. Harrison was doing this to show Hooch that he didn't like the way Hooch delayed shipments of likker to jack up the price. Harrison was showing him that he had real power, and all Hooch had was money. Well, let Harrison play at being a powerful man. Hooch knew some things, too. He knew that someday the

Wobbish country would petition the U.S. Congress in Phil-adelphia to become a state. And when it did, a certain William Henry Harrison would have his little heart set on being governor. And Hooch had seen enough elections back in Suskwahenny and Pennsylvania and Appalachee to know that you can't get votes without silver dollars to pass around. Hooch would have those silver dollars. And when the time came, he might pass around those silver dol-lars to Harrison voters; and then again he might not. He just might not. He might help another man sit in the gov-ernor's mansion, someday when Carthage was a real city and Wobbish was a real state, and then Harrison would have to sit there the rest of his life and remember what it was like to be able to lock people up, and he would grind his teeth in anger at how men like Hooch took all that away from him.

That's how Hooch kept himself entertained, sitting in that lock-up room for two long days and nights.

Then they hauled him out and brought him into court—unshaven, dirty, his hair wild, and his clothes all wrin-kled up. General Harrison was the judge, the jury was all in uniform, and the defense attorney was—Andrew Jack-son! It was plain Governor Bill was trying to make Hooch get mad and start in ranting, but Hooch wasn't born yes-terday. He knew that whatever Harrison had in mind, it wouldn't do no good to yell about it. Just sit tight and put up with it.

It took only a few minutes.

Hooch listened with a straight face as a young lieuten-ant testified that all Hooch's whisky had been sold to the sutler at exactly the price it sold for last time. According to the legal papers, Hooch didn't make a penny more from having kept them waiting four months between shipments. Well, thought Hooch, that's fair enough, Harrison's letting me know how he wants things run. So he didn't say a word.

Harrison looked as merry as you please, behind his magisterial solemnity. Enjoy yourself, thought Hooch. You can't make me mad.

But he *could,* after all. They took 220 dollars right off the top and handed it over to Andrew Jackson right there in court. Counted out eleven gold twenty-dollar coins. That caused Hooch physical pain, to see that fiery metal dropping into Jackson's hands. He couldn't keep his silence then. But he did manage to keep his voice low and mild-sounding. "It don't seem regular to me," he said, "to have the plaintiff acting as defense attorney."

"Oh, he's not your defense attorney on the debt charges," said His Honor Judge Harrison. "He's just your defense attorney on the likker charges." Then Harrison grinned and gaveled that matter closed.

The likker business didn't take much longer. Jackson carefully presented all the same invoices and receipts to prove that every keg of whisky was sold to the sutler of Carthage Fort, and not a speck of it to any Reds. "Though I will say," said Jackson, "that the amount of whisky represented by these receipts seems like enough for three years for an army ten times this size."

"We've got a bunch of hard-drinking soldiers," said Judge Harrison. "And I reckon that likker won't last six months. But not a drop to the Reds, Mr. Jackson, you may be sure!"

Then he dismissed all charges against Hooch Palmer, alias Ulysses Brock. "But let this be a lesson to you, Mr. Palmer," said Harrison in his best judicial voice. "Justice on the frontier is swift and sure. See to it you pay your debts. And avoid even the appearance of evil."

"Sure enough," said Hooch cheerfully. Harrison had rolled him over good, but everything had worked out fine. Oh, the 220 dollars bothered him, and so did the two days in jail, but Harrison didn't mean for Hooch to suffer much.

Because what Jackson didn't know, and no one else saw fit to mention, was that Hooch Palmer happened to have the contract as sutler for the U.S. Army in Wobbish Territory. All those documents that proved he hadn't sold the likker to the Reds *really* showed that he sold the likker to himself—and at a profit, too. Now Jackson would head on home and Hooch would settle down in the sutler's store, selling likker to the Reds at extortionate prices, splitting the profits with Governor Bill and watching the Reds die like flies. Harrison had played his little joke on Hooch, right enough, but he'd played an even bigger one on old Hickory.

Hooch made sure to be at the wharf when they ferried Jackson back across the Hio. Jackson had brought along two big old mountain boys with rifles, no less. Hooch took note that one of them looked to be half Red himself, probably a Cherriky half-breed—there was lots of that kind of thing in Appalachee, White men actually *marrying* squaws like as if they was real women. And both those rifles had "Eli Whitney" stamped on the barrel, which meant they was made in the state of Irrakwa, where this Whitney fellow set up shop making guns so fast he made the price drop; and the story was that all his workmen was *women,* Irrakwa *squaws,* if you can believe it. Jackson could talk all he wanted about pushing the Reds west of the Mizzipy, but it was already too late. Ben Franklin did it, by letting the Irrakwa have their own state up north, and Tom Jefferson made it worse by letting the Cherriky be full voting citizens in Appalachee when they fought their revolution against the King. Treat them Reds like citizens and they start to figure they got the same rights as a White man. There was no way to have an orderly society if *that* sort of thing caught on. Why, next thing you know them Blacks'd start trying to get out of being slaves, and first thing you know you'd sit down at the bar in a saloon and you'd look to your left and there'd be a *Red,* and you'd look to your right and there'd be a *Black,* and that was just plain against nature.

There went Jackson, thinking he was going to save the White man from the Red, when he was traveling with a half-breed and toting Red-made rifles. Worst of all, Jackson had eleven gold coins in his saddle pouch, coins that properly belonged to Hooch Palmer. It made Hooch so mad he couldn't think straight.

So Hooch hotted up that saddle pouch, right where the metal pin held it onto the saddle. He could feel it from here, the leather charring, turning ash-black and stiff around that pin. Pretty soon, as the horse walked along, that bag would drop right off. But since they was likely to notice it, Hooch figured he wouldn't stop with the pouch. He hotted up a whole lot of other places on that saddle, and on the other men's saddles, too. When they reached the other shore they mounted up and rode off, but Hooch knew they'd be riding bareback before they got back to Nashville. He most sincerely hoped that Jackson's saddle would break in such a way and at such a time that old Hickory would land on his butt or maybe even break his arm. Just thinking about the prospect made Hooch pretty cheerful. Every now and then it was kind of fun to be a spark. Take some pompous holy-faced lawyer down a peg.

Truth is, an honest man like Andrew Jackson just wasn't no match for a couple of scoundrels like Bill Harrison and Hooch Palmer. It was just a crying shame that the army didn't give no medals to soldiers who likkered their enemies to death instead of shooting them. Cause if they did, Harrison and Palmer would both be heroes, Hooch knew that for sure.

As it was, Hooch reckoned Harrison would find a way to make himself a hero out of all this anyway, while Hooch would end up with nothing but money. Well, that's how it goes, thought Hooch. Some people get the fame, and some people get the money. But I don't mind, as long as I'm not one of the people who end up with nothing at all. I sure never want to be one of them. And if I am, they're sure going to be sorry.

TA-KUMSAW

gone, and Hooch, some people get the nope, just some
people get the nopes. You don't know nothing, as I'm not
one of the people tore up with nothing at all. I want
me everyone in be square this. And if I am, they're sure
going to be sorry.

2

*

TA-KUMSAW

While Hooch was watching Jackson cross the river, Ta-Kumsaw watched the White whisky trader and knew what he did. So did any other Red man who cared to watch—sober Red man, anyway. White man does a lot of things Red man don't understand, but when he fiddle with fire, water, earth, and air, he can't hide it from a Red man.

Ta-Kumsaw didn't *see* the saddle leather burn on Jackson's horse. He didn't feel the heat. What he saw was like a stirring, a tiny whirlwind, sucking his attention out across the water. A twisting in the smoothness of the land. Most Red men couldn't feel such things as keen as Ta-Kumsaw. Ta-Kumsaw's little brother, Lolla-Wossiky, was the only one Ta-Kumsaw ever knew who felt it more. Very much more. He knew all those whirlpools, those eddies in the stream. Ta-Kumsaw remembered their father, Pucky-Shinwa, he spoke of Lolla-Wossiky, that he would be shaman, and Ta-Kumsaw would be war-leader.

That was before Lying-Mouth Harrison shot Pucky-Shinwa right before Lolla-Wossiky's eyes. Ta-Kumsaw was off hunting that day, four-hands walk to the north, but he felt the murder like a gun fired right behind him. When a White man laid a hex or a curse or cast a doodlebug, it felt to Ta-Kumsaw like an itch under his skin, but when a White man killed, it was like a knife stabbing.

He was with another brother, Methowa-Tasky, and he called to him. "Did you feel it?"

Methowa-Tasky's eyes went wide. He had not. But even then, even at that age—not yet thirteen—Ta-Kumsaw had no doubt of himself. He felt it. It was true. A murder had been done, and he must go to the dying man.

He led the way, running through the forest. Like all Red men in the old days, his harmony with the woodland was complete. He did not have to think about where he placed his feet; he knew that the twigs under his feet would soften and bend, the leaves would moisten and not rustle, the branches he brushed aside would go back quick to their right place and leave no sign he passed. Some White men prided themselves that they could move as quiet as a Red, and in truth some of them could—but they did it by moving slow, careful, watching the ground, stepping around bushes. They never knew how little thought a Red man took for making no sound, for leaving no trace.

What Ta-Kumsaw thought of was not his steps, not himself at all. It was the green life of the woodland all around him, and in the heart of it, before his face, the black whirlpool sucking him downward, stronger, faster, toward the place where the living green was torn open like a wound to let a murder through. Long before they got there, even Methowa-Tasky could feel it. There on the ground lies their father, a bullet through his face. And by him, silent and unseeing, stands Lolla-Wossiky, ten years old.

Ta-Kumsaw carried his father's body home across his shoulders, like a deer. Methowa-Tasky led Lolla-Wossiky by the hand, for otherwise the boy would not move. Mother greeted them with great wails of grief, for she also felt the death, but did not know it was her own husband until her sons brought him back. Mother tied her husband's corpse to Ta-Kumsaw's back; then Ta-Kumsaw climbed the tallest tree, untied his father's corpse from his back, and bound it to the highest branch he could reach.

It would have been very bad if he had climbed beyond his strength, and his father's body had fallen from his grasp. But Ta-Kumsaw did not climb beyond his strength. He tied his father to a branch so high the sun touched his father's face all day. The birds and insects would eat of him; the sun and air would dry him; the rain would wash the last of him downward to the earth. This was how Ta-Kumsaw gave his father back to the land.

But what could they do with Lolla-Wossiky? He said nothing, he wouldn't eat unless someone fed him, and if you didn't take his hand and lead him, he would stay in one place forever. Mother was frightened at what had happened to her son. Mother loved Ta-Kumsaw very much, more than any other mother in the tribe loved any other son; but even so, she loved Lolla-Wossiky more. Many times she told them all how baby Lolla-Wossiky cried the first time the air grew bitter cold each winter. She could never get him to stop, no matter how she covered him with bearskins and buffalo robes. Then one winter he was old enough to talk, and he told her why he cried. "All the bees are dying," he said. That was Lolla-Wossiky, the only Shaw-Nee who ever felt the death of bees.

That was the boy standing beside his father when Colonel Bill Harrison shot him dead. If Ta-Kumsaw felt that murder like a knife wound, half a day's journey away, what did Lolla-Wossiky feel, standing so close, and already so sensitive? If he cried for the death of bees in winter, what did he feel when a White man murdered his father before his eyes?

After a few years, Lolla-Wossiky finally began to speak again, but the fire was gone from his eyes, and he was careless. He put his own eye out by accident, because he tripped and fell on the short jagged stump of a broken bush. Tripped and fell! What Red man ever did that? It was like Lolla-Wossiky lost all feeling for the land; he was dull as a White man.

Or maybe, Ta-Kumsaw thought, maybe the sound of that ancient gunshot still rings in his head so loud he can't hear anything else now; maybe that old pain is still so sharp that he can't feel the tickling of the living world. Pain all the time till the first taste of whisky showed Lolla-Wossiky how to take away the sharp edge of it.

That was why Ta-Kumsaw never beat Lolla-Wossiky for likkering, though he would beat any other Shaw-Nee, even his brothers, even an old man, if he found him with the White man's poison in his hand.

But the White man never guessed at what the Red man saw and heard and felt. The White man brought death and emptiness to this place. The White man cut down wise old trees with much to tell; young saplings with many lifetimes of life ahead; and the White man never asked, Will you be glad to make a lodgehouse for me and my tribe? Hack and cut and chop and burn, that was the White man's way. Take from the forest, take from the land, take from the river, but put nothing back. The White man killed animals he didn't need, animals that did him no harm; yet if a bear woke hungry in the winter and took so much as a single young pig, the White man hunted him down and killed him in revenge. He never felt the balance of the land at all.

No wonder the land hated the White man! No wonder all the natural things of the land rebelled against his step: crackling underfoot, bending the wrong way, shouting out to the Red man, Here was where the enemy stood! Here came the intruder, through these bushes, up this hill! The White man joked that Reds could even track a man on water, then laughed as if it wasn't true. But it *was* true, for when a White man passed along a river or a lake, it bubbled and foamed and rippled loud for hours after he had passed.

Now Hooch Palmer, poison-seller, sly killer, now he stands making his silly fire on another White man's saddles, thinking no one knows. These White men with their weak little knacks. These White men with their hexes and their wardings. Didn't they know their hexes only fended off *unnatural* things? If a thief comes, knowing he does wrong, then a good strong fending hex makes his fear grow till he cries out and runs away. But the Red man never is a thief. The Red man belongs wherever he is in this land. To him the hex is just a cold place, a stirring in the air, and nothing more. To him a knack is like a fly, buzz buzz buzz. Far above this fly, the power of the living land is a hundred hawks, watching, circling.

Ta-Kumsaw watched Hooch turn away, return to the fort. Soon Hooch sells his poison in earnest. Most of the Red men gathered here will be drunk. Ta-Kumsaw will stay, keeping watch. He does not have to speak to anyone. They only see him, and those with any pride left will turn away without likkering. Ta-Kumsaw is not a chief yet. But Ta-Kumsaw is not to be ignored. Ta-Kumsaw is the pride of the Shaw-Nee. All other Red men of every tribe must measure themselves against him. Whisky-Reds are very small inside when they see this tall strong Red man.

He walked to the place where Hooch had stood, and let his calm replace the twisting Hooch put there. Soon the buzzing, furious insects quieted. The smell of the likkery man settled. Again the water lapped the shore with accidental song.

How easy to heal the land after the White man passes. If all the White men left today, by tomorrow the land would be at rest, and in a year it would not show any sign the White man ever came. Even the ruins of the White man's buildings would be part of the land again, making homes for small animals, crumbling in the grip of the hungering vines. White man's metal would be rust; White man's stone work would be low hills and small caves; White man's murders would be wistful, beautiful notes in the song of the redbird—for the redbird remembered everything, turning it into goodness when it could.

All day Ta-Kumsaw stood outside the fort, watching Red men go in to buy their poison. Men and women from every tribe—Wee-Aw and Kicky-Poo, Potty-Wottamee and Chippy-Wa, Winny-Baygo and Pee-Orawa—they went in carrying pelts or baskets and came out with no more than cups or jugs of likker, and sometimes with nothing more than what they already had in their bellies. Ta-Kumsaw said nothing, but he could feel how the Reds who drank this poison were cut off from the land. They did not twist the green of life the way the White man did; rather it was as if they did not exist at all. The Red man who drank whisky was already dead, as far as the land knew. No, not even dead, for they give nothing back to the land at all. I stand here to watch them be ghosts, thought Ta-Kumsaw, not dead and not alive. He said this only inside his head, but the land felt his grief, and the breeze answered him by weeping through the leaves.

Come dusk, a redbird walks on the dirt in front of Ta-Kumsaw.

Tell me a story, says the redbird in its silent way, its eyes cocked upward at the silent Red man.

You know my story before I tell it, says Ta-Kumsaw silently. You feel my tears before I shed them. You taste my blood before it is spilled.

Why do you grieve for Red men who are not of the Shaw-Nee?

Before the White man came, says Ta-Kumsaw silently, we did not see that all Red men were alike, brothers of the land, because we thought all creatures were this way; so we quarreled with other Red men the way the bear quarrels with the cougar, the way the muskrat scolds the beaver. Then the White man came, and I saw that all Red men are like twins compared to the White man.

What is the White man? What does he do?

The White man is like a human being, but he crushes all other living things under his feet.

Then why, O Ta-Kumsaw, when I look into your heart, why is it that you do not wish to hurt the White man, that you do not wish to kill the White man?

The White man doesn't know the evil that he does. The White man doesn't feel the peace of the land, so how can he tell the little deaths he makes? I can't blame the White man. But I can't let him stay. So when I make him leave this land, I won't hate him.

If you are free of hate, O Ta-Kumsaw, you will surely drive the White man out.

I'll cause him no more pain than it takes to make him go away.

The redbird nods. Once, twice, three times, four. It flutters up to a branch as high as Ta-Kumsaw's head. It sings a new song. In this song Ta-Kumsaw hears no words; but he hears his own story being told. From now on, his story is in the song of every redbird in the land, for what one redbird knows, all remember.

Whoever watched Ta-Kumsaw all that time had no idea of what he said and saw and heard. Ta-Kumsaw's face showed nothing. He stood where he had been standing; a redbird landed near him, stayed awhile, sang, and went away.

Yet this moment turned Ta-Kumsaw's life; he knew it right away. Until this day he had been a young man. His strength and calm and courage were admired, but he spoke only as any Shaw-Nee could speak, and having spoken, he

then kept still and older men decided. Now he would decide for himself, like a true chief, like a war chief. Not a
chief of the Shaw-Nee, or even a chief of the Red men of
this north country, but rather the chief of all Red tribes
in the war against the White man. He knew for many
years that such a war must come; but until this moment he
had thought that it would be another man, a chief like
Cornstalk, Blackfish, or even a Cree-Ek or Chok-Taw
from the south. But the redbird came to *him,* Ta-Kumsaw,
and put him in the song. Now wherever Ta-Kumsaw went
throughout the land that knew the redbird song, his name
would be well known to the wisest Red men. He was war
chief of all Red men who loved the land; the land had
chosen him.

As he stood there near the bank of the Hio, he felt like
he was the face of the land. The fire of the sun, the breath
of the air, the strength of the earth, the speed of the water,
all reached into him and looked out on the world through
his eyes. I am the land; I am the hands and feet and
mouth and voice of the land as it struggles to rid itself of
the White man.

These were his thoughts.

He stood there until it was fully dark. The other Red
men had returned to their lodges or their cabins to
sleep—or to lie drunken and as good as dead till morning. Ta-Kumsaw came out of his redbird trance and heard
laughter from the Red village, laughter and singing from
the White soldiers inside the fort.

Ta-Kumsaw walked away from the place where he had
stood so many hours. His legs were stiff, but he did not
stagger; he forced his legs to move smoothly, and the
ground yielded gently under his feet. The White man had
to wear rough heavy boots to walk far in this land, because
the dirt scuffed and tore at his feet; the Red man could
wear the same moccasins for years, because the land was

gentle and welcomed his step. As he moved, Ta-Kumsaw felt soil, wind, river, and lightning all moving with him; the land within him, all things living, and he the hands and feet and face of the land.

There was a shout inside the fort. And more shouts:

"Thief! Thief!"

"Stop him!"

"He's got a keg!"

Curses, howls. Then the worst sound: a gunshot. Ta-Kumsaw waited for the sting of death. It didn't come.

A shadowy man rose above the parapet. Whatever man it was, he balanced a keg on his shoulders. For a moment he teetered on the very peak of the stockade poles, then jumped down. Ta-Kumsaw knew it was a Red man because he could jump from three man-heights, holding a heavy keg, and make almost no sound upon landing.

On purpose maybe, or maybe not, the fleeing thief ran straight to Ta-Kumsaw and stopped before him. Ta-Kumsaw looked down. By starlight he knew the man.

"Lolla-Wossiky," he said.

"Got a keg," said Lolla-Wossiky.

"I should break that keg," said Ta-Kumsaw.

Lolla-Wossiky cocked his head like the redbird and regarded his brother. "Then I'd have to take another."

The White men chasing Lolla-Wossiky came to the gate, clamoring for the guard to open it. I have to remember this, thought Ta-Kumsaw. This is a way to get them to open the gate for me. Even as he thought that, however, he also put his arm around his brother, keg and all. Ta-Kumsaw felt the green land like a second heartbeat, strong within him, and as he held his brother, the same power of the land flowed into Lolla-Wossiky. Ta-Kumsaw heard him gasp.

The Whites ran out of the fort. Even though Ta-Kumsaw and Lolla-Wossiky stood in the open, in plain sight, the

White soldiers did not see them. Or no, they *saw;* they simply did not notice the two Shaw-Nee. They ran past, shouting and firing randomly into the woods. They gathered near the brothers, so close they could have lifted an arm and touched them. But they did not lift their arms; they did not touch the Red men.

After a while the Whites gave up the search and returned to the fort, cursing and muttering.

"It was that one-eye Red."

"The Shaw-Nee drunk."

"Lolla-Wossiky."

"If I find him, I'll kill him."

"Hang the thieving devil."

They said these things, and there was Lolla-Wossiky, not a stone's throw from them, holding the keg on his shoulder.

When the last White man was inside the fort, Lolla-Wossiky giggled.

"You laugh with the White man's poison on your shoulders," said Ta-Kumsaw.

"I laugh with my brother's arm across my back," answered Lolla-Wossiky.

"Leave that whisky, Brother, and come with me," said Ta-Kumsaw. "The redbird heard my story, and remembers me in her song."

"Then I will listen to that song and be glad all my life," said Lolla-Wossiky.

"The land is with me, Brother. I'm the face of the land, the land is my breath and blood."

"Then I will hear your heartbeat in the pulse of the wind," said Lolla-Wossiky.

"I will drive the White man back into the sea," said Ta-Kumsaw.

In answer, Lolla-Wossiky began to weep; not drunken weeping, but the dry, heavy sobs of a man burdened down with grief. Ta-Kumsaw tried to tighten his embrace, but his brother pushed him away and staggered off, still carrying the keg, into the darkness and the trees.

Ta-Kumsaw did not follow him. He knew why his brother was grieving: because the land had filled Ta-Kumsaw with power, power enough to stand among the drunken Whites and seem as invisible as a tree. And Lolla-Wossiky knew that by rights whatever power Ta-Kumsaw had, Lolla-Wossiky should have had ten times that power. But the White man had stolen it from Lolla-Wossiky with murders and likker, until Lolla-Wossiky wasn't man enough to have the redbird learn his song or the land fill up his heart.

Never mind, never mind, never mind.

The land has chosen me to be its voice, and so I must begin to speak. I will no longer stay here, trying to shame the wretched drunks who have already been killed by their thirst for the White man's poison. I will give no more warnings to White liars. I will go to the Reds who are still alive, still men, and gather them together. As one great people we will drive the White man back across the sea.

3

DE MAUREPAS

Frederic, the young Comte de Maurepas, and Gilbert, the aging Marquis de La Fayette, stood together at the railing of the canal barge, looking out across Lake Irrakwa. The sail of the *Marie-Philippe* was plainly visible now; they had been watching for hours as it came closer across this least and lowest of the Great Lakes.

Frederic could not remember when he had last been so humiliated on behalf of his nation. Perhaps the time when Cardinal What's-his-name had tried to bribe Queen Marie-Antoinette. Oh but of course Frederic had only been a boy, then, a mere twenty-five years old, callow and young, without experience of the world. He had thought that no greater humiliation could come to France than to have it known that a cardinal would actually believe that the Queen could be bribed with a diamond necklace. Or bribed at all, for that matter. Now, of course, he understood that the real humiliation was that a French cardinal would be so stupid as to suppose that bribing the Queen was worth doing; the most she could do was influence the King, and since old King Louis never influenced anybody, there you were.

Personal humiliation was painful. Humiliation of one's family was much worse. Humiliation of one's social standing was agony to bear. But humiliation of one's nation was the most excruciating of human miseries.

Now here he stood on a miserable canal barge, an *American* canal barge, tied at the verge of an *American* canal, waiting to greet a French general. Why wasn't it a French canal? Why hadn't the French been the first to engineer those clever locks and build a canal around the Canadian side of the falls?

"Don't fume, my dear Frederic," murmured La Fayette.

"I'm not fuming, my dear Gilbert."

"Snorting, then. You keep snorting."

"Sniffing. I have a cold." Canada certainly was a repository for the dregs of French society, Frederic thought for the thousandth time. Even the nobility that ended up here was embarrassing. This Marquis de La Fayette, a member of the—no, a *founder* of the Club of the Feuillants, which was almost the same as saying he was a declared traitor to King Charles. Democratic twaddle. Might as well be a Jacobin like that terrorist Robespierre. Of course they exiled La Fayette to Canada, where he could do little harm. Little harm, that is, except to humiliate France in this unseemly manner—

"Our new general has brought several staff officers with him," said La Fayette, "and all their luggage. It makes no sense to disembark and make the miserable portage in wagons and carriages, when it can all be carried by water. It will give us a chance to become acquainted."

Since La Fayette, in his normal crude way (disgrace to the aristocracy!), insisted on being blunt about the matter at hand, Frederic would have to stoop to his level and speak just as plainly. "A French general should not have to travel on foreign soil to reach his posting!"

"But my dear Frederic, he'll never set foot on American soil, now, will he! Just boat to boat, on water all the way."

La Fayette's simper was maddening. To make light of this smudge on the honor of France. Why, oh, why couldn't Frederic's father have remained in favor with the king just a little longer, so Frederic could have stayed in France long enough to win promotion to some elegant posting, like Lord of the Italian March or something—did they have such a posting?—anyway, somewhere with decent food and music and dancing and theatre—ah, Moliere! In Europe, where he could face a civilized enemy like the Austrians or the Prussians or even—though it stretched the meaning of the word *civilized*—the English. Instead here he was, trapped forever—unless Father wormed his way back into the King's favor—facing a constant ragtag invasion of miserable uneducated Englishmen, the worst, the utter dregs of English society, not to mention the Dutch and Swedes and Germans—oh, it did not bear thinking about. And even worse were the allies! Tribes of Reds who weren't even heretics, let alone Christians—they were *heathen,* and half the military operation in Detroit consisted of buying those hideous bloody trophies—

"Why, my dear Frederic, you really are taking a chill," said La Fayette.

"Not a bit."

"You shivered."

"I *shuddered.*"

"You must stop pouting and make the best of this. The Irrakwa have been very cooperative. They provided us with the governor's own barge, free of charge, as a gesture of goodwill."

"The governor! The *governor?* You mean that fat hideous red-skinned heathen *woman?*"

"She can't help her red skin, and she isn't heathen. In

fact she's a Baptist, which is almost like being Christian, only louder."

"Who can keep track of these English heresies?"

"I think there's something quite elegant about it. A woman as governor of the state of Irrakwa, and a Red at that, accepted as the equal of the governors of Suskwahenny, Pennsylvania, New Amsterdam, New Sweden, New Orange, New Holland—"

"I think sometimes you prefer those nasty little United States to your own native land."

"I am a Frenchman to the heart," said La Fayette mildly. "But I admire the American spirit of egalitarianism."

Egalitarianism again. The Marquis de La Fayette was like a pianoforte that had but a single key. "You forget that our enemy in Detroit is American."

"*You* forget that our enemy is the horde of illegal squatters, no matter what nation they come from, who have settled in the Red Reserve."

"That's a quibble. They're all Americans. They all pass through New Amsterdam or Philadelphia on their way west. So you encourage them here in the east—they all know how much you admire their anti-monarchist philosophy—and then I have to pay for their scalps when the Reds massacre them out west."

"Now, now, Frederic. Even in humor, you mustn't accuse me of being anti-monarchist. M. Guillotin's clever meat-slicing machine awaits anyone convicted of *that*."

"Oh, do be serious, Gilbert. They'd never use it against a marquis. They don't cut off the heads of aristocrats who propound these insane democratic ideas. They just send them to Quebec." Frederic smiled—he couldn't resist driving home the nail. "The ones they really despise, they send to Niagara."

"Then what in the world did *you* do—to get sent to Detroit?" murmured La Fayette.

More humiliation. Would it never end?

The *Marie-Philippe* was near enough for them to see individual sailors and hear them shouting as the ship made its final tack into Port Irrakwa. The lowest of the Great Lakes, Irrakwa was the only one that could be visited by oceangoing vessels—the Niagara Falls saw to that. In the last three years, since the Irrakwa finished their canal, almost all the shipping that needed to be transported past the falls into Lake Canada came to the American shore and was taken up the Niagara Canal. The French portage towns were dying; an embarrassing number of Frenchmen had moved across the lake to live on the American side, where the Irrakwa were only too happy to put them to work. And the Marquis de La Fayette, supposedly the supreme governor of all Canada south and west of Quebec, didn't seem to mind at all. If Frederic's father ever got back into King Charles's good graces, Frederic would see to it that La Fayette was the first aristocrat to feel the Guillotin knife. What he had done here in Canada was plain treason.

As if he could read Frederic's mind, La Fayette patted his shoulder and said, "Very soon, now, just be patient." For a moment Frederic thought, insanely, that La Fayette was calmly prophesying his own execution for treason.

But La Fayette was merely talking about the fact that at last the *Marie-Philippe* was near enough to heave a line to the wharf. The Irrakwa stevedores caught the line and affixed it to the windlass, and then chanted in their unspeakable language as they towed the ship close in. As soon as it was in place, they began unloading cargo on the one side, and passengers on the other.

"Isn't that ingenious, how they speed the transfer of cargo," said La Fayette. "Unload it on those heavy cars, which sit on rails—rails, just like mining carts!—and then the horses tow it right up here, smooth and easy as you please. On rails you can carry a much heavier load than on regular wagons, you know. Stephenson explained it to me the last time I was here. It's because you don't have to steer." On and on he blathered. Sure enough, within moments he was talking again about Stephenson's steam engine, which La Fayette was convinced would replace the horse. He had built some in England or Scotland or somewhere, but now he was in America, and do you think La Fayette would invite Stephenson to build his steam wagons in Canada? Oh, no—La Fayette was quite content to let him build them for the Irrakwa, mumbling some idiotic excuse like: The Irrakwa are already using steam engines for their spinning wheels, and all the coal is on the American side—but Frederic de Maurepas knew the truth. La Fayette believed that the steam engine, pulling cars on railed roads, would make commerce and travel infinitely faster and cheaper—and he thought it would be better for the world if it were built within the borders of a *democracy!* Of course Frederic did not believe the engines would ever be as fast as horses, but that didn't matter—La Fayette *did* believe in them, and so the fact that he didn't bring them to Canada was pure treason.

He must have been forming the word with his lips. Either that or La Fayette could hear other men's thoughts—Frederic had heard rumors that La Fayette had a knack for that. Or perhaps La Fayette merely guessed. Or perhaps the devil told him—there's a thought! Anyway, La Fayette laughed aloud and said, "Frederic, if I had Stephenson build his railroad in Canada, you'd have me cashiered for wasting money on nonsense. As it is, if you made a report accusing me of treason for encouraging Stephenson to remain in Irrakwa, they'd call you home and lock you up in a padded room!"

"Treason? I accuse you?" said Frederic. "It's the farthest thought from my mind." Still, he crossed himself, on the off-chance that it was the devil who had told La Fayette. "Now, haven't we had enough of watching the stevedores loading cargo? I believe we have an officer to greet."

"Why are you so eager to meet him now?" asked La Fayette. "Yesterday you kept reminding me that he *is* a commoner. He even entered the service as a corporal, I think you said."

"He's a general now, and His Majesty has seen fit to send him to us." Frederic spoke with stiff propriety. Still La Fayette insisted on smiling with amusement. Someday, Gilbert, someday.

Several officers in full army dress uniform were milling about on the wharf, but none was of general rank. The hero of the battle of Madrid was obviously waiting to make a grand entrance. Or did he expect a Marquis and the son of a Comte to come and meet *him* in his cabin? Unthinkable.

And, in fact, he did not think it. The officers stepped back, and from their position by the railing of the canal barge de Maurepas and La Fayette could see him step off the *Marie-Philippe* onto the wharf.

"Why, he's not a very large man, is he," said Frederic.

"They aren't very tall in the south of France."

"South of France!" said Frederic scornfully. "He's from Corsica, my dear Gilbert. That's hardly even French at all. More like Italian."

"He defeated the Spanish army in three weeks, while his superior officer was indisposed with dysentery," La Fayette reminded him.

"An act of subordination for which he should have been cashiered," said Frederic.

"Oh, I quite agree with you," said La Fayette. "Only, you see, he did win the war, and as long as King Charles was adding the crown of Spain to his collection of headgear, he thought it would be churlish to court-martial the soldier who won it for him."

"Discipline above all. Everybody must know his place and stay in it, or there will be chaos."

"No doubt. Well, they *did* punish him. They made him a general, but they sent him *here*. Didn't want him involved with the Italian campaign. His Majesty wouldn't mind being Doge of Venice, but this General Bonaparte might get carried away, capture the College of Cardinals, and make King Charles pope."

"Your sense of humor is a crime."

"Frederic, look at the man."

"I *am* looking at him."

"Then *don't* look at him. Look at everyone else. Look at his officers. Have you ever seen soldiers show so much love for their commander?"

Frederic reluctantly tore his gaze from the Corsican general and looked at the underlings who walked quietly behind. Not like courtiers—there was no sense of jockeying for position. It was like—it was like—Frederic couldn't find words for it—

"It's as if each man knows that Bonaparte loves him, and values him."

"A ridiculous system, if that's what his system is," said Frederic. "You cannot control your underlings if you don't keep them in constant fear of losing their position."

"Let's go meet him."

"Absurd! He must come to us!"

But La Fayette, as usual, did not hesitate between the word and the deed—he was already on the wharf, striding the last few yards to stand before Bonaparte and receive his salute. Frederic, however, knew his station in life, and knew Bonaparte's as well, and Bonaparte would have to come to *him*. They might make Bonaparte a general, but they could never make him a gentleman.

La Fayette was fawning, of course. "General Bonaparte,

we're honored to have you here. I only regret that we cannot offer you the amenities of Paris—"

"My lord Governor," said Bonaparte—naturally getting the form of address all wrong, "I have never known the amenities of Paris. All my happiest moments have been in the field."

"And the happiest moments, too, for France, are when you are in the field. Come, meet General de Maurepas. He will be your superior officer in Detroit."

Frederic heard the slight pause before La Fayette said the word *superior*. Frederic knew when he was being ridiculed. I will remember every slight, Gilbert, and I will repay.

The Irrakwa were very efficient at transferring cargo; it wasn't an hour before the canal barge was under way. Naturally, La Fayette spent the first afternoon telling Bonaparte all about Stephenson's steam engine. Bonaparte made a show of being interested, asking all about the possibilities of troop transport, and how quickly track could be laid behind an advancing army, and how easily these railed roads might be disrupted by enemy action—but it was all so tedious and boring that Frederic could not imagine how Bonaparte kept it up. Of course an officer had to *pretend* to be interested in everything a Governor said, but Bonaparte was taking it to extremes.

Before too long the conversation obviously excluded Frederic, but he didn't mind. He let his thoughts wander, remembering that actress, What's-her-name, who did such an exquisite job of that part, whatever it was, or was she a ballerina? He remembered her legs, anyway, such graceful legs, but she refused to come to Canada with him, even though he assured her he loved her and promised to set her up in a house even nicer than the one he would build for his wife. If only she had come. Of course, she might have died of fever, the way his wife did. So perhaps it was all for the best. Was she still on the stage in Paris? Bonaparte would not know, of course, but one of his junior officers might have seen her. He would have to inquire.

They supped at Governor Rainbow's table, of course, since that was the only table on the canal boat. The governor had sent her regrets that she could not visit the distinguished French travelers, but she hoped her staff would make them comfortable. Frederic, supposing this meant an Irrakwa chef, had braced himself for another tedious Red meal of tough deer gristle—one could hardly call such fare *venison*—but instead the chef was, of all things, a Frenchman! A Huguenot, or rather the grandson of Huguenots, but he didn't hold grudges, so the food was superb. Who would have imagined good French food in a place like this—and not the spicy Acadian style, either.

Frederic did try to take a more active part in the conversation at supper, once he had finished off every scrap of food on the table. He tried his best to explain to Bonaparte the almost impossible military situation in the southwest. He counted off the problems one by one—the undisciplined Red allies, the unending flow of immigrants. "Worst of all is our own soldiers, though. They are a determinedly superstitious lot, as the lower classes always are. They see omens in everything. Some Dutch or German settler puts a hex on his door and you practically have to beat our soldiers to get them to go in."

Bonaparte sipped his coffee (barbaric fluid! but he seemed to relish it exactly as the Irrakwa did), then leaned back in his chair, regarding Frederic with his steady, piercing eyes. "Do you mean to say that you accompany foot soldiers in house-to-house searches?"

Bonaparte's condescending attitude was outrageous, but before Frederic could utter the withering retort that was just on the tip of his tongue, La Fayette laughed aloud. "Napoleon," he said, "my dear friend, that is the nature of our supposed enemy in this war. When the largest city in fifty miles consists of four houses and a smithy, you don't conduct house-to-house searches. Each house *is* the enemy fortress."

Napoleon's forehead wrinkled. "They don't concentrate their forces into armies?"

"They have never fielded an army, not since General Wayne put down Chief Pontiac years ago, and that was an English army. The U.S. has a few forts, but they're all along the Hio."

"Then why are those forts still standing?"

La Fayette chuckled again. "Haven't you read reports of how the English king fared in his war against the Appalachee rebels?"

"I was otherwise engaged," said Bonaparte.

"You needn't remind us you were fighting in Spain," said Frederic. "We would all have gladly been there, too."

"Would you?" murmured Bonaparte.

"Let me summarize," said La Fayette, "what happened to Lord Cornwallis's army when he led it from Virginia to try to reach the Appalachee capital of Franklin, on the upper Tennizy River."

"Let *me*," said Frederic. "Your summaries are usually longer than the original, Gilbert."

La Fayette looked annoyed at Frederic's interruption, but after all, La Fayette was the one who had insisted they address each other as brother generals, by first names. If La Fayette wanted to be treated like a marquis, he should insist on protocol. "Go ahead," said La Fayette.

"Cornwallis went out in search of the Appalachee army. He never found it. Lots of empty cabins, which he burned— but they can build new ones in a day. And every day a half-dozen of his soldiers would be killed or wounded by musketry."

"Rifle fire," corrected La Fayette.

"Yes, well, these Americans prefer the rifled barrel," said Frederic.

"They can't volley properly, rifles are so slow to load," said Bonaparte.

"They don't volley at all, unless they outnumber you," said La Fayette.

"I'm telling it," said Frederic. "Cornwallis got to Franklin and realized that half his army was dead, injured, or protecting his supply lines. Benedict Arnold—the Appalachee general—had fortified the city. Earthworks, balustrades, trenches all up and down the hillsides. Lord Cornwallis tried to lay a siege, but the Cherriky moved so silently that the Cavalier pickets never heard them bringing in supplies during the night. Fiendish, the way those Appalachee Whites worked so closely with the Reds—made them citizens, right from the start, if you can imagine, and it certainly paid off for them this time. Appalachee troops also raided Cornwallis's supply lines so often that after less than a month it became quite clear that Cornwallis was the besieged, not the besieger. He ended up surrendering his entire army, and the English King had to grant Appalachee its independence."

Bonaparte nodded gravely.

"Here's the cleverest thing," said La Fayette. "After he surrendered, Cornwallis was brought into Franklin City and discovered that all the families had been moved out long before he arrived. That's the thing about these Americans on the frontier. They can pick up and move anywhere. You can't pin them down."

"But you can kill them," said Bonaparte.

"You have to catch them," said La Fayette.

"They have fields and farms," said Bonaparte.

"Well, yes, you could try to find every farm," said La Fayette. "But when you get there, if anyone's at home you'll find it's a simple farm family. Not a soldier among them.

There's no *army*. But the minute you leave, someone is shooting at you from the forest. It might be the same humble farmer, and it might not."

"An interesting problem," said Bonaparte. "You never know your enemy. He never concentrates his forces."

"Which is why we deal with the Reds," said Frederic. "We can't very well go about murdering innocent farm families ourselves, can we?"

"So you pay the Reds to kill them for you."

"Yes. It works rather well," said Frederic, "and we have no plans to do anything different."

"*Well?* It works *well?*" said Bonaparte scornfully. "Ten years ago there weren't five hundred American households west of the Appalachee Mountains. Now there's ten thousand households between the Appalachees and the My-Ammy, and more moving farther west all the time."

La Fayette winked at Frederic. Frederic hated him when he did that. "Napoleon read our dispatches," La Fayette said cheerfully. "Memorized our estimates of American settlements in the Red Reserve."

"The King wants this American intrusion into French territory stopped, and stopped at once," said Bonaparte.

"Oh he does?" asked La Fayette. "What an odd way he has of showing it."

"Odd? He sent me," said Bonaparte. "That means he expects victory."

"But you're a general," said La Fayette. "We already have generals."

"Besides," said Frederic, "you're not in command. *I'm* in command."

"The Marquis has the supreme military authority here," said Bonaparte.

Frederic understood completely: La Fayette also had the authority to put Bonaparte in command over Frederic, if he desired. He cast an anxious look toward La Fayette, who was complacently spreading goose-liver paste on his bread. La Fayette smiled benignly. "General Bonaparte is under *your* command, Frederic. That will not change. Ever. I hope that's clear, my dear Napoleon."

"Of course," said Napoleon. "I would not dream of changing that. You should know that the King is sending more than generals to Canada. Another thousand soldiers will be here in the spring."

"Yes, well, I'm impressed to learn that he's promised to send more troops again—haven't we heard a dozen such promises before, Frederic? I'm always reassured to hear another promise from the King." La Fayette took the last sip from his wineglass. "But the fact is, my dear Napoleon, we already have soldiers, too, who do nothing but sit in garrison at Fort Detroit and Fort Chicago, paying for scalps with bourbon. Such a waste of bourbon. The Reds drink it like water and it kills them."

"If we don't need generals and we don't need soldiers," asked Bonaparte condescendingly, "what *do* you think we need to win this war?"

Frederic couldn't decide if he hated Bonaparte for speaking so rudely to an aristocrat, or loved him for speaking so rudely to the detestable Marquis de La Fayette.

"To win? Ten thousand French settlers," said La Fayette. "Match the Americans man for man, wife for wife, child for child. Make it impossible to do business in that part of the country without speaking French. Overwhelm them with numbers."

"No one would come to live in such wild country," said Frederic, as he had said so many times before.

"Offer them free land and they'd come," said La Fayette.

"Riff-raff," said Frederic. "We hardly need more riff-raff."

Bonaparte studied La Fayette's face a moment in silence. "The commercial value of these lands is the fur trade," said Bonaparte quietly. "The King was very clear on that point. He wants no European settlement at all outside the forts."

"Then the King will lose this war," said La Fayette cheerfully, "no matter how many generals he sends. And with that, gentlemen, I think we have done with supper."

La Fayette arose and left the table immediately.

Bonaparte turned to face Frederic, who was already standing up to leave. He reached out his hand and touched Frederic's wrist. "Stay, please," he said. Or no, actually he merely said, "Stay," but it felt to Frederic that he was saying *please,* that he really *wanted* Frederic to remain with him, that he loved and honored Frederic—

But he couldn't, no, he couldn't, he was a commoner, and Frederic had nothing to say to him—

"My lord de Maurepas," murmured the Corsican corporal. Or did he say merely "Maurepas," while Frederic simply imagined the rest? Whatever his words, his voice was rich with respect, with trust, with hope—

So Frederic stayed.

Bonaparte said almost nothing. Just normal pleasantries. We should work well together. We can serve the King properly. I will help you all I can.

But to Frederic, there was so much more than words. A promise of future honor, of returning to Paris covered with glory. Victory over the Americans, and above all putting La Fayette in his place, triumphing over the democratic traitorous marquis. He and this Bonaparte could do it, together. Patience for a few years, building up an army of Reds so large that it provokes the Americans to raise an army, too; then we can defeat that American army and go home. That's all it will take. It was almost a fever of hope and trust that filled Frederic's heart, until—

Until Bonaparte took his hand away from Frederic's wrist.

It was as if Bonaparte's hand had been his connection to a great source of life and warmth; with the touch removed, he grew cold, weary. But still there was Bonaparte's smile, and Frederic looked at him and remembered the feeling of promise he had had a moment before. How could he have ever thought working with Bonaparte would be anything but rewarding? The man knew his place, that was certain. Frederic would merely *use* Bonaparte's undeniable military talents, and together they would triumph and return to France in glory—

Bonaparte's smile faded, and again Frederic felt a vague sense of loss.

"Good evening," said Bonaparte. "I will see you in the morning, sir."

The Corsican left the room.

If Frederic could have seen his face, he might have recognized his own expression: it was identical to the look of love and devotion that all Bonaparte's junior officers had worn. But he could not see his face. That night he went to bed feeling more at peace, more confident, more hopeful and excited than he had felt in all his years in Canada. He even felt—what, what is this feeling, he wondered—ah yes. Intelligent. He even felt intelligent.

IT WAS DEEP night, but the canalmen were hard at work, using their noisy steam engine to pump water into the lock. It was an engineering marvel, the steepest system of locks on any canal in the world. The rest of the world did not know it. Europe still thought of America as a land of savages. But the enterprising United States of America, inspired by the example of that old wizard Ben Franklin, was encouraging invention and industry. Rumor had it that a man named Fulton had a working steam-powered boat plying up and down the Hudson—a steamboat that King Charles had been offered, and refused to fund! Coal mines were plunging into the earth in Suskwahenny and Appalachee. And here in the state of Irrakwa, the Reds were outdoing the Whites at their own game, building canals, steam-powered cars to run on railed roads, steam-powered spinning wheels that spat out the cotton of the Crown Colonies and turned it into fine yarns that rivaled anything in Europe—at half the cost. It was just beginning, just starting out, but already more than half the boats that came up the St. Lawrence River were bound for Irrakwa, and not for Canada at all.

La Fayette stood at the rail until the lock was filled and the fires of the steam engine were allowed to die. Then the clop, clop, clop of the canal horses and the boat slid forward again through the water. La Fayette left the rail and walked quietly up the stairs to his room. By dawn, they would be at Port Buffalo. De Maurepas and Bonaparte would go west to Detroit. La Fayette would return to the Governor's mansion in Niagara. There he would sit, issuing orders and watching Parisian policies kill any future for the French in Canada. There was nothing La Fayette could do to keep the Americans, Red and White together, from surpassing Canada and leaving it behind. But he *could* do a few things to help change France into the kind of nation that could reach out to the future as boldly as America was doing.

In his own quarters, La Fayette lay on his bed, smiling. He could imagine what Bonaparte had done tonight, alone in the room with poor empty-headed Freddie. The young Comte de Maurepas was doubtless completely charmed. The same thing might well have happened to La Fayette, but he had been warned about what Bonaparte could do, about his knack for making people trust their lives to him. It was a good knack for a general to have, as long as he only used it on his soldiers, so they'd be willing to die for him. But Bonaparte used it on everybody, if he thought

344 Orson Scott Card

he could get away with it. So La Fayette's good friend Robespierre had sent him a certain jeweled amulet. The antidote to Bonaparte's charm. And a vial of powder, too— the final antidote to Bonaparte, if he could be controlled no other way.

Don't worry, Robespierre, my dear fellow, thought La Fayette. Bonaparte will live. He thinks he is manipulating Canada to serve his ends, but I will manipulate him to serve the ends of democracy. Bonaparte does not suspect it now, but when he returns to France he will be ready to take command of a revolutionary army, and use his knack to end the tyranny of the ruling class instead of using it to add meaningless crowns to King Charles's most unworthy head.

For La Fayette's knack was not to read other men's thoughts, as de Maurepas suspected, but it was nearly that. La Fayette knew upon meeting them what other men and women wanted most. And knowing that, everything else could be guessed at. La Fayette already knew Napoleon better than Napoleon knew himself. He knew that Napoleon Bonaparte wanted to rule the world. And maybe he'd achieve it. But for now, here in Canada, La Fayette would rule Napoleon Bonaparte. He fell asleep clutching the amulet that kept him safe.

4

LOLLA-WOSSIKY

When Lolla-Wossiky left Ta-Kumsaw standing by the gate of Fort Carthage, he knew what his brother thought. Ta-Kumsaw thought he was going off with his keg to drink and drink and drink.

But Ta-Kumsaw didn't know. White Murderer Harrison didn't know. Nobody knew about Lolla-Wossiky. This keg would last him two months maybe. A little bit now, a little bit then. Careful, careful, never spill a drop, drink just *this* much, close it tight, make it last. Maybe even three months.

Always before he had to stay close to White Murderer Harrison's fort, to get the cups of dribbling likker from the dark brown jug. Now, though, he had plenty to make his journey, his great north journey to meet his dream beast.

Nobody knew that Lolla-Wossiky had a dream beast. White man didn't know cause White man had no dream beast, White man slept all the time and never woke up. Red man didn't know cause Red man saw Lolla-Wossiky and thought he was a likker Red, going to die, had no dream beast, never wake up.

Lolla-Wossiky knew though. Lolla-Wossiky knew that light up north, he saw it come five years back. He knew it was his dream beast calling, but he never could go. He started five, six, twelve times north, but then the likker would seep out of his blood and then the noise would come back, terrible black noise that hurt him so bad all the time. When the black noise came it was like a hundred tiny knives in his head, twisting, twisting, so he couldn't feel the land no more, couldn't even see his dream beast light, had to go back, find the likker, still the noise so he could *think*.

This last was the very worst time. No likker came for a long, long time, and for two months at the end even White Murderer Harrison didn't have much for him, maybe one cup in a week, never enough to last more than a few hours, maybe a day. Two long months of black noise all the time.

Black noise made it so Lolla-Wossiky couldn't walk right. Everything wiggles, ground bumps up and down, how can you walk when the land looks like water? So everybody thought Lolla-Wossiky was drunk, stagger like a whisky-Red, fall down all the time. Where does he get the likker? they all ask. Nobody has likker but Lolla-Wossiky still gets drunk, how does he do it? Not one person has eyes to see that Lolla-Wossiky isn't drunk at all. Don't they hear how he talks, clear talking, not drunk-talk? Don't they smell he got no likker-stink? Nobody guesses, nobody reckons, nobody calcalates, nobody figures. They know Lolla-Wossiky always needs likker. Never nobody thinks maybe Lolla-Wossiky has pain so bad he hopes to die.

And when he closes his eye to stop the world from rippling like the river, they all think he's asleep and they say things. Oh, they say things they don't want no Red to hear. Lolla-Wossiky figured that out very quick and so when the black noise got so bad he wanted to go lie down on the bottom of the river to shut out the noise forever, instead he staggered to White Murderer Harrison's office and fell down on the floor by his door and listened. Black noise was very loud, but it wasn't ear noise, so he could still hear voices even with the roaring of the black noise in his head. He thought very hard to hear every word under the door. He knew all that White Murderer Harrison said to everybody.

Lolla-Wossiky never told anybody what he heard.

Lolla-Wossiky never told anybody anything true. They never believed him anyway. You're drunk, Lolla-Wossiky. Shame on you, Lolla-Wossiky. Even when he wasn't drunk, even when he hurt so bad he wanted to kill everything alive to make it go away, even then they said, Too bad to see even a Red get so awful drunk. And Ta-Kumsaw, standing there never saying anything or when he did, being so strong and right, when Lolla-Wossiky was so weak and wrong.

North north north went Lolla-Wossiky, chanting to himself. North a thousand steps before I take a little drink. North with the black noise so loud I don't know where north is, but still north because I don't dare to stop.

Very dark night. Black noise so bad the land says nothing to Lolla-Wossiky. Even the white light of the dream beast is far off and seems to come from everywhere at the same time. One eye sees night, other eye sees black noise. Have to stop. Have to stop.

Very carefully Lolla-Wossiky found a tree, put down the keg, sat down and leaned against the tree, keg between his legs. Very slowly because he couldn't see, he felt the keg all over to make sure of the bung. Tap tap tap with the tommy-hawk, tap, tap, tap till the bung was loose. Slowly he wiggled it out with his fingers. Then he leaned over and put his mouth over the bunghole, tight as a kiss, tight as a baby on the nipple, that's how tight; then up with the keg, very slow, very slow, not very high, there's the taste, there's the likker, one swallow, two swallows, three swallows, four.

Four is all. Four is the end. Four is the true number, the whole number, the square number. Four swallows.

He put the bung back into the keg and tapped it into place, tight. Already the likker is getting to his head. Already the black noise is fading, fading.

Into silence. Into beautiful green silence.

But the green also goes away, fading with the black. Every time it goes this way. The land sense, the green vision that every Red has, nobody ever saw it clearer than Lolla-Wossiky. But now when it comes, right behind it comes the black noise every time. And when the black noise goes, when the likker chases it off, right behind it goes away the green living silence every time.

Lolla-Wossiky is left like a White man then. Cut off from the land. Ground crunching underfoot. Branches snagging. Roots tripping. Animals running away.

Lolla-Wossiky hoped, hoped for years to find just the right amount of likker to drink, to still the black noise and still leave the green vision. Four swallows, that was as close as he ever came. It left the black noise just out of reach, just behind the nearest tree. But it also left the green where he could just touch it. Just reach it. So he could pretend to be a true Red instead of a whisky-Red, which was really a White.

Tonight, though, he had been without likker so long, two months except for a cup now and then, that four swallows was too strong for him. The green was gone with the black. But he didn't care, not today. Didn't care, had to sleep.

WHEN HE WOKE up in the morning, the black noise was just coming back. He wasn't sure whether the sun or the noise woke him, and he didn't care. Tap on the bung, four swallows, tap it closed. This time the land sensed stayed close by, he could feel it a little. Enough to find the rabbit in the hole.

Thick old stick. Cut it here, slice it, slice it, so splintery burrs of wood stuck out in every direction.

Lolla-Wossiky knelt down in front of the rabbit hole.

"I am very hungry," he whispered. "And I am not very strong. Will you give me meat?"

He strained to hear the answer, strained to know if it was right. But it was too far off, and rabbits were very quiet in their land-voice. Once, he remembered, he could hear all the voices, and from miles and miles away. Maybe if the black noise ever went away, he could hear again. But for now, he had no way of knowing if the rabbits gave consent or not.

So he didn't know if he had the right or not. Didn't know if he was taking like a Red man, just what the land offered, or stealing like a White man, murdering whatever it pleased him to kill. He had no choice. He thrust the stick into the burrow, twisting it. He felt it quiver, heard the squeal, and pulled it out, still twisting. Little rabbit, not a big one, just a little rabbit squirming to get away from the splinters, but Lolla-Wossiky was quick, just at the moment the rabbit was at the burrow mouth, ready to get free and run, Lolla-Wossiky had his hand there, held the rabbit by the head, lifted it quickly into the air and gave it a snap and a shake. It came down dead, little rabbit, and Lolla-Wossiky carried it away from the burrow, back to the keg, because it is very bad, it makes an empty place in the land, if you skin a baby animal where its kin can see or hear you.

He did not make a fire. Too dangerous, and there was no time to smoke the meat, not this close to White Murderer Harrison's fort. There wasn't much meat anyway; he ate it all, raw so it took chewing but the flavor was very strong and good. If you can't smoke meat, Red man knows, carry all you can in your belly. He tucked the hide into the waist of his loincloth, hoisted the keg over his shoulder, and started north. The white light was on ahead of him, dream beast calling, dream beast urging him on. I will wake you up, said the dream beast. I will end your dream.

White man heard about dream beasts. White man thought the Red man went out into the forest and had dreams. Stupid White man, never understood. All of life at first is a long sleep, a long dream. You fall asleep at the moment you are born, and never wake up, never wake up until finally one day the dream beast calls you. You go then, into the forest, sometimes only a few steps, sometimes to the edge of the world. You go until you meet the beast who calls you. The beast is not in a dream. The beast wakes you up from the dream. The beast shows you who you are, teaches you your place in the land. Then you go home awake, awake at last, and tell the shaman and your mother and your sisters who the dream beast was. A bear? A badger? A bird? A fish? A hawk or an eagle? A bee or a wasp? The shaman will tell you stories and help you choose your woke-up name. Your mother and sisters will name all your children, whether they have been born yet or not.

All of Lolla-Wossiky's brothers met their dream beasts long ago. Now his mother was dead, his two sisters were gone to live with another tribe. Who would name his children?

I know, said Lolla-Wossiky. I know. Lolla-Wossiky will never have children, this old one-eyed whisky-Red. But Lolla-Wossiky will find his dream beast. Lolla-Wossiky will wake up. Lolla-Wossiky will have his woke-up name.

Then Lolla-Wossiky will see if he should live or die. If the black noise goes on, and waking up teaches him nothing more than he knows now, Lolla-Wossiky will go sleep in the river and let it roll him to the sea, far away from the land and the black noise. But if waking up teaches him some reason to live on, black noise or not, then Lolla-

Wossiky will live, many long years of drink and pain, pain and drink.

Lolla-Wossiky drank four swallows every morning, four swallows every night, and then went to sleep hoping that when the dream beast woke him up, he then could die.

ONE DAY HE stood on the banks of a clearwater stream, with the black noise thick in his vision and loud in his ears. A great brown bear stood in the water. It slapped the face of the water and a fish flew into the air. The bear caught it in his teeth, chomped twice, and swallowed. It was not the eating that Lolla-Wossiky cared about. It was the bear's eyes.

The bear had one eye missing, just like Lolla-Wossiky. This made Lolla-Wossiky wonder if the bear could be his dream beast. But that could not be. The white light that called him was still north and somewhat west of this place. So this bear was not the dream beast, it was part of the dream.

Still, it might have a message for Lolla-Wossiky. This bear might be here because the land wanted to tell Lolla-Wossiky a story.

This is the first thing Lolla-Wossiky noticed: When the bear caught the fish in his jaws, he was looking with his single eye, seeing the glimmer of sunlight shining on the fish. Lolla-Wossiky knew about this, cause Lolla-Wossiky tilted his head to one side just like the bear.

This is the second thing Lolla-Wossiky noticed: When the bear looked into the water to see the fish swimming, so he could slap at it, he looked with the other eye, with the eye that wasn't there. Lolla-Wossiky didn't understand this. It was very strange.

This is the last thing Lolla-Wossiky noticed: As he watched the bear, his own good eye was closed. And when he opened his eye, the river was still there, the sunlight was still there, the fishes still danced into the air and then disappeared, but the bear was gone. Lolla-Wossiky could see the bear only if he closed his good eye.

Lolla-Wossiky drank two swallows from the keg, and the bear went away.

ONE DAY LOLLA-WOSSIKY crossed a White man's road, and felt it like a river moving under his feet. The current of the road swept him along. He staggered with it, then caught the stride and jogged along, the keg on his shoulder. A Red man never walked on the White man's road— the dirt was packed too hard in dry weather, mud too deep in rain, and the wagon wheel ruts reached out like White man's hands to turn the Red man's ankle, trip him up, break him down. This time, though, the ground was soft like spring grass on a riverbank, as long as Lolla-Wossiky ran along the road the right direction. Not toward the light anymore, cause the light was soft around him, and he knew the dream beast was very very close.

The road three times went over water—two little streams and a big one—and each time there was a bridge, made of great heavy logs and sturdy planks, with a roof like a White man's house. Lolla-Wossiky stood on the first bridge a long time. He never heard of such a thing. Here he was standing in the place where water was supposed to be, and yet the bridge was so heavy and strong, the walls so thick, that he couldn't see or hear the water at all.

And the river hated it. Lolla-Wossiky could hear how angry it was, how it wanted to reach up and tear the bridge away. White man's ways, thought Lolla-Wossiky, White man has to conquer, tear things away from the land.

Yet standing on the bridge, he noticed something else. Even though the likker was mostly gone from his body, the black noise was quieter on the bridge. He could hear more of the green silence than he had in a long time. As if the black noise came partly from the river. How can that be? River got no anger against Red man. And no White-built thing can bring the Red man closer to the land. Yet that was what happened in this place. Lolla-Wossiky hurried on down the road; maybe when his dream beast woke him up, he'd understand this thing.

Road poured out into a place of meadows and a few White man's buildings. Lots of wagons. Horses posted and tied, grazing on the meadow grass. Sound of metal hammers ringing, chopping of axes in the wood, screech of saws going back and forth, all kinds of White-man forest-killing sounds. A White man's town.

But *not* a White man's town. Lolla-Wossiky stopped at the edge of the open land. Why is this White man's town different, what's missing that I expect to see?

The stockade. There was no stockade.

Where did the White men go to hide? Where did they lock up drunken Reds and White man thieves? Where did they hide their guns?

"Lift! Lift! Lift!" White man's voice ringing out loud as a bell in the thick air of a summer afternoon.

Up a grassy hill, maybe half a mile off, a strange wooden thing was rising up. Lolla-Wossiky couldn't see the men raising it cause the angle was wrong; they were all hid up behind the brow of the hill. But he could see a new-wood frame go up, poles at the high end to raise it into place.

"Side wall now! Lift! Lift! Lift!"

Now another frame rose up, slowly, slowly, sideways to the first. When both frames were standing straight, they met just so along one edge. For the first time Lolla-Wossiky saw men. White boys scrambled up the frames and raised their hammers and brought them down like tommy-hawks to beat the wood into submission. After they pounded for a while, they stood up, three of them, standing on the very top of the wall frames, their hammers raised up high like spears just pulled from the body of the wild buffalo. The poles that had pushed the walls in place were pulled away. The walls stood, holding each other in place. Lolla-Wossiky heard a cheer.

Then suddenly the White men all appeared on the brow of the hill. Did they see me? Will they come to make me go away or lock me up? No, they were just going down the hill to where their horses and their wagons stood. Lolla-Wossiky melted into the woods.

He drank four swallows from the keg, then climbed into a tree and settled the keg into a place where three thick branches split apart. Nice and tight, nice and safe. Leaves nice and thick; nobody see it from the ground, not even Red man.

Lolla-Wossiky took the long way round, but pretty soon there he was on the hill where the new walls stood. Lolla-Wossiky looked a long time, but he couldn't understand what this building was going to be. It was the new way of building, those frame walls, like White Murderer Harrison's new mansion, but it was very big. Bigger than anything Lolla-Wossiky ever saw White men build, taller than the stockade.

First the strange bridges, tight as houses. Now this strange building, tall as trees. Lolla-Wossiky walked out from the shelter of the forest onto the open meadow, rocking back and forth because the ground never stayed level when he had likker in him. When he reached the building, he stepped up onto the wooden floor. White man's floor, White man's walls, but it didn't feel like any White man building Lolla-Wossiky ever saw. Big open space inside. Walls very high. First time ever he saw White man build something that wasn't closed in and dark. In this place a Red man still maybe glad to be here.

"Who's that? Who are you?"

Lolla-Wossiky turned around so fast he almost fell. A

tall White man stood at the edge of the building. The floor was up so high it met this man at the waist. He wasn't in buckskin like a hunter, or in uniform like a soldier. He was dressed like a farmer maybe, only he was clean. In fact Lolla-Wossiky never saw such a man in Carthage City.

"Who are you?" demanded the man again.

"Red man," said Lolla-Wossiky.

"It's getting on dusk, but it sure ain't night yet. I'd have to be blind not to know you're Red. But I know the Reds close by and you ain't from around here."

Lolly-Wossiky laughed. What White man ever knew one Red from another so well he could say who was from close by and who was from far away?

"You got a name, Red man?"

"Lolla-Wossiky."

"You're likkered, ain't you. I can smell it, and you don't walk too good."

"Very likkered. Whisky-Red."

"Who gave you that likker! You tell me! Where'd you get that likker?"

Lolla-Wossiky was confused. White man never asked him where he got his likker before. White man always knew. "From White Murderer Harrison," he said.

"Harrison's two hundred miles southeast of here. What did you call him?"

"Governor Bill Harrison."

"You called him White Murderer Harrison."

"This Red very drunk."

"I can see that. But you sure didn't get drunk at Fort Carthage and then walk all this way without sobering up. Now where'd you get that likker?"

"You going to lock me up?"

"Lock you—now where would I lock you up, tell me that? You really are from Fort Carthage, aren't you. Well, I'll tell you, Mr. Lolla-Wossiky, we got no place to lock up drunk Reds around here, cause around here Reds don't get drunk. And if they do, we find the White man who gave him likker and that White man gets a flogging. So you tell me right now where you got that likker."

"My whisky," said Lolla-Wossiky.

"Maybe you better come with me."

"Lock me up?"

"I told you, we don't—listen, you hungry?"

"Reckon so," said Lolla-Wossiky.

"You got a place to eat?"

"Eat wherever I am."

"Well, tonight you come on down and eat at my house."

Lolla-Wossiky didn't know what to say. Was this a White man joke? White man jokes were very hard to understand.

"Aren't you hungry?"

"Reckon so," said Lolla-Wossiky again.

"Well, come on, then!"

Another White man came up the hill. "Armor-of-God!" he called. "Your good wife wondered where you were."

"Just a minute, Reverend Thrower. I think maybe we got us company for supper."

"Who is that? Why, Armor-of-God, I daresay that's a Red."

"He says his name's Lolla-Wossiky. He's a Shaw-Nee. He's also drunk as a skunk."

Lolla-Wossiky was very surprised. This White man knew he was a Shaw-Nee without asking. From his hair, plucked out except the tall strip down the middle? Other Reds did this. The fringe on his loincloth? White man never saw these things.

"A Shaw-Nee," said the new-come White man. "Aren't they a particularly savage tribe?"

"Well, now, I don't know, Reverend Thrower," said Armor-of-God. "What they are is a particularly *sober* tribe. By which I mean they don't get so likkered as some of these others. Some folks think that the only safe Red is a whisky-Red, so they see all these sober Shaw-Nee and they think that makes them dangerous."

"This one seems not to have that problem."

"I know. I tried to find out who gave him his whisky, and he won't tell me."

Reverend Thrower addressed Lolla-Wossiky. "Don't you know that whisky is the devil's tool and the downfall of the Red man?"

"I don't think he talks English enough to know what you're talking about, Reverend."

"Likker very bad for Red man," said Lolla-Wossiky.

"Well, maybe he *does* understand," said Armor-of-God, chuckling. "Lolla-Wossiky, if you know how bad likker is, how come you stink of cheap whisky like an Irish barroom?"

"Likker very bad for Red man," said Lolla-Wossiky, "but Red man thirsty all the time."

"There's a simple scientific explanation for that," said Reverend Thrower. "Europeans have had alcoholic beverages for so long that they've built up a tolerance. Europeans who desperately hunger for alcohol tend to die younger, have fewer children, provide less well for those children they do have. The result is that most Europeans have a resistance to alcohol built into them. But you Reds have never built up that tolerance."

"Very damn right," said Lolla-Wossiky. "True-talking White man, how come White Murderer Harrison not kill you yet?"

"Well, now, will you listen to that," said Armor-of-God. "That's the second time he called Harrison a murderer."

"He also swore, which I do not appreciate."

"If he's from Carthage, he learned to talk English from a class of White man that thinks words like 'damn' are punctuation, if you catch my drift, Reverend. But listen, Lolla-Wossiky. This man here, he's Reverend Philadelphia Thrower, and he's a minister of the Lord Jesus Christ, so mind you don't use no bad language around him."

Lolla-Wossiky hadn't the faintest idea what a minister was—there was no such thing in Carthage City. The best he could think of was that a minister was like a governor, only nicer.

"Will you live in this very big house?"

"Live here?" asked Thrower. "Oh, no. This is the Lord's house."

"Who?"

"The Lord Jesus Christ."

Lolla-Wossiky had heard of Jesus Christ. White man called out that name all the time, mostly when they were angry or lying. "Very angry man," said Lolla-Wossiky. "He live here?"

"Jesus Christ is a loving and forgiving Lord," said Reverend Thrower. "He won't live here the way a White man lives in a house. But when good Christians want to worship—to sing hymns and pray and hear the word of the Lord—we'll come together in this place. It's a church, or it will be."

"Jesus Christ talks here?" Lolla-Wossiky thought it might be interesting to meet this very important White man face to face.

"Oh, no, not in person. I speak *for* him."

From below the hill came a woman's voice. "Armor! Armor Weaver!"

Armor-of-God came alert. "Supper's ready, and there she is calling out, she hates when she has to do that. Come on, Lolla-Wossiky. Drunk or not, if you want supper you can come and get it."

"I hope you will," said Reverend Thrower. "And when

supper is done, I hope to be able to teach you the words of the Lord Jesus."

"Very most first thing," said Lolla-Wossiky. "You promise not to lock me up. I don't want lock-up, I got to find dream beast."

"We won't lock you up. You can walk out of my house any time." Armor-of-God turned to Reverend Thrower. "You can see what these Reds learn about White men from William Henry Harrison. Likker and lock-ups."

"I am more moved by his pagan beliefs. A dream beast! Is this their idea of gods?"

"The dream beast isn't God, it's an animal they dream about that teaches them things," explained Armor. "They always take a long journey till they have the dream and come home. That explains what he's doing two hundred miles from the main Shaw-Nee settlements on the lower My-Ammy."

"Dream beast *real*," said Lolla-Wossiky.

"Right," said Armor-of-God. Lolla-Wossiky knew he was saying that only to avoid offending him.

"This poor creature is obviously in dire need of the gospel of Jesus," said Thrower.

"Looks to me like he's in more need of supper at the moment. Gospel is learned best on a full belly, wouldn't you say?"

Thrower chuckled. "I don't think it says that anywhere in the Bible, Armor-of-God, but I dare say you're correct."

Armor-of-God put his hands on his hips and asked Lolla-Wossiky again. "You coming or not?"

"Reckon so," said Lolla-Wossiky.

LOLLA-WOSSIKY'S BELLY WAS full, but it was White man's food, soft and smooth and overcooked, and it grumbled inside him. Thrower went on and on with very strange words. The stories were good, but Thrower kept going on about original sin and redemption. One time when Lolla-Wossiky thought he understood, he said, "What a silly god, he makes everybody born bad to go to burning hell. Why so mad? All his fault!" But this made Thrower get very upset and talk longer and faster, so after that Lolla-Wossiky did not offer any of his thoughts.

The black noise came back louder and louder the more Thrower talked. Whisky wearing off? It was very quick for the likker to go out of him. And when Thrower left one time to go empty himself, the black noise got quieter. Very strange—Lolla-Wossiky never before noticed anybody making the black noise louder or softer by coming or going.

But maybe that was because he was here in the dream beast place. He knew this was the place because the white light was all around him when he looked, and he couldn't see where to go. Don't be surprised at bridges that make black noise soft and White minister who makes black noise loud. Don't be surprised at Armor-of-God with his landface picture who feeds Red man and doesn't sell likker or even give likker.

While Thrower was outside, Armor-of-God showed Lolla-Wossiky the map. "This is a picture of the whole land around here. Up to the northwest, there's the big lake—the Kicky-Poo call it Fat Water. Right there, Fort Chicago—it's a French outpost."

"French. One cup of whisky for a White man scalp."

"That's the going rate, all right," said Armor-of-God. "But the Reds around here don't take scalps. They trade fair with me, and I trade fair with them, and we don't go shooting down Reds and they don't go killing White folks for the bounty. You understand me? You start getting thirsty, you think about this: There was a whisky-Red from the Wee-Aw tribe here some four year back, he killed him a little Danish boy out in the woods. Do you think it was White men tracked him down? Reckon not; you know a White man's got no hope to find no Red in these woods, specially not farmers and such like us. No, it was Shaw-Nee and Otty-Wa who found him two hours after the boy turned up missing. And do you think it was White men punished that whisky-Red? Reckon not; they set that Wee-Aw down and said, 'You want to show brave?' and when he said yes, they took six hours killing him."

"Very kind," said Lolla-Wossiky.

"*Kind?* I reckon not," said Armor-of-God.

"Red man kills White boy for whisky, I never let him show brave, he die—uh! Like that, quick like rattlesnake, no man him."

"I got to say you Reds think real strange," said Armor. "You mean it's a favor when you torture somebody to death?"

"Not *somebody.* Enemy. Catch enemy, he shows brave before he dies so then his spirit flies back to home. Tell his mother and sisters he died brave, they sing songs and scream for him. He doesn't show brave, then his spirit falls flat on the dirt and you step on him, grind him in, he never goes home, nobody remembers his name."

"It's a good thing Thrower's out at the privy right now, or I reckon he'd wet his pants over *that* doctrine." Thrower squinted at Lolla-Wossiky. "You mean they *honored* that Wee-Aw who killed that little boy?"

"Very bad thing, killing little boy. But maybe Red man knows about whisky-Red, very thirsty, making crazy. Not like killing man to take his house or his woman or his land, like White man all the time."

"I got to say, the more I learn about you Reds, the more it kind of starts to make sense. I better read the Bible more every night before I turn Red myself."

Lolla-Wossiky laughed and laughed.

"What's so funny?"

"Many Red men turn White and then die. But never does a White man turn Red. I have to tell this story, everybody laugh."

"You Reds have a sense of humor like I just don't understand." Armor patted the map. "Here's us, right here just downriver from where the Tippy-Canoe flows into the Wobbish. All these dots, they're White man's farms. And these circles, they're Red villages. This one's Shaw-Nee, this one's Winny-Baygo, see how it goes?"

"White Murderer Harrison tells Reds that you make this land-face picture so you can find Red villages. Killing everybody, he says."

"Well, that's just the kind of lie I'd expect him to tell. So you heard about me afore you came up here, did you? Well, I hope you don't believe his lies."

"Oh, no. Nobody believes White Murderer Harrison."

"Good thing."

"Nobody believes any White man. All lies."

"Well, not me, you understand that? Not me. Harrison wants to be governor so bad that he'll tell any lie he can to get power and keep it."

"He says you want to be governor, too."

Armor paused at that. Looked at the map. Looked at the door to the kitchen, where his wife was washing up. "Well, I reckon he didn't lie about that. But my idea of what it means to be governor and his are two different things. I want to be governor so Red men and White men can live together in peace here, farming the land side by side, going to the same schools so someday there ain't no difference between Red and White. But Harrison, he wants to get rid of the Red man altogether."

If you make the Red man just like the White man, then he won't be Red no more. Harrison's way or Armor's way, you end up with no Red men at the end. Lolla-Wossiky thought of this, but he didn't say it. He knew that even though turning all the Red men White would be very bad, killing them all with likker the way Harrison planned, or killing them and driving them off the land the way Jackson planned, those were even worse. Harrison was a very bad man. Armor wanted to be a good man, he just didn't know how. Lolla-Wossiky understood this, so he didn't argue with Armor-of-God.

Armor went on showing him the map. "Down here's Fort Carthage, it's got a square, cause it's a town. I put a square for us, too, even though we're not rightly a town yet. We're calling it Vigor Church, on account of that church we're building."

"Church for building. Why Vigor?"

"Oh, the first folks settled here, the ones who cut the road and made the bridges, the Miller family. They live on up behind the church, way along the road there. My wife is their oldest girl, in fact. They named this place Vigor on account of their oldest son was named Vigor. He drowned in the Hatrack River clear back near Suskwa-henny, on their way coming here. So they named the place after him."

"Your wife, very pretty," said Lolla-Wossiky.

It took Armor just a few seconds to answer that, he looked so surprised. And in the shop in back, where they ate the meal, his wife Eleanor must have been listening, cause she was suddenly standing there in the doorway.

"Nobody ever called me pretty," she said softly.

Lolla-Wossiky was baffled. Most White women had narrow faces, no cheekbones, sick-looking skin. Eleanor was darker, wide-faced, high cheekbones.

"I think you're pretty," said Armor. "I really do."

Lolla-Wossiky didn't believe him, and neither did Eleanor, though she smiled and went away from the door. He never had thought she was pretty, that was plain.

And after a moment, Lolla-Wossiky understood why. She was pretty like a *Red* woman. So naturally White men who never saw straight thought her pretty was very ugly.

This also meant that Armor-of-God was married to a woman he thought was ugly. But he didn't shout at her or hit her, like a Red man with an ugly squaw. This was a good thing, Lolla-Wossiky decided.

"You very happy," said Lolla-Wossiky.

"That's because we're Christians," said Armor-of-God. "You'd be happy, too, if you was Christian."

"I won't never be happy," said Lolla-Wossiky. He meant to say, "Till I hear green silence again, till black noise goes away." But no use saying that to a White man, they didn't know that half the things going on in the world were plain invisible to them.

"Yes you will," said Thrower. He strode into the room with all kinds of energy, ready to tackle this heathen all over again. "You accept Jesus Christ as your savior, and you will have true happiness."

Now, that was a promise worth looking into. That was a good reason to talk about this Jesus Christ. Maybe Jesus Christ was Lolla-Wossiky's dream beast. Maybe he would make the black noise go away and make Lolla-Wossiky happy again like he was before White Murderer Harrison blew up the world with black noise from his gun.

"Jesus Christ makes me wake up?" asked Lolla-Wossiky.

"Come follow me, he said, and I will make you fishers of men," answered Thrower.

"He waking me up? He making me happy?"

"Eternal joy, in the bosom of the Heavenly Father," said Thrower.

None of this made any sense, but Lolla-Wossiky decided to go ahead anyway on the chance that it would wake him up and *then* he'd understand what Thrower was talking about. Even though Thrower made the black noise louder, maybe he also had the cure for it.

So that night Lolla-Wossiky slept out in the woods, took his four swallows of whisky in the morning, and staggered on up to the church. Thrower was annoyed that Lolla-Wossiky was drunk, and Armor once again insisted on knowing who gave him likker. Since all the other men who were doing the church-raising were gathered around, Armor made a speech, with a whole bunch of threats in it. "If I find out who's likkering up these Reds, I swear I'll burn his house down and make him go live with Harrison down on the Hio. Up here we're Christian folk. Now I can't stop you from putting those hexes on your houses and making those spells and conjures, even though they show lack of faith in the Lord, but I *sure* can stop you from poisoning the folk that the Lord saw fit to put on this land. Do you understand me?"

All the White folk nodded and said yes and that's right and reckon so.

"Nobody here gave me whisky," said Lolla-Wossiky.

"Maybe he carried it with him in a cup!" said one of the men.

"Maybe he's got him a still in the woods!" said another. They all laughed.

"Please be reverent," said Thrower. "This heathen is accepting the Lord Jesus Christ. He shall be covered with the water of baptism as was Jesus himself. Let this mark the beginning of a great missionary labor among the Red men of the American forest!"

Amen, murmured the men.

Well, the water was cold, and that's about all Lolla-Wossiky noticed, except that when Thrower sprinkled it on him the black noise just got louder. Jesus Christ didn't show up, so he wasn't the dream beast after all. Lolla-Wossiky was disappointed.

But Reverend Thrower wasn't. That was the strange thing about White men. They just seemed not to notice what went on around them. Here Thrower performed a baptism that didn't do a lick of good, and he went strutting around the rest of the day like he had just called a buffalo into a starving village in the dead of winter.

Armor-of-God was just as blind. At noon, when Eleanor brought dinner up the hill to the workmen, they let Lolla-Wossiky eat with them. "Can't turn away a Christian, can we?" said one. But none of them was too happy about sitting next to Lolla-Wossiky, probably because he stank of liquor and sweat and he staggered when he walked. It ended up that Armor-of-God sat with Lolla-Wossiky off a ways from the others, and they talked about this and that.

Till Lolla-Wossiky asked him, "Jesus Christ, he don't like hexes?"

"That's right. *He* is the way, and all this beseeching and suchlike is blasphemy."

Lolla-Wossiky nodded gravely. "Painted hex no good. Paint never was alive."

"Painted, carved, same thing."

"Wooden hex, a little strong. Tree used to be alive."

"Doesn't matter to me, wooden or painted, I won't have no hexes in my house. No conjures, no come-hithers, no fendings, no wardings, none of that stuff. A good Christian relies on prayer, and that's that. The Lord is my shepherd, I shall not want."

Lolla-Wossiky knew then that Armor-of-God was just as blind as Thrower. Because Armor-of-God's house was the strongest-hexed house Lolla-Wossiky ever saw. That was part of the reason Lolla-Wossiky was impressed with Armor, that his house was actually well protected, because he understood enough to make his hexes out of living things. Arrangements of living plants hanging on the porch, seeds with the life in them sitting in carefully placed jars, garlics, stains of berry juices, all so strongly placed that even with the likker in him to dull the black noise, Lolla-Wossiky could feel the pushing and pulling of the fendings and wardings and hexes.

Yet Armor-of-God didn't have the faintest idea that his house had any hexes at all. "My wife Eleanor, her folks always had hexes. Her little brother Al Junior, he's that six-year-old wrassling with the blond-headed Swedish boy there—see him? He's a real hex-carver, they say."

Lolla-Wossiky looked at the boy, but couldn't exactly see him. He saw the yellow-hair boy he was tussling with, but the other boy just couldn't come clear for him, he didn't know why.

Armor was still talking. "Don't that make you sick? That young, and already he's being turned away from Jesus. Anyway, it was real hard for Eleanor to give up those hexes and such. But she did it. Gave me her solemn oath, or we never would've got married."

At that moment Eleanor, the pretty wife that White men thought was ugly, came up to take away the dinner basket. She heard the last words that her husband said, but she gave no sign that it meant anything to her. Except that when she took Lolla-Wossiky's bowl from him, and looked him in the eye, he felt like she was asking him. Did you see those hexes?

Lolla-Wossiky smiled at her, his biggest smile, so she'd know he didn't have any plan to tell her husband.

She smiled back, hesitantly, untrustingly. "Did you like the food?" she asked him.

"Everything cooked too much," said Lolla-Wossiky. "Blood taste all gone."

Her eyes went wide. Armor only laughed and clapped Lolla-Wossiky on the shoulder. "Well, that's what it means to be civilized. You give up drinking blood, and that's a fact. I hope your baptism sets you on the right road—it's plain you've been a long time on the wrong one."

"I wondered," said Eleanor—and she stopped, glanced down at Lolla-Wossiky's loincloth, and then looked at her husband.

"Oh, yes, we talked about that last night. I've got some old trousers and a shirt I don't use anymore, and Eleanor's making me new ones anyway, so I thought, now that you're baptized, you really ought to start dressing like a Christian."

"Very hot day," said Lolla-Wossiky.

"Yes, well, Christians believe in modesty of dress, Lolla-Wossiky." Armor laughed and hit him on the shoulder again.

"I can bring the clothes up this afternoon," said Eleanor.

Lolla-Wossiky thought this was a very stupid idea. Red men always looked stupid dressed in White man's clothes. But he didn't want to argue with them because they were trying to be very friendly. And maybe the baptism would work after all, if he put on White man's clothes. Maybe then the black noise would go away.

So he didn't answer. He just looked at where the yellow-hair boy was running around in circles, shouting, "Alvin! Ally!" Lolla-Wossiky tried very hard to see the boy that he was chasing. He saw a foot touching the ground and raising dust, a hand moving through the air, but never quite saw the boy himself. Very strange thing.

Eleanor was waiting for him to answer. Lolla-Wossiky said nothing, since he was now watching the boy who wasn't there. Finally Armor-of-God laughed and said, "Bring the clothes up, Eleanor. We'll dress him like a Christian, all right, and maybe tomorrow he can lend a hand on building the church, start learning a Christian trade. Get a saw into his hand."

Lolla-Wossiky didn't actually hear that last, or he might

have taken off into the woods right away. He had seen what happened to Red men who started using White man's tools. The way they got cut off from the land, bit by bit, every time they hefted that metal. Even guns. A Red man starts using guns for hunting, he's half White the first time he pulls the trigger; only thing a Red man can use a gun for is killing White men, that's what Ta-Kumsaw always said, and he was right. But Lolla-Wossiky didn't hear Armor talk about wanting Lolla-Wossiky to use a saw because he had just made the most remarkable discovery. When he closed his good eye, he could see that boy. Just like the one-eyed bear in the river. Open his eye, and there was the yellow-head boy chasing and shouting, but no Alvin Miller Junior. Close his eye, and there was nothing but the black noise and the traces of the green—and then, right in the middle, there was the boy, bright and shining with light as if he had the sun in his back pocket, laughing and playing with a voice like music.

And then he didn't see him at all.

Lolla-Wossiky opened his eye. There was Reverend Thrower. Armor and Eleanor were gone—all the men were back to work on the church. It was Thrower who made the boy disappear, that was plain enough. Or maybe not—because now, with Thrower standing by him, Lolla-Wossiky could see the boy with his good eye. Just like any other child.

"Lolla-Wossiky, it occurs to me that you really ought to have a Christian name. I've never baptized a Red before, and so I just thoughtlessly used your uncivilized nomenclature. You're supposed to take a new name, a Christian name. Not necessarily a saint's name—we're not Papists—but something to suggest your new commitment to Christ."

Lolla-Wossiky nodded. He knew he would need a new name, if the baptism turned out to work after all. Once he met his dream beast and went back home, he would get a name. He tried to explain this to Thrower, but the White minister didn't really understand. Finally, though, he grasped the idea that Lolla-Wossiky *wanted* a new name and meant to get one soon, so he was mollified.

"While we're both right here, by the way," said Thrower, "I wondered if I might examine your head. I am working on developing some orderly categorizations for the infant science of phrenology. It is the idea that particular talents and propensities in the human soul are reflected in or perhaps even caused by protuberances and depressions in the shape of the skull."

Lolla-Wossiky didn't have any idea what Thrower was talking about, so he nodded silently. This usually worked with White men who were talking nonsense, and Thrower was no exception. The end of it was that Thrower felt all over Lolla-Wossiky's head, stopping now and then to make sketches and notes on a piece of paper, muttering things like "Interesting," "Ha!" and "So much for *that* theory." When it was over, Thrower thanked him. "You've contributed greatly to the cause of science, Mr. Wossiky. You are living proof that a Red man does not necessarily have the bumps of savagery and cannibalism. Instead you have the normal array of knacks and lacks that any human has. Red men are not intrinsically different from White men, at least not in any simple, easily categorized way. In fact, you have every sign of being quite a remarkable speaker, with a profoundly developed sense of religion. It is no accident that you are the first Red man to accept the gospel in my ministry here in America. I must say that your phrenological pattern has many great similarities to my own. In short, my dear new-baptized Christian, I would not be surprised if you ended up being a missionary of the gospel yourself. Preaching to great multitudes of Red men and women and bringing them to an understanding of heaven. Contemplate that vision, Mr. Wossiky. If I am not mistaken, it is your future."

Lolla-Wossiky barely caught the gist of what Thrower said. Something about him being a preacher. Something about telling the future. Lolla-Wossiky tried to make sense of this, but it didn't work.

By nightfall, Lolla-Wossiky was dressed in White man's clothes, looking like a fool. His likker had worn off and he hadn't had a chance to dodge back into the woods and get his four swallows, so the black noise was getting very bad. Worse yet, it looked to be a rainy night, so he couldn't see with his eye, and with the black noise as bad as it was, his land sense couldn't lead him to his keg, either.

The result was that he was staggering worse than when he had likker in him, the ground heaved and tossed so much under his feet. He fell over trying to get out of his chair at Armor's supper table. Eleanor insisted that he had to spend the night there. "We can't have him sleep in the woods, not when it rains," she said, and as if to buttress her point there was a clap of thunder and rain started pelting the roof and walls. Eleanor made up a bed on the floor of the kitchen while Thrower and Armor went around the house closing shutters. Gratefully Lolla-Wossiky crawled to the bed, not even removing the stiff uncomfortable trousers and shirt, and lay down, his eye closed, trying to endure the stabbing in his head, the pain of the black noise like knives cutting out his brain slice by slice.

As usual, they thought he was asleep.

"He seems drunker than he did this morning," said Thrower.

"I know he never left the hill," said Armor. "There's not a chance he got a drink anywhere."

"I've heard it said that when a drunk becomes sober," said Thrower, "at first he acts more drunk than when he has alcohol in him."

"I hope that's all it is," said Armor.

"I daresay he was somewhat disappointed at the baptism today," said Thrower. "Of course it's impossible to understand what a savage is feeling, but—"

"I wouldn't call him a savage, Reverend Thrower," said Eleanor. "I think in his own way he's civilized."

"You might as well call a badger civilized, then," said Thrower. "In his own *way,* anyway."

"I mean to say," Eleanor said, her voice even quieter and meeker-sounding, but therefore carrying all the more weight, "that I saw him reading."

"Turning pages you mean," said Thrower. "He couldn't be *reading.*"

"No. He read, and his lips formed the words," she said. "The signs on the wall in the front room, where we serve customers. He read the words."

"It's possible, you know," said Armor. "I know for a fact that the Irrakwa read just as good as any White men. I been there to do business often enough, and you can bet you have to read the fine print on the contracts they write up. Red men can learn to read, and that's a fact."

"But this one, this drunk—"

"Who knows what he can become, when the likker ain't in him?" said Eleanor.

Then they went away to the other room, and left the house for a while, walking Thrower home to the cabin he was staying in before the rain got so bad he had to stay the night.

Alone in the house, Lolla-Wossiky tried to make sense of things. Baptism alone hadn't wakened him from his dream. Nor had White man's clothes. Maybe going without likker for a night would do it, like Eleanor suggested, though it made him crazy with pain so he couldn't sleep.

Whatever happened, though, he knew that the dream

beast was waiting somewhere near here. The white light was suffused all around him now; this was the waking place for Lolla-Wossiky. Maybe if he stayed away from the church hill today, maybe if he wandered in the woods around Vigor Church, then the dream beast could find him.

One thing was sure. He wasn't going to spend another night without whisky. Not when he had a keg out in a crotch of a tree that could take away the black noise and let him sleep.

LOLLA-WOSSIKY WALKED EVERYWHERE in the woods. He saw many animals, but they all ran from him; he was so drunk or so bound up in the black noise that he never was part of the land, and they ran from him just as if he were White.

Discouraged, he began to drink more than four swallows, even though he knew he would run out of whisky too fast. He walked less and less in the forest, more and more along the White man's paths and roads, showing up at farmhouses in the middle of the day. The women sometimes screamed and ran away, carrying a baby and leading children off into the woods. Other women pointed guns at him and made him leave. Some of them fed him and talked about Jesus Christ. Finally Armor-of-God told him not to visit the farms when the men were away, working on the church.

So there was nothing left for Lolla-Wossiky to do. He knew he was close to the dream beast, but he couldn't find it. He couldn't walk in the forest because the animals ran from him and he stumbled and fell all the time, more and more, until he feared he might break a bone and die of starvation because he couldn't even call small animals to feed him. He couldn't visit the farms because the men were angry. So he lay on the commons, sleeping from drunkenness or trying to endure the pain of the black noise, one or the other.

Sometimes he worked up the energy to go up the hill and see the men working on the church. Whenever he got there, some man would call out, "Here comes the Red Christian!" and Lolla-Wossiky knew that there was malice and ridicule in the voices that said it and the voices that laughed.

He was not at the church the day the roof-beam fell. He was sleeping on the grass of the commons, near the porch of Armor's house, when he heard the crash. It startled him awake, and the black noise came back harsher than ever, even though he had drunk eight swallows that morning and ought to be drunk till noon. He lay there holding his head until men started coming down from the hill, cursing and muttering about the strange thing that happened.

"What happened?" Lolla-Wossiky asked. He had to know, because whatever it was, it had made the black noise worse than it had been in years. "Was a man killed?" He knew that a gunshot made the black noise in the first place. "Did White Murderer Harrison shoot somebody?"

At first they paid him no attention, because they thought he was drunk, of course. But finally someone told him what happened.

They had been laying the first ridgebeam in place, high on top of the building, when the central ridgepole shivered and tossed the ridgebeam up in the air. "Came down flat, just like God's own foot stepping on the earth, and wouldn't you know, there was that little Alvin Junior, Al Miller's boy, right under the beam. Well, we thought he was dead. The boy just stood there, the beam landed smack—you must have heard the noise, that's why it sounded like a gun to you—but you won't believe this. That ridgebeam split right in half, right in the very place where Alvin was standing, split right in two and landed on this side and that side of him, didn't touch a hair on his head."

"Something strange about that boy," said a man.

"He's got a guardian angel, that's what he's got," said another.

Alvin Junior. The boy he couldn't see with his eye open.

There was no one at the church when Lolla-Wossiky got there. The ridgebeam was also gone, everything swept out, no sign of the accident. But Lolla-Wossiky was not looking with his eye. He could feel it, almost as soon as he got within sight of the church. A whirlpool, not fast at the edges, but stronger and stronger the closer he came. A whirlwind of light, and the closer he got, the weaker the black noise became. Until he stood on the church floor, in the spot that he knew was where the boy was standing. How did he know? The black noise was quieter. Not gone, the pain not healed, but Lolla-Wossiky could feel the green land again, just a little, not like it used to be, but he could feel the small life under the floor, a squirrel in the meadow not far off, things he hadn't felt, drunk or sober, in all the years since the gun blew the black noise into his head.

Lolla-Wossiky turned around and around, seeing nothing but the walls of the church. Until he closed his eye. Then he saw the whirlwind, yes, white light spinning and spinning around him, and the black noise retreating. He was in the end of his own dream now, and he could see with his eye closed, see clearly. There was a shining path ahead of him, a road as bright as the noonday sky, dazzling like meadow snow on a clear day. He knew already, without opening his eye to see, where the path would lead. Up the hill, down the other side, up a higher hill, to a house not far from a stream, a house where lived a White boy who was only visible to Lolla-Wossiky with his eye closed.

HIS SILENT STEP had returned to him, now that the black noise had backed off a bit. He walked around the house, around and around. No one heard him. Inside laughter, shouting, screaming. Happy children, quarreling children. Stern voices of parents. Except for the language, it could be his village. His own sisters and brothers in the happy days before White Murderer Harrison took his father's life.

The White father, Alvin Miller, came out to the privy. Not long after, the boy himself came, running, as if he was afraid. He shouted at the privy door. With his eye open, Lolla-Wossiky only knew that someone was standing there, shouting. With his eye closed, he saw the boy clearly, radiant, and heard his voice like birdsong across a river, all music, even though what he said was silly, foolish, like a child.

"If you don't come out I'll do it right in front of the door so you'll step in it when you come out!"

Then silence, as the boy grew more worried, hitting himself on the top of his head with his own fist, as if to say, Stupid, stupid, stupid. Something changed in Al Junior's expression; Lolla-Wossiky opened his eye to see that the father had come out, was saying something.

The boy answered him, ashamed. The father corrected him. Lolla-Wossiky closed his eye.

"Yes sir," said the boy.

Again the father must be speaking, but with his eye closed Lolla-Wossiky did not hear the father.

"Sorry, Papa."

Then the father must have walked away, because little Alvin went into the privy. Muttering, so soft no one could hear. But Lolla-Wossiky heard. "Well, if you'd just build another outhouse I'd be fine."

Lolla-Wossiky laughed. Foolish boy, foolish father, like all boys, like all fathers.

The boy finished and went into the house.

Here I am, said Lolla-Wossiky silently. I followed the

shining path, I came to this place, I saw silly White family things; now where is my dream beast?

And again he saw the white light gather, inside the house, following the boy up the stairs. For Lolla-Wossiky there were no walls. He saw the boy being very careful, as if he were watching for an enemy, for some attack. When he reached the bedroom he ducked inside, closed his door quickly behind him. Lolla-Wossiky saw him so clearly that he thought he could almost hear his thoughts; and then, because he thought it, and because this was near the end of his dream, almost to the time of waking, he *did* hear the boy's thoughts, or at least felt his feelings. It was his sisters he was afraid of. A silly quarrel, begun with teasing, but malicious now—he was afraid of their vengeance.

It came as he stripped off his clothes and pulled his nightshirt over his head. Stinging! Insects, thought the boy. Spiders, scorpions, tiny snakes! He pulled the nightshirt off, slapped himself, cried out from the pain, the surprise, the fear.

But Lolla-Wossiky could feel the land well enough to know there were no insects. Not on his body, not in the shirt. Though there were many living creatures there. Small life, little animals. Roaches, hundreds of them living in the walls and floors.

Not in *all* the walls and floors, though. Just in Alvin Junior's room. All gathered to his room.

Was it enmity? Roaches were too small for hate. They knew only three feelings, those little creatures. Fear, hunger, and the third sense, the land sense. The trust in how things ought to be. Did the boy feed them? No. They came to him for the other thing. Lolla-Wossiky could hardly believe it, but he felt it in the roaches and couldn't doubt. The boy had called them somehow. The boy had the land sense, at least enough to call these small creatures.

Call them why? Who wanted roaches? But he was only a boy. There didn't have to be sense in it. Just the discovery that the little life would come when you called it. Red boys learned this, but always with their father or a brother, always out on the first hunt. Kneel and speak silently to the life you need to take, and ask it if this is a good time, and if it is willing to die to make your life strong. Is it your time to die? asks the Red boy. And if the life consents, it will come.

This is what the boy did. Except it wasn't so simple. He didn't call the roaches to die for his need, because he had no need. No, he called them and kept them safe. He protected them. It was like a treaty. There were certain places the roaches didn't go. Into Alvin's bed. Into his brother Calvin's little bed. Into Alvin's clothing, folded on the stool. And in return Alvin never killed them. They were safe in his room. It was a sanctuary, a reserve. A very silly thing, a child playing with things he didn't understand.

But the marvel of it was—this was a White boy, doing something beyond even a Red man's reach. When did the Red man ever say to the bear, come and live with me and I will keep you safe? When did the bear ever believe such a thing? No wonder the light was centered on this boy. This wasn't the foolish knack of the White man Hooch, or even the strong living hexes of the woman Eleanor. This wasn't the Red man's power to fit himself into the pattern of the land. No, Alvin didn't fit himself into anything. The land fit itself to him. If he wanted the roaches to live a certain way, to make a bargain, then that was how the land ordered itself. In this small place, for this time, with these tiny lives, Alvin Junior had commanded and the land obeyed.

Did the boy understand how miraculous this was?

No, no, he had no idea. How could he know? What White man could even understand it?

And now, because he didn't understand, Alvin Junior was destroying the delicate thing that he had done. The insects that had bitten him were metal pins that his sisters had poked into his nightshirt. Now he could hear them laughing behind their wall. Because he had been very frightened, now he was very angry. Get even, get back at them; Lolla-Wossiky could feel his childish rage. He only did one little thing to tease them, and they pay him back by scaring him, poking him a hundred times and making him bleed. Get even, give them such a scare—

Alvin Junior sat on the edge of the bed, angrily taking the pins out of his nightshirt, saving them—White men were so careful with all their useless metal tools, even such tiny ones as those. As he sat there he saw the roaches scurrying along the walls, running in and out of cracks in the floor, and he saw his vengeance.

Lolla-Wossiky felt him making the plan in his mind. Then Alvin knelt on the floor and explained it softly to the roaches. Because he was a child, and a White boy with no one to teach him, Alvin thought he had to say the words aloud, that the roaches somehow understood his language. But no—it was the order of things, the way he arranged the world in his mind.

And in his mind he lied to them. Hunger, he told them. And in the other room, food. He showed them food if they went under the wall into the sisters' room and climbed on the beds and the bodies there. Food if they hurried, food for all of them. It was a lie, and Lolla-Wossiky wanted to shout at him not to do this.

If a Red man knelt and called to prey that he didn't need, the prey would know his lie and wouldn't come. The lie itself would cut the Red man from the land, make him walk alone awhile. But this White boy could lie with such force and strength that the tiny minds of the roaches believed him. They scurried, a hundred, a thousand of them under the walls, into the other room.

Alvin Junior heard something, and he was delighted. But Lolla-Wossiky was angry. He opened his eye, so he didn't have to see Alvin Junior's glee at his revenge. Instead now he heard the sisters screaming as the roaches climbed all over them. And then the parents and brothers rushing into their room. And the stomping. The stomping, the smashing, the murders of the roaches. Lolla-Wossiky closed his eye and felt the deaths, each one a pinprick. It had been so long with the black noise masking all the deaths behind one vast memory of murder that Lolla-Wossiky had forgotten what the small pains felt like.

Like the death of bees.

Roaches, useless animals, eating up garbage, making filthy rustling noises in their dens, loathsome when they crawled on the skin; but part of the land, part of the life, part of the green silence, and their death was an evil noise, their useless murder because they believed in a lie.

This is why I came, Lolla-Wossiky realized. The land brought me here, knowing that this boy had such power, knowing that there was no one to teach him how to use it, no one to teach him to wait to feel the need of the land before changing it. No one to teach him how to be Red instead of White.

I didn't come for my own dream beast, but to be the dream beast for this boy.

The noise settled. The sisters, the brothers, the parents went back to sleep. Lolla-Wossiky pressed his fingers into the cracks between the logs, climbed carefully, his eye closed so that the land would guide him instead of trusting in himself. The boy's shutters were open, and Lolla-Wossiky thrust his elbows over the sill and hung there, looking in.

First with his eye open. He saw a bed, a stool with

clothes neatly folded, and at the foot of the bed, a cot. The
window opened onto the space between the bed and the cot.
In the bed, a shape, boy-sized, unidentifiable.

Lolla-Wossiky closed his eye again. Alvin lay in the
bed. Lolla-Wossiky felt the heat of the boy's excitement
like a fever. He had been so afraid of being caught, so ex-
hilarated at his victory, and now lay trembling, trying to
breathe calmly, trying to stifle laughter.

His eye open again, Lolla-Wossiky scrambled up onto
the sill and swung onto the floor. He expected Alvin to
notice him, to cry out; but the shape of the boy lay still in
the bed; there was no sound.

The boy couldn't see him when his eye was open, any
more than he could see the boy. This was the end of
the dream, after all, and Lolla-Wossiky was dream beast
for the boy. It was Lolla-Wossiky's duty to give visions to
the boy, not to be seen as himself, a whisky-Red with one
eye missing.

What vision will I show him?

Lolla-Wossiky reached inside his White man's trousers
to where he still wore his loincloth, and pulled his knife
from its sheath. He held both his hands high, the one holding the knife. Then he closed his eye.

The boy still didn't see him; his eyes were closed.
So Lolla-Wossiky gathered the white light he could feel
around him, gathered it close to himself, so that he could
feel himself shining brighter and brighter. The light came
from his skin, so he tore open the breast of the White man's
shirt he wore, then raised his hands again. Now, even
through closed eyelids, the boy could see the brightness,
and he opened his eyes.

Lolla-Wossiky felt the boy's terror at the sight of the apparition he had become: a bright and shining Red man,
one-eyed, with a sharp knife in his hand. But it wasn't fear
Lolla-Wossiky wanted. No one should fear his own dream

beast. So he sent the light outward to the boy, to include him, and with the light he sent calm, calm, don't be scared.

The boy relaxed a little, but still wriggled up in his bed, so he was sitting up, leaning against the wall.

It was time to begin to wake the boy from his life of sleep. How did Lolla-Wossiky know what to do? No man, Red or White, had ever been another man's dream beast. Yet he knew without thinking what he ought to do. What the boy needed to see and feel. Whatever came to Lolla-Wossiky's mind that felt right to do, that was what he did.

Lolla-Wossiky took his shining knife and brought the blade against his other palm—and cut. Sharp, hard, deep, so blood leapt from the wound, rushed down his forearm to gather and pool in his sleeve. Quickly it began to drip on the floor.

The pain came suddenly, a moment later; Lolla-Wossiky knew at once how to take the pain and make it into a picture and put it into the boy's mind. The picture of his sisters' room as a small weak creature saw it. Rushing in, hungering, hungering, looking for the food, certain that the food was there; on the soft body was the promise, climb the body, find the food. But great hands slapped and brushed, and the small creature was thrown onto the floor. The floor shook with giant footfalls, a sudden shadow, the agony of death.

Again and again, each small life, hungering, trusting, and then betrayed, crushed, battered.

Many lived, but they cowered, they scurried, they fled. The sisters' room, the room of death, yes, they fled from there. But better to stay there and die than run into the other room, the room of lies. Not words, there were no words in the small creature's life, there were no thoughts that could be named as thoughts. But the fear of death in the one place was not as strong as another kind of fear, the fear of a world gone crazy, a place where anything could happen, where nothing could be trusted, where nothing was certain. A terrible place.

Lolla-Wossiky ended the vision. The boy was pressing his hands against his eyes, sobbing desperately. Lolla-Wossiky had never seen anyone so tortured by remorse; the vision Lolla-Wossiky had given him was stronger than any dream a man could imagine for himself. I am a terrible dream beast, thought Lolla-Wossiky. He will wish I hadn't wakened him. In dread of his own strength, Lolla-Wossiky opened his eye.

At once the boy disappeared, and Lolla-Wossiky knew that the boy would think that Lolla-Wossiky had also disappeared. What now? he thought. Am I here to make this boy crazy? To give him a terrible thing, as bad as the black noise was to me?

He could see from the shaking of the bed, the movement of the bedclothes, that the boy was still crying passionately. Lolla-Wossiky closed his eye, and again sent the light to the boy. Calm, calm.

The boy's weeping became a whimper, and he looked again at Lolla-Wossiky, who was still shining with a dazzling light.

Lolla-Wossiky didn't know what to do. While he was silent and uncertain, Alvin began to speak, to plead. "I'm sorry, I'll never do it again, I'll—"

Babbling on and on. Lolla-Wossiky pushed more light at him, to help him see better. It came to the boy almost as a question. What will you never do again?

Alvin couldn't answer, didn't know. What was it he actually did? Was it because he sent the roaches to die?

He looked at the Shining Man and saw an image of a Red kneeling before a deer, calling it to come and die; the deer came, trembling, afraid; the Red loosed his arrow and it stood quivering on the deer's flank; the deer's legs wobbled, and it fell. It wasn't the dying or the killing that was his sin, because dying and killing were a part of life.

Was it the power he had? The knack he had for making things go just where he wanted, to break just at the right place, or fit together so tight that they joined forever without any gluing or hammering. The knack he had for making things do what he wanted, arrange themselves in the right order. Was it that?

Again he looked at the Shining Man, and now he saw a vision of himself pressing his hands against a stone, and the stone melted like butter under his hands, came out in just the shape he wanted, smooth and whole, fell from the side of the mountain and rolled away, a perfect ball, a perfect sphere, growing and growing until it was a whole world, shaped just the way his hands had made it, with trees and grass springing up in its face, and animals running and leaping and flying and swimming and crawling and burrowing on and above and beneath the ball of stone that he had made. No, it wasn't a terrible power, it was a glorious one, if he only knew how to use it.

If it isn't the dying and it isn't the power, what did I do wrong?

This time the Shining Man didn't show him anything. This time Alvin didn't have the answer come to him in a vision. This time he studied it out in his mind. He felt like he couldn't understand, he was too stupid to understand, and then suddenly he knew.

It was because he did it for himself. It was because the roaches thought he was doing it for them, and really he was doing it for himself. Hurting the roaches, his sisters, everyone, making everyone suffer and all for what? Because Alvin Miller Junior was angry and wanted to get *even*—

Now he looked at the Shining Man and saw a fire leap from his single eye and strike him in the heart. "I'll never use it for myself again," murmured Alvin Junior, and when he said the words he felt as though his heart were on fire, it burned so hot inside. And then the Shining Man disappeared again.

Lolla-Wossiky stood panting, his head spinning. He felt weak, weary. He had no idea what the boy had been thinking. He only knew what visions to send him, and then at the end, no vision at all, just to stand there, that's all he was to do, stand there and stand there until, suddenly, he sent a strong pulse of fire at the boy and buried it in his heart.

And now what? Twice now he had closed his eye and appeared to the boy. Was he through? He knew that he was not.

For the third time Lolla-Wossiky closed his eye. Now he could see that the boy was much brighter than *he* was; that the light had passed from him into the child. And then he understood—he was the boy's dream beast, yes, but the boy was also his. Now it was time for him to wake up from his dream life.

He took three steps and knelt beside the bed, his face only a little way from the boy's small and frightened face, which now shone so brightly that Lolla-Wossiky could hardly see that it was a child and not a man who looked at him. What do I want from him? Why am I here? What can he give me, this powerful child?

"Make all things whole," Lolla-Wossiky whispered. He spoke, not in English, but in Shaw-Nee.

Did the boy understand? Alvin raised his small hand, reached out gently and touched Lolla-Wossiky's cheek, under the broken eye. Then he raised his finger until it touched the slack eyelid.

There was a cracking sound in the air, and a spark of light. The boy gasped and drew back his hand. Lolla-Wossiky didn't see him, though, because suddenly the boy was invisible. But Lolla-Wossiky had no care for what he saw, for what he *felt* was the most impossible thing of all:

Silence. Green silence. The black noise was utterly, completely gone. His land-sense had returned, and the ancient injury was healed.

Lolla-Wossiky knelt there, gasping for breath, as the land returned to him the way that it had been before. All these years had passed; he had forgotten how strong it was, to see in all directions, hear the breath of every animal, smell the scent of every plant. A man who has been dry and thirsty until he was at the point of death, and suddenly cold water pours down his throat so fast he can't swallow, can't breathe; it's what he longed for, but much too strong, much too sudden, can't contain it, can't endure it—

"It didn't work," the boy whispered. "I'm sorry."

Lolla-Wossiky opened his good eye, and now for the first time saw the boy as a natural man. Alvin was staring at his bad eye. Lolla-Wossiky wondered why; he reached up, touched his missing eye. The lid still hung over an empty socket. Then he understood. The boy thought that was what he was supposed to heal. No, no, don't be disappointed, child, you healed me from the *deep* injury; what do I care about this tiny wound? I never lost my sight; it was my land-sense that was gone, and you gave it back to me.

He meant to shout all this to the boy, cry out and sing for the joy of it. But it was all too strong for him. The words never came to his lips. He couldn't even send him visions now because both of them were now awake. The dream was over. They had each been dream beast for the other.

Lolla-Wossiky seized the boy with both hands, pulled him close, kissed him on the forehead, hard and strong, like a father to a son, like brothers, like true friends the day before they die. Then he ran to the window, swung out and dropped to the ground. The earth yielded to his feet

as it did to other Red men, as it hadn't done for him in so
many years; the grass rose up stronger where he stepped;
the bushes parted for him, the leaves softened and yielded
as he ran among the trees; and now he did cry out, shouted,
sang, caring not at all who heard him. Animals didn't run
from him, as they used to; now they came to hear his song;
songbirds awoke to sing with him; a deer leapt from the
wood and ran beside him through a meadow, and he rested
his hand upon her flank.

He ran until he had no breath, and in all that time he met
no enemy, he felt no pain; he was whole again, in every
way that mattered. He stood on the bank of the Wobbish
River, across from the mouth of the Tippy-Canoe, panting,
laughing, gasping for air.

Only then did he realize that his hand was still dripping
blood from where he had cut himself to give pain to the
White boy. His pants and shirt were thick with it. White
man's clothing! I never needed it. He stripped it off and
flung it into the river.

A funny thing happened. The clothing didn't move. It
sat on the surface of the water, not sinking, not sliding left-
ward with the current.

How could this be? Wasn't the dream over? Wasn't he
fully awake yet?

Lolla-Wossiky closed his eye.

Immediately he saw a terrible thing and shouted in fear.
As soon as he closed his eye, he saw the black noise again,
a great sheet of it, hard and frozen. It was the river. It was
the water. It was made of death.

He opened his eye, and it was water again, but still his
clothing didn't move.

He closed his eye, and saw that where the clothing was,
light sparkled on the surface of the black. It pooled, it
shone, it dazzled. It was his own blood shining.

Now he could see that the black noise wasn't a thing. It

was nothing. Emptiness. The place where the land ended, and emptiness began; it was the edge of the world. But where his own blood sparkled, it was like a bridge across nothingness. Lolla-Wossiky knelt, his eye still closed, and reached out with his cut and still-bleeding hand, touched the water.

It was solid, warm and solid. He smeared his blood across the surface, and it made a platform. He crawled out onto the platform. It was smooth and hard as ice, only warm, welcoming.

He opened his eye. It was a river again, except that under him it was solid. Wherever his blood had touched, the water was hard and smooth.

He crawled out to where the clothing was, slid it ahead of him. All the way out to the middle of the river he crawled, and beyond the middle, making a thin, glowing bridge of blood to the other side.

What he was doing was impossible. The boy had done much more than heal him. He had changed the order of things. It was frightening and wonderful. Lolla-Wossiky looked down into the water between his hands. His own one-eyed reflection looked back up at him. Then he closed his eye, and a whole new vision leapt to view.

He saw himself standing in a clearing, speaking to a hundred Red men, a thousand, from every tribe. He saw them build a city of lodges, a thousand, five thousand, ten thousand Reds, all of them strong and whole, free of the White man's likker, the White man's hate. In his vision they called him the Prophet, but he insisted that he was not that at all. He was only the door, the open door. Step through, he said, and be strong, one people, one land.

The door. Tenskwa-Tawa.

In his vision, his mother's face appeared, and she said that word to him. Tenskwa-Tawa. It is your name now, for the dreamer is awake.

And more, he saw much more that night, staring downward into the solid water of the Wobbish River, he saw so much that he could never tell it all; in that hour on the water he saw the whole history of the land, the life of every man and woman, White or Red or Black, who ever set foot on it. He saw the beginning and he saw the end. Great wars and petty cruelties, all the murderings of men, all the sins; but also all the goodness, all the beauty.

And above all, a vision of the Crystal City. The city made of water as solid and as clear as glass, water that would never melt, formed into crystal towers so high that they should have cast shadows seven miles across the land. But because they were so pure and clear they cast no shadow at all, the sunlight passed unblocked through every inch and yard and mile of it. Wherever a man or woman stood, they could look deep into the crystal and see all the visions that Lolla-Wossiky saw now. Perfect understanding, that was what they had, seeing with eyes of pure sunlight and speaking with the voice of lightning.

Lolla-Wossiky, who from now on would be named Tenskwa-Tawa, did not know if he would build the Crystal City, or live in it, or even see it before he died. It was enough to do the first things that he saw in the solid water of the Wobbish River. He looked and looked until his mind couldn't see more. Then he crawled across to the far shore, climbed onto the bank, and walked until he came to the meadow he had seen in the vision.

This was where he would call the Reds together, teach them what he saw in his vision, and help them to be, not the strongest, but strong; not the largest, but large; not the freest, but free.

A CERTAIN KEG in the crotch of a certain tree. All summer it was hidden from view. But the rain still found it, and the heat of high summer, and the insects, and the teeth of salt-hungry squirrels. Wetting, drying, heating, cooling; no keg can last forever in such conditions. It split, just a little, but enough; the liquid inside seeped out, drop by drop; in a few hours the keg was empty.

It didn't matter. No one ever looked for it. No one ever missed it. No one mourned when it broke apart from ice in the winter, the fragments tumbling down the tree into the snow.

5

A SIGN

When word started spreading about a one-eyed Red man who was called the Prophet, Governor Bill Harrison laughed and said, "Why, that ain't nobody but my old friend Lolla-Wossiky. When he runs out of that likker keg he stole from me, he'll quit seeing visions."

After a little while, though, Governor Harrison took note of how much store was set by the Prophet's words, and how the Reds spoke his name as reverent as a true Christian says the name of Jesus, and it got him somewhat alarmed. So he called together all the Reds around Carthage City—it was nigh onto a whisky day, so there wasn't no shortage of audience for him—and he gave them a speech. And in that speech he said one particular thing:

"If old Lolla-Wossiky is really a Prophet, then he ought to do us a miracle, to show he's got more to him than just talk. You ought to make him cut off a hand or a foot and then put it back—that'd prove he was a prophet now, wouldn't it? Or better still, make him put out an eye and then heal it back. What's that you say? You mean he *already* had his eye put out? Well then he's ripe for a miracle, wouldn't you say? I say that as long as he's only got one eye, he ain't no prophet!"

Word of that came to the Prophet while he was teaching in a meadow that sloped gently down to the banks of the Tippy-Canoe, not a mile above where it poured into the waters of the Wobbish. It was some whisky-Reds brought that challenge, and they wasn't above mocking the Prophet and saying, "We came to see you make your eye whole."

The Prophet looked at them with his one good eye, and he said, "With this eye I see two Red men, weak and sick, slaves of likker, the kind of men who would mock me with the words of the man who killed my father." Then he closed his good eye, and he said, "With this eye I see two children of the land, whole and strong and beautiful, who love wives and children, and do good to all creatures." Then he opened his eye again and said, "Which eye is sick, and which eye sees true?" And they said to him, "Tenskwa-Tawa, you are a true prophet, and both your eyes are whole."

"Go tell White Murderer Harrison that I have performed the sign he asked for. And tell him another sign that he didn't ask for. Tell him that one day a fire will start in his own house. No man's hand will set this fire. Only rain will put out this fire, and before the fire dies, it will cut off something he loves more than a hand or a foot or an eye, and he will not have the power to restore it, either."

6

POWDER KEG

H ooch was astounded. "You mean you *don't want* the whole shipment?"

"We ain't used up what you sold us last time, Hooch," said the quartermaster. "Four barrels, that's all we want. More than we need, to tell the truth."

"I come down the river from Dekane, loaded up with likker, not stopping to sell any at the towns along the way, I make that *sacrifice* and you tell me—"

"Now, Hooch, I reckon we all know what kind of sacrifice that was." The quartermaster smirked a little. "I think you'll still recover your costs, pretty much, and if you don't, well, it just means you ain't been careful with the profits you've made off us afore."

"Who else is selling to you?"

"Nobody," said the quartermaster.

"I been coming to Carthage City for nigh on seven years now, and the last four years I've had a monopoly—"

"And if you'll pay heed, you'll remember that in the old days it used to be Reds what bought most of your likker."

Hooch looked around, walked away from the quartermaster, stood on the moist grassy ground of the riverbank. His flatboat rocked lazily on the water. There wasn't a Red

to be seen, not a one, and that was a fact. But it wasn't no
conspiracy, Hooch knew that. Reds had been slacking off
the last few times he came. Always there used to be a few
drunks, though.

He turned and shouted at the quartermaster. "You telling me there ain't no whisky-Reds left!"

"Sure there's whisky-Reds. But we ain't run out of
whisky yet. So they're all off somewhere lying around being drunk."

Hooch cussed a little. "I'm going to see the Gov about
this."

"Not today you ain't," said the quartermaster. "He's got
himself a right busy schedule."

Hooch grinned nastily. "Oh, his schedule ain't too busy
for *me*."

"It sure is, Hooch. He said it real specific."

"I reckon he might *think* his schedule is too busy, boy,
but I reckon it just ain't so."

"Suit yourself," said the quartermaster. "Want me to unload the four barrels I got here?"

"No I don't," he said. Then he shouted at his pole-boys,
most specially at that Mike Fink, cause he looked to be
the most likely to do murder if need be. "Anybody tries to
lay a hand on that whisky, I want to see four bullet holes
in their body before we chuck him in the water!"

The poleboys laughed and waved, except Mike Fink,
who just sort of screwed his face up a little tighter. That
was one mean old boy. They said you could tell which men
had ever tried to wrassle Mike Fink, cause they got no
ears. They said, if you want to get away from Fink with
one ear still on your head, you got to wait till he's chewing on your first ear and then shoot him twice to distract
him while you get away. A real good riverboy. But it made
Hooch a little nervy to think what Fink might do if Hooch
didn't have a payroll for him. Bill Harrison was going to

pay for this whole load of likker, or there'd be real trouble.

Walking into the stockade, Hooch noticed a few things. The sign was the same one Harrison put up four years ago; it was getting ratty-looking now, weathered up, but nobody changed it. Town wasn't growing either. Everything had lost that new look, and now it was plain shabby.

Not like the way things were going back in Hio Territory. What used to be little stockade towns like this were turning into real towns, with painted houses, even a few cobbled streets. Hio was booming, at least the eastern part of it, close on to Suskwahenny, and folks speculated on how it wasn't far from statehood.

But there wasn't no boom going on in Cathage City.

Hooch walked along the main street inside the stockade. Still plenty of soldiers, and they still looked to have pretty good discipline, had to give Governor Bill credit for that. But where there used to be whisky-Reds sprawled all over the place, now there was river-rat types, uglier-looking than Mike Fink, unshaved, with a whisky stink as bad as any likkered-up Red ever had. Four old buildings had been turned into saloons, too, and they were doing good business in the middle of the afternoon.

That's why, thought Hooch. That's the trouble. Carthage City's gone and turned into a river town, a saloon town. Nobody wants to live around here, with all these river rats. It's a whisky town.

But if it's a whisky town, Governor Bill ought to be buying whisky from me instead of this business about only wanting four barrels.

"You can wait if you want, Mr. Palmer, but the Governor won't see you today."

Hooch sat on the bench outside Harrison's office. He noticed that Harrison had switched offices with his adjutant. Gave up his nice big office in exchange for what? Smaller space, but—all interior walls. No windows. Now, that meant something. That meant Harrison didn't like having people look in on him. Maybe he was even afraid of getting himself killed.

Hooch sat there for two hours, watching soldiers come in and out. He tried not to get mad. Harrison did this now and then, making somebody sit around and wait so by the time they got in they was so upset they couldn't think straight. And sometimes he did it so a body'd get in a huff and go away. Or start to feeling small and unimportant, so Harrison could do some bullying. Hooch knew all this, so he tried to stay calm. But when it got on to evening, and the soldiers started changing shifts and going off duty, it was more than he could stand.

"What do you think you're doing?" he demanded of the corporal who sat at the front desk.

"Going off duty," said the corporal.

"But I'm still here," said Hooch.

"You can go off duty too, if you like," said the corporal.

That smart-mouthed answer was like a slap in the face. Time was these boys all tried to suck up to Hooch Palmer. Times were changing too fast. Hooch didn't like it at all. "I could buy your old mother and sell her at a profit," said Hooch.

That got to him. That corporal didn't look bored no more. But he didn't let himself haul off and take a swing, neither. Just stood there, more or less at attention, and said, "Mr. Palmer, you can wait here all night and wait here all day tomorrow, and you ain't going to get in to see His Excellency the Governor. And you just sitting here waiting all day is proof you're just too plain dumb to catch on to how things are."

So it was Hooch lost his temper and took a swing. Well, not a swing exactly. More like a kick, cause Hooch never did learn no rules about fighting like a gentleman. His idea of a duel was to wait behind a rock for his enemy to pass by, shoot him in the back, and run like hell. So that corporal got Hooch's big old boot in his knee, which bent his leg backward in a way it wasn't meant to go. That corporal screamed bloody murder, which he had a right to, and not just from the pain—after a kick like that, his leg would never be any good again. Hooch probably shouldn't've kicked him there, he knew, but that boy was so snooty. Practically begged for it.

Trouble was, the corporal wasn't exactly alone. First yelp he made, all of a sudden there was a sergeant and four soldiers, bayonets at the ready, popping right out of the Governor's office and looking mad as hornets. The sergeant ordered two of his boys to carry the corporal to the infirmary. The others put Hooch under arrest. But it wasn't gentlemanly like that last time, four years before. This time the butts of their muskets got bumped into Hooch's body in a few places, sort of accidentally, and Hooch had him some boot prints in various places on his clothes, can't say how they got there. He ended up locked in a jail cell—no storage room this time. They left him with his clothes and a lot of pain.

No doubt about it. Things had changed around here.

That night six other men were put in lock-up, three of them drunks, three for brawling. Not one was Red. Hooch listened to them talking. It's not like any of them was particularly bright, but Hooch couldn't believe that they didn't talk about beating up no Reds, or making fun with some of them or something. It was like Reds had practically disappeared from the vicinity.

Well, maybe that was true. Maybe the Reds had all took off, but wasn't that what Governor Harrison hoped for? With the Reds gone, why wasn't Carthage City prosperous, full of White settlers?

The only inkling Hooch got was something one of the brawlers said. "I reckon I'm broke till tax season." The others whooped and hollered a little. "I got to say I don't mind government service, but it sure ain't steady work."

Hooch knew better than to ask them what they meant. No need to call attention to himself. He sure didn't want word getting around about how he looked all beat up the night he spent in jail. That kind of idea starts spreading and pretty soon everybody thinks he can beat a body up, and Hooch didn't reckon to start all over as a common street brawler, not at his age.

In the morning the soldiers came for him. Different ones, and this time they wasn't so careless with their feet and their musket butts. They just marched Hooch on out of the jail and now, finally, he got to see Bill Harrison.

But not in his office. It was in his own Governor's mansion, in a cellar room. And the way they got there was peculiar. The soldiers—must have been a dozen of them—just marched along behind the house, when all of a sudden one of them dashed over, flung up the cellar door, and two others half dragged Hooch down the steps. Cellar door slammed shut almost before their heads were clear of it, and in all that time the soldiers just kept right on marching, as if nothing was happening. Hooch didn't like that at all. It meant that Harrison didn't want anybody to see that Hooch was with him. Which meant this meeting could get pretty ugly, cause Harrison could deny it ever happened. Oh, the *soldiers* knew, of course, but they all knew about a certain corporal who got his knee bent the wrong way last night; they weren't about to testify on Hooch Palmer's behalf.

Harrison was his old self, though, smiling and shaking Hooch by the hand and clapping him on the shoulder. "How are you, Hooch?"

"I been better, Gov. How's your wife? And that little boy of yours?"

"She's healthy as you could hope for, a refined lady like her being out here on the frontier. And my little boy, he's quite a soldier, we even stitched him up a little uniform, you should see him strutting on parade."

"It's talk like that makes me think I ought to take a wife someday."

"I heartily recommend it. Oh, here, Hooch, what am I thinking of? You set down, set down right there."

Hooch sat. "Thanks, Bill."

Harrison nodded, satisfied. "It's good to see you, it's been so long."

"Wisht I'd've seen you yesterday," said Hooch.

Harrison smiled ruefully. "Well, I get busy. Didn't my boys tell you I had a full-up schedule?"

"Schedule never used to be full for *me*, Bill."

"You know how it gets sometimes. Real busy, and what can I do about it?"

Hooch shook his head. "Now, Bill, we've lied to each other just about long enough, I think. What happened was part of a plan, and it wasn't *my* plan."

"What are you talking about, Hooch?"

"I'm saying maybe that corporal didn't want his leg broke, but I have a feeling his job was to get me swinging at him."

"His job was to see that nobody disturbed me unless they were on my schedule, Hooch. That's the only plan I know about." Harrison looked sad. "Hooch, I got to tell you, this is real ugly. Assaulting an officer of the U.S. Army."

"A corporal ain't no officer, Bill."

"I only wish I could ship you back to Suskwahenny for trial, Hooch. They got lawyers there, and juries, and so on. But the trial has to be *here*, and juries around here ain't too partial to folks who go around breaking corporals' knees."

"Suppose you stop the threats and tell me what you really want?"

"Want? I ain't asking for favors, Hooch. Just concerned about a friend of mine who's got himself in trouble with the law."

"It must be something real sickening or you'd bribe me to do it instead of trying to strong-arm me. It must be something that you think I wouldn't be willing to do unless you scare me to death, and I keep trying to imagine what *you* think is so bad that you think I wouldn't do it. It ain't much of a list, Bill."

Harrison shook his head. "Hooch, you got me wrong. Just plain wrong."

"This town is dying, Bill," said Hooch. "Things ain't working out like you planned. And I think it's cause you done some real dumb things. I think the Reds started going away—or maybe they all died off—and you made the stupid mistake of trying to make up for all that lost likker income by bringing in the scum of the earth, the worst kind of White man, the river rats who spent the night in jail with me. You've used them to collect taxes, right? Farmers don't like taxes. They specially don't like taxes when they're collected by scum like this."

Harrison poured himself three fingers of whisky in a tumbler and drank off half of it in a single gulp.

"So you been losing your whisky-Reds, and you been losing your White farmers, and all you got left is your soldiers, the river rats, and whatever money you can steal from the United States Army appropriation for peace-keeping in the west."

Harrison drank the rest of the whisky and belched.

"What that means is you've been unlucky and you've

been stupid, and somehow you think you can make me get you out of it."

Harrison poured another three fingers into the glass. But instead of drinking it, he hauled off and threw it into Hooch's face. The whisky splashed in his eyes, the tumbler bounced off his forehead, and Hooch found himself rolling on the floor trying to dig the alcohol out of his eyes.

A while later, with a wet cloth pressed against his forehead, Hooch was sitting in the chair again, acting a lot more meek and reasonable. But that was because he knew Harrison had a flush and his own hand was just two pair. Get out of here alive and then just see what comes next, right?

"I wasn't stupid," Harrison said.

No, you're the smartest governor Carthage ever had, I'm surprised you ain't King. That's what Hooch *would've* said. But he was keeping his mouth shut.

"It was that Prophet. That Red up north. Building his Prophetstown right across the Wobbish from Vigor Church—you can't tell me that's just a coincidence. It's Armor-of-God, that's what it is, trying to take the state of Wobbish away from me. Using a *Red* to do it, too. I knew that a lot of Reds were going north, everybody knew that, but I still had me my whisky-Reds, them as hadn't died off. And with fewer Reds around here—especially the Shaw-Nee, when they left—well, I thought I'd get more White settlers. And you're wrong about my tax collectors. They didn't run the White settlers off. It was Ta-Kumsaw."

"I thought it was the Prophet."

"Don't get smart with me, Hooch, I don't have much patience these days."

Why didn't you warn me before you threw the glass? No, no, don't say nothing to make him mad. "Sorry, Bill."

"Ta-Kumsaw's been real smart. He doesn't kill White

folks. He just shows up at their farms with fifty Shaw-Nee. Doesn't shoot anybody, but when you got fifty painted-up warriors all around your house, these White folks didn't exactly figure it was smart to start shooting. So the White farmers watched while the Shaw-Nee opened every gate, every stable, every coop. Let them animals go on out. Horses, pigs, milk cows, chickens. Just like Noah bringing beasts into the ark, the Shaw-Nee walk into the woods and the animals trot on right behind. Just like that. Never see them again."

"You can't tell me they never round up at least some of their stock."

"All gone. Never find even their tracks. Never even a feather from a chicken. That's what run the White farmers off, is knowing that any day, all their animals can disappear."

"Shaw-Nee eating them or something? Ain't no chicken smart enough to live long in the woods. It's just Christmastime for foxes, that's all it is."

"How should I know? White folks come to me, they say, Get our animals back, or kill the Reds what took them. But my soldiers, my scouts, nobody can find where Ta-Kumsaw's people are. No villages at all! I tried raiding a Caska-Skeeaw village up the Little My-Ammy, but all that did was convince more Reds to leave, didn't even slow down what Ta-Kumsaw was doing."

Hooch could imagine what that raid on the Caska-Skeeaw village was like. Old men, women, children, their corpses shot up and half-burnt—Hooch knew how Harrison dealt with Reds.

"And then last month, here comes the Prophet. I knew he was coming—even the whisky-Reds couldn't talk about nothing else. Prophet's coming. Got to go see the Prophet. Well, I tried to find out where he was going to be, where he was going to give a speech, I even had some of my tame

Reds try to find out for me, but no dice, Hooch. Not a clue. Nobody knew. Just one day the word went through the whole town, Prophet's here. Where? Just come on, Prophet's here. No one ever said where. I swear these Reds can talk without talking, if you know what I mean."

"Bill, tell me you had spies there, or I'll start to thinking you lost your touch."

"Spies? I went myself, how's that? And do you know how? Ta-Kumsaw sent me an invitation, if that don't beat all. No soldiers, no guns, just me."

"And you *went?* He could've captured you and—"

"He gave me his word. Ta-Kumsaw may be a Red, but he keeps his word."

Hooch thought that was kind of funny. Harrison, the man who prided himself on never keeping a promise to a Red man, but he still counted on Ta-Kumsaw keeping a promise to him. Well, he got back alive, didn't he? So Ta-Kumsaw was as good as his word.

"I went there. Must've been every Red in the whole My-Ammy country there. Must've been ten thousand. Squatting around in this old abandoned cornfield—there's plenty of them in these parts, you can bet, thanks to Ta-Kumsaw. If I'd had my two cannon there and a hundred soldiers, I could've ended the whole Red problem, then and there."

"Too bad you didn't," said Hooch.

"Ta-Kumsaw wanted me to sit right up front, but I wouldn't. I hung back and I listened. The Prophet got up, stood on an old stump in the field, and he talked and talked and talked."

"You understand any of it? I mean, you don't talk Shaw-Nee."

"He was talking English, Hooch. Too many different tribes there, the only language they all knew was English. Oh, sometimes he talked in that Red gibberish, but there was plenty of English. Talking about the destiny of the Red

man. Stay pure from White contamination. Live all together and fill up a part of the land so the White man will
have his place and the Red man will have *his*. Build a
city—a crystal city, he said, it sounded real pretty except
these Reds can't even build a proper shed, I hate to think
how they'd do at building a city out of glass! But most of
all, he said, Don't drink likker. Not a drop. Give it up, stay
away from it. Likker is the chain of the White man, the
chain and the whip, the chain and the whip and the knife.
First he'll catch you, then he'll whip you, then he'll kill
you, likker will, and when the White man's killed you with
his whisky, he'll come in and steal your land, destroy it,
make it unfit, dead, useless."

"Sounds like he made a real impression on you, Bill,"
said Hooch. "Sounds like you memorized the speech he
gave."

"Memorized? He talked for three straight hours. Talked
about visions of the past, visions of the future. Talked
about—oh, Hooch, it was *crazy* stuff, but those Reds were
drinking it up like, like—"

"Whisky."

"Like whisky except it was *instead* of whisky. They all
went with him. Pretty near all of them, anyway. Only ones
left are a few whisky-Reds that're bound to die soon. And
of course my tame Reds, but that's different. And some
wild Reds across the Hio."

"Went with him where?"

"Prophetstown! That's what kills me, Hooch. They all
go up to Prophetstown, or thereabouts, right across the
river from Vigor Church. And that's exactly where all the
Whites are going! Well, not all to Vigor Church, but up
into the lands where Armor-of-Hell Weaver has his maps.
They're in cahoots, Hooch, I promise you that. Ta-Kumsaw,
Armor-of-God Weaver, and the Prophet."

"Sounds like."

"The worst thing is I had that Prophet here in my own office must be a thousand times, I could have killed that boy and saved myself more trouble—but you never know, do you?"

"You know this Prophet?"

"You mean you *don't* know who it is?"

"I don't know that many Reds by name, Bill."

"How about if I tell you that he's only got one eye?"

"You ain't saying it's Lolla-Wossiky!"

"Reckon so."

"That one-eyed drunk?"

"God's own truth, Hooch. Calls himself Tenskwa-Tawa now. It means 'the open door' or something. I'd like to shut that door. I *should've* killed him when I had the chance. But I figured when he ran off—he ran off, you know, stole a keg and took off into the woods—"

"I was here that night, I helped chase him."

"Well when he didn't come back, I figured he probably drank himself to death off that keg. But there he is telling Reds how he used to have to drink all the time, but God sent him visions and he's never had another drink."

"Send me visions, I'd give up drinking, too."

Harrison took another swallow of whisky. From the jug, this time, since the tumbler was on the floor in the corner of the room. "You see my problem, Hooch."

"I see you got lots of problems, Bill, and I don't know how any of them has a thing to do with me, except you weren't joking when you had the quartermaster tell me you only wanted four barrels."

"Oh, it's got more to do with you than that, count on it, Hooch. More than that. Because I ain't beat. The Prophet's took away all my whisky-Reds, and Ta-Kumsaw's got my White citizens scared, but I ain't quitting."

"No, you're no quitter," said Hooch. You're a slimy sneaky snake of a man, but you're no quitter. Didn't *say* that, of course, cause Harrison was bound to take it wrong—but to Hooch, it was all praise. His kind of man.

"It's Ta-Kumsaw and the Prophet, simple as that. I got to kill them. No, no, I take it back. I got to *beat* them and kill them. I got to take them on and make them both look like fools and *then* kill them."

"Good idea. I'll handle the betting on it."

"I bet you would. Stand there taking bets. Well, I can't just take my soldiers up north to Vigor Church and wipe out Prophetstown, cause Armor-of-God would fight me every step of the way, probably get the army detachment at Fort Wayne to back him up. Probably get my commission stripped or something. So I've got to arrange things so the people in Vigor Church, all along the Wobbish, they all beg me to come up and get rid of them Reds."

Now, at last, Hooch understood what this was all about. "You want a provocation."

"That's my boy, Hooch. That's my boy. I want some Reds to go up north and make some real trouble, and *tell* everybody that Ta-Kumsaw and the Prophet told them to do it. Blame it all on them."

Hooch nodded. "I see. It couldn't be just running off their cows or nothing like that. No, the only thing that'll get those people up north screaming for Red blood is something real ugly. Like capturing children and torturing them to death and then signing Ta-Kumsaw's name on them and leaving them where they'll be found. Something like that."

"Well, I wouldn't go so far as to tell anybody to do something awful like *that,* Hooch. In fact I don't reckon I'd give them specific instructions at all. Just tell them to do something that'd rile up the Whites up north, and then spread the word that Ta-Kumsaw ordered it."

"But you wouldn't be surprised if it turned out to be rape and torture."

"I wouldn't want them to touch any White women, Hooch. That's out of line."

"Oh, that's right, pure truth," said Hooch. "So it's definitely torturing children. *Boy* children."

"Like I said, I wouldn't ever tell somebody to do a thing like that."

Hooch nodded a little, his eyes closed. Harrison might not tell somebody to do it, but he sure wasn't telling him not to do it, either. "And of course it couldn't be any Reds from around here, could it, Bill, cause they're all gone, and your tame Reds are the most worthless scum that ever lived on the face of the earth."

"Pretty much, that's true."

"So you need Reds from south of the river. Reds who still haven't heard the Prophet's preaching, so they still want likker. Reds who still have brains enough to do the job right. Reds who have the blood thirst to kill children real slow. And you need my cargo as a bribe."

"Reckon so, Hooch."

"You got it, Bill. Dismiss charges against me, and you got all my likker free. Just give me enough money to pay off my poleboys so they don't knife me on the way home, I hope that ain't too much to ask."

"Now, Hooch, you know that ain't all I need."

"But Bill, that's all I'll do."

"I can't be the one to go ask them, Hooch. I can't be the one to go tell them Cree-Eks or Choc-Taws what I need done. It's got to be somebody else, somebody who if it gets found out I can say, I never told him to do that. He used his own whisky to do it, I didn't have any idea."

"Bill, I understand you, but you guessed right from the start. You actually found something so low that I won't be part of it."

Harrison glowered at him. "Assaulting an officer is a

hanging offense in this fort, Hooch. Didn't I make that clear?"

"Bill, I've lied, cheated, and sometimes killed to get ahead in the world. But one thing I've never done is bribe somebody to go steal some mother's children and torture them to death. I honestly never did that, and I honestly never will."

Harrison studied Hooch's face and saw that it was true. "Well, don't that beat all. There's actually a sin so bad that Hooch Palmer won't do it, even if he dies because of it."

"You won't kill me, Bill."

"Oh yes I will, Hooch. There's two reasons I will. First, you gave me the wrong answer to my request. And second, you heard my request in the first place. You're a dead man, Hooch."

"Fine with me," said Hooch. "Make it a real scratchy rope, too. A good and tall gallows, with a twenty-foot drop. I want a hanging that folks'll remember for a long time."

"You'll get a tree limb and we'll raise the rope up slow, so you strangle instead of breaking your neck."

"Just so it's memorable," said Hooch.

Harrison called in some soldiers and had them take Hooch back to jail. This time they did a little kicking and poking, so Hooch had a whole new batch of bruises, and maybe a broken rib.

He also didn't have much time.

So he lay down real calm on the floor of the jail. The drunks were gone, but the three brawlers were still there, using all the cots; the floor was all that was available. Hooch didn't much care. He knew Harrison would give him an hour or two to think about it, then take him out and put the rope around his neck and kill him. He might pretend to give him one last chance, of course, but he wouldn't mean it, because now he wouldn't trust Hooch.

Hooch had told him no, and so he'd never trust him to carry out the assignment if he let him go.

Well, Hooch planned to use the time wisely. He started out pretty simply. He closed his eyes and let some heat build up inside him. A spark. And then he sent that spark outside himself. It was like what doodlebugs said they did, sending out their bug to go searching underground and see what it could see. He set his spark to searching and pretty soon he found what he was looking for. Governor Bill's own house. His spark was too far away by now for him to find some particular spot in the house. And his aim couldn't be too tight. So instead he just pumped all his hate and rage and pain into the spark, built it hotter and hotter and hotter. He let himself go like he never done before in his life. And he kept pushing it and pushing it until he started hearing that most welcome sound.

"Fire! Fire!" The shouts came from outside, from far away, but more and more people took up the cry. Gunshots went off—distress signals.

The three brawlers heard it, too. One of them stepped on Hooch where he was lying on the floor, they were in such a hurry. Stood at the door, they did, rattling and shouting at the guard. "Let us out! Don't go trying to fight that fire without letting us out first! Don't let us die in here!"

Hooch hardly noticed the man stepping on him, he already hurt so bad. Instead he just lay there, using his spark again, only this time heating up the metal inside the lock of the jail door. Now his aim was tight and his spark could get much hotter.

The guard came in and put his key in the lock, turned it, opened the door. "You boys can come on out," he said. "Sergeant said so, we need you to help with the fire brigade."

Hooch struggled to his feet, but the guard straight-armed him and shoved him back into the cell. Hooch wasn't surprised. But he made the spark go hotter yet, so hot that now the iron of the lock melted inside. It even glowed red a little. The guard slammed the door shut and went to turn the key. By now it was so hot that it burned his hand. He cussed and went for his shirttail to try and grab the key, but Hooch kicked the door open, knocking the guard down. He stomped the guard in the face and kicked his head, which probably broke his neck, but Hooch didn't think of that as murder. He thought of it as justice, cause the guard had been all set to leave him locked in his cell to burn to death.

Hooch walked on out of the jail. Nobody paid him much attention. He couldn't see the mansion from here, but he could see the smoke rising. Sky was low and grey. Probably it'd rain before it burned the stockade. Hooch sure hoped not, though. Hoped the whole place burned to the ground. It was one thing to want to kill off Reds, that was fine with Hooch, he and Harrison saw eye to eye on that. Kill them with likker if you can, bullets if you can't. But you don't go killing White folks, you don't go hiring Reds to torture White babies. Maybe to Harrison it was all part of the same thing. Maybe to him it was like White soldiers having to die in a war with Reds, only the soldiers'd just be a little younger. All in a good cause, right? Maybe Harrison could think that way, but Hooch couldn't. It actually took him by surprise, to tell the truth. He was more like Andrew Jackson than he ever supposed. He had a line he wouldn't cross. He drew it in a different place than old Hickory did, but still, he had a line, and he'd die before he crossed it.

Of course he didn't reckon to die if he could help it. He couldn't go out the stockade gate, cause the bucket line to the river would go through there and he'd be seen. But it was easy enough to climb up to the parapet. The soldiers weren't exactly keeping a lookout. He clambered over the wall and dropped down outside the fort. Nobody saw him. He walked the ten yards into the woods, then made his way—slowly, cause his ribs hurt pretty bad and he was a little weak from so much sparking, it took something out of him—through the woods to the riverbank.

He came out of the woods on the far side of the open area around the wharf. There was his flatboat, still loaded up with all his kegs. And his poleboys standing around, watching the bucket brigade dipping into the river some thirty yards farther upstream. It didn't surprise Hooch a bit that his poleboys weren't over there helping with the buckets. They weren't exactly the public-spirited type.

Hooch walked out onto the wharf, beckoning for the poleboys to come join him. He jumped down to the flatboat; stumbled a little, from being weak and hurting. He turned around to tell his boys what was happening, why they had to push off, but they hadn't followed. They just stood there on the bank, looking at him. He beckoned again, but they didn't make a move to come.

Well, then, he'd go without them. He was even moving toward the rope, to cast off and pole himself away, when he realized that not all the poleboys were on shore. No, there was one missing. And he knew right where that missing boy would be. Right there on the flatboat, standing right behind him, reaching out his hands—

Mike Fink wasn't the knifing kind. Oh, he'd knife you if he had to, but he'd rather kill with his bare hands. He used to say something about killing with a knife, some comparison with whores and a broomstick. Anyway, that's why Hooch knew that it wouldn't be a knife. That it wouldn't be quick. Harrison must've known Hooch might get away, so he bought off Mike Fink, and now Fink would kill him sure.

Sure, but slow. And slow gave Hooch time. Time to make sure he didn't die alone.

So as the fingers closed around his throat and cinched tight, much tighter than Hooch ever imagined, clamping him so he thought his head would get wrung right off, he forced himself to make his spark go, to find that keg, that one place, he knew right where the place was on the flatboat, to hot up that keg, as hot as he could, hotter, hotter—

And he waited for the explosion, waited and waited, but it never came. It felt like Fink's fingers had pressed through the front of his throat clear to the spine, and he felt all his muscles just give way, he felt himself kicking, his lungs heaving to try to suck in air that just wouldn't come, but he kept his spark going till the last second, waiting for the gunpowder keg to blow.

Then he died.

Mike Fink hung on to him for another whole minute after he was dead, maybe just cause he liked the feel of a dead man dangling from his hands. Hard to tell with Mike Fink. Some folks said he was as nice a man as you could hope to find, when he was in the mood. Sure that's what Mike thought of himself. He *liked* to be nice and have friends and drink real sociable. But when it came to killing, well, he liked that too.

But you can't just hang on to a dead body forever. For one thing, somebody's going to start complaining about it or maybe puking. So he shoved Hooch's body off into the water.

"Smoke," said one of the poleboys, pointing.

Sure enough, there was smoke coming out of the middle of the pile of kegs.

"It's the gunpowder keg!" shouted one of them.

Well, the poleboys took off running to get away from the explosion, but Mike Fink just laughed and laughed. He walked over and started unloading kegs, hoisting them onto the wharf, unloading them until he got to the middle where there was a keg with a fuse coming out of it. He didn't pick *that* one up with his hands, though. He tipped it over with his heel, then kind of rolled it along till it was on the open area around the edge of the boat.

By now the poleboys had come back to see what was going on, since it looked pretty much like Mike Fink wasn't going to blow up after all. "Hatchet," Mike called out, and one of the boys tossed him the one he kept in a sheath at his belt. It took a few good whacks, but the top finally sprung off the keg, and a whole cloud of steam came up. The water inside was so hot it was still boiling.

"You mean it wasn't gunpowder after all?" asked of the boys. Not a bright one, but then not many rivermen was famous for brains.

"Oh, it was gunpowder when he set it down here," said Mike. "Back in Suskwahenny. But you don't think Mike Fink'd go all the way down the Hio River on the same flatboat with a keg of powder with a fuse coming out of it, do you?"

Then Mike jumped off the boat up onto the wharf and bellowed at the top of his voice, so loud that they heard him clear inside the fort, so loud that the bucket brigade stopped long enough to listen.

"My name is Mike Fink, boys, and I'm the meanest low-down son of an alligator that ever bit off the head of a buffalo! I eat growed men's ears for breakfast and bears' ears for supper, and when I'm thirsty I can drink enough to stop Niagara from falling. When I piss folks get on flatboats and float downstream for fifty mile, and when I fart the Frenchmen catch the air in bottles and sell it for perfume. I'm Mike Fink, and this my flatboat, and if you miserable little pukes ever put that fire out, there's a free pint of whisky in it for every one of you!"

Then Mike Fink led the poleboys over and joined the bucket brigade, and they slowed the fire down until the rain came and put it out.

414 Orson Scott Card

That night, with all the soldiers drinking and singing, Mike Fink was sitting up sober as you please, feeling pretty good about finally being in the likker business for himself. Only one of the poleboys was with him now, the youngest fellow, who kind of looked up to Fink. The boy was setting there playing with the fuse that used to go into a gunpowder keg.

"This fuse wasn't lit," said the poleboy.

"No, I reckon not," said Mike Fink.

"Well, how'd the water get to boiling then?"

"Reckon Hooch had a few tricks up his sleeve. Reckon Hooch had something to do with the fire in the fort."

"You knew that, didn't you?"

Fink shook his head. "Nope, just lucky. I'm just plain lucky. I just get a feeling about things, like I had a feeling about that gunpowder keg, and I just do what I feel like doing."

"You mean like a knack?"

In answer, Fink stood up and pulled down his trousers. There on his left buttock was a sprawl of a tattoo, six-sided and dangerous-looking. "My mama had that poked on when I wasn't a month old. Said that'd keep me safe so I'd live out my whole natural life." He turned and showed the boy the other buttock. "And that one she said was to help me make my fortune. I didn't know how it'd work, and she died without telling me, but as near as I can tell it makes me lucky. Makes it so I just kind of know what I ought to do." He grinned. "Got me a flatboat now, and a cargo of whisky, don't I?"

"Is the Governor really going to give you a medal for killing Hooch?"

"Well, for catching him, anyhow, looks like."

"I don't guess the Gov looked too bothered that old Hooch was dead, though."

"Nope," said Fink. "No, I reckon not. No, me and the

Gov, we're good friends now. He says he's got some things need doing, that only a man like me can do."

The poleboy looked at him with adoration in his eighteen-year-old eyes. "Can I help you? Can I come with you?"

"You ever been in a fight?"

"A lot of fights!"

"You ever bit off an ear?"

"No, but I gouged out a man's eye once."

"Eyes are easy. Eyes are soft."

"And I butted a man's head so he lost five teeth."

Fink considered that for a few seconds. Then he grinned and nodded. "Sure, you come along with me, boy. By the time I'm through, there ain't a man woman or child within a hundred mile of this river who won't know my name. Do you doubt that, boy?"

The boy didn't doubt it.

In the morning, Mike Fink and his crew pushed off for the south bank of the Hio, loaded with a wagon, some mules, and eight kegs of whisky. Bound to do a little trading with the Reds.

In the afternoon, Governor William Harrison buried the charred remains of his second wife and their little boy, who had the misfortune of being in the nursery together, dressing the boy in his little parade uniform, when the room burst into flames.

A fire in his own house, set by no hand, which cut off what he loved the most, and no power on earth could bring them back.

7

CAPTIVES

Alvin Junior never felt small except when he was setting on the back of a big old horse. Not to say he wasn't a good rider—he and horses got along pretty good, they never throwing him and he never whipping them. It's just that his legs stuck way out on both sides, and since he was riding with a saddle on this trip, the stirrup had to be hiked up so far they punched new holes in the leather so he could ride. Al was looking forward to the day he growed up to be man-size. Other folks might tell him he was right big for his age, but that didn't amount to nothing in Alvin's opinion. When your age is ten, big for your age ain't nothing like being big.

"I don't like it," said Faith Miller. "Don't like sending my boys off in the middle of all these Red troubles."

Mother always worried, but she had good cause. All his life Al was kind of clumsy, always having accidents. Things turned out fine in the end, but it was nip and tuck a lot of the time. Worst was a few months ago, when the new millstone fell on his leg and gave it a real ugly break. It looked like he was going to die, and he pretty much expected to himself. Would have, too. Surely would have. Even though he knew he had the power to heal himself.

Ever since the Shining Man came to him in his room that night when he was six, Al had never used his knack to help himself. Cutting stone for his father, that he could do, cause it would help everybody. He'd run his fingers on the stone, get the feel of it, find the hidden places in the stone where it could break, and then set it all in order, just make it go that way; and the stone would come out, just right, just the way he asked. But never for his own good.

Then with his leg broke and the skin tore up, everybody knowed he was bound to die. And Al never would've used his knack for fixing things to heal himself, never would've tried, except old Taleswapper was there. Taleswapper asked him, why don't you fix your leg yourself? And so Al told him what he never told a soul before, about the Shining Man. Taleswapper believed him, too, didn't think he was crazy or dreaming. He made Al think back, think real hard, and remember what the Shining Man said. And when Al remembered, it come to him that it was Al himself who said that about never doing it for himself. The Shining Man just said, "Make all things whole."

Make all things whole. Well, wasn't his leg part of "all things"? So he fixed it, best he could. There was a lot more to it than that, but all in all he used his own power, with the help of his family, to heal himself. That's why he was alive.

But during those days he looked death in the face and he wasn't as scared of it as he thought he'd be. Lying there with death seeping through his bone, he began to feel like his body was just a kind of lean-to, a shelter he lived in during bad weather till his house was built. Like them shanty cabins new folks built till they could get a log house set up proper. And if he died, it wouldn't be awful at all. Just different, and maybe better.

So when his ma went on and on about the Reds and how dangerous it was and how they might get killed, he didn't give no heed. Not because he thought that she was wrong, but because he didn't much care whether he died or not.

Well, no, that wasn't quite so. He had a lot of things to do, though he didn't know yet what they were, and so he'd be *annoyed* about dying. He sure didn't *plan* to die. It just didn't fill him up with fear like it did some folks.

Al's big brother Measure was trying to get Ma to ease off and not get herself all worked up. "We'll be all right, Mama," said Measure. "All the trouble's down south, and we'll be on good roads all the way."

"Folks disappear every week on those good roads," she said. "Those French up in Detroit are buying scalps, they don't never let up on that, don't matter one bit what Ta-Kumsaw and his savages are doing, it only takes one arrow to kill you—"

"Ma," said Measure. "If you're a-scared of Reds getting us, you ought to *want* us to go. I mean there's ten thousand Reds at *least* living in Prophetstown right across the river. It's the biggest city west of Philadelphia right now, and every one of them is a Red. We're getting *away* from Reds by going east—"

"That one-eyed Prophet don't worry me," she said. "He never talks about killing. I just think you shouldn't—"

"It don't matter what you think," said Pa.

Ma turned to face him. He'd been slopping the hogs out back, but now he was come around to say good-bye. "Don't you tell me it don't matter what I—"

"It don't matter what I think, neither," said Pa. "It don't matter what anybody thinks, and you know it."

"Then I don't see why the good Lord gave us brains, then, if that's how things are, Alvin Miller!"

"Al's going east to Hatrack River to be an apprentice blacksmith," said Pa. "I'll miss him, you'll miss him, everybody except maybe Reverend Thrower's going to miss the boy, but the papers are signed and Al Junior is going.

So instead of jawing how you don't want them to go, kiss the boys good-bye and wave them off."

If Pa'd been milk she would've curdled him on the spot, she gave him such a look. "I'll kiss my boys, and I'll wave them off," she said. "I don't need you to tell me that. I don't need you to tell me anything."

"I reckon not," said Pa. "But I'll tell you anyway, and I reckon you'll return the favor, just like you always done." He reached up a hand to shake with Measure, saying good-bye like a man does. "You get him there safe and come right back," he told Measure.

"You know I will," said Measure.

"Your ma's right, it's dangerous every step of the way, so keep your eyes open. We named you right, you got such keen eyes, boy, so use them."

"I will, Pa."

Ma said her good-bye to Measure while Pa came on over to Al. He gave Al a good stinging slap on the leg and shook *his* hand, too, and that felt good, Pa treating him like a man, just like Measure. Maybe if Al wasn't sitting up on a horse, Pa would've roughed his hair like a little boy, but then maybe he wouldn't have, either, and it still felt grown-up, all the same.

"I ain't scared of the Reds," said Al. He spoke real soft, so Ma wouldn't hear. "But I sure wish I didn't have to go."

"I know it, Al," said Pa. "But you got to. For your own good."

Then Pa got that faraway sad look on his face, which Al Junior had seen before more than once, and never understood. Pa was a strange man. It took Al a long time to realize that, since for the longest time while Al was just little, Pa was Pa, and he didn't try to understand him.

Now Al was getting older, and he began to compare his father to the other men around. To Armor-of-God Weaver, for instance, the most important man in town, always talking about peace with the Red man, sharing the land with him, mapping out Red lands and White lands— everybody listened to him with respect. Nobody listened to Pa that way, considering his words real serious, maybe arguing a little, but knowing that what he said was *important.* And Reverend Thrower, with his highfalutin educated way of talking, shouting from his pulpit about death and resurrection and the fires of hell and the rewards of heaven, everybody listened to *him,* too. It was different from the way they listened to Armor, cause it was always about religion and so it didn't have nothing to do with little stuff like farming and chores and how folks lived. But *respect.*

When Pa talked, other folks listened to him, all right, but they just scoffed sometimes. "Oh, Alvin Miller, you just go on, don't you!" Al noticed that, and it made him mad at first. But then he realized that when folks was in trouble and needed help, they didn't go to Reverend Thrower, no sir, and they didn't go to Armor-of-God, cause neither of them knew all that much about how to solve the kind of problems folks had from time to time. Thrower might tell them how to stay out of hell, but that wasn't till they was dead, and Armor might tell them how to keep peace with the Reds, but that was politics except when it was war. When they had a quarrel about a boundary line, or didn't know what to do about a boy that always sassed his ma no matter how many lickings he got, or when the weevils got their seed corn and they didn't have nothing to plant, they come to Al Miller. And he'd say his piece, just a few words usually, and they'd go off shaking their heads and saying, "Oh, Alvin Miller, you just go on, don't you!" But then they'd go ahead and settle that boundary line and build them a stone fence there; and they'd let their smart-mouth boy move on out of the house and take up as a hired man on a neighbor's farm; and come planting time a half-dozen folks'd come by with sacks of "spare" seed cause Al Miller mentioned they might be a little shy.

When Al Junior compared his pa to other men, he knew Pa was strange, knew Pa did things for reasons known only to himself. But he also knew that Pa could be trusted. Folks might give their respect to Armor-of-God and Reverend Philadelphia Thrower, but they *trusted* Al Miller.

So did Al Junior. Trusted his pa. Even though he didn't want to leave home, even though having been so close to death he felt like apprenticing and suchlike was a waste of time—what did it matter what his trade was, would there be smiths in heaven?—still he knew that if Pa said it was right for him to go, then Al would go. The way folks always knew that if Al Miller said, "Just do this and it'll work out," why, they should do the thing he said, and it'd work out like he said.

He had told Pa he didn't want to go; Pa had said, Go anyway, it's for your own good. That's all Alvin Junior needed to hear. He nodded his head and did what Pa said, not cause he had no spunk, not cause he was scared of his pa like other boys he knew. He just knew his pa well enough to trust his judgment. Simple as that.

"I'll miss you, Pa." And then he did a crazy fool thing, which if he stopped to think about it he never would've done. He reached down and tousled his *father's* hair. Even while he was doing it, he thought, Pa's going to slap me silly for treating him like a boy! Pa's eyebrows *did* go up, and he reached up and caught Al Junior's hand by the wrist. But then he got him a twinkle in his eye and laughed loud and said, "I reckon you can do that *once,* Son, and live."

Pa was still laughing when he stepped back to give Ma space to say her good-bye. She had tears running down her face, but she didn't have no last-minute list of *do*s and *don't*s for him, the way she had for Measure. She just kissed his hand and clung on to it, and looked him in the eye and said, "If I let you go today, I'll never see you with my natural eyes again, as long as I live."

"No, Ma, don't say that," he told her. "Nothing bad's going to happen to me."

"You just remember me," she said. "And you keep that amulet I gave you. You wear that all the time."

"What's it do?" he asked, taking it from his pocket again. "I don't know this kind."

"Never you mind, you just keep it close to you all the time."

"I will, Ma."

Measure walked his horse up beside Al Junior's. "We best be going now," he said. "We want to get to country we don't see every day before we bed down tonight."

"Don't you do that," said Pa sternly. "We arranged for you to stay with the Peachee family tonight. That's as far as you need to get in one day. Don't want you to spend a night in the open when you don't have to."

"All right, all right," said Measure, "but we at least ought to get there before supper."

"Go on then," said Ma. "Go on then, boys."

They only got a rod or so on the way before Pa came running out and caught Measure's horse by the bridle, and Al Junior's, too. "Boys, you remember! Cross rivers at the bridges. You hear me? Only at the bridges! There's bridges at every river on this road, between here and Hatrack River."

"I know, Pa," said Measure. "I helped build them all, you know."

"Use them! That's all I'm saying. And if it rains, you stop, you find a house and stop, you hear me? I don't want you out in the water."

They both pledged most solemnly not to get near anything wet. "Won't even stand downstream from the horses when they spurt," said Measure.

Pa shook a finger at him. "Don't you make light," he said.

Finally they got on their way, not looking back cause that was awful luck, and knowing that Ma and Pa went back into the house well before they was out of sight, cause it was calling for a long separation if you watched a long time when folks were leaving, and if you watched them clear out of sight it was a good chance somebody'd die before you ever saw them again. Ma took that real serious. Going inside quick like that was the last thing she'd be able to do to help protect her boys on their way.

AL AND MEASURE stopped in a stretch of woods between Hatchs' and Bjornsons' farms, where the last storm knocked down a tree half onto the road. They could get by all right, being on horseback as they were, but you don't leave a thing like that for somebody else to find. Maybe somebody in a wagon, hurrying to make home before dark on a stormy night, maybe that's who'd come by next, and find the road blocked. So they stopped and ate the lunch Ma packed for them, and then set to work with their hatchets, cutting it free from the few taut strands of wood that clung to the ragged stump. They were wishing for a saw long before they were done, but you don't carry a saw with you on a three-hundred-mile trip on horseback. A change of clothes, a hatchet, a knife, a musket for hunting, powder and lead, a length of rope, a blanket, and a few odd tokens and amulets for wardings and fendings. Much more than that and you'd have to bring a wagon or a pack horse.

After the trunk was free, they tied both horses to it and pulled it out of the way. Hard work, sweaty work, cause the horses weren't used to pulling as a team and they bothered each other. Tree kept snagging up on them, too, and they had to keep rolling it and chopping away branches. Now, Al knew he could've used his knack to change the wood of that tree inside, to make it split apart in all the right places. But that wouldn't have been right, he knew. The Shining Man wouldn't've stood for that—it would've been pure selfishness, pure laziness, and no good to anybody. So he hacked and tugged and sweated right alongside Measure. And it wasn't so bad. It was *good* work, and when it was all done it was no more than an hour. It was time well spent.

They talked somewhat during the work, of course. Some of the conversation turned on the stories about Red massacres down south. Measure was pretty skeptical. "Oh, I hear those stories, but the bloody ones are all things somebody heard from somebody else about somebody else. The folks who actually lived down there and got run out, all they ever say is that Ta-Kumsaw come and run off their pigs and chickens, that's all. Not a one ever said nothing about no arrows flying or folks getting killed."

Al, being ten years old, was more inclined to believe the stories, the bloodier the better. "Maybe when they kill somebody, they kill the whole family so nobody talks about it."

"Now you think about it, Al. That don't make sense. Ta-Kumsaw wants all the White people out of there, don't he? So he wants them scared to death, so they pack up and move, don't he? So wouldn't he leave one alive to tell about it, if he was doing massacres? Wouldn't somebody've found some *bodies,* at least?"

"Well where do the stories come from, then?"

"Armor-of-God says Harrison's telling lies, to try to get people het up against the Reds."

"Well, he couldn't very well lie about them burning down his house and his stockade. People could plain *see* if it got burnt, couldn't they? And he couldn't very well lie about it killing his wife and his little boy, could he?"

"Well of course it *did* burn, Al. But maybe it wasn't fire arrows from Ta-Kumsaw started that fire. You ever think of that?"

"Governor Harrison isn't going to burn down his own house and kill his own family just so he can get people hot against the Reds," said Al. "That's plain dumb."

And they speculated on and on about Red troubles in the south part of the Wobbish country, because that was the most important topic of conversation around, and since nobody knowed anything accurate anyway, everybody's opinion was as good as anybody else's.

Seeing how they weren't more than a half mile from two different farms, in country they'd visited four or five times a year for ten years, it never even came to mind they ought to keep their eyes open for trouble. You just don't keep too wary that close to home, not even when you're talking about Red massacres and stories about murders and torture. Fact is, though, careful or not there wasn't much they could've done. Al was coiling ropes and Measure was cinching up the saddles when all of a sudden there was about a dozen Reds around them. One minute nobody but crickets and mice and a bird here and there, the next minute Reds all painted up.

It took a few seconds even at that for them to be afraid. There was a lot of Reds in Prophetstown, and they came pretty regular to trade at Armor-of-God's store. So Alvin spoke before he even hardly looked at them. "Howdy," said Alvin.

They didn't howdy him back. They had paint all over their faces.

"These ain't no howdy Reds," said Measure softly. "They got muskets."

That made it sure these weren't no Prophetstown Reds.

The Prophet taught his followers never to use White man's weapons. A true Red didn't need to hunt with a gun, because the land knew his need, and the game would come near enough to kill with a bow. Only reason for a Red to have a gun, said the Prophet, was to be a murderer, and murdering was for White men. That's what he said. So it was plain these weren't Reds that put much store in the Prophet.

Alvin was looking one right in the face. Al must've showed his fear, cause the Red got a glint in his eye and smiled a little. The Red reached out his hand.

"Give him the rope," said Measure.

"It's our rope," said Al. As soon as he said it he knew it didn't make no sense. Al handed both ropes to him.

The Red took the coils, gentle as you please. Then he tossed one over the White boys' heads, to another Red, and the whole bunch of them set to work, stripping off the boys' outer clothes and then tying their arms behind them so tight it was pulling on their shoulder joints something painful.

"Why do they want our clothes?" Al asked.

In answer, one of the Reds slapped him hard across the face. He must've liked the sound it made, because he slapped him again. The sting of it brought tears to Al's eyes, but he didn't cry out, partly cause he was so surprised, partly cause it made him mad and he didn't want to give them no satisfaction. Slapping was an idea that caught on real good with the other Reds, cause they started in slapping Measure, too, both of the boys, again and again, till they were half-dazed and their cheeks were bleeding inside and out.

One Red babbled something, and they gave him Al's shirt. He slashed at it with his knife, and then rubbed it on Al's bleeding face. Must not have got enough blood on it, because he took his knife and slashed right across Al's forehead. The blood just gushed out, and a second later the pain hit Al and for the first time he *did* cry out. It felt like he'd been laid open right to the bone, and the blood was running down in his eyes so he couldn't see. Measure yelled for them to leave Al alone, but there wasn't no chance of that. Everybody knew that once a Red started in to cutting on you, you were bound to end up dead.

Minute Al cried out and the blood started coming, them Reds started laughing and making little hooting sounds. This bunch was out for real trouble, and Al thought back to all the stories he heard. Most famous one was probably about Dan Boone, a Pennsylvania man who tried to settle in the Crown Colonies for a while. That was back when the Cherriky were against the White man, and one day Dan Boone's boy got kidnapped. Boone wasn't a half hour behind them Reds. It was like they were playing with him. They'd stop and cut off parts of the boy's skin, or poke out an eye, something to cause bad pain and make him scream. Boone heard his boy screaming, and followed, him and his neighbors, armed with their muskets and half-mad with rage. They'd reach the place where the boy'd been tortured, and the Reds were gone, not a trace of a track in the wood, and then there'd come another scream. Twenty miles they went that day, and finally at nightfall they found the boy hanging from three different trees. They say Boone never forgot that, he could never look a Red in the eye after that without thinking on that twenty-mile day.

Al had that twenty-mile day on his mind now, too, hearing them Reds laugh, feeling the pain, just the start of the pain, knowing that whatever these Reds were after, they wanted it to start with two dead White boys, and they wouldn't mind a little noise along the way. Keep still, he told himself. Keep still.

They rubbed his slashed-up shirt on his face, and Measure's hacked up clothes, too. While they were doing that,

Al kept his mind on other things. Only time he ever tried to heal himself was that busted leg of his, and then he was lying down, resting, plenty of time to study it out, to find his way to all those small places where there was broken veins and heal them up, knit together the skin and bone. This time he was a-scared and getting pushed this way and that, not calm, not resting. But he still managed to find the biggest veins and arteries, make them close up. Last time they wiped his face on a shirt, his forehead didn't gush blood down to cover his eyes again. It was still bleeding, but just a trickle now, and Al tipped his head up so the blood would ooze on down his temples, and leave his eyes clear to see.

They hadn't cut Measure yet. He was looking at Al, and there was a sick look on Measure's face. Al knew his brother well enough to guess what he was thinking, about how Ma and Pa trusted Al into Measure's keeping, and now look how he let them down. That was crazy, to blame himself. They could've done what they were doing now at any cabin or house in the whole countryside, and weren't nobody could stop them. If Al and Measure hadn't been going off on a long trip, they might still have been on this very road at this very time anyhow. But Al couldn't say nothing like that to Measure, couldn't do much except to smile.

Smile and, as best he could, work on healing up his own wound. Making everything in his forehead go back to the way it was supposed to be. He kept at it, finding it easier and easier to do, while he watched what the Reds were doing.

They didn't talk much. They pretty much knew what to do. They got the blood-smeared clothes and tied them to the saddles. Then with a knife one of them carved the English letters for "Ta-Kumsaw" in one of the saddle seats, and "Prophet" in the other. For a second Al was surprised that he could write English, but then he saw him checking how he made the letters, comparing them to a paper he had folded up in the waistband of his loincloth. A paper.

Then, while two of them held each horse by the bridle, another Red jabbed the horse's flanks with a knife, little cuts, not all that deep, but enough to make them crazy with pain, kicking out, bucking, rearing up. The horses knocked down the Reds holding them and took off, ran away, heading—as the Reds knowed they would—on up the road toward home.

A message, that's what it was. These Reds wanted to be followed. They wanted a whole bunch of White folks to get their muskets and horses and follow. Like Daniel Boone in the story. Follow the sound of screaming. Go crazy from the sound of their children dying.

Well Alvin decided then and there that, live or die, he and Measure wouldn't let Reds make his parents hear what Daniel Boone heard. There wasn't a chance in the world of them getting away. Even if Al made the rope come apart—which he could do easy enough—there wasn't no way two White boys could outrun Reds in the forest. No, these Reds had them as long as they wanted. But Al knew ways to keep them from doing things to them. And it would be all right to do it, too, to use his knack, because it wouldn't just be for himself. It would be for his brother, and for his family, and in a funny way he knew it would be for the Reds, too, because if there was something real, if some White boys really did get tortured to death, then there'd be a war, there'd be a real knockdown-drag-out fight between Reds and Whites, and a lot of people on both sides would die. As long as he didn't kill anybody, then, it would be all right for Al to use his knack.

With the horses gone, the Reds tied thongs around Al's and Measure's necks. Then they pulled on the thongs to drag them along. Measure was a big man, taller than any of the Reds, so as they led him they made him bend over. It was hard for him to run, and the thong was real tight on him. Al was getting pulled along behind him, so he could see how Measure was being treated, could hear him choking a little. It was a simple thing for Al, though, to get inside that thong and stretch it out, stretch it and stretch it, so it was loose around Measure's neck, and long enough that Measure could run pretty much upright. It happened slow enough that the Reds didn't really notice it. But Al knew that they'd notice what he was doing soon enough.

Everybody knew that Reds didn't leave footprints. And when Reds took White captives, they usually carried them, slung by their arms and legs like dressed-out deer, so the clumsy White folks wouldn't leave no tracks. These Reds meant to be followed, then, cause they were letting Al and Measure leave tracks and traces every step they took.

But they didn't mean it to be *too* easy to find them. After they'd gone forever, it felt like—a couple of hours at least—they came to a brook and walked on upstream a ways, and then ran on another half mile or maybe a mile before they finally stopped in a clearing and built a fire.

No farms close by, but that didn't mean much. By now the horses were home with the bloody clothing and the wounds in the horses' flanks and those names carved into the saddles. By now every White man in the whole area was bringing his family in to Vigor Church, where a few men could protect them while the rest went out searching for the missing boys. By now Ma was pale with terror, Pa raging for the other men to hurry, hurry, not a minute to waste, got to find the boys, if you don't come now I'll go on alone! And the others saying, Calm down, calm down, can't do no good by yourself, we'll catch them, you bet. Nobody admitting what they all knew—that Al and Measure were as good as dead.

But Al didn't plan to be dead. No sir. He planned to be absolutely alive, him and Measure both.

The Reds built up the fire good and hot, and it sure wasn't no cook fire. Since the sun was shining bright and hard already, it made Al and Measure sweat something awful, even in their short summer underwear. They sweated even more when the Reds cut even that much off them, popping off the buttons down the front and slicing it right down the back, so they were naked right down to the ground they sat on.

It was about then that one of the Reds noticed Al's forehead. He took a big hank of underwear cloth and wiped at Al's face, rubbing pretty hard to get the dried blood off. Then he started jabbering at the others. They all gathered around to see. Then they checked Measure's forehead, too. Well, Al knew what they were looking for. And he knew they wouldn't find it. Cause he had healed up his own forehead without a scar, not a mark on his own face. And of course no mark on Measure, either, since he wasn't cut. That'd make them think a little.

But it wasn't healing that Al was depending on to save them. It was too hard, too slow—they could sure cut faster than Al could heal, and that was the truth. It was a lot faster for him to use that knack he had on things like stone and metal, which was all the same straight through; living flesh, on the other hand, was complicated with all kinds of little stuff that he had to get right in his head before he could change it and make it whole.

So when one of the Reds sat down in front of Measure, brandishing a knife, Al didn't wait for him to start cutting. He got that knife into his head, the steel of the blade—White man's knife, just like they were carrying White man's muskets. He found the edge of it, the point, and flattened it out, smoothed it, rounded it.

The Red laid that knife up against Measure's bare chest

and tried to cut. Measure braced himself for the pain to start. But that knife made no more mark on Measure than if it was a spoon.

Al almost laughed to see that Red pull his knife away and look at it, try to see what was wrong. He ran the edge against his own finger, to test it; Al thought of making the blade razor sharp right then, but no, no, the rule was to use his knack to make things right, not to cause injury. The others gathered round to look at the knife. Some of them mocked the knife's owner, probably thinking he hadn't kept the edge sharp. But Al spent that time finding all the other steel edges that those Red men had and making them round and smooth. They couldn't've cut a pea pod in half with them knives when Al was through.

Sure enough, all the others pulled out their knives to try them, running the edges against Al or Measure first, and finally yelling and shouting and accusing each other, quarreling over whose fault it was, probably.

But they had a job to do, didn't they? They were supposed to torture these White boys and make them scream, or at least hack them up bad enough that when their folks found the bodies they'd thirst for revenge.

So one of the Reds took his old-fashioned stone-edged tommy-hawk and brandished it in front of Al's face, waving it around so he'd get good and scared. Al used the time to soften up the stone, weaken the wood, loosen the thongs that held it all together. By the time the Red got to lifting it up ready to do some real business, like smashing Al in the face with it, it crumbled apart in his hand. The wood was rotted clear through, the stone fell to the ground as gravel, and even the thong was split and frayed through. That Red man shouted and jumped back like as if he had a rattler a-biting at him.

Another one had a steel-blade hatchet, and he didn't

waste no time waving it around, he just laid out Measure's hand on a rock and whacked it down, meaning to cut Measure's fingers off. This was easy stuff to Al, though. Hadn't he cut whole millstones, when the need was? So the hatchet struck and rang on the stone, and Measure gasped at the sight of it, sure it'd take his fingers clean off; but when the Red picked up the hatchet, there was Measure's hand just like before, not marked a bit, while the hatchet had finger-shaped depressions in the blade, like it was made of cool butter or wet cake-soap.

Them Reds, they howled, they looked at each other with fear in their eyes, fear and anger at the strange things going on. Alvin couldn't know it, being White, but the thing that made this worst of all for them was they couldn't feel it like they felt a White man's spells or charms or doodles. A White man put a hex, they felt it like a bump in their land-sense; a beseeching was a nasty stink; a warding was a buzz when they came close. But this that Alvin did, it didn't interrupt the land at all, their sense of how things ought to be didn't show them nothing different going on. It was like all the natural laws had changed on them, and suddenly steel was soft and flesh was hard, rock was brittle and leather weak as grass. They didn't look to Al or Measure as the cause of what was going on. It was some natural force doing it, as best they could figure.

All that Alvin saw was their fear and anger and confusion, which pleased him well enough. He wasn't cocky, though. He knew there was some things he didn't know how to handle. Water was the main one; if they took it in their heads to drown the boys, Al wouldn't know how to stop them, or save himself or Measure. He was only ten, and being bound by rules he didn't understand, he hadn't figured out what-all his knack was good for, or how it worked. Maybe there was things within his power that could be right spetackler, if he only knowed how, but the point was he didn't know, and so he only did the things that were within his reach.

This much was on his side—they didn't think of drowning. But they thought of fire. Most likely they were planning that from the start—folks told tales of finding torture victims in the Red wars back in New England, their blackened feet in the cooling ashes of a fire, where they had to watch their own toes char until the pain and bleeding and madness of it killed them. Alvin saw them stoking up the fire, putting hot-burning branches on it to make it flare. He didn't know how to take the heat out of a fire, he'd never tried. So he thought as fast as he could, and while they were picking Measure up by his armpits and dragging him to the fire, Al got inside the firewood and broke it up, made it crumble into dust, so it burnt up fast, all at once, in a fire so fast it made a loud clap and a puff of bright hot light shot upward. It rose so fast that it made a wind blow in from all directions onto the place where the fire had been, and it made a whirlwind for a second or two, whipping around, sucking up the ashes and then puffing them out to drift down like dust.

Just like that, nothing left of the fire at all except dust settling fine as mist all over the clearing.

Oh, they howled, they jumped and danced and beat on their own shoulders and chests. And while they were carrying on like an Irish funeral, Al loosened the ropes on him and Measure, hoping against hope that they might even get away after all before their folks and neighbors found them and started in with shooting and killing and dying.

Measure felt the ropes loosening, of course, and looked sharp at Alvin; up to then he'd been almost as crazy with what was happening as the Reds. Of course, he knew right off that it was Alvin doing it, but it wasn't as if Alvin could explain what he was planning—it took Measure by surprise same as the others. Now, though, he looked at Alvin and nodded, starting to twist his arms out of the ropes. None of the Reds had noticed so far, and maybe they could get a running start, or maybe—just maybe—the Reds were so upset they wouldn't even try to follow.

Right then, though, everything changed. There was a hooting sound from the forest, and then it got picked up by what sounded like three hundred owls, all in a circle. Measure must have thought for a second that Al was causing *that* to happen, too, the way he looked at his little brother—but the Reds knew what it was, and stopped their carrying on right away. From the fear on their faces, though, Al figured it must be something good, maybe even something like rescue.

From the forest all around the clearing there stepped out dozens, then a hundred Reds. These were all carrying bows—not a musket among them—and the way they dressed and had their hair, Al reckoned them to be Shaw-Nee, and followers of the Prophet. It was about the last thing Al expected, truth to tell. It was White faces he wanted to see, not more Red ones.

One Red stepped out of the mass of the newcomers, a tall strong man with a face as hard and sharp as stone, it looked like. He fired off a couple of harsh-sounding words, and immediately their captors began babbling, jabbering, *pleading*. It was like a bunch of children, Al thought, doing something they knew they shouldn't ought to, and then their pa comes along and catches them at it. Having been caught in such mischief himself sometimes, he almost felt a little sympathy, till he remembered that what his captors had had in mind was cruel death for him and his brother. Just because they ended up without a scratch didn't mean them Reds weren't guilty of the bad intent.

Then one word stuck out of all the yammering—a name: Ta-Kumsaw. Al looked at Measure to see if he'd heard, and

Measure was looking at him, raising his eyebrows, asking the same thing. They both mouthed the name at the same time. Ta-Kumsaw.

Did this mean Ta-Kumsaw was in charge of all this? Was he angry at the captors because they failed at the torture, or because they'd captured White boys at all? There wasn't no explanation from the Reds, that was sure. All that Al could know for sure was what they *did*. The new-come Reds took all the muskets away from the gun-toters, and then led them off into the woods. Only about a dozen Reds stayed with Al and Measure. Among them was Ta-Kumsaw.

"They say you have fingers made of steel," said Ta-Kumsaw.

Measure looked at Al for him to answer, and Al couldn't think of anything to say. He was sure reluctant about telling this Red what it was he done. So it was Measure answered him after all, by raising his hands and wiggling his fingers. "Just regular fingers near as I can tell," he said.

Ta-Kumsaw reached out and took him by the hand—a strong, hard grip, it must have been, cause Measure tried to pull away and couldn't. "Iron skin," said Ta-Kumsaw. "Can't cut with knife. Can't burn. Boys made of stone."

He pulled Measure up to a standing position and, with his free hand, slapped him hard on the upper part of the arm. "Stone boy, throw me on the dirt!"

"I can't wrassle you," said Measure. "I don't want a fight with nobody."

"Throw me!" commanded Ta-Kumsaw. And he adjusted his grip, put out his foot, and waited until Measure put out his own foot to join him. Facing off, man to man, the way the Reds did in their games. Only this wasn't no game, not to these boys who'd been looking death in the face and didn't have no guarantee that it still wasn't just around the corner.

Al didn't know what he ought to do, but he was in a mood for doing something, coming on the heels of all his changing of things. So it was almost without a thought of the consequences that the very moment Measure and Ta-Kumsaw started to push and pull on each other, Al made the dirt come all loose under Ta-Kumsaw's feet, so his own pushing made him fall ass over elbow in the dirt.

The other Reds had been kind of laughing and joshing about the wrassle, but when they saw the greatest chief of all the tribes, a man whose name was known from Boston to New Orleans, when they saw him smash on the ground like that they kind of left off laughing. Truth to tell there wasn't a sound in that clearing. Ta-Kumsaw picked himself up and looked at the dirt under his feet, scraping on it with his foot. It was solid enough now, of course. But he stepped a few feet away, onto the grass, and held out his hand again.

This time Measure had a little more confidence, and reached out to take his hand—but at the last second, Ta-Kumsaw snatched his own hand away. He stood very still, not looking at Measure or Al or anybody, just looking into space, his face all hard and set. Then he turned to the other Reds and fired off a volley of words, spitting them out with all the Ss and Ks and Xs of Shaw-Nee talk. Al and the other children of Vigor Church used to imitate Red talk by saying things like "boxy talksy skock woxity" and laughing till their sides ached. But it didn't sound too funny the way Ta-Kumsaw said it, and when he was done Al and Measure found themselves getting pulled along by them thongs again. And when the rags of their underjohns fell down and started tripping them up, Ta-Kumsaw came back and tore them off the boys, ripping that fabric to shreds with his bare hands, his face all angry. Neither Al nor Measure felt like mentioning that they was left pretty near naked by this time, considering that the only wearing apparel left on them was the thong around their neck; it just didn't seem like a good time to complain. Where Ta-Kumsaw was taking them they had no idea, and since they also had no choice about going, there wasn't much point in asking, either.

Al and Measure never ran so long or so far in their lives. Hour after hour, mile after mile, never going too terrible fast, but never stopping, neither. Moving like this, a Red could travel faster on foot than a White usually could on horseback, unless he was making his nag run all the way. Which wasn't too good on the horse. And the horse had to stay on cleared roads. While Reds—Reds didn't even need a *path*.

Al noticed real quick that running through the woods was different for the Reds than it was for him and Measure. The only sound he heard was his and Measure's footfalls. Al being near the back, he could see how things went with Measure. The Red who was pulling Measure would push a branch with his body, and the branch would bend to make way. But the next second when Measure tried to push through, it would snatch at his skin and then break off. Reds would step on roots or twigs and there'd be no sound, nothing snagging their feet; Al would step on the same spot, and he'd trip up, stumble, the thong catching at his neck; or the twig would snap under his bare foot, or the rough bark of the root would tear at his skin. Al, on account of being just a boy, was used to walking around barefoot a good deal of the time, so the soles of his feet were somewhat toughened up. But Measure'd been in growed-man's boots for some years now, and Al could see that after maybe half a mile Measure was bleeding.

One thing he could do, Al reckoned, was help his brother's feet to heal up. He tried to start, to find his way into his brother's body the way he'd found his way into the stone and the steel and the wood. Running along like that, though, it was hard to concentrate. And living flesh was just too complicated.

Al wasn't the kind to give up. No, he just tried a different way. Since it was running that distracted him, he just quit thinking about running. Didn't look at the ground. Didn't try to step where the Red ahead of him stepped, just didn't think about it at all. Like trimming an oil lamp, he trimmed his own wick, as they say, letting his eyes focus on nothing, thinking about nothing, letting his body work like a pet animal that could be let to have its own head and go its own way.

He had no notion that he was doing what doodlebugs do, when they let their bug go out of their head and travel on its own. And anyway it wasn't the same, on account of there wasn't no doodlebug in the natural world who ever tried to doodle while he was running with a thong around his neck.

Now, though, he didn't have a speck of trouble getting into Measure's body, finding the sore places, the bleeding cuts on his feet, the ache in his legs, the pain in his side. Healing the feet, toughing them up, callusing them, that was easy enough. For the others, Al felt how Measure's body was craving for him to breathe more, deeper, faster; so Al got into his lungs and cleared them, opened them into the deepest places. Now when Measure sucked in air, his body got more of a use out of it, like it could wring out each rag of air to get the very last drop of good out of it. Al didn't even half understand what he was doing—but he knowed it worked, cause the pain in Measure's body began to ease, he didn't weary so much, he didn't gasp for breath.

As he returned to himself, Al noticed that in the whole time he was helping Measure, he didn't step on no twig that broke or get smacked by some snaggy branch flipping back from the Red in front of him. Now, though, he was getting poked and tripped and snapped as much as ever. He thought right off, it was happening just the same all along, only I didn't hardly notice cause I wasn't rightly paying attention to my own skin. But even as he decided that was true and even mostly believed it, he also realized that the sound of the world had changed. Now it was just breathing and pale-skinned feet thumping on the dirt or swishing through ancient dead leaves. A bird sound now and then, a fly buzzing. Nothing remarkable, except that Al could remember, just as plain as anything, that until he came back from fixing up Measure's body he could hear something else, a kind of music, a kind of—green music. Well, that didn't make no sense. There wasn't no way music could have a color to it, that was plain crazy. So Al put that out of his mind, just didn't think about it. Without thinking about it, though, he was still longing to hear it again. Hear it or see it or smell it, however it came into him, he wanted it back again.

And one more little thing. Until he went out of himself to help Measure, his own body wasn't doing all that well, neither; in fact he was near wore out. But now he was all right, his body was doing fine, he was breathing deep, his legs and arms felt like he could go on forever, sturdy in their motion as trees were in their stillness. Now maybe that was because in healing Measure, he also somehow healed himself—but he didn't rightly believe that, cause he always knew what he did and what he didn't do. No, to Al Junior's thinking, his body was doing better because of something else. And that something else, either it was part of the green music, or it caused the music, or they both were caused by the same thing. As near as Al could figure.

Running along like that, Al and Measure didn't have no chance to talk till getting on nightfall, when they came to a Red village on the curve of a dark deep river. Ta-Kumsaw led them right into the middle of the village and then walked off and left them. The river was just down the slope from them, maybe a hundred yards of grassy ground.

"Think we could make it down to the river without them catching us?" whispered Measure.

"No," said Al. "And anyways I can't swim. Pa never let me near the water."

Then all the Red women and children come out of the stick-and-mud huts they lived in and pointed at them two naked Whites, man and boy, and laughed and threw sods at them. At first Al and Measure tried to dodge, but it just made them laugh harder and run around and around, throwing wet dirt from different angles, trying to catch them in the face or the crotch. Finally Measure just sat down on the grass, put his face to his knees, and let them throw all they wanted. Al did the same. Finally somebody barked a few words and the sod-throwing stopped. Al looked up in time to see Ta-Kumsaw walking away, and a couple of his fighting men come out to watch and make sure nothing else happened.

"That was the farthest I ever run in my whole life," said Measure.

"Me too," said Al.

"Right at the start there I thought I was like to die, I was so tired," said Measure. "Then I got my second wind. I didn't think I had it in me."

Al didn't say nothing.

"Or did you have something to do with that?"

"Maybe some," said Al.

"I never know what you can do, Alvin."

"Me neither," said Al, and it was the truth.

"When that hatchet come down on my fingers I thought that was the end of my working days."

"Just be glad they didn't try to drownd us."

"You and water again," said Measure. "Well I'm glad you done what you done, Al. Though I *will* say it might've worked out better if you hadn't made the chief slip like that when he was set to arm-wrassle me."

"Why not?" said Al. "I didn't want him to hurt you—"

"There's no way you should know it, Al, so don't blame yourself. But that kind of wrassling ain't to hurt a body, it's kind of a test. Of manliness and quickness and what all. If he beat me, but I put up a fair fight, then I'd have his respect, and if I beat him fair, why, there's respect in that, too. Armor told me about it. They do it all the time."

Alvin thought about this. "So when I made him fall, was that real bad?"

"I don't know. Depends on why they think it happened. Might be they'll think it means that God is on my side or something."

"Do they believe in God?"

"They've got a Prophet, don't they? Just like in the Bible. Anyway I just hope they don't think it means I'm a coward and a cheater. Things won't go so good for me then."

"Well I'll tell them it was me done it," said Al.

"Don't you dare," said Measure. "The only thing saved us was they didn't know it was you doing them changes on the knives and hatchets and such. If they knowed it was you, Al, they would've hacked your head open, mashed you flat and then done what they wanted with me. Only thing that saved you was they didn't know what was causing it."

Then they got to talking about how worried Pa and Ma would be, speculating on how Ma would be so mad, or maybe she'd be too worried to be angry at Pa, and there must be men out looking for them by now even if the horses never came home, cause when they didn't show up for supper at the Peachees they wouldn't waste a minute giving the warning.

"They'll be talking about war with the Reds," said Measure. "I know that much—there's plenty of folks from down Carthage way who hate Ta-Kumsaw already, from his running off their livestock earlier this year."

"But it was Ta-Kumsaw who saved us," said Al.

"Or that's how it looks, anyway. But I notice he didn't take us home, or even ask us where home *was*. And how did he happen to come along right at that very minute, if he wasn't part of it himself? No, Al, I don't know what's going on, but Ta-Kumsaw didn't save us, or if he did he saved us for his own reasons, and I don't know as how I trust him to do good for us. For one thing, I really ain't much for setting around naked in the middle of a Red village."

"Me neither. And I'm hungry."

It wasn't long, though, before Ta-Kumsaw himself came out with a pot of corn mash. It was almost funny, seeing that tall Red man, who carried himself like a king, toting a pot like one of the Red women. But after that first surprise, Al realized that when Ta-Kumsaw did it, pot-toting looked downright noble.

He set down the pot in front of Al and Measure, and then took a couple of strips of Red-weave cloth from around his neck. "Wrap up," he said, and handed each of them a strip. Neither one of them knowed the first thing about tying on a loincloth, beginning with the fact that Ta-Kumsaw was still holding the deerskin belts that were supposed to hold them on. Ta-Kumsaw laughed at how confused they were, and then made Al stand up. He dressed Al himself, and that showed Measure how it was done so he could cover himself, too. It wasn't like proper clothes, but it was sure better than being buck naked.

Then Ta-Kumsaw sat down on the grass, the pot between

him and them, and showed them how to eat the mash—dipping in his hand, pulling out a tepid, jelly-thick glop of it and smacking it into his open mouth. Tasted so bland that Alvin like to gagged on it. Measure saw it, and said, "Eat." So Alvin ate, and once he got some swallowed he could feel how much his belly wanted more, even though it still took real persuasion to get his throat to take on the job of transportation.

When they had the pot cleaned right down to the bottom, Ta-Kumsaw set it aside. He looked at Measure for a while. "How did you make me fall down, White coward?" he said.

Al was all for speaking up right then, but Measure answered too quick and loud. "I ain't no coward, Chief Ta-Kumsaw, and if you wrassle me now it'll be fair and square."

Ta-Kumsaw smiled grimly. "So you can make me fall down with all these women and children watching?"

"It was me," said Alvin.

Ta-Kumsaw turned his head, slowly, the smile not leaving his face—but not so grim now, neither. "Very small boy," he said. "Very worthless child. You can make the ground loose under my feet?"

"I just got a knack," said Alvin. "I didn't know you weren't aiming to hurt him."

"I saw a hatchet," said Ta-Kumsaw. "Finger-marks like this." He waved his finger to show the kind of pattern Measure's fingers had left in the blade of the hatchet. "You did that?"

"It ain't right to cut a man's fingers off."

Ta-Kumsaw laughed out loud. "Very good!" Then he leaned in close. "White men's knacks, they make noise, very much noise. But you, what you do is so quiet nobody sees it."

Al didn't know what he was talking about.

In the silence, Measure spoke up bold as you please. "What you plan to do with us, Chief Ta-Kumsaw?"

"Tomorrow we run again," he said.

"Well why don't you think about letting us run toward home? There's got to be a hundred of our neighbors out now, mad as hornets. There's going to be a lot of trouble if you don't let us go home."

Ta-Kumsaw shook his head. "My brother wants you."

Measure looked at Alvin, then back at Ta-Kumsaw. "You mean the Prophet?"

"Tenskwa-Tawa," said Ta-Kumsaw.

Measure looked plain sick. "You mean after he built up his Prophetstown for four years, nobody causing him a lick of trouble, White man and Red man getting along real good, now he goes around taking Whites captive and torturing them and—"

Ta-Kumsaw clapped his hands once, loudly. Measure fell silent. "Chok-Taw took you! Chok-Taw tried to kill you! My people don't kill except to defend our land and our families from White thieves and murderers. And Tenskwa-Tawa's people, they don't kill at all."

That was the first Al ever heard of there being a split between Ta-Kumsaw's people and the Prophet's people.

"Then how'd you know where we were?" demanded Measure. "How'd you know how to find us?"

"Tenskwa-Tawa saw you," said Ta-Kumsaw. "Told me to hurry and get you, save you from the Chok-Taw, bring you to Mizogan."

Measure, who knew more about Armor-of-God's maps than Alvin did, recognized the name. "That's the big lake, where Fort Chicago is."

"We don't go to Fort Chicago," said Ta-Kumsaw. "We go to the holy place."

"A church?" asked Alvin.

Ta-Kumsaw laughed. "You White people, when you

make a place holy you build walls so nothing of the land can get in. Your god is nothing and nowhere, so you build a church with nothing alive inside, a church that could be anywhere, it doesn't matter—nothing and nowhere."

"Well what *does* make a place holy?" asked Alvin.

"Because that's where the Red man talks to the land, and the land answers." Ta-Kumsaw grinned. "Sleep now. We will go when it's still dark."

"It's going to be mighty cool tonight," said Measure.

"Women will bring you blankets. Warriors don't need them. This is summer." Ta-Kumsaw walked a few steps away, then turned back to Alvin. "Weaw-Moxiky ran behind you, White boy. He saw what you did. Don't try to keep the secret from Tenskwa-Tawa. He will know when you lie." Then the chief was gone.

"What's he talking about?" asked Measure.

"I wisht I knew," said Al. "I'm going to have trouble telling the truth when I don't know what the truth *is*."

The blankets came soon enough. Al snuggled close to his big brother, for courage more than warmth. He and Measure whispered awhile, trying to puzzle things out. If Ta-Kumsaw wasn't in on this from the start, how come them Chok-Taw cut his and the Prophet's names into the saddle? And even if that was a lie, it was going to look real bad that Ta-Kumsaw finally did end up with the captives, and then up and took them to Lake Mizogan instead of just letting them go home. It was going to take some tall talking to keep this from turning into a war.

Finally, though, they fell silent, weary to the bone from all their running, not to mention their work moving the tree and the plain terror when the Chok-Taw was out to torture them. Measure started snoring lightly. And Alvin, he found himself drifting. In the very last moments before sleep, he heard that green music again, or saw it, or anyhow knew that it was there. But before he could even listen, he dozed off. Dozed off and slept real peaceful, what with the night breeze blowing cool off the river, the blanket and the warmth of Measure's body keeping him warm, the night-sounds of the animals, the cries of a hungry infant from a hut somewhere; all of it was part of the green music flowing through his head.

8

RED-LOVER

They gathered in the clearing, some thirty White men, grim-faced and angry and tired from walking through the woods. The trail was easy enough to follow, but it seemed like the branches grabbed at them and the roots tripped them up—the forest was never kind to a White man. Then there was an hour lost when the trail reached a stream, and they had to go up and down the stream to find where the Reds took them boys out of the water and up onto land again. Old Alvin Miller like to went crazy when he saw they dragged the boys through water—it took his son Calm about ten minutes to get him quiet and able to go on. The man was just mad with fear.

"Shouldn't've sent him away, I never should've let him go," he kept saying.

And Calm kept saying, "Could've happened anywhere, don't blame yourself, we'll find them all right, they're still walking ain't they?" All kinds of talk, but mostly it was his voice that soothed Al Miller, it was his manner—some folks even said it was his knack, that his ma named him straight for what he could best do.

Now they were in the clearing, and trails led off about five different ways, and all of them plumb disappeared after a few steps. They found the boys' tore-up underwear a few steps into the woods heading northwest. Nobody figured they ought to show that to Al Miller, so by the time he got there—him bringing up the rear at that point, with Calm by his side—the underjohns were tucked away out of sight.

"We'll never track them from here," said Armor-of-God. "The boys aren't leaving no footprints now—which don't mean nothing, Mr. Miller, so don't you fret." Armor called his father-in-law *Mr. Miller* ever since Al throwed him out of the house into the snow that time he came to say Al Junior was dying cause the family committed the sin of using hexes and beseechings. It just don't seem right to call a man *Pa* after he heaves you off his porch. "They might be toting the boys, or they might be stepping after them, kind of wiping out their prints. We all know if a Red don't want to leave a trail, there ain't no trail."

"We all know about Reds," said Al Miller. "And what they do to White boys when they—"

"So far all we know is they're trying to scare us," said Armor.

"Doing a good job so far," said one of the Swedes. "Scared mostly to death, my family and me."

"Besides, everybody knows Armor-of-God here is a Red-lover."

Armor looked around, trying to see who said that. "If by Red-lover you mean I think Reds are human beings just like Whites, then it's true. But if you mean I like Reds *better* than Whites, then you best work up some courage to step out here and say it to my face, so I can mash your face into the bark of a tree."

"No need to quarrel," said Reverend Thrower, panting. He wasn't much for exercise, was Thrower, so he only just now caught up with the rest of them. "The Lord God loves all his children, even the heathens. Armor-of-God is a good Christian. But we all know that if it ever comes to fighting between Christian and heathen, Armor-of-God will stand on the side of righteousness."

The crowd murmured their agreement. After all, they all liked Armor; he'd loaned most of them money or given them credit at his store, and never nagged them for payment—a good many of them might not have made it through their first few years in Wobbish country if it wasn't for Armor. Grateful or not, though, they all knew he treated Reds like they was almost White, which was a bit suspicious at a time like this.

"It's coming to fighting right now," said a man. "We don't have to track down these Reds. We got their names on the saddles, carved right in."

"Now just wait a minute!" said Armor-of-God. "You just think a minute! In all this time Prophetstown's been a-growing there across the Wobbish from Vigor Church, has any Red so much as stole a thing from you? Slapped one of your children? Snatched a pig? Done any single bad thing to any one of you?"

"I think stealing Al Miller's boys is a pretty bad thing!" said a man.

"I'm talking about the Reds in Prophetstown! You know they never done nothing wrong, you *know* that! And you know why, too. You know it's cause the Prophet tells them to live in peace, keep to their own land and do no harm to the White man."

"That ain't what Ta-Kumsaw says!"

"Well even if they *did* want to do some terrible crime against White folks—which I ain't saying—is there any one of you thinks Ta-Kumsaw or Tenskwa-Tawa is so blamed stupid he's going to sign his name?"

"They're proud of killing White folks!"

"If the Red man was smart, he'd be White!"

"See what I mean about Red-lovers?"

Armor-of-God knew these people, and he knew that most of them were still with him. Even the grumblers weren't about to go off half-cocked; they'd sit tight until the whole group decided on action. So let them call him a Red-lover, that was fine, when men was scared and mad they said things that later they repented of. As long as they waited. As long as they didn't jump into war against the Reds.

Cause Armor had his suspicions about this whole thing. It was just too easy, the way them horses was sent on home with names carved in the saddle. It wasn't the way Reds did things, even the bad ones that would kill you soon as look at you. Armor knew enough about Reds to know they only tortured to give a man a chance to show brave, not to terrorize people. (Or most Reds, anyway—there were stories about the Irrakwa before they got civilized.) So whoever did this wasn't acting like a natural Red. Armor was near convinced it was a hired-out job. The French in Detroit had been trying to cause war between Reds and American settlers for years—it might've been them. And it might have been Bill Harrison. Oh yes, it might well have been that man, down there like a spider in his fort on the Hio. Armor thought that was the most likely thing. Course he wouldn't dare to say it out loud, cause folks would think he was just jealous of Bill Harrison, which was true—he *was* jealous. But he also knew that Harrison was a wicked man, who'd do anything to make things go his way. Maybe even get some wild Reds to come up and kill a few White boys near Prophetstown. After all, it was Tenskwa-Tawa who got most of the Reds from Harrison's part of the country to lay off whisky and come to Prophetstown. And it was Ta-Kumsaw who ran off half the White settlers down there. It looked to Armor like Harrison was behind this, a lot more likely than the French.

But he couldn't say none of this, cause there was no

proof. He just had to try to keep things calm, till some real evidence showed up.

Which might be right now. They'd brought along old Tack Sweeper, wheezing his way with the best of them—it was remarkable how vigorous he was, for a man whose lungs sounded like a baby's rattle when he breathed. Tack Sweeper had him a knack, which wasn't all that reliable, he was the first to say. But sometimes it worked remarkable well. What he did was stand around in a place for a while with his eyes closed and sort of see the things that happened there in the past. Just quick little visions, a few faces. Like that time they was afraid maybe Jan de Vries killed hisself on purpose, or maybe was murdered, Tack was able to see how it was an accident when his gun went off in his own face, so they could bury him in the church-yard and not have to worry about hunting for no killer.

So the hope was Tack could tell them something about what happened in this clearing. He shooed them all back to the edges of the wood, so they'd be out of the way. Then he walked around in the middle, his eyes closed, moving slow. "You boys shouldn't have got so mad here," he said after a while. "All I can see is you all jawing." They laughed, kind of embarrassed. They should've knowed better than to mess up the memories of a place before Tack got there.

"It don't look good. I keep seeing them Red faces. Knife, all kind of knives getting slashed on folks' skin. A hatchet falling."

Al Miller moaned.

"It's all just a mess here, so much happened," said Tack. "I can't see right. No. No, I can—one man. A Red man, I know his face, I seen him—he's just standing there, just still as you please, I know that face."

"Who is it?" said Armor-of-God. But he knew, he had that sickening feeling of dread, oh he knew.

"Ta-Kumsaw," said Tack. He opened his eyes wide and looked at Armor, almost apologetic. "I wouldn't've believed it either, Armor," he said. "I always kind of thought Ta-Kumsaw was the bravest man I ever knew. But he was here, and he was in charge. I see him standing there, and telling people what to do. He stood right here. I can see him so clear cause there wasn't nobody else stood exactly in that place for so long. And he was mad. Ain't no mistake about it."

Armor believed it. They all did—they all knew Tack was a truthful man, and if he said he was sure, then he was sure. But there had to be some reason. "Maybe he come and saved the boys, did you think of that? Maybe he come and stopped some band of wild Reds from—"

"Red-lover!" somebody shouted.

"You know Ta-Kumsaw! He's no coward, and stealing them boys was a cowardly thing to do, you *know* that man!"

"Nobody ever knows a Red man."

"Ta-Kumsaw didn't take those boys!" insisted Armor-of-God. "I know it!"

Then everybody fell silent, cause old Al Miller was pushing his way forward, out to where Armor-of-God was standing. Faced down his son-in-law, he did, with a face like living hell he was so mad. "You don't know nothing, Armor-of-God Weaver. You are the most worthless scum ever formed on the top of a chamber pot. First you married my daughter and wouldn't let her work no hexes cause you were so cock-eyed sure it was the devil's work. Then you let all these Reds stay around here all the time. And when we thought of building a stockade you said, No, if we build a stockade that just gives them French something to attack and burn down, we'll be *friends* with the Reds and then they'll leave us alone, we'll *trade* with the Reds. Well look what it got us! Look what you done for us! Ain't we all glad we listened to you now! I don't think you're no Red-lover, Armor-of-God, I just think you're the blamedest fool ever to cross the Hio and come out west, and the only folks dumber than you is *us* if we listen to you for another minute!"

Then Al Miller turned to face the other men, who were looking at him with awe in their face like they just seen majesty for the first time in their lives. "We done it Armor's way for ten years here. But I've done with that. I lost one boy in the Hatrack River on my way here, and this town is named for him. Now I lost two other boys. I only got me five sons left, but I tell you I'll put guns in their hands myself, and lead them all into the middle of Prophetstown and blast them Reds into hell, even if it means we all die! You hear me?"

They heard him, oh yes they did. They heard and shouted back. This was the word they wanted right now, the word of hate and anger and revenge, and nobody better to give it to them than Al Miller, who was normally a peaceable man, never picked a quarrel with nobody. Him being the father of the captured boys just made it all the stronger when he spoke.

"The way I see it," said Al Miller, "Bill Harrison was right all along. Ain't no way the Red man and the White man can share this land. And I tell you something else. It ain't me that's leaving. There's too much blood of mine been shed here now for me to pack up and go away. I'm staying, either on this land or in it."

Me too, said all them boys. That's the truth, Al Miller. We're staying.

"Thanks to Armor here, we got no stockade and we got no U.S. Army fort closer than Carthage City. If we fight right now, we might lose everything and everybody. So let's hold off the Reds as best we can and send for help. A dozen men down to Carthage City and beg Bill Harrison to send us up an army, and maybe bring his cannon if he can. My two boys are gone, and a thousand Reds for each of my sons won't be enough getting even for me!"

THE DOZEN RIDERS set on their way south first thing the next morning. They left from the commons, which was crowded with wagons as more and more families from outlying farms came in to town to put up with close-in friends and kinfolk. But Al Miller wasn't there to see them off. Yesterday his words set them all in motion, but that was all the leadership they'd get from him. He didn't want to be in charge. He just wanted his boys back.

In the church, Armor-of-God sat on the front pew, despondent. "We're making the most terrible mistake," he said to Reverend Thrower.

"That's what men do," said Thrower, "when they make their decisions without the help of the Lord."

"It wasn't Ta-Kumsaw, I know it. Nor the Prophet either."

"He's no Prophet, not of God, anyway," said Thrower.

"He's no killer, either," said Armor. "Maybe Tack was right, maybe somehow Ta-Kumsaw's got something to do with this. But I know one thing. Ta-Kumsaw's no killer. Even when he was a young man, during General Wayne's war, there was a bunch of Reds all set to burn a bunch of captives to death, the way they did in those days—Chippy-Wa, I think they were. And along comes Ta-Kumsaw, all by himself, just this one lone Shaw-Nee, and he makes them stop. We want the White man to respect us, to treat us as a nation, he says to them. White man won't respect us if we act like this! We got to be civilized. No scalps, no torture, no burning, no killing captives. That's what he says to them. He's stuck to that ever since. He kills in battle, yes, but in all his raids down south he didn't kill one soul, do you realize that? If Ta-Kumsaw's got them boys, then they're as safe as if their mama had them home in bed."

Thrower sighed. "I suppose you know these Reds better than I do."

"I know them better than anybody." He laughed bitterly. "So they call me a Red-lover and don't listen to a word I say. Now they're calling for that whisky-dealing tyrant from Carthage City to come up here and take over. No matter what he does he'll be a hero. They'll make him governor for real, then. Heck, they'll probably make him President, if Wobbish ever joins the U.S.A."

"I don't know this Harrison. He can't be the devil you make him out to be."

Armor laughed. "Sometimes, Reverend, I think you are as trusting as a little child."

"Which is how the Lord told us to be. Armor-of-God, be patient. All things will work out as the Lord intends."

Armor buried his face in his hands. "I sure hope so, Reverend. I sure do. But I keep thinking about Measure, as good a man as you can hope to find, and that boy Alvin, that sweet-faced boy, and how much store his papa sets by him, and—"

Thrower's face went grim. "Alvin Junior," he muttered. "Who would have imagined that the Lord would do his work through the hands of heathens?"

"What are you talking about?" asked Armor.

"Nothing, Armor, nothing. Just that everything about this may be exactly, *exactly* what the Lord intends."

UP THE HILL at the Miller house, Al still sat at the breakfast table. He didn't eat no supper the night before, and when he tried to eat breakfast he like to gagged on the food. Faith cleared it all away, and now she stood behind him, rubbing his shoulders. She never once said to him, I told you not to send them. But they both knew it. It hung between them like a sword, and neither dared reach out to the other for fear of it.

The silence broke when Wastenot came in, a rifle over his shoulder. He set it beside the front door, swung a chair between his legs, and sat and looked at his parents. "They're gone, down to fetch the army."

To his surprise, his father only lowered his head and rested it on his arms, which were crossed on the table.

Mother looked at him, her face haggard with worry and grief. "Since when did you learn how to use that thing?"

"Me and Wantnot been practicing," he said.

"And you're going to kill Reds with it?"

Wastenot was surprised at the loathing in her voice. "I sure hope so," he said.

"And when all the Reds are dead, and you pile all their bodies together, will Measure and Alvin somehow wriggle out of that pile and come on home to me?"

Wastenot shook his head.

"Last night some Red went home to his family, all proud because he killed him some White boys yesterday." Her voice caught when she said it, but she went on all the same, cause when Faith Miller had aught to say, it got said. "And maybe his wife or his mama patted him and kissed him and made him supper. But don't you ever walk through that door and tell me you killed a Red man. Cause you won't get no supper, boy, and you won't get no kiss, and you won't get no pat, and no word, and no home, and no mama, you hear me?"

He heard, all right, but he didn't like it. He stood up and walked back to the door and picked up the gun. "You think what you like, Mama," he said, "but this is a war, and I *am* going to kill me some Reds, and I'm going to come back home, and I'm going to own up to it proud as can be. And if that means you don't want to be my mama no more, then you might as well stop being my mama now, and not wait till I come back." He opened the door, but stopped before slamming it shut behind him. "Cheer up, Mama. Maybe I won't come back at all."

He never talked that way to his mother in his life, and he wasn't real sure that it felt good to do it now. But she was being crazy, not understanding that it was war now, that them Reds had declared it open season on White folks and so there wasn't no more choice about it.

What bothered him most, though, as he got on his horse and rode out to David's place, was that he couldn't exactly be sure but he thought, he just suspected anyway, that Papa was crying. If that didn't beat all. Yesterday Papa was so hot against the Reds, and now Mama talked against fighting, and Papa just sat there and cried. Maybe it was getting old that made Papa like that. But that wasn't Wastenot's business, not now. Maybe Papa and Mama didn't want to kill them as took their sons—but Wastenot knew what he was going to do to them as took his brothers. Their blood was his blood, and whoever shed his blood was going to shed some of their own, too, a gallon for every drop.

9

LAKE MIZOGAN

In his whole life Alvin never saw so much water all in one place. He stood on the top of a sand dune, looking out over the lake. Measure stood beside him, a hand resting on Al's shoulder.

"Pa told me to keep you away from water," said Measure, "and now look where they bring you."

The wind was hot and hard, gusting sometimes and shooting sand around like tiny arrows. "Brought you, too," said Al.

"Look, there's a real storm coming."

Off in the southwest, the clouds got black and ugly. Not one of them summer-shower storms. Lightning crackled along the face of the clouds. The thunder came much later, muffled by distance. While Alvin was watching, he felt suddenly like he could see much wider, much farther than before, like he could see the twisting and churning in the clouds, feel the hot and cold of it, the icy air swooping down, the hot air shooting upward, all writhing in a vast circle of the sky.

"Tornado," said Al. "There's a tornado in that storm."

"I don't see one," said Measure.

"It's coming. Look how the air is spinning there. Look at that."

"I believe you, Al. But it's not like there's any place to hide around here."

"Look at all these people," said Alvin. "If it hits us here—"

"When did you learn how to tell the weather?" asked Measure. "You never done that before."

Al didn't have an answer to that. He never *had* felt a storm inside himself like this. It was like the green music he'd heard last night, all kinds of strange things happening now that he was captured by these Reds. But he couldn't waste another minute trying to think about why he knew—it was enough that he knew it. "I've got to warn somebody."

Alvin took off down the dune, sliding so that each step was like leaping off the face of the hill, then landing on one foot and leaping again. He'd never run downhill so fast before. Measure chased after him, shouting, "They told us to stay up there till—" The wind gusted and whipped away his words. Now they were off the hill, the sand was even worse; the wind lifted big sheets of sand off the dunes, hurled it a ways, then let it fall. Al had to close his eyes, shield them with his hand, turn his face out of the wind—whatever it took to keep the sand from blinding him as he ran to the group of Reds gathered at the edge of the water.

Ta-Kumsaw was easy to spot, and not just cause he was so big. The other Reds left a space around him, and he stood there like a king. Al ran right up to him. "Tornado coming!" he yelled. "There's tornadoes in that cloud!"

Ta-Kumsaw leaned his head back and laughed; the wind was so loud Al barely heard him. Then Ta-Kumsaw reached over Al's head, to touch the shoulder of another Red standing there. "This is the boy!" shouted Ta-Kumsaw.

Al looked at the man Ta-Kumsaw touched. He didn't carry himself like a king at all—nothing like Ta-Kumsaw. He was stooped somewhat, and one eye was missing, the lid just hanging empty over nothing. He looked taut, his arms wiry rather than muscled, his legs downright scrawny. But as Al sat there looking up into his face, he knew him. There wasn't no mistake.

The wind died down for just a minute.

"Shining Man," said Al.

"Roach boy," said Tenskwa-Tawa, Lolla-Wossiky, the Prophet.

"You're real," said Al. Not a dream, not a vision. A real man who had stood there at the foot of his bed, vanishing and reappearing, his face shining like sunlight so it hurt to look at him. But it was the same man. "I didn't heal you!" said Al. "I'm sorry."

"Yes you did," said the Prophet.

Then Al remembered why he'd come running down the dune, busting into a conversation between the two greatest Reds in the whole world, these brothers whose names were known to every White man, woman, and child west of the Appalachee Mountains. "Tornadoes!" he said.

As if to answer him, the wind whipped up again, howling now. Al turned around, and what he'd seen and felt was coming true. There were four twisters forming, hanging down out of the storm like snakes hanging from trees, slithering lower toward the ground, their heads ready to strike. They were all four coming right toward them, but not touching the ground yet.

"Now!" shouted the Prophet.

Ta-Kumsaw handed his brother a flint-tipped arrow. The Prophet sat down in the sand and jammed the point of the arrow into the sole of his left foot, then his right foot. Blood oozed copiously from the wounds. Then he did the same to his hands, jabbing himself so deep in the palm that it was bleeding on the top side of his hands, too.

Almost without thinking, Al cried out and started to cast his mind into the Prophet's body, to heal the wounds.

"No!" cried the Prophet. "This is the power of the Red man—the blood of his body—the fire of the land!"

Then he turned and started walking out into Lake Mizogan.

No, not *into* the lake. *Onto* it. Alvin couldn't hardly believe it, but under the Prophet's bloody feet the water became smooth and flat as glass, and the Prophet was standing on it. His blood pooled on the surface, deep red. A few yards away, the water became loose and choppy, wind-whipped waves rushing toward the smooth place and then just flattening, calming, becoming smooth.

The Prophet kept walking, farther out onto the water, his bloody footprints marking the smooth path through the storm.

Al looked back at the tornadoes. They were close now, almost overhead. Al could feel them twisting inside *him,* as if he were part of the clouds, and these were the great raging emotions of his own soul.

Out on the water, the Prophet raised his hands and pointed at one of the twisters. Almost immediately, the other three twisters rose up, sucked back up into the clouds and disappeared. But the other came nearer, until it was directly over the Prophet, maybe a hundred feet up. It was near enough that around the edges of the Prophet's glassy smooth path, the water was leaping up, as if it wanted to dive upward into the clouds; the water started to circle, too, twisting around and around with the wind under the twister.

"Come!" shouted the Prophet.

Alvin couldn't hear him, but he saw his eyes—even from that far away—saw his lips move, and knew what the

Prophet wanted. Alvin didn't hesitate. He stepped out onto the water.

By now, of course, Measure was caught up with him, and when Al started walking onto the warm, smooth glass of the Prophet's path, Measure shouted at him, grabbed at him. Before he could touch the boy, though, the Reds had him, pulled him back; he screamed at Alvin to come back, don't go, don't go onto the water—

Alvin heard him, and Alvin was as scared as he could be. But the Shining Man was waiting for him under the mouth of the tornado, standing on the water. Inside himself Al felt such a longing, like Moses when he saw the burning bush—I have to stop and see this thing, said Moses, and that's what Alvin was saying, I have to go and see what this is. Because this wasn't the kind of thing that happened in the natural universe, and that was the truth. There wasn't no beseeching or hex or witchery he ever heard of that could call a tornado and turn a stormy lake into glass. Whatever this Red man was doing, it was the most important thing Al ever saw or ever was likely to see in his life.

And the Prophet loved him. That was one thing Al didn't have no doubt of. The Shining Man had stood once at the foot of his bed and taught him. Al remembered that the Shining Man cut himself then, too. Whatever the Prophet was doing, he used his own blood and pain to do it with. There was a real majesty to that. Under the circumstances, Al can't be much blamed for feeling kind of worshipful as he walked out onto the water.

Behind him, the path loosened up, dissolved, disappeared. He felt the waves licking at his heels. It scared him, but as long as he walked forward there wasn't no harm done to him. And finally he stood with the Prophet, who reached out and took Alvin's hands in his. "Stand with me," shouted the Prophet. "Stand here in the eye of the land, and see!"

Then the tornado sank quickly downward; the water leaped up, rising like a wall around them. They were in the very center of the tornado, getting sucked upward—

Until the Prophet reached out one bloody hand and touched the waterspout, and it, too, went smooth and hard as glass. No, not glass. It was as clear and clean as a drop of dew on a spiderweb. There wasn't no storm now. Just Al and the Shining Man, in the middle of a tower of crystal, bright and transparent.

Only instead of being like a window that showed what was happening outside, Al couldn't see the lake or the storm or the shore through the crystal wall. Instead he saw other things.

He saw a wagon caught in a flooding river, a tree floating down like a battering ram, and a young man leaping out onto the tree, rolling it over, turning it from the wagon. And then the man tangling in the roots of the tree, getting smashed against a boulder, then rolling and tumbling downstream, all the time struggling to live, to breathe just a while longer, keep breathing, keep breathing—

He saw a woman bearing a baby, and a little girl who stood nearby reached out and touched her belly. She shouted something, and the midwife reached in her hand and took the baby's head, pulled it out. The mother tore and bled. The little girl reached under and pulled something off the baby's face; the baby cried. The man in the river heard that cry, somehow, knew that he had lived long enough, and so he died.

Al didn't know what to make of it. Until he heard the Prophet whisper in his ear: "The first thing you see in here is the day you are born."

The baby was Alvin Junior; the man who died was his brother, Vigor. Who was the girl who took the birth caul off his face? Al never saw her before in his life.

"I will show you," said the Prophet. "This stays only a

little while, and I have things to see for myself, but I will show you." He took Alvin by the hand and together they rose upward through the column of glass.

It didn't feel like flying, not like the soaring of a bird; it was as if there wasn't no up or down. The Prophet pulled him upward, but Al couldn't figure how the Prophet pulled *himself.* Didn't matter. There were so many things to see. Wherever he hung in the air, he could look in any direction and see something else through the wall of the tower. Until he realized that every moment of time, every human life must be visible through this tower wall. How could you find your way through here? How could you look for any one particular story in the hundreds, thousands, millions of moments of past time?

The Prophet stopped, hoisted the boy up until he could see what the Prophet was seeing, their cheeks pressed together, their breath mingling, the Prophet's heartbeat loud in Alvin's ear.

"Look," said the Prophet.

What Alvin saw was a city, shining in sunlight. Towers of ice, it looked like, or clear glass, because when the sun set behind the city its light didn't so much as dim, and the city cast no shadow on the meadowland around it. Inside that city there were people, like bright shadows moving here and there, going up and down the towers without stairs or wings. More important than what he saw, though, was what he felt, looking at that place. Not peace, no, there was nothing quiet about what he felt. It was excitement, his heart pumping fast as a horse in full gallop. The people there, they weren't perfect—they were sometimes angry, sometimes sad. But nobody was hungry, and nobody was ignorant, and nobody had to do something just because somebody else made them do it. "Where is that city!" whispered Alvin.

"I don't know," said the Prophet. "Every time I come

here, I see it in a different shape. Sometimes these tall thin towers, sometimes big crystal mounds, sometimes just people living on a sea of crystal fire. I think this city was built many times in the past. I think it will be built again."

"Are you going to build it? Is that what Prophetstown is for?"

Tears came from the Prophet's eyes—spilling from his one good eye, oozing out of the slack lid of the other. "Red man can't build this place alone," he said. "We are part of the land, and this city is more than the land alone. The land is good and bad, life and death all together, the green silence."

Alvin thought of his sense of green music, but he didn't say nothing, cause the Prophet was saying things he wanted to hear, and Al was smart enough to know that sometimes it's better to listen than to talk.

"But this city," said the Prophet, "the crystal city is light without dark, clean without dirty, healthy without sick, strong without weak, plenty without hungry, drink without thirst, life without death."

"The people in that place, they aren't all happy," said Alvin. "They don't live forever."

"Ah," said the Prophet. "You don't see the same that I see."

"What I see is, they're building it." Al frowned. "At one end they're building it, and at the other end, it's falling down."

"Ah," said the Prophet. "The city I see will never fall."

"Well what's the difference? How come we don't see the same thing?"

"I don't know, Roach Boy. I never showed this to anybody. Now go back down, wait for me below. I have things to see before time starts again."

Just thinking about going down made Alvin start to sink, until he was clear to the bottom, on the shiny clear floor. Floor? It could have been the ceiling for all he knowed. There was light coming up from there just like it was shining through the other walls, and he saw pictures there, too.

He saw a huge cloud of dust spin faster and faster, but instead of spitting out dust it sucked it all in, and suddenly it started glowing, and then it caught fire, and it was the sun, just as plain as could be. Alvin knew somewhat about the planets, cause Thrower talked about them, so he wasn't surprised to see them glowing points of light that pretty soon got dim. And after a while instead of dust mixed with darkness, it was all either worlds or empty space, pretty much. He saw the Earth, so small, but then he came closer and he saw how big it was, spinning so fast, one face of the Earth lit up from sunlight, the other face dark. He stood in the sky, it seemed, looking down on the lit place, but he could see all that was going on. First bare rock, spouting volcanoes; then out of the ocean, plants spreading out, growing tall, ferns and trees. He saw fish leaping in the sea, crawly life on the shore where the tide came in, and then bugs and other small critters, hopping and nibbling on leaves and catching each other and eating each other up. Them animals kept getting bigger and bigger, so fast Alvin couldn't follow the changes, just the Earth spinning and him watching, huge monstrous creatures like he never heard of, with long snakey necks some of them, and teeth and jaws to tear down trees with a single bite, it looked like. And then they were gone, and there were elephants and antelopes and tigers and horses, all the life of the earth, getting more and more like what Alvin thought animals ought to look like. But nowhere in all this did he see a man. He found apes and hairy things that hit each other with rocks, things that walked on their hind legs but looked about as dumb as frogs.

And then he *did* see some folks, though he wasn't sure

at first cause they were Black and he hadn't seen but one Black man in his life, a slave owned by a peddler from the Crown Colonies, who happened to come through Vigor Church maybe two years back. But they looked like human people, all right, Black or not, and they were pulling fruit down out of trees and berries off of bushes, feeding each other, a passel of pickaninnies following in their tracks. Two of the young ones got to fighting, and the big one killed the little one. The papa came back then, and kicked the one who did the killing, made him go away. Then he picked up the dead one and brought him back to the mama, both of them crying, and they laid that dead child down and covered him up with rocks. Then they gathered up their family and walked on, and after just a few steps they were eating again, and the tears stopped, and they went on, just went on. These are folks, that's sure, thought Alvin. This is just the way human people are.

The Earth kept turning, and by the time it come round again there was all kinds of folks, dark ones in the hot countries, light ones in the cold countries, with all shades in between. Except when America came under the light of the sun. In America folks was pretty much all the same kind, all Red, whether they lived north or south, hot or cold, wet or dry. And the land was at peace, compared to the other part of the world. It was strange for him to see, because when the big part of the land came by, with all its different races and nations, why, it changed with every sweep of the Earth, whole countries moved from one place to another, everything always shuffling around, and wars every minute, everywhere. The smaller land, America, it had some wars, too, but it was all slower, gentler. The people lived in a different rhythm. The land had its own heartbeat, its own life.

From time to time more people would come from the old world—fishermen, mostly. Off course, led astray by storms, running from enemies. They'd come, and for a time they'd live their old-world life in America, trying to build fast, and breed fast, and kill as much as they could. Like a sickness. But then they'd either join in with the Reds and disappear, or get killed off. None of them ever kept up their old-world ways.

Until now, thought Alvin. Now when we came, we were just too strong. Like getting a couple of colds maybe, and you begin to think you won't never get real sick, and then you get a dose of smallpox and you know that you were never truly sick before at all.

Alvin felt a hand on his shoulder.

"So there is where you looked," said the Prophet. "What did you see?"

"I think I saw the whole creation of the world," said Al. "Just like in the Bible. I think I saw—"

"I know what you saw. We all see this, all who have ever come to this place."

"I thought you said I was the first you brought."

"This place—there are many doors inside. Some walk in through fire. Some walk in through water. Some through being buried in the earth. Some by falling through the air. They come to this place and see. They go back and tell what they remember, as much of it as they understood, and tell it, as much as they have words to say, and others listen and remember, as much as they can understand. This is the seeing place."

"I don't want to leave," said Alvin.

"No, and neither does the other one."

"Who? Is there somebody else here?"

The Prophet shook his head. "Not his body. But I feel him in me, looking out of my eye." He tapped the cheekbone under his good eye. "Not this eye, the other."

"Can't you tell who it is?"

"White," he said. "It doesn't matter. Whoever it is did

no harm. I think maybe—will do a good thing. Now we go."

"But I want to know all the stories in this place!"

The Prophet laughed. "You could live forever and not see all the stories. They change faster than a man can see."

"How will I ever come here again? I want to see everything, all of it!"

"I will never bring you back," said the Prophet.

"Why? Did I do something wrong?"

"Hush, Roach Boy. I will never bring you back, because I will never come here myself again. This is the last time. I have seen the end of all my dreams."

For the first time, Alvin realized how sad the Prophet looked. His face was haggard with grief.

"I saw you in this place. I saw that I had to bring you here. I saw you in the hands of the Chok-Taw. I sent my brother to get you, bring you back."

"Is it cause you brought me here that you can't never come here again yourself?"

"No. The land has chosen. The end will be soon." He smiled, but it was a ghastly smile. "Your preacher, Reverend Thrower, he said to me once—if your foot gets sick, cut it off. Right?"

"I don't remember that."

"I do," said the Prophet. "This part of the land, it is already sick. Cut it off, so the rest of the land can live."

"What do you mean?" Alvin conjured up pictures in his mind, about pieces of the land breaking off and falling into the sea.

"Red man will go west of the Mizzipy. White man will stay east. Red part of land will live. White part of land will be very dead, cut off. Full of smoke and metal, guns and death. Red men who stay in the east will turn White. And White men won't come west of the Mizzipy."

"There's already White men west of the Mizzipy. Trappers and traders, mostly, but a few farmers with their families."

"I know," said the Prophet. "But what I see here today—I know how to make the White man never come west again, and how to make the Red man never stay east."

"How're you going to do that?"

"If I tell," said the Prophet, "then it won't happen. Some things in this place, you can't tell, or it changes, and they go away."

"Is it the crystal city?" asked Alvin.

"No," said the Prophet. "It is the river of blood. It is the forest of iron."

"Show me!" demanded the boy. "Let me see what you saw!"

"No," said the Prophet. "You wouldn't keep the secret."

"Why wouldn't I? If I give my word I won't break it!"

"You could give your word all day, Roach Boy, but if you saw the vision you would cry out in fear and pain. And you would tell your brother. You would tell your family."

"Is something going to happen to them?"

"Not one of your family will die," said the Prophet. "All safe and healthy when this is over."

"Show me!"

"No," said the Prophet. "I will break the tower now, and you will remember what we did and said here. But the only way you'll ever come back and see these things is if you find the crystal city."

The Prophet knelt down at the place where the wall met the floor. He pushed his bloody fingers into the wall and lifted. The wall rose up, dissolved, turned to wind. They were surrounded now by the scene they left so many hours before, it seemed. The water, the storm, the twister rising back up into the clouds above them. Lightning flashed all around them, and the rain came down, so fast it made the shore disappear. The rain that landed on the crystal place where they stood turned to crystal, too, became part of the floor under them.

The Prophet went to the edge nearest the shore, and stepped out onto the rough water. It went hard under his foot, but it still undulated slowly—it wasn't as firm as the platform. The Prophet reached back, took Alvin's hand, pulled him out onto the new path he was making on the surface of the lake. It wasn't near as smooth as before, and the farther they walked the rougher it got, the more it moved, the slicker it got so it was hard to go up and over the waves.

"We stayed too long!" cried the Prophet.

Alvin could feel the black water under the thin shell of crystal, roiling with hate. Nothingness out of an ancient nightmare, wanting to break through the crystal, get hold of Al, suck him down, drown him, tear him to pieces, to the tiniest pieces of all, and discard him into the darkness.

"It wasn't me!" shouted Alvin.

The Prophet turned around, picked him up, lifted him to his shoulders. The rain beat down on him, the wind tried to tear him from the Prophet's shoulders. Alvin clung tight to Tenskwa-Tawa's hair. He could feel that now the Prophet's feet were sinking down into the water more and more with every step. Behind them there wasn't a trace of a path, all of it gone, the waves rising higher and higher.

The Prophet stumbled, fell; Alvin fell too, forward, knowing he was going to drown—

And found himself sprawled on the wet sand of the beach, the water licking up around him, sucking sand out from under him, trying to pull him back out into the water. Then strong hands under his arms, pulling him away, up the beach, up toward the dunes.

"He's out there, the Prophet!" Alvin shouted. Or thought he shouted—his voice was just a whisper, and he hardly made a sound. It wouldn't have mattered, the wind being so loud. He opened his eyes and they were whipped full of sand and rain.

Then Measure's lips were against his ear, yelling to him. "The Prophet's all right! Ta-Kumsaw pulled him out! I thought you were dead for sure, when that twister sucked you up! Are you all right?"

"I saw everything!" Alvin cried. But he was so feeble now that he couldn't make a sound, and he gave it up, let his body go limp, and collapsed into exhausted sleep.

10

GATLOPP

Measure saw little of Alvin—too little. After the episode with the tornado on the lake, Measure would have thought Alvin would be awake to his danger here, eager to get away. Instead he seemed to care for nothing but to be with the Prophet, listening to his stories and the perverse poetic wisdom he dispensed.

Once when Alvin was actually with him long enough to set and talk, Measure asked him why he bothered. "Even when them Reds talk English I can't understand them. Talk about the land like it was a person, things about taking only the life that offers itself, the land dying east of the Mizzipy—it ain't dying here, Al, as any fool can see. And even if it's got smallpox, black death, and ten thousand hangnails, there ain't no doctor knows how to cure it."

"Tenskwa-Tawa *does* know how," said Alvin.

"Then let him do it, and let's get on home."

"Another day, Measure."

"Ma and Pa'll be worried sick, they think we're dead!"

"Tenskwa-Tawa says the land is working out its own course."

"There you go again! Land is land, and it ain't got a

thing to do with Pa getting a bunch of the boys together combing through the woods to find us!"

"Go on without me, then."

But Measure wasn't ready to do *that* yet. He didn't have no particular wish to face Ma if he came home without Alvin. "Oh, he was fine when I left him. Just playing around with tornadoes and walking on water with a one-eyed Red. Didn't want to come home just yet, you know how them ten-year-old boys are." No, Measure wasn't ripe to come home just now, not if he didn't have Alvin in tow. And it was sure he couldn't take Alvin against his will. The boy wouldn't even listen to talk of escape.

The worst of it was that while everybody liked Alvin just fine, jabbering to him in English and Shaw-Nee, not a soul there would so much as talk to Measure, except Ta-Kumsaw himself, and the Prophet, who talked all the time whether anybody was listening or not. It got powerful lonely, walking around all day. And not walking far, either. Nobody talked to him, but if he started heading away from the dunes toward the woods, somebody'd shoot off an arrow. It'd land with a thud in the sand right by him. They sure trusted their aim a lot better than Measure did. He kept thinking about arrows drifting a little this way or that and hitting him.

Escape *was* a silly idea, when Measure gave it serious thought. They'd track him down in no time. But what he couldn't figure was why they didn't want him to go. They weren't doing nothing with him. He was completely use-less. And they swore they had no plans to kill him or even break him up a little.

Fourth day at the dunes, though, it finally came to a head. He went to Ta-Kumsaw and plain *demanded* that he be let go. Ta-Kumsaw looked annoyed, but that was pretty normal for him. This time, though, Measure didn't back down.

"Don't you know it's plain stupid for you to keep us here? It ain't like we disappeared without a trace, you know. Our horses must have been found by now with your name all over them."

That was the first time Measure realized that Ta-Kumsaw didn't have a notion about them horses. "My name isn't on horses."

"On their saddles, Chief. Don't you know? Them Chok-Taw who took us—if they weren't your own boys, which I ain't quite satisfied about either, if you want to know—they carved your name into the saddle on my horse and then jabbed the horse so it'd run. The Prophet's name was carved in Alvin's saddle. They must've gone home right away."

Ta-Kumsaw's face seemed to turn dark, his eyes flashing like lightning. If you want to see a sky-god, thought Measure, this is what he looks like. "All the Whites," said Ta-Kumsaw. "They'll think I stole you."

"You didn't know?" asked Measure. "Well if that don't beat all. I thought you Reds knew everything, the way you carry on. I even tried to mention it to some of your boys, but they just turn their backs on me. And all the time none of you knowed it."

"*I* didn't know," said Ta-Kumsaw. "But someone did." He stalked off, as best you can do that in loose sand; then he turned back around. "Come on, I want you!"

So Measure followed him to the bark-covered wigwam where the Prophet held Bible classes or whatever it was he did all day. Ta-Kumsaw wasn't shy about showing how angry he was. Didn't say a thing—just walked around the wigwam, kicking away the rocks that helped anchor it to the sand. Then he picked up one end of it and started lifting. "Needs two men for this," he said.

Measure squatted down next to him, got a grip, and counted to three. Then he heaved. Ta-Kumsaw didn't, so the wigwam only lifted about six inches and dropped back down.

Measure grunted from the exertion and glared at Ta-Kumsaw. "Why didn't you lift?"

"You only got to three," said Ta-Kumsaw.

"That's the count, Chief. One, two, three."

"You Whites are such fools. Every man knows four is the strong number."

Ta-Kumsaw counted to four. This time they lifted together, got it up, tipped it clean over. By now, of course, whoever was inside knew what was going on, but nobody shouted or nothing. And when the wigwam lay on its back like a stranded turtle, there sat the Prophet and Alvin and a few Reds, cross-legged on blankets on the sand, the one-eyed Red still talking away like as if nothing had happened at all.

Ta-Kumsaw started bellowing in Shaw-Nee, and the Prophet answered him, mildly at first, but louder and louder as time went on. It was quite a row, the sort of yelling that in Measure's experience always came to blows. But not with these two Reds. Just yelled for a half hour and then stood there, facing each other, breathing hard, saying nothing at all. The silence was only a few minutes, but it felt longer than the shouting.

"You understand any of this?" asked Measure.

"I just know that the Prophet said Ta-Kumsaw was coming today, and he'd be very angry."

"Well, if he knowed, why didn't he do something to change it?"

"Oh, he's real careful about that. He's got everything going just the way it needs to, for the land to be divided right between White and Red. If he goes and changes something because he knows what's going to happen, he might undo everything, mess it all up. So he knows what's going to happen, but he don't tell a soul who might change it."

"Well, what good does it do to know the future if you ain't going to do nothing about it?"

"Oh, he does things," said Alvin. "He just doesn't necessarily tell folks what he's doing. That's why he made the crystal tower when that storm came by. To make sure the vision was still the way it was supposed to be, to make sure things hadn't gotten themselves off the right path."

"What's all *this* about? Why are they fighting?"

"You tell *me,* Measure. You're the one helped him turn over the wigwam."

"Beats me. I just told him about his and the Prophet's names being carved on our saddles."

"He knowed that," said Alvin.

"Well, he sure acted like he didn't hear of it before."

"I told the Prophet myself, the night after he took me into the tower."

"Didn't it come to your mind that maybe the Prophet didn't tell Ta-Kumsaw?"

"Why not?" asked Alvin. "Why wouldn't he tell it?"

Measure nodded wisely. "I have a feeling that's the very question Ta-Kumsaw's asking his brother about right now."

"It's crazy not to tell," said Alvin. "I figured Ta-Kumsaw must've sent somebody by now to tell our folks we were all right."

"You know what I think, Al? I think your Prophet's been playing us all for fools. I don't even have a guess as to why, but I think he's working out some plan, and part of that plan is keeping us from going home. And since that means all our family and neighbors and all are going to be up in arms about it, you can figure it out. The Prophet wants to get a real hot little shooting war going here."

"No!" said Alvin. "The Prophet says no man can kill another man who doesn't want to die, that it's as wrong to kill a White man as it is to kill a wolf or a bear that you don't want for food."

"Maybe he wants us for food. But he's going to *have* a war if we don't get home and tell our kin that we're safe."

That was right when Ta-Kumsaw and the Prophet fell silent. And it was Measure who broke the silence. "Think you boys are about set to let us go home?" he asked.

The Prophet immediately sank down into a cross-legged position, sitting on a blanket across from the two Whites. "Go home, Measure," said the Prophet.

"Not without Alvin."

"Yes without Alvin," said the Prophet. "If he stays in this part of the country, he will die."

"What are you talking about?"

"What I saw with my eyes!" said the Prophet. "The things to come. If Alvin goes home now, he'll be dead in three days. But *you* go, Measure. Today in the afternoon is a very perfect time for you to go."

"What are you going to do with Alvin? You think he's going to be any safer with *you?*"

"Not with *me,*" said the Prophet. "With my brother."

"This is all a stupid idea!" shouted Ta-Kumsaw.

"My brother is going to make many visits. With the French at Detroit, with the Irrakwa, the Appalachee nation, with the Chok-Taw and the Cree-Ek, every kind of Red man, every kind of White who might stop a very bad war from happening."

"If I talk to Reds, Tenskwa-Tawa, I'll talk to them about coming to fight with me and drive the White men back across the mountains, back into their ships, back into the sea!"

"Talk about whatever you want," said Tenskwa-Tawa. "But leave this afternoon, and take the White boy who walks like a Red man."

"No," said Ta-Kumsaw.

Grief swept across Tenskwa-Tawa's face, and he moaned sharply. "Then all the land will die, not just a part. If you don't do what I say today, then White man will kill all the land, from one ocean to the other, from north to south, all the land dead! And Red men will die except a very few who will live on tiny pieces of ugly desert land, like prisons, live there all their lives, because you did not obey what I saw in my vision!"

"Ta-Kumsaw does not obey these mad visions! Ta-Kumsaw is the face of the land, the voice of the land! The redbird told me, and you know that, Lolla-Wossiky!"

The Prophet whispered. "Lolla-Wossiky is dead."

"The voice of the land doesn't obey a one-eyed whisky-Red."

The Prophet was stung to the heart, but he kept his face impassive. "You are the voice of the land's anger. You will stand in battle against a mighty army of Whites. I tell you this will happen before the first snow falls. If the White boy Alvin is not with you, then you will die in defeat."

"And if he *is* with me?"

"Then you will live," said the Prophet.

"I'm glad to go," said Alvin. When Measure started to argue, Alvin touched his arm. "You can tell Ma and Pa I'm all right. But I *want* to go. The Prophet told me, I can learn more from Ta-Kumsaw than any other man in the whole world."

"Then I'm going with you, too," said Measure. "I gave my word to Pa and Ma both."

The Prophet looked coldly at Measure. "You will go back to your own people."

"Then Alvin comes with me."

"You are not the one who says," the Prophet retorted.

"And you are? Why, because your boys got all the arrows?"

Ta-Kumsaw reached out, touched Measure on the shoulder. "You are not a fool, Measure. Someone has to go back and tell your people that you and Alvin aren't dead."

"If I leave him behind, how do I *know* he ain't dead, tell me that?"

"You know," said Ta-Kumsaw, "because I say that while I live no Red man will hurt this boy."

"And while he's with you, nobody can hurt *you,* either, is that it? My little brother's a hostage, that's all—"

Measure could see that Ta-Kumsaw and Tenskwa-Tawa were both about as mad as they could be without killing him, and he knew he was so mad he was ready to break his hand on somebody's face. And it might've come to that, too, except Alvin stood up, all ten years and sixty inches of him, and took charge.

"Measure, you know better than anybody that I can take care of myself. You just tell Pa and Ma about what I did with them Chok-Taw, and they'll see that I'm fit. They were sending me off anyway, weren't they? To be a prentice to blacksmith. Well, I'm going to serve as prentice for a little while to Ta-Kumsaw, that's all. And everybody knows that except for maybe Tom Jefferson, Ta-Kumsaw is the greatest man in America. If I can somehow keep Ta-Kumsaw alive, then that's my duty. And if you can stop a war from happening by going home, then that's your duty. Don't you see?"

Measure *did* see, right enough, and he even agreed. But he also knew that he was going to have to face his parents. "There's a story in the Bible, about Joseph, the son of Jacob. He was his father's favorite son, but his brothers hated him and sold him into slavery, and then they took some of his clothes and soaked them in goat's blood and tore them up and came and told their father, Look, he got hisself et by lions. And his father tore his clothes and he just wouldn't stop grieving, not ever."

"But you're going to tell them I *ain't* dead."

"I'm going to tell them I saw you turn a hatchet head soft as butter, walk on the water, fly up into a tornado—that'll just make them feel all safe and warm, knowing you're tucked into such a common ordinary life with these here Reds."

Ta-Kumsaw interrupted. "You are a coward," he said. "You're afraid to tell the truth to your father and mother."

"I made an oath to them," said Measure.

"You're a coward. You take no risk. No danger. You want Alvin with you to keep you safe!"

That was just too much for Measure. He swung out with his right arm, aiming to connect with Ta-Kumsaw's smile. It didn't surprise him that Ta-Kumsaw blocked the blow—but it was kind of a shock that he caught Measure's wrist so easy, twisted it. Measure got even madder, punched at Ta-Kumsaw's stomach, and this time he *did* connect. But the chief's belly was about as soft as a stump, and he snagged Measure's other hand and held them both.

So Measure did what any good wrassler knows to do. He popped his knee up right between Ta-Kumsaw's legs.

Now, Measure had done that only twice before, and both times he did it, the other fellow got right down on the ground, writhing like a half-squished worm. Ta-Kumsaw just stood there, rigid, like he was soaking up the pain, getting madder and madder. Since he was still holding on to Measure's arms, Measure had a good notion that he was about to die, ripped right in half down the middle—that's how mad Ta-Kumsaw looked.

Ta-Kumsaw let go of Measure's arms.

Measure took his arms back, rubbed his wrists where the chief's fingermarks were white and sore. The chief looked angry, all right, but it was Alvin he was mad at. He turned and looked down at that boy like he was ready to peel off Alvin's skin and feed it to him raw.

"You did your filthy White man's tricks in me," he said.

"I didn't want neither of you getting hurt," said Alvin.

"You think I'm a coward like your brother? You think I'm afraid of pain?"

"Measure ain't no coward!"

"He threw me to the ground with White man's tricks."

Measure didn't like hearing that same accusation. "You know I didn't ask him to do that! I'll take you now, if you want! I'll fight you fair and square!"

"Strike a man with your knee?" said Ta-Kumsaw. "You don't know how to fight like a man."

"I'll face you any way you want," said Measure.

Ta-Kumsaw smiled. "Gatlopp, then."

By now a whole bunch of Reds had gathered round, and when they heard the word *gatlopp,* they started hooting and laughing.

There wasn't a White in America who hadn't heard stories about how Dan Boone ran the gatlopp and just kept on running, that first time he escaped from the Reds; but there was other stories, about Whites who got beat to death. Taleswapper told about it somewhat, the time he visited last year. It's like a jury trial, he said, where the Reds hit you hard or easy depending on how much they think you deserve to die. If they think you're a brave man, they'll strike you hard to test you with pain. But if they think you're a coward, they'll break your bones so you never get out of the gatlopp alive. The chief can't tell the gatlopp how hard to strike, or where. It's just about the most democratic and vicious system of justice ever seen.

"I see you're afraid of that," said Ta-Kumsaw.

"Of course I am," said Measure. "I'd be a fool not to, specially with your boys already thinking I'm a coward."

"I'll run the gatlopp before you," said Ta-Kumsaw. "I'll tell them to strike me as hard as they strike you."

"They won't do it," said Measure.

"They will if I ask them," said Ta-Kumsaw. He must

have seen the disbelief on Measure's face, cause then he said, "And if they don't, I'll run the gatlopp again."

"And if they kill me, will you die?"

Ta-Kumsaw looked up and down Measure's body. Lean and strong, Measure knew he was, from chopping trees and firewood, toting pails, lifting hay, and hoisting grain bags in the mill. But he wasn't *tough*. His skin was burnt something awful from being near naked in the sun out here on the dunes, even though he tried to use a blanket to cover up. Strong but soft, that's what Ta-Kumsaw found when he studied Measure's body.

"The blow that would kill you," said Ta-Kumsaw, "it might bruise me."

"So you admit it ain't fair."

"Fair is when two men face the same pain. Courage is when two men face the same pain. You don't want fair, you want easy. You want safe. You're a coward. I knew you wouldn't do it."

"I'll do it," said Measure.

"And you!" cried Ta-Kumsaw, pointing at Alvin. "You touch nothing, you heal nothing, you cure nothing, you don't take away pain!"

Alvin didn't say a word, just looked at him. Measure knew that look. It was the expression Alvin got on his face whenever he had no intention of doing a thing you said.

"Al," said Measure. "You better promise me not to meddle."

Al just set his lips and didn't speak.

"You better promise me not to meddle, Alvin Junior, or I just won't go home."

Alvin promised. Ta-Kumsaw nodded and walked away, talking in Shaw-Nee to his boys. Measure felt sick with fear.

"Why are you afraid, White man?" asked the Prophet.

"Cause I'm not stupid," said Measure. "Only a stupid man wouldn't be scared to run the gatlopp."

The Prophet just laughed and walked off.

Alvin was sitting in the sand again, writing or drawing or something with his finger.

"You ain't mad at me, are you, Alvin? Cause I got to tell you, you can't be half as mad at *me* as I am at *you*. You got no duty to these Reds, but you sure got a duty to your ma and pa. Things being how they are, I can't make you do nothing, but I can tell you I'm ashamed of you for siding with them against me and your kin."

Al looked up, and there was tears in his eyes. "Maybe I *am* siding with my kin, did you think of that?"

"Well you sure got a funny way of doing it, seeing as how you'll keep Ma and Pa worried sick for months, no doubt."

"Don't you think about anything bigger than our family? Don't you think maybe the Prophet's working out a plan to save the lives of thousands of Reds and Whites?"

"That's where we're different," said Measure. "I don't believe there *is* anything bigger than our family."

Alvin was still writing as Measure walked away. It didn't even occur to Measure what Alvin wrote in the sand. He saw, but he didn't *look*, he didn't read it. Now, though, the words came to his mind. RUN AWAY NOW, that's what Al was writing. A message to him? Why didn't he say it with his mouth, then? Nothing made sense. The writing probably wasn't for him. And he *sure* wasn't going to run away and have Ta-Kumsaw and all them Reds sure he was a coward forever. What difference would it make if he ran away now? The Reds'd catch him in a minute, there in the woods, and then he'd run the gatlopp anyway, only it'd even be worse for him.

The warriors formed two lines in the sand. They were carrying heavy branches fallen or cut from trees. Measure watched as an old man took the beads from around Ta-Kumsaw's neck, then pulled off his loincloth. Ta-Kumsaw turned to Measure and grinned. "White man is naked when he has no clothes. Red man is never naked in his own land. The wind is my clothing, the fire of the sun, the dust of the earth, the water of rain. I wear all these. I am the voice and the face of the land!"

"Just get on with it," said Measure.

"I know someone who says a man like you has no poetry in his soul," said Ta-Kumsaw.

"And I know plenty of people who say that a man like you has no soul at all."

Ta-Kumsaw glared at him, barked a few words to his men, and then stepped between the lines.

He walked slowly, his chin high and arrogant. The first Red struck him a blow across his thighs, using the skinny end of a branch. Ta-Kumsaw snatched the branch out of his hands, turned it around, and made him strike again, this time in the chest, a harsh blow that drove the air out of Ta-Kumsaw's lungs. Measure could hear the grunting sound from where he stood.

The lines ran up the face of a dune, so that progress up the hill was slow. Ta-Kumsaw never paused as the blows came. His men were stern-faced, dutiful. They were helping him show courage, and so they gave him pain—but no damaging blows. His thighs and belly and shoulders took the worst of it. Nothing on his shins, nothing in his face. But that didn't mean he had it easy. Measure could see his shoulders, bloody from the rough bark of the branches. He imagined himself receiving every blow that fell, and knew that they'd strike him harder. I'm a royal fool, he said to himself. Here I am matching courage with the noblest man in America, as everybody knows.

Ta-Kumsaw reached the end, turned, faced Measure from the top of the dune. His body was dripping with blood, and he was smiling. "Come to me, brave White man," he called.

Measure didn't hesitate. He started toward the gatlopp. It was a voice from behind that stopped him. The Prophet, shouting in Shaw-Nee. The Reds looked at him. When he was finished, Ta-Kumsaw spat. Measure, not knowing what had been said, started forward again. When he got to the first Red, he expected at least as hard a blow as Ta-Kumsaw got. But there was nothing. He took another step. Nothing. Maybe to show their contempt they meant to hit him in the back, but he climbed higher and higher up the dune, and still there was not a blow, not a move.

He should have been relieved, he knew, but instead he was angry. They gave Ta-Kumsaw help in showing his courage, and now they were making Measure's passage through the gatlopp a walk of shame instead of honor. He whirled around and faced the Prophet, who stood at the bottom of the dune, his arm across Alvin's shoulders.

"What did you say to them?" Measure demanded.

"I told them that if they killed you, everyone would say Ta-Kumsaw and the Prophet kidnapped these boys and murdered them. I told them that if they marked you in any way, when you went home everybody would say we tortured you."

"And I say I want a fair chance to prove I'm not a coward!"

"The gatlopp is a stupid idea, for men who forget their duty."

Measure reached down and grabbed a club from a Red man's hand. He struck his own thighs with it, again, again, trying to draw blood. It hurt, but not very bad, because whether he wanted to or not, his arms flinched at causing pain to his own self. So he thrust the branch back into the warrior's arms and demanded, "Hit me!"

"The bigger a man is, the more people he serves," said the Prophet. "A small man serves himself. Bigger is to serve your family. Bigger is to serve your tribe. Then your people. Biggest of all, to serve all men, and all lands. For yourself, you show courage. For your family, your tribe, your people, my people—for the land and all people in it, you walk this gatlopp with no mark on you."

Slowly, Measure turned around, walked up the dune to Ta-Kumsaw, untouched. Again Ta-Kumsaw spat on the ground, this time at Measure's feet.

"I ain't no coward," said Measure.

Ta-Kumsaw walked away. Walked, slipped, slid down the dune. The warriors of the gatlopp also walked away. Measure stood at the top of the hill, feeling ashamed, angry, used.

"Go!" shouted the Prophet. "Walk south from here!"

He handed a pouch to Alvin, who scrambled up the dune and gave it to Measure. Measure opened it. It contained pemmican and dried corn, so he could suck on it on his way.

"You coming with me?" Measure asked.

"I'm going with Ta-Kumsaw," said Alvin.

"I could've made it through the gatlopp," said Measure.

"I know," said Alvin.

"If he wasn't going to let me go through it," said Measure, "how come the Prophet allowed it to happen at all?"

"He ain't telling," said Alvin. "But something terrible's going to happen. And he *wants* it to happen. If you'd've went before, when I told you to run away—"

"They would've caught me, Al."

"It was worth a try. Now when you leave, you're doing just what he wants."

"He plans for me to get killed or something?"

"He promised me you'd live through this, Measure. And all the family. Him and Ta-Kumsaw, too."

"Then what's so terrible?"

"I don't know. I'm just scared of what's going to happen. I think he's sending me with Ta-Kumsaw to save my life."

One more time, it was worth a try. "Alvin, if you love me, come with me now."

Alvin started to cry. "Measure, I love you, but I can't go." Still crying, he ran down the dune. Not wanting to watch him out of sight, Measure started walking. Almost due south, a little bit east. He wouldn't have no trouble finding the way. But he felt sick with dread, and with shame for having let them talk him into leaving without his brother. I failed at everything here. I'm pretty near useless.

He walked the rest of that day and spent the night in a pile of leaves in a hollow. Next day he walked till late afternoon, when he came to a south-flowing creek. It would flow into the Tippy-Canoe or the Wobbish, one or the other. It was too deep to walk down the middle, and too overgrown to walk alongside. So he just kept the stream within earshot and made his own way through the forest. He wasn't no Red, that was for sure. He got scratched up by bushes and branches and bit by insects, none of which felt too good on his sunburnt skin. He also kept running into thickets and having to back out. Like the land was his enemy, slowing him down. He kept wishing for a horse and a good road.

Hard as it was to go through the woods, though, he *was* up to it. Partly cause Alvin toughened up his feet for him. Partly cause of the way he seemed to breathe deeper than ever before. But it was more than that. Strength was wound in among his muscles in a way he never felt in his life. Never so alive as now. And he thought, If I had a horse right now, I think maybe I'd be wishing I was on foot.

It was late afternoon on the second day when he heard a splashing sound in the river. There was no mistaking it— horses were being walked in the stream. That meant White men, maybe even folks from Vigor Church, still searching for him and Alvin.

He scrambled his way to the stream, getting scratched

something awful on the way. They were headed down-stream, away from him, four men on horseback. It wasn't till he was already out into the stream, yelling to bust his head off that he noticed they were wearing the green uniform of the U.S. Army. He never heard of them coming up in these parts. This was the country where White folks didn't go much, on account of not wanting to rile up the French at Fort Chicago.

They heard him right off, and wheeled their horses around to see him. Almost quick as they saw him, three of them had their muskets up to the ready.

"Don't shoot!" Measure cried.

The soldiers rode toward him, making pretty slow progress as their horses had some trouble breasting the water.

"Don't shoot, for heaven's sake," Measure said. "You can see I ain't armed, I don't even have a knife."

"He talks English real good, don't he?" said one soldier to another.

"Of course I do! I'm a White man."

"Now don't that beat all," said another soldier. "First time I ever heard one of them claim to be White."

Measure looked down at his own skin. It was a vivid red color from his sunburn, much lighter than any true Red man. He *was* wearing a loincloth, and he looked pretty wild and dirty. But his beard was growing somewhat, wasn't it? For the first time Measure found himself wishing he was a hairy man, with thick heavy beard and lots of chest hair. Then there'd be no mistake, since Reds didn't grow much. As it was, though, they wouldn't see his light-colored mustache hair or the few little hairs on his chin till they were up close.

And they weren't taking no chances, either. Only one rode right up to him. The others hung back, their muskets out, ready to open fire in case Measure had some boys lying in ambush on the riverbank. He could see that the man riding toward him was plumb scared to death, looking this way and that, waiting to see a Red man flitch an arrow at him. Kind of an idiot, Measure decided, since there wasn't no chance of seeing a Red man in the woods till his arrow was already in you.

The soldier didn't come right to him. He circled around, got beside him. Then he looped a rope and tossed it to Measure. "You hitch this around your chest, under your arms," said the soldier.

"What for?"

"So I can lead you along."

"The hell I will," said Measure. "If I thought you were going to drag me along by a rope in the middle of a creek, I'd've stayed on dry land and walked home myself."

"If you don't put this rope around you in five seconds, them boys are going to blow your head off."

"What are you talking about?" Measure demanded. "I'm Measure Miller. I was captured with my little brother, Alvin, almost a week ago, and I'm just going home to Vigor Church."

"Well, ain't that a real pretty story?" said the soldier. He drew back the rope, sopping wet, and cast it again. This time it hit Measure in the face. Measure caught at it, held it in his hand. The soldier drew his sword. "Get ready to shoot, boys!" shouted the soldier. "It's that renegade, all right!"

"Renegade! I—" Then it finally occurred to Measure that something had gone real bad with this. They knew who he was, and they still wanted to take him prisoner. With three muskets and a sword close by, they had a fair chance of maybe even killing him if he tried to run away. This was the U.S. Army, wasn't it? Once they got him to an officer, he could explain and all this would get cleared up. So he put the rope over his head, and pulled the loop around his chest.

It wasn't too bad as long as they were in the water;

sometimes he just floated along. But pretty soon they got out and then they made him walk along behind as they picked their way through the woods. They were looping east, around behind Vigor Church.

Measure tried talking, but they told him to shut up. "I tell you, we been told we can bring in renegades like you alive or dead. White man dressed like a Red—we know what you are."

From their conversation he was able to gather a few things. They were on a scout-around from General Harrison. It made Measure sick, to think things had got to the point where they'd call on that likker-dealing scoundrel to come north. And he got here awful fast, too.

They spent the night camped in a clearing. They made so much noise that Measure thought it was a wonder they didn't have every Red in the whole country nosing around before morning.

The next day, he flat refused to be dragged along on a rope. "I'm near naked, I got no weapons, and you can kill me or let me ride." They could talk about bringing him in alive or dead and not caring which, but he knew that that was talk. These were a crude bunch, but they didn't hanker much after killing White men in cold blood. So he ended up on horseback, holding one of them around the waist. Pretty soon they reached country that had some roads and trails, and they made good time.

Just after noon they reached an army camp. Not much of an army, maybe a hundred in uniform and another two hundred marching and drilling on a parade ground that used to be a pasture. Measure couldn't remember the name of the family that lived here. They were new folks, just come up from the area around Carthage. Turned out it didn't matter who they were, though. It was General Harrison had their house for his headquarters, and these scouts led him straight to Harrison.

"Ah," said Harrison. "One of the renegades."

"I'm no renegade," said Measure. "They been treating me like a prisoner this whole way. I swear the Reds treated me better than your White soldiers."

"I ain't surprised much," said Harrison. "They treated you real nice, I'm sure. Where's the other renegade?"

"Other renegade? You mean my brother Alvin? You know who I am, and you ain't letting me go home?"

"You answer *my* questions, and then I'll give some thought to answering yours."

"My brother Alvin ain't here, and he ain't coming, and from what I see before me I'm real glad he didn't come."

"Alvin? Ah, yes, they told me you were claiming to be Measure Miller. Well, we know that Measure Miller was murdered by Ta-Kumsaw and the Prophet."

Measure spat on the floor. "You *know* that? From a few tore-up bloody clothes? Well you don't fool me. Do you think I don't see what you're doing?"

"Take him to the cellar," said Harrison. "Be real gentle with him."

"You don't *want* folks to know I'm alive, cause then they'll see they don't need you up here!" shouted Measure. "I wouldn't be surprised if you got them Chok-Taw to capture us in the first place!"

"If that's true," said Harrison, "then if I were you I'd watch how I talked and what I said. I'd be real worried about getting home alive, *ever*. Now look at yourself, boy. Skin red as a redbird, wearing a loincloth, looking wild as a real bad dream. No, I reckon if it turned out you was shot dead by mistake, nobody'd blame us, not a soul."

"My father'd know," said Measure. "You can't fool him with a lie like that, Harrison. And Armor-of-God, he'll—"

"Armor-of-God? That pathetic weakling? The one who keeps telling people that Ta-Kumsaw and the Prophet are innocent, and we shouldn't be getting ready to wipe them out? Nobody listens to him no more, Measure."

"They will. Alvin's alive, and you'll never catch *him*."

"Why not?"

"Cause he's with Ta-Kumsaw."

"Ah, and where is that?"

"Not around *here,* you can bet."

"You've seen him? And the Prophet?"

The hungry look in Harrison's eyes made Measure kind of step back and hold his tongue. "I seen what I seen," said Measure. "And I'll say what I say."

"Say what I ask, or you'll be dead," said Harrison.

"Kill me, and I won't say nothing at all. But I'll tell you this. I saw the Prophet call a tornado out of a storm. I saw him walk on water. I saw him prophesy, and his prophecies all come true. He knows everything you plan to do. You think you're doing what *you* want, but you'll end up serving his purpose, you watch and see."

"What an idea," said Harrison, chuckling. "By that reckoning, boy, it serves his purpose for you to be in my hands, don't it?" He waved his hands, and the soldiers dragged him out of the house and down into the root cellar. They treated him real gentle on the way—kicked him and knocked him down and all they could before they threw him down the steps and barred the door behind him.

Since these folks came from Carthage country, the cellar door had a lock, as well as the bar. Down with the carrots, potatoes, and spiders, Measure tested that door as best he could. His whole body was one big ache. All the scratches and the sunburn were nothing compared to the raw skin inside his thighs from riding behind with bare legs. And that was nothing compared to the pain from the kicks and bashes they gave him on the way here.

Measure didn't waste no more time. He knew what was going on well enough to know Harrison couldn't let him

out alive. He had those scouts out *looking* for him and
Alvin. If they turned up alive, it would undo all his plans,
and that'd be a real shame, cause things were going just
right for Harrison. After all these years, here he was at
Vigor Church, training the local men to be soldiers, while
nobody was listening to Armor-of-God at all. Measure
didn't much like the Prophet, but compared to Harrison
the Prophet was a saint.

Or was he? The Prophet had him wait for the gatlopp—
why? So he'd leave in the afternoon two days ago, instead
of morning. So he'd reach the Tippy-Canoe just when them
soldiers were riding down. Otherwise he would've come
to Prophetstown and then hopped on over into Vigor
Church without seeing a soldier. They'd never have found
him, if he hadn't heard them and called out to them himself. Was this all part of the Prophet's plan?

Well, so what if it was? Maybe the Prophet's plan was a
good thing, and maybe it wasn't—so far Measure didn't
think too highly of it. But he sure wasn't going to sit around
in a root cellar waiting to see how the plan worked out.

He burrowed his way through the potatoes to the back
of the cellar. There was more spiderwebs in his face and
hair than he cared for, but this wasn't a time to worry about
tidiness. Pretty soon he cleared him a space at the back,
with the potatoes pushed mostly to the front. When they
opened the doors, they'd just see a lot of potatoes. Not a
sign of his digging.

The root cellar was the normal kind. Dug out, timbered
over, roofed, and then the roof covered up with all the dirt
from the hole. He could dig into the back wall and come
up behind the cellar, and they couldn't see a thing from
the house at all. It was bare-hands digging, but this was
rich Wobbish soil. He'd come out looking more like a
Black than a Red, but he didn't much care.

Trouble was, the back wall wasn't dirt, it was wood.

They'd walled it in, right to the bottom. Tidy folks. The floor was dirt, all right. But that meant digging down under the wall before he could tunnel up. Instead of being something he could do overnight, it'd take days. And any time, they might catch him digging. Or just plain drag him out and shoot him. Or maybe even bring back them Chok-Taws, to do what they started—leave him looking like Ta-Kumsaw and the Prophet had him tortured. All possible.

Home wasn't ten miles away. That's what plain drove him crazy. So close to home, and they didn't even guess it, had no idea they ought to come to help. He remembered that torch girl from Hatrack River, years ago, the one who saw them stuck in the river and sent help. That's who I need right now, I need me a torch, somebody who'd find me and send help.

But that wasn't too likely. Not for Measure. If it was Alvin, now, there'd be eight miracles, whatever it took to get him out safe. But for Measure, there'd be just whatever he could work up for hisself.

He broke a fingernail half off in the first ten minutes of digging. The pain was real bad, and he knew he was bleeding. If they dragged him out now, they'd know he was making a tunnel. But it was his only chance. So he kept digging, pain and all, every now and then stopping to toss out a potato that rolled down into the hole.

Pretty soon he took off his loincloth and used it in his work. He'd loosen up the soil with his hands, then pile it onto the cloth and use that to hoist it up out of the hole. It wasn't as good as having a spade, but it sure beat moving the dirt out one handful at a time. What did he have, days? Hours?

11

RED BOY

It wasn't an hour after Measure left. Ta-Kumsaw stood atop a dune, the White boy Alvin beside him. And in front of him, Tenskwa-Tawa. Lolla-Wossiky. His brother, the boy who once cried for the death of bees. A prophet, supposedly. Speaking the will of the land, supposedly. Speaking words of cowardice, surrender, defeat, destruction.

"This is the oath of the land at peace," said the Prophet. "To take none of the White man's weapons, none of the White man's tools, none of the White man's clothing, none of the White man's food, none of the White man's drink, and none of the White man's promises. Above all, never to take a life that doesn't offer itself to die."

The Reds who heard him had heard it all before, as had Ta-Kumsaw. Most of those who had come to Mizogan with them had already refused the Prophet's covenant of weakness. They took a different oath, the oath of the land's anger, the oath that Ta-Kumsaw offered them. Every White must live under Red man's law, or leave the land, or die. A White man's weapons can be used, but only to defend Reds against murder and theft. No Red man will torture or kill a prisoner—man, woman, or child. Above all, the death of no Red will go unavenged.

Ta-Kumsaw knew that if all the Reds of America took his oath, they could still defeat the White man. Whites had only made such inroads because the Reds could never unite under one leader. The Whites could always ally themselves with a tribe or two, who would lead them through the trackless forest and help them find their enemy. If Reds had not turned renegade—like the unspeakable Irrakwa, the half-White Cherriky—then the White man could not have survived here in the land. They would have been swallowed up, lost, as had happened to every other group that came from the old world.

When the Prophet finished his challenge, there were only a handful who took his oath, who would go back with him. He seemed sad, Ta-Kumsaw thought. Weighed down. He turned his back on the ones who remained—on the warriors, who would fight the White man.

"Those men are yours," said the Prophet. "I wish there weren't so many."

"Mine, yes, but I wish there weren't so few."

"Oh, you'll find allies enough. Chok-Taw, Cree-Ek, Chicky-Saw, the vicious Semmy-Noll of the Oky-Fenoky. Enough to raise the greatest army of Reds ever seen in this land, all thirsting for White man's blood."

"Stand at my side in that battle," said Ta-Kumsaw.

"You'll lose your cause by killing," said the Prophet. "I'll win my cause."

"By dying."

"If the land calls for my death, I'll answer."

"And all your people with you."

The Prophet shook his head. "I've seen what I've seen. The people of my oath are as much a part of the land as the bear or the buffalo, the squirrel or the beaver, the turkey or the pheasant or the grouse. All those animals have stood still to take your arrow, haven't they? Or stretched out their neck for your knife. Or lain down their head for your tommy-hawk."

"They're animals, meant to be meat."

"They're alive, meant to live until they die, and when they die, die so that others can live."

"Not me. Not *my* people. We won't stretch out our neck for the White man's knife."

The Prophet took Ta-Kumsaw by the shoulders, tears streaming down his face. He pressed his cheek against Ta-Kumsaw's cheek, putting his tears on his brother's face.

"Come find me across the Mizzipy, when all this is done," said the Prophet.

"I'll never let the land be divided," said Ta-Kumsaw. "The east doesn't belong to the White man."

"The east will die," said the Prophet. "Follow me west, where the White man will never go."

Ta-Kumsaw said nothing.

The White boy Alvin touched the Prophet's hand. "Tenskwa-Tawa, does that mean I can never go west?"

The Prophet laughed. "Why do you think I'm sending you with Ta-Kumsaw? If anyone can turn a White boy Red, Ta-Kumsaw can."

"I don't want him," said Ta-Kumsaw.

"Take him or die," said the Prophet.

Then the Prophet walked down the slope of the dune, to the dozen men who waited for him, their palms dripping blood to seal the covenant. They walked off along the shore of the lake, to where their families waited. Tomorrow they'd be back in Prophetstown. Ripe to be slaughtered.

Ta-Kumsaw waited until the Prophet had disappeared behind a dune. Then he cried out to the hundreds who remained. "When will the White man have peace?"

"When he leaves!" they shouted. "When he dies!"

Ta-Kumsaw laughed and held out his arms. He felt their love and trust like the heat of the sun on a winter's day. Lesser men had felt that heat before, but it had oppressed them, because they weren't worthy of the trust they had been given. Not Ta-Kumsaw. He had measured himself, and he knew that there was no task ahead of him that he couldn't accomplish. Only treachery could keep him from victory. And Ta-Kumsaw was very good at knowing a man's heart. Knowing if he could be trusted. Knowing if he was a liar. Hadn't he known Governor Harrison from the beginning? A man like that couldn't hide from him.

They left only minutes later. A few dozen men led the women and children to the new place where their wandering village would settle. They stayed no more than three days in any place—a permanent village like Prophetstown was an invitation to a massacre. The only thing that kept the Prophet safe was sheer numbers. Ten thousand Reds lived there now, more than had ever lived in any one place before. And it *was* a miraculous place, Ta-Kumsaw knew it. The maize grew up six ears to the stalk, thicker and milkier than any corn had ever been before. Buffalo and deer wandered into the city from a hundred miles around, walked to the cooking fires, and lay down waiting for the knife. When the geese flew overhead, a few from every flock would come to land on the Wobbish and the Tippy-Canoe, waiting for the arrow. The fish swam up from the Hio to leap into the nets of Prophetstown.

All that would mean nothing, if the White man ever brought his cannons to fire grapeshot and shrapnel through the fragile wigwams and lodges of the Red city. The searing metal would cut through the delicate walls—that deadly driven rain would not be held out by sticks and mud. Every Red man in Prophetstown would regret his oath on that day.

Ta-Kumsaw led them through the forest. The White boy

ran directly behind him. Ta-Kumsaw deliberately set a killing pace, twice as fast as they had run before, bringing the boy and his brother to Mizogan. They had two hundred miles to Fort Detroit, and Ta-Kumsaw was determined to cover that distance in a single day. No White man could do it—no White man's horse, either. A mile every five minutes, on and on, the wind whipping through the topknot of his hair. It would kill a man to run so fast for half an hour, except that the Red man called on the strength of the land to help him. The ground pushed back against his feet, adding to his strength. The bushes parted, making paths; space appeared where there was no space; Ta-Kumsaw raced across streams and rivers so quickly that his feet did not touch the bottom of the stream, merely sank just deep enough to find purchase on the water itself. His hunger to arrive at Fort Detroit was so strong that the land answered by feeding him, giving him strength. And not just Ta-Kumsaw, but every man behind him, every Red man who knew the feel of the land within him, he found the same strength as his leader, stepped in the same path, footfall by footfall, like one great soul walking a long slender highway through the wood.

I will have to carry the White boy, thought Ta-Kumsaw. But the footsteps behind him—for Whites made noise when they ran—kept up, falling into a rhythm identical with his own.

That, of course, was not possible. The boy's legs were too short, he had to take more strides to cover the same ground. Yet each step of Ta-Kumsaw's was matched so closely that he heard the sound of the White boy's feet as if they were his own.

Minute after minute, mile after mile, hour after hour, the boy kept on.

The sun set behind them, over the left shoulder. The stars came out, but no moon, and the night was dark under the trees. Still they didn't slow, found their way easily through the wood, because it wasn't their own eyes or their own mind finding the way, it was the land itself drawing them through the safe places in the darkness. Several times in the night, Ta-Kumsaw noticed that the boy was no longer making noise. He called out in Shaw-Nee to the man who ran behind the White boy Alvin, and always the man answered, "He runs."

The moon came up, casting patches of dim light onto the forest floor. They overtook a storm—the ground grew moist under their feet, then wet; they ran through showers, heavy rain, showers again, and then the land was dry. They never slackened their pace. The sky in the east turned grey, then pink, then blue, and the sun leapt upward. The day was warming and the sun already three hands above the horizon when they saw the smoke of cookfires, then the slack fleur-de-lis flag, and finally the cross of the cathedral. Only then did they slow down. Only then did they break the perfect unison of their step, loose the grip of the land in their minds, and come to rest in a meadow so near the town that they could hear the organ playing in the cathedral.

Ta-Kumsaw stopped, and the boy stopped behind him. How had Alvin, a White boy, traveled like a Red man through the night? Ta-Kumsaw knelt before the boy. Though Alvin's eyes were open, he seemed not to see anything. "Alvin," said Ta-Kumsaw, speaking English. The boy didn't answer. "Alvin, are you asleep?"

Several warriors gathered around. They were all somewhat quiet and spent from the journey. Not exhausted, because the land replenished them along the way. Their quiet was more from awe at having been so closely tied to the land; such a journey was known to be a holy thing, a gift from the land to its noblest children. Many a Red had set out on such a journey and been turned away, forced to stop and sleep and rest and eat, stopped by darkness or bad weather, because his need for the journey wasn't great enough, or his journey was contrary to what the land itself needed. Ta-Kumsaw, though, had never been refused; they all knew it. This was much of the reason Ta-Kumsaw was held in as high esteem as his brother. The Prophet did miraculous things, but no one saw his visions; he could only tell about them. What Ta-Kumsaw did, though, his warriors did with him, felt with him.

Now, though, they were as puzzled by the White boy as Ta-Kumsaw was. Had Ta-Kumsaw sustained the boy by his own power? Or had the land, unbelievably, reached out and supported a White child for his own sake?

"Is he White like his skin, or Red in his heart?" asked one. He spoke Shaw-Nee, and not in the quick way, but rather in the slow and holy language of the shamans.

To Ta-Kumsaw's surprise, Alvin responded to his words, looking at the man who spoke instead of staring straight ahead. "White," murmured Alvin. He spoke English.

"Does he speak our language?" asked a man.

Alvin appeared confused by the question. "Ta-Kumsaw," he said. He looked up to see the angle of the sun. "It's morning. Was I asleep?"

"Not asleep," said Ta-Kumsaw in Shaw-Nee. Now the boy appeared not to understand at all. "Not asleep," Ta-Kumsaw repeated in English.

"I feel like I was asleep," he said. "Only I'm standing up."

"You don't feel tired? You don't want to rest?"

"Tired? Why would I be tired?"

Ta-Kumsaw didn't want to explain. If the boy didn't know what he had done, then it was a gift of the land. Or perhaps there was something to what the Prophet had said about him. That Ta-Kumsaw should teach him to be Red. If he could match grown Shaw-Nee, step for step, in such a run as that, perhaps this boy of all Whites could learn to feel the land.

Ta-Kumsaw stood and spoke to the others. "I'm going into the city, with only four others."

"And the boy," said one. Others repeated his words. They all knew the Prophet's promise to Ta-Kumsaw, that as long as the boy was with him he wouldn't die. Even if he were tempted to leave the boy behind, they'd never let him do it.

"And the boy," Ta-Kumsaw agreed.

Detroit was not a fort like the pathetic wooden stockades of the Americans. It was made of stone, like the cathedral, with huge cannon pointing outward toward the river that connected Lake Huron and Lake St. Clair with Lake Canada, and smaller cannon aimed inland, ready to fend off attackers on land.

But it was the city, not the fort, that impressed them. A dozen streets of houses, wooden ones, with shops and stores, and in the center of all, a cathedral so massive that it made a mockery of Reverend Thrower's church. Black-robed priests went about their business like crows in the streets. The swarthy Frenchmen didn't show the same hostility toward Reds that Americans often seemed to have. Ta-Kumsaw understood that this was because the French in Detroit weren't there to settle. They didn't think of Reds as rivals for possession of the land. The French here were all biding their time till they went back to Europe, or at least back to the White-settled lands of Quebec and Ontario across the river; except the trappers, of course, and for them the Reds were not enemies, either. Trappers held Reds in awe, trying to learn how Reds found game so easily, when the trappers had such a devilish time knowing where to lay their snares. They thought, as White men always do, that it was some kind of trick the Reds performed, and if they only studied Red men long enough, these White trappers would learn how to do it. They would never learn. How could the land accept the kind of man who would kill every beaver in a pond, just for the pelts, leaving the meat to rot, and no beaver left to bear young? No wonder the bears killed these trappers whenever they could. The land rejected them.

When I have driven the Americans from the land west of the mountains, thought Ta-Kumsaw, then I will drive out the Yankees from New England, and the Cavaliers from the Crown Colonies. And when they're all gone, I'll turn to the Spanish of Florida and the French of Canada. Today I'll make use of you for my own purpose, but tomorrow I'll drive you out, too. Every White face that stays in this land will stay here because it's dead. And in that day, beavers will die only when the land tells them it's the time and place to die.

The French commander in Detroit was officially de Maurepas, but Ta-Kumsaw avoided him whenever he could. It was only the second man, Napoleon Bonaparte, who was worth talking to.

"I heard you were at Lake Mizogan," said Napoleon. He spoke in French, of course, but Ta-Kumsaw had learned French at the same time he was learning English, and from the same person. "Come, sit down." Napoleon looked with vague interest at the White boy Alvin, but said nothing to him.

"I was there," said Ta-Kumsaw. "So was my brother."

"Ah. But was there an army?"

"The seed of one," said Ta-Kumsaw. "I gave up arguing with Tenskwa-Tawa. I'll make an army out of other tribes."

"When!" demanded Napoleon. "You come here two, three times each year, you tell me you're going to have an army. Do you know how long I've waited? Four years, four miserable years of exile."

"I know how many years," said Ta-Kumsaw. "You'll have your battle."

"Before my hair turns grey? Tell me that! Do I have to be dying of old age before you'll call out a general rising of the Reds? You know how helpless I am. La Fayette and de Maurepas won't let me go more than fifty miles from here, won't give me any troops at all. There has to be an army first, they say. The Americans have to have some main force that you can fight with. Well, the only thing that will cause those miserably independent bastards to unite is *you*."

"I know," said Ta-Kumsaw.

"You promised me an army of ten thousand Reds, Ta-Kumsaw. Instead I keep hearing about a city of ten thousand *Quakers*!"

"Not Quakers."

"If they renounce war it amounts to the same thing." Suddenly Napoleon let his voice become soft, loving, persuasive. "Ta-Kumsaw, I need you, I depend on you, don't fail me."

Ta-Kumsaw laughed. Napoleon learned long ago that his tricks worked on White men, but not half so well on Reds, and on Ta-Kumsaw not at all. "You care nothing for me, and I care nothing for you," said Ta-Kumsaw. "You want one battle and a victory, so you can go home a hero to Paris. I want one battle and a victory, so I can strike terror into White men's hearts and bring together an even greater army of Reds under my command, to sweep the land south of here and drive the Englishmen back across the mountains. One battle, one victory—that's why we work together, and when that's done I'll never think of you again, and you'll never think of me."

Napoleon was angry, but he laughed. "Half true," he said. "I won't care about you, but I'll think of you. I've learned from you, Ta-Kumsaw. That love of a commander makes men fight better than love of country, and love of country better than the hope of glory, and the hope of glory better than looting, and looting better than wages. But best of all is to fight for a cause. A great and noble dream. I've always had the love of my men. They would die for me. But for a cause, they'd let their wives and children die and think it was worth the price."

"How did you learn that from me?" said Ta-Kumsaw. "That's my brother's talk, not mine."

"Your brother? I thought he didn't think anything was worth dying for."

"No, he's very free with dying. It's killing he won't do."

Napoleon laughed, and Ta-Kumsaw laughed with him. "You're right, you know. We're not friends. But I do like you. What puzzles me is this—when you've won, and all the White men are gone, you really mean to walk away and let all the tribes go back to the way they were before, separate, quarreling, weak."

"Happy. That's how we were before. Many tribes, many languages, but one living land."

"Weak," said Napoleon again. "If I ever brought all of *my* land under my flag, Ta-Kumsaw, I'd hold them together so long and so tightly that they'd become one great people, great and strong. And if I ever do that, you can count on this. We'll be back, and take your land away from you, just like every other land on Earth. Count on it."

"That's because you are evil, General Bonaparte. You want to bend everything and everybody to your obedience."

"That isn't evil, foolish savage. If everybody obeyed me, then they'd be happy and safe, at peace, and, for the first time in all of history, free."

"Safe, unless they opposed you. Happy, unless they hated you. Free, unless they wanted something contrary to your will."

"Imagine, a Red man philosophizing. Do those peasant squatters south of here know that you've read Newton, Voltaire, Rousseau, and Adam Smith?"

"I don't think they know I can read their languages."

Napoleon leaned across his desk. "We'll destroy them, Ta-Kumsaw, you and I together. But you have to bring me an army."

"My brother prophesies that we'll have that army before the year ends."

"A prophecy?"

"All his prophecies come true."

"Does he say we'll win?"

Ta-Kumsaw laughed. "He says you'll be known as the greatest European general who ever lived. And I will be known as the greatest Red."

Napoleon ran his fingers through his hair and smiled, almost boyish now; he could pass from menacing to friendly to adorable in moments. "That seems to dodge the question. Dead men can be called great, too."

"But men who lose battles are never called great, are they? Noble, perhaps, even heroic. But not great."

"True, Ta-Kumsaw, true. But your brother is being coy. Oracular. Delphic."

"I don't know those words."

"Of course you don't. You're a savage." Napoleon poured wine. "I forget myself. Wine?"

Ta-Kumsaw shook his head.

"I suppose none for the boy," said Napoleon.

"He's only ten," said Ta-Kumsaw.

"In France, that means we water the wine half and half. What are you doing with a White boy, Ta-Kumsaw? Are you capturing children now?"

"This White boy," said Ta-Kumsaw, "he's more than he seems."

"In a loincloth he doesn't look like much. Does he understand French?"

"Not a word," said Ta-Kumsaw. "I came to ask you—can you give us guns?"

"No," said Napoleon.

"We can't fight bullets with arrows," said Ta-Kumsaw.

"La Fayette refuses to authorize us to issue you any guns. Paris agrees with him. They don't trust you. They're afraid any guns they give you might someday be turned against us."

"Then what good will it do me to raise an army?"

Napoleon smiled, sipped his wine. "I've been speaking to some Irrakwa traders."

"The Irrakwa are the urine of sick dogs," said Ta-Kumsaw. "They were cruel, vicious animals before the White man came, and they are worse now."

"Odd. The English seemed to find them to be kindred spirits. And La Fayette adores them. All that matters now, though, is this: They manufacture guns, in large numbers, cheaply. Not the most *reliable* weapons, but they use exactly the same size ammunition. It means they can make balls that fit the barrel more tightly, with better aim. And yet they sell them for less."

"You'll buy them for us?"

"No. *You'll* buy them."

"We don't have money."

"Pelts," said Napoleon. "Beaver pelts. Minks. Deer-hides and buffalo leather."

Ta-Kumsaw shook his head. "We can't ask these animals to die for the sake of guns."

"Too bad," said Napoleon. "You Reds have a knack for hunting, I've been told."

"True Reds do. The Irrakwa don't. They've used White man's machines so long now that they're dead to the land, just like White men. Or they'd go and get the pelts they want for themselves."

"There's something else they want. Besides pelts," said Napoleon.

"We don't have anything they want."

"Iron," said Napoleon.

"We don't have iron."

"No. But they know where it is. In the upper reaches of the Mizzipy, and along the Mizota. Up near the west end of High Water Lake. All they want is your promise that you won't harm their boats bringing iron ore back to Irrakwa, or their miners as they dig it out of the earth."

"Peace for the future, in exchange for guns now?"

"Yes," said Napoleon.

"Aren't they afraid that I'll turn the guns against *them*?"

"They ask you to promise that you won't."

Ta-Kumsaw considered this. "Tell them this. I promise that if they give us guns, not one of the guns will ever be used against any Irrakwa. All my men will take this oath. And we will never attack any of their boats on the water, or their miners as they dig in the earth."

"You mean that?" asked Napoleon.

"If I said it, I meant it," said Ta-Kumsaw.

"As much as you hate them?"

"I hate them because the land hates them. When the White man is gone, and the land is strong again, not sick, then earthquakes can swallow up miners, and storms can sink boats, and the Irrakwa will become true Red men again or they will die. Once the White man is gone, the land will be stern with its children who remain."

The meeting was soon finished after that. Ta-Kumsaw got up and shook hands with the general. Alvin surprised them both by also stepping forward and offering his hand.

Napoleon shook hands with him, amused. "Tell the boy he keeps dangerous company," he said.

Ta-Kumsaw translated. Alvin looked at him with wide eyes. "Does he mean *you*?" he asked.

"I think so," said Ta-Kumsaw.

"But *he's* the most dangerous man in the world," said Alvin.

Napoleon laughed when Ta-Kumsaw translated the boy's words. "How can I be dangerous? A little man stuck away out here in the middle of the wilderness, when the center of the world is Europe, great wars are fought there and I have no part in them!"

Ta-Kumsaw didn't need to translate—the boy understood from Napoleon's tone and expression. "He's so dangerous because he makes people love him without deserving it."

Ta-Kumsaw felt the truth in the boy's words. That was what Napoleon did to White men, and it *was* dangerous, dangerous and evil and dark. Is this the man I rely on to help me? To be my ally? Yes, he is, because I have no choice. Ta-Kumsaw didn't translate what the boy said, even though Napoleon insisted. So far the French general had not attempted to cast his spell on the boy. If he knew the boy's words, he might try, and it just might capture Alvin. Ta-Kumsaw was coming to appreciate what the boy was. Perhaps the boy was too strong for Napoleon to charm him. Or perhaps the boy would become an adoring slave like de Maurepas. Better not to find out. Better to take the boy away.

Alvin insisted on seeing the cathedral. One priest looked horrified to see men in loincloths come into the place, but another rebuked him and welcomed them inside. Ta-Kumsaw was always amused by the statues of the saints. Whenever possible, the statues were shown being tortured in the most gruesome ways. White could talk all day about how barbaric it was, the Red practice of torturing captives so they could show courage. Yet whose statues did they kneel at to pray? People who showed courage under torture. There was no making sense of White men.

He and Alvin talked about this on their way out of the city, not hurrying at all now. He also explained to the boy something of how they were able to run so far, so quickly. And how remarkable it was for a White boy to keep up with them.

Alvin seemed to understand how Red men lived within the land; at least he tried. "I think I felt that. While I was running. It's like I'm not in myself. My thoughts are wandering all over. Like dreaming. And while I'm gone, something else is telling my body what to do. Feeding it, using it, taking it wherever it wants to go. Is that what you feel?"

That wasn't at all what Ta-Kumsaw felt. When the land came into *him*, it was like he was more alive than ever; not absent from his body, but more strongly present in it than at any other time. But he didn't explain this to the boy. Instead he turned the question back to Alvin. "You say it's like dreaming. What did you dream last night?"

"I dreamed again about a lot of the visions I saw when I was in the crystal tower with the Shining—with the Prophet."

"The Shining Man. I know you call him that—he told me why."

"I dreamed those things again. Only it was different. I could see some things more clearly now, and other things I forgot."

"Did you dream anything you *hadn't* seen before?"

"*This* place. The statues in the cathedral. And that man we visited, the general. And something even stranger. A big hill, almost round—no, with eight sides. I remember that, it was real clear. A hill with eight straight sides to it, sloping down. Inside it there was a whole city, lots of little rooms, like in anthills, only people-sized. Or anyway bigger than ants. And I was on top of it, wandering around in all these strange trees—they had silver leaves, not green—and I was looking for my brother. For Measure."

Ta-Kumsaw said nothing for a long time. But he thought many things. No White man had ever seen that place—the land was still strong enough to keep them from finding *that*. Yet this boy had dreamed of it. And a dream of Eight-Face Mound never came by chance. It always meant something. It always meant the same thing.

"We have to go there," Ta-Kumsaw said.

"Where?"

"To the hill you dreamed of," said Ta-Kumsaw.

"There *is* such a place?"

"No White man has ever seen it. For a White man to stand there would be—filthy." Alvin didn't answer that. What could he say? Ta-Kumsaw swallowed hard. "But if you dream of it, you have to go."

"What is it?"

Ta-Kumsaw shook his head. "The place you dreamed of. That's all. If you want to know more, dream again."

It was near night when they reached the camp; wigwams had been erected, because it looked like more rain tonight. The others insisted that Ta-Kumsaw share a hut with Alvin, for his safety's sake. But Ta-Kumsaw didn't want to. The boy made him afraid. The land was doing things with this boy, and not giving Ta-Kumsaw any idea what was happening.

But when you saw yourself at the Eight-Face Mound in your dreams, you had no choice but to go. And since Alvin could never find the way alone, Ta-Kumsaw had to take him.

He could never explain it to the others, and even if he could, he wouldn't do it. Word would get out that Ta-Kumsaw had taken a White to the ancient holy place, and then many Reds would refuse to listen to Ta-Kumsaw anymore.

So in the morning he told the others he was taking the boy off to teach him, as the Prophet had told him he must. "Meet me in five days where the Pickawee flows into the Hio," he told them. "From there we'll go south to talk to the Chok-Taw and the Chicky-Saw."

Take us with you, they said. You won't be safe alone. But he didn't answer them, and soon enough they gave up. He set off at a run, and once again Alvin fell in step behind him, matching him stride for stride. It was almost as far again as the journey from Mizogan to Detroit. By nightfall they would be at the edge of the Land of Flints. Ta-Kumsaw planned to sleep there, and find dreams of his own, before daring to lead a White boy to Eight-Face Mound.

12

❧

CANNONS

Measure heard them coming only seconds before the door swung open and light flooded the root cellar. Time enough to dump out the dirt and tuck his loincloth into the deerhide belt, then scramble forward onto the potatoes. The breechclout was so filthy it was like wearing dirt, but this wasn't a time to get finicky.

They didn't waste no time on prison inspection, so they didn't see the hole that was now reaching a good two feet under the back wall. Instead they reached in and drug him out by the armpits, slamming the root cellar doors shut behind him. The light was so sudden it dazzled him, and he couldn't make out who had him, or how many they were. Didn't much matter. Anyone local would have known him right off, so they had to be Harrison's boys, and once he knew that, he knew it wasn't nothing good going to happen to him.

"Like a pig," said Harrison. "Disgusting. You look like a Red."

"You put me in a hole in the ground," said Measure. "I ain't about to come out clean."

"I gave you one long night to think about it, boy," said

Harrison. "Now you got to make up your mind. There's two ways you can be useful to me. One is alive, you telling all about how they tortured your brother to death, him screaming every second. You make it a good story, and you tell all about how Ta-Kumsaw and the Prophet were there, getting their own hands into the boy's blood. You tell a story like that, and it's worth keeping you alive."

"Ta-Kumsaw saved my life from *your* Chok-Taw Reds," said Measure. "That's the only story I'll tell. Except to mention how you *wanted* me to tell another story."

"That's what I thought," said Harrison. "Fact is, even if you lied to me and promised to tell the story my way, I reckon I wouldn't've believed you. So we both agree—it's the other choice."

Measure knew Harrison meant to produce his body, with the evidence of torture on it. Dead, he couldn't tell anybody who did the cutting and burning. Well, thought Measure, you'll see I die as brave as any man.

But because he wasn't one to welcome death with both hands, he thought he'd give talking a bit more of a try. "You let me go and call off this war, Harrison, and I'll keep my mouth shut. Just let me wander in, and you allow as how it was all a terrible mistake and take your boys on home and leave Prophetstown in peace, and I won't tell a word otherwise. That's a lie I'm glad to tell."

Harrison hesitated just a moment, and Measure allowed himself to hope he might actually have some spark of godliness left in him, to turn away from the sin of murder before it was fully done. Then Harrison smiled, shook his head, and waved his hand at a big ugly riverman standing right up against the wall.

"Mike Fink, this here's a renegade White boy, who has joined in with all the evil doings of Ta-Kumsaw and his gang of child-killers and wife-rapers. I hope you'll break several of his bones."

Fink stood there, contemplating. "I reckon he'll make a powerful lot of noise, Gov."

"Well, jam in a gag on him." Harrison took a kerchief out of his own coat pocket. "Here, stuff this in his mouth and tie it there."

Fink complied. Measure tried to keep his eyes off him, tried to calm the dread that made his belly so tight and his bladder so full. The kerchief filled his mouth so full he choked on it. He only got control of himself by breathing slow and steady through his nose. Fink tied his own red scarf so tight around Measure's face that it forced the gag down into his throat even farther; again it took all his concentration just to breathe evenly and stop from gagging and retching. If he did that, he'd sure breathe that kerchief right down into his lungs, and then he *would* die.

Which was a crazy thought, seeing as how Harrison meant to have him dead no matter what. Maybe choking on a kerchief would be better than the pain Fink meant to cause. But Measure had too strong a spark of life to choose to die like that. Pain or not, when he died he'd go out gasping, not smothering himself just to get off easy.

"Breaking his bones ain't the way Reds do it." Fink was being helpful. "They usually cut and burn."

"Well, we don't have time for cutting, and you can burn the body after he's dead. The point of this is to have a colorful corpse, Mike, not to cause this boy pain. We're not savages, or at least some of us aren't."

Mike chuckled, then reached out, took Measure by the shoulder, and kicked his feet out from under him. Measure never felt so helpless in his life as in that moment when he fell. Fink didn't have an inch of height or reach on him, and Measure knew a few wrassling tricks, but Fink never even tried to grapple with him. Just a grab and a kick, and Measure was on the floor.

"Don't you need to tie him first?" asked Harrison.

In answer, Fink picked up Measure's left leg so fast and high that Measure slid across the floor and his buttocks lifted right into the air. No chance to get leverage, no chance to kick. Then Fink brought Measure's leg down across his own thigh hard and sharp. His leg bones snapped like dry kindling wood. Measure screamed into the gag, then nearly inhaled the kerchief gasping for breath. He never felt pain like that in all his life. For one crazy moment he thought, This is how Alvin felt when that millstone fell on his leg.

"Not in here," said Harrison. "Take him out back. Do it in the root cellar."

"How many bones you want me to break?" asked Fink.

"All of them."

Fink picked Measure up by an arm and a leg and practically tossed him up over his shoulders. Despite the pain, Measure tried to lay in a punch or two, but Fink jerked down on his arm, breaking it right at the elbow.

Measure was barely conscious the rest of the way outside. He heard somebody in the distance call, "Who you got there!"

Fink yelled back, "Caught us a Red spy, sneaking around!"

The voice from the distance sounded familiar to Measure, but he couldn't concentrate well enough to remember who it was. "Tear him apart!" he shouted.

Fink didn't answer. He didn't set Measure down to open the root cellar doors, even though they were low and at a slant, so you had to reach out and down, then pull them up. Fink just hooked the toe of his boot under the door and flipped it up. It moved so fast it banged on the ground and rebounded so as to nearly close again, but by then Fink was already stepping into the cellar; the door hit his thigh and bounced right open again. Measure just heard it as banging and a little jostling, which made his leg and his elbow hurt all the more. Why haven't I fainted yet, he wondered. Now's as good a time as any.

But he never did faint. Both legs broken above and below the knee, his fingers bent back and disjointed, his hands crushed, his arms broken above and below the elbows—through all that he stayed awake, though the pain eventually got kind of far away, more like the memory of pain than pain itself. If you hear one cymbal crash, it's loud; two or three cymbal crashes at once are louder yet. But along about the twentieth cymbal crash, it don't get louder, you just get deafer, and you hardly hear any of them at all. That's how it was for Measure.

There was a sound of cheering in the distance.

Somebody ran up. "Governor says finish up real quick, he wants you right away."

"I'll be done in a minute," said Fink. "Except for the burning."

"Save it till later," the man said. "Hurry!"

Fink dropped Measure, then stomped his chest till his ribs were pretty much broke, bending in and out any which way. Then he picked him up by the arm and the hair and bit off his ear. Measure felt it tear away with one last desperate surge of anger. Then Fink gave his head a sharp twist. Measure heard his own neck snap. Fink flung him onto the potatoes. He rolled down the backside and into the hole he dug. Only when his face was in the dirt did the pain stop and darkness come.

Fink flipped the doors shut with his foot, slid the bar into place, and headed back to the house. The cheering out front was louder. Harrison met him coming out of his office. "Never mind about that now," Harrison said. "There's no need for a corpse to keep things hot around here. The cannon just got here, and we'll attack in the morning."

Harrison rushed out to the front porch, and Mike Fink followed him. Cannon? What did cannons have to do with needing or not needing a corpse? What did he think Mike was, an assassin? Killing Hooch was one thing, and killing a man in a fair fight was something else. But killing a young man with a gag in his mouth, that was altogether different. When he bit off that ear it just didn't feel right. It wasn't no trophy of a fair fight. Took the heart right out of him. He didn't even bother biting off the other ear.

Mike stood there beside Harrison, watching the horses pull the four cannon right along, brisk as you please. He knew how Harrison would use the guns, he'd heard him planning it. Two here, two there, so they rake the whole Red city from both sides. Grape and canister, to rip and tear the bodies of the Reds, women and children right along with the men.

It ain't my kind of a fight, thought Mike. Like that man out back. No challenge at all, like stomping baby frogs. You can do it, and not think twice. But you don't pick up the dead frogs, stuff them, and hang them on the wall, you just don't do that.

It ain't my kind of fight.

13

EIGHT-FACE MOUND

There was a different feel to the land around Licking River. Alvin didn't notice right off, mostly cause he was running with his wick trimmed, so to speak. Didn't notice much at all. It was one long dream as he ran. But as Ta-Kumsaw led him into the Land of Flints, there was a change in the dream. All around him, no matter what he saw in his dream, there was little sparks of deep-black fire. Not like the nothingness that always lurked at the edges of his vision. Not like the deep black that sucked light into itself and never let it go. No, this black shone, it gave off sparks.

And when they stopped running, and Alvin came to himself again, those black fires may have faded just a bit but they were still there. Without so much as thinking, Alvin walked toward one, a black blaze in a sea of green, reached down and picked it up. A flint. A good big one.

"A twenty-arrow flint," said Ta-Kumsaw.

"It shines black and burns cold," said Alvin.

Ta-Kumsaw nodded. "You want to be a Red boy? Then make arrowheads with me."

Alvin caught on quick. He had worked with stone before. When he cut a millstone, he wanted smooth, flat surfaces. With flint, it was the edge, not the face that counted. His first two arrowheads were clumsy, but then he was able to feel his way into the stone and find the natural creases and folds, and then break them apart. For his fourth arrowhead, he didn't chip at all. Just used his fingers and gently pulled the arrowhead away from the flint.

Ta-Kumsaw's face showed no expression. That's what most White folks thought he looked like all the time. They thought Red men, and most especially Ta-Kumsaw, never *felt* nothing cause they never let nobody *see* their feelings. Alvin had seen him laugh, though, and cry, and all the other faces that a man can show. So he knowed that when Ta-Kumsaw showed nothing on his face, that meant he was feeling a whole lot of things.

"I worked with stone a lot before," said Alvin. He felt like he was sort of apologizing.

"Flint isn't *stone,*" said Ta-Kumsaw. "Pebbles in the river, boulders, those are stone. This is living rock, rock with fire in it, the hard earth that the land gives to us freely. Not hewn out and tortured the way White men do with iron." He held up Alvin's fourth arrowhead, the one he cajoled out of the flint with his fingers. "Steel can never have an edge this sharp."

"It's just about as perfect an edge as I ever saw," said Al.

"No chip marks," said Ta-Kumsaw. "No pressing. A Red man would see this flint and say, The land grew the flint this way."

"But you know better," said Al. "You know it's just a knack I got."

"A *knack* bends the land," said Ta-Kumsaw. "Like a snag in the river churns the water on the river's face. So it is with the land when a White uses his knack. Not you."

Alvin puzzled on that for a minute. "You mean you can see where other folks did their doodlebug or beseeching or hex or charm?"

"Like the bad stink when a sick man loosens his bowel," said Ta-Kumsaw. "But you—what you do is clean. Like part of the land. I thought I would teach you how to be Red. Instead the land gives you arrowheads like a gift."

Again, Alvin felt like apologizing. It seemed to make Ta-Kumsaw angry, that he could do the things he did. "It ain't like I asked anybody for this," he said. "I was just the seventh son of a seventh son, and the thirteenth child."

"These numbers—seven, thirteen—you Whites care about them, but they're nothing in the land. The land has true numbers. One, two, three, four, five, six—these numbers you can find when you stand in the forest and look around you. Where is seven? Where is thirteen?"

"Maybe that's why they're so strong," said Alvin. "Maybe cause they ain't natural."

"Then why does the land love this unnatural thing that you do?"

"I don't know, Ta-Kumsaw. I'm only ten going on eleven."

Ta-Kumsaw laughed. "Ten? Eleven? Very weak numbers."

They spent the night there, in the borders of the Land of Flints. Ta-Kumsaw told Alvin the story of that place, how it was the best flint country in the whole land. No matter how many flints the Reds came and took away, more always came out of the ground, just lying there to get picked up. In years gone by, every now and then some tribe would try to own the place. They'd bring their warriors and kill anyone else who came for flints. That way they figured they'd have arrows and the other tribes wouldn't have any. But it never worked right. Cause as soon as that tribe won its battles and held the land, the flints just plain disappeared. Not a one. Members of that tribe would search and search, and never find a thing. They'd go away, and another tribe would come in, and there'd be flints again, as many as ever.

"It belongs to everybody, this place. All Reds are at peace here. No killing, no war, no quarrels—or the tribe has no flints."

"I wish the whole world was a place like that," said Alvin.

"Listen to my brother long enough, White boy, and you'll start to think it is. No, no, don't explain to me. Don't defend him. He takes his road, I take mine. I think his way will kill more people, Red or White, than mine."

In the night, Alvin dreamed. He saw himself walk all the way around Eight-Face Mound, until he found a place where a path seemed to lead up the steep hill. He climbed, then, and came to the top. The silver-leafed trees shook in the breeze, blinding him as the sun shone off them. He walked to one tree, and in it there was a nest of redbirds. Every tree the same, a single redbird nest.

Except one tree. It was different from the others. It was older, gnarled, with spreading branches instead of the up-reaching kind. Like a fruit tree. And the leaves were gold, not silver, so they didn't shine so bright, but they were soft and deep. In the tree, he saw round white fruit, and he knew that it was ripe. But when he reached out his hand to take the fruit, and eat it, he could hear laughter, jeering. He looked around him and saw everybody he ever knowed in his whole life, laughing at him. Except one— Taleswapper. Taleswapper was standing there, and he said, "Eat." Alvin reached up and plucked a single fruit out of the tree and took it to his lips and bit into it. It was juicy and firm, and the taste was sweet and bitter, salt and sour all at once, so strong it made him tingle all over—but good, a taste he wanted to hold inside him forever.

He was about to take a second bite when he saw that the fruit was gone from his hand, and not a one hung from the tree. "One bite is all you need for now," said Taleswapper. "Remember how it tastes."

"I'll never forget," said Alvin.

Everybody was still laughing, louder than ever; but Alvin paid them no mind. He'd took him a bite of the fruit, and all he wanted now was to bring his family to the same tree, and let them eat; to bring everybody he ever knowed, and even strangers, too, and let them taste it. If they'd just taste it, Alvin figured, they'd know.

"What would they know?" asked Taleswapper.

Al couldn't think what it was. "Just know," he said. "Know everything. Everything that's good."

"That's right," said Taleswapper. "With the first bite, you *know.*"

"What about the second bite?"

"With the second bite, you live forever," said Taleswapper. "And that isn't a thing you'd better plan on doing, my boy. Don't ever imagine you can live forever."

Alvin woke up that morning with the taste of the fruit still in his mouth. He had to force himself to believe that it was just a dream. Ta-Kumsaw was already up. He had a low fire going, and he had called two fish out of the Licking River. Now they were spitted with sticks down their mouths. He handed one to Alvin.

But Alvin didn't want to eat. If he did, the taste of the fruit would go out of his mouth. He'd begin to forget, and he wanted to remember. Oh, he knowed that he'd have to eat sometime—a body can get remarkable thin saying no to food all the time. But today, for now, he didn't want to eat.

Still, he held the spit and watched the trout sizzle. Ta-Kumsaw talked, telling him about calling fish and other animals when you need to eat. Asking them to come. If the land wants you to eat, then they come; or maybe some other animal, it doesn't matter, just so you eat what the land gives you. Alvin thought about the fish he was roasting. Didn't the land know he wasn't going to eat this morning? Or did it send this fish to tell him he ought to eat after all?

Neither one. Because just at the moment the fish were ready to eat, they heard the crashing and thumping that told them a White man was coming.

Ta-Kumsaw sat very still, but he didn't so much as pull out his knife. "If the land brings a White man *here,* then he isn't my enemy," said Ta-Kumsaw.

In a few seconds, the White man stepped into the clearing. His hair was white, where he wasn't bald. He was carrying his hat. He had a slack-looking pouch over his shoulder, and no weapon at all. Alvin knew right off what was in that pouch. A change of clothes, a few snatches of food, and a book. A third of the book contained single sentences, where folks had written down the most important thing they ever saw happen with their own eyes. The last two-thirds of the book, though, were sealed with a leather strap. That was where Taleswapper wrote down his own stories, the ones he believed and thought were important.

Cause that's who it was, Taleswapper, who Alvin never thought to see again in his life. And suddenly, seeing that old friend, Alvin knew why two fish came at Ta-Kumsaw's call. "Taleswapper," Alvin said, "I hope you're hungry, cause I got a fish here that I roasted for you."

Taleswapper smiled. "I'm right glad to see you, Alvin, and right glad to see that fish."

Alvin handed him the spit. Taleswapper sat him down in the grass, across the fire from Alvin and Ta-Kumsaw. "Thank you kindly, Alvin," said Taleswapper. He pulled out his knife and neatly began flaking off slices of fish. They sizzled his lips, but he just licked and smacked and made short work of the trout. Ta-Kumsaw also ate his, and

Alvin watched them both. Ta-Kumsaw never took his eyes off Taleswapper.

"This is Taleswapper," Alvin said. "He's the man who taught me how to heal."

"I didn't teach you," said Taleswapper. "I just gave you some idea how to teach yourself. And persuaded you that you ought to try." Taleswapper directed his next sentence at Ta-Kumsaw. "He was set to let himself die before he'd use his knack to heal himself, can you believe that?"

"And this is Ta-Kumsaw," said Alvin.

"Oh, I knew that the minute I saw you. Do you know what a legend you are among White people? You're like Saladin during the Crusade—they admire you more than they admire their own leaders, even though they know you're sworn to fight until you've driven the last White man out of America."

Ta-Kumsaw said nothing.

"I've met maybe two dozen children named after you, most of them boys, all of them White. And stories—about you saving White captives from being burned to death, about you bringing food to people you drove out of their homes, so they wouldn't starve. I even believe some of those stories."

Ta-Kumsaw finished his fish and laid the spit in the fire.

"I also heard a story as I was coming here, about how you captured two Whites from Vigor Church and sent their bloody torn-up clothes to their parents. How you tortured them to death to show how you meant to destroy every White—man, woman, and child. How you said the time for being civilized was past, and now you'd use pure terror to drive the White man out of America."

For the first time since Taleswapper arrived, Ta-Kumsaw spoke. "Did you believe *that* story?"

"Well, I didn't," said Taleswapper. "But that's because I already knew the truth. You see, I got a message from a girl I knew—a young lady now, she is. It was a letter." He took a folded letter from his coat, three sheets of paper covered with writing. He handed them to Ta-Kumsaw.

Without looking at it, Ta-Kumsaw handed the letter to Alvin. "Read it to me," he said.

"But you can read English," said Alvin.

"Not here," said Ta-Kumsaw.

Alvin looked at the letter, at all three pages of it, and to his surprise he couldn't read it either. The letters all looked familiar. When he studied them out, he could even name them—T-H-E-M-A-K-E-R-N-E-E-D-S-Y-O-U, that's how it started, but it made no sense to Al at all, he couldn't even say for sure what language it was in. "I can't read it either," he said, and handed it back to Taleswapper.

Taleswapper studied it for a minute, then laughed and put it back into his coat pocket. "Well, that's a story for my book. A place where a man can't read."

To Alvin's surprise, Ta-Kumsaw smiled. "Even you?"

"I know what it says, because I read it before," said Taleswapper. "But I can't make out a single word of it today. Even when I know what the word is supposed to be. What *is* this place?"

"We're in the Land of Flints," said Alvin.

"We're in the shadow of Eight-Face Mound," said Ta-Kumsaw.

"I didn't think a White man could get here," said Taleswapper.

"Neither did I," said Ta-Kumsaw. "But here is a White boy, and there is a White man."

"I dreamed you last night," said Alvin. "I dreamed I was on top of Eight-Face Mound, and you were with me, explaining things to me."

"Don't count on it," said Taleswapper. "I doubt there's a thing on Eight-Face Mound that I could explain to anybody."

"How did you come here," asked Ta-Kumsaw, "if you didn't know you were coming to the Land of Flints?"

"She told me to come up the Musky-Ingum, and when I saw a white boulder on the right, I should take the fork that led left. She said I'd find Alvin Miller Junior sitting with Ta-Kumsaw by a fire, roasting fish."

"Who told you all this?" asked Alvin.

"A woman," said Taleswapper. "A torch. She told me you saw her in a vision, Alvin, inside a crystal tower, not more than a week ago by now. She was the one who pulled the caul from your face, when you were born. She's been watching you ever since, in the way a torch sees. She went inside that tower with you and saw out of your eyes."

"The Prophet *said* someone was with us," said Alvin.

"She looked out of *his* eye, too," said Taleswapper, "and she saw all his futures. The Prophet will die. Tomorrow morning. Shot by your own father's gun, Alvin."

"No!" cried Alvin.

"Unless," said Taleswapper. "Unless Measure comes in time to show your father that he's alive, that Ta-Kumsaw and the Prophet never harmed him, or you either."

"But Measure left days ago!"

"That's right, Alvin. But he got captured by Governor Harrison's men. Harrison has him, and today, maybe even right now, one of Harrison's men is killing him. Breaking his bones, breaking his neck. Tomorrow Harrison will attack Prophetstown with his cannon, killing everybody. Every soul. So much blood that the Tippy-Canoe will flow scarlet and the Wobbish will flow red clear to the Hio."

Ta-Kumsaw leaped to his feet. "I have to go back. I have to—"

"You know how far you are," said Taleswapper. "You know where your warriors are. Even if you ran all night and all day, as fast as you Reds can go—"

"Noon tomorrow," said Ta-Kumsaw.

"He'll be dead already," said Taleswapper.

Ta-Kumsaw shouted in anguish, so loud that several birds cried out and flew away from the meadow.

"Now, hold your horses, just wait a minute. If there were nothing we could do, she wouldn't very well have sent me on this chase, now, would she? Don't you see we're acting out a plan that's bigger than all of us? Why did it happen that Alvin and Measure were the two boys that Harrison's hired Chok-Taw kidnapped? How do you happen to be here, and me also, at the very day when we're most needed?"

"They need us *there*," said Ta-Kumsaw.

"I don't think so," said Taleswapper. "I think that if they needed us there, then there we'd be. They need us *here*."

"You're like my brother, trying to make me fit into his plans!"

"I wish I *were* like your brother. He has visions and sees what's going on, while all I get is a letter from a torch. But here I am, and here you are, and if we weren't supposed to be here, we just plain wouldn't, whether you like it or not."

Alvin didn't like this talk of what was supposed to happen. Who was doing all this supposing? What did Taleswapper mean—they were all poppets on sticks? Was somebody making them move any old way, whatever he felt ought to happen? "If somebody's so all-fired in charge of everything," said Alvin, "he hasn't been doing too good a job of it, getting us into a fix like this."

Taleswapper grinned. "You really don't take to religion, do you, boy?"

"I just don't think anybody's making us do anything."

"Nor did I say so," said Taleswapper. "I'm just saying things never get so bad we can't do something to make them better."

"Well I'll be glad to take suggestions. What did this torch lady think I ought to do?" asked Alvin.

"She said you're supposed to climb the mountain and heal Measure. Don't ask me more than that—that's all she said. There isn't a mountain worthy of the name in these parts, and Measure's in the root cellar behind Vinegar Riley's house—"

"I know that place," said Alvin. "I been there. But I can't—I mean I've never tried to heal somebody who wasn't right there in front of me."

"Enough talking," said Ta-Kumsaw. "Eight-Face Mound called you in a dream, White boy. This man came to tell you to go up the mountain. Everything begins when you climb the Mound. If you can."

"Some things end on Eight-Face Mound," said Taleswapper.

"What does a White man know about this place?" asked Ta-Kumsaw.

"Not a thing," said Taleswapper. "But I knelt by the bed of a dying Irrakwa woman, many years ago, and she told me that the most important thing in her life was, she was the last Irrakwa ever to stand inside Eight-Face Mound."

"The Irrakwa have all turned White in their hearts," said Ta-Kumsaw. "Eight-Face Mound would never let them in now."

"But I'm White," said Alvin.

"Very good problem," said Ta-Kumsaw. "The Mound will tell you the answer. Maybe the answer is you don't go up and everybody dies. Come."

He led them along the path the land opened up for them, until they came to a steep hill, thickly grown with trees and brambles. There was no path. "This is Red Man's Face," said Ta-Kumsaw. "This is where Red men climb. The path is gone. You can't climb here."

"Where, then?" asked Alvin.

"How do I know?" said Ta-Kumsaw. "The story is that if you climb a different face, you find a different Mound. The story is that if you climb the Builders' Face, you find their ancient city, still alive on the Mound. If you climb the Beasts' Face, you find a land where a giant buffalo is king, a strange animal with horns that come out of his mouth and a nose like a terrible snake, and huge cougars with teeth as long as spears all bow before him and worship. Who knows if these stories are true? No one climbs those faces now."

"Is there a White Man's Face?" asked Alvin.

"Red Man, Medicine, Builder, Beast. Four other faces we don't know their names," said Ta-Kumsaw. "Maybe one of them is White Man's Face. Come."

He led them around the hill. The Mound rose on their left hand. No path opened. Alvin recognized everything they saw. His dream last night was true, at least this much: Taleswapper was with him, and he circled the Mound before climbing.

They came to the last of the unknown faces. No path. Alvin made as if to go on to the next face.

"No use," said Ta-Kumsaw. "All eight faces, none will let us up. The next is Red Man's Face again."

"I know," said Alvin. "But here's the path."

There it was, straight as an arrow. Right on the edge shared by Red Man's Face and the unknown face beside it.

"You *are* half Red," said Ta-Kumsaw.

"Go on up," said Taleswapper.

"In my dream you were with me up there," said Alvin.

"Maybe so," said Taleswapper. "But the fact is, I can't see this path the two of you are talking about. It looks just like all the rest of the faces. So I reckon I'm not invited."

"Go," said Ta-Kumsaw. "Hurry."

"You come with me, then," said Alvin. "You see the path, don't you?"

"I didn't dream of the Mound," said Ta-Kumsaw. "And what you see there, it will be half what the Red man sees, and half a new place that I should never see. Go now, don't waste time anymore. My brother and your brother will die unless you do whatever it is the land brought you here to do."

"I'm thirsty," said Al.

"Drink there," said Ta-Kumsaw, "if the Mound offers you water. Eat if the Mound offers you food."

Al set his feet on the path and scrambled up the hill. It was steep, but there were roots to grab, plenty of footholds, and before long the path crested, leveled, and the underbrush ended.

He had thought the Mound was a single hill, with eight slopes. Now, though, he could see that each of the eight slopes was a separate Mound, arranged to form a deep bowl in the middle. The valley seemed much too large, the farthest Mounds much too far away. Hadn't Alvin walked around the entire Mound this morning with Ta-Kumsaw and Taleswapper? Eight-Face Mound was much more inside than it seemed to be outside.

He walked carefully down the grassy slope. It was tufted, irregular, the grass cool, the soil moist and firm. It seemed much farther going down than it had been going up. When he finally reached the valley floor, he stood on the verge of a meadow, with silver-leafed trees, just like in his dream. So his dream had been true, showing him a real place that he could not have imagined.

But how was he supposed to find Measure and heal him? What did the Mound have to do with anything at all? It was afternoon now, they'd taken so long circling the Mound—Measure might already be dying, and he didn't have any idea how to go about helping him.

He couldn't think of anything to do but walk. He thought he'd cross the valley and see one of the other mounds, but it was the strangest thing. No matter how far he walked, no matter how many silver-leafed trees he passed, the mound he walked toward was always just as far away. It made him afraid—would he be trapped up here forever?—and he hurried back in the direction he started from. In just a few minutes he reached the place where his footprints came down the slope. Surely he had walked away from that spot for much longer than that. A couple more tries convinced him that the valley went on forever in every direction except the one he came from. In *that* direction, it was just like he was always in the very center of the Mound, no matter how far he'd walked to get where he was.

Alvin looked for the gold-leafed tree with the pure white fruit, but he couldn't find it, and he wasn't surprised. The taste of the fruit was still in his mouth from the dream the night before. He wouldn't get another taste of it, waking or dreaming, because the second bite would make him live forever. He didn't mind much, not getting that bite. Death didn't breathe all that heavy down the neck of a boy his age.

He heard water. A brook, clear cold water flowing rapidly over stones. It was impossible, of course. The valley of Eight-Face Mound was completely enclosed. If water ran so fast here, why didn't the valley fill right up to make a lake? Why wasn't there a single stream running off the mound outside? Where would such a stream come from, anyway? The mound was man-made, like all the other mounds scattered all through the country, though none of the others was so old. You don't get springs coming out of man-made hills. It made him suspicious of this water, to have it be so impossible. Come to think of it, though, quite a few impossible things had happened to him in his life, and this was far from being the most peculiar.

Ta-Kumsaw said to drink if the mound offered him water, so he knelt and drank, plunging his face right into the water and sucking the water straight into his mouth. It didn't take away the taste of the fruit. If anything, it was stronger after he drank.

He knelt on the bank, studying the opposite shore of the brook. The water was flowing differently there. In fact, it was lapping the shore like ocean waves, and once that thought occurred to Alvin he saw that the *shape* of the opposite shore was just like the map of the east coast that Armor-of-God showed him. The memory came back clear and sharp. Here where the shore bowed outward, that was Carolina in the Crown Colonies. This deep bay was the Chase-a-pick, and here was the mouth of the Potty-Mack, which made the border between the United States and the Crown Colonies.

Alvin stood and stepped across the stream.

It was just grass. He didn't see no rivers or towns, no boundaries, no roads. But from the coast, he could pretty much guess where the Hio country was, and where this very mound would be. He took two steps, and all of a sudden there he saw Ta-Kumsaw and Taleswapper, setting on the ground in front of him, looking up at him as surprised as could be.

"You climbed up after all," said Alvin.

"Nothing of the sort," said Taleswapper. "We've been right here since you left."

"Why did you come back down?" asked Ta-Kumsaw.

"But I ain't down at all," said Alvin. "I'm down here in the valley of the mound."

"Valley?" asked Ta-Kumsaw.

"We're down here below the mound," said Taleswapper.

Then Alvin understood. Not so as to put it into words, but well enough to use it, to use what the mound had given him. He could travel across the face of the land like this, a hundred miles in a step, and see the people that he needed to see. The people that he knew. Measure. Alvin touched his forehead in salute to the two men who waited for him, then took a small step. They disappeared.

He found the town of Vigor Church easy enough. First person he saw was Armor-of-God, kneeling in prayer. Alvin didn't say nothing to him, for fear Armor might take it as a vision of the dead. Where would Armor be, though? In his own house? In that case Vinegar Riley's place would be back this way, east of town. He turned around.

He saw his own father, setting with Mother. Pa was smoothing out some musket balls he'd cast. And Ma was whispering to him, all urgent. She was angry, and so was Pa. "Women and children, that's what they are in that town. Even if the Prophet and Ta-Kumsaw killed our boys, them women and children there didn't do it. You'll be no better than them if you raise a hand against them. I won't see you come back into this house, I'll never see you again if you kill one soul of them. I swear it, Alvin Miller."

Pa just kept on polishing, except once when he said, "They killed my boys."

Alvin tried to answer, opened his mouth to say, "But I ain't dead, Pa!"

It didn't work. He couldn't say a word. He wasn't brought up here to give a vision to his parents, neither. It was Measure he had to find, or Pa's own musket ball would kill the Shining Man.

It wasn't far, not even a step. Alvin just inched his feet forward, and Ma and Pa disappeared. He caught a glimpse of Calm and David, shooting their guns—probably at targets. And Wastenot and Wantnot, ramming something—ramming shot down the barrel of a cannon. Glimpses of other folks, though because he didn't know or care about them he didn't see them clear. Finally he saw Measure.

He had to be dead. His neck was broke, judging from the angle of his head, and his arms and legs were all broke, too. Alvin didn't dare move, or he'd travel a mile in an instant, and Measure would disappear just like the others. Alvin just stood there, and sent his spark out into the body of his brother, lying before him on the ground.

Alvin never felt such pain in all his life. It wasn't Measure's pain, it was his own. It was Alvin's sense of how things ought to be, of the right shape of things; inside Measure's body, nothing was going right. Parts of him were dying, the blood was packed into his belly and crushing his own life out, his brain wasn't connected to his body no more, it was the most terrible mess Alvin ever saw, everything wrong, so wrong that it hurt him to see it, a pain so sharp he cried out. But Measure didn't hear him. Measure was beyond hearing. If Measure wasn't dead he was half an inch from being dead, and that was sure.

Alvin went to his heart first. It was still pumping, but there wasn't much blood left in the veins; it was all lost in Measure's chest and belly. That was the first thing Alvin had to mend, heal up the blood vessels and get the blood back where it belonged, flowing in its channels.

Time, it all took time. All the broken ribs, the cut-up organs. All the bones, joining them without so much as a hand to help move something into the right place—some of the bones were so out of line that he couldn't heal them at all. He'd have to wait until Measure woke up enough to help him.

So Alvin got inside Measure's brain, the nerves running down his spine, and healed it all, put it back the way it had to be.

Measure woke with one long, terrible scream of agony. He was alive and the pain was back, sharper and clearer than it ever was before. I'm sorry, Measure. I can't heal you up without letting the pain come back. And I got to heal you, or too many innocent folks are dead.

Alvin didn't even notice that it was already night, and half his work still lay ahead of him.

14

TIPPY-CANOE

In Prophetstown, no one but the children slept that night. The adults all felt the circling White army; the hidings and hexes cast by the White troops were like trumpets and banners to the land-sense of the Reds.

Not all of them found they had the courage to keep their oath, now that iron-and-fire death was hours away. But they kept the oath this far: They gathered their families and slipped out of Prophetstown, passing silently between companies of White soldiers, who neither heard nor saw them. Knowing they could not die without defending themselves, they left, so that not one Red would mar the perfection of the Prophet's refusal to fight.

Tenskwa-Tawa was not surprised that some left; he was surprised that so many stayed. Almost all. So many who believed in him, so many who would prove that trust in blood. He dreaded the morning; the pain of a single murder close at hand had cursed him with the black noise for many years. True, it was his father who was killed, so the pain was more; but did he love the people of Prophetstown any less than he had loved his father?

Yet he had to fend off the black noise, keep his wits about him, or all their deaths would be in vain. If their dying accomplished nothing, he wouldn't have them do it. So many times he had searched the crystal tower, trying to find some way to approach this day, some path that would lead to something good. The best that he could find was the land divided, Red west of the Mizzipy, White to the east. Even that, though, could be found only through the narrowest of paths. So much depended on the White boys, so much on Tenskwa-Tawa, so much on White Murderer Harrison himself. For in all the paths in which Harrison showed any mercy, the massacre of Tippy-Canoe did nothing to stop the destruction of the Reds, and, with them, the land. In all those paths, the Red men dwindled, confined to tiny preserves of desolate land, until the whole land was White, and therefore brutalized into submission, stripped and cut and ravished, giving vast amounts of food that was only an imitation of the true harvest, poisoned into life by alchemical trickery. Even the White man suffered in those visions of the future, but it would be many generations before he realized what he had done. Yet here—Prophetstown—there was a day—tomorrow— when the future could be turned onto an unlikely path, but a better one. One that would lead to a living land after all, even if it was truncated; one that would lead someday to a crystal city catching sunlight and turning it into visions of truth for all who lived within it.

That was Tenskwa-Tawa's hope, that he could cling to the bright vision through all of tomorrow's pain, and so turn that pain, that blood, that black noise of murder, to an event that would change the world.

Even before the first detectable rays of light rose above the horizon, Tenskwa-Tawa felt the coming dawn. He felt it partly in the stirring of life to the east. He could feel it from farther off than any other Red. He felt it also, though, from the movements among the Whites as they prepared to light the matches for their cannon. Four fires, hidden and therefore revealed by spells and witchery. Four cannon, poised to rake the city, end to end.

Tenskwa-Tawa walked through the city, humming softly. They heard him, and awakened their children. The White men thought to kill them in their sleep, faceless within their wigwams and lodges. Instead, they emerged in the darkness, walking surefooted to the broad meadow of the meeting ground. There wasn't room enough for all of them even to sit. They stood, families together, father and mother with their children in the circle of their embrace, waiting for the White man to spill their blood.

"The earth will not soak up your blood," Tenskwa-Tawa had promised them. "It will flow into the river, and I will hold it there, all the power of all your lives and all your deaths, and I will use it to keep the land alive, and bind the White man to the lands he has already captured and begun to kill."

So now Tenskwa-Tawa made his way to the bank of the Tippy-Canoe, watching the meadow fill up with his people, of whom so many would die before him because they believed in his words.

"STAND WITH ME today, Mr. Miller," said General Harrison. "It's your kin whose blood we'll avenge today. I want you to have the honor of firing the first bullet in this war."

Mike Fink watched as the hot-eyed miller carefully rammed wad and shot down his musket barrel. Mike knew the thirst for murder in his eyes. It was a kind of madness that came on a man, and it made him dangerous, made him able to do things beyond his normal reach. Mike was just as glad that miller didn't know just when and how his boy had died. Oh, Governor Bill hadn't never told him right out who that young man was, but Mike Fink wasn't a boy in short pants, and he knew all right. Harrison played a deep game, but one thing was sure. He'd do anything to raise himself higher and put more land and people under his control. And Mike Fink knew that Harrison would only keep him around as long as he was useful.

The funny thing was, you see, that Mike Fink didn't think of himself as a murderer. He thought of life as a contest, and dying was what happened to those who came out second best, but it wasn't the same as murder, it was a fair fight. Like how he killed Hooch—Hooch didn't have to be so careless. Hooch could have noticed Mike wasn't on the shore with the other poleboys, Hooch could have been watchful and wary, and if he had been, why, Mike Fink might well have died. So Hooch lost his life because he lost the contest—the contest he and Mike were both playing for.

But that boy yesterday, he wasn't a player. He wasn't in the contest at all. He just wanted to go home. Mike Fink never wrassled a man who didn't want a fight, and he never killed a man who wasn't set to kill him first if he got a chance. Yesterday was the first time he had ever killed somebody just cause he was told to, and he didn't like it, didn't like it one bit. Mike could see now that Governor Bill *thought* he had killed Hooch that same way, just because he was told to. But it wasn't so. And today Mike Fink looked at the young man's father, with all that rage in his eyes, and he said to that man—but silently, so nobody could hear—he said, I'm with you, I agree with you that the man who killed your boy should die.

Trouble was, Mike Fink was that man. And he was plain ashamed.

Same thing with them Red men in Prophetstown. What kind of contest was it, to wake them up with grapeshot whistling through their own houses, setting them afire, cutting into their bodies, the bodies of children and women and old men?

Not my kind of fight, thought Mike Fink.

The first light of dawn came into the sky. Prophetstown was still nothing but shadows, but it was time. Alvin Miller aimed his musket right into the thick of the houses, and then he fired.

A few seconds later, the cannons banged out their answer. Maybe a few more seconds, and the first flame appeared in the town.

The cannons fired again. Yet not a soul ran screaming out of the wigwams. Not even the ones that were afire.

Didn't anybody else notice it? Didn't they realize that the Reds were all gone out of Prophetstown? And if they were gone, that meant they knew all about this morning's attack. And if they knew, that meant they might be ready, lying in ambush. Or maybe they all escaped, or maybe—

Mike Fink's lucky amulet was nearly burning him, it felt so hot. He knew what that meant. Time to go. Something real bad was going to happen to him if he stayed.

So he slid off down the line of soldiers—or what passed for soldiers, since there hadn't been more than a day or two for training some of these raw farmers. Nobody paid no heed to Mike Fink. They were too busy watching the wigwams burn. Some of them had finally noticed that nobody seemed to be in the Red city, and they were talking about it, worried. Mike said nothing, kept moving along the line, down toward the creek.

The cannon were all on the high ground; they sounded farther away. Mike emerged from the trees into the cleared ground that ran down to the river. There he stopped short and stared. The dawn was still just a grey streak in the distance, but there was no mistaking what he saw. Thousands and thousands of Reds, standing shoulder to shoulder in the meadow. Some were crying softly—no doubt stray shrapnel and musket balls had come this far, since two of the cannons were on the opposite side of the city from here, firing this direction. But they weren't making a move to defend themselves. It wasn't an ambush. They had no weapons. These Red folks were all lined up to die.

There was maybe a dozen canoes up and down the bank of the river. Mike Fink pushed one out into the water and rolled himself aboard. Downstream, that's where he'd go, all the way down the Wobbish to the Hio. It wasn't war today, it was massacre, and that just wasn't Mike Fink's kind of fight. Nearly everybody's got a thing so bad he just won't do it.

IN THE DARKNESS of the root cellar, Measure couldn't see if Alvin was really there or not. But he could hear his voice, soft but urgent, riding in over the crest of the pain. "I'm trying to fix you, Measure, but I need your help."

Measure couldn't answer. Speech wasn't one of the things he could manage right at the moment.

"I've fixed your neck, and some of your ribs, and the guts that got tore up," said Alvin. "And your left arm bones were pretty much in a line, so they're all right, can you feel that?"

It was true that there wasn't no pain coming from Measure's left arm. He moved it. It jostled the whole rest of his body, but it could move, it had some strength in it.

"Your ribs," said Alvin. "Poking out. You got to push them back in place."

Measure pushed on one and nearly fainted from the pain. "I can't."

"You got to."

"Make it not hurt."

"Measure, I don't know how. Not without making it so you can't *move*. You just got to stand it. Everything you get back in place, I can fix it, and then it won't hurt no more, but first you got to straighten it, you got to."

"You do it."

"I can't."

"Just reach out and do it, Alvin, you're big for ten, you can do it."

"I can't."

"I once cut your bone for you, to save your life, I once did that."

"Measure, I can't do it cause I ain't *there*."

This made no sense to Measure. So he knew he was dreaming. Well, if he was dreaming, why didn't he come up with some dream where things didn't hurt so bad?

"Push on the bone, Measure."

Alvin just wouldn't go away. So Measure pushed, and it hurt him. But Alvin was as good as his word. Soon after, the place where he straightened out the bone didn't hurt no more.

It took so long. He was so tore up that it seemed there just wasn't no end to the pain. But in between times, while Alvin was making things heal up where he just fixed the bones, Measure explained to Alvin what had happened to him, and Alvin told him what *he* knew, and pretty soon Measure understood that there was a lot more to this than saving the life of one young man in a root cellar.

Finally, finally it was over. Measure couldn't hardly believe it. He had hurt so much for so many hours that it felt downright strange not to hurt anywhere.

He heard the thump, thump of cannon firing. "Can you hear that, Alvin?" he asked.

Alvin couldn't.

"The shooting's started. The cannon."

"Then run, Measure. Go as fast as you can."

"Alvin, I'm in a root cellar. They barred the door."

Alvin cussed with a couple of words that Measure didn't know the boy had ever heard.

"Alvin, I got me a hole half-dug here in the back. You

got such a knack with stone, I wondered if you could loosen things up for me here, so I could dig out real fast."

And that's how it worked out. Measure rolled himself into the hole and just closed his eyes and pawed at the dirt above his head. It was nothing like digging the day before, rubbing his fingers raw on the dirt. It just fell away, slid off him; when he reached up to dig more, the dirt slipped under his shoulders, and *there* it firmed right up, so that he didn't even have to think about moving the dirt out of the hole, it was just filling up underneath him. He kicked, and his legs jostled the dirt loose, so his whole body was rising up the same way.

Swimming through dirt, that's what I'm doing, he thought, and he started to laugh, it was so easy and so strange.

His laugh was finished in the open air. He was on top, just behind the root cellar. The sky was pretty light—the sun would be up in just a minute or so. The booming of the cannon had stopped. Did that mean it was over, too late? Maybe, though, they were just letting the guns cool. Or moving them to another place. Or maybe the Reds even managed to capture the guns—

But would that be good news? Right or wrong, his brothers and his father were with them guns, and if the Reds won this battle, some of his kin might die. It was one thing to know that the Reds were in the right and the Whites in the wrong; it was something else to wish defeat on your own family, defeat and maybe death. He had to stop the battle, and so he ran, like he never done before. Alvin's voice was gone, now, but Measure didn't need to be encouraged. He fair to flew down that road.

He met two people on the way. One was Mrs. Hatch, who was driving her wagon along the road, loaded down with supplies. When she saw Measure, she screamed—he was wearing a loincloth and filthy as could be, and she couldn't be blamed for thinking he was a Red all set to scalp her. She was off that wagon and running before Measure could so much as call her name. Well, that was fine with him. He nearly tore the horse from the wagon, he worked so fast, and then he was riding bareback, galloping along the road hoping that the horse wouldn't trip and spill him.

The other person he met along the way was Armor-of-God. Armor was kneeling in the middle of the common green, out front of his store, praying his heart out while the cannon roared and the muskets crackled across the river. Measure hailed him, and Armor looked up with a face like as if he'd seen Jesus resurrected. "Measure!" he shouted. "Stop, stop!"

Measure was all set to go on, to say he had no time, but then Armor was out in the middle of the way, and the horse was shy to go around him, so he *did* stop. "Measure, are you an angel or alive?"

"Alive, no thanks to Harrison. Tried to murder me, he did. I'm alive and so is Alvin. This whole thing was Harrison's doing, and I've got to put a stop to it."

"Well you can't go like that," said Armor. "Wait, I said! You can't just show up wearing a loincloth and covered up with dirt like that, somebody's going to think you're a Red and shoot you on the spot!"

"Then hop on this horse behind me, and give me your clothing on the way!"

So Measure hoisted Armor-of-God onto the horse behind him, and they rode out to the river crossing.

Peter Ferryman's wife was there to run the winch. One look at Measure was enough to tell her all she needed to know. "Hurry," she said. "It's so bad, the river's running scarlet."

On the ferry, Armor stripped off his clothes while Measure ducked himself in the water, blood and all, to wash some of the dirt away. He didn't come out clean, but at least he looked somewhat like a White man. Still wet, he put on Armor's shirt and trousers, and then his waistcoat. They didn't fit too good, Armor being a smaller man, but Measure shrugged on the coat all the same. While he did, he said, "Sorry to leave you with just your summerjohns."

"I'd stand naked half the day in front of all the ladies in church if it would stop this massacre," said Armor. If he said more, Measure didn't hear it, cause he was already on his way.

NOTHING WAS THE way Alvin Miller Senior thought that it would be. He'd imagined shooting his musket at the same screaming savages who cut up and killed his boys. But the city turned up empty, and they found the Reds all gathered in Speaking Meadow, just like they was ready for a sermon from the Prophet. Miller never knowed there was so many Reds in Prophetstown, cause he never seen them all in the same place like this. But they were Reds, weren't they? So he shot his musket all the same, just like the other men, firing and reloading, hardly looking at whether his shot hit anything. How could he miss, them all standing together so close? The bloodlust was on him then, he was crazy with anger and the power to kill. He didn't notice how some of the other men were getting quieter. Shooting less often. He just loaded and fired, loaded and fired, stepping a yard or two closer every time, out from the cover of the forest, out into the open; only when the cannon got moved into place did he stop shooting, make way for them, watched them mow great swaths through the mass of Reds.

That was the first time he really noticed what all was happening to the Reds, what they were doing, what they *weren't* doing. They weren't screaming. They weren't fighting back. They were just standing there, men and women and children, just looking out at the White men who were killing them. Not a one even turned his back to the hail of shrapnel. Not a parent tried to shield a child from the blast. They just stood, waited, died.

The grapeshot carved gaps in the crowd; the only thing to stop the spray of metal was human bodies. Miller saw them fall. Them as could, got up again, or at least knelt, or raised their heads above the mass of corpses so that the next blast would take them and kill them.

What is it, do they want to die?

Miller looked around him. He and the men with him were standing in a sea of corpses—they had already walked out to where the outer edges of the crowd of Reds had been. Right at his feet, the body of a boy no older than Alvin lay curled, his eye blown out by a musket ball. Maybe my own musket ball, thought Miller. Maybe I killed this boy.

During the lulls between cannon volleys, Miller could hear men crying. Not the Reds, the ones still living, huddled in an ever-smaller mass down toward the river. No, the men crying were his neighbors, White men standing beside him, or behind the line. Some of them were talking, pleading. Stop it, they said. Please, stop it.

Please stop. Were they talking to the cannon? Or to the Red men and women, who insisted on standing there, not trying to escape, not crying out in fear? Or to their children, who faced the guns as bravely as their parents? Or did they speak to the terrible gnawing pain in their own hearts, to see what they had done, were doing, would yet do?

Miller noticed that the blood didn't soak into the grass of the meadow. As it poured out of the wounds of those most recently hit, it formed rivulets, streams, great sheets of blood flowing down the slope of the meadow, toward the Tippy-Canoe Creek. The morning sunlight on this bright clear day shone vivid red from the water of the creek.

While he was watching, all at once the water of the creek went smooth as glass. The sunlight didn't dance on the water now, it reflected like a mirror, near blinding him. But he could still see a solitary Red man walking on the water, just like Jesus in the story, standing on the water in the middle of the creek.

It wasn't just a whimper behind him anymore. It was a shout, from more and more men. Stop shooting! Stop it! Put down your guns! And then others, talking about the man standing on the water.

A bugle sounded. The men fell silent. "Time to finish them, men!" shouted Harrison. He was on a prancing stallion at the head of the meadow, leading the way down the blood-slick hill. None of the farmer folk were with him, but his uniformed soldiers formed a line and came along, bayonets fixed. Where once ten thousand Reds had stood, there was just a field of bodies, and maybe a thousand, a ragged remnant, gathered near the water at the bottom of the hill.

That was the moment when a tall young White man ran from the wood at the bottom of the hill, dressed in a suit too small, his feet bare, his coat and waistcoat all unbuttoned, his hair wet and tousled, and face grimy and wet. But Miller knew him, knew him before he heard his voice.

"Measure!" he cried. "It's my boy Measure!"

He threw down his musket and ran out into the field of corpses, down the hill toward his son.

"My boy Measure! He's alive! You're alive!"

Then he slipped in the blood, or maybe he tripped on a body, but whatever happened he fell, his hands splashing into a river of blood, spattering his chest and face.

He heard Measure's voice, not ten yards away, shouting out so every man could hear him. "The Reds who captured me were hired by Harrison. Ta-Kumsaw and

Tenskwa-Tawa saved me. When I came home two days ago, Harrison's soldiers captured me and wouldn't let me tell you the truth. He even tried to kill me." Measure spoke slow and clear, so every word carried, every sound was understood. "He knew all the time. This whole thing, Harrison planned it all along. The Reds are innocent. You're killing innocent people."

Miller stood up from the bloody field and raised his hands high over his head, thick blood running from his scarlet hands. A cry was wrung from his throat, forced out by anguish, by despair. "What have I done! What have I done!" The cry was echoed by a dozen, a hundred, three hundred voices.

And there was General Harrison on his prancing horse, out in front of everybody. Even his own soldiers had thrown down their guns by now.

"It's a lie!" cried Harrison. "I never saw this boy! Someone has played a terrible trick on me!"

"It ain't no trick!" shouted Measure. "Here's his kerchief—they stuffed it in my mouth yesterday, to gag me while they broke my bones!"

Miller could see the kerchief clearly in his son's hand. It had the WHH embroidered in large, clear letters in the corner. Every man in that army had seen his handkerchiefs.

And now some of Harrison's own soldiers spoke up. "It's true! We brought this boy to Harrison two days ago."

"We didn't know he was one of the boys they all said the Reds had killed!"

A high, howling cry floated over the meadow. They all looked down to where the one-eyed Prophet stood on the solid, scarlet water of the Tippy-Canoe.

"Come to me, my people!" he said.

The surviving Reds walked, slowly, steadily toward the water. They walked across it, then gathered on the other side.

"All my people, come!"

The corpses rustled, moved. The White men standing among them cried out in terror. But the dead were not rising up to walk—only the wounded who still breathed, they were the ones who rose up, staggered. Some of them tried to carry children, babies—they had no strength for it.

Miller saw and felt the blood on his own hands. He had to do something, didn't he? So he reached out to a struggling woman, whose husband leaned against her for support, meaning to take the baby from her arms and carry it for her. But when he came near, she looked into his face, and he saw his own reflection in her eyes—his face haggard, White, spattered with blood, his hands dripping with blood. Tiny as it was, he saw that reflection as clear as if it had been on a mirror held in front of his own face. He couldn't touch her baby, not with hands like his.

Some of the other White men on the hill also tried to help, but they must have seen something like what Miller saw, and they recoiled as if they had been burned.

Maybe a thousand wounded got up and tried to reach the creek. Many of them collapsed and died before they got there. Those that reached the water walked, staggered, crawled across; they were helped by the Reds on the other side.

Miller noticed something peculiar. All those wounded Reds, all the uninjured ones, they had walked on this meadow, they had walked across the blood-red river, and yet there wasn't a spot of blood on their hands or feet.

"All my people, all who died— Come home, says the land!"

All around them, the meadow was strewn with bodies— by far the majority of those who had stood there as living families only an hour before. Now, at the Prophet's words, these bodies seemed to shudder, to crumble; they collapsed and sank into the grass of the meadow. It took

perhaps a minute, and they were gone, the grass springing up lush and green. The last of the blood skittered down
the slope like beads of water on a hot griddle and became
part of the bright red creek.

"Come to me, my friend Measure." The Prophet spoke
quietly, and held out his hand.

Measure turned his back on his father and walked down
the grassy slope to the water's edge.

"Walk to me," said the Prophet.

"I can't walk on the blood of your people," he said.

"They gave their blood to lift you up," said the Prophet.
"Come to me, or take the curse that will fall on every
White man in that meadow."

"I reckon I'll stay here, then," said Measure. "If I'd've
been in their place, I don't figure I'd've done a thing different than what they did. If they're guilty, so am I."

The Prophet nodded.

Every White man there felt something warm and wet
and sticky on his hands. Some of them cried out when they
saw. From elbow to hands, they dripped with blood. Some
tried to wipe it off on their shirts. Some searched for
wounds that might be bleeding, but there were no wounds.
Just bloody hands.

"Do you want your hands to be clean of the blood of my
people?" asked the Prophet. He wasn't shouting anymore,
but they all heard him, every word. And yes, yes, they
wanted their hands to be clean.

"Then go home and tell this story to your wives and
children, to your neighbors, to your friends. Tell the whole
story. Leave nothing out. Don't say that someone fooled
you—you all knew when you fired on people who had no
weapons that what you did was murder. No matter whether
you thought some of us might have committed some crime.
When you shot at babies in their mothers' arms, little children, old men and women, you were murdering us because

we were Red. So tell the story as it happened, and if you tell it true, your hands will be clean."

There wasn't a man on that meadow who wasn't weeping or trembling or faint with shame. To tell of this day's work to their wives and children, their parents, their brothers and sisters, that seemed unbearable. But if they didn't, these bloody hands would tell the story for them. It was more than they could bear to think of.

But the Prophet wasn't through. "If some stranger comes along, and you don't tell him the whole story before you sleep, then the blood will come back on your hands, and stay there until you do tell him. That's how it will be for the rest of your lives—every man and woman that you meet will have to hear the true story from your lips, or your hands will be filthy again. And if you ever, for any reason, kill another human being, then your hands and face will drip with blood forever, even in the grave."

They nodded, they agreed. It was justice, simple justice. They couldn't give back the lives of those they killed, but they could make sure no lie was ever told about the way that they were killed. No one could ever claim that Tippy-Canoe was a victory, or even a battle. It was a massacre, and White men committed it, and not one Red raised a hand in violence or defense. No excuse, no softening; it would be known.

Only one thing remained—the guilt of the man on the prancing stallion.

"White Murderer Harrison!" called the Prophet. "Come to me!"

Harrison shook his head, tried to turn his horse; the reins slipped from his bloody hands, and the horse walked briskly down the hill. All the White men watched him silently, hating him for how he lied to them, stirred them up, found the murder in their hearts and called it forth. The horse brought him to the water's edge. He looked downward at the one-eyed Red who had once sat under his table and begged for drops of whiskey from his cup.

"Your curse is the same," said the Prophet, "except that your story is much longer and uglier to tell. And you won't wait for strangers to come along before you speak—every day of your life you'll have to find someone who has never heard the story from your lips before, and tell it to him—every day!—or your hands will drip with blood. And if you decide to hide, and live with blood-soaked hands rather than find new people to tell, you'll feel the pain of my people's wounds, one new wound each day, until you tell the story again, once for every day you missed. Don't try to kill yourself, either—you can't do it. You'll wander from one end of this White man's land to the other. People will see you coming and hide, dreading the sound of your voice; you'll beg them to stop and listen to you. They'll even forget your old name, and call you by the name you earned today. Tippy-Canoe. That's your new name, White Murderer Harrison. Your true name, till you die a natural death as an old, old man."

Harrison bent onto the mane of the horse and wept into his bloody hands. But his were tears of fury, not grief or shame. Tears of rage that all his plans had gone awry. He would kill the Prophet even now, if he could. He would search far and wide for some witch or wizard who could break this curse. He couldn't bear to let this miserable one-eyed Red defeat him.

Measure spoke to the Prophet from the shore. "Where will you go now, Tenskwa-Tawa?"

"West," said Tenskwa-Tawa. "My people, all who still believe in me, we'll go west of the Mizzipy. When you tell your story, tell White men this—that west of the Mizzipy is Red man's land. Don't come there. The land can't bear the touch of a White man's foot. You breathe out death;

your touch is poison; your words are lies; the living land won't have you."

He turned his back, walked to the Reds waiting for him on the other shore, and helped an injured child walk up the far slope into the trees. Behind him, the water of the Tippy-Canoe began to flow again.

Miller walked down the slope to where his son stood on the bank of the creek. "Measure," he said, "Measure, Measure."

Measure turned and reached out his hands to embrace his father. "Alvin's alive, Father, far to the east of us. He's with Ta-Kumsaw, and he—"

But Miller hushed him, held his son's hands out. They dripped blood, just like Miller's own. Miller shook his head. "It's my fault," he said. "All my fault."

"Not all, Father," said Measure. "There's fault enough for everyone to share."

"But not for you, Son. That's *my* shame on your hands."

"Well, then, maybe you'll feel it less, for having two of us to carry it." Measure reached out and took his father by the shoulders, held him close. "We've seen the worst that men can do, Pa, and been the worst that men can be. But that don't mean that someday we won't see the best, too. And if we can never be perfect after this, well, we can still be pretty good, can't we?"

Maybe, thought Miller. But he doubted it. Or maybe he just doubted that he'd ever believe it, even if it were true. He'd never look into his own heart again and like what he found there.

They waited there on the riverbank for Miller's other sons. They came with bloody hands—David, Calm, Wastenot, Wantnot. David held his hands in front of him and wept. "I wish that I had died with Vigor in the Hatrack River!"

"No you don't," said Calm.

"I'd be dead, but I'd be clean."

The twins said nothing, but held each other's cold and slimy hands.

"We need to go home," said Measure.

"No," said Miller.

"They'll be worried," said Measure. "Ma, the girls, Cally."

Miller remembered his parting from Faith. "She said that if I—if this—"

"I know how Ma talks, but I also know your children need their pa, and she won't keep you out."

"I'll have to tell her. What we did."

"Yes, and the girls and Cally, too. We each have to tell them, and Calm and David have their wives to tell. Best do it now, and clean our hands, and get on with our lives. All of us at once, all of us together. And I have a story to tell you, too, about me and Alvin. When we've done with this tale, I'll tell mine, is that good? Will you stay for that?"

Armor met them at the Wobbish. The ferry was already on the other side, still unloading, and other men had took all the boats they used for crossing last night. So they stood and waited.

Measure stripped off his bloody coat and trousers, but Armor wouldn't put them on. Armor didn't make no accusations, but none of the others would look at their brother-in-law. Measure took him aside and told him about the curse while the ferry was slowly drawn back across the river. Armor listened, then walked to Miller, whose back was to him, looking at the far shore.

"Father," said Armor-of-God.

"You were right, Armor," said Miller, still not looking at him. He held up his hands. "Here it is, the proof that you were right."

"Measure tells me that I have to hear the story once from all of you," said Armor, turning to include them all in his speech. "But then you'll never hear another word of it from me. I'm still your son and brother, if you'll have me; my wife is your daughter and your sister, and you're the only kin I have out here."

"To your shame," whispered David.

"Don't punish me because my hands are clean," said Armor.

Calm held out a bloody hand. Armor took it without hesitation, shook firmly, then let go.

"Look at that," said Calm. "You touch us, it comes off on you."

In answer, Armor held out that same stained hand to Miller. After a while, Miller took it. The handshake lasted till the ferry came. Then they headed on home.

15

TWO-SOUL MAN

Taleswapper woke at dawn, instantly aware that something was wrong. It was Ta-Kumsaw, sitting on the grass, his face toward the west, rocking back and forth and breathing heavily, as if he was enduring a dull and heavy ache. Was he ill?

No. Alvin had failed. The slaughter had begun. Ta-Kumsaw's pain was not from his own body. It was Ta-Kumsaw's people dying, somewhere afar off, and what he felt was not grief or pity, it was the pain of their deaths. Even for a Red man as gifted as Ta-Kumsaw, to feel death from so far away meant that many, many souls had gone on to their reward.

As he had so many times before, Taleswapper addressed a few silent words to God, which always came down to this question: Why do you put us to so much trouble, when it all comes to nought in the end? Taleswapper couldn't bear the futility of it. Ta-Kumsaw and Alvin racing across country in their way, Taleswapper making the best time a White man can make, and Alvin going onto Eight-Face Mound, and what does it come to? Does it save a life? So many are dying now that Ta-Kumsaw can feel it from clear away by the Wobbish.

And, as usual, God had nothing much to say to Taleswapper when his questioning was done.

Taleswapper had no wish to interrupt Ta-Kumsaw. Or rather he guessed that Ta-Kumsaw had no particular wish to get into conversation with a White man at this particular moment. Yet he felt a vision growing within him. Not a vision such as prophets were rumored to see, not a vision of inward eyes. To Taleswapper visions came as words, and he did not know what the vision was until his own words told him. Even then, he knew that he was not a prophet; his visions were never such as would change the world, only the sort of thing that records it, that *understands* the world. Now, however, he took no thought of whether his visions were worthy or not. It came, and he must record it. Yet because the writing of words had been taken from him in this place, he could not write it down. What was there, then, but to speak the words aloud?

So Taleswapper spoke, forming the words into couplets as he said them because that was how visions ought to be expressed, in poetry. It was a confusing tale at first, and Taleswapper could not decide whether it was God or Satan whose terrible light blinded him as the words tumbled forth. He only knew that whichever one it was, whichever one had brought such slaughter to the world, he richly deserved Taleswapper's anger, and so he wasn't bashful about lashing him with language.

It all came down to these words rushing forth in a stream so intense that Taleswapper hardly breathed, certainly made no sensible break in the rhythms of his speech, his voice growing louder and louder as the lines were wrung from him and dashed out against the harsh wall of air around him, as if he dared God to hear him and resent his resentment:

When I had my defiance given
The sun stood trembling in heaven
The moon that glowed remote below
Became leprous and white as snow
And every soul of men on the earth
Felt affliction and sorrow and sickness and dearth
God flamed in my path and the Sun was hot
With the bows of my mind and the arrows of thought
My bowstring fierce with ardor breathes
My arrows glow in their golden sheaves
My brothers and father march before
The heavens drop with human gore—

"Stop!"

It was Ta-Kumsaw. Taleswapper waited with his mouth open, more words, more anguish waiting to pour from him. But Ta-Kumsaw was not to be disobeyed.

"It's finished," said Ta-Kumsaw.

"All dead?" whispered Taleswapper.

"I can't feel life from here," said Ta-Kumsaw. "I can feel death—the world is torn like an old cloth, it can never be mended." Despair gave way immediately to cold hate. "But it can be cleaned."

"If I could have prevented it, Ta-Kumsaw—"

"Yes, you're a good man, Taleswapper. There are others, too, among your kind. Armor-of-God Weaver is such a man. And if all White men came like you, to learn this land, then there'd be no war between us."

"There *is* no war between you and me, Ta-Kumsaw."

"Can you change the color of your skin? Can I change mine?"

"It isn't our skin, but our hearts—"

"When we stand with all the Red men on one side of the field, and all the White men on the other side of the field, where will you stand?"

"In the middle, pleading with both sides to—"

"You will stand with your people, and I will stand with mine."

How could Taleswapper argue with him? Perhaps he would have the courage to refuse such a choice. Perhaps not. "Pray God it never comes to such a pass."

"It already has, Taleswapper." Ta-Kumsaw nodded. "From this day's work, I will have no trouble gathering my army of Red men at last."

The words leapt from Taleswapper before he could stop them: "Then it's a terrible work you've chosen, if the death of so many good folk helps it along!"

Ta-Kumsaw answered with a roar, springing on Taleswapper all at once, knocking him back, flat on the grass of the meadow. Ta-Kumsaw's right hand clutched Taleswapper's hair; his left pressed against Taleswapper's throat. "All White men will die, all who don't escape across the sea!"

Yet it was not murder he intended. Even in his rage, Ta-Kumsaw did not press so hard as to strangle Taleswapper. After a moment the Red man pushed off and rolled away, burying his face in the grass, his arms and legs spread out to touch the earth with as much of his body as he could.

"I'm sorry," Taleswapper whispered. "I was wrong to say that."

"Lolla-Wossiky!" cried Ta-Kumsaw. "I did not want to be right, my brother!"

"Is he alive?" asked Taleswapper.

"I don't know," said Ta-Kumsaw. He turned his head to press his cheek against the grass; his eyes, though, bored at Taleswapper as if to kill him with a look. "Taleswapper, the words you were saying. What did they mean? What did you see?"

"I saw nothing," said Taleswapper. And then, though he

only learned the truth as the words came out, he said, "It was Alvin's vision I was speaking. It's what *he* saw. My brothers and father march before. The heavens drop with human gore. His vision, my poem."

"And where is the boy?" asked Ta-Kumsaw. "All night on that Mound, and where is he now?" Ta-Kumsaw jumped to his feet, orienting himself toward Eight-Face Mound, toward the very center of it. "No one stays there through the whole night, and now the sun is rising and he hasn't come." Ta-Kumsaw abruptly turned to face Taleswapper. "He can't come down."

"What do you mean?"

"He needs me," said Ta-Kumsaw. "I can feel it. A terrible wound is in him. All his strength is bleeding into the earth."

"What's on that hill! What wounded him?"

"Who knows what a White boy finds inside?" said Ta-Kumsaw. Then he turned to face the Mound again, as if he had felt a new summoning. "Yes," he said, then walked quickly toward the Mound.

Taleswapper followed, saying nothing about the incongruity—Ta-Kumsaw vowing to make war against Whites until all were dead or gone from this land, and yet hurrying back to Eight-Face Mound to save a White boy.

They stood together at the place where Alvin climbed.

"Can you see the place?" asked Taleswapper.

"There is no path," said Ta-Kumsaw.

"But you saw it yesterday," said Taleswapper.

"Yesterday there was a path."

"Then some other way," said Taleswapper. "Your own way onto the Mound."

"Another way would not take me to the same place."

"Come now, Ta-Kumsaw, the Mound is big, but not so big you can't find someone up there in an hour of looking."

Ta-Kumsaw gazed disdainfully at Taleswapper.

Abashed, Taleswapper spoke less confidently. "So you have to take the same path to reach the same place?"

"How do I know?" asked Ta-Kumsaw. "I never heard of one going up the Mound, and another following by the same path."

"Don't you ever go here in twos or threes?"

"This is the place where the land speaks to all creatures who live here. The speech of the land is grass and trees; the adornment is beasts and birds."

Taleswapper noted that when he wished to, Ta-Kumsaw could speak the English language like any White man. No: like a well-educated White man. Adornment. Where in the Hio country could he learn a word like that? "So we can't get in?"

Ta-Kumsaw's face showed no expression.

"Well, I say we go up anyway. We know the road he took—let's take it, whether we can see it or not."

Ta-Kumsaw said nothing.

"Are you just going to stand here, then, and let him die up there?"

In answer, Ta-Kumsaw took a single step that brought him face to face—no, breast to breast—with Taleswapper. Ta-Kumsaw gripped his hand, threw his other arm around Taleswapper, held him close. Their legs were tangled; Taleswapper for a moment imagined how they must look, if there had been anyone to see them—whether someone would know which leg belonged to which man, they were so close together. He felt the Red man's heart beating, its rhythm more commanding within Taleswapper's body than the unsensed beat of his own hot pulse. "We are not two men," whispered Ta-Kumsaw. "Not Red and White men here, with blood between us. We are one man with two souls, a Red soul and a White soul, one man."

"All right," said Taleswapper. "Let it be as you say."

Still holding Taleswapper tightly, Ta-Kumsaw turned within the embrace; their heads pressed against each other, their ears so close-joined Taleswapper could hear nothing but Ta-Kumsaw's pulse like the pounding of ocean waves inside his ear. But now, their bodies so tightly joined that they seemed to have a single heartbeat, Taleswapper could see a clear path leading up the face of the Mound.

"Do you—" began Ta-Kumsaw.

"I see it," said Taleswapper.

"Stay this close to me," said Ta-Kumsaw. "Now we are like Alvin—a Red soul and a White soul in a single body."

It was awkward, even ridiculous, to attempt to climb the Mound this way. Yet when their movement up the path jostled them apart, even the tiniest fraction, the path seemed to grow more difficult, hidden behind an errant growth of some vine, some bush, some dangling limb. So Taleswapper clung to Ta-Kumsaw as tightly as the Red man clung to him, and together they made their difficult way up the hill.

At the top Taleswapper was astonished to see that instead of a single Mound, they were at the crest of a ring of eight separate Mounds, with an octagonal valley between them. More important, Ta-Kumsaw was also surprised. He seemed uncertain; his grip on Taleswapper was not as tight; he was no longer in control.

"Where does a White man go in this place?" asked Ta-Kumsaw.

"Down, of course," said Taleswapper. "When a White man sees a valley, he goes down into it, to find what's there."

"Is this how it always is for you?" asked Ta-Kumsaw. "Not knowing where you are, where anything is?"

Only then did Taleswapper realize that Ta-Kumsaw lacked his land-sense here. He was as blind as a White man in this place.

"Let's go down," said Taleswapper. "And look—we don't have to cling so tightly now. It's a grassy hill, and we don't need a path."

They crossed a stream and found him in a meadow, with a mist low on the ground around them. Alvin was not injured, but he lay trembling—as if fevered, though his brow was cool—and his breathing was shallow and quick. As Ta-Kumsaw had said: dying.

Taleswapper touched him, caressed him, then shook him, trying to wake the boy. Alvin showed no sign that he was aware of them. Ta-Kumsaw was no help. He sat beside the boy, holding his hand, whining so softly that Taleswapper doubted he knew he was making a sound.

But Taleswapper was not one to give in to despair, if in fact that was what Ta-Kumsaw was feeling. He looked around. Nearby was a tree, looking like spring, its leaves so yellow-green that in the light of dawn they might have been made of thin-hammered gold. Hanging from the tree was a light-colored fruit. No, a *white* fruit. And suddenly, as soon as he saw it, Taleswapper smelled it, pungent and sweet, so that he could almost taste it.

He acted, not thinking what he would do, but doing it. He walked to the tree, plucked the fruit, carried it back to Alvin where he lay on the ground, a child so small. Taleswapper passed it under Alvin's nose, so the odor of it might be like smelling salts, and revive him. Alvin's breathing suddenly became great deep gasps. His eyes opened, his lips parted, and from gritted teeth came a whine almost exactly like Ta-Kumsaw's keening; almost exactly like a kicked dog.

"Take a bite," said Taleswapper.

Ta-Kumsaw reached out, snatched Alvin's lower jaw in one hand and upper jaw in the other, his fingers interlaced at Alvin's teeth, and with great effort prised Alvin's jaws apart. Taleswapper thrust the fruit between Alvin's teeth; Ta-Kumsaw forced the jaws closed again. The fruit broke open, spilling clear fluid into Alvin's mouth and dribbling down his cheek into the grass. Slowly, with great effort, Alvin began to chew. Tears flowed from his eyes. He swallowed. Suddenly he reached out his hands, caught Taleswapper by the neck and Ta-Kumsaw by the hair, and pulled himself up to a sitting position. Clinging to them both, drawing their faces so close to his that they all breathed each other's breath, Alvin wept until their faces all were wet, and because Ta-Kumsaw and Taleswapper were also weeping, none could be sure whose tears cast a glaze across the skin of each man's face.

Alvin said little, but enough. He told them all that happened at Tippy-Canoe Creek that day, of blood in the river, a thousand survivors crossing on the water made smooth and hard; blood on White men's hands, and on one man's hands in particular.

"Not enough," said Ta-Kumsaw.

Taleswapper offered no argument. It was not for a White man to tell Ta-Kumsaw that the killers of his people had received a punishment exactly proportioned to their sin. Besides, Taleswapper wasn't sure he believed it himself.

Alvin told them how he had spent the evening and the night before, restoring Measure from the edge of death; and how he spent the morning, taking away the immeasurable agony as nine thousand innocent deaths shouted in the Prophet's mind—nine thousand times that one black shout that years before had maddened him. Which was harder—healing Measure or healing Lolla-Wossiky? "It was like you said," Alvin whispered to Taleswapper. "I just can't build that brick wall faster than it breaks down." Then, exhausted but at peace now, Alvin slept.

Taleswapper and Ta-Kumsaw faced each other, Alvin curled between them, his breathing soft and slow.

"I know his wound now," Ta-Kumsaw said. "His grief is for his own people, with their bloody hands."

"His grief was for the dead and the living too," said Taleswapper. "If I know Alvin, his deepest wound was thinking that he failed, that if he'd just tried harder, he might have got Measure there in time to stop it before the first shot was fired."

"White men grieve for White men," Ta-Kumsaw said.

"Lie to yourself if you like," said Taleswapper, "but lies don't fool me."

"But Red men don't grieve at all," said Ta-Kumsaw. "Red men will put White blood into the ground for the blood spilled today."

"I thought you served the land," said Taleswapper. "Don't you realize what happened today? Don't you remember where we are? You've seen a part of Eight-Face Mound you never knew existed, and why? Because the land let us into this place together, because—"

Ta-Kumsaw held up one hand. "To save this boy."

"Because Red and White can share this land if we—"

Ta-Kumsaw reached out his hand and touched his fingers to Taleswapper's lips.

"I'm not a farmer who wants to hear stories of faraway places," Ta-Kumsaw said. "Go tell your tales to someone who wants to hear them."

Taleswapper slapped Ta-Kumsaw's hand away. He had meant merely to push the Red man's arm, but instead he struck with too much force, throwing Ta-Kumsaw off balance. Ta-Kumsaw immediately leapt to his feet; Taleswapper did the same.

"Here is where it starts!" shouted Ta-Kumsaw.

Between them, at their feet, Alvin stirred.

"A Red man angered you, and you struck him, just like a White man, no patience—"

"You told me to be silent, you said my tales were—"

"Words, that's what I gave you, words and a soft touch, and you answered me with a blow." Ta-Kumsaw smiled. It was a terrifying smile, like a tiger's teeth out of the darkness of the jungle, his eyes glowing, his skin bright as flame.

"I'm sorry, I didn't mean—"

"White man never means anything, just couldn't help himself, it was all a *mistake*. That's what you think, isn't it, White Liar! Alvin's people killed my people because of a *mistake*, because they thought two White boys were dead. For the sake of two White boys they lashed out, just like you did, and they killed nine thousand of my people, babies and mothers, old men and stripling boys, their cannon—"

"I heard what Alvin said."

"Don't you like *my* story? Don't you want to hear it? You are White, Taleswapper. You are like all White men, quick to ask forgiveness, slow to give it; always expecting patience, but flaring up like a spark when the wind rises—you burn down a forest because you tripped on a root!" Ta-Kumsaw turned and began to walk quickly back the way they came.

"How can you leave without me!" cried Taleswapper after him. "We have to leave here together!"

Ta-Kumsaw stopped, turned around, tipped back his head, and laughed without mirth. "I don't need a path to get *down*, White Liar!" Then he was off again, running.

Alvin was awake, of course.

"I'm sorry, Alvin," said Taleswapper. "I didn't mean—"

"No," said Alvin. "Let me guess what he did. He touched you like this." Alvin touched Taleswapper's lips, just as Ta-Kumsaw had.

"Yes."

"That's what a Shaw-Nee mama does to shut up a little boy who's making too much noise. But I'll bet if one Red man did that to another—he was provoking you."

"I shouldn't have hit him."

"Then he would've done something else till you did."

Taleswapper had nothing to answer to that. Seemed to him the boy was probably right. Certainly right. The one thing Ta-Kumsaw could not bear today was being a White man's companion in peace.

Alvin slept again. Taleswapper explored, but found nothing strange. Just stillness and peace. He couldn't even tell now which tree it was the fruit came from. They all looked silvery green to him now, and no matter how far he walked in any direction, he ended up no farther from Alvin than a few minutes' walk. A strange place, not a place a man could map in his mind, not a place that a man could master. Here the land gives you what it wants to give, and no more.

It was near sunset when Alvin roused again, and Taleswapper helped him to his feet.

"I'm walking like a newborn colt," said Alvin. "I feel so weak."

"You only did half the labors of Hercules in the last twenty-four hours," said Taleswapper.

"Her what?"

"Hercules. A Greek."

"I got to find Ta-Kumsaw," said Alvin. "I shouldn't have let him go, but I was so tired."

"You're White, too," said Taleswapper. "Think he'll want you with him?"

"Tenskwa-Tawa prophesied," said Alvin. "As long as I'm with him, Ta-Kumsaw won't die."

Taleswapper supported Alvin as they walked to the one place that let them approach; they climbed the gentle grassy rise between Mounds and crested the hill. They stopped and looked down. Taleswapper saw no path—just thorns, vines, bushes, brambles. "I can't get down through that."

Alvin looked up at him, puzzled. "There's a path as plain as day."

"For you, maybe," said Taleswapper. "Not for me."

"You got in here," said Alvin.

"With Ta-Kumsaw," said Taleswapper.

"He got out."

"I'm no Red man."

"I'll lead."

Alvin started out with a few bold steps, as easy as if he was on a Sunday jaunt on the commons. But to Taleswapper it looked like the briars opened wide for him and closed up tight right after. "Alvin!" he called. "Stay with me!"

Alvin came and took him by the hand. "Follow tight behind," he said.

Taleswapper tried, but still the brambles snapped back and tore at his face, cut him sore. With Alvin going before, Taleswapper could make his way, but he felt like he was being flayed from behind. Even deerskin was no match for thorns like daggers, limbs that snapped back at him like a bo'sun's lash. He could feel blood running down his arms, his back, his legs. "I can't go any more, Alvin!" said Taleswapper.

"I see him," said Alvin.

"Who?"

"Ta-Kumsaw. Wait here."

He let go of Taleswapper's hand; he was gone for a moment, and Taleswapper was alone with the brambles. He tried not to move, but even his breathing seemed to provoke more stings and stabs.

Alvin was back. He took Taleswapper by the hand. "Follow me tight. One more step."

Taleswapper steeled himself and took the step.

"Down," said Alvin.

Taleswapper obeyed Alvin's tugging and knelt, though

he feared that he'd never be able to rise again through the briars that closed over his head.

Then Alvin led his hand until it touched another hand, and suddenly the brambles cleared a little, and Taleswapper could see Ta-Kumsaw lying there, blood seeping from hundreds of wounds on his nearly naked body. "He got this far alone," said Alvin.

Ta-Kumsaw opened his eyes, rage burning. "Leave me here," he whispered.

In answer, Taleswapper cradled Ta-Kumsaw's head in his other arm. As more of their bodies touched, the briars seemed to sag and fall away; now Taleswapper could see a kind of path where he hadn't seen one before.

"No," said Ta-Kumsaw.

"We can't get down from here without each other's help," said Taleswapper. "Like it or not, if you're going to get your vengeance against the White man, you need a White man's help."

"Then leave me here," whispered Ta-Kumsaw. "Save your people by leaving me to die."

"I can't get down without you," said Taleswapper.

"Good," said Ta-Kumsaw.

Taleswapper noticed that Ta-Kumsaw's wounds looked much fewer. And those that were left were scabbed over, nearly healed. Then he realized that his own injuries didn't hurt anymore. He looked around. Alvin sat nearby, leaning against a tree trunk, his eyes closed, looking like somebody just flogged him, he was so spent and dreary.

"Look what we cost him, healing us," said Taleswapper.

Ta-Kumsaw's face showed his surprise, for once; surprise, then anger. "I didn't ask you to heal me!" he cried. He tore himself out of Taleswapper's grasp and tried to reach toward Alvin. But suddenly there were brambles twining around his arm, and Ta-Kumsaw cried out, not in pain, but in fury. "I won't be forced!" he cried.

"Why should you be the only man who isn't?" said Taleswapper.

"I'll do what I set out to do, and nothing else, whatever the land says!"

"The words of the blacksmith in his forge," said Taleswapper. "The farmer cutting down the trees, he says that."

"Don't you dare compare me to a White man!"

But the brambles bound him tight, till Taleswapper again made his painful way to Ta-Kumsaw, and embraced him. Again Taleswapper felt his own wounds heal, saw Ta-Kumsaw's vanish as quickly as the vines themselves had let go and dropped away. Alvin was looking at them with such pleading, as if to say, How much more strength will you steal from me, before you do what you know you have to do?

With a final anguished cry, Ta-Kumsaw turned and embraced Taleswapper as fully as before. Together they made their way down a wide path to the bottom of the Mound. Alvin stumbled after them.

They slept that night where they had the night before, but it was a troubled sleep. In the morning, Taleswapper wordlessly packed up his few goods, including the book whose letters made no sense. Then he kissed Alvin on the head and walked away. He said nought to Ta-Kumsaw, and Ta-Kumsaw said no more to him. They both knew what the land had said, and they both knew that for the first time in his life, Ta-Kumsaw was going against what was good for the land and satisfying a different need. Taleswapper didn't even try to argue against him anymore. He knew that Ta-Kumsaw would follow his path no matter what, no matter if it left him pierced with a thousand bleeding wounds. He only hoped that Alvin had the strength to stay with him all the way, and keep him alive when all hope was gone.

About noon, after walking almost due west all morning, Taleswapper stopped and pulled his book out of his pack. To his relief, he could read the words again. He unsealed the back two-thirds of the book, the pages where he did his own writing, and spent the rest of the afternoon writing all that had happened to him, all that Alvin had told him, all that he feared for the future. He also wrote the words of the poem that had come to him the morning before, the verses that came from his mouth but Alvin's vision. The poem was still right and true, but even as he read the words in his book, the power of them faded. It was the closest he had ever come to being a prophet himself; but now the gift had left him. It was never his gift at all, anyway. Just as he and Ta-Kumsaw had walked on the meadow without seeing anything special, never guessing that for Alvin it had been a map of the whole continent, so now Taleswapper had the words written down in his book and had no notion anymore of the power behind them.

Taleswapper couldn't travel like a Red man, through the night, sleeping on his feet. So it took him more than a few days to get all the way west to the town of Vigor Church, where he knew there'd be a lot of folks with a long and bitter tale to tell him. If ever a folk needed such a man as Taleswapper to hear their tale, it was them. Yet if ever there was a story that Taleswapper was loath to listen to, it was theirs. Still, he didn't shy from calling on them. He could bear it. There'd be plenty more dark tales to tell before Ta-Kumsaw was through; might as well get started now, so as not to fall behind.

16

LA FAYETTE

Gilbert de La Fayette sat at his vast table, looking into the grain of the wood. Several letters lay before him. One was a letter from de Maurepas to King Charles. Obviously, Freddie had been won over by Napoleon. The letter was full of praise for the little general and his brilliant strategy.

So soon we are going to win the decisive victory, Your Majesty, and glorify your name. General Bonaparte refuses to be bound by European military tradition. He is training our troops to fight like Reds, even as he lures the so-called Americans into fighting in the open field, like Europeans. As Andrew Jackson gathers his American army, we also gather an army of men who have better claim to the name American. Ta-Kumsaw's ten thousand will stand with us as we destroy the ten thousand of Old Hickory. Ta-Kumsaw will thus avenge the blood of the slaughter at Tippy-Canoe, while we destroy the American army and subjugate the land from the Hio to Huron Lake. In all this, we loyally give the glory to Your Majesty, for it was your insight in sending General Bonaparte here that has made this great conquest possible. And if you now send us two thousand more Frenchmen, to stiffen our line and provoke the Americans into further rashness, your act will be seen as the key intervention in our battle.

It was an outrageous letter for a mere Comte—and one out of favor—to send to his King. Yet Gilbert knew how the letter would be received. For King Charles was also under Napoleon's spell, and he would read praise of the little Corsican with agreement, with joy.

If only Napoleon were only a vain posturer with a gift for seducing the loyalty of his betters. Then La Fayette could watch his inevitable destruction without soiling his own hands. Napoleon and de Maurepas would lead the French army to disaster, such a disaster as might well bring down a government, and lead to a curbing of the King's authority, even an expulsion of the monarchy, as the English so wisely did a century and a half before.

But Napoleon was exactly what he seduced Freddie and Charlie into thinking he was: a brilliant general. Gilbert knew that Napoleon's plan would succeed. The Americans would march northward, convinced that they faced only Reds. At the last moment, they would find themselves in combat with the French army, disciplined, well-armed, and fanatically loyal to Napoleon. The Americans would be forced to array themselves like a European army. Under their attack, the French would slowly, carefully retreat. When American discipline collapsed in the pursuit, *then* the Reds would attack in devastating numbers, completely surrounding the Americans. Not one American would escape alive—and almost no French lives would be lost.

It was audacious. It was dangerous. It involved exposing French troops to serious risk of destruction, as they would be vastly outnumbered by the Americans. It required implicit trust in the Reds. But Gilbert knew that Napoleon's trust in Ta-Kumsaw was justified.

Ta-Kumsaw would have his revenge. De Maurepas would have his escape from Detroit. Even La Fayette could probably claim enough credit from such a victory to come home and live in comfort and dignity on his ancestral lands. Above all, Napoleon would become the most loved and trusted figure in the military. King Charles would surely grant him a title and lands, and send him out a-conquering in Europe, making King Charles ever richer and more powerful and the people ever more willing to endure his tyranny.

So Gilbert carefully tore de Maurepas's letter into tiny fragments.

The second letter was from Napoleon himself to Gilbert. It was candid, even brutal, in its assessment of the situation. Napoleon had come to realize that while Gilbert de La Fayette was immune to his intoxicating charm, he was a sincere admirer and, indeed, a friend. I *am* your friend, Napoleon. Yet I am more a friend of France than of any man. And the path I have in mind for you is far greater than being the mere toady of a stupid King.

Gilbert reread the key paragraph of Napoleon's letter.

De Maurepas merely echoes what I say, which is comfortable but tedious. I shudder to think what would happen if he were ever in command. His idea of alliance with the Reds is to put them in uniform and stand them in rows like ninepins. What foolishness! How can King Charles consider himself anything but a halfwit, forcing me to serve *under* such an idiot as Freddie? But to Charles, Freddie no doubt seems like the soul of wit—after all, he does know how to appreciate the ballet. In Spain I won a victory for Charles that he did not deserve, and yet he is so spineless that he lets his jealous courtiers maneuver me to Canada, where my allies are savages and my officers are fools. Charlie doesn't deserve the victory I'll bring him. But then, Gilbert my friend, the royal blood has grown thin and weak in the years since Louis Fourteen. I'd urge you to burn this letter, except that Charlie loves me so well that I think he could read it word for word and not take offense! And if he did take offense, how would he dare punish me? What would his stature be in Europe, if I hadn't helped old Wooden-head to a case of dysentery so I could win the war in Spain, instead of losing it, as would surely have happened without me?

Napoleon's vanity was insufferable, but primarily because it was so fully justified. Every word in this letter was true, if rash; but Gilbert had carefully cultivated this candor in Napoleon. Napoleon had obviously longed for someone to admire him sincerely, without Napoleon diddling with his affections. He had found such a one—truly he had—in Gilbert, the only real friend Napoleon would ever have. And yet. And yet.

Gilbert carefully folded Napoleon's letter and enclosed it in his own, a simple note that said:

Your Majesty, please do not be harsh with this gifted young man. He has the arrogance of youth; there is no treason in his heart, I know it. Nevertheless, I will be guided by you, as always, for you will always know the proper balance between justice and mercy. Your humble servant, Gilbert.

King Charles would be livid, of course. Even if Napoleon was right, and Charlie was inclined to be indulgent, the courtiers would never let such an opportunity pass.

There would be such a howl for Napoleon's head that even King Charles could not resist cashiering the boy.

Another letter, the most painful one, was again in Gilbert's own hand, this time addressed to Frederic, Comte de Maurepas. Gilbert had written it long ago, almost as soon as Napoleon arrived in Canada. Soon it would be time to send it.

> On the eve of such momentous events, my dear Freddie, I think you should wear this amulet. It was given me by a holy man to fend the lies and deceptions of Satan. Wear it at all times, my friend, for I think your need for it is greater far than mine.

Freddie need not know that the "holy man" was Robespierre—de Maurepas would certainly never wear it then. Gilbert drew the amulet from the bosom of his shirt, where it dangled on a golden chain. What will de Maurepas do when Napoleon has no power over him? Why, he will act his true self again, that is what he will do.

Gilbert had sat thus for half an hour, knowing that the time of decision had arrived. The amulet would not be sent yet—only at the cusp of events would Napoleon suddenly lose his influence over Freddie. But the letter to the King must be sent now, if there was to be time for it to reach Versailles, and the inevitable response to return to Canada before the springtime battle with the Americans.

Am I a traitor, to work for the defeat of my King and country? No, I am not, most certainly I am not. For if I thought it would do my beloved France even an ounce of good, I would help Napoleon win his victory over the Americans, even if it meant crippling the cause of liberty in this new land. For though I am a Feuillant, a democrat, even a Jacobin in my darkest heart, and even though my love for America is greater than that of any man save perhaps Franklin or Washington, who are dead, or Jefferson among the living—despite all that, I am a Frenchman first, and what care I for liberty in any corner of God's world, if there is none in France?

No, I do this because a terrible, humiliating defeat in Canada is exactly what France needs, especially if it can be seen that the defeat is caused by King Charles's direct intervention. Such a direct intervention as removing popular and brilliant Bonaparte from command on the eve of battle, and replacing him with an ass like de Maurepas, all for the sake of Charlie's own vanity.

For there was one last letter, this one in code, seemingly innocuous in its babbling about hunting and the tedium of life in Niagara. But hidden within it was the entire text of both Napoleon's and Frederic's letters, to be published to withering effect as soon as the news of French defeat reached Paris. Almost as quickly as Napoleon's original letter reached the King, Robespierre would have this ciphered letter in his hands.

But what of my oath to the king? What sort of plotting is this? I was meant to be a general, to lead armies in battle; or a Governor, to move the machinery of state for the good of the people. Instead I am reduced to plotting, backstabbing, deception, betrayal. I am a Brutus, willing to betray all for the sake of a loyalty to the people. And yet—I pray that history will be kind to me, and let it be known that but for me King Charles would have called himself Charlemagne Second and used Napoleon to subjugate Europe in a new French Empire. Instead, with God's help, because of me France will set an example of peacefulness and liberty to all the world.

He lit his wax candle, let it drip to fasten closed the letter to the King and the letter to his trusted neighbor, and then pressed his seal into both. He called in his aide, who put them in the mail pouch, then left to carry them to the ship—the last ship that was sure to make it down the river and on to France before winter.

Only the letter to de Maurepas remained, that and the amulet. How I regret having you, he said to the amulet. If only I, too, could have been deceived by Napoleon, and rejoiced as he made his inevitable way into history. Instead I am thwarting him, for how can a general, be he as brilliant as Caesar, possibly thrive in the democracy Robespierre and I will create in France?

All seeds are planted, all traps are set.

For another hour Gilbert de La Fayette sat trembling in his chair. Then he arose, dressed in his finest clothing, and spent the evening watching a wretched farce by a fifth-rate company, the finest that poor Niagara could get from Mother France. At the end he stood and applauded, which, because he was Governor, guaranteed the company financial success in Canada; applauded long and vigorously, as the rest of the audience was forced to keep applauding with him; clapped his hands until his arms were sore, until the amulet was slick with sweat on his chest, until he felt the heat of his exertion burning through his shoulders and back, until he could clap no more.

17

BECCA'S LOOM

Winter'd been going on half Alvin's life, it seemed like. Used to be he liked snowy times, peeking out his window through the craze of frost, looking at the sun dazzling off the smooth unbroken sea of snow. But then, in those days he could always get inside where it was warm, eat Ma's cooking, sleep in a soft bed. Not that he was suffering so much now; what with learning Red ways for doing things, Alvin wasn't bad off.

It had just been going on for too many months. Almost a year since that spring morning when Alvin set out with Measure for the trip to Hatrack River. That had seemed such a long journey then; now, to Alvin, it was no more than a day's jaunt by comparison with the traveling he had done. They been south so far the Reds spoke Spanish more than English when they talked White man talk. They been west to the foggy bottom lands near the Mizzipy. They talked to Cree-Ek, Chok-Taw, the "uncivilized" Cherriky folk of the bayou country. And north to the highest reaches of the Mizzipy where the lakes were so many and all hooked on that you could go everywhere by canoe.

It went the same with every village they visited. "We

know about you, Ta-Kumsaw, you come to talk war. We don't want war. But—if the White man comes here, we fight."

And then Ta-Kumsaw explaining that by the time the White man comes to their village, it's too late, they'll be alone, and the Whites will be like a hailstorm, pounding them into the dirt. "We must make ourselves into one army. We still can be stronger than they are if we do."

It was never enough. A few young men would nod, would wish to say yes, but the old men, they didn't want war, they didn't want glory, they wanted peace and quiet, and the White man was still far away, still a rumor.

Then Ta-Kumsaw would turn to Alvin, and say, "Tell them what happened at Tippy-Canoe."

By the third telling, Alvin knew what would happen when he told the tale the tenth time, the hundredth time, every time. Knew it as soon as the Reds seated around the fire turned to look at him, with distaste because he was White, with interest because he was the White boy who traveled with Ta-Kumsaw. No matter how simple he made the tale, no matter how he included the fact that the Whites of Wobbish Territory thought that Ta-Kumsaw had kidnapped and tortured him and Measure, the Reds still listened to it with grief and grim fury. And at the end, the old men would be gripping handfuls of soil in their hands, tearing at the ground as if to turn loose some terrible beast inside the earth; and the young men would be drawing their flint-edged knives gently across their own thighs, drawing faint lines of blood, teaching their knives to be thirsty, teaching their own bodies to seek out pain and love it.

"When the snow is gone from the banks of the Hio," said Ta-Kumsaw.

"We will be there," said the young men, and the old men nodded their consent. The same in every village, every tribe. Oh, sometimes a few spoke of the Prophet and urged peace; they were scorned as "old women"; though as far as Alvin could see, the old women seemed most savage of all in their hate.

Yet Alvin never complained that Ta-Kumsaw was using him to heat up anger against his own race. After all, the story Alvin had to tell was true, wasn't it? He couldn't deny to tell it, not to anybody, not for any reason, no more than his family could deny to speak under the Prophet's curse. Not that blood would appear on Alvin's hands if he refused to tell. He just felt like the same burden was on him like it was on all the Whites who beheld the massacre at Tippy-Canoe. The story of Tippy-Canoe was true, and if every Red who heard that tale became filled with hate and wanted vengeance, wanted to kill every White man who didn't sail back to Europe, why, would that be a reason for Alvin to try to keep them from knowing? Or wasn't that their natural right, to know the truth so as to be able to let the truth lead them to do good or evil, as they chose?

Not that Alvin could talk about natural rights and such out loud. There wasn't much chance for conversation. Sure enough, he was always with Ta-Kumsaw, never more than an arm's length off. But Ta-Kumsaw almost never spoke to Alvin, and when he did it was things like "Catch a fish" or "Come with me now." Ta-Kumsaw made it plain that he had no friendship for Alvin now, and in fact he didn't much want a White along with him. Ta-Kumsaw walked fast, in his Red man's way, and never looked back to see if Alvin was with him or not. The only time he ever seemed to care that Alvin was there was when he turned to him and said, "Tell what happened at Tippy-Canoe."

One time, after they left a village so het up against Whites they were looking with interest at Alvin's own scalp, Alvin got to feeling defiant and he said, "Why don't you have me tell them about how you and I and Taleswapper all got into Eight-Face Mound?" Ta-Kumsaw's only answer was to walk so fast that Alvin had to run all day just keeping up.

Traveling with Ta-Kumsaw was like traveling alone, when it came to company. Alvin couldn't remember ever being so lonely in his life. So why don't I leave, he asked himself. Why do I keep going with him? It ain't like it's fun, and I'm helping him start a war against my own folks, and it's getting colder all the time, like as if the sun gave up shining and the world was supposed to be grey bare trees and blinding snow from one end to the other, and he don't even want me here.

Why did Alvin go on? It was partly Tenskwa-Tawa's prophecy that Ta-Kumsaw never would die if Alvin stuck close by. Alvin might not like Ta-Kumsaw's company, but Alvin knew he was a great and good man, and if Alvin could somehow help keep him alive, then it was his duty to give it a try as best he could.

But it was also more than that, more than the duty he felt to the Prophet, to care for his brother; more than the need he felt to act out the terrible punishment of his family by telling the tale of Tippy-Canoe all over the Red man's country. Alvin couldn't exactly find it in words to tell himself inside his head as he ran along through the woods, lost in a halfway dream, the green of the forest guiding his footsteps and filling his head with the music of the earth. No, that wasn't a word time. But it was a time of understanding without words, of having a sense of rightness about what he was doing, a feeling that Alvin was like the oil on the axle of a wagon wheel that was carrying great events forward. I might just get myself all used up, I might get burned away by the heat of the wheel rubbing on the axle, but the world is changing, and somehow I'm part of what's helping it go forward. Ta-Kumsaw's building something, bringing together Red men to make something out of them.

It was the first time Alvin understood that something could be built out of people, that when Ta-Kumsaw talked them Reds into feeling with one heart and acting with one mind, they became something bigger than just a few people; and building something like that, it was against the Unmaker, wasn't it? Just like Alvin always used to make little baskets by weaving grass. The grass was nothing but grass by itself, but all wove together it was something more than grass.

Ta-Kumsaw's making something new where there wasn't nothing, but the new thing won't come to be without me.

That filled him with fear of helping make something he didn't understand; but it also filled him with eagerness to see the future. So he pressed on, pushed forward, wore himself down, talked to Reds who started out suspicious and ended up filled with hate, and stared most of every day at the back of Ta-Kumsaw running ahead of him ever deeper into the forest. The green of the wood turned gold and red, then black with the rains of autumn on the bare trees, and finally grey and white and still. And all his worry, all his discouragement, all his confusion, all his grief for the terrible things he saw coming and the terrible things he'd seen in the past—all turned into a weary distaste for winter, an impatience for the season to change, for the snow to melt and spring to come, and then summer.

Summer, when he could look back and think of all this as the past. Summer, when he'd know pretty much how it all turned out, for good or ill, and not have this sickening snow-white dread in the back of his mind, masking all his other feelings the way snow masked the earth beneath it.

Until one day Alvin noticed that the air *was* somewhat warm, and the snow had slacked off the grass and dirt and was purely gone from the tree limbs, and there was a flash of red where a certain bird was getting itself ready to find him a wife and nestle in for egg season. And on that very day, Ta-Kumsaw turned eastward, up over a ridge of hills, and stood perched atop a rock looking down on a valley of White men's farms in the northern part of the White man's state of Appalachee.

It was a sight Alvin had never seen before in his life. Not like the French city of Detroit, people all packed in together, nor like the sparse settlements of the Wobbish country, with each farm carved out like a gouge in the greenwood forest. Here the trees were all disciplined, lined up in rows to mark off one farmer's field from another. Only on the hills skirting the valley were the trees somewhat wild again. And as the ground softened today, there were farmers out cutting the earth open with their plows, just as gentle and shallow on the face of the earth as those Red warriors' flint knives against their thighs, teaching the blade to thirst, teaching the earth to bear, so that like the blood that seeped upward under the Red men's knives, the wheat or maize or rye or oats would seep upward, make a thin film of life across the skin of the earth, an open wound all summer until harvest blades made another kind of cut. Then the snow again, it would form like a scab, to heal the earth until the next year's injury. This whole valley was like that, broken like an old horse.

I shouldn't feel like this, thought Alvin. I should be glad to see White lands again. There was curls of smoke from a hundred chimneys up and down the valley. There was folks there, children getting outside to play after being penned up the whole of winter, men sweating into the chilly air of early spring as they did their tasks, hardworking animals raising a steam from their nostrils and off their hot, heaving flanks. This was like home, wasn't it? This was what Armor and Pa and every other White man wanted to turn the Wobbish country into, wasn't it? This was civilization, one household butting up into the next one, all elbows jostling, all the land parceled out till nobody had no doubt at all who owned every inch of it, who had the right to use it and who was trespassing and better move along.

But after this year of being with Reds practically every minute and hardly seeing a White man except for Measure, for a while, and Taleswapper for a day or two, why, Alvin didn't see that valley with White eyes. He saw it like a Red man, and so to Alvin it looked like the end of the world.

"What're we doing here?" Alvin asked Ta-Kumsaw.

In answer, Ta-Kumsaw just walked right down from the mountain and on into the White man's valley, just like he had a right. Alvin couldn't figure, but he followed tight.

To Alvin's surprise, as they traipsed right through a field half-plowed, the farmer didn't so much as yell at them to mind the furrows, he just looked up, squinted at them, and then waved. "Howdy, Ike!" he called.

Ike?

And Ta-Kumsaw raised his hand in greeting and walked on.

Alvin like to laughed out loud. Ta-Kumsaw, being known to civilized farmers in a place like this, known so well that a White man could tell who he was at such a distance! Ta-Kumsaw, the most ferocious hater of Whites in all the woodland, being called by a White man's name?

But Alvin knew better than to ask for explanation. He just followed close behind till Ta-Kumsaw finally came to where he was going.

It looked to be a house like any other house, maybe a speck older. Big, anyway, and added onto in a jumbly way. Maybe that corner of the house was the original cabin, with a stone foundation, and then they added that wing onto it bigger than the log house, so the cabin no doubt got turned into a kitchen, and then another wing across the front of the cabin, only this time two stories high, with an attic, and then an add-on in the back of the cabin, right across the roof of it, keeping the gable shape and framing it with shaped timbers, which were whitewashed clean enough once, but now were peeling off the paint and showing grey wood through. The whole history of this valley in that house—desperately just throwing up enough of a cabin to keep rain off between battling the forest; then a measure of peace to add a room or two for comfort; then some prosperity, and more children, and a need to put a grand two-story face on things, and finally three generations in that house, and building not for pride but just for space, just for rooms to put folks into.

Such a house it was, a house that held the whole story of the White man's victorious war against the land in its shape.

And up walks Ta-Kumsaw to a small and shabby-looking door in the back, and he doesn't so much as knock, he just opens the door and goes inside.

Well, Alvin saw that, and for the first time he didn't know what to do. By habit he wanted to follow Ta-Kumsaw right into the house, the way he'd followed him into a hundred mud-daubed Red man's huts. But by even older habit he knew you don't just walk right into a house like *this*, with a proper door and all. You go round to the front and knock polite, and wait for folks to invite you in.

So Alvin stood at the back door, which Ta-Kumsaw of course didn't even bother to close, watching the first flies of spring wander into the hallway. He could almost hear his mother yelling about people leaving doors open so the flies would come in and drive everybody crazy all night, buzzing when folks are trying to sleep. And so Alvin, thinking that way, did what Ma always had them do: He stepped inside and closed the door behind him.

But he dared go no farther into the house than that back hall, with some heavy coats on pegs and dirt-crusted boots in a jumble by the door. It felt too strange to move. He'd been hearing the greensong of the forest for so many months that it was deafening, the silence when it was near gone, near completely killed by the cacophony of the jammering life on a White man's farm in spring.

"Isaac," said a woman's voice.

One of the White noises stopped. Only then did Alvin realize that it had been an actual noise he was hearing with his ears, not the life-noises he heard with his Red senses. He tried to remember what it was. A rhythm, and banging, regular rhythm like—like a loom. It was a loom he'd been hearing. Ta-Kumsaw must've just walked hisself right into the room where some woman was weaving. Only he wasn't no stranger here, she knew him by the same name as that farmer fellow out in the fields. Isaac.

"Isaac," she said again, whoever she was.

"Becca," said Ta-Kumsaw.

A simple name, no reason for Alvin's heart to start a-pounding. But the *way* Ta-Kumsaw said it, the way he spoke—it was such a tone of voice that was meant to make hearts pound. And more: Ta-Kumsaw spoke it, not with the strange-twisted vowels of Red men talking English, but with as true an accent as if he was from England. Why, he sounded more like Reverend Thrower than Alvin would have thought possible.

No, no, it wasn't Ta-Kumsaw at all, it was another man, a White man in the same room with the White woman, that's all. And Alvin walked softly down the hall to find where the voices were, to see the White man whose presence would explain all.

Instead he stood in an open door and looked into a room where Ta-Kumsaw stood holding a White woman by her shoulders, looking down into her face, and her looking up into his. Saying not a word, just looking at each other. Not a White man in the room.

"My people are gathering at the Hio," said Ta-Kumsaw, in his strange English-sounding voice.

"I know," said the woman. "It's already in the fabric." Then she turned to look at Alvin in the doorway. "And you didn't come alone."

Alvin never saw eyes like hers before. He was still too young to hanker after women like he remembered Wastenot and Wantnot doing when they both hit fourteen at a gallop. So it wasn't any kind of man-wishing-for-a-woman feeling that he had, looking at her eyes. He just looked into them like he sometimes looked into a fire, watching the flames dance, not asking for them to make sense, just watching the sheer randomness of it. That was what her eyes were like, as if those eyes had seen a hundred thousand things happen, and they were all still swirling around inside those eyes, and no one had ever bothered or maybe even known how to get those visions out and make sensible stories out of them.

And Alvin feared mightily that she had some power of witchery that she used to turn Ta-Kumsaw into a White man.

"My name is Becca," said the woman.

"His name is Alvin," said Ta-Kumsaw; or rather, said Isaac, for it sure didn't sound like Ta-Kumsaw anymore. "He's a miller's son from the Wobbish country."

"He's that thread I saw running through the fabric out of place." She smiled at Alvin. "Come here," she said. "I want to see the legendary Boy Renegado."

"Who's that?" asked Alvin. "The Boy Rainy God—"

"Renegado. There are stories all through Appalachee, don't you know that? About Ta-Kumsaw, who appears one day in the Osh-Kontsy country and the next day in a village on the banks of the Yazoo, stirring up Reds to do massacre and torture. And always with him is a White boy who urges the Reds to be ever more brutal, who teaches them the secret methods of torture that used to be practiced by the Papist Inquisitions in Spain and Italy."

"That ain't so," said Alvin.

She smiled. The flames of her eyes danced.

"They must hate me," said Alvin. "I don't even know what a Inky-zitchum is."

"Inquisition," said Isaac.

Alvin felt a sick dread in his heart. If folks were telling such tales about him, why, folks would regard him as a criminal, a monster, practically. "I'm only going along with—"

"I know what you're doing, and why," said Becca. "Around here we all know Isaac well enough to disbelieve such lies about him and you both."

But Alvin didn't care about "around here." What he cared about was back home in Wobbish country.

"Don't worry yourself," said Becca. "Nobody knows who this legendary White boy is. Certainly not one of the two Innocents that Ta-Kumsaw chopped to bits in the forest. Certainly not Alvin or Measure. Which one *are* you, by the way?"

"Alvin," said Isaac.

"Oh, yes," said Becca. "You already told me that. I have such a hard time holding people's names in my head."

"Ta-Kumsaw didn't chop nobody up."

"As you might guess, Alvin, we didn't believe that story here, either."

"Oh." Alvin didn't know what to say, and since he'd been living like a Red for so long, he did what Reds do when they have nothing to say, something that a White man hardly ever thinks of doing. He said nary a thing at all.

"Bread and cheese?" asked Becca.

"You're too kind. Thank you," said Isaac.

If that didn't beat all. Ta-Kumsaw saying thank you like a fine gentleman. Not that he wasn't noble and fair-spoke among his kind. But in White man's language he was always so cold, so unflowered in his talk. Till now. Witchery.

Becca rang a little bell.

"It's simple fare, but we live simply in this house. And I especially in this room. Which is fitting—it's such a simple place."

Alvin looked around. She was right. It only just now occurred to him that this room was the original log cabin, with its one remaining window casting southern light into the room. Around it the walls were all still rough old wood; he just hadn't noticed, from all the cloth draped here and there, hanging on hooks, piled up on furniture, rolled up in bolts. A strange kind of cloth, lots of color in it but the color making no pattern or sense, just weaving this way, that way, changing shades and colors, a broad streak of blue, a few narrow strands of green, all twisting in and out of each other.

Somebody came into the room to answer Becca's bell, an older man from the sound of his voice; she sent him for food, but Alvin didn't even know what he looked like, he couldn't take his eyes off the cloth. What was so much cloth for? Why would somebody make it such a bright and ugly unorganized set of colors?

And where did it end?

He walked over to where maybe a dozen bolts of cloth were standing in a corner, leaning on each other, and he realized that each bolt grew out of the one before. Somebody'd taken the end of cloth from one bolt and wrapped it around itself to start the next one, so the cloth spooled off the end of one bolt, then leapt up and plunged right down into the center of the next, one after the other, making a chain of fabric. It wasn't a bunch of different cloths, it was all one cloth, rolled up until it was almost too heavy to move, and then the next bolt started right up, with never a scissor touching the cloth. Alvin began to wander around the room, his fingers tracing the pattern of the cloth, following its path up over hooks on the wall, down into folds stacked up on the floor. He followed, he followed, until finally, just as the old man returned with the bread and cheese, he found the end of the cloth. It was feeding out the front of Becca's loom.

All that time, Ta-Kumsaw had been talking to Becca in his Isaac voice, and she to him in her deep melodious way of speech, which had just the slightest hint of foreignness to it, like some of the Dutch in the area around Vigor Church, who'd been in America all their lives but still had a trace of the old country in their talk. Only now, with Alvin standing by the loom and the food on a low table with three chairs around it, only now did he pay attention to what they were saying, and that only because he wanted so badly to ask Becca what all this cloth was *for,* seeing as how she must have been weaving at it for more than a year, to have it so long, without never once taking shears to it to make something out of it. It was what Ma always called a shameful waste, to have something and make no use of it, like Dally Framer's pretty singing voice, which she sang with all day at home but wouldn't ever join in singing hymns at church.

"Eat," said Ta-Kumsaw. And when he spoke so bluntly to Alvin, his voice lost that Englishness; he was the real Ta-Kumsaw again. It set Alvin's mind to rest, knowing that there wasn't some witchery at work, that Ta-Kumsaw just had two different ways of talking; but of course that also set more questions into Alvin's mind, about how Ta-Kumsaw ever learned such talk. Alvin never even heard so much as a rumor about Ta-Kumsaw having White friends in Appalachee, and you'd think a tale like that would be known. Though it wasn't hard to guess why Ta-Kumsaw wouldn't want it noised around much. What would all those het-up Reds think if they saw Ta-Kumsaw here and now? What would it do to Ta-Kumsaw's war?

And come to think of it, how could Ta-Kumsaw wage such a war, if he had true White friends like the folk of this valley? Surely the land was dead here, at least as the Reds knew it. How could Ta-Kumsaw bear it? It left such a hunger in Alvin that even though he packed bread and cheese down his throat till his belly poked out, he still felt a gnawing inside him, a need to get back to the woodland and feel the song of the land inside himself.

The meal was filled with Becca's pleasant chatter about doings in the valley, her saying names that meant nothing to Alvin, except any one of them could have been the name of a body back in Vigor Church—there was even folks named Miller, which was natural, seeing how a valley this size no doubt had more than one miller's worth of grain to grind.

The old man came back to clear away.

"Did you come to see my cloth?" asked Becca.

Ta-Kumsaw nodded. "That's half why I came."

Becca smiled, and led him to the loom. She sat on her weaving stool and gathered the newest cloth up into her lap. She started about three yards from the lip of the loom. "Here," she said. "The gathering of your folk to Prophets-town."

Alvin saw how she passed her hand over a whole bunch of threads that seemed to climb out of their proper warp and migrate across the cloth to gather up near the edge.

"Reds from every tribe," she said. "The strongest of your people."

Even though the fibers tended to be greenish, they were indeed heavier than most threads, strong and taut. Becca fed the cloth farther down her lap. The gathering grew stronger and clearer, and the threads turned brighter green. How could threads change color that way? And how with the machinery of the loom could the warp shift like that?

"And now the Whites that gathered against them," she said.

And sure enough, another group of threads, tighter to start with, but gathering, knotting up a little. To Alvin's eyes it looked like the cloth was a ruin, the threads all tangled and bunched—who'd wear a shirt made of such stuff as that?—and the colors made no sense, all jumbled together without no effort to make a pattern or any kind of regular order.

Ta-Kumsaw reached out his hand and pulled the cloth toward himself. Pulled until he exposed a place were all those pure green threads just went slack and then stopped, most of them. The warp of the cloth was spare and thin, then, maybe one thread for every ten there used to be, like a worn-down raggedy patch in the elbow of an old shirt, so when you bent your elbow maybe a dozen threads made lines across your skin one direction, and no threads at all the other way.

If the green threads stood for Prophetstown, there couldn't be no mistake what was going on here. "Tippy-Canoe," Alvin murmured. Now he knew the order of this cloth.

Becca bent over the cloth and tears dropped from her eyes straight down on it.

Tearless, Ta-Kumsaw pulled the cloth again, steadily. Alvin saw the rest of the green threads, the few that remained from the massacre at Tippy-Canoe, migrate to the edge of the cloth and stop. The cloth was narrower by that many threads. Only now there was another gathering, and the threads were not green. They were mostly black.

"Black with hate," said Becca. "You are gathering your people with hate."

"Can you imagine conducting a war with love?" asked Ta-Kumsaw.

"That's a reason to refuse to make war at all," she said gently.

"Don't talk like a White woman," said Ta-Kumsaw.

"But she is one," said Alvin, who thought she made perfect sense.

They both looked at Alvin, Ta-Kumsaw impassively, Becca with—amusement? Pity? Then they returned to the cloth.

Very quickly they came to where the cloth hung over the beam, then fed out of the loom. Along the way, the black threads of Ta-Kumsaw's army worked closer together, knotted, intertwined. And other threads, some blue, some yellow, some black, all gathered in another place, the fabric bunching up something awful. It was thicker, but it didn't seem to Alvin that it was a speck stronger. Weaker, if anything. Less useful. Less trustworthy.

"This cloth ain't going to be worth much, if this goes on," said Alvin.

Becca smiled grimly. "Truer words were never spoken, lad."

"If this is about a year's worth of story," said Alvin, "you must have two hundred years all gathered up here."

Becca cocked her head. "More than that," she said.

"How do you find out all that's going on, to make it all go into the cloth?"

"Oh, Alvin, there's some things folks just do, without knowing how," she said.

"And if you change the threads around, can't you make things go different?" Alvin had in mind a careful rearrangement, spreading the threads out more even-like, and getting those black threads farther apart from each other.

"It doesn't work like that," she said. "I don't make things happen, with what I do here. Things that happen, they change *me*. Don't fret about it, Alvin."

"But there wasn't even White folks in this part of America more than two hundred years ago. How can this cloth go farther back?"

She sighed. "Isaac, why did you bring him to plague me with questions?"

Ta-Kumsaw smiled at her.

"Lad, will you tell no one?" she asked. "Will you keep it secret who I am and what I do?"

"I promise."

"I weave, Alvin. That's all. My whole family, from before we even remember, we've been weavers."

"That your name, then? Becca Weaver? My brother-in-law, Armor-of-God, his pa's a Weaver, and—"

"Nobody *calls* us weavers," said Becca. "If they had any name for us at all, they'd call us—no."

She wouldn't tell him.

"No, Alvin, I can't put such a burden on you. Because you'd want to come. You'd want to come and see—"

"See what?" asked Alvin.

"Like Isaac here. I should never have told him, either."

"He kept the secret, though. Never breathed a word."

"He didn't keep it secret from himself, though. He came to see."

"See what?" Alvin asked again.

"See how long are the threads a-flowing up into my loom."

Only then did Alvin notice the back end of the loom, where the warp threads were gathered into place by a rack of fine steel wires. The threads weren't colored at all. They were raw white. Cotton? Surely not wool. Linen, maybe. With all the colors in the finished cloth, he hadn't really noticed what it was made of.

"Where do the colors come from?" asked Alvin.

No one answered.

"Some of the threads go slack."

"Some of them end," said Ta-Kumsaw.

"Many of them end," said Becca. "And many begin. It's the pattern of life."

"What do you see, Alvin?" asked Ta-Kumsaw.

"If these black threads are your folk," said Alvin, "then I'd say there's a battle coming, and a lot are going to die. Not like Tippy-Canoe, though. Not as bad."

"That's what I see, too," said Ta-Kumsaw.

"And these other colors all bunched up, what are they? An army of White folk?"

"Word is that a man named Andrew Jackson of the western Tennizy country is gathering up an army. They call him Old Hickory."

"I know the man," said Ta-Kumsaw. "He doesn't stay in the saddle too well."

"He's been doing with White folks what you've been doing with Red, Isaac. He's been going up and down the western country, rousting people out and haranguing them about the Red Menace. About *you*, Isaac. For every Red soldier you've gathered, he's recruited two Whites. And he figures you'll go north, to join with a French army. He knows all your plans."

"He knows nothing," said Ta-Kumsaw. "Alvin, tell me, how many threads of this White army end?"

"A lot. More, maybe. I don't know. It's about even."

"Then it tells me nothing."

"It tells you that you'll have your battle," said Becca. "It tells you that there'll be more blood and suffering in the world, thanks to you."

"But it says nothing of victory," said Ta-Kumsaw.

"It never does."

Alvin wondered if you could just tie another thread onto

the end of one of the broken ones, and save somebody's life. He looked for the spools of thread from which the warp was formed, but he couldn't find them. The threads hung down from the back beam of the loom, taut like there was a heavy weight hanging on them, but Alvin couldn't see where the threads came from. They didn't touch the floor. They didn't exactly stop, either. He looked this far, and there they were, hanging tight and long; and he looked this much farther, and there weren't no threads, nothing there at all. The threads were just coming out of nowhere, and there was no way the human eye could see or make sense of how they started.

But Alvin, he could see with other eyes, inward eyes, the way he studied into the tiny workings of the human body, into the cold inward currents of stone. And with that hidden vision he looked into a single thread and traced its shape, following how the fibers wound around and through, twisting and gripping each other to make the strength of the yarn. This time he could just keep following the thread. Just keep on following until finally, far beyond the place where the threads all disappeared to natural eyes, the thread ended. Whosoever soul that thread bespoke, he had a good long life ahead of him, before he died.

All these threads must end, when the person dies. And somehow a new thread must start up when a baby got born. Another thread coming out of nowhere.

"It never ends," said Becca. "I'll grow old and die, Alvin, but the cloth will go on."

"Do you know which thread is you?"

"No," she said. "I don't want to know."

"I reckon I'd like to see. I want to know how many years I got."

"Many," said Ta-Kumsaw. "Or few. All that matters is what you do with however many years you have."

"It does too matter how long I live," said Alvin. "Don't go saying it don't, cause you don't believe that yourself."

Becca laughed.

"Miss Becca," said Alvin, "what do you do this for, if you don't make things happen?"

She shrugged. "It's a work. Everybody has a work to do, and this is mine."

"You could go out and weave things for folks to wear."

"To wear and then wear out," she said. "And no, Alvin, I can't go out."

"You mean you stay indoors all the time?"

"I stay here, always," she said. "In this room, with my loom."

"I begged you once to go with me," said Isaac.

"And I begged you once to stay." She smiled up at him.

"I can't live forever where the land is dead."

"And I can't live a moment away from my cloth. The way the land lives in your mind, Isaac, that is how the lives of all the souls of America live in mine. But I love you. Even now."

Alvin felt like he shouldn't be there. It was like they forgot he was there, even though he'd just been talking to them. It finally dawned on him that they'd probably rather be alone. So he moved away, walked over to the cloth again, and again began tracing its path, the opposite direction this time, scanning quickly but carefully, up the walls, through the bolts and piles, searching for the earliest end of the cloth.

Couldn't find it. In fact, he must have been looking the wrong direction or got himself twisted up, because pretty soon he found himself on the same familiar path he had followed, the path that first led him to the loom. He reversed direction, and after a short time he found himself again on the path to the loom. He could no more search backward to find the oldest end of the cloth than he could search forward to find where the newest threads were coming from.

He turned again to Ta-Kumsaw and Becca. Whatever whispered conversation they had carried on was over. Ta-Kumsaw sat cross-legged on the floor in front of her, his head bowed. She was stroking his hair with gentle hands.

"This cloth is older than the oldest part of this house," said Alvin.

Becca didn't answer.

"This cloth's been going on forever."

"As long as men and women have known how to weave, this cloth has passed through the loom."

"But not this loom. This loom's new," said Alvin.

"We change looms from time to time. We build the new one around the old. It's what the men of our kind do."

"This cloth is older than the oldest White settlements in America," said Alvin.

"It was once a part of a larger cloth. But one day, back in our old country, we saw a large portion of the threads moving off the edge of the cloth. My great-great-great-great-great-great-grandfather built a new loom. We had the threads we needed. They pulled away from the old cloth; we continued it from there. It's still connected up—that's what you're seeing."

"But now it's here."

"It's here *and* there. Don't try to understand it, Alvin. I gave up long ago. But isn't it good to know that all of the threads of life are being woven into one great cloth?"

"Who's weaving the cloth for the Red folk that went west with Tenskwa-Tawa?" asked Alvin. "Those threads went off the cloth."

"That's not your business," said Becca. "We'll just say that another loom was built, and carried west."

"But Ta-Kumsaw said no White folk would ever cross the river to the west. The Prophet said it, too."

Ta-Kumsaw turned slowly on the floor, without getting up. "Alvin," he said, "you're only a boy."

"And I was only a girl," Becca reminded him, "when I first loved you." She turned to Alvin. "It's my daughter who carried the loom into the west. She could go because she's only half White." She again stroked Ta-Kumsaw's hair. "Isaac is my husband. My daughter Wieza is his daughter."

"Mana-Tawa," said Ta-Kumsaw.

"I thought for a time that Isaac would choose to stay here, to live with us. But then I watched as his thread moved away from us, even though his body still was with us. I knew he would go to be with his people. I knew why he had come to us, alone from the forest. There is a hunger deeper than the Red man's hunger for the song of the living forest, deeper than a blacksmith's yearning for the hot wet iron, deeper even than a doodlebug's longing for the hollow heart of the earth. That hunger brought Ta-Kumsaw to our house. My mother was still the weaver at the loom then. I taught Ta-Kumsaw to read and write; he rushed through my father's library, and read every other book in the valley, and we sent for more books from Philadelphia and he read those. He chose his own name, then, for the man who wrote the *Principia*. When we came of age, he married me. I had a baby. He left. When Wieza was three, he came back, built a loom, and took her west over the mountain to live with his people."

"And you let your own daughter go?"

"Just like one of my ancestors sat at her old loom and let her daughter go, across the ocean to this land, her with a new loom and her watchful father beside her, yes, I let her go." Becca smiled sadly at Alvin. "We all have our work, but there's no good work that doesn't have its cost. By the time Isaac took her, I was already in this room. Everything that happened has been good."

"You didn't even ask how your daughter was doing when he got here! You still haven't asked."

"I didn't have to ask," said Becca. "No harm comes to the keepers of the loom."

"Well, if your daughter's gone, who's going to take your place?"

"Perhaps another husband will come here, by and by. One who'll stay in this house, and make another loom for me, and yet another for a daughter not yet born."

"And what happens to you then?"

"So many questions, Alvin," said Ta-Kumsaw. But his voice was soft and tired and English-sounding; Alvin wasn't in awe of the Ta-Kumsaw who read White men's books, and so he paid no heed to the mild rebuke.

"What happens to you when your daughter takes your place?"

"I don't know," said Becca. "But the story is that we go to the place where the threads come from."

"What do you do there?"

"We spin."

Alvin tried to imagine Becca's mother, and her grandmother, and the women before that, all in a line, he tried to imagine how many there'd be, all of them working their spinning wheels, winding out threads from the spindle, yarn all raw and white, which would just go somewhere, go on and disappear somewhere until it broke. Or maybe when it broke they held the whole thing, a whole human life, in their hands, and then tossed it upward until it was caught by a passing wind, and then dropped down and got snagged up in somebody's loom. A life afloat on the wind, then caught and woven into the cloth of humanity; born at some arbitrary time, then struggling to find its way into the fabric, weaving into the strength of it.

And as he imagined this, he also imagined that he understood something about that fabric. About the way it grew stronger the more tightly woven in each thread became. The ones that skipped about over the top of the cloth, dipping into the weft only now and then, they added little to the strength, though much to the color, of the cloth. While some whose color hardly showed at all, they were deeply wound among the threads, holding all together. There was a goodness in those hidden binding threads. Forever from then on, Alvin would see some quiet man or woman, little noticed and hardly thought of by others, who nevertheless went a-weaving through the life of village, town, or city, binding up, holding on, and Alvin would silently salute such folk, and do them homage in his heart, because he knew how their lives kept the cloth strong, the weave tight.

He also remembered the many threads that ended at the point where Ta-Kumsaw's battle was to take place. It was as if Ta-Kumsaw had taken shears to the cloth.

"Ain't there a way to heal things up?" asked Alvin. "Ain't there a hope of keeping this battle from ever happening, so those threads don't all get broke?"

Becca shook her head. "Even if Isaac refused to go, the battle would take place without him. No, the threads aren't broken by anything Isaac did. They broke the moment some Red man chose a course of action that would surely end in his death in battle; you and Isaac weren't going around spreading death, if that's what worries you. No more than Old Hickory's been killing people. You were just going spreading choices. They didn't have to believe in you. They didn't have to choose to die."

"But they didn't know that's what they was choosing."

"They knew," said Becca. "We always know. We don't admit it to ourselves, not until the very moment of death, but in that moment, Alvin, we see all the life before us and we understand how we chose, every day of our lives, the manner of our death."

"What if something just happens to fall on somebody's head and mashes him?"

"He chose to be in a place where such things happen. And he wasn't looking up."

"I don't believe it," said Alvin. "I think folks can always change what's coming, and I think some things happen that ain't nobody ever chose to happen."

Becca smiled at him, reached out her arm. "Come here, Alvin. Let me hold you close to me. I love your simple faith, child. I want to hold on to that faith, even if I can't believe it."

So she held him for a time, and her arm around him felt so much like his own mama's, strong and gentle, that he cried a little. In fact he cried a good deal more than he would ever have meant to cry, if he'd meant to cry at all. And he knew better than to ask to see his own thread, even though he imagined his thread would be easy to find—the one thread born in the White man's section of the cloth, but migrating over and becoming green. Surely becoming green, like the Prophet's people did.

One thing he was also sure of, so sure that he didn't even ask, though heaven knows he wasn't shy about asking any question popped into his head: He was sure that Becca knew which thread was Ta-Kumsaw's, and knew as well that his and Ta-Kumsaw's threads were all bound up with each other, for a while at least. As long as Alvin was with him, Ta-Kumsaw'd be alive. Alvin knew that there was two endings to the prophecy: the one in which Alvin died first, leaving Ta-Kumsaw by himself, in which case he'd die too; or the one in which neither one of them died and their threads went on until they disappeared. There might've been a third way it could come out: Alvin might just up and leave Ta-Kumsaw. But then if he did that, he wouldn't be Alvin anymore, so there wasn't no point in considering that as a possibility, cause it wasn't one.

Alvin slept the night on a mat on the library floor, after reading a few pages in a book by a man named Adam Smith. Where Ta-Kumsaw slept, Alvin didn't know or care to ask. What a man does with his wife is no affair for children, Alvin knew; but he wondered if the main reason Ta-Kumsaw had come back here wasn't his wish to see the loom, but the hungering that Becca spoke of. The need to make another daughter to care for Becca's loom. It wasn't a bad idea, in Alvin's mind, to have the cloth of White America in the hands of a Red man's daughter.

In the morning Ta-Kumsaw led him away, back into the forest. They did not speak of Becca, or anything else; it was back to the old way, with Ta-Kumsaw speaking only to get things done. Alvin never heard him speak in his Isaac voice again, so that Alvin began to wonder if he really heard it.

On the north bank of the Hio, near where the Wobbish empties into it, the Red army gathered, more Reds than Alvin knew existed in the whole world. More people than Alvin had ever imagined together in the same place at the same time.

Because such a company was bound to get hungry, the animals also came to them, sensing their need and fulfilling what they all was born for. Did the forest know that all its hopes of withstanding White men's axes depended on Ta-Kumsaw's victory?

No, Alvin decided, the forest was just doing what it always did—making shift to feed its own.

It was raining and the breeze was cool on the morning they set out from the Hio, bound northward. But what was rain to Red men? The messenger had come from the French in Detroit. It was time to join forces, and lure Old Hickory's army north.

18

❧

DETROIT

It was a glorious time for Frederic, Comte de Maurepas. Far from living in hell here in Detroit, with none of the amenities of Paris, he found the exhilaration of, for once, being part of something larger than himself. War was afoot, the fort was stirring, the heathen Reds were gathering from the far corners of the wilderness, and soon, under de Maurepas's command, the French would destroy the ragtag American army Old Chestnut had brought north of the Maw-Mee. Old Willow? Whatever they called him.

Of course a part of him was rather unnerved by all this. Frederic had never been a man of action, and now so much action was going on that he could hardly fathom it. It bothered him sometimes that Napoleon was letting the savages fight from behind trees. Surely Europeans, even the barbarous Americans, should be courteous enough not to let the Reds take unfair advantage of their ability to hide in the woods. But never mind. Napoleon was sure it would work out. What could go wrong, really? Everything was working as Napoleon said it would. Even Governor La Fayette, traitorous effete Feuillant dog that he was, seemed enthusiastic about the battle ahead. He had even sent another ship with more troops, which Frederic had seen pull into harbor not ten minutes ago.

"My lord," said Whoever-it-was, the servant who handled things in the evening. He was announcing somebody, of all things.

"Who?" Who is it visiting at such an ungodly hour?

"A messenger from the Governor."

"In," said Frederic. He was feeling too pleasant to bother keeping the man cooling his heels for a while. After all, it was evening—no need to pretend to be hard at work at an hour like this. After four o'clock, in fact!

The man came in, smart in his uniform. A major officer, in fact. Frederic should know his name, probably, but then he wasn't anybody, hadn't even a cousin with a title. So Frederic waited, not greeting him.

The major held two letters in his hand. He laid one on Frederic's table.

"Is the other for me as well?"

"Yes, sir. But I have the Governor's instructions to give you that one first, to wait while you read it in my presence, and then decide whether to give you the other."

"The Governor's instructions! To make me wait to receive my mail until I've read his letter first?"

"The second letter is not addressed to you, my lord," said the major. "So it is not your mail. But I think you will want to see it."

"What if I'm weary of work, and choose to read the letter tomorrow?"

"Then I have still another letter, which I will read to your soldiers if you don't read the first letter within five minutes. That third letter relieves you of command and places me in charge of Fort Detroit, under the authority of the Governor."

"Audacious! Offensive! To address me in this manner!"

"I but repeat the words of the Governor, my lord. I urge you, read his letter. It can do you no harm, and not reading it will have devastating effect."

Unbearable. Who did the Governor think he was? Well, in fact, he was a Marquis. But then, La Fayette was actually farther out of favor with the King than—

"Five minutes, my lord."

Seething, Frederic opened the letter. It was heavy; when he unfolded it, a metal amulet on a chain spilled onto the desk, clattering.

"What is *this?*"

"The letter, my lord."

Frederic scanned it quickly. "An amulet! Holy man! What am I to make of this? Has La Fayette become superstitious?" Yet despite his bravado, Frederic knew at once that he would put on the amulet. A ward against Satan! He had heard of such amulets, priceless beyond compare, for all had been touched by the finger of the Holy Mother herself, giving them their power. Could this be such a one? He opened the chain and lowered it over his head.

"Inside," said the major.

Frederic looked at him a moment in bafflement, then realized what was expected and tucked the amulet into his shirt. Now it was out of sight.

"There," he said. "I'm wearing it."

"Excellent, my lord," said the major. He held out the other letter.

It was not fastened shut, but it *had* been sealed, and Frederic was astonished to see that it was His Majesty's great seal imprinted in the wax. It was addressed to the Marquis de La Fayette. It contained the order for Napoleon Bonaparte to be placed under immediate arrest, to be returned to Paris in irons to stand trial for treason, sedition, disloyalty, and malfeasance.

"DO YOU THINK your pleading moves me?" said de Maurepas.

"I should hope that the justice of my arguments would move you," said Napoleon. "Tomorrow will be the battle. Ta-Kumsaw expects to take his orders from me; only I understand fully what is expected of the French army in this engagement."

"Only you? What is this sudden vanity of yours, to believe that only you are capable of command, that only you understand?"

"But of course *you* understand, my lord de Maurepas. Only it is for you to be concerned with the broader picture, while I—"

"Save your breath," said de Maurepas. "I am no longer deceived. Your witchery, your satanic influence, it floats past me like bubbles in the air, it means nothing to me. I am stronger than you thought. I have secret strengths!"

"It's good that you do, since all you have in public is idiocy," said Napoleon. "The defeat you will suffer without me will mark you as the champion fool in the history of the French army. Whenever anyone suffers an ignominious and avoidable disaster, they will laugh at him and say that he committed a Maurepas!"

"Enough," said de Maurepas. "Treason, sedition, malfeasance, *and* if that weren't enough, now insubordination. M. Guillotin will have business with you, I'm quite certain, my vain little bantam cock. Go, try your spurs on His Majesty, see how deep they dig when your limbs are in irons and your head is forfeit."

THE BETRAYAL WAS not obvious till morning, but then it was swift and complete. It began when the French quartermaster refused to issue gunpowder to Ta-Kumsaw's people. "I have my orders," he said.

When Ta-Kumsaw tried to see Napoleon, they laughed at him. "He won't see you now, or ever," he was told.

What about de Maurepas, then?

"He is a Comte. He does not treat with savages. He is not a lover of beasts, like little Napoleon."

Only then did Alvin notice that all the Frenchman they were dealing with today were the very ones that Napoleon had been circumventing; all the officers Napoleon preferred and trusted were not to be found. Napoleon had fallen.

"Bows and arrows," said an officer. "That's what your braves excel with, isn't it? With bullets you would cause more damage to your own men than to the enemy."

Ta-Kumsaw's scouts told him that the American army would arrive by noon. Ta-Kumsaw immediately deployed his men to harass the enemy. But now, without the range of muskets, they could do little more than annoy Old Hickory's army with the stings of feeble arrows fired from too far off, where they had meant to cripple the Americans with an irresistible storm of metal. And because the bowmen had to come so close to the Americans in order to fire, many of them were killed.

"Don't stand near me," Ta-Kumsaw told Alvin. "They all know of the prophecy. They'll think my courage only comes because I know I cannot die."

So Alvin stood farther off, but never so far that he didn't see deeply into Ta-Kumsaw's body, ready to heal any wound. What he could not heal was the fear and anger and despair that already gathered in Ta-Kumsaw's soul. Without gunpowder, without Napoleon, the sure victory had become a chancy thing at best.

The basic tactics were successful. Old Hickory spotted the trap at once, but the terrain forced him to fall into it or retreat, and he knew that retreat would be disaster. So he marched his army boldly between the hills filled with Reds, funneling into the narrow ground where French cannon and musketry would rake the Americans while the Reds killed any who tried to flee. The victory would be complete. Except that the Americans were supposed to be demoralized, confused, and their numbers deeply reduced by the Red men shooting at them all the way here.

The tactics were successful, except that when the American army came in view of the French, and hesitated before the muzzles of nine cannon loaded with canister, and two thousand muskets arrayed to sweep and double-sweep the field, the French incomprehensibly began to move back. It was as if they did not trust the impregnability of their own position. They did not even try to withdraw the cannon. They retreated as if they feared immediate destruction.

The course of the battle was predictable, then. Old Hickory knew what to do with opportunity. His soldiers ignored the Reds and fell on the retreating Frenchmen, slaughtering all who did not run, seizing their cannon and muskets, their powder and shot. Within an hour they had used the French artillery to break down the fortress walls in three places; Americans streamed into Detroit; there was bloody fighting in the streets.

Ta-Kumsaw should have left then. He should have let the Americans destroy the French, should have taken his men to safety. Perhaps he felt a duty to help the French, even after they had betrayed him. Perhaps he saw a glimmer of hope that with the Americans involved in battle, his army of Reds might win a victory after all. Or perhaps he knew that never again would he have the power to gather all the fighting men of every tribe; if he retreated now, with the battle unfought, who would follow him again? And if they would not follow him, they would follow no one, and the

White men would nibble their way to conquest, devouring now this tribe, now that. Ta-Kumsaw surely knew that it was either victory now, however unlikely, or the struggle would be over for all time, and any of his people who weren't slaughtered outright would either escape into the west, a strange land to them, lacking in forest; or would remain as a diminished people, living like White men instead of Red, the forest forever silent. Whether he hoped for victory or not, he could not surrender to such a future, not without a fight.

So armed with bows and arrows, clubs and knives, the Reds attacked the American army from behind. At first they reaped the Whites in bloody harvest, clubbing them to the ground, piercing them with flints. Ta-Kumsaw shouted at them to take muskets, powder, ammunition from the dead, and many Reds obeyed. But then Old Hickory got the disciplined core of his men into action. The guns were turned. And the Reds, exposed on the open field, were felled in great swathes of grapeshot.

By evening, the sun going down, Detroit was on fire and the smoke filled the nearby wood. In that choking darkness stood Ta-Kumsaw with a few hundred of his own Shaw-Nee. Other tribes made isolated stands here and there; most despaired and fled into the forest, where no White man could follow. Old Hickory himself led the final assault against Ta-Kumsaw's wooded fortress, bringing with him the thousand Americans who weren't busy looting the French city and smashing the idols in the Papist cathedral.

The bullets came from all directions, it seemed. But through it all Ta-Kumsaw stood upright, shouting to his men, urging them to fight on with muskets stolen from fallen Americans in the first attack. For fifteen minutes that seemed like forever, Ta-Kumsaw fought like a madman, and his Shaw-Nee fought and died beside him. Ta-

Kumsaw's body blossomed with scarlet wounds; blood streaked down his back and belly; one arm hung limp by his side. No one knew how he found the strength to stand, he had so many wounds in him. But Ta-Kumsaw was made of flesh like any other man, and at last he fell in the smoky dusk, bearing half a dozen wounds, any one of which would surely have been fatal by itself.

When Ta-Kumsaw fell, the firing slackened. It was as if the Americans knew that they had only to kill that one man, and they would break the spirit of the Red man, now and forever. The dozen surviving Shaw-Nee warriors crept away in the smoke and the darkness, to bear the bitter news of Ta-Kumsaw's death to every Shaw-Nee village, and eventually to every hut where Red men and women lived. The great battle was hopeless; White men could not be trusted, French or American, and so Ta-Kumsaw's great plan could never have succeeded. Yet the Red men remembered that at least for a time they had united under one great man, had become a single people, had dreamed of victory. So Ta-Kumsaw was remembered in song as Red villages and families moved west across the Mizzipy to join the Prophet; he was remembered in stories told beside brick hearths, by families who wore clothing and worked at jobs like White men, but still remembered that once there was another way to live, and the greatest of all the forest Reds had been a man called Ta-Kumsaw, who died trying to save the woodland and the ancient, doomed Red way of life.

It was not only Reds who remembered Ta-Kumsaw. Even as they fired muskets at his shadowy figure in the woods, the American soldiers admired him. He was a great hero out of olden times. Americans were all farmers and shopkeepers at heart; Ta-Kumsaw lived a story like Achilles or Odysseus, Caesar or Hannibal, David or the Maccabees. "He can't die," they murmured as they saw him take bullets and still not fall. And when at last he did fall, they searched for his body and did not find it.

"The Shaw-Nee dragged him off," said Old Hickory, and that was that. He wouldn't even let them search for the Renegado Boy, figuring that such a White traitor was no doubt as faithless as the French and snuck off during the fight. Leave be, said Old Hickory, and who was going to argue with the old man? He won them the victory, didn't he? He broke the back of Red resistance once and for all, didn't he? Old Hickory, Andy Jackson—they wanted to make him King but they'd have to settle for President someday. Yet in the meantime they could not forget Ta-Kumsaw, and rumors spread that he was alive somewhere, crippled by his wounds, waiting to get healed up and lead a great Red invasion from across the Mizzipy, from the swamps of the South, or from some secret hidden fastness in the Appalachee Mountains.

ALL THROUGH THE battle Alvin worked with all his might to keep Ta-Kumsaw alive. As each new bullet tore through flesh, Alvin mended broken arteries, trying to hold Ta-Kumsaw's blood inside him. The pain he had no time for, but Ta-Kumsaw seemed not to mind the savage injuries he took. Alvin crouched down in his hiding place between a standing tree and a fallen one, his eyes closed, watching Ta-Kumsaw only with his inward eyes, seeing his flesh from the inside out. Alvin saw none of the images that would haunt Ta-Kumsaw's legends. Alvin never even noticed as bullets sent a spray of leaf bits and chips of wood falling on him. He even took a sharp stinging bullet in the back of his left hand and hardly felt it, he was concentrating so hard on keeping Ta-Kumsaw on his feet.

But one thing Alvin saw: Beyond the edges of his vision, just out of reach, there was the Unmaker like a transparent shadow, shimmering fingers slicing through the wood. Ta-Kumsaw, him Alvin could heal. But who could heal the greenwood? Who could heal the tearing apart of tribe from tribe, Red from Red? All that Ta-Kumsaw had built was shivered apart in that single fraction of an hour, and all Alvin could do was keep a single man alive. A great man, true, a man who had changed the world, who had built something, even if it was something that in the end led to more harm and suffering; Ta-Kumsaw was a builder, and yet even as Alvin saved his life, he knew that Ta-Kumsaw's building days were done. Likely enough the Unmaker didn't begrudge Alvin his friend's life. What was Ta-Kumsaw, compared to what the Unmaker was consuming at this feast? Just like Taleswapper had said so long ago, the Unmaker could tear down, eat through, use up, and crush things faster than any one man could ever hope to build.

All the time, though Alvin scarcely noticed *where* Ta-Kumsaw was what with worrying about what was going on inside him, the Red man circled Alvin's hiding place like he was a dog tied to a tree, winding around and getting closer and closer. So when the bullets finally became too much for Alvin and the blood flowed so fast from dozens of wounds that Alvin couldn't stanch them all, it was into Alvin's sheltered place that Ta-Kumsaw fell, sprawling across Alvin's body, knocking the wind out of the boy.

Alvin scarce heard the search go on around him. He was too busy healing wounds, binding up torn flesh, connecting severed nerves and straightening broken bones. In desperation to save Ta-Kumsaw's life he opened his eyes and cut into the Red man's flesh with his own flint knife, prying bullets out and then healing up where he had cut. And all the time it was like the smoke gathered above them, making it impossible for anyone to see into the little shel-tered place where the Unmaker had got Alvin holed up in hiding.

It was afternoon next day when Alvin awoke. Ta-Kumsaw lay beside him, weak and spent, but whole. Alvin was filthy and itchy and he had to void himself; gingerly he pulled himself out from under Ta-Kumsaw, who felt so light, as if he was half made of air. The smoke was gone now, but Alvin still felt invisible, walking around in broad daylight dressed like a Red man. He could hear drunken singing from the American camp near the ruins of Detroit. Stray smoke still drifted through the trees. And every-where Alvin walked were the bodies of Red men cast like wet straw on the forest floor. It stank of death.

Alvin found a brook and drank, trying not to imagine some dead body lying in it upstream. He washed his face and hands, dipped his head into the water to cool his brain, the way he used to do at home after a hard day's work. Then he went back to wake Ta-Kumsaw and bring him here to drink.

Ta-Kumsaw was already awake. Already standing over the body of a fallen friend. His head was tipped back, his mouth open, as if he uttered a cry so deep and loud that human ears couldn't hear the sound of it, could only feel the earth trembling with the vibration of the shout. Alvin ran to him and flung his arms around him, clinging to him like the child he was, only it was Alvin doing the comfort-ing, Alvin whispering, "You done your best, you done all that could be done."

And Ta-Kumsaw answered not at all, though his silence was an answer, too, like as if he was saying, I'm alive, which means I didn't do enough.

They walked away in the afternoon, not even bothering to conceal themselves. Some White men later woke up with hangovers, swearing they saw visions of Ta-Kumsaw and the Renegado Boy walking through the corpses of the Red army, but nobody paid them mind. And what did it matter? Ta-Kumsaw wasn't no danger to the Whites now. He'd broken against them like a great wave, but they stood against him; he thought to shatter them, but they broke him and his people into spray, and if some drops of it still clung, what did that matter? They had no power anymore. It was all spent in one brutal, futile blow.

Alvin spoke not a word to Ta-Kumsaw all the way south to the headwaters of the My-Ammy, and Ta-Kumsaw spoke nary a word to him as they dug out a canoe together. Alvin made the wood soft in the right places, so it took scarce half an hour, and another half hour to shape a good paddle. Then they dragged the canoe to the river's edge. Only with the canoe half in the water did Ta-Kumsaw stop and turn to Alvin, reach out a hand and touch his face. "If all White men were true like you, Alvin, I would never have been their enemy."

And as Alvin watched Ta-Kumsaw paddle steadily down the river out of sight, it occurred to him that it just didn't feel like Ta-Kumsaw had lost. It was as if the battle wasn't *about* Ta-Kumsaw. It was about White men, and their worthiness to have this land. They might think they won, they might think the Red man slunk away or bowed his head in defeat, but in fact it was the White man who lost, because when Ta-Kumsaw paddled down the Wobbish to the Hio, down the Hio to the Mizzipy, and crossed the fogs of the river to the other side, he was taking the land with him, the greensong; what the White man had won with so much blood and dishonesty was not the living land of the Red man, but the corpse of that land. It was decay that the White man won. It would turn to dust in his hands, Alvin knew it.

But I'm a White man, not a Red, whatever anybody might say. And rotting underfoot or not, this land is all the land we have, and our people all the people that we've got. So Alvin walked along the shore of the Wobbish, heading downriver, knowing that where the Tippy-Canoe discharged itself into the larger stream, there he'd find his pa and ma, his brothers and his sisters, all a-waiting there to find out what had happened to him in the year since he set out to become a prentice blacksmith back at Hatrack River.

19

HOMECOMING

Napoleon did not wear irons on his way back to France. He slept in the second cabin, and ate at table with Governor La Fayette, who was only too glad to have him. In the hot afternoons of the Atlantic crossing, La Fayette confided all his plans of revolution to Napoleon, his dearest friend, and Napoleon offered helpful advice on how to make the revolution go much faster and more effectively.

"The best thing about all these sad events," said La Fayette the day the lookout first spied the coast of Bretagne, "is that we are friends now, and the revolution is assured of success because you are a part of it. To think that once I mistrusted you, figuring you to be a tool of the King. A tool of Charles! But soon all France will know you for the hero that you are, and blame the King and Freddie for the sacking of Detroit. All that territory in the hands of Protestants and savages, while we are here to offer a better way, a truer leadership to the people of France. Ah, Napoleon, I have yearned for such a man as you through all my years of planning for democracy. All we have needed, we Feuillants, was a leader, a man who could guide us, a man who could lead France to true freedom." And La Fayette sighed and sank deeper into the cushions of his chair.

Through all this Napoleon listened with satisfaction, yes, but also sadness. For he had thought that La Fayette was immune to his charm because of some great inward strength. Now he knew that it was only a foolish amulet, that La Fayette was like any ordinary man when it came to resisting Napoleon; and now that the amulet lay buried in a mass grave outside Detroit, no doubt still chained to the moldering vertebrae of Frederic de Maurepas, Napoleon knew that he would never find his equal in this world, unless it was God himself, or Nature. There would be no man to deny him, that much was sure. So he listened to La Fayette's babbling with a wistful longing for the kind of man he once thought La Fayette could be.

The men on deck bustled and hurried and made ten thousand noises, for they were heaving in to land; Napoleon was home in France at last.

TA-KUMSAW DID NOT need to fear the thick fog that descended as he reached the Hio's mouth, pouring into the Mizzipy and getting lost in those stronger currents. He knew the way: west, and any shore would be his refuge, his safety, the end of his life.

For that's all that he could see ahead of him now. The land west of the Mizzipy was his brother's land, the place where White man would not come. The land itself, the water, every living thing would work to bar those White who were foolish enough to think that the Red men could be defeated again. But it was the Prophet's gifts the Red folk needed now, not those of a warrior like Ta-Kumsaw. He might be a figure of legend in the east, among fallen Reds and foolish Whites, but in the west they would know him for what he was. A failure, a bloody-handed man who led his people to destruction.

The water lapped at his canoe. He heard a redbird singing not far off. The fog grew whiter, dazzling; then broke, and the sun shone bright, blinding him. In three paddlestrokes his canoe nosed the shore, and there, to his surprise, was a man silhouetted in the late afternoon sun, standing on the bank. The man sprang down and took the end of Ta-Kumsaw's canoe and pulled it tight against the riverbank, then helped Ta-Kumsaw out of the little boat. Ta-Kumsaw couldn't see his face, his eyes were so bedazzled; but he knew who it was all the same, from the touch of the hand. And then the voice, murmuring, "Let the canoe drift away. There'll be no more crossing to the other side, my brother."

"Lolla-Wossiky," cried Ta-Kumsaw. Then he wept and knelt at his brother's feet, clinging to his knees. All the anguish, all the grief spilled out of him, while above him Lolla-Wossiky, called Tenskwa-Tawa, called the Prophet, sang to him a song of melancholy, a song about the death of bees.

THINGS WERE CHANGED somewhat when Alvin got to town. There was a sign right out on the Wobbish Road, saying:

> *Pass by, stranger, if you can.*
> *Or hear a tale unfit for ears of man.*

Well Alvin knew the purpose of that sign. But he was no stranger here.

Or was he? As he made his way along the little spur of the road toward Vigor Church, he saw that new buildings had been put up, new houses built. Folks were living pretty much cheek-by-jowl here now, and Vigor Church was a proper town. But no one greeted him in the road, and even the children a-playing in the commons had no word for him; no doubt their parents taught them not to welcome strangers, or maybe they just were sick of hearing their fathers and older brothers telling their awful tale to whatever stranger came to call. Better not to welcome any man or woman here.

And the past year had changed Alvin. He was taller, yes, but also he knew that his walk was different, more like a Red man, unaccustomed to the feel of a White man's road beneath his feet, wishing for the greenwood song, which was near extinguished in these parts. Maybe I *am* a stranger here these days. Maybe I seen and done too much this last year to ever come back and be Alvin Junior anymore.

Even with the changes in the town, Alvin knew his way. This much hadn't changed: There was still bridges over every little stream on the roadway up to his father's house. Alvin tried to feel the old way, feel the anger of the water against him. But the black evil that once was his enemy, it hardly knew him either, now that he walked like a Red man, all at one with the living world. Never mind, thought Alvin. As the land gets tame and broken, I'll be White again in my step, and the Unmaker will find me. Just as he broke the Red man's healing hold on this land, he'll try to break me too, and if Ta-Kumsaw wasn't strong enough or Tenskwa-Tawa wise enough to stand against the old Unmaker, what will I ever do?

Just make my way, day by day, like the old hymn said. Make my way, day by day, Lord above, light and love, in my grief bring relief, fill my cup, lift me up, heal my soul, make me whole, Amen. Amen.

Cally was a-standing there right on the porch, doing nothing, like as if he was just watching out in case Alvin Junior should come home today, and maybe that's what he was doing, maybe it was. Anyway it was Cally shouted out, Cally who knew him at once despite all changes in him.

"Alvin! Ally! Alvin Junior! He's home! You're home!"

First one to come at his call, running around the house with his sleeves up and the ax still trailing from his hand, was Measure. Soon as he saw it was truly Alvin, he dropped the ax and took Alvin Junior by the shoulders, looked him over for any harm, and Alvin done the same, looking for any scars on Measure. None at all, healed proper. But Measure found some deeper injuries in Alvin, and softly said, "You got older, Al." To which Alvin had nary a thing to say, it being true, and for a moment they just stared into each other's eyes, each knowing how far down the long road of the Red man's suffering and exile the other had walked; no other White man could ever know what they knew.

Then Ma came out onto the porch and Pa out of the mill and up to the house, and oh, there was hugging and kissing and crying and laughing and shouting and silence. They didn't kill the fatted calf, but there was a young pig didn't see another sunrise. Cally ran to the brothers' farms and Armor-of-God's store and gave notice what was up, and soon all the family was gathered to greet Alvin Junior, who they knew wasn't dead but had given up hope of seeing again.

And then, as it was getting late, there came a time when Pa hid his hands in his pockets, and the other menfolk all grew still, and then the womenfolk, till Alvin nodded and said, "I know the tale you have to tell. So tell it now, all of you, and then I'll tell you my part in it."

They did, and he did, and there was more weeping, of grief this time instead of joy. This valley of the Wobbish was all the home they'd ever know now; it was the only way they could bear to live, all the folk who'd done murder at Tippy-Canoe, was right among each other and seeing no strangers. Where could they go and live in peace, what with having to tell all comers what it was they done? "So we got to stay, Al Junior. But not you or Cally, you know. And maybe your apprenticeship is still a thing that we can do, what do you think?"

"Time to think of that later," said Ma. "Time for all those questions later. He's home, that's all for now, you hear me? He's home, who I never thought to lay eyes on again. Thank the Lord God that he didn't make me a prophet, when I said I'd never lay eyes on my sweet little Alvin anymore."

Alvin hugged his ma back just as hard as she hugged him. He didn't tell her that her prophecy was true. That it wasn't her sweet little Alvin who'd come home this time. Let her find that out on her own. Right now it was enough that the year was over, that he'd seen the unwinding of all the great changes, that now, however different it might be, however bitter, life could go on in a steady path, with no more breaking of the ground underfoot.

At night in his own bed, Alvin listened to the distant greensong, still warm and beautiful, still bright and hopeful even though the forest was getting so sparse, even though the future was so dim. Cause there's no fear of future in the song of life, just the ever-joyful present moment. That's all I want right now, thought Alvin. The present moment, which is good enough.